TALES OF HENRY JAMES

THE TEXTS OF THE STORIES
THE AUTHOR ON HIS CRAFT
BACKGROUND AND CRITICISM

≫ A NORTON CRITICAL EDITION ≪

TALES OF HENRY JAMES

THE TEXTS OF THE STORIES
THE AUTHOR ON HIS CRAFT
BACKGROUND AND CRITICISM

≫ ≪

Selected and Edited by
CHRISTOF WEGELIN
UNIVERSITY OF OREGON

W • W • Norton & Company
New York   London

813
J27 Ywe2

Library of Congress Cataloging in Publication Data
James, Henry, 1843–1916.
    Tales of Henry James.
    (A Norton critical edition)
    Bibliography: p.
    I. James, Henry, 1843–1916—Criticism and interpreta-
tion—Addresses, essays, lectures.   I. Wegelin, Christof,
1911–   .   II. Title.
PS2111.W44   1983   813.4   83-13367

ISBN 0-393-01824-5

ISBN 0-393-95359-9 (pbk.)

W. W. Norton & Company, Inc.,
500 Fifth Avenue, New York, N.Y. 10110
W. W. Norton & Company Ltd.,
37 Great Russell Street, London WC1B 3NU

4 5 6 7 8 9 0

PERMISSIONS

Jacques Barzun: "James the Melodramatist," *Kenyon Review*, 5 (Autumn 1943), 508–515, 517–521. Reprinted in *The Energies of Art: Studies of Authors Classic and Modern* (New York: Harper & Brothers, Publishers), 227–244. © 1956 by Jacques Barzun. Reprinted by permission of the author.

Wayne Booth: Reprinted from *The Rhetoric of Fiction*, pages 354–364 by Wayne C. Booth by permission of The University of Chicago Press. © 1961 by The University of Chicago.

Edwin H. Cady: From *The Light of Common Day: Realism in American Fiction*, 1971. © Edwin H. Cady. All rights reserved. Reprinted by permission of the author.

Clifton Fadiman: From *The Short Stories of Henry James* selected and edited by Clifton Fadiman. Copyright 1945 by Random House, Inc. Reprinted by permission of the publisher.

David Daiches: Portion of "Sensibility and Technique" by David Daiches, *The Kenyon Review*, Volume V No. 4, Autumn, 1943. Copyright 1943 by Kenyon College. Reprinted by permission of the author and *The Kenyon Review*.

Leon Edel: "Henry James: The Americano-European Legend" reprinted by permission of the author and University of Toronto Press.

Henry James: "The Jolly Corner," in *The Novels and Tales of Henry James*, New York Edition. Copyright 1909 Charles Scribner's Sons; copyright renewed 1937 Henry James. Reprinted with the permission of Charles Scribner's Sons. Prefaces to *The Middle Years*, "The Beast in the Jungle," "The Jolly Corner," *Daisy Miller*, "Brooksmith," "The Real Thing," from *The Novels and Tales of Henry James*, New York Edition. Copyright 1909 Charles Scribner's Sons; copyright renewed 1937 Henry James. Reprinted with the permission of Charles Scribner's Sons. From *The Notebooks of Henry James*, edited by F. O. Matthiessen and Kenneth B. Murdock. Copyright 1947 by Oxford University Press, Inc. renewed 1974 by Kenneth B. Murdock and Mrs. Peters Putnam. Reprinted by permission. Two letters, "To Eliza Lynn Linton" and "To Mrs. F. H. Hill" from *The Selected Letters of Henry James*, cited by Leon Edel. Copyright 1955 by Leon Edel. Reprinted by permission of Farrar, Straus and Giroux, Inc., and William Morris Agency, Inc., on behalf of Leon Edel.

Mildred Hartsock: "Unweeded Garden: A View of *The Aspern Papers*," from *Studies in Short Fiction*, 5 (1967), 60–68. Reprinted by permission of the editor. From "Henry James and the Cities of the Plain," from *Modern Language Quarterly*, 29 (1968), 298, 299, 305–6, copyright 1968 by the University of Washington. Reprinted by permission of the Estate of Mildred Hartsock and *Modern Language Quarterly*.

Earle Labor: "James's 'The Real Thing': Three Levels of Meaning," *College English*, 23 (February 1962), 376–378. Reprinted by permission of the National Council of Teachers of English.

Carol Ohmann: From "Daisy Miller: A Study of Changing Intentions" by Carol Ohmann, *American Literature*, 1964, 36, 1–11. Copyright © 1964, Duke University Press (Durham, North Carolina). Reprinted by permission of Duke University Press.

Katherine Anne Porter: "The Days Before" excerpted from the book *The Collected Essays and Occasional Writings of Katherine Anne Porter*. Copyright © 1943 by Katherine Anne Porter. Originally published in Kenyon Review. Reprinted by permission of DELACORTE PRESS/SEYMOUR LAWRENCE and Isabel Bayley, Literary Trustee for Katherine Anne Porter.

Philip Rahv: "Daisy Miller" commentary by Philip Rahv from *The Great Short Novels of Henry James*, copyright 1944 by The Dial Press, Inc. Reprinted by permission of Doubleday & Company, Inc.

Krishna Baldev Vaid: Reprinted by permission of the publishers from *Technique in the Tales of Henry James*, by Krishna Baldev Vaid, Cambridge, Massachusetts: Harvard University Press, Copyright © 1964 by the President and Fellows of Harvard College.

Christof Wegelin: From Christof Wegelin, *The Image of Europe in Henry James*, © 1958, SMU Press. Reprinted by permission of the Southern Methodist University Press.

Contents

Preface   ix

The Texts of the Stories
  Daisy Miller: A Study (1878)   3
  An International Episode (1878)   51
  The Aspern Papers (1888)   112
  The Pupil (1891)   188
  Brooksmith (1891)   225
  The Real Thing (1892)   239
  The Middle Years (1893)   260
  The Beast in the Jungle (1903)   277
  The Jolly Corner (1908)   313

The Author on His Craft
  Editor's Commentary   343
  Henry James • The Art of Fiction   345
  Henry James • From His Notebooks
    [On the origin of "Brooksmith"]   362
    [On the origin of "The Aspern Papers"]   363
    [On the origin of "The Real Thing"]   364
    [On the origin of "The Middle Years"]   366
    [On the origin of "The Beast in the Jungle"]   367
    [Regarding "The Jolly Corner" in retrospect]   368
  Henry James • From His Prefaces
    [On "Daisy Miller"]   368
    [On "The Aspern Papers"]   371
    [On "The Pupil"]   376
    [On "Brooksmith" and "The Real Thing"]   379
    [On "The Middle Years"]   380
    [On "The Beast in the Jungle"]   381
    [On "The Jolly Corner"]   383
  Henry James • From His Letters
    To Eliza Lynn Linton (ca. August 1880)   383
    To Mrs. F. H. Hill (March 21, 1879)   385

Background

Katherine Anne Porter • The Days Before   391
Leon Edel • Henry James: The Americano-European
        Legend   405

Criticism

David Daiches • Sensibility and Technique (Preface to a
        Critique)   419
Jacques Barzun • James the Melodramatist   424
F. O. Matthiessen and Kenneth B. Murdock • [How
        His Ideas Came to Him]   433
Christof Wegelin • Revision and Style   435
Philip Rahv • Daisy Miller   442
Carol Ohmann • Daisy Miller: A Study of Changing
        Intentions   443
Christof Wegelin • [An International Episode]   452
Wayne C. Booth • "The Purloining of the Aspern Papers"
        or "The Evocation of Venice"?   455
Mildred Hartsock • Unweeded Garden: A View of
        The Aspern Papers   463
Mildred Hartsock • [The Pupil]   470
Earle Labor • James's "The Real Thing": Three Levels of
        Meaning   472
Krishna Baldev Vaid • The Beast in the Jungle   475
Edwin H. Cady • [The Beast in the Jungle]   481
Krishna Baldev Vaid • The Jolly Corner   484

Selected Bibliography   489

Preface

Henry James published his first story in 1864 and in the half-century that followed produced twenty novels and a hundred and twelve shorter narratives which he usually called tales. Although probably best known for his novels, he took his shorter works just as seriously: when he came to represent his life's work in the so-called New York Edition he called it *The Novels and Tales of Henry James.* Some of the novels are short and some of the tales very long, so that the distinction between them may seem arbitrary. Of course length is not the only difference between novels and what today we call short stories. But publishing conditions forced James to be concerned with questions of length, and the nine tales in the present collection illustrate his range in this regard. "Brooksmith," with barely eight thousand words, is one of James's shortest tales; "The Aspern Papers," with almost forty thousand, approaches novel length. The nine tales also exemplify other formal variations. They are told from different points of view, for instance, in the first or third person, by narrators either detached from the action or participating in it to varying degrees. Some of James's favorite subjects and themes are here—the international scene, problems encountered by writers and artists, the human being haunted by visible and invisible ghosts, the exposure of children in the adult world, tyranny in its many guises, among them the willingness to make use of others, which is the closest approach Jamesian characters make to villainy.

The nine stories span most of James's long career. They are reproduced here as they first appeared in books (all but one originally appeared in magazines) and presumably as proofread by the author himself. The texts here presented therefore illustrate the development of his prose style. Occasional inconsistencies in spelling, e.g., *dependant* in "The Middle Years" and *dependent* in "The Beast in the Jungle," have been left standing. But rare typographical errors have been corrected silently, quotation marks have been brought into consistent accord with American usage—double instead of single— and the occasional and now strange printing of contractions—e.g., "had n't" for "hadn't" or "did n't" for "didn't"—normalized.

James was also a practicing critic throughout his career, and his essay "The Art of Fiction" is here offered as an early statement of principles which he never abandoned. Although the essay speaks of novelists and novels, it concerns fiction in general, including short forms. Problems of length and other technical problems of short fiction are discussed in the prefaces which James wrote much later for the New York Edition. There he often "remounts the stream of time" or "the stream of composition" to recall the source of a particular story, the *donnée* or "germ" from which it evolved, and sometimes the thought processes by which it did so. Most of the passages in the prefaces which bear on the tales in this collection, as well as pertinent passages from James's notebooks and letters, are included in the section entitled "The Author on His Craft."

James continues to receive more critical attention than most other American authors. Some general essays on his background and his work, as well as essays on individual stories, are here reproduced. In selecting them my aim has been to enlarge and sharpen the reader's sense of James's mind and artistry. Choosing a few pages out of the enormous mass available has made painful decisions necessary, and readers dismayed by omissions must draw what comfort they can from the editor's fellowship.

The staffs of the University of Oregon Library, of the Department of Rare Books and Special Collections of the Princeton University Library, and of the University of Oregon English Department have been helpful in many ways. Substantial assistance and advice has come from colleagues and students, among them above all Heather Derby, E. G. Moll, Jeffrey Porter, A. K. Weatherhead, and Oliver Willard, and from W. W. Norton's own Barry Wade. To all of them thanks.

C. W.

The Texts of
The Stories

Daisy Miller: A Study

(1878)†

I

At the little town of Vevey, in Switzerland, there is a particularly comfortable hotel. There are, indeed, many hotels; for the entertainment of tourists is the business of the place, which, as many travellers will remember, is seated upon the edge of a remarkably blue lake[1]—a lake that it behoves every tourist to visit. The shore of the lake presents an unbroken array of establishments of this order, of every category, from the "grand hotel" of the newest fashion, with a chalk-white front, a hundred balconies, and a dozen flags flying from its roof, to the little Swiss *pension* of an elder day, with its name inscribed in German-looking lettering upon a pink or yellow wall, and an awkward summer-house in the angle of the garden. One of the hotels at Vevey, however, is famous, even classical, being distinguished from many of its upstart neighbours by an air both of luxury and of maturity. In this region, in the month of June, American travellers are extremely numerous; it may be said, indeed, that Vevey assumes at this period some of the characteristics of an American watering-place. There are sights and sounds which evoke a vision, an echo, of Newport and Saratoga.[2] There is a flitting hither and thither of "stylish" young girls, a rustling of muslin flounces, a rattle of dance-music in the morning hours, a sound of high-pitched voices at all times. You receive an impression of these things at the excellent inn of the "Trois Couronnes,"[3] and are transported in fancy to the Ocean House or to Congress Hall. But at the "Trois Couronnes," it must be added, there are other features that are much at variance with these suggestions: neat German waiters, who look like secretaries of legation; Russian princesses sitting in the garden; little Polish boys walking about, held by the hand, with their governors; a view of the snowy crest of the Dent du Midi and the picturesque towers of the Castle of Chillon.[4]

I hardly know whether it was the analogies or the differences that

†"Daisy Miller: A Study" first appeared in the *Cornhill Magazine* of June and July 1878. Its first appearance in a book was in America in Harper's Half-Hour Series as volume I of *Daisy Miller: A Study/An International Episode/Four Meetings*, published in November 1878. James was in England at the time and did not supervise this edition. The text reprinted here follows the first English Edition published under the same title by Macmillan and Co. in February 1879.

1. Lake Geneva.

2. Newport, Rhode Island, and Saratoga Springs, New York, were resorts.
3. "Three Crowns." The Ocean House and Congress Hall were hotels in Newport and Saratoga, respectively.
4. A medieval castle built on a small rocky island in Lake Geneva, made famous among English speakers by Byron's poem "The Prisoner of Chillon" (1816). The Dent du Midi is a mountain south of Vevey (hence its name: "tooth of the south").

were uppermost in the mind of a young American, who, two or three years ago, sat in the garden of the "Trois Couronnes," looking about him, rather idly, at some of the graceful objects I have mentioned. It was a beautiful summer morning, and in whatever fashion the young American looked at things, they must have seemed to him charming. He had come from Geneva the day before, by the little steamer, to see his aunt, who was staying at the hotel—Geneva having been for a long time his place of residence. But his aunt had a headache—his aunt had almost always a headache—and now she was shut up in her room, smelling camphor, so that he was at liberty to wander about. He was some seven-and-twenty years of age; when his friends spoke of him, they usually said that he was at Geneva, "studying." When his enemies spoke of him they said—but, after all, he had no enemies; he was an extremely amiable fellow, and universally liked. What I should say is, simply, that when certain persons spoke of him they affirmed that the reason of his spending so much time at Geneva was that he was extremely devoted to a lady who lived there—a foreign lady—a person older than himself. Very few Americans—indeed I think none—had ever seen this lady, about whom there were some singular stories. But Winterbourne had an old attachment for the little metropolis of Calvinism;[5] he had been put to school there as a boy, and he had afterwards gone to college there—circumstances which had led to his forming a great many youthful friendships. Many of these he had kept, and they were a source of great satisfaction to him.

After knocking at his aunt's door and learning that she was indisposed, he had taken a walk about the town, and then he had come in to his breakfast. He had now finished his breakfast; but he was drinking a small cup of coffee, which had been served to him on a little table in the garden by one of the waiters who looked like an *attaché*. At last he finished his coffee and lit a cigarette. Presently a small boy came walking along the path—an urchin of nine or ten. The child, who was diminutive for his years, had an aged expression of countenance, a pale complexion, and sharp little features. He was dressed in knickerbockers, with red stockings, which displayed his poor little spindleshanks; he also wore a brilliant red cravat. He carried in his hand a long alpenstock, the sharp point of which he thrust into everything that he approached—the flower-beds, the garden-benches, the trains of the ladies' dresses. In front of Winterbourne he paused, looking at him with a pair of bright, penetrating little eyes.

"Will you give me a lump of sugar?" he asked, in a sharp, hard little voice—a voice immature, and yet, somehow, not young.

Winterbourne glanced at the small table near him, on which his coffee-service rested, and saw that several morsels of sugar remained.

5. Geneva, where the French reformer Jean Calvin (1509–64), the founder of the theologi- cal system of Calvinism, organized a Protestant republic.

"Yes, you may take one," he answered; "but I don't think sugar is good for little boys."

This little boy stepped forward and carefully selected three of the coveted fragments, two of which he buried in the pocket of his knickerbockers, depositing the other as promptly in another place. He poked his alpenstock, lance-fashion, into Winterbourne's bench, and tried to crack the lump of sugar with his teeth.

"Oh, blazes; it's har-r-d!" he exclaimed, pronouncing the adjective in a peculiar manner.

Winterbourne had immediately perceived that he might have the honour of claiming him as a fellow-countryman. "Take care you don't hurt your teeth," he said, paternally.

"I haven't got any teeth to hurt. They have all come out. I have only got seven teeth. My mother counted them last night, and one came out right afterwards. She said she'd slap me if any more came out. I can't help it. It's this old Europe. It's the climate that makes them come out. In America they didn't come out. It's these hotels."

Winterbourne was much amused. "If you eat three lumps of sugar, your mother will certainly slap you," he said.

"She's got to give me some candy, then," rejoined his young interlocutor. "I can't get any candy here—any American candy. American candy's the best candy."

"And are American little boys the best little boys?" asked Winterbourne.

"I don't know. I'm an American boy," said the child.

"I see you are one of the best!" laughed Winterbourne.

"Are you an American man?" pursued this vivacious infant. And then, on Winterbourne's affirmative reply—"American men are the best," he declared.

His companion thanked him for the compliment; and the child, who had now got astride of his alpenstock, stood looking about him, while he attacked a second lump of sugar. Winterbourne wondered if he himself had been like this in his infancy, for he had been brought to Europe at about this age.

"Here comes my sister!" cried the child, in a moment. "She's an American girl."

Winterbourne looked along the path and saw a beautiful young lady advancing. "American girls are the best girls," he said, cheerfully, to his young companion.

"My sister ain't the best!" the child declared. "She's always blowing at me."

"I imagine that is your fault, not hers," said Winterbourne. The young lady meanwhile had drawn near. She was dressed in white muslin, with a hundred frills and flounces, and knots of pale-coloured ribbon. She was bare-headed; but she balanced in her hand a large parasol, with a deep border of embroidery; and she was strikingly, admirably pretty. "How pretty they are!" thought Winterbourne, straightening himself in his seat, as if he were prepared to rise.

The young lady paused in front of his bench, near the parapet of the garden, which overlooked the lake. The little boy had now converted his alpenstock into a vaulting-pole, by the aid of which he was springing about in the gravel, and kicking it up not a little.

"Randolph," said the young lady, "what *are* you doing?"

"I'm going up the Alps," replied Randolph. "This is the way!" And he gave another little jump, scattering the pebbles about Winterbourne's ears.

"That's the way they come down," said Winterbourne.

"He's an American man!" cried Randolph, in his little hard voice.

The young lady gave no heed to this announcement, but looked straight at her brother. "Well, I guess you had better be quiet," she simply observed.

It seemed to Winterbourne that he had been in a manner presented. He got up and stepped slowly towards the young girl, throwing away his cigarette. "This little boy and I have made acquaintance," he said, with great civility. In Geneva, as he had been perfectly aware, a young man was not at liberty to speak to a young unmarried lady except under certain rarely-occurring conditions; but here at Vevey, what conditions could be better than these?—a pretty American girl coming and standing in front of you in a garden. This pretty American girl, however, on hearing Winterbourne's observation, simply glanced at him; she then turned her head and looked over the parapet, at the lake and the opposite mountains. He wondered whether he had gone too far; but he decided that he must advance farther, rather than retreat. While he was thinking of something else to say, the young lady turned to the little boy again.

"I should like to know where you got that pole," she said.

"I bought it!" responded Randolph.

"You don't mean to say you're going to take it to Italy."

"Yes, I am going to take it to Italy!" the child declared.

The young girl glanced over the front of her dress, and smoothed out a knot or two of ribbon. Then she rested her eyes upon the prospect again. "Well, I guess you had better leave it somewhere," she said, after a moment.

"Are you going to Italy?" Winterbourne inquired, in a tone of great respect.

The young lady glanced at him again.

"Yes, sir," she replied. And she said nothing more.

"Are you—a—going over the Simplon?" Winterbourne pursued, a little embarrassed.

"I don't know," she said. "I suppose it's some mountain. Randolph, what mountain are we going over?"

"Going where?" the child demanded.

"To Italy," Winterbourne explained.

"I don't know," said Randolph. "I don't want to go to Italy. I want to go to America."

"Oh, Italy is a beautiful place!" rejoined the young man.

"Can you get candy there?" Randolph loudly inquired.

"I hope not," said his sister. "I guess you have had enough candy, and mother thinks so too."

"I haven't had any for ever so long—for a hundred weeks!" cried the boy, still jumping about.

The young lady inspected her flounces and smoothed her ribbons again; and Winterbourne presently risked an observation upon the beauty of the view. He was ceasing to be embarrassed, for he had begun to perceive that she was not in the least embarrassed herself. There had not been the slightest alteration in her charming complexion; she was evidently neither offended nor fluttered. If she looked another way when he spoke to her, and seemed not particularly to hear him, this was simply her habit, her manner. Yet, as he talked a little more, and pointed out some of the objects of interest in the view, with which she appeared quite unacquainted, she gradually gave him more of the benefit of her glance; and then he saw that this glance was perfectly direct and unshrinking. It was not, however, what would have been called an immodest glance, for the young girl's eyes were singularly honest and fresh. They were wonderfully pretty eyes; and, indeed, Winterbourne had not seen for a long time anything prettier than his fair countrywoman's various features—her complexion, her nose, her ears, her teeth. He had a great relish for feminine beauty; he was addicted to observing and analysing it; and as regards this young lady's face he made several observations. It was not at all insipid, but it was not exactly expressive; and though it was eminently delicate Winterbourne mentally accused it—very forgivingly—of a want of finish. He thought it very possible that Master Randolph's sister was a coquette; he was sure she had a spirit of her own; but in her bright, sweet, superficial little visage there was no mockery, no irony. Before long it became obvious that she was much disposed towards conversation. She told him that they were going to Rome for the winter—she and her mother and Randolph. She ask him if he was a "real American"; she wouldn't have taken him for one; he seemed more like a German—this was said after a little hesitation, especially when he spoke. Winterbourne, laughing, answered that he had met Germans who spoke like Americans; but that he had not, so far as he remembered, met an American who spoke like a German. Then he asked her if she would not be more comfortable in sitting upon the bench which he had just quitted. She answered that she liked standing up and walking about; but she presently sat down. She told him she was from New York State—"if you know where that is." Winterbourne learned more about her by catching hold of her small, slippery brother and making him stand a few minutes by his side.

"Tell me your name, my boy," he said.

"Randolph C. Miller," said the boy, sharply. "And I'll tell you her name"; and he levelled his alpenstock at his sister.

"You had better wait till you are asked!" said this young lady, calmly.

"I should like very much to know your name," said Winterbourne.

"Her name is Daisy Miller!" cried the child. "But that isn't her real name; that isn't her name on her cards."

"It's a pity you haven't got one of my cards!" said Miss Miller.

"Her real name is Annie P. Miller," the boy went on.

"Ask him *his* name," said his sister, indicating Winterbourne.

But on this point Randolph seemed perfectly indifferent; he continued to supply information with regard to his own family. "My father's name is Ezra B. Miller," he announced. "My father ain't in Europe; my father's in a better place than Europe."

Winterbourne imagined for a moment that this was the manner in which the child had been taught to intimate that Mr. Miller had been removed to the sphere of celestial rewards. But Randolph immediately added, "My father's in Schenectady. He's got a big business. My father's rich, you bet."

"Well!" ejaculated Miss Miller, lowering her parasol and looking at the embroidered border. Winterbourne presently released the child, who departed, dragging his alpenstock along the path. "He doesn't like Europe," said the young girl. "He wants to go back."

"To Schenectady, you mean?"

"Yes; he wants to go right home. He hasn't got any boys here. There is one boy here, but he always goes round with a teacher; they won't let him play."

"And your brother hasn't any teacher?" Winterbourne inquired.

"Mother thought of getting him one, to travel round with us. There was a lady told her of a very good teacher; an American lady—perhaps you know her—Mrs. Sanders. I think she came from Boston. She told her of this teacher, and we thought of getting him to travel round with us. But Randolph said he didn't want a teacher travelling round with us. He said he wouldn't have lessons when he was in the cars. And we *are* in the cars about half the time. There was an English lady we met in the cars[6]—I think her name was Miss Featherstone; perhaps you

6. Railroad cars.

know her. She wanted to know why I didn't give Randolph lessons—give him "instruction," she called it. I guess he could give me more instruction than I could give him. He's very smart."

"Yes," said Winterbourne; "he seems very smart."

"Mother's going to get a teacher for him as soon as we get to Italy. Can you get good teachers in Italy?"

"Very good, I should think," said Winterbourne.

"Or else she's going to find some school. He ought to learn some more. He's only nine. He's going to college." And in this way Miss Miller continued to converse upon the affairs of her family, and upon other topics. She sat there with her extremely pretty hands, ornamented with very brilliant rings, folded in her lap, and with her pretty eyes now resting upon those of Winterbourne, now wandering over the garden, the people who passed by, and the beautiful view. She talked to Winterbourne as if she had known him a long time. He found it very pleasant. It was many years since he had heard a young girl talk so much. It might have been said of this unknown young lady, who had come and sat down beside him upon a bench, that she chattered. She was very quiet, she sat in a charming tranquil attitude; but her lips and her eyes were constantly moving. She had a soft, slender, agreeable voice, and her tone was decidedly sociable. She gave Winterbourne a history of her movements and intentions, and those of her mother and brother, in Europe, and enumerated, in particular, the various hotels at which they had stopped. "That English lady in the cars," she said—"Miss Featherstone—asked me if we didn't all live in hotels in America. I told her I had never been in so many hotels in my life as since I came to Europe. I have never seen so many—it's nothing but hotels." But Miss Miller did not make this remark with a querulous accent; she appeared to be in the best humour with everything. She declared that the hotels were very good, when once you got used to their ways, and that Europe was perfectly sweet. She was not disappointed—not a bit. Perhaps it was because she had heard so much about it before. She had ever so many intimate friends that had been there ever so many times. And then she had had ever so many dresses and things from Paris. Whenever she put on a Paris dress she felt as if she were in Europe.

"It was a kind of a wishing-cap," said Winterbourne.

"Yes," said Miss Miller, without examining this analogy; "it always made me wish I was here. But I needn't have done that for dresses. I am sure they send all the pretty ones to America; you see the most frightful things here. The only thing I don't like," she proceeded, "is the society. There isn't any society; or, if there is, I don't know where it keeps itself. Do you? I suppose there is some society somewhere, but I haven't seen anything of it. I'm very fond of society, and I have always had a great deal of it. I don't mean only in Schenectady, but in New

York. I used to go to New York every winter. In New York I had lots of society. Last winter I had seventeen dinners given me; and three of them were by gentlemen," added Daisy Miller. "I have more friends in New York than in Schenectady—more gentlemen friends; and more young lady friends too," she resumed in a moment. She paused again for an instant; she was looking at Winterbourne with all her prettiness in her lively eyes and in her light, slightly monotonous smile. "I have always had," she said, "a great deal of gentlemen's society."

Poor Winterbourne was amused, perplexed, and decidedly charmed. He had never yet heard a young girl express herself in just this fashion; never, at least, save in cases where to say such things seemed a kind of demonstrative evidence of a certain laxity of deportment. And yet was he to accuse Miss Daisy Miller of actual or potential *inconduite*, [7] as they said at Geneva? He felt that he had lived at Geneva so long that he had lost a good deal; he had become dishabituated to the American tone. Never, indeed, since he had grown old enough to appreciate things, had he encountered a young American girl of so pronounced a type as this. Certainly she was very charming; but how deucedly sociable! Was she simply a pretty girl from New York State—were they all like that, the pretty girls who had a good deal of gentlemen's society? Or was she also a designing, an audacious, an unscrupulous young person? Winterbourne had lost his instinct in this matter, and his reason could not help him. Miss Daisy Miller looked extremely innocent. Some people had told him that, after all, American girls were exceedingly innocent; and others had told him that, after all, they were not. He was inclined to think Miss Daisy Miller was a flirt—a pretty American flirt. He had never, as yet, had any relations with young ladies of this category. He had known, here in Europe, two or three women—persons older than Miss Daisy Miller, and provided, for respectability's sake, with husbands—who were great coquettes—dangerous, terrible women, with whom one's relations were liable to take a serious turn. But this young girl was not a coquette in that sense; she was very unsophisticated; she was only a pretty American flirt. Winterbourne was almost grateful for having found the formula that applied to Miss Daisy Miller. He leaned back in his seat; he remarked to himself that she had the most charming nose he had ever seen; he wondered what were the regular conditions and limitations of one's intercourse with a pretty American flirt. It presently became apparent that he was on the way to learn.

"Have you been to that old castle?" asked the young girl, pointing with her parasol to the far-gleaming walls of the Château de Chillon.

7. Misconduct.

"Yes, formerly, more than once," said Winterbourne. "You too, I suppose, have seen it?"

"No; we haven't been there. I want to go there dreadfully. Of course I mean to go there. I wouldn't go away from here without having seen that old castle."

"It's a very pretty excursion," said Winterbourne, "and very easy to make. You can drive, you know, or you can go by the little steamer."

"You can go in the cars," said Miss Miller.

"Yes; you can go in the cars," Winterbourne assented.

"Our courier[8] says they take you right up to the castle," the young girl continued. "We were going last week; but my mother gave out. She suffers dreadfully from dyspepsia. She said she couldn't go. Randolph wouldn't go either; he says he doesn't think much of old castles. But I guess we'll go this week, if we can get Randolph."

"Your brother is not interested in ancient monuments?" Winterbourne inquired, smiling.

"He says he don't care much about old castles. He's only nine. He wants to stay at the hotel. Mother's afraid to leave him alone, and the courier won't stay with him; so we haven't been to many places. But it will be too bad if we don't go up there." And Miss Miller pointed again at the Château de Chillon.

"I should think it might be arranged," said Winterbourne. "Couldn't you get some one to stay—for the afternoon—with Randolph?"

Miss Miller looked at him a moment; and then, very placidly—"I wish *you* would stay with him!" she said.

Winterbourne hesitated a moment. "I would much rather go to Chillon with you."

"With me?" asked the young girl, with the same placidity.

She didn't rise, blushing, as a young girl at Geneva would have done; and yet Winterbourne, conscious that he had been very bold, thought it possible she was offended. "With your mother," he answered very respectfully.

But it seemed that both his audacity and his respect were lost upon Miss Daisy Miller. "I guess my mother won't go, after all," she said. "She don't like to ride round in the afternoon. But did you really mean what you said just now; that you would like to go up there?"

"Most earnestly," Winterbourne declared.

"Then we may arrange it. If mother will stay with Randolph, I guess Eugenio will."

"Eugenio?" the young man inquired.

"Eugenio's our courier. He doesn't like to stay with Randolph; he's

8. Man hired to take charge of travel arrangements.

the most fastidious man I ever saw. But he's a splendid courier. I guess he'll stay at home with Randolph if mother does, and then we can go to the castle."

Winterbourne reflected for an instant as lucidly as possible—"we" could only mean Miss Daisy Miller and himself. This programme seemed almost too agreeable for credence; he felt as if he ought to kiss the young lady's hand. Possibly he would have done so—and quite spoiled the project; but at this moment another person—presumably Eugenio—appeared. A tall, handsome man, with superb whiskers, wearing a velvet morning-coat and a brilliant watch-chain, approached Miss Miller, looking sharply at her companion. "Oh, Eugenio!" said Miss Miller, with the friendliest accent.

Eugenio had looked at Winterbourne from head to foot; he now bowed gravely to the young lady. "I have the honour to inform mademoiselle that luncheon is upon the table."

Miss Miller slowly rose. "See here, Eugenio," she said. "I'm going to that old castle, any way."

"To the Château de Chillon, mademoiselle?" the courier inquired. "Mademoiselle has made arrangements?" he added, in a tone which struck Winterbourne as very impertinent.

Eugenio's tone apparently threw, even to Miss Miller's own apprehension, a slightly ironical light upon the young girl's situation. She turned to Winterbourne, blushing a little—a very little. "You won't back out?" she said.

"I shall not be happy till we go!" he protested.

"And you are staying in this hotel?" she went on. "And you are really an American?"

The courier stood looking at Winterbourne, offensively. The young man, at least, thought his manner of looking an offence to Miss Miller; it conveyed an imputation that she "picked up" acquaintances. "I shall have the honour of presenting to you a person who will tell you all about me," he said smiling, and referring to his aunt.

"Oh, well, we'll go some day," said Miss Miller. And she gave him a smile and turned away. She put up her parasol and walked back to the inn beside Eugenio. Winterbourne stood looking after her; and as she moved away, drawing her muslin furbelows over the gravel, said to himself that she had the *tournure*[9] of a princess.

II

He had, however, engaged to do more than proved feasible, in promising to present his aunt, Mrs. Costello, to Miss Daisy Miller. As soon as the former lady had got better of her headache he waited upon her in her apartment; and, after the proper inquiries in regard to her

9. Figure, looks.

health, he asked her if she had observed, in the hotel, an American family—a mamma, a daughter, and a little boy.

"And a courier?" said Mrs. Costello. "Oh, yes, I have observed them. Seen them—heard them—and kept out of their way." Mrs. Costello was a widow with a fortune; a person of much distinction, who frequently intimated that, if she were not so dreadfully liable to sick-headaches, she would probably have left a deeper impress upon her time. She had a long pale face, a high nose, and a great deal of very striking white hair, which she wore in large puffs and *rouleaux*[1] over the top of her head. She had two sons married in New York, and another who was now in Europe. This young man was amusing himself at Homburg,[2] and, though he was on his travels, was rarely perceived to visit any particular city at the moment selected by his mother for her own appearance there. Her nephew, who had come up to Vevey expressly to see her, was therefore more attentive than those who, as she said, were nearer to her. He had imbibed at Geneva the idea that one must always be attentive to one's aunt. Mrs. Costello had not seen him for many years, and she was greatly pleased with him, manifesting her approbation by initiating him into many of the secrets of that social sway which, as she gave him to understand, she exerted in the American capital.[3] She admitted that she was very exclusive; but, if he were acquainted with New York, he would see that one had to be. And her picture of the minutely hierarchical constitution of the society of that city, which she presented to him in many different lights, was, to Winterbourne's imagination, almost oppressively striking.

He immediately perceived, from her tone, that Miss Daisy Miller's place in the social scale was low. "I am afraid you don't approve of them," he said.

"They are very common," Mrs. Costello declared. "They are the sort of Americans that one does one's duty by not—not accepting."

"Ah, you don't accept them?" said the young man.

"I can't, my dear Frederick. I would if I could, but I can't."

"The young girl is very pretty," said Winterbourne, in a moment.

"Of course she's pretty. But she is very common."

"I see what you mean, of course," said Winterbourne, after another pause.

"She has that charming look that they all have," his aunt resumed. "I can't think where they pick it up; and she dresses in perfection—no, you don't know how well she dresses. I can't think where they get their taste."

"But, my dear aunt, she is not, after all, a Comanche savage."

"She is a young lady," said Mrs. Costello, "who has an intimacy

1. Coils.
2. A German resort near Frankfurt am Main.
3. The social capital, i.e., New York.

with her mamma's courier?"

"An intimacy with the courier?" the young man demanded.

"Oh, the mother is just as bad! They treat the courier like a familiar friend—like a gentleman. I shouldn't wonder if he dines with them. Very likely they have never seen a man with such good manners, such fine clothes, so like a gentleman. He probably corresponds to the young lady's idea of a Count. He sits with them in the garden, in the evening. I think he smokes."

Winterbourne listened with interest to these disclosures; they helped him to make up his mind about Miss Daisy. Evidently she was rather wild. "Well," he said, "I am not a courier, and yet she was very charming to me."

"You had better have said at first," said Mrs. Costello with dignity, "that you had made her acquaintance."

"We simply met in the garden, and we talked a bit."

"*Tout bonnement!*[4] And pray what did you say?"

"I said I should take the liberty of introducing her to my admirable aunt."

"I am much obliged to you."

"It was to guarantee my respectability," said Winterbourne.

"And pray who is to guarantee hers?"

"Ah, you are cruel!" said the young man. "She's a very nice girl."

"You don't say that as if you believed it," Mrs. Costello observed.

"She is completely uncultivated," Winterbourne went on. "But she is wonderfully pretty, and, in short, she is very nice. To prove that I believe it, I am going to take her to the Château de Chillon."

"You two are going off there together? I should say it proved just the contrary. How long had you known her, may I ask, when this interesting project was formed? You haven't been twenty-four hours in the house."

"I had known her half-an-hour!" said Winterbourne, smiling.

"Dear me!" cried Mrs. Costello. "What a dreadful girl!"

Her nephew was silent for some moments.

"You really think, then," he began, earnestly, and with a desire for trustworthy information—"you really think that—" But he paused again.

"Think what, sir?" said his aunt.

"That she is the sort of young lady who expects a man—sooner or later—to carry her off?"

"I haven't the least idea what such young ladies expect a man to do. But I really think that you had better not meddle with little American girls that are uncultivated, as you call them. You have lived too long out of the country. You will be sure to make some great mistake. You

4. Quite simply. Just like that!

are too innocent."

"My dear aunt, I am not so innocent," said Winterbourne, smiling and curling his moustache.

"You are too guilty, then!"

Winterbourne continued to curl his moustache, meditatively. "You won't let the poor girl know you then?" he asked at last. "Is it literally true that she is going to the Château de Chillon with you?"

"I think that she fully intends it."

"Then, my dear Frederick," said Mrs. Costello, "I must decline the honour of her acquaintance. I am an old woman, but I am not too old—thank Heaven—to be shocked!"

"But don't they all do these things—the young girls in America?" Winterbourne inquired.

Mrs. Costello stared a moment. "I should like to see my granddaughters do them!" she declared, grimly.

This seemed to throw some light upon the matter, for Winterbourne remembered to have heard that his pretty cousins in New York were "tremendous flirts." If, therefore, Miss Daisy Miller exceeded the liberal license allowed to these young ladies, it was probable that anything might be expected of her. Winterbourne was impatient to see her again, and he was vexed with himself that, by instinct, he should not appreciate her justly.

Though he was impatient to see her, he hardly knew what he should say to her about his aunt's refusal to become acquainted with her; but he discovered, promptly enough, that with Miss Daisy Miller there was no great need of walking on tiptoe. He found her that evening in the garden, wandering about in the warm starlight, like an indolent sylph, and swinging to and fro the largest fan he had ever beheld. It was ten o'clock. He had dined with his aunt, had been sitting with her since dinner, and had just taken leave of her till the morrow. Miss Daisy Miller seemed very glad to see him; she declared it was the longest evening she had ever passed.

"Have you been all alone?" he asked.

"I have been walking round with mother. But mother gets tired walking round," she answered.

"Has she gone to bed?"

"No; she doesn't like to go to bed," said the young girl. "She doesn't sleep—not three hours. She says she doesn't know how she lives. She's dreadfully nervous. I guess she sleeps more than she thinks. She's gone somewhere after Randolph; she wants to try to get him to go to bed. He doesn't like to go to bed."

"Let us hope she will persuade him," observed Winterbourne.

"She will talk to him all she can; but he doesn't like her to talk to him," said Miss Daisy, opening her fan. "She's going to try to get

Eugenio to talk to him. But he isn't afraid of Eugenio. Eugenio's a splendid courier, but he can't make much impression on Randolph! I don't believe he'll go to bed before eleven." It appeared that Randolph's vigil was in fact triumphantly prolonged, for Winterbourne strolled about with the young girl for some time without meeting her mother. "I have been looking round for that lady you want to introduce me to," his companion resumed. "She's your aunt." Then, on Winterbourne's admitting the fact, and expressing some curiosity as to how she had learned it, she said she had heard all about Mrs. Costello from the chambermaid. She was very quiet and very *comme il faut*;[5] she wore white puffs; she spoke to no one, and she never dined at the *table d'hôte.*[6] Every two days she had a headache. "I think that's a lovely description, headache and all!" said Miss Daisy, chattering along in her thin, gay voice. "I want to know her ever so much. I know just what *your* aunt would be; I know I should like her. She would be very exclusive. I like a lady to be exclusive; I'm dying to be exclusive myself. Well, we *are* exclusive, mother and I. We don't speak to every one—or they don't speak to us. I suppose it's about the same thing. Any way, I shall be ever so glad to know your aunt."

Winterbourne was embarrassed. "She would be most happy," he said; "but I am afraid those headaches will interfere."

The young girl looked at him through the dusk. "But I suppose she doesn't have a headache every day," she said, sympathetically.

Winterbourne was silent a moment. "She tells me she does," he answered at last—not knowing what to say.

Miss Daisy Miller stopped and stood looking at him. Her prettiness was still visible in the darkness; she was opening and closing her enormous fan. "She doesn't want to know me!" she said, suddenly. "Why don't you say so? You needn't be afraid. I'm not afraid!" And she gave a little laugh.

Winterbourne fancied there was a tremor in her voice; he was touched, shocked, mortified by it. "My dear young lady," he protested, "she knows no one. It's her wretched health."

The young girl walked on a few steps, laughing still. "You needn't be afraid," she repeated. "Why should she want to know me?" Then she paused again; she was close to the parapet of the garden, and in front of her was the starlit lake. There was a vague sheen upon its surface, and in the distance were dimly-seen mountain forms. Daisy Miller looked out upon the mysterious prospect, and then she gave another little laugh. "Gracious! she *is* exclusive!" she said. Winterbourne wondered whether she was seriously wounded; and for a moment almost wished that her sense of injury might be such as to make it becoming in him to attempt to reassure and comfort her. He

5. Proper.
6. Meal of several courses eaten at a common table in the hotel dining room.

had a pleasant sense that she would be very approachable for consolatory purposes. He felt then, for the instant, quite ready to sacrifice his aunt, conversationally; to admit that she was a proud, rude woman, and to declare that they needn't mind her. But before he had time to commit himself to this perilous mixture of gallantry and impiety, the young lady, resuming her walk, gave an exclamation in quite another tone. "Well; here's mother! I guess she hasn't got Randolph to go to bed." The figure of a lady appeared, at a distance, very indistinct in the darkness, and advancing with a slow and wavering movement. Suddenly it seemed to pause.

"Are you sure it is your mother? Can you distinguish her in this thick dusk?" Winterbourne asked.

"Well!" cried Miss Daisy Miller, with a laugh, "I guess I know my own mother. And when she has got on my shawl, too! She is always wearing my things."

The lady in question, ceasing to advance, hovered vaguely about the spot at which she had checked her steps.

"I am afraid your mother doesn't see you," said Winterbourne. "Or perhaps," he added—thinking, with Miss Miller, the joke permissible—"perhaps she feels guilty about your shawl."

"Oh, it's a fearful old thing!" the young girl replied, serenely. "I told her she could wear it. She won't come here, because she sees you."

"Ah, then," said Winterbourne, "I had better leave you."

"Oh no; come on!" urged Miss Daisy Miller.

"I'm afraid your mother doesn't approve of my walking with you."

Miss Miller gave him a serious glance. "It isn't for me; it's for you—that is, it's for *her*. Well; I don't know who it's for! But mother doesn't like any of my gentlemen friends. She's right down timid. She always makes a fuss if I introduce a gentleman. But I *do* introduce them—almost always. If I didn't introduce my gentlemen friends to mother," the young girl added, in her little soft, flat monotone, "I shouldn't think I was natural."

"To introduce me," said Winterbourne, "you must know my name." And he proceeded to pronounce it.

"Oh, dear; I can't say all that!" said his companion, with a laugh. But by this time they had come up to Mrs. Miller, who, as they drew near, walked to the parapet of the garden and leaned upon it, looking intently at the lake and turning her back upon them. "Mother!" said the young girl, in a tone of decision. Upon this the elder lady turned round. "Mr. Winterbourne," said Miss Daisy Miller, introducing the young man very frankly and prettily. "Common" she was, as Mrs. Costello had pronounced her; yet it was a wonder to Winterbourne that, with her commonness, she had a singularly delicate grace.

Her mother was a small, spare, light person, with a wandering eye, a very exiguous nose, and a large forehead, decorated with a certain amount of thin, much-frizzled hair. Like her daughter, Mrs. Miller was dressed with extreme elegance; she had enormous diamonds in her ears. So far as Winterbourne could observe, she gave him no greeting—she certainly was not looking at him. Daisy was near her, pulling her shawl straight. "What are you doing, poking round here?" this young lady inquired; but by no means with that harshness of accent which her choice of words may imply.

"I don't know," said her mother, turning towards the lake again.

"I shouldn't think you'd want that shawl!" Daisy exclaimed.

"Well—I do!" her mother answered, with a little laugh.

"Did you get Randolph to go to bed?" asked the young girl.

"No; I couldn't induce him," said Mrs. Miller, very gently. "He wants to talk to the waiter. He likes to talk to that waiter."

"I was telling Mr. Winterbourne," the young girl went on; and to the young man's ear her tone might have indicated that she had been uttering his name all her life.

"Oh, yes!" said Winterbourne; "I have the pleasure of knowing your son."

Randolph's mamma was silent; she turned her attention to the lake. But at last she spoke. "Well, I don't see how he lives!"

"Anyhow, it isn't so bad as it was at Dover," said Daisy Miller.

"And what occurred at Dover?" Winterbourne asked.

"He wouldn't go to bed at all. I guess he sat up all night—in the public parlour. He wasn't in bed at twelve o'clock: I know that."

"It was half-past twelve," declared Mrs. Miller, with mild emphasis.

"Does he sleep much during the day?" Winterbourne demanded.

"I guess he doesn't sleep much," Daisy rejoined.

"I wish he would!" said her mother. "It seems as if he couldn't."

"I think he's real tiresome," Daisy pursued.

Then, for some moments, there was silence. "Well, Daisy Miller," said the elder lady, presently, "I shouldn't think you'd want to talk against your own brother!"

"Well, he *is* tiresome, mother," said Daisy, quite without the asperity of a retort.

"He's only nine," urged Mrs. Miller.

"Well, he wouldn't go to that castle," said the young girl. "I'm going there with Mr. Winterbourne."

To this announcement, very placidly made, Daisy's mamma offered no response. Winterbourne took for granted that she deeply disapproved of the projected excursion; but he said to himself that she was a simple, easily-managed person, and that a few deferential protestations would take the edge from her displeasure. "Yes," he began; "your daughter has kindly allowed me the honour of being her guide."

Mrs. Miller's wandering eyes attached themselves, with a sort of appealing air, to Daisy, who, however, strolled a few steps farther, gently humming to herself. "I presume you will go in the cars," said her mother.

"Yes; or in the boat," said Winterbourne.

"Well, of course, I don't know," Mrs. Miller rejoined. "I have never been to that castle."

"It is a pity you shouldn't go," said Winterbourne, beginning to feel reassured as to her opposition. And yet he was quite prepared to find that, as a matter of course, she meant to accompany her daughter.

"We've been thinking ever so much about going," she pursued; "but it seems as if we couldn't. Of course Daisy—she wants to go round. But there's a lady here—I don't know her name—she says she shouldn't think we'd want to go to see castles *here*; she should think we'd want to wait till we got to Italy. It seems as if there would be so many there," continued Mrs. Miller, with an air of increasing confidence. "Of course, we only want to see the principal ones. We visited several in England," she presently added.

"Ah, yes! in England there are beautiful castles," said Winterbourne. "But Chillon, here, is very well worth seeing."

"Well, if Daisy feels up to it—," said Mrs. Miller, in a tone impregnated with a sense of the magnitude of the enterprise. "It seems as if there was nothing she wouldn't undertake."

"Oh, I think she'll enjoy it!" Winterbourne declared. And he desired more and more to make it a certainty that he was to have the privilege of a *tête-à-tête* with the young lady, who was still strolling along in front of them, softly vocalising. "You are not disposed, madam," he inquired, "to undertake it yourself?"

Daisy's mother looked at him, an instant, askance, and then walked forward in silence. Then—"I guess she had better go alone," she said, simply.

Winterbourne observed to himself that this was a very different type of maternity from that of the vigilant matrons who massed themselves in the forefront of social intercourse in the dark old city at the other end of the lake. But his meditations were interrupted by hearing his name very distinctly pronounced by Mrs. Miller's unprotected daughter.

"Mr. Winterbourne!" murmured Daisy.

"Mademoiselle!" said the young man.

"Don't you want to take me out in a boat?"

"At present?" he asked.

"Of course!" said Daisy.

"Well, Annie Miller!" exclaimed her mother.

"I beg you, madam, to let her go," said Winterbourne, ardently; for he had never yet enjoyed the sensation of guiding through the summer starlight a skiff freighted with a fresh and beautiful young girl.

"I shouldn't think she'd want to," said her mother. "I should think she'd rather go indoors."

"I'm sure Mr. Winterbourne wants to take me," Daisy declared. "He's so awfully devoted!"

"I will row you over to Chillon, in the starlight."

"I don't believe it!" said Daisy.

"Well!" ejaculated the elderly lady again.

"You haven't spoken to me for half-an-hour," her daughter went on.

"I have been having some very pleasant conversation with your mother," said Winterbourne.

"Well; I want you to take me out in a boat!" Daisy repeated. They had all stopped, and she had turned round and was looking at Winterbourne. Her face wore a charming smile, her pretty eyes were gleaming, she was swinging her great fan about. No; it's impossible to be prettier than that, thought Winterbourne.

"There are half-a-dozen boats moored at that landing-place," he said, pointing to certain steps which descended from the garden to the lake. "If you will do me the honour to accept my arm, we will go and select one of them."

Daisy stood there smiling; she threw back her head and gave a little light laugh. "I like a gentleman to be formal!" she declared.

"I assure you it's a formal offer."

"I was bound I would make you say something," Daisy went on.

"You see it's not very difficult," said Winterbourne. "But I am afraid you are chaffing me."

"I think not, sir," remarked Mrs. Miller, very gently.

"Do, then, let me give you a row," he said to the young girl.

"It's quite lovely, the way you say that!" cried Daisy.

"It will be still more lovely to do it."

"Yes, it would be lovely!" said Daisy. But she made no movement to accompany him; she only stood there laughing.

"I should think you had better find out what time it is," interposed her mother.

"It is eleven o'clock, madam," said a voice, with a foreign accent, out of the neighbouring darkness; and Winterbourne, turning, perceived the florid personage who was in attendance upon the two ladies. He had apparently just approached.

"Oh, Eugenio," said Daisy, "I am going out in a boat!"

Eugenio bowed. "At eleven o'clock, mademoiselle?"

"I am going with Mr. Winterbourne. This very minute."

"Do tell her she can't," said Mrs. Miller to the courier.

"I think you had better not go out in a boat, mademoiselle," Eugenio declared.

Winterbourne wished to Heaven this pretty girl were not so familiar with her courier; but he said nothing.

"I suppose you don't think it's proper!" Daisy exclaimed. "Eugenio doesn't think anything's proper."

"I am at your service," said Winterbourne.

"Does mademoiselle propose to go alone?" asked Eugenio of Mrs. Miller.

"Oh, no; with this gentleman!" answered Daisy's mamma.

The courier looked for a moment at Winterbourne—the latter thought he was smiling—and then, solemnly, with a bow, "As mademoiselle pleases!" he said.

"Oh, I hoped you would make a fuss!" said Daisy. "I don't care to go now."

"I myself shall make a fuss if you don't go," said Winterbourne.

"That's all I want—a little fuss!" And the young girl began to laugh again.

"Mr. Randolph has gone to bed!" the courier announced, frigidly.

"Oh, Daisy; now we can go!" said Mrs. Miller.

Daisy turned away from Winterbourne, looking at him, smiling and fanning herself. "Good night," she said; "I hope you are disappointed, or disgusted, or something!"

He looked at her, taking the hand she offered him. "I am puzzled," he answered.

"Well; I hope it won't keep you awake!" she said, very smartly; and, under the escort of the privileged Eugenio, the two ladies passed towards the house.

Winterbourne stood looking after them; he was indeed puzzled. He lingered beside the lake for a quarter of an hour, turning over the mystery of the young girl's sudden familiarities and caprices. But the only very definite conclusion he came to was that he should enjoy deucedly "going off" with her somewhere.

Two days afterwards he went off with her to the Castle of Chillon. He waited for her in the large hall of the hotel, where the couriers, the servants, the foreign tourists were lounging about and staring. It was not the place he would have chosen, but she had appointed it. She came tripping downstairs, buttoning her long gloves, squeezing her folded parasol against her pretty figure, dressed in the perfection of a soberly elegant travelling-costume. Winterbourne was a man of imagination and, as our ancestors used to say, of sensibility; as he looked at her dress and, on the great staircase, her little rapid, confiding step, he felt as if there were something romantic going forward. He could have believed he was going to elope with her. He passed out with her among all the idle people that were assembled there; they were all looking at her very hard; she had begun to chatter as soon as she joined him. Winterbourne's preference had been that they should be conveyed to Chillon in a carriage; but she expressed a lively wish to go in the little steamer; she declared that she had a passion for steamboats. There was always such a lovely breeze upon the water, and you saw such lots of people. The sail was not long, but Winterbourne's companion found time to say a great many things. To the young man himself their little excursion was so much of an escapade—an adventure—that, even allowing for her habitual sense of freedom, he had some expectation of seeing her regard it in the same way. But it must be confessed that, in this particular, he was disappointed. Daisy Miller was extremely animated, she was in charming spirits; but she was apparently not at all excited; she was not fluttered; she avoided neither his eyes nor those of any one else; she blushed neither when she looked at him nor when she saw that people were looking at her. People continued to look at her a great deal, and Winterbourne took much satisfaction in his pretty companion's distinguished air. He had been a little afraid that she would talk loud, laugh overmuch, and even, perhaps, desire to move about the boat a good deal. But he quite forgot his fears; he sat smiling, with his eyes upon her face, while, without moving from her place, she delivered herself of a great number of original reflections. It was the most charming garrulity he had ever heard. He had assented to the idea that she was "common;" but was she so, after all, or was he simply getting used to her commonness? Her conversation was chiefly of what metaphysicians term the objective cast; but every now and then it took a subjective turn.

"What on *earth* are you so grave about?" she suddenly demanded, fixing her agreeable eyes upon Winterbourne's.

"Am I grave?" he asked. "I had an idea I was grinning from ear to ear."

"You look as if you were taking me to a funeral. If that's a grin, your ears are very near together."

"Should you like me to dance a hornpipe on the deck?"

"Pray do, and I'll carry round your hat. It will pay the expenses of our journey."

"I never was better pleased in my life," murmured Winterbourne.

She looked at him a moment, and then burst into a little laugh. "I like to make you say those things! You're a queer mixture!"

In the castle, after they had landed, the subjective element decidedly prevailed. Daisy tripped about the vaulted chambers, rustled her skirts in the corkscrew staircases, flirted back with a pretty little cry and a shudder from the edge of the *oubliettes*,[7] and turned a singularly well-shaped ear to everything Winterbourne told her about the place. But he saw that she cared very little for feudal antiquities, and that the dusky traditions of Chillon made but a slight impression upon her.

---

7. Secret dungeons with trapdoors at the top.

They had the good fortune to have been able to walk about without other companionship than that of the custodian; and Winterbourne arranged with this functionary that they should not be hurried—that they should linger and pause wherever they chose. The custodian interpreted the bargain generously—Winterbourne, on his side, had been generous—and ended by leaving them quite to themselves. Miss Miller's observations were not remarkable for logical consistency; for anything she wanted to say she was sure to find a pretext. She found a great many pretexts in the rugged embrasures of Chillon for asking Winterbourne sudden questions about himself—his family, his previous history, his tastes, his habits, his intentions—and for supplying information upon corresponding points in her own personality. Of her own tastes, habits and intentions Miss Miller was prepared to give the most definite, and indeed the most favourable, account.

"Well; I hope you know enough!" she said to her companion, after he had told her the history of the unhappy Bonivard.[8] "I never saw a man that knew so much!" The history of Bonivard had evidently, as they say, gone into one ear and out of the other. But Daisy went on to say that she wished Winterbourne would travel with them and "go round" with them; they might know something, in that case. "Don't you want to come and teach Randolph?" she asked. Winterbourne said that nothing could possibly please him so much; but that he had unfortunately other occupations. "Other occupations? I don't believe it!" said Miss Daisy. "What do you mean? You are not in business." The young man admitted that he was not in business; but he had engagements which, even within a day or two, would force him to go back to Geneva. "Oh, bother!" she said, "I don't believe it!" and she began to talk about something else. But a few moments later, when he was pointing out to her the pretty design of an antique fireplace, she broke out irrelevantly, "You don't mean to say you are going back to Geneva?"

"It is a melancholy fact that I shall have to return to Geneva to-morrow."

"Well, Mr. Winterbourne," said Daisy; "I think you're horrid!"

"Oh, don't say such dreadful things!" said Winterbourne—"just at the last."

"The last!" cried the young girl; "I call it the first. I have half a mind to leave you here and go straight back to the hotel alone." And for the next ten minutes she did nothing but call him horrid. Poor Winterbourne was fairly bewildered; no young lady had as yet done him the honour to be so agitated by the announcement of his movements. His companion, after this, ceased to pay any attention to the curiosities of Chillon or the beauties of the lake; she opened fire upon the mysteri-

8. Sixteenth-century prisoner in the Castle of Chillon and hero of Byron's poem. Inciden- tally, Byron scratched his own name into one of the stone pillars of the castle.

ous charmer in Geneva, whom she appeared to have instantly taken it for granted that he was hurrying back to see. How did Miss Daisy Miller know that there was a charmer in Geneva? Winterbourne, who denied the existence of such a person, was quite unable to discover; and he was divided between amazement at the rapidity of her induction and amusement at the frankness of her *persiflage*. She seemed to him, in all this, an extraordinary mixture of innocence and crudity. "Does she never allow you more than three days at a time?" asked Daisy, ironically. "Doesn't she give you a vacation in summer? There's no one so hard worked but they can get leave to go off somewhere at this season. I suppose, if you stay another day, she'll come after you in the boat. Do wait over till Friday, and I will go down to the landing to see her arrive!" Winterbourne began to think he had been wrong to feel disappointed in the temper in which the young lady had embarked. If he had missed the personal accent, the personal accent was now making its appearance. It sounded very distinctly, at last, in her telling him she would stop "teasing" him if he would promise her solemnly to come down to Rome in the winter.

"That's not a difficult promise to make," said Winterbourne. "My aunt has taken an apartment in Rome for the winter, and has already asked me to come and see her."

"I don't want you to come for your aunt," said Daisy; "I want you to come for me." And this was the only allusion that the young man was ever to hear her make to his invidious kinswoman. He declared that, at any rate, he would certainly come. After this Daisy stopped teasing. Winterbourne took a carriage, and they drove back to Vevey in the dusk; the young girl was very quiet.

In the evening Winterbourne mentioned to Mrs. Costello that he had spent the afternoon at Chillon, with Miss Daisy Miller.

"The Americans—of the courier?" asked this lady.

"Ah, happily," said Winterbourne, "the courier stayed at home."

"She went with you all alone?"

"All alone."

Mrs. Costello sniffed a little at her smelling-bottle. "And that," she exclaimed, "is the young person you wanted me to know!"

III

Winterbourne, who had returned to Geneva the day after his excursion to Chillon, went to Rome towards the end of January. His aunt had been established there for several weeks, and he had received a couple of letters from her. "Those people you were so devoted to last summer at Vevey have turned up here, courier and all," she wrote. "They seem to have made several acquaintances, but the courier continues to be the most *intime.*[9] The young lady, however, is also very intimate with some third-rate Italians, with whom she rackets about in a way that makes much talk. Bring me that pretty novel of Cherbuliez's—'Paule Méré'[1]—and don't come later than the 23rd."

In the natural course of events, Winterbourne, on arriving in Rome, would presently have ascertained Mrs. Miller's address at the American banker's and have gone to pay his compliments to Miss Daisy. "After what happened at Vevey I certainly think I may call upon them," he said to Mrs. Costello.

"If, after what happens—at Vevey and everywhere—you desire to keep up the acquaintance, you are very welcome. Of course a man may know every one. Men are welcome to the privilege!"

"Pray what is it that happens—here, for instance?" Winterbourne demanded.

"The girl goes about alone with her foreigners. As to what happens farther, you must apply elsewhere for information. She has picked up half-a-dozen of the regular Roman fortune-hunters, and she takes them about to people's houses. When she comes to a party she brings with her a gentleman with a good deal of manner and a wonderful moustache."

"And where is the mother?"

"I haven't the least idea. They are very dreadful people."

Winterbourne meditated a moment. "They are very ignorant—very innocent only. Depend upon it they are not bad."

"They are hopelessly vulgar," said Mrs. Costello. "Whether or no being hopelessly vulgar is being 'bad' is a question for the metaphysicians. They are bad enough to dislike, at any rate; and for this short life that is quite enough."

The news that Daisy Miller was surrounded by half-a-dozen wonderful moustaches checked Winterbourne's impulse to go straightway to see her. He had perhaps not definitely flattered himself that he had made an ineffaceable impression upon her heart, but he was annoyed at hearing of a state of affairs so little in harmony with an image that had lately flitted in and out of his own meditations; the image of a very pretty girl looking out of an old Roman window and asking herself urgently when Mr. Winterbourne would arrive. If, however, he determined to wait a little before reminding Miss Miller of his claims to her consideration, he went very soon to call upon two or three other friends. One of these friends was an American lady who had spent

9. Familiar, intimate.
1. Novel (published in 1865) by Victor Cherbuliez (1829–99) of Geneva. It deals with the love of a weak man for an exceptional woman and reflects the author's accumulated resentments of Genevan self-righteousness. James reviewed Cherbuliez's fiction favorably in *The North American Review*, October 1873. He mentions *Paule Méré* only briefly but refers to the heroine as "a delightfully tender conception" though perhaps "not absolutely natural."

several winters at Geneva, where she had placed her children at school. She was a very accomplished woman and she lived in the Via Gregoriana.[2] Winterbourne found her in a little crimson drawing-room, on a third floor; the room was filled with southern sunshine. He had not been there ten minutes when the servant came in, announcing "Madame Mila!" This announcement was presently followed by the entrance of little Randolph Miller, who stopped in the middle of the room and stood staring at Winterbourne. An instant later his pretty sister crossed the threshold; and then, after a considerable interval, Mrs. Miller slowly advanced.

"I know you!" said Randolph.

"I'm sure you know a great many things," exclaimed Winterbourne, taking him by the hand. "How is your education coming on?"

Daisy was exchanging greetings very prettily with her hostess; but when she heard Winterbourne's voice she quickly turned her head. "Well, I declare!" she said.

"I told you I should come, you know," Winterbourne rejoined smiling.

"Well—I didn't believe it," said Miss Daisy.

"I am much obliged to you," laughed the young man.

"You might have come to see me!" said Daisy.

"I arrived only yesterday."

"I don't believe that!" the young girl declared.

Winterbourne turned with a protesting smile to her mother; but this lady evaded his glance, and seating herself, fixed her eyes upon her son. "We've got a bigger place than this," said Randolph. "It's all gold on the walls."

Mrs. Miller turned uneasily in her chair. "I told you if I were to bring you, you would say something!" she murmured.

"I told *you*!" Randolph exclaimed. "I tell *you*, sir!" he added jocosely, giving Winterbourne a thump on the knee. "It *is* bigger, too!"

Daisy had entered upon a lively conversation with her hostess; Winterbourne judged it becoming to address a few words to her mother. "I hope you have been well since we parted at Vevey," he said.

Mrs. Miller now certainly looked at him—at his chin. "Not very well, sir," she answered.

"She's got the dyspepsia," said Randolph. "I've got it too. Father's got it. I've got it worst!"

This announcement, instead of embarrassing Mrs. Miller, seemed to relieve her. "I suffer from the liver," she said. "I think it's the climate; it's less bracing than Schenectady, especially in the winter

2. A fashionable street near the head of the Spanish Steps.

season. I don't know whether you know we reside at Schenectady. I was saying to Daisy that I certainly hadn't found any one like Dr. Davis, and I didn't believe I should. Oh, at Schenectady, he stands first; they think everything of him. He has so much to do, and yet there was nothing he wouldn't do for me. He said he never saw anything like my dyspepsia, but he was bound to cure it. I'm sure there was nothing he wouldn't try. He was just going to try something new when we came off. Mr. Miller wanted Daisy to see Europe for herself. But I wrote to Mr. Miller that it seems as if I couldn't get on without Dr. Davis. At Schenectady he stands at the very top; and there's a great deal of sickness there, too. It affects my sleep."

Winterbourne had a good deal of pathological gossip with Dr. Davis's patient, during which Daisy chattered unremittingly to her own companion. The young man asked Mrs. Miller how she was pleased with Rome. "Well, I must say I am disappointed," she answered. "We had heard so much about it; I suppose we had heard too much. But we couldn't help that. We had been led to expect something different."

"Ah, wait a little, and you will become very fond of it," said Winterbourne.

"I hate it worse and worse every day!" cried Randolph.

"You are like the infant Hannibal,"[3] said Winterbourne.

"No, I ain't!" Randolph declared, at a venture.

"You are not much like an infant," said his mother. "But we have seen places," she resumed, "that I should put a long way before Rome." And in reply to Winterbourne's interrogation, "There's Zurich," she observed; "I think Zurich is lovely; and we hadn't heard half so much about it."

"The best place we've seen is the City of Richmond!" said Randolph.

"He means the ship," his mother explained. "We crossed in that ship. Randolph had a good time on the City of Richmond."

"It's the best place I've seen," the child repeated. "Only it was turned the wrong way."

"Well, we've got to turn the right way some time," said Mrs. Miller, with a little laugh. Winterbourne expressed the hope that her daughter at least found some gratification in Rome, and she declared that Daisy was quite carried away. "It's on account of the society—the society's splendid. She goes round everywhere; she has made a great number of acquaintances. Of course she goes round more than I do. I must say they have been very sociable; they have taken her right in. And then she knows a great many gentlemen. Oh, she thinks there's nothing like

3. Hannibal (247 to 183 or 182 B.C.), the Carthaginian general who led his army, including a train of elephants, across the Alps into Italy. Hannibal hated Rome from childhood on, when his father fought the Romans in Sicily and lost.

Rome. Of course, it's a great deal pleasanter for a young lady if she knows plenty of gentlemen."

By this time Daisy had turned her attention again to Winterbourne. "I've been telling Mrs. Walker how mean you were!" the young girl announced.

"And what is the evidence you have offered?" asked Winterbourne, rather annoyed at Miss Miller's want of appreciation of the zeal of an admirer who on his way down to Rome had stopped neither at Bologna nor at Florence, simply because of a certain sentimental impatience. He remembered that a cynical compatriot had once told him that American women—the pretty ones, and this gave a largeness to the axiom—were at once the most exacting in the world and the least endowed with a sense of indebtedness.

"Why, you were awfully mean at Vevey," said Daisy. "You wouldn't do anything. You wouldn't stay there when I asked you."

"My dearest young lady," cried Winterbourne, with eloquence, "have I come all the way to Rome to encounter your reproaches?"

"Just hear him say that!" said Daisy to her hostess, giving a twist to a bow on this lady's dress. "Did you ever hear anything so quaint?"

"So quaint, my dear?" murmured Mrs. Walker, in the tone of a partisan of Winterbourne.

"Well, I don't know," said Daisy, fingering Mrs. Walker's ribbons. "Mrs. Walker, I want to tell you something."

"Motherr," interposed Randolph, with his rough ends to his words, "I tell you you've got to go. Eugenio'll raise something!"

"I'm not afraid of Eugenio," said Daisy, with a toss of her head. "Look here, Mrs. Walker," she went on, "you know I'm coming to your party."

"I am delighted to hear it."

"I've got a lovely dress."

"I am very sure of that."

"But I want to ask a favour—permission to bring a friend."

"I shall be happy to see any of your friends," said Mrs. Walker, turning with a smile to Mrs. Miller.

"Oh, they are not my friends," answered Daisy's mamma, smiling shyly, in her own fashion. "I never spoke to them!"

"It's an intimate friend of mine—Mr. Giovanelli," said Daisy, without a tremor in her clear little voice or a shadow on her brilliant little face.

Mrs. Walker was silent a moment, she gave a rapid glance at Winterbourne. "I shall be glad to see Mr. Giovanelli," she then said.

"He's an Italian," Daisy pursued, with the prettiest serenity. "He's a great friend of mine—he's the handsomest man in the world—except Mr. Winterbourne! He knows plenty of Italians, but he wants to know some Americans. He thinks ever so much of Americans. He's tremendously clever. He's perfectly lovely!"

It was settled that this brilliant personage should be brought to Mrs. Walker's party, and then Mrs. Miller prepared to take her leave. "I guess we'll go back to the hotel," she said.

"You may go back to the hotel, mother, but I'm going to take a walk," said Daisy.

"She's going to walk with Mr. Giovanelli," Randolph proclaimed.

"I am going to the Pincio,"[4] said Daisy, smiling.

"Alone, my dear at this hour?" Mrs. Walker asked. The afternoon was drawing to a close—it was the hour for the throng of carriages and of contemplative pedestrians. "I don't think it's safe, my dear," said Mrs. Walker.

"Neither do I," subjoined Mrs. Miller. "You'll get the fever as sure as you live. Remember what Dr. Davis told you!"

"Give her some medicine before she goes," said Randolph.

The company had risen to its feet; Daisy, still showing her pretty teeth, bent over and kissed her hostess. "Mrs. Walker, you are too perfect," she said. "I'm not going alone; I am going to meet a friend."

"Your friend won't keep you from getting the fever," Mrs. Miller observed.

"Is it Mr. Giovanelli?" asked the hostess.

Winterbourne was watching the young girl; at this question his attention quickened. She stood there smiling and smoothing her bonnet-ribbons; she glanced at Winterbourne. Then, while she glanced and smiled, she answered without a shade of hesitation, "Mr. Giovanelli—the beautiful Giovanelli."

"My dear young friend," said Mrs. Walker, taking her hand, pleadingly, "don't walk off to the Pincio at this hour to meet a beautiful Italian."

"Well, he speaks English," said Mrs. Miller.

"Gracious me!" Daisy exclaimed, "I don't want to do anything improper. There's an easy way to settle it." She continued to glance at Winterbourne. "The Pincio is only a hundred yards distant, and if Mr. Winterbourne were as polite as he pretends he would offer to walk with me!"

Winterbourne's politeness hastened to affirm itself, and the young girl gave him gracious leave to accompany her. They passed downstairs before her mother, and at the door Winterbourne perceived Mrs. Miller's carriage drawn up, with the ornamental courier whose acquaintance he had made at Vevey seated within. "Good-bye, Eugenio!" cried Daisy, "I'm going to take a walk." The distance from the Via Gregoriana to the beautiful garden at the other end of the Pincian Hill is, in fact, rapidly traversed. As the day was splendid, however, and the concourse of vehicles, walkers, and loungers

4. A hill with a fine view of Rome.

numerous, the young Americans found their progress much delayed. This fact was highly agreeable to Winterbourne, in spite of his consciousness of his singular situation. The slow-moving, idly-gazing Roman crowd bestowed much attention upon the extremely pretty young foreign lady who was passing through it upon his arm; and he wondered what on earth had been in Daisy's mind when she proposed to expose herself, unattended, to its appreciation. His own mission, to her sense, apparently, was to consign her to the hands of Mr. Giovanelli; but Winterbourne, at once annoyed and gratified, resolved that he would do no such thing.

"Why haven't you been to see me?" asked Daisy. "You can't get out of that."

"I have had the honour of telling you that I have only just stepped out of the train."

"You must have stayed in the train a good while after it stopped!" cried the young girl, with her little laugh. "I suppose you were asleep. You have had time to go to see Mrs. Walker."

"I knew Mrs. Walker—" Winterbourne began to explain.

"I knew where you knew her. You knew her at Geneva. She told me so. Well, you knew me at Vevey. That's just as good. So you ought to have come." She asked him no other question than this; she began to prattle about her own affairs. "We've got splendid rooms at the hotel; Eugenio says they're the best rooms in Rome. We are going to stay all winter—if we don't die of the fever; and I guess we'll stay then. It's a great deal nicer than I thought; I thought it would be fearfully quiet; I was sure it would be awfully poky. I was sure we should be going round all the time with one of those dreadful old men that explain about the pictures and things. But we only had about ι week of that, and now I'm enjoying myself. I know ever so many people, and they are all so charming. The society's extremely select. There are all kinds—English, and Germans, and Italians. I think I like the English best. I like their style of conversation. But there are some lovely Americans. I never saw anything so hospitable. There's something or other every day. There's not much dancing; but I must say I never thought dancing was everything. I was always fond of conversation. I guess I shall have plenty at Mrs. Walker's—her rooms are so small." When they had passed the gate of the Pincian Gardens, Miss Miller began to wonder where Mr. Giovanelli might be. "We had better go straight to that place in front," she said, "where you look at the view."

"I certainly shall not help you to find him," Winterbourne declared.

"Then I shall find him without you," said Miss Daisy.

"You certainly won't leave me!" cried Winterbourne.

She burst into her little laugh. "Are you afraid you'll get lost—or run over? But there's Giovanelli, leaning against that tree. He's staring at the women in the carriages: did you ever see anything so cool?"

Winterbourne perceived at some distance a little man standing with folded arms, nursing his cane. He had a handsome face, an artfully poised hat, a glass in one eye and a nosegay in his button-hole. Winterbourne looked at him a moment and then said, "Do you mean to speak to that man?"

"Do I mean to speak to him? Why, you don't suppose I mean to communicate by signs?"

"Pray understand, then," said Winterbourne, "that I intend to remain with you."

Daisy stopped and looked at him, without a sign of troubled consciousness in her face; with nothing but the presence of her charming eyes and her happy dimples. "Well, she's a cool one!" thought the young man.

"I don't like the way you say that," said Daisy. "It's too imperious."

"I beg your pardon if I say it wrong. The main point is to give you an idea of my meaning."

The young girl looked at him more gravely, but with eyes that were prettier than ever. "I have never allowed a gentleman to dictate to me, or to interfere with anything I do."

"I think you have made a mistake," said Winterbourne. "You should sometimes listen to a gentleman—the right one?"

Daisy began to laugh again. "I do nothing but listen to gentlemen!" she exclaimed. "Tell me if Mr. Giovanelli is the right one."

The gentleman with the nosegay in his bosom had now perceived our two friends, and was approaching the young girl with obsequious rapidity. He bowed to Winterbourne as well as to the latter's companion; he had a brilliant smile, an intelligent eye; Winterbourne thought him not a bad-looking fellow. But he nevertheless said to Daisy— "No, he's not the right one."

Daisy evidently had a natural talent for performing introductions; she mentioned the name of each of her companions to the other. She strolled along with one of them on each side of her; Mr. Giovanelli, who spoke English very cleverly—Winterbourne afterwards learned that he had practised the idiom upon a great many American heiresses—addressed her a great deal of very polite nonsense; he was extremely urbane, and the young American, who said nothing, reflected upon that profundity of Italian cleverness which enables people to appear more gracious in proportion as they are more acutely disappointed. Giovanelli, of course, had counted upon something more intimate; he had not bargained for a party of three. But he kept his temper in a manner which suggested far-stretching intentions. Winterbourne flattered himself that he had taken his measure. "He is not a gentleman," said the young American; "he is only a clever imitation of one. He is a music-master, or a penny-a-liner, or a third-rate artist. Damn his good looks!" Mr. Giovanelli had certainly a very pretty face; but Winterbourne felt a superior indignation at his own lovely fellow-countrywoman's not knowing the difference between a spurious gentleman and a real one. Giovanelli chattered and jested and made himself wonderfully agreeable. It was true that if he was an imitation the imitation was very skillful. "Nevertheless," Winterbourne said to himself, "a nice girl ought to know!" And then he came back to the question whether this was in fact a nice girl. Would a nice girl—even allowing for her being a little American flirt—make a rendezvous with a presumably low-lived foreigner? The rendezvous in this case, indeed, had been in broad daylight, and in the most crowded corner of Rome; but was it not impossible to regard the choice of these circumstances as a proof of extreme cynicism? Singular though it may seem, Winterbourne was vexed that the young girl, in joining her *amoroso*, [5] should not appear more impatient of his own company, and he was vexed because of his inclination. It was impossible to regard her as a perfectly well-conducted young lady; she was wanting in a certain indispensable delicacy. It would therefore simplify matters greatly to be able to treat her as the object of one of those sentiments which are called by romancers "lawless passions." That she should seem to wish to get rid of him would help him to think more lightly of her, and to be able to think more lightly of her would make her much less perplexing. But Daisy, on this occasion, continued to present herself as an inscrutable combination of audacity and innocence.

She had been walking some quarter of an hour, attended by her two cavaliers, and responding in a tone of very childish gaiety, as it seemed to Winterbourne, to the pretty speeches of Mr. Giovanelli, when a carriage that had detached itself from the revolving train drew up beside the path. At the same moment Winterbourne perceived that his friend Mrs. Walker—the lady whose house he had lately left—was seated in the vehicle and was beckoning to him. Leaving Miss Miller's side, he hastened to obey her summons. Mrs. Walker was flushed; she wore an excited air. "It is really too dreadful," she said. "That girl must not do this sort of thing. She must not walk here with you two men. Fifty people have noticed her."

Winterbourne raised his eyebrows. "I think it's a pity to make too much fuss about it."

"It's a pity to let the girl ruin herself!"

"She is very innocent," said Winterbourne.

"She's very crazy!" cried Mrs. Walker. "Did you ever see anything so imbecile as her mother? After you had all left me, just now, I could not sit still for thinking of it. It seemed too pitiful, not even to attempt

5. Beau, sweetheart.

to save her. I ordered the carriage and put on my bonnet, and came here as quickly as possible. Thank heaven I have found you!"

"What do you propose to do with us?" asked Winterbourne, smiling.

"To ask her to get in, to drive her about here for half-an-hour, so that the world may see she is not running absolutely wild, and then to take her safely home."

"I don't think it's a very happy thought," said Winterbourne; "but you can try."

Mrs. Walker tried. The young man went in pursuit of Miss Miller, who had simply nodded and smiled at his interlocutrix in the carriage and had gone her way with her own companion. Daisy, on learning that Mrs. Walker wished to speak to her, retraced her steps with a perfect good grace and with Mr. Giovanelli at her side. She declared that she was delighted to have a chance to present this gentleman to Mrs. Walker. She immediately achieved the introduction, and declared that she had never in her life seen anything so lovely as Mrs. Walker's carriage-rug.

"I am glad you admire it," said this lady, smiling sweetly. "Will you get in and let me put it over you?"

"Oh, no, thank you," said Daisy. "I shall admire it much more as I see you driving round with it."

"Do get in and drive with me," said Mrs. Walker.

"That would be charming, but it's so enchanting just as I am!" and Daisy gave a brilliant glance at the gentlemen on either side of her.

"It may be enchanting, dear child, but it is not the custom here," urged Mrs. Walker, leaning forward in her victoria with her hands devoutly clasped.

"Well, it ought to be, then!" said Daisy. "If I didn't walk I should expire."

"You should walk with your mother, dear," cried the lady from Geneva, losing patience.

"With my mother dear!" exclaimed the young girl. Winterbourne saw that she scented interference. "My mother never walked ten steps in her life. And then, you know," she added with a laugh, "I am more than five years old."

"You are old enough to be more reasonable. You are old enough, dear Miss Miller, to be talked about."

Daisy looked at Mrs. Walker, smiling intensely. "Talked about? What do you mean?"

"Come into my carriage and I will tell you."

Daisy turned her quickened glance again from one of the gentlemen beside her to the other. Mr. Giovanelli was bowing to and fro, rubbing down his gloves and laughing very agreeably; Winterbourne thought it a most unpleasant scene. "I don't think I want to know what you mean," said Daisy presently. "I don't think I should like it."

Winterbourne wished that Mrs. Walker would tuck in her carriage-rug and drive away; but this lady did not enjoy being defied, as she afterwards told him. "Should you prefer being thought a very reckless girl?" she demanded.

"Gracious me!" exclaimed Daisy. She looked again at Mr. Giovanelli, then she turned to Winterbourne. There was a little pink flush in her cheek; she was tremendously pretty. "Does Mr. Winterbourne think," she asked slowly, smiling, throwing back her head and glancing at him from head to foot, "that—to save my reputation—I ought to get into the carriage?"

Winterbourne coloured; for an instant he hesitated greatly. It seemed so strange to hear her speak that way of her "reputation." But he himself, in fact, must speak in accordance with gallantry. The finest gallantry, here, was simply to tell her the truth; and the truth, for Winterbourne, as the few indications I have been able to give have made him known to the reader, was that Daisy Miller should take Mrs. Walker's advice. He looked at her exquisite prettiness; and then he said very gently, "I think you should get into the carriage."

Daisy gave a violent laugh. "I never heard anything so stiff! If this is improper, Mrs. Walker," she pursued, "then I am all improper, and you must give me up. Good-bye; I hope you'll have a lovely ride!" and, with Mr. Giovanelli, who made a triumphantly obsequious salute, she turned away.

Mrs. Walker sat looking after her, and there were tears in Mrs. Walker's eyes. "Get in here, sir," she said to Winterbourne, indicating the place beside her. The young man answered that he felt bound to accompany Miss Miller; whereupon Mrs. Walker declared that if he refused her this favour she would never speak to him again. She was evidently in earnest. Winterbourne overtook Daisy and her companion and, offering the young girl his hand, told her that Mrs. Walker had made an imperious claim upon his society. He expected that in answer she would say something rather free, something to commit herself still farther to that "recklessness" from which Mrs. Walker had so charitably endeavoured to dissuade her. But she only shook his hand, hardly looking at him, while Mr. Giovanelli bade him farewell with a too emphatic flourish of the hat.

Winterbourne was not in the best possible humour as he took his seat in Mrs. Walker's victoria. "That was not clever of you," he said candidly, while the vehicle mingled again with the throng of carriages.

"In such a case," his companion answered, "I don't wish to be clever, I wish to be *earnest!*"

"Well, your earnestness has only offended her and put her off."

"It has happened very well," said Mrs. Walker. "If she is so perfectly determined to compromise herself, the sooner one knows it the better; one can act accordingly."

"I suspect she meant no harm," Winterbourne rejoined.

"So I thought a month ago. But she has been going too far."

"What has she been doing?"

"Everything that is not done here. Flirting with any man she could pick up; sitting in corners with mysterious Italians; dancing all the evening with the same partners; receiving visits at eleven o'clock at night. Her mother goes away when visitors come."

"But her brother," said Winterbourne, laughing, "sits up till midnight."

"He must be edified by what he sees. I'm told that at their hotel every one is talking about her, and that a smile goes round among the servants when a gentleman comes and asks for Miss Miller."

"The servants be hanged!" said Winterbourne angrily. "The poor girl's only fault," he presently added, "is that she is very uncultivated."

"She is naturally indelicate," Mrs. Walker declared. "Take that example this morning. How long had you known her at Vevey?"

"A couple of days."

"Fancy, then, her making it a personal matter that you should have left the place!"

Winterbourne was silent for some moments; then he said, "I suspect, Mrs. Walker, that you and I have lived too long at Geneva!" And he added a request that she should inform him with what particular design she had made him enter her carriage.

"I wished to beg you to cease your relations with Miss Miller—not to flirt with her—to give her no farther opportunity to expose herself—to let her alone, in short."

"I'm afraid I can't do that," said Winterbourne. "I like her extremely."

"All the more reason that you shouldn't help her to make a scandal."

"There shall be nothing scandalous in my attentions to her."

"There certainly will be in the way she takes them. But I have said what I had on my conscience," Mrs. Walker pursued. "If you wish to rejoin the young lady I will put you down. Here, by-the-way, you have a chance."

The carriage was traversing that part of the Pincian Garden which overhangs the wall of Rome and overlooks the beautiful Villa Borghese.[6] It is bordered by a large parapet, near which there are several seats. One of the seats, at a distance, was occupied by a gentleman and a lady, towards whom Mrs. Walker gave a toss of her head. At the same moment these persons rose and walked towards the parapet. Winter-

6. A seventeenth-century palace in a large park.

bourne had asked the coachman to stop; he now descended from the carriage. His companion looked at him a moment in silence; then, while he raised his hat, she drove majestically away. Winterbourne stood there; he had turned his eyes towards Daisy and her cavalier. They evidently saw no one; they were too deeply occupied with each other. When they reached the low garden-wall they stood a moment looking off at the great flat-topped pine-clusters of the Villa Borghese; then Giovanelli seated himself familiarly upon the broad ledge of the wall. The western sun in the opposite sky sent out a brilliant shaft through a couple of cloud-bars; whereupon Daisy's companion took her parasol out of her hands and opened it. She came a little nearer and he held the parasol over her; then, still holding it, he let it rest upon her shoulder, so that both of their heads were hidden from Winterbourne. This young man lingered a moment, then he began to walk. But he walked—not towards the couple with the parasol; towards the residence of his aunt, Mrs. Costello.

IV

He flattered himself on the following day that there was no smiling among the servants when he, at least, asked for Mrs. Miller at her hotel. This lady and her daughter, however, were not at home; and on the next day after, repeating his visit, Winterbourne again had the misfortune not to find them. Mrs. Walker's party took place on the evening of the third day, and in spite of the frigidity of his last interview with the hostess Winterbourne was among the guests. Mrs. Walker was one of those American ladies who, while residing abroad, make a point, in their own phrase, of studying European society; and she had on this occasion collected several specimens of her diversely-born fellow-mortals to serve, as it were, as text-books. When Winterbourne arrived Daisy Miller was not there; but in a few moments he saw her mother come in alone, very shyly and ruefully. Mrs. Miller's hair, above her exposed-looking temples, was more frizzled than ever. As she approached Mrs. Walker, Winterbourne also drew near.

"You see I've come all alone," said poor Mrs. Miller. "I'm so frightened; I don't know what to do; it's the first time I've ever been to a party alone—especially in this country. I wanted to bring Randolph or Eugenio, or some one, but Daisy just pushed me off by myself. I ain't used to going round alone."

"And does not your daughter intend to favour us with her society?" demanded Mrs. Walker, impressively.

"Well, Daisy's all dressed," said Mrs. Miller, with that accent of the dispassionate, if not of the philosophic, historian with which she always recorded the current incidents of her daughter's career. "She got dressed on purpose before dinner. But she's got a friend of hers there; that gentleman—the Italian—that she wanted to bring. They've got going at the piano; it seems as if they couldn't leave off. Mr. Giovanelli sings splendidly. But I guess they'll come before very long," concluded Mrs. Miller hopefully.

"I'm sorry she should come—in that way," said Mrs. Walker.

"Well, I told her that there was no use in her getting dressed before dinner if she was going to wait three hours," responded Daisy's mamma. "I didn't see the use of her putting on such a dress as that to sit round with Mr. Giovanelli."

"This is most horrible!" said Mrs. Walker, turning away and addressing herself to Winterbourne. "*Elle s'affiche.*[7] It's her revenge for my having ventured to remonstrate with her. When she comes I shall not speak to her."

Daisy came after eleven o'clock, but she was not, on such an occasion, a young lady to wait to be spoken to. She rustled forward in radiant loveliness, smiling and chattering, carrying a large bouquet and attended by Mr. Giovanelli. Every one stopped talking, and turned and looked at her. She came straight to Mrs. Walker. "I'm afraid you thought I never was coming, so I sent mother off to tell you. I wanted to make Mr. Giovanelli practise some things before he came; you know he sings beautifully, and I want you to ask him to sing. This is Mr. Giovanelli; you know I introduced him to you; he's got the most lovely voice and he knows the most charming set of songs. I made him go over them this evening, on purpose; we had the greatest time at the hotel." Of all this Daisy delivered herself with the sweetest, brightest audibleness, looking now at her hostess and now round the room, while she gave a series of little pats, round her shoulders, to the edges of her dress. "Is there any one I know?" she asked.

"I think every one knows you!" said Mrs. Walker pregnantly, and she gave a very cursory greeting to Mr. Giovanelli. This gentleman bore himself gallantly. He smiled and bowed and showed his white teeth, he curled his moustaches and rolled his eyes, and performed all the proper functions of a handsome Italian at an evening party. He sang, very prettily, half-a-dozen songs, though Mrs. Walker afterwards declared that she had been quite unable to find out who asked him. It was apparently not Daisy who had given him his orders. Daisy sat at a distance from the piano, and though she had publicly, as it were, professed a high admiration for his singing, talked, not inaudibly, while it was going on.

"It's a pity these rooms are so small; we can't dance," she said to Winterbourne, as if she had seen him five minutes before.

"I am not sorry we can't dance," Winterbourne answered; "I don't dance."

"Of course you don't dance; you're too stiff," said Miss Daisy. "I

7. She advertises herself (seeks notoriety, makes a show of herself).

hope you enjoyed your drive with Mrs. Walker."

"No, I didn't enjoy it; I preferred walking with you."

"We paired off, that was much better," said Daisy. "But did you ever hear anything so cool as Mrs. Walker's wanting me to get into her carriage and drop poor Mr. Giovanelli; and under the pretext that it was proper? People have different ideas! It would have been most unkind; he had been talking about that walk for ten days."

"He should not have talked about it at all," said Winterbourne; "he would never have proposed to a young lady of this country to walk about the streets with him."

"About the streets?" cried Daisy, with her pretty stare. "Where then would he have proposed to her to walk? The Pincio is not the streets, either; and I, thank goodness, am not a young lady of this country. The young ladies of this country have a dreadfully pokey time of it, so far as I can learn; I don't see why I should change my habits for *them*."

"I am afraid your habits are those of a flirt," said Winterbourne gravely.

"Of course they are," she cried, giving him her little smiling stare again. "I'm a fearful, frightful flirt! Did you ever hear of a nice girl that was not? But I suppose you will tell me now that I am not a nice girl."

"You're a very nice girl, but I wish you would flirt with me, and me only," said Winterbourne.

"Ah! thank you, thank you very much; you are the last man I should think of flirting with. As I have had the pleasure of informing you, you are too stiff."

"You say that too often," said Winterbourne.

Daisy gave a delighted laugh. "If I could have the sweet hope of making you angry, I would say it again."

"Don't do that; when I am angry I'm stiffer than ever. But if you won't flirt with me, do cease at least to flirt with your friend at the piano; they don't understand that sort of thing here."

"I thought they understood nothing else!" exclaimed Daisy.

"Not in young unmarried women."

"It seems to me much more proper in young unmarried women than in old married ones," Daisy declared.

"Well," said Winterbourne, "when you deal with natives you must go by the custom of the place. Flirting is a purely American custom; it doesn't exist here. So when you show yourself in public with Mr. Giovanelli and without your mother—"

"Gracious! poor mother!" interposed Daisy.

"Though you may be flirting, Mr. Giovanelli is not; he means something else."

"He isn't preaching, at any rate," said Daisy with vivacity. "And if you want very much to know, we are neither of us flirting; we are too good friends for that; we are very intimate friends."

"Ah!" rejoined Winterbourne, "if you are in love with each other it is another affair."

She had allowed him up to this point to talk so frankly that he had no expectation of shocking her by this ejaculation; but she immediately got up, blushing visibly, and leaving him to exclaim mentally that little American flirts were the queerest creatures in the world. "Mr. Giovanelli, at least," she said, giving her interlocutor a single glance, "never says such very disagreeable things to me."

Winterbourne was bewildered; he stood staring. Mr. Giovanelli had finished singing; he left the piano and came over to Daisy. "Won't you come into the other room and have some tea?" he asked, bending before her with his decorative smile.

Daisy turned to Winterbourne, beginning to smile again. He was still more perplexed, for this inconsequent smile made nothing clear, though it seemed to prove, indeed, that she had a sweetness and softness that reverted instinctively to the pardon of offences. "It has never occurred to Mr. Winterbourne to offer me any tea," she said, with her little tormenting manner.

"I have offered you advice," Winterbourne rejoined.

"I prefer weak tea!" cried Daisy, and she went off with the brilliant Giovanelli. She sat with him in the adjoining room, in the embrasure of the window, for the rest of the evening. There was an interesting performance at the piano, but neither of these young people gave heed to it. When Daisy came to take leave of Mrs. Walker, this lady conscientiously repaired the weakness of which she had been guilty at the moment of the young girl's arrival. She turned her back straight upon Miss Miller and left her to depart with what grace she might. Winterbourne was standing near the door; he saw it all. Daisy turned very pale and looked at her mother, but Mrs. Miller was humbly unconscious of any violation of the usual social forms. She appeared, indeed, to have felt an incongruous impulse to draw attention to her own striking observance of them. "Good night, Mrs. Walker," she said; "we've had a beautiful evening. You see if I let Daisy come to parties without me, I don't want her to go away without me." Daisy turned away, looking with a pale, grave face at the circle near the door; Winterbourne saw that, for the first moment, she was too much shocked and puzzled even for indignation. He on his side was greatly touched.

"That was very cruel," he said to Mrs. Walker.

"She never enters my drawing-room again," replied his hostess.

Since Winterbourne was not to meet her in Mrs. Walker's drawing-room, he went as often as possible to Mrs. Miller's hotel. The ladies were rarely at home, but when he found them the devoted Giovanelli was always present. Very often the polished little Roman was in the drawing-room with Daisy alone, Mrs. Miller being apparently constantly of the opinion that discretion is the better part of the surveillance. Winterbourne noted, at first with surprise, that Daisy on these occasions was never embarrassed or annoyed by his own entrance; but he very presently began to feel that she had no more surprises for him; the unexpected in her behaviour was the only thing to expect. She showed no displeasure at her *tête-à-tête* with Giovanelli being interrupted; she could chatter as freshly and freely with two gentlemen as with one; there was always in her conversation, the same odd mixture of audacity and puerility. Winterbourne remarked to himself that if she was seriously interested in Giovanelli it was very singular that she should not take more trouble to preserve the sanctity of their interviews, and he liked her the more for her innocent-looking indifference and her apparently inexhaustible good humour. He could hardly have said why, but she seemed to him a girl who would never be jealous. At the risk of exciting a somewhat derisive smile on the reader's part, I may affirm that with regard to the women who had hitherto interested him it very often seemed to Winterbourne among the possibilities that, given certain contingencies, he should be afraid—literally afraid—of these ladies. He had a pleasant sense that he should never be afraid of Daisy Miller. It must be added that this sentiment was not altogether flattering to Daisy; it was part of his conviction, or rather of his apprehension, that she would prove a very light young person.

But she was evidently very much interested in Giovanelli. She looked at him whenever he spoke; she was perpetually telling him to do this and to do that; she was constantly "chaffing" and abusing him. She appeared completely to have forgotten that Winterbourne had said anything to displease her at Mrs. Walker's little party. One Sunday afternoon, having gone to St. Peter's with his aunt, Winterbourne perceived Daisy strolling about the great church in company with the inevitable Giovanelli. Presently he pointed out the young girl and her cavalier to Mrs. Costello. This lady looked at them a moment through her eyeglass, and then she said:

"That's what makes you so pensive in these days, eh?"

"I had not the least idea I was pensive," said the young man.

"You are very much pre-occupied, you are thinking of something."

"And what is it," he asked, "that you accuse me of thinking of?"

"Of that young lady's—Miss Baker's, Miss Chandler's—what's her name?—Miss Miller's intrigue with that little barber's block."[8]

"Do you call it an intrigue," Winterbourne asked—"an affair that goes on with such peculiar publicity?"

"That's their folly," said Mrs. Costello, "it's not their merit."

"No," rejoined Winterbourne, with something of that pensiveness

8. A wooden head on which wigs are fitted.

to which his aunt had alluded. "I don't believe that there is anything to be called an intrigue."

"I have heard a dozen people speak of it; they say she is quite carried away by him."

"They are certainly very intimate," said Winterbourne.

Mrs. Costello inspected the young couple again with her optical instrument. "He is very handsome. One easily sees how it is. She thinks him the most elegant man in the world, the finest gentleman. She has never seen anything like him; he is better even than the courier. It was the courier probably who introduced him, and if he succeeds in marrying the young lady, the courier will come in for a magnificent commission."

"I don't believe she thinks of marrying him," said Winterbourne, "and I don't believe he hopes to marry her."

"You may be very sure she thinks of nothing. She goes on from day to day, from hour to hour, as they did in the Golden Age. I can imagine nothing more vulgar. And at the same time," added Mrs. Costello, "depend upon it that she may tell you any moment that she is 'engaged.' "

"I think that is more than Giovanelli expects," said Winterbourne.

"Who is Giovanelli?"

"The little Italian. I have asked questions about him and learned something. He is apparently a perfectly respectable little man. I believe he is in a small way a *cavaliere avvocato.* [9] But he doesn't move in what are called the first circles. I think it is really not absolutely impossible that the courier introduced him. He is evidently immensely charmed with Miss Miller. If she thinks him the finest gentleman in the world, he, on his side, has never found himself in personal contact with such splendour, such opulence, such expensiveness, as this young lady's. And then she must seem to him wonderfully pretty and interesting. I rather doubt whether he dreams of marrying her. That must appear to him too impossible a piece of luck. He has nothing but his handsome face to offer, and there is a substantial Mr. Miller in that mysterious land of dollars. Giovanelli knows that he hasn't a title to offer. If he were only a count or a *marchese!* [1] He must wonder at his luck at the way they have taken him up."

"He accounts for it by his handsome face, and thinks Miss Miller a young lady *qui se passe ses fantaisies!*" [2] said Mrs. Costello.

"It is very true," Winterbourne pursued, "that Daisy and her mamma have not yet risen to that stage of—what shall I call it?—of culture, at which the idea of catching a count or a *marchese* begins. I believe that they are intellectually incapable of that conception."

9. Gentleman lawyer. 2. Who lives according to her whims.
1. Marquis.

"Ah! but the *cavaliere* can't believe it," said Mrs. Costello.

Of the observation excited by Daisy's "intrigue," Winterbourne gathered that day at St. Peter's sufficient evidence. A dozen of the American colonists in Rome came to talk with Mrs. Costello, who sat on a little portable stool at the base of one of the great pilasters. The vesper-service was going forward in splendid chants and organ-tones in the adjacent choir, and meanwhile, between Mrs. Costello and her friends, there was a great deal said about poor little Miss Miller's going really "too far." Winterbourne was not pleased with what he heard; but when, coming out upon the great steps of the church, he saw Daisy, who had emerged before him, get into an open cab with her accomplice and roll away through the cynical streets of Rome, he could not deny to himself that she was going very far indeed. He felt very sorry for her—not exactly that he believed that she had completely lost her head, but because it was painful to hear so much that was pretty and undefended and natural assigned to a vulgar place among the categories of disorder. He made an attempt after this to give a hint to Mrs. Miller. He met one day in the Corso[3] a friend—a tourist like himself—who had just come out of the Doria Palace, where he had been walking through the beautiful gallery. His friend talked for a moment about the superb portrait of Innocent X. by Velasquez, which hangs in one of the cabinets of the palace, and then said, "And in the same cabinet, by-the-way, I had the pleasure of contemplating a picture of a different kind—that pretty American girl whom you pointed out to me last week." In answer to Winterbourne's inquiries, his friend narrated that the pretty American girl—prettier than ever—was seated with a companion in the secluded nook in which the great papal portrait is enshrined.

"Who was her companion?" asked Winterbourne.

"A little Italian with a bouquet in his button-hole. The girl is delightfully pretty, but I thought I understood from you the other day that she was a young lady *du meilleur monde*."[4]

"So she is!" answered Winterbourne; and having assured himself that his informant had seen Daisy and her companion but five minutes before, he jumped into a cab and went to call on Mrs. Miller. She was at home; but she apologised to him for receiving him in Daisy's absence.

"She's gone out somewhere with Mr. Giovanelli," said Mrs. Miller. "She's always going round with Mr. Giovanelli."

"I have noticed that they are very intimate," Winterbourne observed.

3. An avenue in the center of Rome. On it is the Doria Palace, an eighteenth-century mansion with a picture gallery containing, among other masterpieces, a portrait of Pope Innocent X by the Spanish painter Velasquez (1599–1660).
4. Of the best society.

"Oh! it seems as if they couldn't live without each other!" said Mrs. Miller. "Well, he's a real gentleman, anyhow. I keep telling Daisy she's engaged!"

"And what does Daisy say?"

"Oh, she says she isn't engaged. But she might as well be!" this impartial parent resumed. "She goes on as if she was. But I've made Mr. Giovanelli promise to tell me, if *she* doesn't. I should want to write to Mr. Miller about it—shouldn't you?"

Winterbourne replied that he certainly should; and the state of mind of Daisy's mamma struck him as so unprecedented in the annals of parental vigilance that he gave up as utterly irrelevant the attempt to place her upon her guard.

After this Daisy was never at home, and Winterbourne ceased to meet her at the houses of their common acquaintance, because, as he perceived, these shrewd people had quite made up their minds that she was going too far. They ceased to invite her, and they intimated that they desired to express to observant Europeans the great truth that, though Miss Daisy Miller was a young American lady, her behaviour was not representative—was regarded by her compatriots as abnormal. Winterbourne wondered how she felt about all the cold shoulders that were turned towards her, and sometimes it annoyed him to suspect that she did not feel at all. He said to himself that she was too light and childish, too uncultivated and unreasoning, too provincial, to have reflected upon her ostracism or even to have perceived it. Then at other moments he believed that she carried about in her elegant and irresponsible little organism a defiant, passionate, perfectly observant consciousness of the impression she produced. He asked himself whether Daisy's defiance came from the consciousness of innocence or from her being, essentially, a young person of the reckless class. It must be admitted that holding oneself to a belief in Daisy's "innocence" came to seem to Winterbourne more and more a matter of fine-spun gallantry. As I have already had occasion to relate, he was angry at finding himself reduced to chopping logic about this young lady; he was vexed at his want of instinctive certitude as to how far her eccentricities were generic, national, and how far they were personal. From either view of them he had somehow missed her, and now it was too late. She was "carried away" by Mr. Giovanelli.

A few days after his brief interview with her mother, he encountered her in that beautiful abode of flowering desolation known as the Palace of the Cæsars. The early Roman spring had filled the air with bloom and perfume, and the rugged surface of the Palatine[5] was muffled with tender verdure. Daisy was strolling along the top of one of those great mounds of ruin that are embanked with mossy marble and paved with

5. A hill park in the center of Rome filled with historical monuments.

monumental inscriptions. It seemed to him that Rome had never been so lovely as just then. He stood looking off at the enchanting harmony of line and colour that remotely encircles the city, inhaling the softly humid odours and feeling the freshness of the year and the antiquity of the place reaffirm themselves in mysterious interfusion. It seemed to him also that Daisy had never looked so pretty; but this had been an observation of his whenever he met her. Giovanelli was at her side, and Giovanelli, too, wore an aspect of even unwonted brilliancy.

"Well," said Daisy, "I should think you would be lonesome!"

"Lonesome?" asked Winterbourne.

"You are always going round by yourself. Can't you get any one to walk with you?"

"I am not so fortunate," said Winterbourne, "as your companion."

Giovanelli, from the first, had treated Winterbourne with distinguished politeness; he listened with a deferential air to his remarks; he laughed, punctiliously, at his pleasantries; he seemed disposed to testify to his belief that Winterbourne was a superior young man. He carried himself in no degree like a jealous wooer; he had obviously a great deal of tact; he had no objection to your expecting a little humility of him. It even seemed to Winterbourne at times that Giovanelli would find a certain mental relief in being able to have a private understanding with him—to say to him, as an intelligent man, that, bless you, *he* knew how extraordinary was this young lady, and didn't flatter himself with delusive—or at least *too* delusive—hopes of matrimony and dollars. On this occasion he strolled away from his companion to pluck a sprig of almond blossom, which he carefully arranged in his button-hole.

"I know why you say that," said Daisy, watching Giovanelli. "Because you think I go round too much with *him!*" And she nodded at her attendant.

"Every one thinks so—if you care to know," said Winterbourne.

"Of course I care to know!" Daisy exclaimed seriously. "But I don't believe it. They are only pretending to be shocked. They don't really care a straw what I do. Besides, I don't go round so much."

"I think you will find they do care. They will show it—disagreeably."

Daisy looked at him a moment. "How—disagreeably?"

"Haven't you noticed anything?" Winterbourne asked.

"I have noticed you. But I noticed you were as stiff as an umbrella the first time I saw you."

"You will find I am not so stiff as several others," said Winterbourne, smiling.

"How shall I find it?"

"By going to see the others."

"What will they do to me?"

"They will give you the cold shoulder. Do you know what that means?"

Daisy was looking at him intently; she began to colour. "Do you mean as Mrs. Walker did the other night?"

"Exactly!" said Winterbourne.

She looked away at Giovanelli, who was decorating himself with his almond-blossom. Then looking back at Winterbourne—"I shouldn't think you would let people be so unkind!" she said.

"How can I help it?" he asked.

"I should think you would say something."

"I do say something;" and he paused a moment. "I say that your mother tells me that she believes you are engaged."

"Well, she does," said Daisy very simply.

Winterbourne began to laugh. "And does Randolph believe it?" he asked.

"I guess Randolph doesn't believe anything," said Daisy. Randolph's scepticism excited Winterbourne to farther hilarity, and he observed that Giovanelli was coming back to them. Daisy, observing it too, addressed herself again to her countryman. "Since you have mentioned it," she said, "I *am* engaged.". . . Winterbourne looked at her; he had stopped laughing. "You don't believe it!" she added.

He was silent a moment; and then, "Yes, I believe it!" he said.

"Oh, no, you don't," she answered. "Well, then—I am not!"

The young girl and her cicerone were on their way to the gate of the enclosure, so that Winterbourne, who had but lately entered, presently took leave of them. A week afterwards he went to dine at a beautiful villa on the Cælian Hill,[6] and, on arriving, dismissed his hired vehicle. The evening was charming, and he promised himself the satisfaction of walking home beneath the Arch of Constantine and past the vaguely-lighted monuments of the Forum.[7] There was a waning moon in the sky, and her radiance was not brilliant, but she was veiled in a thin cloud-curtain which seemed to diffuse and equalise it. When, on his return from the villa (it was eleven o'clock), Winterbourne approached the dusky circle of the Colosseum,[8] it occurred to him, as a lover of the picturesque, that the interior, in the pale moonshine, would be well worth a glance. He turned aside and walked to one of the empty arches, near which, as he observed, an open carriage—one of the little Roman street-cabs—was stationed. Then he passed in among the cavernous shadows of the great structure, and emerged upon the clear and silent arena. The place had never seemed to him more impressive. One-half of the gigantic circus

6. One of the seven hills on which ancient Rome was built.
7. The ruins of the center of pre-Christian Rome. The Arch of Constantine, erected to

celebrate the emperor's victory over a rival in A.D. 312, is adorned with bas-reliefs depicting scenes from the lives of Roman emperors.
8. The ancient Roman amphitheater.

was in deep shade; the other was sleeping in the luminous dusk. As he stood there he began to murmur Byron's famous lines, out of "Manfred";[9] but before he had finished his quotation he remembered that if nocturnal meditations in the Colosseum are recommended by the poets, they are deprecated by the doctors. The historic atmosphere was there, certainly; but the historic atmosphere, scientifically considered, was no better than a villanous miasma. Winterbourne walked to the middle of the arena, to take a more general glance, intending thereafter to make a hasty retreat. The great cross in the centre was covered with shadow; it was only as he drew near it that he made it out distinctly. Then he saw that two persons were stationed upon the low steps which formed its base. One of these was a woman, seated; her companion was standing in front of her.

Presently the sound of the woman's voice came to him distinctly in the warm night-air. "Well, he looks at us as one of the old lions or tigers may have looked at the Christian martyrs!" These were the words he heard, in the familiar accent of Miss Daisy Miller.

"Let us hope he is not very hungry," responded the ingenious Giovanelli. "He will have to take me first; you will serve for dessert!"

Winterbourne stopped, with a sort of horror; and, it must be added, with a sort of relief. It was as if a sudden illumination had been flashed upon the ambiguity of Daisy's behaviour and the riddle had become easy to read. She was a young lady whom a gentleman need no longer be at pains to respect. He stood there looking at her—looking at her companion, and not reflecting that though he saw them vaguely, he himself must have been more brightly visible. He felt angry with himself that he had bothered so much about the right way of regarding Miss Daisy Miller. Then, as he was going to advance again, he checked himself; not from the fear that he was doing her injustice, but from a sense of the danger of appearing unbecomingly exhilarated by this sudden revulsion from cautious criticism. He turned away towards the entrance of the place; but as he did so he heard Daisy speak again.

"Why, it was Mr. Winterbourne! He saw me—and he cuts me!"

What a clever little reprobate she was, and how smartly she played an injured innocence! But he wouldn't cut her. Winterbourne came forward again, and went towards the great cross. Daisy had got up; Giovanelli lifted his hat. Winterbourne had now begun to think simply of the craziness, from a sanitary point of view, of a delicate young girl lounging away the evening in this nest of malaria. What if she *were* a clever little reprobate? that was no reason for her dying of

9. The lines begin: "I stood within the Coliseum's wall,/Midst the chief relics of almighty Rome;/The trees which grew along the broken arches/Waved dark in the blue midnight. . . ." (act III, scene iv).

the *perniciosa*.[1] "How long have you been there?" he asked, almost brutally.

Daisy, lovely in the flattering moonlight, looked at him a moment. Then—"All the evening," she answered gently . . . "I never saw anything so pretty."

"I am afraid," said Winterbourne, "that you will not think Roman fever very pretty. This is the way people catch it. I wonder," he added, turning to Giovanelli, "that you, a native Roman, should countenance such a terrible indiscretion."

"Ah," said the handsome native, "for myself, I am not afraid."

"Neither am I—for you! I am speaking for this young lady."

Giovanelli lifted his well-shaped eyebrows and showed his brilliant teeth. But he took Winterbourne's rebuke with docility. "I told the Signorina it was a grave indiscretion; but when was the Signorina ever prudent?"

"I never was sick, and I don't mean to be!" the Signorina declared. "I don't look like much, but I'm healthy! I was bound to see the Colosseum by moonlight; I shouldn't have wanted to go home without that; and we have had the most beautiful time, haven't we, Mr. Giovanelli? If there has been any danger, Eugenio can give me some pills. He has got some splendid pills."

"I should advise you," said Winterbourne, "to drive home as fast as possible and take one!"

"What you say is very wise," Giovanelli rejoined. "I will go and make sure the carriage is at hand." And he went forward rapidly.

Daisy followed with Winterbourne. He kept looking at her; she seemed not in the least embarrassed. Winterbourne said nothing; Daisy chattered about the beauty of the place. "Well, I *have* seen the Colosseum by moonlight!" she exclaimed. "That's one good thing." Then, noticing Winterbourne's silence, she asked him why he didn't speak. He made no answer; he only began to laugh. They passed under one of the dark archways; Giovanelli was in front with the carriage. Here Daisy stopped a moment, looking at the young American. "*Did* you believe I was engaged the other day?" she asked.

"It doesn't matter what I believed the other day," said Winterbourne, still laughing.

"Well, what do you believe now?"

"I believe that it makes very little difference whether you are engaged or not!"

He felt the young girl's pretty eyes fixed upon him through the thick gloom of the archway; she was apparently going to answer. But Giovanelli hurried her forward. "Quick, quick," he said; "if we get in by midnight we are quite safe."

1. Pernicious fever, i.e., malaria.

Daisy took her seat in the carriage, and the fortunate Italian placed himself beside her. "Don't forget Eugenio's pills!" said Winterbourne, as he lifted his hat.

"I don't care," said Daisy, in a little strange tone, "whether I have Roman fever or not!" Upon this the cab-driver cracked his whip, and they rolled away over the desultory patches of the antique pavement.

Winterbourne—to do him justice, as it were—mentioned to no one that he had encountered Miss Miller, at midnight, in the Colosseum with a gentleman; but nevertheless, a couple of days later, the fact of her having been there under these circumstances was known to every member of the little American circle, and commented accordingly. Winterbourne reflected that they had of course known it at the hotel, and that, after Daisy's return, there had been an exchange of jokes between the porter and the cab-driver. But the young man was conscious at the same moment that it had ceased to be a matter of serious regret to him that the little American flirt should be "talked about" by low-minded menials. These people, a day or two later, had serious information to give: the little American flirt was alarmingly ill. Winterbourne, when the rumour came to him, immediately went to the hotel for more news. He found that two or three charitable friends had preceded him, and that they were being entertained in Mrs. Miller's salon by Randolph.

"It's going round at night," said Randolph—"that's what made her sick. She's always going round at midnight. I shouldn't think she'd want to—it's so plaguey dark. You can't see anything here at night, except when there's a moon. In America there's always a moon!" Mrs. Miller was invisible; she was now, at least, giving her daughter the advantage of her society. It was evident that Daisy was dangerously ill.

Winterbourne went often to ask for news of her, and once he saw Mrs. Miller, who, though deeply alarmed, was—rather to his surprise—perfectly composed, and, as it appeared, a most efficient and judicious nurse. She talked a good deal about Dr. Davis, but Winterbourne paid her the compliment of saying to himself that she was not, after all, such a monstrous goose. "Daisy spoke of you the other day," she said to him. "Half the time she doesn't know what she's saying, but that time I think she did. She gave me a message: she told me to tell you. She told me to tell you that she never was engaged to that handsome Italian. I am sure I am very glad; Mr. Giovanelli hasn't been near us since she was taken ill. I thought he was so much of a gentleman; but I don't call that very polite! A lady told me that he was afraid I was angry with him for taking Daisy round at night. Well, so I am; but I suppose he knows I'm a lady. I would scorn to scold him. Any way, she says she's not engaged. I don't know why she wanted you to know; but she said to me three times—'Mind you tell Mr. Winterbourne.' And then she told me to ask if you remembered the time you went to that castle, in Switzerland. But I said I wouldn't give any such messages as that. Only, if she is not engaged, I'm sure I'm glad to know it."

But, as Winterbourne had said, it mattered very little. A week after this the poor girl died; it had been a terrible case of the fever. Daisy's grave was in the little Protestant cemetery, in an angle of the wall of imperial Rome, beneath the cypresses and the thick spring-flowers. Winterbourne stood there beside it, with a number of other mourners; a number larger than the scandal excited by the young lady's career would have led you to expect. Near him stood Giovanelli, who came nearer still before Winterbourne turned away. Giovanelli was very pale; on this occasion he had no flower in his button-hole; he seemed to wish to say something. At last he said, "She was the most beautiful young lady I ever saw, and the most amiable." And then he added in a moment, "And she was the most innocent."

Winterbourne looked at him, and presently repeated his words, "And the most innocent?"

"The most innocent!"

Winterbourne felt sore and angry. "Why the devil," he asked, "did you take her to that fatal place?"

Mr. Giovanelli's urbanity was apparently imperturbable. He looked on the ground a moment, and then he said, "For myself, I had no fear; and she wanted to go."

"That was no reason!" Winterbourne declared.

The subtle Roman again dropped his eyes. "If she had lived, I should have got nothing. She would never have married me, I am sure."

"She would never have married you?"

"For a moment I hoped so. But no. I am sure."

Winterbourne listened to him; he stood staring at the raw protuberance among the April daisies. When he turned away again Mr. Giovanelli, with his light slow step, had retired.

Winterbourne almost immediately left Rome; but the following summer he again met his aunt, Mrs. Costello, at Vevey. Mrs. Costello was fond of Vevey. In the interval Winterbourne had often thought of Daisy Miller and her mystifying manners. One day he spoke of her to his aunt—said it was on his conscience that he had done her injustice.

"I am sure I don't know," said Mrs. Costello. "How did your injustice affect her?"

"She sent me a message before her death which I didn't understand at the time. But I have understood it since. She would have appreciated one's esteem."

"Is that a modest way," asked Mrs. Costello, "of saying that she would have reciprocated one's affection?"

Winterbourne offered no answer to this question; but he presently said, "You were right in that remark that you made last summer. I was booked to make a mistake. I have lived too long in foreign parts."

Nevertheless, he went back to live at Geneva, whence there continue to come the most contradictory accounts of his motives of sojourn: a report that he is "studying" hard—an intimation that he is much interested in a very clever foreign lady.

An International Episode

(1878)†

I

Four years ago—in 1874—two young Englishmen had occasion to go to the United States. They crossed the ocean at midsummer; and, arriving in New York on the first day of August, were much struck with the fervid temperature of that city. Disembarking upon the wharf, they climbed into one of those huge high-hung coaches which convey passengers to the hotels, and with a great deal of bouncing and bumping, took their course through Broadway. The midsummer aspect of New York is not perhaps the most favourable one; still, it is not without its picturesque and even brilliant side. Nothing could well resemble less a typical English street than the interminable avenue, rich in incongruities, through which our two travellers advanced—looking out on each side of them at the comfortable animation of the sidewalks, the high-coloured, heterogeneous architecture, the huge white marble façades, glittering in the strong, crude light and be-dizened with gilded lettering, the multifarious awnings, banners and streamers, the extraordinary number of omnibuses, horse-cars and other democratic vehicles, the vendors of cooling fluids, the white trousers and big straw-hats of the policemen, the tripping gait of the modish young persons on the pavement, the general brightness, newness, juvenility, both of people and things. The young men had exchanged few observations; but in crossing Union Square, in front of the monument to Washington—in the very shadow, indeed, pro-jected by the image of the *pater patriae*[1]—one of them remarked to the other, "It seems a rum-looking place."

"Ah, very odd, very odd," said the other, who was the clever man of the two.

"Pity it's so beastly hot," resumed the first speaker, after a pause.

"You know we are in a low latitude," said his friend.

"I daresay," remarked the other.

"I wonder," said the second speaker, presently, "if they can give one a bath."

"I daresay not," rejoined the other.

"Oh, I say!" cried his comrade.

This animated discussion was checked by their arrival at the hotel, which had been recommended to them by an American gentleman

† "An International Episode" first appeared in the *Cornhill Magazine* of December 1878 and January 1879. The present text follows the first English book publication: *Daisy Miller: A Study/An International Episode/Four Meetings* (London: Macmillan and Co., 1879), vol. II).
1. The father of the country.

whose acquaintances they made—with whom, indeed, they became very intimate—on the steamer, and who had proposed to accompany them to the inn and introduce them, in a friendly way, to the proprietor. This plan, however, had been defeated by their friend's finding that his "partner" was awaiting him on the wharf, and that his commercial associate desired him instantly to come and give his attention to certain telegrams received from St. Louis. But the two Englishmen, with nothing but their national prestige and personal graces to recommend them, were very well received at the hotel, which had an air of capacious hospitality. They found that a bath was not unattainable, and were indeed struck with the facilities for prolonged and reiterated immersion with which their apartment was supplied. After bathing a good deal—more indeed than they had ever done before on a single occasion—they made their way into the dining-room of the hotel, which was a spacious restaurant, with a fountain in the middle, a great many tall plants in ornamental tubs, and an array of French waiters. The first dinner on land, after a sea-voyage, is under any circumstances a delightful occasion, and there was something particularly agreeable in the circumstances in which our young Englishmen found themselves. They were extremely good-natured young men; they were more observant than they appeared; in a sort of inarticulate, accidentally dissimulative fashion, they were highly appreciative. This was perhaps especially the case with the elder, who was also, as I have said, the man of talent. They sat down at a little table which was a very different affair from the great clattering see-saw in the saloon of the steamer. The wide doors and windows of the restaurant stood open, beneath large awnings, to a wide pavement, where there were other plants in tubs, and rows of spreading trees; and beyond which there was a large shady square, without any palings[2] and with marble-paved walks. And above the vivid verdure rose other façades of white marble and of pale chocolate-coloured stone, squaring themselves against the deep blue sky. Here, outside, in the light and the shade and the heat, there was a great tinkling of the bells of innumerable street-cars, and a constant strolling and shuffling and rustling of many pedestrians, a large proportion of whom were young women in Pompadour-looking[3] dresses. Within, the place was cool and vaguely-lighted; with the plash of water, the odour of flowers and the flitting of French waiters, as I have said, upon soundless carpets.

"It's rather like Paris, you know," said the younger of our two travellers.

"It's like Paris—only more so," his companion rejoined.

"I suppose it's the French waiters," said the first speaker. "Why

2. Unfenced (in contrast with London squares, which often contain a private, fenced little park in the middle).

3. High-waisted and with full skirts.

don't they have French waiters in London?"

"Fancy a French waiter at a club," said his friend.

The young Englishmen stared a little, as if he could not fancy it. "In Paris I'm very apt to dine at a place where there's an English waiter. Don't you know, what's-his-name's, close to the thingumbob? They always set an English waiter at me. I suppose they think I can't speak French."

"No more you can." And the elder of the young Englishmen unfolded his napkin.

His companion took no notice whatever of this declaration. "I say," he resumed, in a moment, "I suppose we must learn to speak American. I suppose we must take lessons."

"I can't understand them," said the clever man.

"What the deuce is *he* saying?" asked his comrade, appealing from the French waiter.

"He is recommending some soft-shell crabs," said the clever man.

And so, in desultory observation of the idiosyncrasies of the new society in which they found themselves the young Englishmen proceeded to dine—going in largely, as the phrase is, for cooling draughts and dishes, of which their attendant offered them a very long list. After dinner they went out and slowly walked about the neighbouring streets. The early dusk of waning summer was coming on, but the heat was still very great. The pavements were hot even to the stout boot-soles of the British travellers, and the trees along the kerb-stone emitted strange exotic odours. The young men wandered through the adjoining square—that queer place without palings, and with marble walks arranged in black and white lozenges. There were a great many benches, crowded with shabby-looking people, and the travellers remarked, very justly, that it was not much like Belgrave Square.[4] On one side was an enormous hotel, lifting up into the hot darkness an immense array of open, brightly-lighted windows. At the base of this populous structure was an eternal jangle of horse-cars, and all round it, in the upper dusk, was a sinister hum of mosquitoes. The ground-floor of the hotel seemed to be a huge transparent cage, flinging a wide glare of gaslight into the street, of which it formed a sort of public adjunct, absorbing and emitting the passers-by promiscuously. The young Englishmen went in with every one else, from curiosity, and saw a couple of hundred men sitting on divans along a great marble-paved corridor, with their legs stretched out, together with several dozen more standing in a *queue*, as at the ticket-office of a railway station, before a brilliantly-illuminated counter, of vast extent. These latter persons, who carried portmanteaux in their hands, had a dejected, exhausted look; their garments were not very fresh, and they

4. A quiet, elegant square in London.

seemed to be rendering some mysterious tribute to a magnificent young man with a waxed moustache and a shirt front adorned with diamond buttons, who every now and then dropped an absent glance over their multitudinous patience. They were American citizens doing homage to an hotel-clerk.

"I'm glad he didn't tell us to go there," said one of our Englishmen, alluding to their friend on the steamer, who had told them so many things. They walked up the Fifth Avenue, where, for instance, he had told them that all the first families lived. But the first families were out of town, and our young travellers had only the satisfaction of seeing some of the second—or perhaps even the third—taking the evening air upon balconies and high flights of doorsteps, in the streets which radiate from the more ornamental thoroughfare. They went a little way down one of these side-streets, and they saw young ladies in white dresses—charming-looking persons—seated in graceful attitudes on the chocolate-coloured steps. In one or two places these young ladies were conversing across the street with other young ladies seated in similar postures and costumes in front of the opposite houses, and in the warm night air their colloquial tones sounded strange in the ears of the young Englishmen. One of our friends, nevertheless—the younger one—intimated that he felt a disposition to intercept a few of these soft familiarities; but his companion observed, pertinently enough, that he had better be careful. "We must not begin with making mistakes," said his companion.

"But he told us, you know—he told us," urged the young man, alluding again to the friend on the steamer.

"Never mind what he told us!" answered his comrade, who, if he had greater talents, was also apparently more of a moralist.

By bed-time—in their impatience to taste of a terrestrial couch again our seafarers went to bed early—it was still insufferably hot, and the buzz of the mosquitoes at the open windows might have passed for an audible crepitation of the temperature. "We can't stand this, you know," the young Englishmen said to each other; and they tossed about all night more boisterously than they had tossed upon the Atlantic billows. On the morrow, their first thought was that they would re-embark that day for England; and then it occurred to them that they might find an asylum nearer at hand. The cave of Æolus[5] became their ideal of comfort, and they wondered where the Americans went when they wished to cool off. They had not the least idea, and they determined to apply for information to Mr. J. L. Westgate. This was the name inscribed in a bold hand on the back of a letter carefully preserved in the pocket-book of our junior traveller. Beneath the address, in the left-hand corner of the envelope, were the words,

5. The god of winds.

"Introducing Lord Lambeth and Percy Beaumont, Esq." The letter had been given to the two Englishmen by a good friend of theirs in London, who had been in America two years previously and had singled out Mr. J. L. Westgate from the many friends he had left there as the consignee, as it were, of his compatriots. "He is a capital fellow," the Englishman in London had said, "and he has got an awfully pretty wife. He's tremendously hospitable—he will do everything in the world for you; and as he knows every one over there, it is quite needless I should give you any other introduction. He will make you see every one; trust to him for putting you into circulation. He has got a tremendously pretty wife." It was natural that in the hour of tribulation Lord Lambeth and Mr. Percy Beaumont should have bethought themselves of a gentleman whose attractions had been thus vividly depicted; all the more so that he lived in the Fifth Avenue and that the Fifth Avenue, as they had ascertained the night before, was contiguous to their hotel. "Ten to one he'll be out of town," said Percy Beaumont; "but we can at least find out where he has gone, and we can immediately start in pursuit. He can't possibly have gone to a hotter place, you know."

"Oh, there's only one hotter place," said Lord Lambeth, "and I hope he hasn't gone there."

They strolled along the shady side of the street to the number indicated upon the precious letter. The house presented an imposing chocolate-coloured expanse, relieved by facings and window-cornices of florid sculpture, and by a couple of dusty rose-trees, which clambered over the balconies and the portico. This last-mentioned feature was approached by a monumental flight of steps.

"Rather better than a London house," said Lord Lambeth, looking down from his altitude, after they had rung the bell.

"It depends upon what London house you mean," replied his companion. "You have a tremendous chance to get wet between the house-door and your carriage."

"Well," said Lord Lambeth, glancing at the burning heavens, "I 'guess'[6] it doesn't rain so much here!"

The door was opened by a long negro in a white jacket, who grinned familiarly when Lord Lambeth asked for Mr. Westgate.

"He ain't at home, sir; he's down town at his o'fice."

"Oh, at his office?" said the visitors. "And when will he be at home?"

"Well, sir, when he goes out dis way in de mo'ning, he ain't liable to come home all day."

This was discouraging; but the address of Mr. Westgate's office was freely imparted by the intelligent black, and was taken down by Percy

6. Lambeth seems conscious of using an American idiom, hence the quotation marks.

Beaumont in his pocket-book. The two gentlemen then returned, languidly, to their hotel, and sent for a hackney-coach; and in this commodious vehicle they rolled comfortably down town. They measured the whole length of Broadway again, and found it a path of fire; and then, deflecting to the left, they were deposited by their conductor before a fresh, light, ornamental structure, ten stories high, in a street crowded with keen-faced, light-limbed young men, who were running about very quickly and stopping each other eagerly at corners and in doorways. Passing into this brilliant building, they were introduced by one of the keen-faced young men—he was a charming fellow, in wonderful cream-coloured garments and a hat with a blue ribbon, who had evidently perceived them to be aliens and helpless—to a very snug hydraulic elevator, in which they took their place with many other persons, and which, shooting upward in its vertical socket, presently projected them into the seventh horizontal compartment of the edifice. Here, after brief delay, they found themselves face to face with the friend of their friend in London. His office was composed of several different rooms, and they waited very silently in one of these after they had sent in their letter and their cards. The letter was not one which it would take Mr. Westgate very long to read, but he came out to speak to them more instantly than they could have expected; he had evidently jumped up from his work. He was a tall, lean personage, and was dressed all in fresh white linen; he had a thin, sharp, familiar face, with an expression that was at one and the same time sociable and business-like, a quick, intelligent eye, and a large brown moustache, which concealed his mouth and made his chin, beneath it, look small. Lord Lambeth thought he looked tremendously clever.

"How do you do, Lord Lambeth—how do you do, sir?" he said, holding the open letter in his hand. "I'm very glad to see you—I hope you're very well. You had better come in here—I think it's cooler"; and he led the way into another room, where there were law-books and papers, and windows wide open beneath striped awnings. Just opposite one of the windows, on a line with his eyes, Lord Lambeth observed the weather-vane of a church steeple. The uproar of the street sounded infinitely far below, and Lord Lambeth felt very high in the air. "I say it's cooler," pursued their host, "but everything is relative. How do you stand the heat?"

"I can't say we like it," said Lord Lambeth; "but Beaumont likes it better than I."

"Well, it won't last," Mr. Westgate very cheerfully declared; "nothing unpleasant lasts over here. It was very hot when Captain Littledale was here; he did nothing but drink sherry-cobblers. He expresses some doubt in his letter whether I shall remember him—as if I didn't remember making six sherry-cobblers for him one day, in about twenty minutes. I hope you left him well; two years having elapsed since then."

"Oh, yes, he's all right," said Lord Lambeth.

"I am always very glad to see your countrymen," Mr. Westgate pursued. "I thought it would be time some of you should be coming along. A friend of mine was saying to me only a day or two ago, 'It's time for the water-melons and the Englishmen.' "

"The Englishmen and the water-melons just now are about the same thing," Percy Beaumont observed, wiping his dripping forehead.

"Ah, well, we'll put you on ice, as we do the melons. You must go down to Newport."

"We'll go anywhere!" said Lord Lambeth.

"Yes, you want to go to Newport[7]—that's what you want to do," Mr. Westgate affirmed. "But let's see—when did you get here?"

"Only yesterday," said Percy Beaumont.

"Ah, yes, by the 'Russia.' Where are you staying?"

"At the 'Hanover,' I think they call it."

"Pretty comfortable?" inquired Mr. Westgate.

"It seems a capital place, but I can't say we like the gnats," said Lord Lambeth.

Mr. Westgate stared and laughed. "Oh, no, of course, you don't like the gnats. We shall expect you to like a good many things over here, but we shan't insist upon your liking the gnats; though certainly you'll admit that, as gnats, they are fine, eh? But you oughtn't to remain in the city."

"So we think," said Lord Lambeth. "If you would kindly suggest something—"

"Suggest something, my dear sir?"—and Mr. Westgate looked at him, narrowing his eyelids. "Open your mouth and shut your eyes! Leave it to me, and I'll put you through. It's a matter of national pride with me that all Englishmen should have a good time; and, as I have had considerable practice, I have learned to minister to their wants. I find they generally want the right thing. So just please to consider yourselves my property; and if any one should try to appropriate you, please to say, 'Hands off; too late for the market.' But let's see," continued the American, in his slow, humorous voice, with a distinctness of utterance which appeared to his visitors to be part of a facetious intention—a strangely leisurely, speculative voice for a man evidently so busy and, as they felt, so professional—"let's see; are you going to make something of a stay, Lord Lambeth?"

---

7. Newport, Rhode Island, was an elegant resort where wealthy New Yorkers escaped from the summer heat, some of them to their own summer places.

"Oh dear no," said the young Englishman; "my cousin was coming over on some business, so I just came across, at an hour's notice, for the lark."

"Is it your first visit to the United States?"

"Oh dear, yes."

"I was obliged to come on some business," said Percy Beaumont, "and I brought Lambeth with me."

"And *you* have been here before, sir?"

"Never—never."

"I thought, from your referring to business—"said Mr. Westgate.

"Oh, you see I'm by way of being a barrister," Percy Beaumont answered. "I know some people that think of bringing a suit against one of your railways, and they asked me to come over and take measures accordingly."

Mr. Westgate gave one of his slow, keen looks again. "What's your railroad?" he asked.

"The Tennessee Central."

The American tilted back his chair a little, and poised it an instant. "Well, I'm sorry you want to attack one of our institutions," he said, smiling. "But I guess you had better enjoy yourself *first!*"

"I'm certainly rather afraid I can't work in this weather," the young barrister confessed.

"Leave that to the natives," said Mr. Westgate. "Leave the Tennessee Central to me, Mr. Beaumont. Some day we'll talk it over, and I guess I can make it square. But I didn't know you Englishmen ever did any work, in the upper classes."

"Oh, we do a lot of work; don't we, Lambeth?" asked Percy Beaumont.

"I must certainly be at home by the 19th of September," said the younger Englishman, irrelevantly, but gently.

"For the shooting, eh? or is it the hunting—or the fishing?" inquired his entertainer.

"Oh, I must be in Scotland," said Lord Lambeth, blushing a little.

"Well, then," rejoined Mr. Westgate, "you had better amuse yourself first, also. You must go down and see Mrs. Westgate."

"We should be so happy—if you would kindly tell us the train," said Percy Beaumont.

"It isn't a train—it's a boat."

"Oh, I see. And what is the name of—a—the—a—town?"

"It isn't a town," said Mr. Westgate, laughing. "It's a—well, what shall I call it? It's a watering-place. In short, it's Newport. You'll see what it is. It's cool; that's the principal thing. You will greatly oblige me by going down there and putting yourself into the hands of Mrs. Westgate. It isn't perhaps for me to say it; but you couldn't be in better hands. Also in those of her sister, who is staying with her. She is very fond of Englishmen. She thinks there is nothing like them."

"Mrs. Westgate or—a—her sister?" asked Percy Beaumont, modestly, yet in the tone of an inquiring traveller.

"Oh, I mean my wife," said Mr. Westgate. "I don't suppose my sister-in-law knows much about them. She has always led a very quiet life; she has lived in Boston."

Percy Beaumont listened with interest. "That, I believe," he said, "is the most—a—intellectual town?"

"I believe it is very intellectual. I don't go there much," responded his host.

"I say, we ought to go there," said Lord Lambeth to his companion.

"Oh, Lord Lambeth, wait till the great heat is over!" Mr. Westgate interposed. "Boston in this weather would be very trying; it's not the temperature for intellectual exertion. At Boston, you know, you have to pass an examination at the city limits; and when you come away they give you a kind of degree."

Lord Lambeth stared, blushing a little; and Percy Beaumont stared a little also—but only with his fine natural complexion; glancing aside after a moment to see that his companion was not looking too credulous, for he had heard a great deal about American humour. "I daresay it is very jolly," said the younger gentleman.

"I daresay it is," said Mr. Westgate. "Only I must impress upon you that at present—to-morrow morning, at an early hour—you will be expected at Newport. We have a house there; half the people in New York go there for the summer. I am not sure that at this very moment my wife can take you in; she has got a lot of people staying with her; I don't know who they all are; only she may have no room. But you can begin with the hotel, and meanwhile you can live at my house. In that way—simply sleeping at the hotel—you will find it tolerable. For the rest, you must make yourself at home at my place. You mustn't be shy, you know; if you are only here for a month that will be a great waste of time. Mrs. Westgate won't neglect you, and you had better not try to resist her. I know something about that. I expect you'll find some pretty girls on the premises. I shall write to my wife by this afternoon's mail, and tomorrow she and Miss Alden will look out for you. Just walk right in and make yourself comfortable. Your steamer leaves from this part of the city, and I will immediately send out and get you a cabin. Then, at half-past four o'clock, just call for me here, and I will go with you and put you on board. It's a big boat; you might get lost. A few days hence, at the end of the week, I will come down to Newport and see how you are getting on."

The two young Englishmen inaugurated the policy of not resisting Mrs. Westgate by submitting, with great docility and thankfulness, to her husband. He was evidently a very good fellow, and he made an impression upon his visitors; his hospitality seemed to recommend itself, consciously—with a friendly wink, as it were—as if it hinted, judicially, that you could not possibly make a better bargain. Lord Lambeth and his cousin left their entertainer to his labours and returned to their hotel, where they spent three or four hours in their respective shower-baths. Percy Beaumont had suggested that they ought to see something of the town; but "Oh, damn the town!" his noble kinsman[8] had rejoined. They returned to Mr. Westgate's office in a carriage, with their luggage, very punctually; but it must be reluctantly recorded that, this time, he kept them waiting so long that they felt themselves missing the steamer and were deterred only by an amiable modesty from dispensing with his attendance and starting on a hasty scramble to the wharf. But when at last he appeared, and the carriage plunged into the purlieus of Broadway, they jolted and jostled to such good purpose that they reached the huge white vessel while the bell for departure was still ringing and the absorption of passengers still active. It was indeed, as Mr. Westgate had said, a big boat, and his leadership in the innumerable and interminable corridors and cabins, with which he seemed perfectly acquainted, and of which any one and every one appeared to have the *entrée,* was very grateful to the slightly bewildered voyagers. He showed them their state-room—a spacious apartment, embellished with gas-lamps, mirrors *en pied*[9] and sculptured furniture—and then, long after they had been intimately convinced that the steamer was in motion and launched upon the unknown stream that they were about to navigate, he bade them a sociable farewell.

"Well, good-bye, Lord Lambeth," he said. "Good-bye, Mr. Percy Beaumont; I hope you'll have a good time. Just let them do what they want with you. I'll come down by-and-by and look after you."

II

The young Englishmen emerged from their cabin and amused themselves with wandering about the immense labyrinthine steamer, which struck them as an extraordinary mixture of a ship and an hotel. It was densely crowded with passengers, the larger number of whom appeared to be ladies and very young children; and in the big saloons, ornamented in white and gold, which followed each other in surprising succession, beneath the swinging gas-lights and among the small side-passages where the negro domestics of both sexes assembled with

8. *The Two Noble Kinsmen* is a play by John Fletcher (1579–1625), probably written in collaboration with Shakespeare. Fletcher collaborated with other playwrights too, among them Francis Beaumont; Beaumont and Fletcher were in fact a popular team contemporary with Shakespeare. Thus a chain of associations links the surname Beaumont with the phrase James uses here to refer to Percy Beaumont's cousin Lord Lambeth—perhaps an accident but, since Renaissance drama was much read in the nineteenth century, more likely one of James's unobtrusive puns.
9. Full-length.

an air of philosophic leisure, every one was moving to and fro and exchanging loud and familiar observations. Eventually, at the instance of a discriminating black, our young men went and had some "supper," in a wonderful place arranged like a theatre, where, in a gilded gallery upon which little boxes appeared to open, a large orchestra was playing operatic selections, and, below, people were handing about bills of fare, as if they had been programmes. All this was sufficiently curious; but the agreeable thing, later, was to sit out on one of the great white decks of the steamer, in the warm, breezy darkness, and, in the vague starlight, to make out the line of low, mysterious coast. The young Englishmen tried American cigars—those of Mr. Westgate—and talked together as they usually talked, with many odd silences, lapses of logic and incongruities of transition; like people who have grown old together and learned to supply each other's missing phrases; or, more especially, like people thoroughly conscious of a common point of view, so that a style of conversation superficially lacking in finish might suffice for a reference to a fund of associations in the light of which everything was all right.

"We really seem to be going out to sea," Percy Beaumont observed. "Upon my word, we are going back to England. He has shipped us off again. I call that 'real mean.' "

"I suppose it's all right," said Lord Lambeth. "I want to see those pretty girls at Newport. You know he told us the place was an island; and aren't all islands in the sea?"

"Well," resumed the elder traveller after a while," if his house is as good as his cigars, we shall do very well."

"He seems a very good fellow," said Lord Lambeth, as if this idea had just occurred to him.

"I say, we had better remain at the inn," rejoined his companion, presently. "I don't think I like the way he spoke of his house. I don't like stopping in the house with such a tremendous lot of women."

"Oh, I don't mind," said Lord Lambeth. And then they smoked awhile in silence. "Fancy his thinking we do no work in England!" the young man resumed.

"I daresay he didn't really think so," said Percy Beaumont.

"Well, I guess they don't know much about England over here!" declared Lord Lambeth, humorously. And then there was another long pause. "He was devilish civil," observed the young nobleman.

"Nothing, certainly, could have been more civil," rejoined his companion.

"Littledale said his wife was great fun," said Lord Lambeth.

"Whose wife—Littledale's?"

"This American's—Mrs. Westgate. What's his name? J. L."

Beaumont was silent a moment. "What was fun to Littledale," he said at last, rather sententiously, "may be death to us."

"What do you mean by that?" asked his kinsman. "I am as good a man as Littledale."

"My dear boy, I hope you won't begin to flirt," said Percy Beaumont.

"I don't care. I daresay I shan't begin."

"With a married woman, if she's bent upon it, it's all very well," Beaumont expounded. "But our friend mentioned a young lady—a sister, a sister-in-law. For God's sake, don't get entangled with her."

"How do you mean, entangled?"

"Depend upon it she will try to hook you."

"Oh, bother!" said Lord Lambeth.

"American girls are very clever," urged his companion.

"So much the better," the young man declared.

"I fancy they are always up to some game of that sort," Beaumont continued.

"They can't be worse than they are in England," said Lord Lambeth, judicially.

"Ah, but in England," replied Beaumont, "you have got your natural protectors. You have got your mother and sisters."

"My mother and sisters—" began the young nobleman, with a certain energy. But he stopped in time, puffing at his cigar.

"Your mother spoke to me about it, with tears in her eyes," said Percy Beaumont. "She said she felt very nervous. I promised to keep you out of mischief."

"You had better take care of yourself," said the object of maternal and ducal solicitude.

"Ah," rejoined the young barrister, "I haven't the expectation of a hundred thousand a year—not to mention other attractions."

"Well," said Lord Lambeth, "don't cry out before you're hurt!"

It was certainly very much cooler at Newport, where our travellers found themselves assigned to a couple of diminutive bed-rooms in a far-away angle of an immense hotel. They had gone ashore in the early summer twilight, and had very promptly put themselves to bed; thanks to which circumstance and to their having, during the previous hours, in their commodious cabin, slept the sleep of youth and health, they began to feel, towards eleven o'clock, very alert and inquisitive. They looked out of their windows across a row of small green fields, bordered with low stone dykes, of rude construction, and saw a deep blue ocean lying beneath a deep blue sky and flecked now and then with scintillating patches of foam. A strong, fresh breeze came in through the curtainless casements and prompted our young men to observe, generously, that it didn't seem half a bad climate. They made other observations after they had emerged from their rooms in pursuit of breakfast—a meal of which they partook in a huge bare hall, where a hundred negroes, in white jackets, were shuffling about upon an uncarpeted floor; where the flies were superabundant and the tables and dishes covered over with a strange, voluminous integument of coarse blue gauze; and where several little boys and girls, who had risen late, were seated in fastidious solitude at the morning repast. These young persons had not the morning paper before them, but they were engaged in languid perusal of the bill of fare.

This latter document was a great puzzle to our friends, who, on reflecting that its bewildering categories had relation to breakfast alone, had an uneasy prevision of an encyclopædic dinner-list. They found a great deal of entertainment at the hotel, an enormous wooden structure, for the erection of which it seemed to them that the virgin forests of the West must have been terribly deflowered. It was perforated from end to end with immense bare corridors, through which a strong draught was blowing—bearing along wonderful figures of ladies in white morning-dresses and clouds of Valenciennes lace, who seemed to float down the long vistas with expanded furbelows, like angels spreading their wings. In front was a gigantic verandah, upon which an army might have encamped—a vast wooden terrace, with a roof as lofty as the nave of a cathedral. Here our young Englishmen enjoyed, as they supposed, a glimpse of American society, which was distributed over the measureless expanse in a variety of sedentary attitudes, and appeared to consist largely of pretty young girls, dressed as if for a *fete champêtre*, [1] swaying to and fro in rocking-chairs, fanning themselves with large straw fans, and enjoying an enviable exemption from social cares. Lord Lambeth had a theory, which it might be interesting to trace to its origin, that it would be not only agreeable, but easily possible, to enter into relations with one of these young ladies; and his companion found occasion to check the young nobleman's colloquial impulses.

"You had better take care," said Percy Beaumont, "or you will have an offended father or brother pulling out a bowie-knife."

"I assure you it is all right," Lord Lambeth replied. "You know the Americans come to these big hotels to make acquaintances."

"I know nothing about it, and neither do you," said his kinsman, who, like a clever man, had begun to perceive that the observation of American society demanded a readjustment of one's standard.

"Hang it, then, let's find out!" cried Lord Lambeth with some impatience. "You know, I don't want to miss anything."

"We will find out," said Percy Beaumont, very reasonably. "We will go and see Mrs. Westgate and make all the proper inquiries."

And so the two inquiring Englishmen, who had this lady's address inscribed in her husband's hand upon a card, descended from the

1. A party in the country, a garden party.

verandah of the big hotel and took their way, according to direction, along a large straight road, past a series of fresh-looking villas, embosomed in shrubs and flowers and enclosed in an ingenious variety of wooden palings. The morning was brilliant and cool, the villas were smart and snug, and the walk of the young travellers was very entertaining. Everything looked as if it had received a coat of fresh paint the day before—the red roofs, the green shutters, the clean, bright browns and buffs of the house-fronts. The flower-beds on the little lawns seemed to sparkle in the radiant air, and the gravel in the short carriage-sweeps to flash and twinkle. Along the road came a hundred little basket-phaetons, in which, almost always, a couple of ladies were sitting—ladies in white dresses and long white gloves, holding the reins and looking at the two Englishmen, whose nationality was not elusive, through thick blue veils, tied tightly about their faces as if to guard their complexions. At last the young men came within sight of the sea again, and then, having interrogated a gardener over the paling of a villa, they turned into an open gate. Here they found themselves face to face with the ocean and with a very picturesque structure, resembling a magnified *chalet*, which was perched upon a green embankment just above it. The house had a verandah of extraordinary width all around it, and a great many doors and windows standing open to the verandah. These various apertures had, in common, such an accessible, hospitable air, such a breezy flutter, within, of light curtains, such expansive thresholds and reassuring interiors, that our friends hardly knew which was the regular entrance, and, after hesitating a moment, presented themselves at one of the windows. The room within was dark, but in a moment a graceful figure vaguely shaped itself in the rich-looking gloom, and a lady came to meet them. Then they saw that she had been seated at a table, writing, and that she had heard them and had got up. She stepped out into the light; she wore a frank, charming smile, with which she held out her hand to Percy Beaumont.

"Oh, you must be Lord Lambeth and Mr. Beaumont," she said. "I have heard from my husband that you would come. I am extremely glad to see you." And she shook hands with each of her visitors. Her visitors were a little shy, but they had very good manners; they responded with smiles and exclamations, and they apologised for not knowing the front door. The lady rejoined, with vivacity, that when she wanted to see people very much she did not insist upon those distinctions, and that Mr. Westgate had written to her of his English friends in terms that made her really anxious. "He said you were so terribly prostrated," said Mrs. Westgate.

"Oh, you mean by the heat?" replied Percy Beaumont. We were rather knocked up, but we feel wonderfully better. We had such a jolly—a—voyage down here. It's so very good of you to mind."

"Yes, so very kind of you," murmured Lord Lambeth.

Mrs. Westgate stood smiling; she was extremely pretty. "Well, I did mind," she said; "and I thought of sending for you this morning, to the Ocean House.[2] I am very glad you are better, and I am charmed you have arrived. You must come round to the other side of the piazza." And she led the way, with a light, smooth step, looking back at the young men and smiling.

The other side of the piazza was, as Lord Lambeth presently remarked, a very jolly place. It was of the most liberal proportions, and with its awnings, its fanciful chairs, its cushions and rugs, its view of the ocean, close at hand, tumbling along the base of the low cliffs whose level tops intervened in lawnlike smoothness, it formed a charming complement to the drawing-room. As such it was in course of use at the present moment; it was occupied by a social circle. There were several ladies and two or three gentlemen, to whom Mrs. Westgate proceeded to introduce the distinguished strangers. She mentioned a great many names, very freely and distinctly; the young Englishmen, shuffling about and bowing, were rather bewildered. But at last they were provided with chairs—low wicker chairs, gilded and tied with a great many ribbons—and one of the ladies (a very young person, with a little snub nose and several dimples) offered Percy Beaumont a fan. The fan was also adorned with pink love-knots; but Percy Beaumont declined it, although he was very hot. Presently, however, it became cooler; the breeze from the sea was delicious, the view was charming, and the people sitting there looked exceedingly fresh and comfortable. Several of the ladies seemed to be young girls, and the gentlemen were slim, fair youths, such as our friends had seen the day before in New York. The ladies were working upon bands of tapestry, and one of the young men had an open book in his lap. Beaumont afterwards learned from one of the ladies that this young man had been reading aloud—that he was from Boston and was very fond of reading aloud. Beaumont said it was a great pity that they had interrupted him; he should like so much (from all he had heard) to hear a Bostonian read. Couldn't the young man be induced to go on?

"Oh, no," said his informant, very freely; "he wouldn't be able to get the young ladies to attend to him now."

There was something very friendly, Beaumont perceived in the attitude of the company; they looked at the young Englishmen with an air of animated sympathy and interest; they smiled, brightly and unanimously, at everything either of the visitors said. Lord Lambeth and his companion felt that they were being made very welcome. Mrs. Westgate seated herself between them, and, talking a great deal to each, they had occasion to observe that she was as pretty as their friend

2. Their hotel.

Littledale had promised. She was thirty years old, with the eyes and the smile of a girl of seventeen, and she was extremely light and graceful, elegant, exquisite. Mrs. Westgate was extremely spontaneous. She was very frank and demonstrative, and appeared always— while she looked at you delightedly with her beautiful young eyes—to be making sudden confessions and concessions, after momentary hesitations.

"We shall expect to see a great deal of you," she said to Lord Lambeth, with a kind of joyous earnestness. "We are very fond of Englishmen here; that is, there are a great many we have been fond of. After a day or two you must come and stay with us; we hope you will stay a long time. Newport's a very nice place when you come really to know it, when you know plenty of people. Of course, you and Mr. Beaumont will have no difficulty about that. Englishmen are very well received here; there are almost always two or three of them about. I think they always like it, and I must say I should think they would. They receive ever so much attention. I must say I think they sometimes get spoiled; but I am sure you and Mr. Beaumont are proof against that. My husband tells me you are a friend of Captain Littledale; he was such a charming man. He made himself most agreeable here, and I am sure I wonder he didn't stay. It couldn't have been pleasanter for him in his own country. Though I suppose it is very pleasant in England, for English people. I don't know myself; I have been there very little. I have been a great deal abroad, but I am always on the Continent. I must say I'm extremely fond of Paris; you know we Americans always are; we go there when we die. Did you ever hear that before? that was said by a great wit.[3] I mean the good Americans; but we are all good; you'll see that for yourself. All I know of England is London, and all I know of London is that place—on that little corner, you know, where you buy jackets—jackets with that coarse braid and those big buttons. They make very good jackets in London, I will do you the justice to say that. And some people like the hats; but about the hats I was always a heretic; I always got my hats in Paris. You can't wear an English hat—at least, I never could—unless you dress your hair *à l'Anglaise*;[4] and I must say that is a talent I never possessed. In Paris they will make things to suit your peculiarities; but in England I think you like much more to have—how shall I say it?—one thing for everybody. I mean as regards dress. I don't know about other things; but I have always supposed that in other things everything was different. I mean according to the people—according to the classes, and all that. I am afraid you will think that I don't take a very favourable view; but you know you can't take a very favourable view in Dover Street, in the month of November. That has always been my fate. Do you know

---

3. Actually Thomas Gold Appleton (1812–84). He was Longfellow's brother-in-law but himself more conversational wit than poet.
4. In the English style.

Jones's Hotel, in Dover Street? That's all I know of Enland. Of course, every one admits that the English hotels are your weak point. There was always the most frightful fog; I couldn't see to try my things on. When I got over to America—into the light—I usually found they were twice too big. The next time I mean to go in the season; I think I shall go next year. I want very much to take my sister; she has never been to England. I don't know whether you know what I mean by saying that the Englishmen who come here sometimes get spoiled. I mean that they take things as a matter of course—things that are done for them. Now, naturally, they are only a matter of course when the Englishmen are very nice. But, of course, they are almost always very nice. Of course, this isn't nearly such an interesting country as England; there are not nearly so many things to see, and we haven't your country life. I have never seen anything of your country life; when I am in Europe I am always on the Continent. But I have heard a great deal about it; I know that when you are among yourselves in the country you have the most beautiful time. Of course, we have nothing of that sort, we have nothing on that scale. I don't apologise, Lord Lambeth; some Americans are always apologising; you must have noticed that. We have the reputation of always boasting and bragging and waving the American flag; but I must say that what strikes me is that we are perpetually making excuses and trying to smooth things over. The American flag has quite gone out of fashion; it's very carefully folded up, like an old tablecloth. Why should we apologise? The English never apologise—do they? No, I must say I never apologise. You must take us as we come—with all our imperfections on our heads. Of course we haven't your country life, and your old ruins, and your great estates, and your leisure-class, and all that. But if we haven't, I should think you might find it a pleasant change—I think any country is pleasant where they have pleasant manners. Captain Littledale told me he had never seen such pleasant manners as at Newport; and he had been a great deal in European society. Hadn't he been in the diplomatic service? He told me the dream of his life was to get appointed to a diplomatic post in Washington. But he doesn't seem to have succeeded. I suppose that in England promotion—and all that sort of thing—is fearfully slow. With us, you know, it's a great deal too fast. You see I admit our drawbacks. But I must confess I think Newport is an ideal place. I don't know anything like it anywhere. Captain Littledale told me he didn't know anything like it anywhere. It's entirely different from most watering-places; it's a most charming life. I must say I think that when one goes to a foreign country, one ought to enjoy the differences. Of course there are differences; otherwise what did one come abroad for? Look for your pleasure in the differences, Lord Lambeth; that's the way to do it; and then I am sure you will find American society—at least Newport society—most charming and most interesting. I wish very much my husband were here; but he's dreadfully confined to New York. I suppose you think that is very strange—for a gentleman. But you see we haven't any leisure-class."

Mrs. Westgate's discourse, delivered in a soft, sweet voice, flowed on like a miniature torrent and was interrupted by a hundred little smiles, glances and gestures, which might have figured the irregularities and obstructions of such a stream. Lord Lambeth listened to her with, it must be confessed, a rather ineffectual attention, although he indulged in a good many little murmurs and ejaculations of assent and deprecation. He had no great faculty for apprehending generalisations. There were some three or four indeed which, in the play of his own intelligence, he had originated, and which had seemed convenient at the moment; but at the present time he could hardly have been said to follow Mrs. Westgate as she darted gracefully about in the sea of speculation. Fortunately she asked for no especial rejoinder, for she looked about at the rest of the company as well, and smiled at Percy Beaumont, on the other side of her, as if he too must understand her and agree with her. He was rather more successful than his companion; for besides being, as we know, cleverer, his attention was not vaguely distracted by close vicinity to a remarkably interesting young girl, with dark hair and blue eyes. This was the case with Lord Lambeth, to whom it occurred after a while that the young girl with blue eyes and dark hair was the pretty sister of whom Mrs. Westgate had spoken. She presently turned to him with a remark which established her identity.

"It's a great pity you couldn't have brought my brother-in-law with you. It's a great shame he should be in New York in these days."

"Oh yes; it's so very hot," said Lord Lambeth.

"It must be dreadful," said the young girl.

"I daresay he is very busy," Lord Lambeth observed.

"The gentlemen in America work too much," the young girl went on.

"Oh, do they? I daresay they like it," said her interlocutor.

"I don't like it. One never sees them."

"Don't you, really?" asked Lord Lambeth. "I shouldn't have fancied that."

"Have you come to study American manners?" asked the young girl.

"Oh, I don't know. I just came over for a lark. I haven't got long." Here there was a pause, and Lord Lambeth began again. "But Mr. Westgate will come down here, will not he?"

"I certainly hope he will. He must help to entertain you and Mr. Beaumont."

Lord Lambeth looked at her a little with his handsome brown eyes.

"Do you suppose he would have come down with us, if we had urged him?"

Mr. Westgate's sister-in-law was silent a moment, and then—"I daresay he would," she answered.

"Really!" said the young Englishman. "He was immensely civil to Beaumont and me," he added.

"He is a dear good fellow," the young lady rejoined. "And he is a perfect husband. But all Americans are that," she continued, smiling.

"Really!" Lord Lambeth exclaimed again; and wondered whether all American ladies had such a passion for generalising as these two.

III

He sat there a good while: there was a great deal of talk; it was all very friendly and lively and jolly. Every one present, sooner or later, said something to him, and seemed to make a particular point of addressing him by name. Two or three other persons came in, and there was a shifting of seats and changing of places; the gentlemen all entered into intimate conversation with the two Englishmen, made them urgent offers of hospitality and hoped they might frequently be of service to them. They were afraid Lord Lambeth and Mr. Beaumont were not very comfortable at their hotel—that it was not, as one of them said, "so private as those dear little English inns of yours." This last gentleman went on to say that unfortunately, as yet, perhaps, privacy was not quite so easily obtained in America as might be desired; still, he continued, you could generally get it by paying for it; in fact you could get everything in America nowadays by paying for it. American life was certainly growing a great deal more private; it was growing very much like England. Everything at Newport, for instance, was thoroughly private; Lord Lambeth would probably be struck with that. It was also represented to the strangers that it mattered very little whether their hotel was agreeable, as every one would want them to make visits; they would stay with other people, and, in any case, they would be a great deal at Mrs. Westgate's. They would find that very charming; it was the pleasantest house in Newport. It was a pity Mr. Westgate was always away; he was a man of the highest ability—very acute, very acute. He worked like a horse and he left his wife—well, to do about as she liked. He liked her to enjoy herself, and she seemed to know how. She was extremely brilliant, and a splendid talker. Some people preferred her sister; but Miss Alden was very different; she was in a different style altogether. Some people even thought her prettier, and, certainly, she was not so sharp. She was more in the Boston style; she had lived a great deal in Boston and she was very highly educated. Boston girls, it was intimated, were more like English young ladies.

Lord Lambeth had presently a chance to test the truth of this proposition; for on the company rising in compliance with a suggestion from their hostess that they should walk down to the rocks and look at the sea, the young Englishman again found himself, as they strolled across the grass, in proximity to Mrs. Westgate's sister. Though she was but a girl of twenty, she appeared to feel the obligation to exert an active hospitality; and this was perhaps the more to be noticed as she seemed by nature a reserved and retiring person, and had little of her sister's fraternising quality. She was perhaps rather too thin, and she was a little pale; but as she moved slowly over the grass, with her arms hanging at her sides, looking gravely for a moment at the sea and then brightly, for all her gravity, at him, Lord Lambeth thought her at least as pretty as Mrs. Westgate, and reflected that if this was the Boston style the Boston style was very charming. He thought she looked very clever; he could imagine that she was highly educated; but at the same time she seemed gentle and graceful. For all her cleverness, however, he felt that she had to think a little what to say; she didn't say the first thing that came into her head; he had come from a different part of the world and from a different society, and she was trying to adapt her conversation. The others were scattering themselves near the rocks; Mrs. Westgate had charge of Percy Beaumont.

"Very jolly place, isn't it?" said Lord Lambeth. "It's a very jolly place to sit."

"Very charming," said the young girl; "I often sit here; there are all kinds of cosy corners—as if they had been made on purpose."

"Ah! I suppose you have had some of them made," said the young man.

Miss Alden looked at him a moment. "Oh no, we have had nothing made. It's pure nature."

"I should think you would have a few little benches—rustic seats and that sort of thing. It might be so jolly to sit here, you know," Lord Lambeth went on.

"I am afraid we haven't so many of those things as you," said the young girl, thoughtfully.

"I daresay you go in for pure nature as you were saying. Nature, over here, must be so grand, you know." And Lord Lambeth looked about him.

The little coast-line hereabouts was very pretty, but it was not at all grand; and Miss Alden appeared to rise to a perception of this fact. "I am afraid it seems to you very rough," she said. "It's not like the coast scenery in Kingsley's novels."[5]

---

5. Neither Charles Kingsley (1819–75) nor his brother Henry (1830–76), both English novelists, was noted for seascapes. But *Westward Ho!* (1855), Charles Kingsley's most popular work, a romantic historical novel of the time of Queen Elizabeth I, contains pictures of the North Devon coast based on the author's childhood memories. They may be what Bessie Alden has in mind.

"Ah, the novels always overdo it, you know," Lord Lambeth rejoined. "You must not go by the novels."

They were wandering about a little on the rocks, and they stopped and looked down into a narrow chasm where the rising tide made a curious bellowing sound. It was loud enough to prevent their hearing each other, and they stood there for some moments in silence. The young girl looked at her companion, observing him attentively but covertly, as women, even when very young, know how to do. Lord Lambeth repaid observation; tall, straight and strong, he was handsome as certain young Englishmen, and certain young Englishmen almost alone, are handsome; with a perfect finish of feature and a look of intellectual repose and gentle good temper which seemed somehow to be consequent upon his well-cut nose and chin. And to speak of Lord Lambeth's expression of intellectual repose is not simply a civil way of saying that he looked stupid. He was evidently not a young man of an irritable imagination; he was not, as he would himself have said, tremendously clever; but, though there was a kind of appealing dulness in his eye, he looked thoroughly reasonable and competent, and his appearance proclaimed that to be a nobleman, an athlete, and an excellent fellow, was a sufficiently brilliant combination of qualities. The young girl beside him, it may be attested without farther delay, thought him the handsomest young man she had ever seen; and Bessie Alden's imagination, unlike that of her companion, was irritable. He, however, was also making up his mind that she was uncommonly pretty.

"I daresay it's very gay here—that you have lots of balls and parties," he said; for, if he was not tremendously clever, he rather prided himself on having, with women, a sufficiency of conversation.

"Oh yes, there is a great deal going on," Bessie Alden replied. "There are not so many balls, but there are a good many other things. You will see for yourself; we live rather in the midst of it."

"It's very kind of you to say that. But I thought you Americans were always dancing."

"I suppose we dance a good deal; but I have never seen much of it. We don't do it much, at any rate, in summer. And I am sure," said Bessie Alden, "that we don't have so many balls as you have in England."

"Really!" exclaimed Lord Lambeth. "Ah, in England it all depends, you know."

"You will not think much of our gaieties," said the young girl, looking at him with a little mixture of interrogation and decision which was peculiar to her. The interrogation seemed earnest and the decision seemed arch; but the mixture, at any rate, was charming. "Those things, with us, are much less splendid than in England."

"I fancy you don't mean that," said Lord Lambeth, laughing.

"I assure you I mean everything I say," the young girl declared. "Certainly, from what I have read about English society, it is very different."

"Ah, well, you know," said her companion, "those things are often described by fellows who know nothing about them. You mustn't mind what you read."

"Oh, I *shall* mind what I read!" Bessie Alden rejoined. "When I read Thackeray and George Eliot, how can I help minding them?"

"Ah, well, Thackeray—and George Eliot," said the young nobleman; "I haven't read much of them."

"Don't you suppose they know about society?" asked Bessie Alden.

"Oh, I daresay they know; they were so very clever. But those fashionable novels," said Lord Lambeth, 'they are awful rot, you know."

His companion looked at him a moment with her dark blue eyes, and then she looked down into the chasm where the water was tumbling about. "Do you mean Mrs. Gore,[6] for instance?" she said presently, raising her eyes.

"I am afraid I haven't read that either," was the young man's rejoinder, laughing a little and blushing. "I am afraid you'll think I am not very intellectual."

"Reading Mrs. Gore is no proof of intellect. But I like reading everything about English life—even poor books. I am so curious about it."

"Aren't ladies always curious?" asked the young man, jestingly.

But Bessie Alden appeared to desire to answer his question seriously. "I don't think so—I don't think we are enough so—that we care about many things. So it's all the more of a compliment," she added, "that I should want to know so much about England."

The logic here seemed a little close; but Lord Lambeth, conscious of a compliment, found his natural modesty just at hand. "I am sure you know a great deal more than I do."

"I really think I know a great deal—for a person who has never been there."

"Have you really never been there?" cried Lord Lambeth. "Fancy!"

"Never—except in imagination," said the young girl.

"Fancy!" repeated her companion. "But I daresay you'll go soon, won't you?"

"It's the dream of my life!" declared Bessie Alden, smiling.

"But your sister seems to know a tremendous lot about London," Lord Lambeth went on.

The young girl was silent a moment. "My sister and I are two very

---

6. Mrs. Catherine Grace Frances Gore (1799–1861), née Moody, author of about sev- enty novels and plays. Thackeray parodied her novels.

different persons," she presently said. "She has been a great deal in Europe. She has been in England several times. She has known a great many English people."

"But you must have known some, too," said Lord Lambeth.

"I don't think that I have ever spoken to one before. You are the first Englishman that—to my knowledge—I have ever talked with."

Bessie Alden made this statement with a certain gravity—almost, as it seemed to Lord Lambeth, an impressiveness. Attempts at impressiveness always made him feel awkward, and he now began to laugh and swing his stick. "Ah, you would have been sure to know!" he said. And then he added, after an instant—"I'm sorry I am not a better specimen."

The young girl looked away; but she smiled, laying aside her impressiveness. "You must remember that you are only a beginning," she said. Then she retraced her steps, leading the way back to the lawn, where they saw Mrs. Westgate come towards them with Percy Beaumont still at her side. "Perhaps I shall go to England next year," Miss Alden continued; "I want to, immensely. My sister is going to Europe, and she has asked me to go with her. If we go, I shall make her stay as long as possible in London."

"Ah, you must come in July," said Lord Lambeth. "That's the time when there is most going on."

"I don't think I can wait till July," the young girl rejoined. "By the first of May I shall be very impatient." They had gone farther, and Mrs. Westgate and her companion were near them. "Kitty," said Miss Alden, "I have given out that we are going to London next May. So please to conduct yourself accordingly."

Percy Beaumont wore a somewhat animated—even a slightly irritated—air. He was by no means so handsome a man as his cousin, although in his cousin's absence he might have passed for a striking specimen of the tall, muscular, fair-bearded, clear-eyed Englishman. Just now Beaumont's clear eyes, which were small and of a pale grey colour, had a rather troubled light, and, after glancing at Bessie Alden while she spoke, he rested them upon his kinsman. Mrs. Westgate meanwhile, with her superfluously pretty gaze, looked at every one alike.

"You had better wait till the time comes," she said to her sister. "Perhaps next May you won't care so much about London. Mr. Beaumont and I," she went on, smiling at her companion, "have had a tremendous discussion. We don't agree about anything. It's perfectly delightful."

"Oh, I say, Percy!" exclaimed Lord Lambeth.

"I disagree," said Beaumont, stroking down his black hair, "even to the point of not thinking it delightful."

"Oh, I say!" cried Lord Lambeth again.

"I don't see anything delightful in my disagreeing with Mrs. Westgate," said Percy Beaumont.

"Well, I do!" Mrs. Westgate declared; and she turned to her sister. "You know you have to go to town. The phaeton is there. You had better take Lord Lambeth."

At this point Percy Beaumont certainly looked straight at his kinsman; he tried to catch his eye. But Lord Lambeth would not look at him; his own eyes were better occupied. "I shall be very happy," cried Bessie Alden. "I am only going to some shops. But I will drive you about and show you the place."

"An American woman who respects herself," said Mrs. Westgate, turning to Beaumont with her bright expository air, "must buy something every day of her life. If she cannot do it herself, she must send out some member of her family for the purpose. So Bessie goes forth to fulfil my mission."

The young girl had walked away, with Lord Lambeth by her side, to whom she was talking still; and Percy Beaumont watched them as they passed towards the house. "She fulfils her own mission," he presently said; "that of being a very attractive young lady."

"I don't know that I should say very attractive," Mrs. Westgate rejoined. "She is not so much that as she is charming when you really know her. She is very shy."

"Oh indeed?" said Percy Beaumont.

"Extremely shy," Mrs. Westgate repeated. "But she is a dear good girl; she is a charming species of girl. She is not in the least a flirt; that isn't at all her line; she doesn't know the alphabet of that sort of thing. She is very simple—very serious. She has lived a great deal in Boston, with another sister of mine—the eldest of us—who married a Bostonian. She is very cultivated, not at all like me—I am not in the least cultivated. She has studied immensely and read everything; she is what they call in Boston 'thoughtful.' "

"A rum sort of girl for Lambeth to get hold of!" his lordship's kinsman privately reflected.

"I really believe," Mrs. Westgate continued, "that the most charming girl in the world is a Boston superstructure upon a New York *fonds*;[7] or perhaps a New York superstructure upon a Boston *fonds*. At any rate it's the mixture," said Mrs. Westgate, who continued to give Percy Beaumont a great deal of information.

Lord Lambeth got into a little basket-phaeton with Bessie Alden, and she drove him down the long avenue, whose extent he had measured on foot a couple of hours before, into the ancient town, as it was called in that part of the world, of Newport. The ancient town was a curious affair—a collection of fresh-looking little wooden houses,

7. Foundation.

painted white, scattered over a hill-side and clustered about a long, straight street, paved with enormous cobble-stones. There were plenty of shops—a large proportion of which appeared to be those of fruit-vendors, with piles of huge water-melons and pumpkins stacked in front of them; and, drawn up before the shops, or bumping about on the cobble-stones, were innumerable other basket-phaetons freighted with ladies of high fashion, who greeted each other from vehicle to vehicle and conversed on the edge of the pavement in a manner that struck Lord Lambeth as demonstrative—with a great many "Oh, my dears," and little quick exclamations and caresses. His companion went into seventeen shops—he amused himself with counting them—and accumulated, at the bottom of the phaeton, a pile of bundles that hardly left the young Englishman a place for his feet. As she had no groom nor footman, he sat in the phaeton to hold the ponies; where, although he was not a particularly acute observer, he saw much to entertain him—especially the ladies just mentioned, who wandered up and down with the appearance of a kind of aimless intentness, as if they were looking for something to buy, and who, tripping in and out of their vehicles, displayed remarkably pretty feet. It all seemed to Lord Lambeth very odd, and bright, and gay. Of course, before they got back to the villa, he had had a great deal of desultory conversation with Bessie Alden.

The young Englishmen spent the whole of that day and the whole of many successive days in what the French call the *intimité* of their new friends.[8] They agreed that it was extremely jolly—that they had never known anything more agreeable. It is not proposed to narrate minutely the incidents of their sojourn on this charming shore; though if it were convenient I might present a record of impressions none the less delectable that they were not exhaustively analysed. Many of them still linger in the minds of our travellers, attended by a train of harmonious images—images of brilliant mornings on lawns and piazzas that overlooked the sea; of innumerable pretty girls; of infinite lounging and talking and laughing and flirting and lunching and dining; of universal friendliness and frankness; of occasions on which they knew every one and everything and had an extraordinary sense of ease; of drives and rides in the late afternoon, over gleaming beaches, on long sea-roads, beneath a sky lighted up by marvellous sunsets; of tea-tables, on the return, informal, irregular, agreeable; of evenings at open windows or on the perpetual verandahs, in the summer starlight, above the warm Atlantic. The young Englishmen were introduced to everybody, entertained by everybody, intimate with everybody. At the end of three days they had removed their luggage from the hotel, and had gone to stay with Mrs. Westgate—a

---

8. In private with their new friends.

step to which Percy Beaumont at first offered some conscientious opposition. I call his opposition conscientious because it was founded upon some talk that he had had, on the second day, with Bessie Alden. He had indeed had a good deal of talk with her, for she was not literally always in conversation with Lord Lambeth. He had meditated upon Mrs. Westgate's account of her sister and he discovered, for himself, that the young lady was clever and appeared to have read a great deal. She seemed very nice, though he could not make out that, as Mrs. Westgate had said, she was shy. If she was shy she carried it off very well.

"Mr. Beaumont," she had said, "please tell me something about Lord Lambeth's family. How would you say it in England?—his position."

"His position?" Percy Beaumont repeated.

"His rank—or whatever you call it. Unfortunately we haven't got a 'Peerage,' like the people in Thackeray."

"That's a great pity," said Beaumont. "You would find it all set forth there so much better than I can do it."

"He is a great noble, then?"

"Oh yes, he is a great noble."

"Is he a peer?"

"Almost."

"And has he any other title than Lord Lambeth?"

"His title is the Marquis of Lambeth," said Beaumont; and then he was silent; Bessie Alden appeared to be looking at him with interest. "He is the son of the Duke of Bayswater," he added, presently.

"The eldest son?"

"The only son."

"And are his parents living?"

"Oh yes; if his father were not living he would be a duke."

"So that when his father dies," pursued Bessie Alden, with more simplicity than might have been expected in a clever girl, "he will become Duke of Bayswater?"

"Of course," said Percy Beaumont. "But his father is in excellent health."

"And his mother?"

Beaumont smiled a little. "The Duchess is uncommonly robust."

"And has he any sisters?"

"Yes, there are two."

"And what are they called?"

"One of them is married. She is the Countess of Pimlico."

"And the other?"

"The other is unmarried; she is plain Lady Julia."

Bessie Alden looked at him a moment. "Is she very plain?"

Beaumont began to laugh again. "You would not find her so

handsome as her brother," he said; and it was after this that he attempted to dissuade the heir of the Duke of Bayswater from accepting Mrs. Westgate's invitation. "Depend upon it," he said, "that girl means to try for you."

"It seems to me you are doing your best to make a fool of me," the modest young nobleman answered.

"She has been asking me," said Beaumont, "all about your people and your possessions."

"I am sure it is very good of her!" Lord Lambeth rejoined.

"Well, then," observed his companion, "if you go, you go with your eyes open."

"Damn my eyes!" exclaimed Lord Lambeth. "If one is to be a dozen times a day at the house, it is a great deal more convenient to sleep there. I am sick of travelling up and down this beastly Avenue."

Since he had determined to go, Percy Beaumont would of course have been very sorry to allow him to go alone; he was a man of conscience, and he remembered his promise to the Duchess. It was obviously the memory of this promise that made him say to his companion a couple of days later that he rathered wondered he should be so fond of that girl.

"In the first place, how do you know how fond I am of her?" asked Lord Lambeth. "And in the second place, why shouldn't I be fond of her?"

"I shouldn't think she would be in your line."

"What do you call my 'line'? You don't set her down as 'fast'?"

"Exactly so. Mrs. Westgate tells me that there is no such thing as the 'fast girl' in America; that it's an English invention and that the term has no meaning here."

"All the better. It's an animal I detest."

"You prefer a blue-stocking."

"Is that what you call Miss Alden?"

"Her sister tells me," said Percy Beaumont, "that she is tremendously literary."

"I don't know anything about that. She is certainly very clever."

"Well," said Beaumont, "I should have supposed you would have found that sort of thing awfully slow."

"In point of fact," Lord Lambeth rejoined, "I find it uncommonly lively."

After this, Percy Beaumont held his tongue; but on August 10th he wrote to the Duchess of Bayswater. He was, as I have said, a man of conscience, and he had a strong, incorruptible sense of the proprieties of life. His kinsman, meanwhile, was having a great deal of talk with Bessie Alden—on the red sea-rocks beyond the lawn; in the course of long island rides, with a slow return in the glowing twilight; on the deep verandah, late in the evening. Lord Lambeth, who had stayed at many houses, had never stayed at a house in which it was possible for a young man to converse so frequently with a young lady. This young lady no longer applied to Percy Beaumont for information concerning his lordship. She addressed herself directly to the young nobleman. She asked him a great many questions, some of which bored him a little; for he took no pleasure in talking about himself.

"Lord Lambeth," said Bessie Alden, "are you an hereditary legislator?"

"Oh, I say," cried Lord Lambeth, "don't make me call myself such names as that."

"But you are a member of Parliament," said the young girl.

"I don't like the sound of that either."

"Doesn't your father sit in the House of Lords?" Bessie Alden went on.

"Very seldom," said Lord Lambeth.

"Is it an important position?" she asked.

"Oh dear no," said Lord Lambeth.

"I should think it would be very grand," said Bessie Alden, "to possess simply by an accident of birth the right to make laws for a great nation."

"Ah, but one doesn't make laws. It's a great humbug."

"I don't believe that," the young girl declared. "It must be a great privilege, and I should think that if one thought of it in the right way—from a high point of view—it would be very inspiring."

"The less one thinks of it the better," Lord Lambeth affirmed.

"I think it's tremendous," said Bessie Alden; and on another occasion she asked him if he had any tenantry. Hereupon it was that, as I have said, he was a little bored.

"Do you want to buy up their leases?" he asked.

"Well—have you got any livings?"[9] she demanded.

"Oh, I say!" he cried. "Have you got a clergyman that is looking out?" But she made him tell her that he had a Castle; he confessed to but one. It was the place in which he had been born and brought up, and, as he had an old-time liking for it, he was beguiled into describing it a little and saying it was really very jolly. Bessie Alden listened with great interest, and declared that she would give the world to see such a place. Whereupon—"It would be awfully kind of you to come and stay there," said Lord Lambeth. He took a vague satisfaction in the circumstance that Percy Beaumont had not heard him make the remark I have just recorded.

Mr. Westgate, all this time, had not, as they said at Newport, "come on." His wife more than once announced that she expected him on the morrow; but on the morrow she wandered about a little,

9. In Great Britain, ecclesiastical offices with incomes attached to them.

with a telegram in her jewelled fingers, declaring it was very tiresome that his business detained him in New York; that he could only hope the Englishmen were having a good time. "I must say," said Mrs. Westgate, "that it is no thanks to him if you are!" And she went on to explain, while she continued that slow-paced promenade which enabled her well-adjusted skirts to display themselves so advantageously, that unfortunately in America there was no leisure-class. It was Lord Lambeth's theory, freely propounded when the young men were together, that Percy Beaumont was having a very good time with Mrs. Westgate, and that under the pretext of meeting for the purpose of animated discussion, they were indulging in practices that imparted a shade of hypocrisy to the lady's regret for her husband's absence.

"I assure you we are always discussing and differing," said Percy Beaumont. "She is awfully argumentative. American ladies certainly don't mind contradicting you. Upon my word I don't think I was ever treated so by a woman before. She's so devilish positive."

Mrs. Westgate's positive quality, however, evidently had its attractions; for Beaumont was constantly at his hostess's side. He detached himself one day to the extent of going to New York to talk over the Tennessee Central with Mr. Westgate; but he was absent only forty-eight hours, during which, with Mr. Westgate's assistance, he completely settled this piece of business. "They certainly do things quickly in New York," he observed to his cousin; and he added that Mr. Westgate had seemed very uneasy lest his wife should miss her visitor—he had been in such an awful hurry to send him back to her. "I'm afraid you'll never come up to an American husband—if that's what the wives expect," he said to Lord Lambeth.

Mrs. Westgate, however, was not to enjoy much longer the entertainment with which an indulgent husband had desired to keep her provided. On August 21st Lord Lambeth received a telegram from his mother, requesting him to return immediately to England; his father had been taken ill, and it was his filial duty to come to him.

The young Englishman was visibly annoyed. "What the deuce does it mean?" he asked of his kinsman. "What am I to do?"

Percy Beaumont was annoyed as well; he had deemed it his duty, as I have narrated, to write to the Duchess, but he had not expected that this distinguished woman would act so promptly upon his hint. "It means," he said, "that your father is laid up. I don't suppose it's anything serious; but you have no option. Take the first steamer; but don't be alarmed."

Lord Lambeth made his farewells; but the few last words that he exchanged with Bessie Alden are the only ones that have a place in our record. "Of course I needn't assure you," he said, "that if you should come to England next year, I expect to be the first person that you inform of it."

Bessie Alden looked at him a little and she smiled. "Oh, if we come to London," she answered, "I should think you would hear of it."

Percy Beaumont returned with his cousin, and his sense of duty compelled him, one windless afternoon, in mid-Atlantic, to say to Lord Lambeth that he suspected that the Duchess's telegram was in part the result of something he himself had written to her. "I wrote to her—as I explicitly notified you I had promised to do—that you were extremely interested in a little American girl."

Lord Lambeth was extremely angry, and he indulged for some moments in the simple language of resentment. But I have said that he was a reasonable young man, and I can give no better proof of it than the fact that he remarked to his companion at the end of half-an-hour—"You were quite right after all. I am very much interested in her. Only, to be fair," he added, "you should have told my mother also that she is not—seriously—interested in me."

Percy Beaumont gave a little laugh. "There is nothing so charming as modesty in a young man in your position. That speech is a capital proof that you are sweet on her."

"She is not interested—she is not!" Lord Lambeth repeated.

"My dear fellow," said his companion, "you are very far gone."

IV

In point of fact, as Percy Beaumont would have said, Mrs. Westgate disembarked on the 18th of May on the British coast. She was accompanied by her sister, but she was not attended by any other member of her family. To the deprivation of her husband's society Mrs. Westgate was, however, habituated; she had made half-a-dozen journeys to Europe without him, and she now accounted for his absence, to interrogative friends on this side of the Atlantic, by allusion to the regrettable but conspicuous fact that in America there was no leisure-class. The two ladies came up to London and alighted at Jones's Hotel, where Mrs. Westgate, who had made on former occasions the most agreeable impression at this establishment, received an obsequious greeting. Bessie Alden had felt much excited about coming to England; she had expected the "associations" would be very charming, that it would be an infinite pleasure to rest her eyes upon the things she had read about in the poets and historians. She was very fond of the poets and historians, of the picturesque, of the past, of retrospect, of mementoes and reverberations of greatness; so that on coming into the great English world, where strangeness and familiarity would go hand in hand, she was prepared for a multitude of fresh emotions. They began very promptly—these tender, fluttering sensations; they began with the sight of the beautiful English landscape, whose dark richness was quickened and brightened by the season; with the carpeted fields and flowering hedge-rows, as she looked at them from the window of the train; with the spires of the rural churches, peeping above the rook-haunted tree-tops; with the oak-studded parks, the ancient homes, the cloudy light, the speech, the manners, the thousand differences. Mrs. Westgate's impressions had of course much less novelty and keenness, and she gave but a wandering attention to her sister's ejaculations and rhapsodies.

"You know my enjoyment of England is not so intellectual as Bessie's," she said to several of her friends in the course of her visit to this country. "And yet if it is not intellectual, I can't say it is physical. I don't think I can quite say what it is, my enjoyment of England." When once it was settled that the two ladies should come abroad and should spend a few weeks in England on their way to the Continent, they of course exchanged a good many allusions to their London acquaintance.

"It will certainly be much nicer having friends there," Bessie Alden had said one day, as she sat on the sunny deck of the steamer, at her sister's feet, on a large blue rug.

"Whom do you mean by friends?" Mrs. Westgate asked.

"All those English gentlemen whom you have known and entertained. Captain Littledale, for instance. And Lord Lambeth and Mr. Beaumont," added Bessie Alden.

"Do you expect them to give us a very grand reception?"

Bessie reflected a moment; she was addicted, as we know, to reflection. "Well, yes."

"My poor sweet child!" murmured her sister.

"What have I said that is so silly?" asked Bessie.

"You are a little too simple; just a little. It is very becoming, but it pleases people at your expense."

"I am certainly too simple to understand you," said Bessie.

"Shall I tell you a story?" asked her sister.

"If you would be so good. That is what they do to amuse simple people."

Mrs. Westgate consulted her memory, while her companion sat gazing at the shining sea. "Did you ever hear of the Duke of Green-Erin?"

"I think not," said Bessie.

"Well, it's no matter," her sister went on.

"It's a proof of my simplicity."

"My story is meant to illustrate that of some other people," said Mrs. Westgate. "The Duke of Green-Erin is what they call in England a great swell; and some five years ago he came to America. He spent most of his time in New York, and in New York he spent his days and his nights at the Butterworths'. You have heard at least of the Butterworths. *Bien.* [1] They did everything in the world for him—they turned

1. French colloquial interjection meaning *"Well!"*

themselves inside out. They gave him a dozen dinner-parties and balls, and were the means of his being invited to fifty more. At first he used to come into Mrs. Butterworth's box at the opera in a tweed travelling-suit; but some one stopped that. At any rate, he had a beautiful time, and they parted the best friends in the world. Two years elapse, and the Butterworths come abroad and go to London. The first thing they see in all the papers—in England those things are in the most prominent place—is that the Duke of Green-Erin has arrived in town for the Season. They wait a little, and then Mr. Butterworth—as polite as ever—goes and leaves a card. They wait a little more; the visit is not returned; they wait three weeks—*silence de mort*[2]—the Duke gives no sign. The Butterworths see a lot of other people, put down the Duke of Green-Erin as a rude, ungrateful man, and forget all about him. One fine day they go to Ascot Races, and there they meet him face to face. He stares a moment and then comes up to Mr. Butterworth, taking something from his pocket-book—something which proves to be a bank-note. 'I'm glad to see you, Mr. Butterworth,' he said, 'so that I can pay you that ten pounds I lost to you in New York. I saw the other day you remembered our bet; here are the ten pounds, Mr. Butterworth. Good-bye, Mr. Butterworth.' And off he goes, and that's the last they see of the Duke of Green-Erin.''

"Is that your story?" asked Bessie Alden.

"Don't you think it's interesting?" her sister replied.

"I don't believe it," said the young girl.

"Ah!" cried Mrs. Westgate, "you are not so simple after all. Believe it or not as you please; there is no smoke without fire."

"Is that the way," asked Bessie after a moment," "that you expect your friends to treat you?"

"I defy them to treat me very ill, because I shall not give them the opportunity. With the best will in the world, in that case, they can't be very disobliging."

Bessie Alden was silent a moment. "I don't see what makes you talk that way," she said. "The English are a great people."

"Exactly; and that is just the way they have grown great—by dropping you when you have ceased to be useful. People say they are not clever; but I think they are very clever."

"You know you have liked them—all the Englishmen you have seen," said Bessie.

"They have liked me," her sister rejoined; "it would be more correct to say that. And of course one likes that."

Bessie Alden resumed for some moments her studies in sea-green. "Well," she said, "whether they like me or not, I mean to like them. And happily," she added, "Lord Lambeth does not owe me ten pounds.''

2. Silence of the grave; i.e., not a word.

During the first few days after their arrival at Jones's Hotel our charming Americans were much occupied with what they would have called looking about them. They found occasion to make a large number of purchases, and their opportunities for conversation were such only as were offered by the deferential London shopmen. Bessie Alden, even in driving from the station, took an immense fancy to the British metropolis, and, at the risk of exhibiting her as a young woman of vulgar tastes, it must be recorded that for a considerable period she desired no higher pleasure than to drive about the crowded streets in a Hansom cab. To her attentive eyes they were full of a strange picturesque life, and it is at least beneath the dignity of our historic muse to enumerate the trivial objects and incidents which this simple young lady from Boston found so entertaining. It may be freely mentioned, however, that whenever, after a round of visits in Bond Street and Regent Street,[3] she was about to return with her sister to Jones's Hotel, she made an earnest request that they should be driven home by way of Westminister Abbey. She had begun by asking whether it would not be possible to take the Tower on the way to their lodgings; but it happened that at a more primitive stage of her culture Mrs. Westgate had paid a visit to this venerable monument, which she spoke of ever afterwards, vaguely, as a dreadful disappointment; so that she expressed the liveliest disapproval of any attempt to combine historical researches with the purchase of hair-brushes and note-paper. The most she would consent to do in this line was to spend half-an-hour at Madame Tussaud's,[4] where she saw several dusty wax effigies of members of the Royal Family. She told Bessie that if she wished to go to the Tower she must get some one else to take her. Bessie expressed hereupon an earnest disposition to go alone; but upon this proposal as well Mrs. Westgate sprinkled cold water.

"Remember," she said, "that you are not in your innocent little Boston. It is not a question of walking up and down Beacon Street." Then she went on to explain that there were two classes of American girls in Europe—those that walked about alone and those that did not. "You happen to belong, my dear," she said to her sister, "to the class that does not."

"It is only," answered Bessie, laughing, "because you happen to prevent me." And she devoted much private meditation to this question of effecting a visit to the Tower of London.

Suddenly it seemed as if the problem might be solved; the two ladies at Jones's Hotel received a visit from Willie Woodley. Such was the social appellation of a young American who had sailed from New York a few days after their own departure, and who, having the privilege of intimacy with them in that city, had lost no time, on his arrival in London, in coming to pay them his respects. He had, in fact, gone to

3. Streets with many fashionable shops.   4. Famous waxwork exhibition.

see them directly after going to see his tailor; than which there can be no greater exhibition of promptitude on the part of a young American who has just alighted at the Charing Cross Hotel. He was a slim, pale youth, of the most amiable disposition, famous for the skill with which he led the "German"[5] in New York. Indeed, by the young ladies who habitually figured in this fashionable frolic he was believed to be "the best dancer in the world;" it was in these terms that he was always spoken of, and that his identity was indicated. He was the gentlest, softest young man it was possible to meet; he was beautifully dressed—"in the English style"—and he knew an immense deal about London. He had been at Newport during the previous summer, at the time of our young Englishmen's visit, and he took extreme pleasure in the society of Bessie Alden, whom he always addressed as "Miss Bessie." She immediately arranged with him, in the presence of her sister, that he should conduct her to the scene of Lady Jane Grey's execution.

"You may do as you please," said Mrs. Westgate. "Only—if you desire the information—it is not the custom here for young ladies to knock about London with young men."

"Miss Bessie has waltzed with me so often," observed Willie Woodley; "she can surely go out with me in a Hansom."

"I consider waltzing," said Mrs. Westgate, "the most innocent pleasure of our time."

"It's a compliment to our time!" exclaimed the young man, with a little laugh, in spite of himself.

"I don't see why I should regard what is done here," said Bessie Alden. "Why should I suffer the restrictions of a society of which I enjoy none of the privileges?"

"That's very good—very good," murmured Willie Woodley.

"Oh, go to the Tower, and feel the axe, if you like!" said Mrs. Westgate. "I consent to your going with Mr. Woodley; but I should not let you go with an Englishman."

"Miss Bessie wouldn't care to go with an Englishman!" Mr. Woodley declared, with a faint asperity that was, perhaps, not unnatural in a young man who, dressing in the manner that I have indicated, and knowing a great deal, as I have said, about London, saw no reason for drawing these sharp distinctions. He agreed upon a day with Miss Bessie—a day of that same week.

An ingenious mind might, perhaps, trace a connection between the young girl's allusion to her destitution of social privileges and a question she asked on the morrow as she sat with her sister at lunch.

"Don't you mean to write to—to any one?" said Bessie.

5. An elaborate kind of dance.

"I wrote this morning to Captain Littledale," Mrs. Westgate replied.

"But Mr. Woodley said that Captain Littledale had gone to India."

"He said he thought he had heard so; he knew nothing about it."

For a moment Bessie Alden said nothing more; then, at last, "And don't you intend to write to—to Mr. Beaumont?" she inquired.

"You mean to Lord Lambeth," said her sister.

"I said Mr. Beaumont because he was so good a friend of yours."

Mrs. Westgate looked at the young girl with sisterly candour. "I don't care two straws for Mr. Beaumont."

"You were certainly very nice to him."

"I am nice to every one," said Mrs. Westgate, simply.

"To every one but me," rejoined Bessie, smiling.

Her sister continued to look at her; then, at last, "Are you in love with Lord Lambeth?" she asked.

The young girl stared a moment, and the question was apparently too humorous even to make her blush. "Not that I know of," she answered.

"Because if you are," Mrs. Westgate went on, "I shall certainly not send for him."

"That proves what I said," declared Bessie, smiling—"that you are not nice to me."

"It would be a poor service, my dear child," said her sister.

"In what sense? There is nothing against Lord Lambeth, that I know of."

Mrs. Westgate was silent a moment. "You *are* in love with him, then?"

Bessie stared again; but this time she blushed a little. "Ah! if you won't be serious," she answered, "we will not mention him again."

For some moments Lord Lambeth was not mentioned again, and it was Mrs. Westgate who, at the end of this period, reverted to him. "Of course I will let him know we are here; because I think he would be hurt—justly enough—if we should go away without seeing him. It is fair to give him a chance to come and thank me for the kindness we showed him. But I don't want to seem eager."

"Neither do I," said Bessie, with a little laugh.

"Though I confess," added her sister, "that I am curious to see how he will behave."

"He behaved very well at Newport."

"Newport is not London. At Newport he could do as he liked; but here, it is another affair. He has to have an eye to consequences."

"If he had more freedom, then, at Newport," argued Bessie, "it is the more to his credit that he behaved well; and if he has to be so careful here, it is possible he will behave even better."

"Better—better," repeated her sister. "My dear child, what is your point of view?"

"How do you mean—my point of view?"

"Don't you care for Lord Lambeth—a little?"

This time Bessie Alden was displeased; she slowly got up from table, turning her face away from her sister. "You will oblige me by not talking so," she said.

Mrs. Westgate sat watching her for some moments as she moved slowly about the room and went and stood at the window. "I will write to him this afternoon," she said at last.

"Do as you please!" Bsesie answered; and presently she turned round. "I am not afraid to say that I like Lord Lambeth. I like him very much."

"He is not clever," Mrs. Westgate declared.

"Well, there have been clever people whom I have disliked," said Bessie Alden; "so that I suppose I may like a stupid one. Besides, Lord Lambeth is not stupid."

"Not so stupid as he looks!" exclaimed her sister, smiling.

"If I were in love with Lord Lambeth, as you said just now, it would be bad policy on your part to abuse him."

"My dear child, don't give me lessons in policy!" cried Mrs. Westgate. "The policy I mean to follow is very deep."

The young girl began to walk about the room again; then she stopped before her sister. "I have never heard in the course of five minutes," she said, "so many hints and innuendoes. I wish you would tell me in plain English what you mean."

"I mean that you may be much annoyed."

"That is still only a hint," said Bessie.

Her sister looked at her, hesitating an instant. "It will be said of you that you have come after Lord Lambeth—that you followed him."

Bessie Alden threw back her pretty head like a startled hind, and a look flashed into her face that made Mrs. Westgate rise from her chair. "Who says such things as that?" she demanded.

"People here."

"I don't believe it," said Bessie.

"You have a very convenient faculty of doubt. But my policy will be, as I say, very deep. I shall leave you to find out this kind of thing for yourself."

Bessie fixed her eyes upon her sister, and Mrs. Westgate thought for a moment there were tears in them. "Do they talk that way here?" she asked.

"You will see. I shall leave you alone."

"Don't leave me alone," said Bessie Alden. "Take me away."

"No; I want to see what you make of it," her sister continued.

"I don't understand."

"You will understand after Lord Lambeth has come," said Mrs. Westgate, with a little laugh.

The two ladies had arranged that on this afternomn Willie Woodley should go with them to Hyde Park,[6] where Bassie Alden expected to derive much entertainment from sitting on a little green chair, under the great trees, beside Rotten Row. The want of a suitable escort had hitherto rendered this pleasure inaccessible; but no escort, now, for such an expedition, could have been more suitable than their devoted young countryman, whose mission in life, it might almost be said, was to find chairs for ladies, and who appeared on the stroke of half-past five with a white camellia in his button-hole.

"I have written to Lord Lambeth, my dear," said Mrs. Westgate to her sister, on coming into the room where Bessie Alden, drawing on her long grey gloves, was entertaining their visitor.

Bessie said nothing, but Willie Woodley exclaimed that his lordship was in town; he had seen his name in the *Morning Post*.

"Do you read the *Morning Post?*" asked Mrs. Westgate.

"Oh yes; it's great fun," Willie Woodley affirmed.

"I want so to see it," said Bessie, "there is so much about it in Thackeray."

"I will send it to you every morning," said Willie Woodley.

He found them what Bessie Alden thought excellent places, under the great trees, beside the famous avenue whose humours had been made familiar to the young girl's childhood by the pictures in *Punch*.[7] The day was bright and warm, and the crowd of riders and spectators and the great procession of carriages were proportionately dense and brilliant. The scene bore the stamp of the London Season at its height, and Bessie Alden found more entertainment in it than she was able to express to her companions. She sat silent, under her parasol, and her imagination, according to its wont, let itself loose into the great changing assemblage of striking and suggestive figures. They stirred up a host of old impressions and preconceptions, and she found herself fitting a history to this person and a theory to that, and making a place for them all in her little private museum of types. But if she said little, her sister on one side and Willie Woodley on the other expressed themselves in lively alternation.

"Look at that green dress with blue flounces," said Mrs. Westgate. "*Quelle toilette!*"[8]

"That's the Marquis of Blackborough," said the young man—"the one in the white coat. I heard him speak the other night in the House of Lords; it was something about ramrods; he called them *wamwods*.

6. A large park in London. Rotten Row (below) was a fashionable horse-riding course. The name derives by corruption from *route dv roi*, French for "the king's road."

7. Famous English comic magazine, published since 1841.
8. What a costume!

He's an awful swell."

"Did you ever see anything like the way they are pinned back?" Mrs. Westgate resumed. "They never know where to stop."

"They do nothing but stop," said Willie Woodley. "It prevents them from walking. Here comes a great celebrity—Lady Beatrice Bellevue. She's awfully fast; see what little steps she takes."

"Well, my dear," Mrs. Westgate pursued, "I hope you are getting some ideas for your *couturière*?"

"I am getting plenty of ideas," said Bessie, "but I don't know that my *couturière*[9] would appreciate them."

Willie Woodley presently perceived a friend on horseback, who drove up beside the barrier of the Row and beckoned to him. He went forward and the crowd of pedestrians closed about him, so that for some ten minutes he was hidden from sight. At last he reappeared, bringing a gentleman with him—a gentleman whom Bessie at first supposed to be his friend dismounted. But at a second glance she found herself looking at Lord Lambeth, who was shaking hands with her sister.

"I found him over there," said Willie Woodley, "and I told him you were here."

And then Lord Lambeth, touching his hat a little, shook hands with Bessie. "Fancy your being here!" he said. He was blushing and smiling; he looked very handsome, and he had a kind of splendour that he had not had in America. Bessie Alden's imagination, as we know, was just then in exercise; so that the tall young Englishman, as he stood there looking down at her, had the benefit of it. "He is hand-somer and more splendid than anything I have ever seen," she said to herself. And then she remembered that he was a Marquis, and she thought he looked like a Marquis.

"Really, you know," he cried, "you ought to have let a man know you were here!"

"I wrote to you an hour ago," said Mrs. Westgate.

"Doesn't all the world know it?" asked Bessie, smiling.

"I assure you I didn't know it!" cried Lord Lambeth. "Upon my honour I hadn't heard of it. Ask Woodley now; had I, Woodley?"

"Well, I think you are rather a humbug," said Willie Woodley.

"You don't believe that—do you, Miss Alden?" asked his lordship. "You don't believe I'm a humbug, eh?"

"No," said Bessie, "I don't."

"You are too tall to stand up, Lord Lambeth," Mrs. Westgate observed. "You are only tolerable when you sit down. Be so good as to get a chair."

He found a chair and placed it sidewise, close to the two ladies. "If I

9. Dressmaker.

hadn't met Woodley I should never have found you," he went on. "Should I, Woodley?"

"Well, I guess not," said the young American.

"Not even with my letter?" asked Mrs. Westgate.

"Ah, well, I haven't got your letter yet; I suppose I shall get it this evening. It was awfully kind of you to write."

"So I said to Bessie," observed Mrs. Westgate.

"Did she say so, Miss Alden?" Lord Lambeth inquired. "I daresay you have been here a month."

"We have been here three," said Mrs. Westgate.

"Have you been here three months?" the young man asked again of Bessie.

"It seems a long time," Bessie answered.

"I say, after that you had better not call me a humbug!" cried Lord Lambeth. "I have only been in town three weeks; but you must have been hiding away. I haven't seen you anywhere."

"Where should you have seen us—where should we have gone?" asked Mrs. Westgate.

"You should have gone to Hurlingham," said Willie Woodley.

"No, let Lord Lambeth tell us," Mrs. Westgate insisted.

"There are plenty of places to go to," said Lord Lambeth—"each one stupider than the other. I mean people's houses; they send you cards."

"No one has sent us cards," said Bessie.

"We are very quiet," her sister declared. "We are here as travellers."

"We have been to Madame Tussaud's," Bessie pursued.

"Oh, I say!" cried Lord Lambeth.

"We thought we should find your image there," said Mrs. Westgate—"yours and Mr. Beaumont's."

"In the Chamber of Horrors?" laughed the young man.

"It did duty very well for a party," said Mrs. Westgate. "All the women were *decolletées*, and many of the figures looked as if they could speak if they tried."

"Upon my word," Lord Lambeth rejoined, "you see people at London parties that look as if they couldn't speak if they tried."

"Do you think Mr. Woodley could find us Mr. Beaumont?" asked Mrs. Westgate.

Lord Lambeth stared and looked round him. "I daresay he could. Beaumont often comes here. Don't you think you could find him, Woodley? Make a dive into the crowd."

"Thank you; I have had enough diving," said Willie Woodley. "I will wait till Mr. Beaumont comes to the surface."

"I will bring him to see you," said Lord Lambeth; "where are you staying?"

"You will find the address in my letter—Jones's Hotel."

"Oh, one of those places just out of Piccadilly? Beastly hole, isn't it?" Lord Lambeth inquired.

"I believe it's the best hotel in London," said Mrs. Westgate.

"But they give you awful rubbish to eat, don't they?" his lordship went on.

"Yes," said Mrs. Westgate.

"I always feel so sorry for the people that come up to town and go to live in those places," continued the young man. "They eat nothing but poison."

"Oh, I say!" cried Willie Woodley.

"Well, how do you like London, Miss Alden?" Lord Lambeth asked, unperturbed by this ejaculation.

"I think it's grand," said Bessie Alden.

"My sister likes it, in spite of the 'poison'!" Mrs. Westgate exclaimed.

"I hope you are going to stay a long time."

"As long as I can," said Bessie.

"And where is Mr. Westgate?" asked Lord Lambeth of this gentleman's wife.

"He's where he always is—in that tiresome New York."

"He must be tremendously clever," said the young man.

"I suppose he is," said Mrs. Westgate.

Lord Lambeth sat for nearly an hour with his American friends; but it is not our purpose to relate their conversation in full. He addressed a great many remarks to Bessie Alden, and finally turned towards her altogether, while Willie Woodley entertained Mrs. Westgate. Bessie herself said very little; she was on her guard, thinking of what her sister had said to her at lunch. Little by little, however, she interested herself in Lord Lambeth again, as she had done at Newport; only it seemed to her that here he might become more interesting. He would be an unconscious part of the antiquity, the impressiveness, the picturesqueness of England; and poor Bessie Alden, like many a Yankee maiden, was terribly at the mercy of picturesqueness.

"I have often wished I were at Newport again," said the young man. "Those days I spent at your sister's were awfully jolly."

"We enjoyed them very much; I hope your father is better."

"Oh dear, yes. When I got to England, he was out grouse-shooting. It was what you call in America a gigantic fraud. My mother had got nervous. My three weeks at Newport seemed like a happy dream."

"America certainly is very different from England," said Bessie.

"I hope you like England better, eh?" Lord Lambeth rejoined, almost persuasively.

"No Englishman can ask that seriously of a person of another country."

Her companion looked at her for a moment. "You mean it's a matter of course?"

"If I were English," said Bessie, "it would certainly seem to me a matter of course that every one should be a good patriot."

"Oh dear, yes; patriotism is everything," said Lord Lambeth, not quite following, but very contented. "Now, what are you going to do here?"

"On Thursday I am going to the Tower."

"The Tower?"

"The Tower of London. Did you never hear of it?"

"Oh yes, I have been there," said Lord Lambeth. "I was taken there by my governess, when I was six years old. It's a rum idea, your going there."

"Do give me a few more rum ideas," said Bessie. "I want to see everything of that sort. I am going to Hampton Court, and to Windsor, and to the Dulwich Gallery."

Lord Lambeth seemed greatly amused. "I wonder you don't go to the Rosherville Gardens."[1]

"Are they interesting?" asked Bessie.

"Oh, wonderful!"

"Are they very old? That's all I care for," said Bessie.

"They are tremendously old; they are all falling to ruins."

"I think there is nothing so charming as an old ruinous garden," said the young girl. "We must certainly go there."

Lord Lambeth broke out into merriment. "I say, Woodley," he cried, "here's Miss Alden wants to go to the Rosherville Gardens!"

Willie Woodley looked a little blank; he was caught in the fact of ignorance of an apparently conspicuous feature of London life. But in a moment he turned it off. "Very well," he said, "I'll write for a permit."

Lord Lambeth's exhilaration increased. "'Gad, I believe you Americans would go anywhere!" he cried.

"We wish to go to Parliament," said Bessie. "That's one of the first things."

"Oh, it would bore you to death!" cried the young man.

"We wish to hear you speak."

"I never speak—except to young ladies," said Lord Lambeth, smiling.

1. Hampton Court is a royal palace, Windsor an ancient castle, Dulwich an art gallery—all in or near London and several centuries old. But the Rosherville Gardens, a popular resort in a suburb of Gravesend at the mouth of the River Thames, were founded in 1843 and lacked the venerable age as well as the historical associations of the places Bessie is excited about. Lord Lambeth seems to be teasing her when he describes them as old enough to be "falling to ruins." Whether James, like the Gardens born in 1843, had himself in mind is an open question.

Bessie Alden looked at him awhile; smiling, too, in the shadow of her parasol. "You are very strange," she murmured. "I don't think I approve of you."

"Ah, now, don't be severe, Miss Alden!" said Lord Lambeth, smiling still more. "Please don't be severe. I want you to like me—awfully."

"To like you awfully? You must not laugh at me, then, when I make mistakes. I consider it my right—as a free-born American—to make as many mistakes as I choose."

"Upon my word, I didn't laugh at you," said Lord Lambeth.

"And not only that," Bessie went on; "but I hold that all my mistakes shall be set down to my credit. You must think the better of me for them."

"I can't think better of you than I do," the young man declared.

Bessie Alden looked at him a moment again. "You certainly speak very well to young ladies. But why don't you address the House? Isn't that what they call it?"

"Because I have nothing to say," said Lord Lambeth.

"Haven't you a great position?" asked Bessie Alden.

He looked a moment at the back of his glove. "I'll set that down," he said, "as one of your mistakes—to your credit." And, as if he disliked talking about his position, he changed the subject. "I wish you would let me go with you to the Tower, and to Hampton Court, and to all those other places."

"We shall be most happy," said Bessie.

"And of course I shall be delighted to show you the Houses of Parliament—some day that suits you. There are a lot of things I want to do for you. I want you to have a good time. And I should like very much to present some of my friends to you, if it wouldn't bore you. Then it would be awfully kind of you to come down to Branches."

"We are much obliged to you, Lord Lambeth," said Bessie. "What is Branches?"

"It's a house in the country. I think you might like it."

Willie Woodley and Mrs. Westgate, at this moment, were sitting in silence, and the young man's ear caught these last words of Lord Lambeth's. "He's inviting Miss Bessie to one of his castles," he murmured to his companion.

Mrs. Westgate, foreseeing what she mentally called "complications," immediately got up; and the two ladies, taking leave of Lord Lambeth, returned, under Mr. Woodley's conduct, to Jones's Hotel.

v

Lord Lambeth came to see them on the morrow, bringing Percy Beaumont with him—the latter having instantly declared his intention of neglecting none of the usual offices of civility. This declaration, however, when his kinsman informed him of the advent of their American friends, had been preceded by another remark.

"Here they are, then, and you are in for it."

"What am I in for?" demanded Lord Lambeth.

"I will let your mother give it a name. With all respect to whom," added Percy Beaumont, "I must decline on this occasion to do any more police duty. Her Grace must look after you herself."

"I will give her a chance," said her Grace's son, a trifle grimly. "I shall make her go and see them."

"She won't do it, my boy."

"We'll see if she doesn't," said Lord Lambeth.

But if Percy Beaumont took a sombre view of the arrival of the two ladies at Jones's Hotel, he was sufficiently a man of the world to offer them a smiling countenance. He fell into animated conversation—conversation, at least, that was animated on her side—with Mrs. Westgate, while his companion made himself agreeable to the younger lady. Mrs. Westgate began confessing and protesting, declaring and expounding.

"I must say London is a great deal brighter and prettier just now than it was when I was here last—in the month of November. There is evidently a great deal going on, and you seem to have a good many flowers. I have no doubt it is very charming for all you people, and that you amuse yourselves immensely. It is very good of you to let Bessie and me come and sit and look at you. I suppose you will think I am very satirical, but I must confess that that's the feeling I have in London."

"I am afraid I don't quite understand to what feeling you allude," said Percy Beaumont.

"The feeling that it's all very well for you English people. Everything is beautifully arranged for you."

"It seems to me it is very well for some Americans, sometimes," rejoined Beaumont.

"For some of them, yes—if they like to be patronised. But I must say I don't like to be patronised. I may be very eccentric and undisciplined and unreasonable; but I confess I never was fond of patronage. I like to associate with people on the same terms as I do in my own country; that's a peculiar taste that I have. But here people seem to expect something else—Heaven knows what! I am afraid you will think I am very ungrateful, for I certainly have received a great deal of attention. The last time I was here, a lady sent me a message that I was at liberty to come and see her."

"Dear me, I hope you didn't go," observed Percy Beaumont.

"You are deliciously *naïf*, I must say that for you!" Mrs. Westgate exclaimed. "It must be a great advantage to you here in London. I suppose that if I myself had a little more *naïveté*, I should enjoy it more. I should be content to sit on a chair in the Park, and see the people pass, and be told that this is the Duchess of Suffolk, and that is the Lord Chamberlain, and that I must be thankful for the privilege of beholding them. I daresay it is very wicked and critical of me to ask for anything else. But I was always critical, and I freely confess to the sin of being fastidious. I am told there is some remarkably superior second-rate society provided here for strangers. *Merci!*[2] I don't want any superior second-rate society. I want the society that I have been accustomed to.

"I hope you don't call Lambeth and me second-rate," Beaumont interposed.

"Oh, I am accustomed to you!" said Mrs. Westgate. "Do you know that you English sometimes make the most wonderful speeches? The first time I came to London, I went out to dine—as I told you, I have received a great deal of attention. After dinner, in the drawing-room, I had some conversation with an old lady; I assure you I had. I forget what we talked about; but she presently said, in allusion to something we were discussing, 'Oh, you know, the aristocracy do so-and-so; but in one's own class of life it is very different.' In one's own class of life! What is a poor unprotected American woman to do in a country where she is liable to have that sort of thing said to her?"

"You seem to get hold of some very queer old ladies; I compliment you on your acquaintance!" Percy Beaumont exclaimed. "If you are trying to bring me to admit that London is an odious place, you'll not succeed. I'm extremely fond of it, and I think it the jolliest place in the world."

"*Pour vous autres.*[3] I never said the contrary," Mrs. Westgate retorted. I make use of this expression because both interlocutors had begun to raise their voices. Percy Beaumont naturally did not like to hear his country abused, and Mrs. Westgate, no less naturally, did not like a stubborn debater.

"Hallo!" said Lord Lambeth; "what are they up to now?" And he came away from the windows, where he had been standing with Bessie Alden.

"I quite agree with a very clever countrywoman of mine," Mrs. Westgate continued, with charming ardour, though with imperfect relevancy. She smiled at the two gentlemen for a moment with terrible brightness, as if to toss at their feet—upon their native heath—the gauntlet of defiance. "For me, there are only two social positions worth speaking of—that of an American lady and that of the Emperor of Russia."

"And what do you do with the American gentlemen?" asked Lord Lambeth.

"She leaves them in America!" said Percy Beaumont.

On the departure of their visitors, Bessie Alden told her sister that Lord Lambeth would come the next day, to go with them to the Tower, and that he had kindly offered to bring his "trap," and drive them thither. Mrs. Westgate listened in silence to this communication, and for some time afterwards she said nothing. But at last, "If you had not requested me the other day not to mention it," she began, "there is something I should venture to ask you." Bessie frowned a little; her dark blue eyes were more dark than blue. But her sister went on. "As it is, I will take the risk. You are not in love with Lord Lambeth: I believe it, perfectly. Very good. But is there, by chance, any danger of your becoming so? It's a very simple question; don't take offence. I have a particular reason," said Mrs. Westgate, "for wanting to know."

Bessie Alden for some moments said nothing; she only looked displeased. "No; there is no danger," she answered at last, curtly.

"Then I should like to frighten them," declared Mrs. Westgate, clasping her jewelled hands.

"To frighten whom?"

"All these people; Lord Lambeth's family and friends."

"How should you frighten them?" asked the young girl.

"It wouldn't be I—it would be you. It would frighten them to think that you should absorb his lordship's young affections."

Bessie Alden, with her clear eyes still overshadowed by her dark brows, continued to interrogate. "Why should that frighten them?"

Mrs. Westgate poised her answer with a smile before delivering it. "Because they think you are not good enough. You are a charming girl, beautiful and amiable, intelligent and clever, and as *bien-élevée*[4] as it is possible to be; but you are not a fit match for Lord Lambeth."

Bessie Alden was immensely disgusted. "Where do you get such extraordinary ideas?" she asked. "You have said some such strange things lately. My dear Kitty, where do you collect them?"

Kitty was, evidently, enamoured of her idea. "Yes, it would put them on pins and needles, and it wouldn't hurt you. Mr. Beaumont is already most uneasy; I could soon see that."

The young girl meditated a moment. "Do you mean that they spy upon him—that they interfere with him?"

"I don't know what power they have to interfere, but I know that a British mamma may worry her son's life out."

It has been intimated that, as regards certain disagreeable things, Bessie Alden had a fund of scepticism. She abstained on the present occasion from expressing disbelief, for she wished not to irritate her sister. But she said to herself that Kitty had been misinformed—that

4. Well brought up.

this was a traveller's tale. Though she was a girl of a lively imagination, there could in the nature of things be, to her sense, no reality in the idea of her belonging to a vulgar category. What she said aloud was—"I must say that in that case I am very sorry for Lord Lambeth."

Mrs. Westgate, more and more exhilarated by her scheme, was smiling at her again. "If I could only believe it was safe!" she exclaimed. "When you begin to pity him, I, on my side, am afraid."

"Afraid of what?"

"Of your pitying him too much."

Bessie Alden turned away impatiently; but at the end of a minute she turned back. "What if I should pity him too much?" she asked.

Mrs. Westgate hereupon turned away, but after a moment's reflection she also faced her sister again. "It would come, after all, to the same thing," she said.

Lord Lambeth came the next day with his trap, and the two ladies, attended by Willie Woodley, placed themselves under his guidance and were conveyed eastward, through some of the duskier portions of the metropolis, to the great turreted donjon which overlooks the London shipping. They all descended from their vehicle and entered the famous enclosure; and they secured the services of a venerable beefeater,[5] who, though there were many other claimants for legendary information, made a fine exclusive party of them and marched them through courts and corridors, through armouries and prisons. He delivered his usual peripatetic discourse, and they stopped and stared, and peeped and stooped, according to the official admonitions. Bessie Alden asked the old man in the crimson doublet a great many questions; she thought it a most fascinating place. Lord Lambeth was in high good-humour; he was constantly laughing; he enjoyed what he would have called the lark. Willie Woodley kept looking at the ceilings and tapping the walls with the knuckle of a pearl-grey glove; and Mrs. Westgate, asking at frequent intervals to be allowed to sit down and wait till they came back, was as frequently informed that they would never come back. To a great many of Bessie's questions— chiefly on collateral points of English history—the ancient warder was naturally unable to reply; whereupon she always appealed to Lord Lambeth. But his lordship was very ignorant. He declared that he knew nothing about that sort of thing, and he seemed greatly diverted at being treated as an authority.

"You can't expect every one to know as much as you," he said.

"I should expect you to know a great deal more," declared Bessie Alden.

"Women always know more than men about names and dates, and that sort of thing," Lord Lambeth rejoined. "There was Lady Jane

5. A yeoman of the royal guard, warden at the Tower of London.

Grey we have just been hearing about, who went in for Latin and Greek and all the learning of her age."

"*You* have no right to be ignorant, at all events," said Bessie.

"Why haven't I as good a right as any one else?"

"Because you have lived in the midst of all these things."

"What things do you mean? Axes and blocks and thumbscrews?"

"All these historical things. You belong to an historical family."

"Bessie is really too historical," said Mrs. Westgate, catching a word of this dialogue.

"Yes, you are too historical," said Lord Lambeth, laughing, but thankful for a formula. "Upon my honour, you are too historical!"

He went with the ladies a couple of days later to Hampton Court, Willie Woodley being also of the party. The afternoon was charming, the famous horse-chestnuts were in blossom, and Lord Lambeth, who quite entered into the spirit of the cockney excursionist, declared that it was a jolly old place. Bessie Alden was in ecstasies; she went about murmuring and exclaiming.

"It's too lovely," said the young girl, "it's too enchanting; it's too exactly what it ought to be!"

At Hampton Court the little flocks of visitors are not provided with an official bellwether, but are left to browse at discretion upon the local antiquities. It happened in this manner that, in default of another informant, Bessie Alden, who on doubtful questions was able to suggest a great many alternatives, found herself again applying for intellectual assistance to Lord Lambeth. But he again assured her that he was utterly helpless in such matters—that his education had been sadly neglected.

"And I am sorry it makes you unhappy," he added in a moment.

"You are very disappointing, Lord Lambeth," she said.

"Ah, now, don't say that!" he cried. "That's the worst thing you could possibly say."

"No," she rejoined; "it is not so bad as to say that I had expected nothing of you."

"I don't know. Give me a notion of the sort of thing you expected."

"Well," said Bessie Alden, "that you would be more what I should like to be—what I should try to be—in your place."

"Ah, my place!" exclaimed Lord Lambeth; "you are always talking about my place."

The young girl looked at him; he thought she coloured a little; and for a moment she made no rejoinder.

"Does it strike you that I am always talking about your place?" she asked.

"I am sure you do it a great honour," he said, fearing he had been uncivil.

"I have often thought about it," she went on after a moment. "I have often thought about your being an hereditary legislator. An hereditary legislator ought to know a great many things."

"Not if he doesn't legislate."

"But you will legislate; it's absurd your saying you won't. You are very much looked up to here—I am assured of that."

"I don't know that I ever noticed it."

"It is because you are used to it, then. You ought to fill the place."

"How do you mean, to fill it?" asked Lord Lambeth.

"You ought to be very clever and brilliant, and to know almost everything."

Lord Lambeth looked at her a moment. "Shall I tell you something?" he asked. "A young man in my position, as you call it—"

"I didn't invent the term," interposed Bessie Alden. "I have seen it in a great many books."

"Hang it, you are always at your books! A fellow in my position, then, does very well, whatever he does. That's about what I mean to say."

"Well, if your own people are content with you," said Bessie Alden, laughing, "it is not for me to complain. But I shall always think that, properly, you should have a great mind—a great character."

"Ah, that's very theoretic!" Lord Lambeth declared. "Depend upon it, that's a Yankee prejudice."

"Happy the country," said Bessie Alden, "where even people's prejudices are so elevated!"

"Well, after all," observed Lord Lambeth, "I don't know that I am such a fool as you are trying to make me out."

"I said nothing so rude as that; but I must repeat that you are disappointing."

"My dear Miss Alden," exclaimed the young man, "I am the best fellow in the world!"

"Ah, if it were not for that!" said Bessie Alden, with a smile.

Mrs. Westgate had a good many more friends in London than she pretended, and before long she had renewed acquaintance with most of them. Their hospitality was extreme, so that, one thing leading to another, she began, as the phrase is, to go out. Bessie Alden, in this way, saw something of what she found it a great satisfaction to call to herself English society. She went to balls and danced, she went to dinners and talked, she went to concerts and listened (at concerts Bessie always listened), she went to exhibitions and wondered. Her enjoyment was keen and her curiosity insatiable, and, grateful in general for all her opportunities, she especially prized the privilege of meeting certain celebrated persons—authors and artists, philosophers and statesmen—of whose renown she had been a humble and distant beholder, and who now, as a part of the habitual furniture of London drawing-rooms, struck her as stars fallen from the firmament and become palpable—revealing also, sometimes, on contact, qualities not to have been predicted of bodies sidereal. Bessie, who knew so many of her contemporaries by reputation, had a good many personal disappointments; but, on the other hand, she had innumerable satisfactions and enthusiasms, and she communicated the emotions of either class to a dear friend, of her own sex, in Boston, with whom she was in voluminous correspondence. Some of her reflections, indeed, she attempted to impart to Lord Lambeth, who came almost every day to Jones's Hotel, and whom Mrs. Westgate admitted to be really devoted. Captain Littledale, it appeared, had gone to India; and of several others of Mrs. Westgate's ex-pensioners—gentlemen who, as she said, had made, in New York, a club-house of her drawing-room—no tidings were to be obtained; but Lord Lambeth was certainly attentive enough to make up for the accidental absences, the short memories, all the other irregularities, of every one else. He drove them in the Park, he took them to visit private collections of pictures, and having a house of his own, invited them to dinner. Mrs. Westgate, following the fashion of many of her compatriots, caused herself and her sister to be presented at the English Court by her diplomatic representative—for it was in this manner that she alluded to the American Minister to England, inquiring what on earth he was put there for, if not to make the proper arrangements for one's going to a Drawing Room.[6]

Lord Lambeth declared that he hated Drawings Rooms, but he participated in the ceremony on the day on which the two ladies at Jones's Hotel repaired to Buckingham Palace in a remarkable coach which his lordship had sent to fetch them. He had on a gorgeous uniform, and Bessie Alden was particularly struck with his appearance—especially when on her asking him, rather foolishly as she felt, if he were a loyal subject, he replied that he was a loyal subject to *her*. This declaration was emphasised by his dancing with her at a royal ball to which the two ladies afterwards went, and was not impaired by the fact that she thought he danced very ill. He seemed to her wonderfully kind; she asked herself, with growing vivacity, why he should be so kind. It was his disposition—that seemed the natural answer. She had told her sister that she liked him very much, and now that she liked him more she wondered why. She liked him for his disposition; to this question as well that seemed the natural answer. When once the impressions of London life began to crowd thickly upon her she completely forgot her sister's warning about the cynicism of public opinion. It had given her great pain at the moment; but there was no particular reason why she should remember it; it corresponded too little with any sensible reality; and it was disagreeable to Bessie to

6. A formal reception at court.

remember disagreeable things. So she was not haunted with the sense of a vulgar imputation. She was not in love with Lord Lambeth—she assured herself of that. It will immediately be observed that when such assurances become necessary the state of a young lady's affections is already ambiguous; and indeed Bessie Alden made no attempt to dissimulate—to herself, of course—a certain tenderness that she felt for the young nobleman. She said to herself that she liked the type to which he belonged—the simple, candid, manly, healthy English temperament. She spoke to herself of him as women speak of young men they like—alluded to his bravery (which she had never in the least seen tested), to his honesty and gentlemanliness; and was not silent upon the subject of his good looks. She was perfectly conscious, moreover, that she liked to think of his more adventitious merits—that her imagination was excited and gratified by the sight of a handsome young man endowed with such large opportunities—opportunities she hardly knew for what, but, as she supposed, for doing great things—for setting an example, for exerting an influence, for conferring happiness, for encouraging the arts. She had a kind of ideal of conduct for a young man who should find himself in this magnificent position, and she tried to adapt it to Lord Lambeth's deportment, as you might attempt to fit a silhouette in cut paper upon a shadow projected upon a wall. But Bessie Alden's silhouette refused to coincide with his lordship's image; and this want of harmony sometimes vexed her more than she thought reasonable. When he was absent it was of course less striking—then he seemed to her a sufficiently graceful combination of high responsibilities and amiable qualities. But when he sat there within sight, laughing and talking with his customary good humour and simplicity, she measured it more accurately, and she felt acutely that if Lord Lambeth's position was heroic, there was but little of the hero in the young man himself. Then her imagination wandered away from him—very far away; for it was an incontestable fact that at such moments he seemed distinctly dull. I am afraid that while Bessie's imagination was thus invidiously roaming, she cannot have been herself a very lively companion; but it may well have been that these occasional fits of indifference seemed to Lord Lambeth a part of the young girl's personal charm. It had been a part of this charm from the first that he felt that she judged him and measured him more freely and irresponsibly—more at her ease and her leisure, as it were—than several young ladies with whom he had been on the whole about as intimate. To feel this, and yet to feel that she also liked him, was very agreeable to Lord Lambeth. He fancied he had compassed that gratification so desirable to young men of title and fortune—being liked for himself. It is true that a cynical counsellor might have whispered to him, "Liked for yourself? Yes; but not so very much!" He had, at any rate, the constant hope of being liked more.

It may seem, perhaps, a trifle singular—but it is nevertheless true—that Bessie Alden, when he struck her as dull, devoted some time, on grounds of conscience, to trying to like him more. I say on grounds of conscience, because she felt that he had been extremely "nice" to her sister, and because she reflected that it was no more than fair that she should think as well of him as he thought of her. This effort was possibly sometimes not so successful as it might have been, for the result of it was occasionally a vague irritation, which expressed itself in hostile criticism of several British institutions. Bessie Alden went to some entertainments at which she met Lord Lambeth; but she went to others at which his lordship was neither actually nor potentially present; and it was chiefly on these latter occasions that she encountered those literary and artistic celebrities of whom mention has been made. After a while she reduced the matter to a principle. If Lord Lambeth should appear anywhere, it was a symbol that there would be no poets and philosophers; and in consequence—for it was almost a strict consequence—she used to enumerate to the young man these objects of her admiration.

"You seem to be awfully fond of that sort of people," said Lord Lambeth one day, as if the idea had just occurred to him.

"They are the people in England I am most curious to see," Bessie Alden replied.

"I suppose that's because you have read so much," said Lord Lambeth, gallantly.

"I have not read so much. It is because we think so much of them at home."

"Oh, I see!" observed the young nobleman. "In Boston."

"Not only in Boston; everywhere," said Bessie. "We hold them in great honour; they go to the best dinner-parties."

"I dare say you are right. I can't say I know many of them."

"It's a pity you don't," Bessie Alden declared. "It would do you good."

"I dare say it would," said Lord Lambeth, very humbly. "But I must say I don't like the looks of some of them."

"Neither do I—of some of them. But there are all kinds, and many of them are charming."

"I have talked with two or three of them," the young man went on, "and I thought they had a kind of fawning manner."

"Why should they fawn?" Bessie Alden demanded.

"I'm sure I don't know. Why, indeed?"

"Perhaps you only thought so," said Bessie.

"Well, of course," rejoined her companion, "that's a kind of thing that can't be proved."

"In America they don't fawn," said Bessie.

"Ah! well, then, they must be better company."

Bessie was silent a moment. "That is one of the things I don't like about England," she said; "your keeping the distinguished people apart."

"How do you mean, apart?"

"Why, letting them come only to certain places. You never see them."

Lord Lambeth looked at her a moment. "What people do you mean?"

"The eminent people—the authors and artists—the clever people."

"Oh, there are other eminent people besides those!" said Lord Lambeth.

"Well, you certainly keep them apart," repeated the young girl.

"And there are other clever people," added Lord Lambeth, simply.

Bessie Alden looked at him, and she gave a light laugh. "Not many," she said.

On another occasion—just after a dinner-party—she told him that there was something else in England she did not like.

"Oh, I say!" he cried; "haven't you abused us enough?"

"I have never abused you at all," said Bessie; "but I don't like your *precedence.*"[7]

"It isn't my precedence!" Lord Lambeth declared, laughing.

"Yes, it is yours—just exactly yours; and I think it's odious," said Bessie.

"I never saw such a young lady for discussing things! Has some one had the impudence to go before you?" asked his lordship.

"It is not the going before me that I object to," said Bessie; "it is their thinking that they have a right to do it—a right that I should recognise."

"I never saw such a young lady as you are for not 'recognising.' I have no doubt the thing is beastly, but it saves a lot of trouble."

"It makes a lot of trouble. It's horrid!" said Bessie.

"But how would you have the first people go?" asked Lord Lambeth. "They can't go last."

"Whom do you mean by the first people?"

"Ah, if you mean to question first principles!" said Lord Lambeth.

"If those are your first principles, no wonder some of your arrangements are horrid," observed Bessie Alden, with a very pretty ferocity. "I am a young girl, so of course I go last; but imagine what Kitty must feel on being informed that she is not at liberty to budge until certain other ladies have passed out!"

"Oh, I say, she is not 'informed'!" cried Lord Lambeth. "No one would do such a thing as that."

"She is made to feel it," the young girl insisted—"as if they were

7. The right, derived from birth or official status, to walk ahead of others in ceremonies or social formalities.

afraid she would make a rush for the door. No, you have a lovely country," said Bessie Alden, "but your precedence is horrid."

"I certainly shouldn't think your sister would like it," rejoined Lord Lambeth, with even exaggerated gravity. But Bessie Alden could induce him to enter no formal protest against this repulsive custom, which he seemed to think an extreme convenience.

VI

Percy Beaumont all this time had been a very much less frequent visitor at Jones's Hotel than his noble kinsman; he had in fact called but twice upon the two American ladies. Lord Lambeth, who often saw him reproached him with his neglect, and declared that although Mrs. Westgate had said nothing about it, he was sure that she was secretly wounded by it. "She suffers too much to speak," said Lord Lambeth.

"That's all gammon," said Percy Beaumont; "there's a limit to what people can suffer!" And, though sending no apologies to Jones's Hotel, he undertook in a manner to explain his absence. "You are always there," he said; "and that's reason enough for my not going."

"I don't see why. There is enough for both of us."

"I don't care to be a witness of your—your reckless passion," said Percy Beaumont.

Lord Lambeth looked at him with a cold eye, and for a moment said nothing. "It's not so obvious as you might suppose," he rejoined, dryly, "considering what a demonstrative beggar I am."

"I don't want to know anything about it—nothing whatever," said Beaumont. "Your mother asks me every time she sees me whether I believe you are really lost—and Lady Pimlico does the same. I prefer to be able to answer that I know nothing about it—that I never go there. I stay away for consistency's sake. As I said the other day, they must look after you themselves."

"You are devilish considerate," said Lord Lambeth. "They never question me."

"They are afraid of you. They are afraid of irritating you and making you worse. So they go to work very cautiously, and, somewhere or other, they get their information. They know a great deal about you. They know that you have been with those ladies to the dome of St. Paul's and—where was the other place?—to the Thames Tunnel."[8]

"If all their knowledge is as accurate as that, it must be very valuable," said Lord Lambeth.

"Well, at any rate, they know that you have been visiting the 'sights of the metropolis.' They think—very naturally, as it seems to me—

8. The first tunnel to connect the north and south sides of the River Thames in London. Saint Paul's Cathedral, in the City of London, was designed by Sir Christopher Wren and built 1675 to 1710.

that when you take to visiting the sights of the metropolis with a little American girl, there is serious cause for alarm." Lord Lambeth responded to this intimation by scornful laughter, and his companion continued, after a pause: "I said just now I didn't want to know anything about the affair; but I will confess that I am curious to learn whether you propose to marry Miss Bessie Alden."

On this point Lord Lambeth gave his interlocutor no immediate satisfaction; he was musing, with a frown. "By Jove," he said, "they go rather too far. They *shall* find me dangerous—I promise them."

Percy Beaumont began to laugh. "You don't redeem your promises. You said the other day you would make your mother call."

Lord Lambeth continued to meditate. "I asked her to call," he said, simply.

"And she declined?"

"Yes, but she shall do it yet."

"Upon my word," said Percy Beaumont, "if she gets much more frightened I believe she will." Lord Lambeth looked at him, and he went on. "She will go to the girl herself."

"How do you mean, she will go to her?"

"She will beg her off, or she will bribe her. She will take strong measures."

Lord Lambeth turned away in silence, and his companion watched him take twenty steps and then slowly return. "I have invited Mrs. Westgate and Miss Alden to Branches," he said, "and this evening I shall name a day."

"And shall you invite your mother and your sisters to meet them?"

"Explicitly!"

"That will set the Duchess off," said Percy Beaumont. "I suspect she will come."

"She may do as she pleases."

Beaumont looked at Lord Lambeth. "You do really propose to marry the little sister, then?"

"I like the way you talk about it!" cried the young man. "She won't gobble me down; don't be afraid."

"She won't leave you on your knees," said Percy Beaumont. "What *is* the inducement?"

"You talk about proposing—wait till I have proposed," Lord Lambeth went on.

"That's right, my dear fellow; think about it," said Percy Beaumont.

"She's a charming girl," pursued his lordship.

"Of course she's a charming girl. I don't know a girl more charming, intrinsically. But there are other charming girls nearer home."

"I like her spirit," observed Lord Lambeth, almost as if he were trying to torment his cousin.

"What's the peculiarity of her spirit?"

"She's not afraid, and she says things out, and she thinks herself as good as any one. She is the only girl I have ever seen that was not dying to marry me."

"How do you know that, if you haven't asked her?"

"I don't know how; but I know it."

"I am sure she asked me questions enough about your property and your titles," said Beaumont.

"She has asked me questions, too; no end of them," Lord Lambeth admitted. "But she asked for information, don't you know."

"Information? Ah, I'll warrant she wanted it. Depend upon it that she is dying to marry you just as much and just as little as all the rest of them."

"I shouldn't like her to refuse me—I shouldn't like that."

"If the thing would be so disagreeable, then, both to you and to her, in Heaven's name leave it alone," said Percy Beaumont.

Mrs. Westgate, on her side, had plenty to say to her sister about the rarity of Mr. Beaumont's visits and the non-appearance of the Duchess of Bayswater. She professed, however, to derive more satisfaction from this latter circumstance than she could have done from the most lavish attentions on the part of this great lady. "It is most marked," she said, "most marked. It is a delicious proof that we have made them miserable. The day we dined with Lord Lambeth I was really sorry for the poor fellow." It will have been gathered that the entertainment offered by Lord Lambeth to his American friends had not been graced by the presence of his anxious mother. He had invited several choice spirits to meet them; but the ladies of his immediate family were to Mrs. Westgate's sense—a sense, possibly, morbidly acute—conspicuous by their absence.

"I don't want to express myself in a manner that you dislike," said Bessie Alden; "but I don't know why you should have so many theories about Lord Lambeth's poor mother. You know a great many young men in New York without knowing their mothers."

Mrs. Westgate looked at her sister, and then turned away. "My dear Bessie, you are superb!" she said.

"One thing is certain," the young girl continued. "If I believed I were a cause of annoyance—however unwitting—to Lord Lambeth's family, I should insist—"

"Insist upon my leaving England," said Mrs. Westgate.

"No, not that. I want to go to the National Gallery again; I want to see Stratford-on-Avon and Canterbury Cathedral. But I should insist upon his coming to see us no more."

"That would be very modest and very pretty of you—but you wouldn't do it now."

"Why do you say 'now'?" asked Bessie Alden. "Have I ceased to be modest?"

"You care for him too much. A month ago, when you said you didn't, I believe it was quite true. But at present, my dear child," said

Mrs. Westgate, "you wouldn't find it quite so simple a matter never to see Lord Lambeth again. I have seen it coming on."

"You are mistaken," said Bessie. "You don't understand."

"My dear child, don't be perverse," rejoined her sister.

"I know him better, certainly, if you mean that," said Bessie. "And I like him very much. But I don't like him enough to make trouble for him with his family. However, I don't believe in that."

"I like the way you say 'however!' " Mrs. Westgate exclaimed. "Come, you would not marry him?"

"Oh no," said the young girl.

Mrs. Westgate, for a moment, seemed vexed. "Why not, pray?" she demanded.

"Because I don't care to," said Bessie Alden.

The morning after Lord Lambeth had had, with Percy Beaumont, that exchange of ideas which has just been narrated, the ladies at Jones's Hotel received from his lordship a written invitation to pay their projected visit to Branches Castle on the following Tuesday. "I think I have made up a very pleasant party," the young nobleman said. "Several people whom you know, and my mother and sisters, who have so long been regrettably prevented from making your acquaintance." Bessie Alden lost no time in calling her sister's attention to the injustice she had done the Duchess of Bayswater, whose hostility was now proved to be a vain illusion.

"Wait till you see if she comes," said Mrs. Westgate. "And if she is to meet us at her son's house the obligation was all the greater for her to call upon us."

Bessie had not to wait long, and it appeared that Lord Lambeth's mother now accepted Mrs. Westgate's view of her duties. On the morrow, early in the afternoon, two cards were brought to the apartment of the American ladies—one of them bearing the name of the Duchess of Bayswater and the other that of the Countess of Pimlico. Mrs. Westgate glanced at the clock. "It is not yet four," she said; "they have come early; they wish to see us. We will receive them." And she gave orders that her visitors should be admitted. A few moments later they were introduced, and there was a solemn exchange of amenities. The Duchess was a large lady, with a fine fresh colour; the Countess of Pimlico was very pretty and elegant.

The Duchess looked about her as she sat down—looked not especially at Mrs. Westgate. "I dare say my son has told you that I have been wanting to come and see you," she observed.

"You are very kind," said Mrs. Westgate, vaguely—her conscience not allowing her to assent to this proposition—and indeed not permitting her to enunciate her own with any appreciable emphasis.

"He says you were so kind to him in America," said the Duchess.

"We are very glad," Mrs. Westgate replied, "to have been able to make him a little more—a little less—a little more comfortable."

"I think he stayed at your house," remarked the Duchess of Bayswater, looking at Bessie Alden.

"A very short time," said Mrs. Westgate.

"Oh!" said the Duchess; and she continued to look at Bessie, who was engaged in conversation with her daughter.

"Do you like London?" Lady Pimlico had asked of Bessie, after looking at her a good deal—at her face and her hands, her dress and her hair.

"Very much indeed," said Bessie.

"Do you like this hotel?"

"It is very comfortable," said Bessie.

"Do you like stopping at hotels?" inquired Lady Pimlico, after a pause.

"I am very fond of travelling," Bessie answered, "and I suppose hotels are a necessary part of it. But they are not the part I am fondest of."

"Oh, I hate travelling!" said the Countess of Pimlico, and transferred her attention to Mrs. Westgate.

"My son tells me you are going to Branches," the Duchess presently resumed.

"Lord Lambeth has been so good as to ask us," said Mrs. Westgate, who perceived that her visitor had now begun to look at her, and who had her customary happy consciousness of a distinguished appearance. The only mitigation of her felicity on this point was that, having inspected her visitor's own costume, she said to herself, "She won't know how well I am dressed!"

"He has asked me to go, but I am not sure I shall be able," murmured the Duchess.

"He had offered us the p—the prospect of meeting you," said Mrs. Westgate.

"I hate the country at this season," responded the Duchess.

Mrs. Westgate gave a little shrug. "I think it is pleasanter than London."

But the Duchess's eyes were absent again; she was looking very fixedly at Bessie. In a moment she slowly rose, walked to a chair that stood empty at the young girl's right hand, and silently seated herself. As she was a majestic, voluminous woman, this little transaction had, inevitably, an air of somewhat impressive intention. It diffused a certain awkwardness, which Lady Pimlico, as a sympathetic daughter, perhaps desired to rectify in turning to Mrs. Westgate.

"I dare say you go out a great deal," she observed.

"No, very little. We are strangers, and we didn't come here for society."

"I see," said Lady Pimlico. "It's rather nice in town just now."

"It's charming," said Mrs. Westgate. "But we only go to see a few people—whom we like."

"Of course one can't like every one," said Lady Pimlico.

"It depends upon one's society," Mrs. Westgate rejoined.

The Duchess, meanwhile, had addressed herself to Bessie. "My son tells me the young ladies in America are so clever."

"I am glad they made so good an impression on him," said Bessie, smiling.

The Duchess was not smiling; her large fresh face was very tranquil. "He is very susceptible," she said. "He thinks every one clever, and sometimes they are."

"Sometimes," Bessie assented, smiling still.

The Duchess looked at her a little and then went on—"Lambeth is very susceptible, but he is very volatile, too."

"Volatile?" asked Bessie.

"He is very inconstant. It won't do to depend on him."

"Ah!" said Bessie; "I don't recognise that description. We have depended on him greatly—my sister and I—and he has never disappointed us."

"He will disappoint you yet," said the Duchess.

Bessie gave a little laugh, as if she were amused at the Duchess's persistency. "I suppose it will depend on what we expect of him."

"The less you expect the better," Lord Lambeth's mother declared.

"Well," said Bessie, "we expect nothing unreasonable."

The Duchess, for a moment, was silent, though she appeared to have more to say. "Lambeth says he has seen so much of you," she presently began.

"He has been to see us very often—he has been very kind," said Bessie Alden.

"I dare say you are used to that. I am told there is a great deal of that in America."

"A great deal of kindness?" the young girl inquired, smiling.

"Is that what you call it? I know you have different expressions."

"We certainly don't always understand each other," said Mrs. Westgate, the termination of whose interview with Lady Pimlico allowed her to give her attention to their elder visitor.

"I am speaking of the young men calling so much upon the young ladies," the Duchess explained.

"But surely in England," said Mrs. Westgate, "the young ladies don't call upon the young men?"

"Some of them do—almost!" Lady Pimlico declared. "When the young men are a great *parti*."[9]

"Bessie, you must make a note of that," said Mrs. Westgate. "My

---

9. A great match or catch.

sister," she added, "is a model traveller. She writes down all the curious facts she hears, in a little book she keeps for the purpose."

The Duchess was a little flushed; she looked all about the room, while her daughter turned to Bessie. "My brother told us you were wonderfully clever," said Lady Pimlico.

"He should have said my sister," Bessie answered—"when she says such things as that."

"Shall you be long at Branches?" the Duchess asked, abruptly, of the young girl.

"Lord Lambeth has asked us for three days," said Bessie.

"I shall go," the Duchess declared, "and my daughter too."

"That will be charming!" Bessie rejoined.

"Delightful!" murmured Mrs. Westgate.

"I shall expect to see a deal of you," the Duchess continued. "When I go to Branches I monopolise my son's guests."

"They must be most happy," said Mrs. Westgate, very graciously.

"I want immensely to see it—to see the Castle," said Bessie to the Duchess. "I have never seen one—in England at least; and you know we have none in America."

"Ah! you are fond of castles?" inquired her Grace.

"Immensely!" replied the young girl. "It has been the dream of my life to live in one."

The Duchess looked at her a moment, as if she hardly knew how to take this assurance, which, from her Grace's point of view, was either very artless or very audacious. "Well," she said, rising, "I will show you Branches myself." And upon this the two great ladies took their departure.

"What did they mean by it?" asked Mrs. Westgate, when they were gone.

"They meant to be polite," said Bessie, "because we are going to meet them."

"It is too late to be polite," Mrs. Westgate replied, almost grimly. "They meant to overawe us by their fine manners and their grandeur, and to make you *lâcher prise*."[1]

"*Lâcher prise?* What strange things you say!" murmured Bessie Alden.

"They meant to snub us, so that we shouldn't dare to go to Branches," Mrs. Westgate continued.

"On the contrary," said Bessie, "the Duchess offered to show me the place herself."

"Yes, you may depend upon it she won't let you out of her sight. She will show you the place from morning till night."

"You have a theory for everything," said Bessie.

1. Let go your hold.

"And you apparently have none for anything."

"I saw no attempt to 'overawe' us," said the young girl. "Their manners were not fine."

"They were not even good!" Mrs. Westgate declared.

Bessie was silent awhile, but in a few moments she observed that she had a very good theory. "They came to look at me!" she said, as if this had been a very ingenious hypothesis. Mrs. Westgate did it justice; she greeted it with a smile and pronounced it most brilliant; while in reality she felt that the young girl's scepticism, or her charity, or, as she had sometimes called it, appropriately, her idealism, was proof against irony. Bessie, however, remained meditative all the rest of that day and well on into the morrow.

On the morrow, before lunch, Mrs. Westgate had occasion to go out for an hour, and left her sister writing a letter. When she came back she met Lord Lambeth at the door of the hotel, coming away. She thought he looked slightly embarrassed; he was certainly very grave. "I am sorry to have missed you. Won't you come back?" she asked.

"No," said the young man, "I can't. I have seen your sister. I can never come back." Then he looked at her a moment, and took her hand. "Good-bye, Mrs. Westgate," he said. "You have been very kind to me." And with what she thought a strange, sad look in his handsome young face, he turned away.

She went in and she found Bessie still writing her letter; that is, Mrs. Westgate perceived she was sitting at the table with the pen in her hand and not writing. "Lord Lambeth has been here," said the elder lady at last.

Then Bessie got up and showed her a pale, serious face. She bent this face upon her sister for some time, confessing silently and, a little, pleading. "I told him," she said at last, "that we could not go to Branches."

Mrs. Westgate displayed just a spark of irritation. "He might have waited," she said with a smile, "till one had seen the Castle." Later, an hour afterwards, she said, "Dear Bessie, I wish you might have accepted him."

"I couldn't," said Bessie, gently.

"He is a dear good fellow," said Mrs. Westgate.

"I couldn't," Bessie repeated.

"If it is only," her sister added, "because those women will think that they succeeded—that they paralysed us!"

Bessie Alden turned away; but presently she added, "They were interesting; I should have liked to see them again."

"So should I!" cried Mrs. Westgate, significantly.

"And I should have liked to see the Castle," said Bessie. "But now we must leave England," she added.

Her sister looked at her. "You will not wait to go to the National Gallery?"

"Not now."

"Nor to Canterbury Cathedral?"

Bessie reflected a moment. "We can stop there on our way to Paris," she said.

Lord Lambeth did not tell Percy Beaumont that the contingency he was not prepared at all to like had occurred; but Percy Beaumont, on hearing that the two ladies had left London, wondered with some intensity what had happened; wondered, that is, until the Duchess of Bayswater came, a little, to his assistance. The two ladies went to Paris, and Mrs. Westgate beguiled the journey to that city by repeating several times, "That's what I regret; they will think they petrified us." But Bessie Alden seemed to regret nothing.

The Aspern Papers

(1888)†

I

I had taken Mrs. Prest into my confidence; in truth without her I should have made but little advance, for the fruitful idea in the whole business dropped from her friendly lips. It was she who invented the short cut, who severed the Gordian knot. It is not supposed to be the nature of women to rise as a general thing to the largest and most liberal view—I mean of a practical scheme; but it has struck me that they sometimes throw off a bold conception—such as a man would not have risen to—with singular serenity. "Simply ask them to take you in on the footing of a lodger"—I don't think that unaided I should have risen to that. I was beating about the bush, trying to be ingenious, wondering by what combination of arts I might become an acquaintance, when she offered this happy suggestion that the way to become an acquaintance was first to become an inmate. Her actual knowledge of the Misses Bordereau was scarcely larger than mine, and indeed I had brought with me from England some definite facts which were new to her. Their name had been mixed up ages before with one of the greatest names of the century, and they lived now in Venice in obscurity, on very small means, unvisited, unapproachable, in a dilapidated old palace on an out-of-the-way canal: this was the substance of my friend's impression of them. She herself had been established in Venice for fifteen years and had done a great deal of good there; but the circle of her benevolence did not include the two shy, mysterious, and as it was somehow supposed, scarcely respectable Americans (they were believed to have lost in their long exile all national quality, besides having had, as their name implied, some French strain in their origin), who asked no favours and desired no attention. In the early years of her residence she had made an attempt to see them, but this had been successful only as regards the little one, as Mrs. Prest called the niece; though in reality, as I afterwards learned, she was considerably the bigger of the two. She had heard Miss Bordereau was ill and had a suspicion that she was in want; and she had gone to the house to offer assistance, so that if there were suffering (and American suffering), she should at least not have it on her conscience. The "little one" received her in the great cold,

† "The Aspern Papers" first appeared in *The Atlantic Monthly* from March to May 1888. The first edition in a book, reprinted here, was *The Aspern Papers/Louisa Pallant/The Modern Warning* (London and New York: Macmillan and Co., 1888), vol. 1.

tarnished Venetian sala,[1] the central hall of the house, paved with marble and roofed with dim cross-beams, and did not even ask her to sit down. This was not encouraging for me, who wished to sit so fast, and I remarked as much to Mrs. Prest. She however replied with profundity, "Ah, but there's all the difference: I went to confer a favour and you will go to ask one. If they are proud you will be on the right side." And she offered to show me their house to begin with—to row me thither in her gondola. I let her know that I had already been to look at it half a dozen times; but I accepted her invitation, for it charmed me to hover about the place. I had made my way to it the day after my arrival in Venice (it had been described to me in advance by the friend in England to whom I owed definite information as to their possession of the papers), and I had besieged it with my eyes while I considered my plan of campaign. Jeffrey Aspern had never been in it that I knew of; but some note of his voice seemed to abide there by a roundabout implication, a faint reverberation.

Mrs. Prest knew nothing about the papers, but she was interested in my curiosity, as she was always interested in the joys and sorrows of her friends. As we went, however, in her gondola, gliding there under the sociable hood with the bright Venetian picture framed on either side by the movable window, I could see that she was amused by my infatuation, the way my interest in the papers had become a fixed idea. "One would think you expected to find in them the answer to the riddle of the universe," she said; and I denied the impeachment only by replying that if I had to choose between that precious solution and a bundle of Jeffrey Aspern's letters I knew indeed which would appear to me the greater boon. She pretended to make light of his genius and I took no pains to defend him. One doesn't defend one's god: one's god is in himself a defence. Besides, to-day, after his long comparative obscuration, he hangs high in the heaven of our literature, for all the world to see; he is a part of the light by which we walk. The most I said was that he was no doubt not a woman's poet: to which she rejoined aptly enough that he had been at least Miss Bordereau's. The strange thing had been for me to discover in England that she was still alive: it was as if I had been told Mrs. Siddons was, or Queen Caroline, or the famous Lady Hamilton,[2] for it seemed to me that she belonged to a generation as extinct. "Why, she must be tremendously old—at least a hundred," I had said; but on coming to consider dates I saw that it was not strictly necessary that she should have exceeded by very much the common span. None the less she was very far advanced in life and her

1. Hallway.
2. Mrs. Sarah Kemble Siddons (1755–1831) was a famous British actress; "Queen Caroline" refers to the queen of either George II (1727–60) or George IV (1820–30); Lady Hamilton (1761?–1815) was the mistress of Admiral Nelson, who defeated the French and Spanish fleets in the Battle of Trafalgar in 1815 but was killed in the course of battle.

relations with Jeffrey Aspern had occurred in her early womanhood.
"That is her excuse," said Mrs. Prest, half sententiously and yet also
somewhat as if she were ashamed of making a speech so little in the
real tone of Venice. As if a woman needed an excuse for having loved
the divine poet! He had been not only one of the most brilliant minds
of his day (and in those years, when the century was young, there
were, as every one knows, many), but one of the most genial men and
one of the handsomest.

The niece, according to Mrs. Prest, was not so old, and she risked
the conjecture that she was only a grand-niece. This was possible; I
had nothing but my share in the very limited knowledge of my English
fellow-worshipper John Cumnor, who had never seen the couple.
The world, as I say, had recognised Jeffrey Aspern, but Cumnor and I
had recognised him most. The multitude, to-day, flocked to his
temple, but of that temple he and I regarded ourselves as the ministers.
We held, justly, as I think, that we had done more for his memory
than any one else, and we had done it by opening lights into his life.
He had nothing to fear from us because he had nothing to fear from
the truth, which alone at such a distance of time we could be interested in establishing. His early death had been the only dark spot in
his life, unless the papers in Miss Bordereau's hands should perversely
bring out others. There had been an impression about 1825 that he
had "treated her badly," just as there had been an impression that he
had "served," as the London populace says, several other ladies in the
same way. Each of these cases Cumnor and I had been able to
investigate, and we had never failed to acquit him conscientiously of
shabby behaviour. I judged him perhaps more indulgently than my
friend; certainly, at any rate, it appeared to me that no man could have
walked straighter in the given circumstances. These were almost
always awkward. Half the women of his time, to speak liberally, had
flung themselves at his head, and out of this pernicious fashion many
complications, some of them grave, had not failed to arise. He was not
a woman's poet, as I had said to Mrs. Prest, in the modern phase of his
reputation; but the situation had been different when the man's own
voice was mingled with his song. That voice, by every testimony, was
one of the sweetest ever heard. "Orpheus and the Mænads!"[3] was the
exclamation that rose to my lips when I first turned over his correspondence. Almost all the Mænads were unreasonable and many of
them insupportable; it struck me in short that he was kinder, more
considerate than, in his place (if I could imagine myself in such a
place!) I should have been.

It was certainly strange beyond all strangeness, and I shall not take

3. The legendary Greek poet and musician Orpheus was pursued and ultimately torn to pieces
by the Maenads, female worshippers of Dionysus (Bacchus).

up space with attempting to explain it, that whereas in all these other lines of research we had to deal with phantoms and dust, the mere echoes of echoes, the one living source of information that had lingered on into our time had been unheeded by us. Every one of Aspern's contemporaries had, according to our belief, passed away; we had not been able to look into a single pair of eyes into which his had looked or to feel a transmitted contact in any aged hand that his had touched. Most dead of all did poor Miss Bordereau appear, and yet she alone had survived. We exhausted in the course of months our wonder that we had not found her out sooner, and the substance of our explanation was that she had kept so quiet. The poor lady on the whole had had reason for doing so. But it was a revelation to us that it was possible to keep so quiet as that in the latter half of the nineteenth century—the age of newspapers and telegrams and photographs and interviewers. And she had taken no great trouble about it either: she had not hidden herself away in an undiscoverable hole; she had boldly settled down in a city of exhibition. The only secret of her safety that we could perceive was that Venice contained so many curiosities that were greater than she. And then accident had somehow favoured her, as was shown for example in the fact that Mrs. Prest had never happened to mention her to me, though I had spent three weeks in Venice—under her nose, as it were—five years before. Mrs. Prest had not mentioned this much to any one; she appeared almost to have forgotten she was there. Of course she had the responsibilities of an editor. It was no explanation of the old woman's having eluded us to say that she lived abroad, for our researches had again and again taken us (not only by correspondence but by personal inquiry) to France, to Germany, to Italy, in which countries, not counting his important stay in England, so many of the too few years of Aspern's career were spent. We were glad to think, at least that in all our publishings (some people consider I believe that we have overdone them), we had only touched in passing and in the most discreet manner on Miss Bordereau's connection. Oddly enough, even if we had had the material (and we often wondered what had become of it), it would have been the most difficult episode to handle.

The gondola stopped, the old palace was there; it was a house of the class which in Venice carries even in extreme dilapidation the dignified name. "How charming! It's gray and pink!" my companion exclaimed; and that is the most comprehensive description of it. It was not particularly old, only two or three centuries; and it had an air not so much of decay as of quiet discouragement, as if it had rather missed its career. But its wide front, with a stone balcony from end to end of the *piano nobile* or most important floor, was architectural enough, with the aid of various pilasters and arches; and the stucco with which in the intervals it had long ago been endued was

rosy in the April afternoon. It overlooked a clean, melancholy, unfre-
quented canal, which had a narrow *riva* or convenient footway on
either side. "I don't know why—there are no brick gables," said Mrs.
Prest, "but this corner has seemed to me before more Dutch than
Italian, more like Amsterdam than like Venice. It's perversely clean,
for reasons of its own; and though you can pass on foot scarcely any
one ever thinks of doing so. It has the air of a Protestant Sunday.
Perhaps the people are afraid of the Misses Bordereau. I daresay they
have the reputation of witches."

I forget what answer I made to this—I was given up to two other
reflections. The first of these was that if the old lady lived in such a big,
imposing house she could not be in any sort of misery and therefore
would not be tempted by a chance to let a couple of rooms. I expressed
this idea to Mrs. Prest, who gave me a very logical reply. "If she didn't
live in a big house how could it be a question of her having rooms to
spare? If she were not amply lodged herself you would lack ground to
approach her. Besides, a big house here, and especially in this *quartier
perdu*, [4] proves nothing at all: it is perfectly compatible with a state of
penury. Dilapidated old palazzi, if you will go out of the way for them,
are to be had for five shillings a year. And as for the people who live in
them—no, until you have explored Venice socially as much as I have
you can form no idea of their domestic desolation. They live on
nothing, for they have nothing to live on." The other idea that had
come into my head was connected with a high blank wall which
appeared to confine an expanse of ground on one side of the house.
Blank I call it, but it was figured over with the patches that please a
painter, repaired breaches, crumblings of plaster, extrusions of brick
that had turned pink with time; and a few thin trees, with the poles of
certain rickety trellises, were visible over the top. The place was a
garden and apparently it belonged to the house. It suddenly occurred
to me that if it did belong to the house I had my pretext.

I sat looking out on all this with Mrs. Prest (it was covered with the
golden glow of Venice) from the shade of our *felze*, [5] and she asked me
if I would go in then, while she waited for me, or come back another
time. At first I could not decide—it was doubtless very weak of me. I
wanted still to think I *might* get a footing, and I was afraid to meet
failure, for it would leave me, as I remarked to my companion,
without another arrow for my bow. "Why not another?" she inquired,
as I sat there hesitating and thinking it over; and she wished to know
why even now and before taking the trouble of becoming an inmate
(which might be wretchedly uncomfortable after all, even if it succeeded), I had not the resource of simply offering them a sum of

4. Forgotten neighborhood.   5. Small cabin of a gondola.

money down. In that way I might obtain the documents without bad nights.

"Dearest lady," I exclaimed, "excuse the impatience of my tone when I suggest that you must have forgotten the very fact (surely I communicated it to you) which pushed me to throw myself upon your ingenuity. The old woman won't have the documents spoken of; they are personal, delicate, intimate, and she hasn't modern notions, God bless her! If I should sound that note first I should certainly spoil the game. I can arrive at the papers only by putting her off her guard, and I can put her off her guard only by ingratiating diplomatic practices. Hypocrisy, duplicity are my only chance. I am sorry for it, but for Jeffrey Aspern's sake I would do worse still. First I must take tea with her; then tackle the main job." And I told over what had happened to John Cumnor when he wrote to her. No notice whatever had been taken of his first letter, and the second had been answered very sharply, in six lines, by the niece. "Miss Bordereau requested her to say that she could not imagine what he meant by troubling them. They had none of Mr. Aspern's papers, and if they had should never think of showing them to any one on any account whatever. She didn't know what he was talking about and begged he would let her alone." I certainly did not want to be met that way.

"Well," said Mrs. Prest, after a moment, provokingly, "perhaps after all they haven't any of his things. If they deny it flat how are you sure?"

"John Cumnor is sure, and it would take me long to tell you how his conviction, or his very strong presumption—strong enough to stand against the old lady's not unnatural fib—has built itself up. Besides, he makes much of the internal evidence of the niece's letter."

"The internal evidence?"

"Her calling him 'Mr. Aspern.' "

"I don't see what that proves."

"It proves familiarity, and familiarity implies the possession of mementoes, of relics. I can't tell you how that 'Mr.' touches me—how it bridges over the gulf of time and brings our hero near to me—nor what an edge it gives to my desire to see Juliana. You don't say 'Mr.' Shakespeare."

"Would I, any more, if I had a box full of his letters?"

"Yes, if he had been your lover and some one wanted them!" And I added that John Cumnor was so convinced, and so all the more convinced by Miss Bordereau's tone, that he would have come himself to Venice on the business were it not that for him there was the obstacle that it would be difficult to disprove his identity with the person who had written to them, which the old ladies would be sure to suspect in spite of dissimulation and a change of name. If they were to ask him point-blank if he were not their correspondent it would be too awkward for him to lie; whereas I was fortunately not tied in that way. I was a fresh hand and could say no without lying.

"But you will have to change your name," said Mrs. Prest. "Juliana lives out of the world as much as it is possible to live, but none the less she has probably heard of Mr. Aspern's editors; she perhaps possesses what you have published."

"I have thought of that," I returned; and I drew out of my pocket-book a visiting-card, neatly engraved with a name that was not my own.

"You are very extravagant; you might have written it," said my companion.

"This looks more genuine."

"Certainly, you are prepared to go far! But it will be awkward about your letters; they won't come to you in that mask."

"My banker will take them in and I will go every day to fetch them. It will give me a little walk."

"Shall you only depend upon that?" asked Mrs. Prest. "Aren't you coming to see me?"

"Oh, you will have left Venice, for the hot months, long before there are any results. I am prepared to roast all summer—as well as hereafter, perhaps you'll say! Meanwhile, John Cumnor will bombard me with letters addressed, in my feigned name, to the care of the *padrona*."

"She will recognise his hand," my companion suggested.

"On the envelope he can disguise it."

"Well, you're a precious pair! Doesn't it occur to you that even if you are able to say you are not Mr. Cumnor in person they may still suspect you of being his emissary?"

"Certainly, and I see only one way to parry that."

"And what may that be?"

I hesitated a moment. "To make love to the niece."

"Ah," cried Mrs. Prest, "wait till you see her!"

II

"I must work the garden—I must work the garden," I said to myself, five minutes later, as I waited, upstairs, in the long, dusky sala, where the bare scagliola floor gleamed vaguely in a chink of the closed shutters. The place was impressive but it looked cold and cautious. Mrs. Prest had floated away, giving me a rendezvous at the end of half an hour by some neighboring watersteps; and I had been let into the house, after pulling the rusty bell-wire, by a little red-headed, white-faced maid-servant, who was very young and not ugly and wore clicking pattens and a shawl in the fashion of a hood. She had not contented herself with opening the door from above by the usual arrangement of a creaking pulley, though she had looked down at me first from an upper window, dropping the inevitable challenge which in Italy precedes the hospitable act. As a general thing I was irritated by this survival of mediæval manners, though as I liked the old I suppose I ought to have liked it; but I was so determined to be genial that I took my false card out of my pocket and held it up to her, smiling as if it were a magic token. It had the effect of one indeed, for it brought her, as I say, all the way down. I begged her to hand it to her mistress, having first written on it in Italian the words, "Could you very kindly see a gentleman, an American, for a moment?" The little maid was not hostile, and I reflected that even that was perhaps something gained. She coloured, she smiled and looked both frightened and pleased. I could see that my arrival was a great affair, that visits were rare in that house, and that she was a person who would have liked a sociable place. When she pushed forward the heavy door behind me I felt that I had a foot in the citadel. She pattered across the damp, stony lower hall and I followed her up the high staircase—stonier still, as it seemed—without an invitation. I think she had meant I should wait for her below, but such was not my idea, and I took up my station in the sala. She flitted, at the far end of it, into impenetrable regions, and I looked at the place with my heart beating as I had known it to do in the dentist's parlour. It was gloomy and stately, but it owed its character almost entirely to its noble shape and to the fine architectural doors—as high as the doors of houses—which, leading into the various rooms, repeated themselves on either side at intervals. They were surmounted with old faded painted escutcheons, and here and there, in the spaces between them, brown pictures, which I perceived to be bad, in battered frames, were suspended. With the exception of several straw-bottomed chairs with their backs to the wall, the grand obscure vista contained nothing else to minister to effect. It was evidently never used save as a passage, and little even as that. I may add that by the time the door opened again through which the maid-servant had escaped, my eyes had grown used to the want of light.

I had not meant by my private ejaculation that I must myself cultivate the soil of the tangled enclosure which lay beneath the windows, but the lady who came toward me from the distance over the hard, shining floor might have supposed as much from the way in which, as I went rapidly to meet her, I exclaimed, taking care to speak Italian: "The garden, the garden—do me the pleasure to tell me if it's yours!"

She stopped, short, looking at me with wonder; and then, "Nothing here is mine," she answered in English, coldly and sadly.

"Oh, you are English; how delightful!" I remarked, ingenuously. "But surely the garden belongs to the house?"

"Yes, but the house doesn't belong to me." She was a long, lean, pale person, habited apparently in a dull-coloured dressing-gown, and she spoke with a kind of mild literalness. She did not ask me to sit down, any more than years before (if she were the niece) she had asked Mrs. Prest, and we stood face to face in the empty pompous hall.

"Well then, would you kindly tell me to whom I must address myself? I'm afraid you'll think me odiously intrusive, but you know I *must* have a garden—upon my honour I must!"

Her face was not young, but it was simple; it was not fresh, but it was mild. She had large eyes which were not bright, and a great deal of hair which was not "dressed," and long fine hands which were—possibly—not clean. She clasped these members almost convulsively as, with a confused, alarmed look, she broke out, "Oh, don't take it away from us; we like it ourselves!"

"You have the use of it then?"

"Oh yes. If it wasn't for that!" And she gave a shy, melancholy smile.

"Isn't it a luxury, precisely? That's why, intending to be in Venice some weeks, possibly all summer, and having some literary work, some reading and writing to do, so that I must be quiet, and yet if possible a great deal in the open air—that's why I have felt that a garden is really indispensable. I appeal to your own experience," I went on, smiling. "Now can't I look at yours?"

"I don't know, I don't understand," the poor woman murmured, planted there and letting her embarrassed eyes wander all over my strangeness.

"I mean only from one of those windows—such grand ones as you have here—if you will let me open the shutters." And I walked toward the back of the house. When I had advanced half-way I stopped and waited, as if I took it for granted she would accompany me. I had been of necessity very abrupt, but I strove at the same time to give her the impression of extreme courtesy. "I have been looking at furnished rooms all over the place, and it seems impossible to find any with a garden attached. Naturally in a place like Venice gardens are rare. It's absurd if you like, for a man, but I can't live without flowers."

"There are none to speak of down there." She came nearer to me, as if, though she mistrusted me, I had drawn her by an invisible thread. I went on again, and she continued as she followed me: "We have a few, but they are very common. It costs too much to cultivate them; one has to have a man."

"Why shouldn't I be the man?" I asked. "I'll work without wages; or rather I'll put in a gardener. You shall have the sweetest flowers in Venice."

She protested at this, with a queer little sigh which might also have been a gush of rapture at the picture I presented. Then she observed, "We don't know you—we don't know you."

"You know me as much as I know you; that is much more, because you know my name. And if you are English I am almost a country-man."

"We are not English," said my companion, watching me helplessly while I threw open the shutters of one of the divisions of the wide high window.

"You speak the language so beautifully: might I ask what you are?" Seen from above the garden was certainly shabby; but I perceived at a glance that it had great capabilities. She made no rejoinder, she was so lost in staring at me, and I exclaimed, "You don't mean to say you are also by chance American?"

"I don't know; we used to be."

"Used to be? Surely you haven't changed?"

"It's so many years ago—we are nothing."

"So many years that you have been living here? Well, I don't wonder at that; it's a grand old house. I suppose you all use the garden," I went on, "but I assure you I shouldn't be in your way. I would be very quiet and stay in one corner."

"We all use it?" she repeated after me, vaguely, not coming close to the window but looking at my shoes. She appeared to think me capable of throwing her out.

"I mean all your family, as many as you are."

"There is only one other; she is very old—she never goes down."

"Only one other, in all this great house!" I feigned to be not only amazed but almost scandalised. "Dear lady, you must have space then to spare!"

"To spare?" she repeated, in the same dazed way.

"Why, you surely don't live (two quiet women—I see *you* are quiet, at any rate) in fifty rooms!" Then with a burst of hope and cheer I demanded: "Couldn't you let me two or three? That would set me up!"

I had now struck the note that translated my purpose and I need not reproduce the whole of the tune I played. I ended by making my interlocutress believe that I was an honourable person, though of course I did not even attempt to persuade her that I was not an eccentric one. I repeated that I had studies to pursue; that I wanted quiet; that I delighted in a garden and had vainly sought one up and down the city; that I would undertake that before another month was over the dear old house should be smothered in flowers. I think it was the flowers that won my suit, for I afterwards found that Miss Tita (for such the name of this high tremulous spinster proved somewhat incongruously to be) had an insatiable appetite for them. When I speak of my suit as won I mean that before I left her she had promised that she would refer the question to her aunt. I inquired who her aunt might be and she answered, "Why, Miss Bordereau!" with an air of surprise, as if I might have been expected to know. There were contradictions like this in Tita Bordereau which, as I observed later, contributed to make her an odd and affecting person. It was the study of the two ladies to live so that the world should not touch them, and yet they had never altogether accepted the idea that it never heard of them. In Tita at any rate a grateful susceptibility to human contact had not died out, and contact of a limited order there would be if I should come to live in the house.

"We have never done anything of the sort; we have never had a lodger or any kind of inmate." So much as this she made a point of saying to me. "We are very poor, we live very badly. The rooms are very bare—that you might take; they have nothing in them. I don't know how you would sleep, how you would eat."

"With your permission, I could easily put in a bed and a few tables and chairs. *C'est la moindre des choses*[6] and the affair of an hour or two. I know a little man from whom I can hire what I should want for a few months, for a trifle, and my gondolier can bring the things round in his boat. Of course in this great house you must have a second kitchen, and my servant, who is a wonderfully handy fellow" (this personage was an evocation of the moment), "can easily cook me a chop there. My tastes and habits are of the simplest; I live on flowers!" And then I ventured to add that if they were very poor it was all the more reason they should let their rooms. They were bad economists—I had never heard of such a waste of material.

I saw in a moment that the good lady had never before been spoken to in that way, with a kind of humorous firmness which did not exclude sympathy but was on the contrary founded on it. She might easily have told me that my sympathy was impertinent, but this by good fortune did not occur to her. I left her with the understanding that she would consider the matter with her aunt and that I might come back the next day for their decision.

""The aunt will refuse; she will think the whole proceeding very *louche!*"[7] Mrs. Prest declared shortly after this, when I had resumed my place in her gondola. She had put the idea into my head and now (so little are women to be counted on) she appeared to take a despondent view of it. Her pessimism provoked me and I pretended to have the best hopes; I went so far as to say that I had a distinct presentiment that I should succeed. Upon this Mrs. Prest broke out, "Oh, I see what's in your head! You fancy you have made such an impression in a quarter of an hour that she is dying for you to come and can be depended upon to bring the old one round. If you do get in you'll count it as a triumph."

I did count it as a triumph, but only for the editor (in the last analysis), not for the man, who had not the tradition of personal

6. That's the least of things.   7. Suspicious, fishy.

conquest. When I went back on the morrow the little maid-servant
conducted me straight through the long sala (it opened there as before
in perfect perspective and was lighter now, which I thought a good
omen) into the apartment from which the recipient of my former visit
had emerged on that occasion. It was a large shabby parlour, with a
fine old painted ceiling and a strange figure sitting alone at one of the
windows. They come back to me now almost with the palpitation they
caused, the successive feelings that accompanied my consciousness
that as the door of the room closed behind me I was really face to face
with the Juliana of some of Aspern's most exquisite and most re-
nowned lyrics. I grew used to her afterwards, though never completely; but as she sat there before me my heart beat as fast as if the
miracle of resurrection had taken place for my benefit. Her presence
seemed somehow to contain his, and I felt nearer to him at that first
moment of seeing her than I ever had been before or ever have been
since. Yes, I remember my emotions in their order, even including a
curious little tremor that took me when I saw that the niece was not
there. With her, the day before, I had become sufficiently familiar,
but it almost exceeded my courage (much as I had longed for the
event) to be left alone with such a terrible relic as the aunt. She was too
strange, too literally resurgent. Then came a check, with the perception that we were not really face to face, inasmuch as she had over her
eyes a horrible green shade which, for her, served almost as a mask. I
believed for the instant that she had put it on expressly, so that from
underneath it she might scrutinise me without being scrutinised
herself. At the same time it increased the presumption that there was a
ghastly death's-head lurking behind it. The divine Juliana as a grinning skull—the vision hung there until it passed. Then it came to me
that she *was* tremendously old—so old that death might take her at any
moment, before I had time to get what I wanted from her. The next
thought was a correction to that; it lighted up the situation. She would
die next week, she would die tomorrow—then I could seize her
papers. Meanwhile she sat there neither moving nor speaking. She
was very small and shrunken, bent forward, with her hands in her lap.
She was dressed in black and her head was wrapped in a piece of old
black lace which showed no hair.

My emotion keeping me silent she spoke first, and the remark she
made was exactly the most unexpected.

III

"Our house is very far from the centre, but the little canal is very
comme il faut."

"It's the sweetest corner of Venice and I can imagine nothing more
charming," I hastened to reply. The old lady's voice was very thin and
weak, but it had an agreeable, cultivated murmur and there was

wonder in the thought that that individual note had been in Jeffrey Aspern's ear.

"Please to sit down there. I hear very well," she said quietly, as if perhaps I had been shouting at her; and the chair she pointed to was at a certain distance. I took possession of it, telling her that I was perfectly aware that I had intruded, that I had not been properly introduced and could only throw myself upon her indulgence. Perhaps the other lady, the one I had had the honour of seeing the day before, would have explained to her about the garden. That was literally what had given me courage to take a step so unconventional. I had fallen in love at sight with the whole place (she herself probably was so used to it that she did not know the impression it was capable of making on a stranger), and I had felt it was really a case to risk something. Was her own kindness in receiving me a sign that I was not wholly out in my calculation? It would render me extremely happy to think so. I could give her my word of honour that I was a most respectable, inoffensive person and that as an inmate they would be barely conscious of my existence. I would conform to any regulations, any restrictions if they would only let me enjoy the garden. Moreover I should be delighted to give her references; guarantees; they would be of the very best, both in Venice and in England as well as in America.

She listened to me in perfect stillness and I felt that she was looking at me with great attention, though I could see only the lower part of her bleached and shrivelled face. Independently of the refining process of old age it had a delicacy which once must have been great. She had been very fair, she had had a wonderful complexion. She was silent a little after I had ceased speaking; then she inquired, "If you are so fond of a garden why don't you go to *terra firma*,[8] where there are so many far better than this?"

"Oh, it's the combination!" I answered, smiling; and then, with rather a flight of fancy, "It's the idea of a garden in the middle of the sea."

"It's not in the middle of the sea; you can't see the water."

I stared a moment, wondering whether she wished to convict me of fraud. "Can't see the water? Why, dear madam, I can come up to the very gate in my boat."

She appeared inconsequent, for she said vaguely in reply to this, "Yes, if you have got a boat. I haven't any; it's many years since I have been in one of the gondolas." She uttered these words as if the gondolas were a curious far-away craft which she knew only by hearsay.

"Let me assure you of the pleasure with which I would put mine at your service!" I exclaimed. I had scarcely said this however before I

---

8. The mainland: Venice sits on islands some two miles from the mainland.

became aware that the speech was in questionable taste and might also do me the injury of making me appear too eager, too possessed of a hidden motive. But the old woman remained impenetrable and her attitude bothered me by suggesting that she had a fuller vision of me than I had of her. She gave me no thanks for my somewhat extravagant offer but remarked that the lady I had seen the day before was her niece; she would presently come in. She had asked her to stay away a little on purpose, because she herself wished to see me at first alone. She relapsed into silence and I asked myself why she had judged this necessary and what was coming yet; also whether I might venture on some judicious remark in praise of her companion. I went so far as to say that I should be delighted to see her again: she had been so very courteous to me, considering how odd she must have thought me—a declaration which drew from Miss Bordereau another of her whimsical speeches.

"She has very good manners; I bred her up myself!" I was on the point of saying that that accounted for the easy grace of the niece, but I arrested myself in time, and the next moment the old woman went on: "I don't care who you may be—I don't want to know; it signifies very little to-day." This had all the air of being a formula of dismissal, as if her next words would be that I might take myself off now that she had had the amusement of looking on the face of such a monster of indiscretion. Therefore I was all the more surprised when she added, with her soft, venerable quaver, "You may have as many rooms as you like—if you will pay a good deal of money."

I hesitated but for a single instant, long enough to ask myself what she meant in particular by this condition. First it struck me that she must have really a large sum in her mind; then I reasoned quickly that her idea of a large sum would probably not correspond to my own. My deliberation, I think, was not so visible as to diminish the promptitude with which I replied, "I will pay with pleasure and of course in advance whatever you may think it proper to ask me."

"Well then, a thousand francs a month," she rejoined instantly, while her baffling green shade continued to cover her attitude.

The figure, as they say, was startling and my logic had been at fault. The sum she had mentioned was, by the Venetian measure of such matters, exceedingly large; there was many an old palace in an out-of-the-way corner that I might on such terms have enjoyed by the year. But so far as my small means allowed I was prepared to spend money, and my decision was quickly taken. I would pay her with a smiling face what she asked, but in that case I would give myself the compensation of extracting the papers from her for nothing. Moreover if she had asked five times as much I should have risen to the occasion; so odious would it have appeared to me to stand chaffering with Aspern's Juliana. It was queer enough to have a question of money with her at all. I assured her that her views perfectly met my own and that on the morrow I should have the pleasure of putting three months' rent into her hand. She received this announcement with serenity and with no apparent sense that after all it would be becoming of her to say that I ought to see the rooms first. This did not occur to her and indeed her serenity was mainly what I wanted. Our little bargain was just concluded when the door opened and the younger lady appeared on the threshold. As soon as Miss Bordereau saw her niece she cried out almost gaily, "He will give three thousand—three thousand tomorrow!"

Miss Tita stood still, with her patient eyes turning from one of us to the other; then she inquired, scarcely above her breath, "Do you mean francs."

"Did you mean francs or dollars?"[9] the old woman asked of me at this.

"I think francs were what you said," I answered, smiling.

"That is very good," said Miss Tita, as if she had become conscious that her own question might have looked over-reaching.

"What do *you* know? You are ignorant," Miss Bordereau remarked; not with acerbity but with a strange, soft coldness.

"Yes, of money—certainly of money!" Miss Tita hastened to exclaim.

"I am sure you have your own branches of knowledge," I took the liberty of saying, genially. There was something painful to me, somehow, in the turn the conversation had taken, in the discussion of the rent.

"She had a very good education when she was young. I looked into that myself," said Miss Bordereau. Then she added, "But she has learned nothing since."

"I have always been with you," Miss Tita rejoined very mildly, and evidently with no intention of making an epigram.

"Yes, but for that!" her aunt declared, with more satirical force. She evidently meant that but for this her niece would never have got on at all; the point of the observation however being lost on Miss Tita, though she blushed at hearing her history revealed to a stranger. Miss Bordereau went on, addressing herself to me: "And what time will you come to-morrow with the money?"

"The sooner the better. If it suits you I will come at noon."

"I am always here but I have my hours," said the old woman, as if her convenience were not to be taken for granted.

---

9. In 1890, two years after publication of the story, the official rate of exchange was about five French francs to the dollar. The lira, the currency of the Kingdom of Italy, to which Venice by that time belonged, was not an international trading currency like the franc. But Venice had been involved in international trade for centuries: this may explain why these Americans in Venice think in francs rather than lire.

"You mean the times when you receive?"

"I never receive. But I will see you at noon, when you come with the money."

"Very good, I shall be punctual;" and I added, "May I shake hands with you, on our contract?" I thought there ought to be some little form, it would make me really feel easier, for I foresaw that there would be no other. Besides, though Miss Bordereau could not today be called personally attractive and there was something even in her wasted antiquity that bade one stand at one's distance, I felt an irresistible desire to hold in my own for a moment the hand that Jeffrey Aspern had pressed.

For a minute she made no answer and I saw that my proposal failed to meet with her approbation. She indulged in no movement of withdrawal, which I half expected; she only said coldly, "I belong to a time when that was not the custom."

I felt rather snubbed but I exclaimed good-humouredly to Miss Tita, "Oh, you will do as well!" I shook hands with her while she replied, with a small flutter, "Yes, yes, to show it's all arranged!"

"Shall you bring the money in gold?" Miss Bordereau demanded, as I was turning to the door.

I looked at her a moment. "Aren't you a little afraid, after all, of keeping such a sum as that in the house?" It was not that I was annoyed at her avidity but I was really struck with the disparity between such a treasure and such scanty means of guarding it.

"Whom should I be afraid of if I am not afraid of you?" she asked with her shrunken grimness.

"Ah well," said I, laughing, "I shall be in point of fact a protector and I will bring gold if you prefer."

"Thank you," the old woman returned with dignity and with an inclination of her head which evidently signified that I might depart. I passed out of the room, reflecting that it would not be easy to circumvent her. As I stood in the sala again I saw that Miss Tita had followed me and I supposed that as her aunt had neglected to suggest that I should take a look at my quarters it was her purpose to repair the omission. But she made no such suggestion; she only stood there with a dim, though not a languid smile, and with an effect of irresponsible, incompetent youth which was almost comically at variance with the faded facts of her person. She was not infirm, like her aunt, but she struck me as still more helpless, because her inefficiency was spiritual, which was not the case with Miss Bordereau's. I waited to see if she would offer to show me the rest of the house, but I did not precipitate the question, inasmuch as my plan was from this moment to spend as much of my time as possible in her society. I only observed at the end of a minute:

"I have had better fortune than I hoped. It was very kind of her to see me. Perhaps you said a good word for me."

"It was the idea of the money," said Miss Tita.

"And did you suggest that?"

"I told her that you would perhaps give a good deal."

"What made you think that?"

"I told her I thought you were rich."

"And what put that idea into your head?"

"I don't know; the way you talked."

"Dear me, I must talk differently now," I declared. "I'm sorry to say it's not the case."

"Well," said Miss Tita, "I think that in Venice the *forestieri*,[1] in general, often give a great deal for something that after all isn't much." She appeared to make this remark with a comforting intention, to wish to remind me that if I had been extravagant I was not really foolishly singular. We walked together along the sala, and as I took its magnificent measure I said to her that I was afraid it would not form a part of my *quartiere*.[2] Were my rooms by chance to be among those that opened into it? "Not if you go above, on the second floor," she answered with a little startled air, as if she had rather taken for granted I would know my proper place.

"And I infer that that's where your aunt would like me to be."

"She said your apartments ought to be very distinct."

"That certainly would be best." And I listened with respect while she told me that up above I was free to take whatever I liked; that there was another staircase, but only from the floor on which we stood, and that to pass from it to the garden-story or to come up to my lodging I should have in effect to cross the great hall. This was an immense point gained; I foresaw that it would constitute my whole leverage in my relations with the two ladies. When I asked Miss Tita how I was to manage at present to find my way up she replied with an access of that sociable shyness which constantly marked her manner.

"Perhaps you can't. I don't see—unless I should go with you." She evidently had not thought of this before.

We ascended to the upper floor and visited a long succession of empty rooms. The best of them looked over the garden; some of the others had a view of the blue lagoon, above the opposite rough-tiled housetops. They were all dusty and even a little disfigured with long neglect, but I saw that by spending a few hundred francs I should be able to convert three or four of them into a convenient habitation. My experiment was turning out costly, yet now that I had all but taken possession I ceased to allow this to trouble me. I mentioned to my companion a few of the things that I should put in, but she replied rather more precipitately than usual that I might do exactly what I

1. Foreigners.   2. Quarters, lodging.

liked; she seemed to wish to notify me that the Misses Bordereau would take no overt interest in my proceedings. I guessed that her aunt had instructed her to adopt this tone, and I may as well say now that I came afterwards to distinguish perfectly (as I believed) between the speeches she made on her own responsibility and those the old lady imposed upon her. She took no notice of the unswept condition of the rooms and indulged in no explanations nor apologies. I said to myself that this was a sign that Juliana and her niece (disenchanting idea!) were untidy persons, with a low Italian standard; but I afterwards recognised that a lodger who had forced an entrance had no *locus standi*[3] as a critic. We looked out of a good many windows, for there was nothing within the rooms to look at, and still I wanted to linger. I asked her what several different objects in the prospect might be, but in no case did she appear to know. She was evidently not familiar with the view—it was as if she had not looked at it for years—and I presently saw that she was too preoccupied with something else to pretend to care for it. Suddenly she said—the remark was not suggested:

"I don't know whether it will make any difference to you, but the money is for me."

"The money?"

"The money you are going to bring."

"Why, you'll make me wish to stay here two or three years." I spoke as benevolently as possible, though it had begun to act on my nerves that with these women so associated with Aspern the pecuniary question should constantly come back.

"That would be very good for me," she replied, smiling.

"You put me on my honour!"

She looked as if she failed to understand this, but went on: "She wants me to have more. She thinks she is going to die."

"Ah, not soon, I hope!" I exclaimed, with genuine feeling. I had perfectly considered the possibility that she would destroy her papers on the day she should feel her end really approach. I believed that she would cling to them till then and I think I had an idea that she read Aspern's letters over every night or at least pressed them to her withered lips. I would have given a good deal to have a glimpse of the latter spectacle. I asked Miss Tita if the old lady were seriously ill and she replied that she was only very tired—she had lived so very, very long. That was what she said herself—she wanted to die for a change. Besides, all her friends were dead long ago; either they ought to have remained or she ought to have gone. That was another thing her aunt often said—she was not at all content.

"But people don't die when they like, do they?" Miss Tita inquired. I took the liberty of asking why, if there was actually enough money to

3. No standing, i.e., no right.

maintain both of them, there would not be more than enough in case of her being left alone. She considered this difficult problem a moment and then she said, "Oh, well, you know, she takes care of me. She thinks that when I'm alone I shall be a great fool, I shall not know how to manage."

"I should have supposed rather that you took care of her. I'm afraid she is very proud."

"Why, have you discovered that already?" Miss Tita cried, with the glimmer of an illumination in her face.

"I was shut up with her there for a considerable time, and she struck me, she interested me extremely. It didn't take me long to make my discovery. She won't have much to say to me while I'm here."

"No, I don't think she will," my companion averred.

"Do you suppose she has some suspicion of me?"

Miss Tita's honest eyes gave me no sign that I had touched a mark. "I shouldn't think so—letting you in after all so easily."

"Oh, so easily! she has covered her risk. But where is it that one could take an advantage of her?"

"I oughtn't to tell you if I knew, ought I?" And Miss Tita added, before I had time to reply to this, smiling dolefully, "Do you think we have any weak points?"

"That's exactly what I'm asking. You would only have to mention them for me to respect them religiously."

She looked at me, at this, with that air of timid but candid and even gratified curiosity with which she had confronted me from the first; and then she said, "There is nothing to tell. We are terribly quiet. I don't know how the days pass. We have no life."

"I wish I might think that I should bring you a little."

"Oh, we know what we want," she went on. "It's all right."

There were various things I desired to ask her: how in the world they did live; whether they had any friends or visitors, any relations in America or in other countries. But I judged such an inquiry would be premature; I must leave it to a later chance. "Well, don't *you* be proud," I contented myself with saying. "Don't hide from me altogether."

"Oh, I must stay with my aunt," she returned, without looking at me. And at the same moment, abruptly, without any ceremony of parting, she quitted me and disappeared, leaving me to make my own way downstairs. I remained a while longer, wandering about the bright desert (the sun was pouring in) of the old house, thinking the situation over on the spot. Not even the pattering little *serva*[4] came to look after me and I reflected that after all this treatment showed confidence.

4. Maidservant, servant girl.

IV

Perhaps it did, but all the same, six weeks later, towards the middle of June, the moment when Mrs. Prest undertook her annual migration, I had made no measureable advance. I was obliged to confess to her that I had no results to speak of. My first step had been unexpectedly rapid, but there was no appearance that it would be followed by a second. I was a thousand miles from taking tea with my hostesses—that privilege of which, as I reminded Mrs. Prest, we both had had a vision. She reproached me with wanting boldness and I answered that even to be bold you must have an opportunity: you may push on through a breach but you can't batter down a dead wall. She answered that the breach I had already made was big enough to admit an army and accused me of wasting precious hours in whimpering in her salon when I ought to have been carrying on the struggle in the field. It is true that I went to see her very often, on the theory that it would console me (I freely expressed my discouragement) for my want of success on my own premises. But I began to perceive that it did not console me to be perpetually chaffed for my scruples, especially when I was really so vigilant; and I was rather glad when my derisive friend closed her house for the summer. She had expected to gather amusement from the drama of my intercourse with the Misses Bordereau and she was disappointed that the intercourse, and consequently the drama, had not come off. "They'll lead you on to your ruin," she said before she left Venice. "They'll get all your money without showing you a scrap." I think I settled down to my business with more concentration after she had gone away.

It was a fact that up to that time I had not, save on a single brief occasion, had even a moment's contact with my queer hostesses. The exception had occurred when I carried them according to my promise the terrible three thousand francs. Then I found Miss Tita waiting for me in the hall, and she took the money from my hand so that I did not see her aunt. The old lady had promised to receive me, but she apparently thought nothing of breaking that vow. The money was contained in a bag of chamois leather, of respectable dimensions, which my banker had given me, and Miss Tita had to make a big fist to receive it. This she did with extreme solemnity, though I tried to treat the affair a little as a joke. It was in no jocular strain, yet it was with simplicity, that she inquired, weighing the money in her two palms: "Don't you think it's too much?" To which I replied that that would depend upon the amount of pleasure I should get for it. Hereupon she turned away from me quickly, as she had done the day before, murmuring in a tone different from any she had used hitherto: "Oh, pleasure, pleasure—there's no pleasure in this house!"

After this, for a long time, I never saw her, and I wondered that the common chances of the day should not have helped us to meet. It could only be evident that she was immensely on her guard against them; and in addition to this the house was so big that for each other we were lost in it. I used to look out for her hopefully as I crossed the sala in my comings and goings, but I was not rewarded with a glimpse of the tail of her dress. It was as if she never peeped out of her aunt's apartment. I used to wonder what she did there week after week and year after year. I had never encountered such a violent *parti pris*[5] of seclusion; it was more than keeping quiet—it was like hunted creatures feigning death. The two ladies appeared to have no visitors whatever and no sort of contact with the world. I judged at least that people could not have come to the house and that Miss Tita could not have gone out without my having some observation of it. I did what I disliked myself for doing (reflecting that it was only once in a way): I questioned my servant about their habits and let him divine that I should be interested in any information he could pick up. But he picked up amazingly little for a knowing Venetian: it must be added that where there is a perpetual fast there are very few crumbs on the floor. His cleverness in other ways was sufficient, if it was not quite all that I had attributed to him on the occasion of my first interview with Miss Tita. He had helped my gondolier to bring me round a boat-load of furniture; and when these articles had been carried to the top of the palace and distributed according to our associated wisdom he organised my household with such promptitude as was consistent with the fact that it was composed exclusively of himself. He made me in short as comfortable as I could be with my indifferent prospects. I should have been glad if he had fallen in love with Miss Bordereau's maid or, failing this, had taken her in aversion; either event might have brought about some kind of catastrophe and a catastrophe might have led to some parley. It was my idea that she would have been sociable, and I myself on various occasions saw her flit to and fro on domestic errands, so that I was sure she was accessible. But I tasted of no gossip from that foundation, and I afterwards learned that Pasquale's affections were fixed upon an object that made him heedless of other women. This was a young lady with a powdered face, a yellow cotton gown and much leisure, who used often to come to see him. She practised, at her convenience, the art of a stringer of beads (these ornaments are made in Venice, in profusion; she had her pocket full of them and I used to find them on the floor of my apartment), and kept an eye on the maiden in the house. It was not for me of course to make the domestics tattle, and I never said a word to Miss Bordereau's cook.

It seemed to me a proof of the old lady's determination to have nothing to do with me that she should never have sent me a receipt for

5. Prejudice (in favor of).

my three months' rent. For some days I looked out for it and then, when I had given it up, I wasted a good deal of time in wondering what her reason had been for neglecting so indispensable and familiar a form. At first I was tempted to send her a reminder, after which I relinquished the idea (against my judgment as to what was right in the particular case), on the general ground of wishing to keep quiet. If Miss Bordereau suspected me of ulterior aims she would suspect me less if I should be businesslike, and yet I consented not to be so. It was possible she intended her omission as an impertinence, a visible irony, to show how she could overreach people who attempted to overreach her. On that hypothesis it was well to let her see that one did not notice her little tricks. The real reading of the matter, I afterwards perceived, was simply the poor old woman's desire to emphasise the fact that I was in the enjoyment of a favour as rigidly limited as it had been liberally bestowed. She had given me part of her house and now she would not give me even a morsel of paper with her name on it. Let me say that even at first this did not make me too miserable, for the whole episode was essentially delightful to me. I foresaw that I should have a summer after my own literary heart, and the sense of holding my opportunity was much greater than the sense of losing it. There could be no Venetian business without patience, and since I adored the place I was much more in the spirit of it for having laid in a large provision. That spirit kept me perpetual company and seemed to look out at me from the revived immortal face—in which all his genius shone—of the great poet who was my prompter. I had invoked him and he had come; he hovered before me half the time; it was as if his bright ghost had returned to earth to tell me that he regarded the affair as his own no less than mine and that we should see it fraternally, cheerfully to a conclusion. It was as if he had said, "Poor dear, be easy with her; she has some natural prejudices; only give her time. Strange as it may appear to you she was very attractive in 1820. Meanwhile are we not in Venice together, and what better place is there for the meeting of dear friends? See how it glows with the advancing summer; how the sky and the sea and the rosy air and the marble of the palaces all shimmer and melt together." My eccentric private errand became a part of the general romance and the general glory—I felt even a mystic companionship, a moral fraternity with all those who in the past had been in the service of art. They had worked for beauty, for a devotion; and what else was I doing? That element was in everything that Jeffrey Aspern had written and I was only bringing it to the light.

I lingered in the sala when I went to and fro; I used to watch—as long as I thought decent—the door that led to Miss Bordereau's part of the house. A person observing me might have supposed I was trying to cast a spell upon it or attempting some odd experiment in hypnotism. But I was only praying it would open or thinking what treasure probably lurked behind it. I hold it singular, as I look back, that I should never have doubted for a moment that the sacred relics were there; never have failed to feel a certain joy at being under the same roof with them. After all they were under my hand—they had not escaped me yet; and they made my life continuous, in a fashion, with the illustrious life they had touched at the other end. I lost myself in this satisfaction to the point of assuming—in my quiet extravagance—that poor Miss Tita also went back, went back as I used to phrase it. She did indeed, the gentle spinster, but not quite so far as Jeffrey Aspern, who was simply heresay to her, quite as he was to me. Only she had lived for years with Juliana, she had seen and handled the papers and (even though she was stupid) some esoteric knowledge had rubbed off on her. That was what the old woman represented—esoteric knowledge; and this was the idea with which my editorial heart used to thrill. It literally beat faster often, of an evening, when I had been out, as I stopped with my candle in the re-echoing hall on my way up to bed. It was as if at such a moment as that, in the stillness, after the long contradiction of the day, Miss Bordereau's secrets were in the air, the wonder of her survival more palpable. These were the acute impressions. I had them in another form, with more of a certain sort of reciprocity, during the hours that I sat in the garden looking up over the top of my book at the closed windows of my hostess. In these windows no sign of life ever appeared; it was as if, for fear of my catching a glimpse of them, the two ladies passed their days in the dark. But this only proved to me that they had something to conceal; which was what I had wished to demonstrate. Their motionless shutters became as expressive as eyes consciously closed, and I took comfort in thinking that at all events though invisible themselves they saw me between the lashes.

I made a point of spending as much time as possible in the garden, to justify the picture I had originally given of my horticultural passion. And I not only spent time, but (hang it! as I said) I spent money. As soon as I had got my rooms arranged and could give the proper thought to the matter I surveyed the place with a clever expert and made terms for having it put in order. I was sorry to do this, for personally I liked it better as it was, with its weeds and its wild, rough tangle, its sweet, characteristic Venetian shabbiness. I had to be consistent, to keep my promise that I would smother the house in flowers. Moreover I formed this graceful project that by flowers I would make my way—I would succeed by big nosegays. I would batter the old women with lilies—I would bombard their citadel with roses. Their door would have to yield to the pressure when a mountain of carnations should be piled up against it. The place in truth had been brutally neglected. The Venetian capacity for dawdling is of the largest, and for a good many days unlimited litter was all my gardener had to show for his ministrations. There was a great digging of holes and carting about of earth, and after a while I grew so impatient that I had thoughts of sending for my bouquets to the nearest stand. But I reflected that the ladies would see through the chinks of their shutters that they must have been bought and might make up their minds from this that I was a humbug. So I composed myself and finally, though the delay was long, perceived some appearances of bloom. This encouraged me and I waited serenely enough till they multiplied. Meanwhile the real summer days arrived and began to pass, and as I look back upon them they seem to me almost the happiest of my life. I took more and more care to be in the garden whenever it was not too hot. I had an arbour arranged and a low table and an armchair put into it; and I carried out books and portfolios (I had always some business of writing in hand), and worked and waited and mused and hoped, while the golden hours elapsed and the plants drank in the light and the inscrutable old palace turned pale and then, as the day waned, began to flush in it and my papers rustled in the wandering breeze of the Adriatic.

Considering how little satisfaction I got from it at first it is remarkable that I should not have grown more tired of wondering what mystic rites of ennui the Misses Bordereau celebrated in their darkened rooms; whether this had always been the tenor of their life and how in previous years they had escaped elbowing their neighbours. It was clear that they must have had other habits and other circumstances; that they must once have been young or at least middleaged. There was no end to the questions it was possible to ask about them and no end to the answers it was not possible to frame. I had known many of my country-people in Europe and was familiar with the strange ways they were liable to take up there; but the Misses Bordereau formed altogether a new type of the American absentee. Indeed it was plain that the American name had ceased to have any application to them—I had seen this in the ten minutes I spent in the old woman's room. You could never have said whence they came, from the appearance of either of them; wherever it was they had long ago dropped the local accent and fashion. There was nothing in them that one recognised, and putting the question of speech aside they might have been Norwegians or Spaniards. Miss Bordereau, after all, had been in Europe nearly threequarters of a century; it appeared by some verses addressed to her by Aspern on the occasion of his own second absence from America—verses of which Cumnor and I had after infinite conjecture established solidly enough the date—that she was even then, as a girl of twenty, on the foreign side of the sea. There was an implication in the poem (I hope not just for the phrase) that he had come back for her sake. We had no real light upon her circumstances at that moment, any more than we had upon her origin, which we believed to be of the sort usually spoken of as modest. Cumnor had a theory that she had been a governess in some family in which the poet visited and that, in consequence of her position, there was from the first something unavowed, or rather something positively clandestine, in their relations. I on the other hand had hatched a little romance according to which she was the daughter of an artist, a painter or a sculptor, who had left the western world when the century was fresh, to study in the ancient schools. It was essential to my hypothesis that this amiable man should have lost his wife, should have been poor and unsuccessful and should have had a second daughter, of a disposition quite different from Juliana's. It was also indispensable 'that he should have been accompanied to Europe by these young ladies and should have established himself there for the remainder of a struggling, saddened life. There was a further implication that Miss Bordereau had had in her youth a perverse and adventurous, albeit a generous and fascinating character, and that she had passed through some singular vicissitudes. By what passions had she been ravaged, by what sufferings had she been blanched, what store of memories had she laid away for the monotonous future?

I asked myself these things as I sat spinning theories about her in my arbour and the bees droned in the flowers. It was incontestable that, whether for right or for wrong, most readers of certain of Aspern's poem's (poems not as ambiguous as the sonnets—scarcely more divine, I think—of Shakespeare) had taken for granted that Juliana had not always adhered to the steep footway of renunciation. There hovered about her name a perfume of reckless passion, an intimation that she had not been exactly as the respectable young person in general. Was this a sign that her singer had betrayed her, had given her away, as we say nowadays, to posterity? Certain it is that it would have been difficult to put one's finger on the passage in which her fair fame suffered an imputation. Moreover was not any fame fair enough that was so sure of duration and was associated with works immortal through their beauty? It was a part of my idea that the young lady had had a foreign lover (and an unedifying tragical rupture) before her meeting with Jeffrey Aspern. She had lived with her father and sister in a queer old-fashioned, expatriated, artistic Bohemia, in the days when the æsthetic was only the academic and the painters who knew the best models for a *contadina*[6] and *pifferaro* wore peaked hats and long hair. It was a society less furnished than the coteries of to-day (in its ignorance of the wonderful chances, the opportunities of the early bird, with which its path was strewn), with tatters of old stuff and fragments of old crockery; so that Miss Bordereau appeared not to have picked up or have inherited many objects of importance. There was no enviable *bric-à-brac*, with its provoking legend of cheapness, in the

6. Country women; a *pifferaro* is a pipe-player.

room in which I had seen her. Such a fact as that suggested bareness, but none the less it worked happily into the sentimental interest I had always taken in the early movements of my countrymen as visitors to Europe. When Americans went abroad in 1820 there was something romantic, almost heroic in it, as compared with the perpetual ferryings of the present hour, when photography and other conveniences have annihilated surprise. Miss Bordereau sailed with her family on a tossing brig, in the days of long voyages and sharp differences; she had her emotions on the top of yellow diligences,[7] passed the night at inns where she dreamed of travellers' tales, and was struck, on reaching the eternal city, with the elegance of Roman pearls and scarfs. There was something touching to me in all that and my imagination frequently went back to the period. If Miss Bordereau carried it there of course Jeffrey Aspern at other times had done so a great deal more. It was a much more important fact, if one were looking at his genius critically, that he had lived in the days before the general transfusion. It had happened to me to regret that he had known Europe at all; I should have liked to see what he would have written without that experience, by which he had incontestably been enriched. But as his fate had ordered otherwise I went with him—I tried to judge how the old world would have struck him. It was not only there, however, that I watched him; the relations he had entertained with the new had even a livelier interest. His own country after all had had most of his life, and his muse, as they said at that time, was essentially American. That was originally what I had loved him for: that at a period when our native land was nude and crude and provincial, when the famous "atmosphere" it is supposed to lack was not even missed, when literature was lonely there and art and form almost impossible, he had found means to live and write like one of the first; to be free and general and not at all afraid; to feel, understand and express everything.

V

I was seldom at home in the evening, for when I attempted to occupy myself in my apartments the lamplight brought in a swarm of noxious insects, and it was too hot for closed windows. Accordingly I spent the late hours either on the water (the moonlight of Venice is famous), or in the splendid square which serves as a vast forecourt to the strange old basilica of Saint Mark.[8] I sat in front of Florian's *café*, eating ices, listening to music, talking with acquaintances: the traveller will remember how the immense cluster of tables and little chairs

7. Stagecoaches.
8. The Piazza San Marco (Saint Mark's Square) is the centerpiece of Venice, famous for its historical and architectural monuments—for the Basilica, a church which dates back to the eleventh century, for its arcades (or covered galleries), which house famous cafés like Florian's, and for its pigeons. It opens out onto the Grand Canal through the Piazzetta, which is flanked by the old Doge's Palace and dominated by twin granite columns guarding the entrance from the water.

stretches like a promontory into the smooth lake of the Piazza. The whole place, of a summer's evening, under the stars and with all the lamps, all the voices and light footsteps on marble (the only sounds of the arcades that enclose it), is like an open-air saloon dedicated to cooling drinks and to a still finer degustation—that of the exquisite impressions received during the day. When I did not prefer to keep mine to myself there was always a stray tourist, disencumbered of his Bädeker,[9] to discuss them with, or some domesticated painter rejoicing in the return of the season of strong effects. The wonderful church, with its low domes and bristling embroideries, the mystery of its mosaic and sculpture, looked ghostly in the tempered gloom, and the sea-breeze passed between the twin columns of the Piazzetta, the lintels of a door no longer guarded, as gently as if a rich curtain were swaying there. I used sometimes on these occasions to think of the Misses Bordereau and of the pity of their being shut up in apartments which in the Venetian July even Venetian vastness did not prevent from being stuffy. Their life seemed miles away from the life of the Piazza, and no doubt it was really too late to make the austere Juliana change her habits. But poor Miss Tita would have enjoyed one of Florian's ices, I was sure; sometimes I even had thoughts of carrying one home to her. Fortunately my patience bore fruit and I was not obliged to do anything so ridiculous.

One evening about the middle of July I came in earlier than usual—I forget what chance had led to this—and instead of going up to my quarters made my way into the garden. The temperature was very high; it was such a night as one would gladly have spent in the open air and I was in no hurry to go to bed. I had floated home in my gondola, listening to the slow splash of the oar in the narrow dark canals, and now the only thought that solicited me was the vague reflection that it would be pleasant to recline at one's length in the fragrant darkness on a garden bench. The odour of the canal was doubtless at the bottom of that aspiration and the breath of the garden, as I entered it, gave consistency to my purpose. It was delicious—just such an air as must have trembled with Romeo's vows when he stood among the flowers and raised his arms to his mistress's balcony. I looked at the windows of the palace to see if by chance the example of Verona[1] (Verona being not far off) had been followed; but everything was dim, as usual, and everything was still. Juliana, on summer nights in her youth, might have murmured down from open windows at Jeffrey Aspern, but Miss Tita was not a poet's mistress any more than I was a poet. This however did not prevent my gratification from being great as I became aware on reaching the end of the garden that Miss Tita was seated in my little bower. At first I only made out an indistinct

9. A popular series of guidebooks published in Germany.   1. The city where Romeo and Juliet lived.

figure, not in the least counting on such an overture from one of my hostesses; it even occurred to me that some sentimental maidservant had stolen in to keep a tryst with her sweetheart. I was going to turn away, not to frighten her, when the figure rose to its height and I recognised Miss Bordereau's niece. I must do myself the justice to say that I did not wish to frighten her either, and much as I had longed for some such accident I should have been capable of retreating. It was as if I had laid a trap for her by coming home earlier than usual and adding to that eccentricity by creeping into the garden. As she rose she spoke to me, and then I reflected that perhaps, secure in my almost inveterate absence, it was her nightly practice to take a lonely airing. There was no trap, in truth, because I had had no suspicion. At first I took for granted that the words she uttered expressed discomfiture at my arrival; but as she repeated them—I had not caught them clearly—I had the surprise of hearing her say, "Oh, dear, I'm so very glad you've come!" She and her aunt had in common the property of unexpected speeches. She came out of the arbour almost as if she were going to throw herself into my arms.

I hasten to add that she did nothing of the kind; she did not even shake hands with me. It was a gratification to her to see me and presently she told me why—because she was nervous when she was out-of-doors at night alone. The plants and bushes looked so strange in the dark, and there were all sorts of queer sounds—she could not tell what they were—like the noises of animals. She stood close to me, looking about her with an air of greater security but without any demonstration of interest in me as an individual. Then I guessed that nocturnal prowlings were not in the least her habit, and I was also reminded (I had been struck with the circumstance in talking with her before I took possession) that it was impossible to over-estimate her simplicity.

"You speak as if you were lost in the backwoods," I said, laughing. "How you manage to keep out of this charming place when you have only three steps to take to get into it, is more than I have yet been able to discover. You hide away mighty well so long as I am on the premises, I know; but I had a hope that you peeped out a little at other times. You and your poor aunt are worse off than Carmelite nuns in their cells. Should you mind telling me how you exist without air, without exercise, without any sort of human contact? I don't see how you carry on the common business of life."

She looked at me as if I were talking some strange tongue and her answer was so little of an answer that I was considerably irritated.

"We go to bed very early—earlier than you would believe." I was on the point of saying that this only deepened the mystery when she gave me some relief by adding, "Before you came we were not so private. But I never have been out at night."

"Never in these fragrant alleys, blooming here under your nose?"

"Ah," said Miss Tita, "they were never nice till now!" There was an unmistakable reference in this and a flattering comparison, so that it seemed to me I had gained a small advantage. As it would help me to follow it up to establish a sort of grievance I asked her why, since she thought my garden nice, she had never thanked me in any way for the flowers I had been sending up in such quantities for the previous three weeks. I had not been discouraged—there had been, as she would have observed, a daily armful; but I had been brought up in the common forms and a word of recognition now and then would have touched me in the right place.

"Why I didn't know they were for me!"

"They were for both of you. Why should I make a difference?"

Miss Tita reflected as if she might be thinking of a reason for that, but she failed to produce one. Instead of this she asked abruptly, "Why in the world do you want to know us?"

"I ought after all to make a difference," I replied. "That question is your aunt's; it isn't yours. You wouldn't ask it if you hadn't been put up to it."

"She didn't tell me to ask you," Miss Tita replied, without confusion; she was the oddest mixture of the shrinking and the direct.

"Well, she has often wondered about it herself and expressed her wonder to you. She has insisted on it, so that she has put the idea into your head that I am unsufferably pushing. Upon my word I think I have been very discreet. And how completely your aunt must have lost every tradition of sociability, to see anything out of the way in the idea that respectable intelligent people, living as we do under the same roof, should occasionally exchange a remark! What could be more natural? We are of the same country and we have at least some of the same tastes, since, like you, I am intensely fond of Venice."

My interlocutress appeared incapable of grasping more than one clause in any proposition, and she declared quickly, eagerly, as if she were answering my whole speech: "I am not in the least fond of Venice. I should like to go far away!"

"Has she always kept you back so?" I went on, to show her that I could be as irrelevant as herself.

"She told me to come out to-night; she has told me very often," said Miss Tita. "It is I who wouldn't come. I don't like to leave her."

"Is she too weak, is she failing?" I demanded, with more emotion, I think, than I intended to show. I judged this by the way her eyes rested upon me in the darkness. It embarrassed me a little, and to turn the matter off I continued genially: "Do let us sit down together comfortably somewhere and you will tell me all about her."

Miss Tita made no resistance to this. We found a bench less

secluded, less confidential, as it were, than the one in the arbour; and we were still sitting there when I heard midnight ring out from those clear bells of Venice which vibrate with a solemnity of their own over the lagoon and hold the air so much more than the chimes of other places. We were together more than an hour and our interview gave, as it struck me, a great lift to my undertaking. Miss Tita accepted the situation without a protest; she had avoided me for three months, yet now she treated me almost as if these three months had made me an old friend. If I had chosen I might have inferred from this that though she had avoided me she had given a good deal of consideration to doing so. She paid no attention to the flight of time—never worried at my keeping her so long away from her aunt. She talked freely, answering questions and asking them and not even taking advantage of certain longish pauses with which they inevitably alternated to say she thought she had better go in. It was almost as if she were waiting for something—something I might say to her—and intended to give me my opportunity. I was the more struck by this as she told me that her aunt had been less well for a good many days and in a way that was rather new. She was weaker; at moments it seemed as if she had no strength at all; yet more than ever before she wished to be left alone. That was why she had told her to come out—not even to remain in her own room, which was alongside; she said her niece irritated her, made her nervous. She sat still for hours together, as if she were asleep; she had always done that, musing and dozing; but at such times formerly she gave at intervals some small sign of life, of interest, liking her companion to be near her with her work. Miss Tita confided to me that at present her aunt was so motionless that she sometimes feared she was dead; moreover she took hardly any food—one couldn't see what she lived on. The great thing was that she still on most days got up; the serious job was to dress her, to wheel her out of her bedroom. She clung to as many of her old habits as possible and she had always, little company as they had received for years, made a point of sitting in the parlour.

I scarcely knew what to think of all this—of Miss Tita's sudden conversion to sociability and of the strange circumstance that the more the old lady appeared to decline toward her end the less she should desire to be looked after. The story did not hang together, and I even asked myself whether it were not a trap laid for me, the result of a design to make me show my hand. I could not have told why my companions (as they could only by courtesy be called) should have this purpose—why they should try to trip up so lucrative a lodger. At any rate I kept on my guard, so that Miss Tita should not have occasion again to ask me if I had an *arrière-pensée*. [2] Poor woman, before we

2. Ulterior motive.

parted for the night my mind was at rest as to *her* capacity for entertaining one.

She told me more about their affairs than I had hoped; there was no need to be prying, for it evidently drew her out simply to feel that I listened, that I cared. She ceased wondering why I cared, and at last, as she spoke of the brilliant life they had led years before, she almost chattered. It was Miss Tita who judged it brilliant; she said that when they first came to live in Venice, years and years before (I saw that her mind was essentially vague about dates and the order in which events had occurred), there was scarcely a week that they had not some visitor or did not make some delightful *passeggio*[3] in the city. They had seen all the curiosities; they had even been to the Lido in a boat (she spoke as if I might think there was a way on foot); they had had a collation, there, brought in three baskets and spread out on the grass. I asked her what people they had known and she said, Oh! very nice ones—the Cavaliere Bombicci and the Contessa Altemura, with whom they had had a great friendship. Also English people—the Churtons and the Goldies and Mrs. Stock-Stock, whom they had loved dearly; she was dead and gone, poor dear. That was the case with most of their pleasant circle (this expression was Miss Tita's own), though a few were left, which was a wonder considering how they had neglected them. She mentioned the names of two or three Venetian old women; of a certain doctor, very clever, who was so kind—he came as a friend, he had really given up practice; of the *avvocato*[4] Pochintesta, who wrote beautiful poems and had addressed one to her aunt. These people came to see them without fail every year, usually at the *capo d'anno*,[5] and of old her aunt used to make them some little present—her aunt and she together: small things that she, Miss Tita, made herself, like paper lamp-shades or mats for the decanters of wine at dinner or those woollen things that in cold weather were worn on the wrists. The last few years there had not been many presents; she could not think what to make and her aunt had lost her interest and never suggested. But the people came all the same; if the Venetians liked you once they liked you for ever.

There was something affecting in the good faith of this sketch of former social glories; the picnic at the Lido had remained vivid through the ages and poor Miss Tita evidently was of the impression that she had had a brilliant youth. She had in fact had a glimpse of the Venetian world in its gossiping, home-keeping, parsimonious, professional walks; for I observed for the first time that she had acquired by contact something of the trick of the familiar, soft-sounding, almost infantile speech of the place. I judged that she had imbibed this

3. Outing, trip. Since this is Venice, where canals serve for streets, these outings are probably by gondola. The island of the Lido is a fashionable beach resort.
4. Lawyer.
5. New Year's Day.

invertebrate dialect, from the natural way the names of things and people—mostly purely local—rose to her lips. If she knew little of what they represented she knew still less of anything else. Her aunt had drawn in—her failing interest in the table-mats and lamp-shades was a sign of that—and she had not been able to mingle in society or to entertain it alone; so that the matter of her reminiscences struck one as an old world altogether. If she had not been so decent her references would have seemed to carry one back to the queer rococo Venice of Casanova.[6] I found myself falling into the error of thinking of her too as one of Jeffrey Aspern's contemporaries; this came from her having so little in common with my own. It was possible, I said to myself, that she had not even heard of him; it might very well be that Juliana had not cared to lift even for her the veil that covered the temple of her youth. In this case she perhaps would not know of the existence of the papers, and I welcomed that presumption—it made me feel more safe with her—until I remembered that we had believed the letter of disavowal received by Cumnor to be in the handwriting of the niece. If it had been dictated to her she had of course to know what it was about; yet after all the effect of it was to repudiate the idea of any connection with the poet. I held it probable at all events that Miss Tita had not read a word of his poetry. Moreover if, with her companion, she had always escaped the interviewer there was little occasion for her having got it into her head that people were "after" the letters. People had not been after them, inasmuch as they had not heard of them; and Cumnor's fruitless feeler would have been a solitary accident.

When midnight sounded Miss Tita got up; but she stopped at the door of the house only after she had wandered two or three times with me round the garden. "When shall I see you again?" I asked, before she went in; to which she replied with promptness that she should like to come out the next night. She added however that she should not come—she was so far from doing everything she liked.

"You might do a few things that *I* like," I said with a sigh.

"Oh, you—I don't believe you!" she murmured, at this, looking at me with her simple solemnity.

"Why don't you believe me?"

"Because I don't understand you."

"That is just the sort of occasion to have faith." I could not say more, though I should have liked to, as I saw that I only mystified her; for I had no wish to have it on my conscience that I might pass for having made love to her. Nothing less should I have seemed to do had I continued to beg a lady to "believe in me" in an Italian garden on a mid-summer night. There was some merit in my scruples, for Miss Tita lingered and lingered: I perceived that she felt that she should not

6. A century before the narrative.

really soon come down again and wished therefore to protract the present. She insisted too on making the talk between us personal to ourselves; and altogether her behaviour was such as would have been possible only to a completely innocent woman.

"I shall like the flowers better now that I know they are also meant for me."

"How could you have doubted it? If you will tell me the kind you like best I will send a double lot of them."

"Oh, I like them all best!" Then she went on, familiarly: "Shall you study—shall you read and write—when you go up to your rooms?"

"I don't do that at night, at this season. The lamplight brings in the animals."

"You might have known that when you came."

"I did know it!"

"And in winter do you work at night?"

"I read a good deal, but I don't often write." She listened as if these details had a rare interest, and suddenly a temptation quite at variance with the prudence I had been teaching myself associated itself with her plain, mild face. Ah yes, she was safe and I could make her safer! It seemed to me from one moment to another that I could not wait longer—that I really must take a sounding. So I went on: "In general before I go to sleep—very often in bed (it's a bad habit, but I confess to it), I read some great poet. In nine cases out of ten it's a volume of Jeffrey Aspern."

I watched her well as I pronounced that name but I saw nothing wonderful. Why should I indeed—was not Jeffrey Aspern the property of the human race?

"Oh, we read him—we *have* read him," she quietly replied.

"He is my poet of poets—I know him almost by heart."

For an instant Miss Tita hesitated; then her sociability was too much for her.

"Oh, by heart—that's nothing!" she murmured, smiling. "My aunt used to know him—to know him"—she paused an instant and I wondered what she was going to say—"to know him as a visitor."

"As a visitor?" I repeated, staring.

"He used to call on her and take her out."

I continued to stare. "My dear lady, he died a hundred years ago!"

"Well," she said, mirthfully, "my aunt is a hundred and fifty."

"Mercy on us!" I exclaimed; "why didn't you tell me before? I should like so to ask her about him."

"She wouldn't care for that—she wouldn't tell you," Miss Tita replied.

"I don't care what she cares for! She *must* tell me—it's not a chance to be lost."

"Oh, you should have come twenty years ago: then she still talked about him."

"And what did she say?" I asked, eagerly.

"I don't know—that he liked her immensely."

"And she—didn't she like him?"

"She said he was a god." Miss Tita gave me this information flatly, without expression; her tone might have made it a piece of trivial gossip. But it stirred me deeply as she dropped the words into the summer night; it seemed such a direct testimony.

"Fancy, fancy!" I murmured. And then, "Tell me this, please—has she got a portrait of him? They are distressingly rare."

"A portrait? I don't know," said Miss Tita; and now there was discomfiture in her face. "Well, good-night!" she added; and she turned into the house.

I accompanied her into the wide, dusky, stone-paved passage which on the ground floor corresponded with our grand sala. It opened at one end into the garden, at the other upon the canal, and was lighted now only by the small lamp that was always left for me to take up as I went to bed. An extinguished candle which Miss Tita apparently had brought down with her stood on the same table with it. "Good-night, good-night!" I replied, keeping beside her as she went to get her light. "Surely you would know, shouldn't you, if she had one?"

"If she had what?" the poor lady asked, looking at me queerly over the flame of her candle.

"A portrait of the god. I don't know what I wouldn't give to see it."

"I don't know what she has got. She keeps her things locked up." and Miss Tita went away, toward the staircase, with the sense evidently that she had said too much.

I let her go—I wished not to frighten her—and I contented myself with remarking that Miss Bordereau would not have locked up such a glorious possession as that—a thing a person would be proud of and hang up in a prominent place on the parlour-wall. Therefore of course she had not any portrait. Miss Tita made no direct answer to this and candle in hand, with her back to me, ascended two or three stairs. Then she stopped short and turned round looking at me across the dusky space.

"Do you write—do you write?" There was a shake in her voice—she could scarcely bring out what she wanted to ask.

"Do I write? Oh, don't speak of my writing on the same day with Aspern's!"

"Do you write about *him*—do you pry into his life?"

"Ah, that's your aunt's question; it can't be yours!" I said, in a tone of slightly wounded sensibility.

"All the more reason then that you should answer it. Do you, please?"

I thought I had allowed for the falsehoods I should have to tell; but I found that in fact when it came to the point I had not. Besides, now that I had an opening there was a kind of relief in being frank. Lastly (it was perhaps fanciful, even fatuous), I guessed that Miss Tita personally would not in the last resort be less my friend. So after a moment's hesitation I answered, "Yes, I have written about him and I am looking for more material. In heaven's name have you got any?"

"*Santo Dio!*"[7] she exclaimed, without heeding my question; and she hurried upstairs and out of sight. I might count upon her in the last resort, but for the present she was visibly alarmed. The proof of it was that she began to hide again, so that for a fortnight I never beheld her. I found my patience ebbing and after four or five days of this I told the gardener to stop the flowers.

VI

One afternoon, as I came down from my quarters to go out, I found Miss Tita in the sala: it was our first encounter on that ground since I had come to the house. She put on no air of being there by accident; there was an ignorance of such arts in her angular, diffident directness. That I might be quite sure she was waiting for me she informed me of the fact and told me that Miss Bordereau wished to see me: she would take me into the room at that moment if I had time. If I had been late for a love-tryst I would have stayed for this, and I quickly signified that I should be delighted to wait upon the old lady. "She wants to talk with you—to know you," Miss Tita said, smiling as if she herself appreciated that idea; and she led me to the door of her aunt's apartment. I stopped her a moment before she had opened it, looking at her with some curiosity. I told her that this was a great satisfaction to me and a great honour; but all the same I should like to ask what had made Miss Bordereau change so suddenly. It was only the other day that she wouldn't suffer me near her. Miss Tita was not embarrassed by my question; she had as many little unexpected serenities as if she told fibs, but the odd part of them was that they had on the contrary their source in her truthfulness. "Oh, my aunt changes," she answered; "it's so terribly dull—I suppose she's tired."

"But you told me that she wanted more and more to be alone."

Poor Miss Tita coloured, as if she found me over-insistent. "Well, if you don't believe she wants to see you—I haven't invented it! I think people often are capricious when they are very old."

"That's perfectly true. I only wanted to be clear as to whether you have repeated to her what I told you the other night."

"What you told me?"

"About Jeffrey Aspern—that I am looking for materials."

"If I had told her do you think she would have sent for you?"

"That's exactly what I want to know. If she wants to keep him to herself she might have sent for me to tell me so."

7. Good Lord!

"She won't speak of him," said Miss Tita. Then as she opened the door she added in a lower tone, "I have told her nothing."

The old woman was sitting in the same place in which I had seen her last, in the same position, with the same mystifying bandage over her eyes. Her welcome was to turn her almost invisible face to me and show me that while she sat silent she saw me clearly. I made no motion to shake hands with her; I felt too well on this occasion that that was out of place for ever. It had been sufficiently enjoined upon me that she was too sacred for that sort of reciprocity—too venerable to touch. There was something so grim in her aspect (it was partly the accident of her green shade), as I stood there to be measured, that I ceased on the spot to feel any doubt as to her knowing my secret, though I did not in the least suspect that Miss Tita had not just spoken the truth. She had not betrayed me, but the old woman's brooding instinct had served her; she had turned me over and over in the long, still hours and she had guessed. The worst of it was that she looked terribly like an old woman who at a pinch would burn her papers. Miss Tita pushed a chair forward, saying to me, "This will be a good place for you to sit." As I took possession of it I asked after Miss Bordereau's health; expressed the hope that in spite of the very hot weather it was satisfactory. She replied that it was good enough—good enough; that it was a great thing to be alive.

"Oh, as to that, it depends upon what you compare it with!" I exclaimed, laughing.

"I don't compare—I don't compare. If I did that I should have given everything up long ago."

I liked to think that this was a subtle allusion to the rapture she had known in the society of Jeffrey Aspern—though it was true that such an allusion would have accorded ill with the wish I imputed to her to keep him buried in her soul. What it accorded with was my constant conviction that no human being had ever had a more delightful social gift than his, and what it seemed to convey was that nothing in the world was worth speaking of if one pretended to speak of that. But one did not! Miss Tita sat down beside her aunt, looking as if she had reason to believe some very remarkable conversation would come off between us.

"It's about the beautiful flowers," said the old lady; "you sent us so many—I ought to have thanked you for them before. But I don't write letters and I receive only at long intervals."

She had not thanked me while the flowers continued to come, but she departed from her custom so far as to send for me as soon as she began to fear that they would not come any more. I noted this; I remembered what an acquisitive propensity she had shown when it was a question of extracting gold from me, and I privately rejoiced at the happy thought I had had in suspending my tribute. She had missed it and she was willing to make a concession to bring it back. At the first sign of this concession I could only go to meet her. "I am afraid you have not had many, of late, but they shall begin again immediately—to-morrow, to-night."

"Oh, do send us some to-night!" Miss Tita cried, as if it were an immense circumstance.

"What else should you do with them? It isn't a manly taste to make a bower of your room," the old woman remarked.

"I don't make a bower of my room, but I am exceedingly fond of growing flowers, of watching their ways. There is nothing unmanly in that: it has been the amusement of philosophers, of statesmen in retirement; even I think of great captains."

"I suppose you know you can sell them—those you don't use," Miss Bordereau went on. "I daresay they wouldn't give you much for them; still, you could make a bargain."

"Oh, I have never made a bargain, as you ought to know. My gardener disposes of them and I ask no questions."

"I would ask a few, I can promise you!" said Miss Bordereau; and it was the first time I had heard her laugh. I could not get used to the idea that this vision of pecuniary profit was what drew out the divine Juliana most.

"Come into the garden yourself and pick them; come as often as you like; come every day. They are for you," I pursued, addressing Miss Tita and carrying off this veracious statement by treating it as an innocent joke. "I can't imagine why she doesn't come down," I added for Miss Bordereau's benefit.

"You must make her come; you must come up and fetch her," said the old woman, to my stupefaction. "That odd thing you have made in the corner would be a capital place for her to sit."

The allusion to my arbour was irreverent; it confirmed the impression I had already received that there was a flicker of impertinence in Miss Bordereau's talk, a strange mocking lambency which must have been a part of her adventurous youth and which had outlived passions and faculties. None the less I asked, "Wouldn't it be possible for you to come down there yourself? Wouldn't it do you good to sit there in the shade, in the sweet air?"

"Oh, sir, when I move out of this it won't be to sit in the air, and I'm afraid that any that may be stirring around me won't be particularly sweet! It will be a very dark shade indeed. But that won't be just yet," Miss Bordereau continued, cannily, as if to correct any hopes that this courageous allusion to the last receptacle of her mortality might lead me to entertain. "I have sat here many a day and I have had enough of arbours in my time. But I'm not afraid to wait till I'm called."

Miss Tita had expected some interesting talk, but perhaps she found it less genial on her aunt's side (considering that I had been sent for with a civil intention) than she had hoped. As if to give the conversation a turn that would put our companion in a light more favourable she said to me, "Didn't I tell you the other night that she had sent me out? You see that I can do what I like!"

"Do you pity her—do you teach her to pity herself?" Miss Bordereau demanded, before I had time to answer this appeal. "She has a much easier life than I had when I was her age."

"You must remember that it has been quite open to me to think you rather inhuman."

"Inhuman? That's what the poets used to call the women a hundred years ago. Don't try that; you won't do as well as they!" Juliana declared. "There is no more poetry in the world—that I know of at least. But I won't bandy words with you," she pursued, and I well remember the old-fashioned, artificial sound she gave to the speech. "You have made me talk, talk! It isn't good for me at all." I got up at this and told her I would take no more of her time; but she detained me to ask, "Do you remember, the day I saw you about the rooms, that you offered us the use of your gondola?" And when I assented, promptly, struck again with her disposition to make a "good thing" of being there and wondering what she now had in her eye, she broke out, "Why don't you take that girl out in it and show her the place?"

"Oh dear aunt, what do you want to do with me?" cried the "girl," with a piteous quaver. "I know all about the place!"

"Well then, go with him as a cicerone!" said Miss Bordereau, with an effect of something like cruelty in her implacable power of retort—an incongruous suggestion that she was a sarcastic, profane, cynical old woman. "Haven't we heard that there have been all sorts of changes in all these years? You ought to see them and at your age (I don't mean because you're so young), you ought to take the chances that come. You're old enough, my dear, and this gentleman won't hurt you. He will show you the famous sunsets, if they still go on—*do* they go on? The sun set for me so long ago. But that's not a reason. Besides, I shall never miss you; you think you are too important. Take her to the Piazza; it used to be very pretty," Miss Bordereau continued, addressing herself to me. "What have they done with the funny old church? I hope it hasn't tumbled down. Let her look at the shops; she may take some money, she may buy what she likes."

Poor Miss Tita had got up, discountenanced and helpless, and as we stood there before her aunt it would certainly have seemed to a spectator of the scene that the old woman was amusing herself at our expense. Miss Tita protested, in a confusion of exclamations and murmurs; but I lost no time in saying that if she would do me the honour to accept the hospitality of my boat I would engage that she should not be bored. Or if she did not want so much of my company the boat itself, with the gondolier, was at her service; he was a capital oar and she might have every confidence. Miss Tita, without definitely answering this speech, looked away from me, out of the window, as if she were going to cry; and I remarked that once we had Miss Bordereau's approval we could easily come to an understanding. We would take an hour, whichever she liked, one of the very next days. As I made my obeisance to the old lday I asked her if she would kindly permit me to see her again.

For a moment she said nothing; then she inquired, "Is it very necessary to your happiness?"

"It diverts me more than I can say."

"You are wonderfully civil. Don't you know it almost kills *me?*"

"How can I believe that when I see you more animated, more brilliant than when I came in?"

"That is very true, aunt," said Miss Tita. "I think it does you good."

"Isn't it touching, the solicitude we each have that the other shall enjoy herself?" sneered Miss Bordereau. "If you think me brilliant to-day you don't know what you are talking about; you have never seen an agreeable woman. Don't try to pay me a compliment; I have been spoiled," she went on. "My door is shut, but you may sometimes knock."

With this she dismissed me and I left the room. The latch closed behind me, but Miss Tita, contrary to my hope, had remained within. I passed slowly across the hall and before taking my way down-stairs I waited a little. My hope was answered; after a minute Miss Tita followed me. "That's a delightful idea about the Piazza," I said. "When will you go—to-night, to-morrow?"

She had been disconcerted, as I have mentioned, but I had already perceived and I was to observe again that when Miss Tita was embarrassed she did not (as most women would have done) turn away from you and try to escape, but came closer, as it were, with a deprecating, clinging appeal to be spared, to be protected. Her attitude was perpetually a sort of prayer for assistance, for explanation; and yet no woman in the world could have been less of a comedian. From the moment you were kind to her she depended on you absolutely; her self-consciousness dropped from her and she took the greatest intimacy, the innocent intimacy which was the only thing she could conceive, for granted. She told me she did not know what had got into her aunt; she had changed so quickly, she had got some idea. I replied that she must find out what the idea was and then let me know; we would go and have an ice together at Florian's and she should tell me while we listened to the band.

"Oh, it will take me a long time to find out!" she said, rather ruefully; and she could promise me this satisfaction neither for that night nor for the next. I was patient now, however, for I felt that I had only to wait; and in fact at the end of the week, one lovely evening after dinner, she stepped into my gondola, to which in honour of the occasion I had attached a second oar.

We swept in the course of five minutes into the Grand Canal; whereupon she uttered a murmur of ecstasy as fresh as if she had been a tourist just arrived. She had forgotten how splendid the great waterway looked on a clear, hot summer evening, and how the sense of floating between marble palaces and reflected lights disposed the mind to sympathetic talk. We floated long and far, and though Miss Tita gave no high-pitched voice to her satisfaction I felt that she surrendered herself. She was more than pleased, she was transported; the whole thing was an immense liberation. The gondola moved with slow strokes, to give her time to enjoy it, and she listened to the plash of the oars, which grew louder and more musically liquid as we passed into narrow canals, as if it were a revelation of Venice. When I asked her how long it was since she had been in a boat she answered, "Oh, I don't know; a long time—not since my aunt began to be ill." This was not the only example she gave me of her extreme vagueness about the previous years and the line which marked off the period when Miss Bordereau flourished. I was not at liberty to keep her out too long, but we took a considerable *giro*[8] before going to the Piazza. I asked her no questions, keeping the conversation on purpose away from her domestic situation and the things I wanted to know; I poured treasures of information about Venice into her ears, described Florence and Rome, discoursed to her on the charms and advantages of travel. She reclined, receptive, on the deep leather cushions, turned her eyes conscientiously to everything I pointed out to her, and never mentioned to me till some time afterwards that she might be supposed to know Florence better than I, as she had lived there for years with Miss Bordereau. At last she asked, with the shy impatience of a child, "Are we not really going to the Piazza? That's what I want to see!" I immediately gave the order that we should go straight; and then we sat silent with the expectation of arrival. As some time still passed, however, she said suddenly, of her own movement, "I have found out what is the matter with my aunt: she is afraid you will go!"

"What has put that into her head?"

"She has had an idea you have not been happy. That is why she is different now."

"You mean she wants to make me happier?"

"Well, she wants you not to go; she wants you to stay."

"I suppose you mean on account of the rent," I remarked candidly.

Miss Tita's candour showed itself a match for my own. "Yes, you know; so that I shall have more."

8. Stroll.

"How much does she want you to have?" I asked, laughing. "She ought to fix the sum, so that I may stay till it's made up."

"Oh, that wouldn't please me," said Miss Tita. "It would be unheard of, your taking that trouble."

"But suppose I should have my own reasons for staying in Venice?"

"Then it would be better for you to stay in some other house."

"And what would your aunt say to that?"

"She wouldn't like it at all. But I should think you would do well to give up your reasons and go away altogether."

"Dear Miss Tita," I said, "it's not so easy to give them up!"

She made no immediate answer to this, but after a moment she broke out: "I think I know what your reasons are!"

"I daresay, because the other night I almost told you how I wish you would help me to make them good."

"I can't do that without being false to my aunt."

"What do you mean, being false to her?"

"Why, she would never consent to what you want. She has been asked, she has been written to. It made her fearfully angry."

"Then she *has* got papers of value?" I demanded, quickly.

"Oh, she has got everything!" sighed Miss Tita, with a curious weariness, a sudden lapse into gloom.

These words caused all my pulses to throb, for I regarded them as precious evidence. For some minutes I was too agitated to speak, and in the interval the gondola approached the Piazzetta. After we had disembarked I asked my companion whether she would rather walk round the square or go and sit at the door of the café; to which she replied that she would do whichever I liked best—I must only remember again how little time she had. I assured her there was plenty to do both, and we made the circuit of the long arcades. Her spirits revived at the sight of the bright shop-windows, and she lingered and stopped, admiring or disapproving of their contents, asking me what I thought of things, theorising about prices. My attention wandered from her; her words of a while before, "Oh, she has got everything!" echoed so in my consciousness. We sat down at last in the crowded circle at Florian's, finding an unoccupied table among those that were ranged in the square. It was a splendid night and all the world was out-of-doors; Miss Tita could not have wished the elements more auspicious for her return to society. I saw that she enjoyed it even more than she told; she was agitated with the multitude of her impressions. She had forgotten what an attractive thing the world is, and it was coming over her that somehow she had for the best years of her life been cheated of it. This did not make her angry; but as she looked all over the charming scene her face had, in spite of its smile of appreciation, the flush of a sort of wounded surprise. She became silent, as if she were thinking with a secret sadness of opportunities, for ever lost, which ought to have been easy; and this gave me a chance to say to her, "Did you mean a while ago that your aunt has a plan of keeping me on by admitting me occasionally to her presence?"

"She thinks it will make a difference with you if you sometimes see her. She wants you so much to stay that she is willing to make that concession."

"And what good does she consider that I think it will do me to see her?"

"I don't know; she thinks it's interesting," said Miss Tita, simply. "You told her you found it so."

"So I did; but every one doesn't think so."

"No, of course not, or more people would try."

"Well, if she is capable of making that reflection she is capable also of making this further one," I went on: "that I must have a particular reason for not doing as others do, in spite of the interest she offers—for not leaving her alone." Miss Tita looked as if she failed to grasp this rather complicated proposition; so I continued, "If you have not told her what I said to you the other night may she not at least have guessed it?"

"I don't know; she is very suspicious."

"But she has not been made so by indiscreet curiosity, by persecution?"

"No, no; it isn't that," said Miss Tita, turning on me a somewhat troubled face. "I don't know how to say it: it's on account of something—ages ago, before I was born—in her life."

"Something? What sort of thing?" I asked, as if I myself could have no idea.

"Oh, she has never told me," Miss Tita answered; and I was sure she was speaking the truth.

Her extreme limpidity was almost provoking, and I felt for the moment that she would have been more satisfactory if she had been less ingenuous. "Do you suppose it's something to which Jeffrey Aspern's letters and papers—I mean the things in her possession—have reference?"

"I daresay it is!" my companion exclaimed, as if this were a very happy suggestion. "I have never looked at any of those things."

"None of them? Then how do you know what they are?"

"I don't," said Miss Tita, placidly. "I have never had them in my hands. But I have seen them when she has had them out."

"Does she have them out often?"

"Not now, but she used to. She is very fond of them."

"In spite of their being compromising?"

"Compromising?" Miss Tita repeated, as if she was ignorant of the meaning of the word. I felt almost as one who corrupts the innocence of youth.

"I mean their containing painful memories."

"Oh, I don't think they are painful."

"You mean you don't think they affect her reputation?"

At this a singular look came into the face of Miss Bordereau's niece—a kind of confession of helplessness, an appeal to me to deal fairly, generously with her. I had brought her to the Piazza, placed her among charming influences, paid her an attention she appreciated, and now I seemed to let her perceive that all this had been a bribe—a bribe to make her turn in some way against her aunt. She was of a yielding nature and capable of doing almost anything to please a person who was kind to her; but the greatest kindness of all would be not to presume too much on this. It was strange enough, as I afterwards thought, that she had not the least air of resenting my want of consideration for her aunt's character, which would have been in the worst possible taste if anything less vital (from my point of view) had been at stake. I don't think she really measured it. "Do you mean that she did something bad?" she asked in a moment.

"Heaven forbid I should say so, and it's none of my business. Besides, if she did," I added, laughing, "it was in other ages, in another world. But why should she not destroy her papers?"

"Oh, she loves them too much."

"Even now, when she may be near her end?"

"Perhaps when she's sure of that she will."

"Well, Miss Tita," I said, "it's just what I should like you to prevent."

"How can I prevent it?"

"Couldn't you get them away from her?"

"And give them to you?"

This put the case very crudely, though I am sure there was no irony in her intention. "Oh, I mean that you might let me see them and look them over. It isn't for myself; there is no personal avidity in my desire. It is simply that they would be of such immense interest to the public, such immeasurable importance as a contribution to Jeffrey Aspern's history."

She listened to me in her usual manner, as if my speech were full of reference to things she had never heard of, and I felt particularly like the reporter of a newspaper who forces his way into a house of mourning. This was especially the case when after a moment she said, "There was a gentleman who some time ago wrote to her in very much those words. He also wanted her papers."

"And did she answer him?" I asked, rather ashamed of myself for not having her rectitude.

"Only when he had written two or three times. He made her very angry."

"And what did she say?"

"She said he was a devil," Miss Tita replied, simply.

"She used that expression in her letter?"

"Oh no; she said it to me. She made me write to him."

"And what did you say?"

"I told him there were no papers at all."

"Ah, poor gentleman!" I exclaimed.

"I knew there were, but I wrote what she bade me."

"Of course you had to do that. But I hope I shall not pass for a devil."

"It will depend upon what you ask me to do for you," said Miss Tita, smiling.

"Oh, if there is a chance of *your* thinking so my affair is in a bad way! I sha'n't ask you to steal for me, nor even to fib—for you can't fib, unless on paper. But the principal thing is this—to prevent her from destroying the papers."

"Why, I have no control of her," said Miss Tita. "It's she who controls me."

"But she doesn't control her own arms and legs, does she? The way she would naturally destroy her letters would be to burn them. Now she can't burn them without fire, and she can't get fire unless you give it to her."

"I have always done everything she has asked," my companion rejoined. "Besides, there's Olimpia."

I was on the point of saying that Olimpia was probably corruptible, but I thought it best not to sound that note. So I simply inquired if that faithful domestic could not be managed.

"Every one can be managed by my aunt," said Miss Tita. And then she observed that her holiday was over; she must go home.

I laid my hand on her arm, across the table, to stay her a moment. "What I want of you is a general promise to help me."

"Oh, how can I—how can I?" she asked, wondering and troubled. She was half surprised, half frightened at my wishing to make her play an active part.

"This is the main thing: to watch her carefully and warn me in time, before she commits that horrible sacrilege."

"I can't watch her when she makes me go out."

"That's very true."

"And when you do too."

"Mercy on us; do you think she will have done anything to-night?"

"I don't know; she is very cunning."

"Are you trying to frighten me?" I asked.

I felt this inquiry sufficiently answered when my companion murmured in a musing, almost envious way, "Oh, but she loves them—she loves them!"

This reflection, repeated with such emphasis, gave me great comfort; but to obtain more of that balm I said, "If she shouldn't intend to destroy the objects we speak of before her death she will probably have made some disposition by will."

"By will?"

"Hasn't she made a will for your benefit?"

"Why, she has so little to leave. That's why she likes money," said Miss Tita.

"Might I ask, since we are really talking things over, what you and she live on?"

"On some money that comes from America, from a lawyer. He sends it every quarter. It isn't much!"

"And won't she have disposed of that?"

My companion hesitated—I saw she was blushing. "I believe it's mine," she said; and the look and tone which accompanied these words betrayed so the absence of the habit of thinking of herself that I almost thought her charming. The next instant she added, "But she had a lawyer once, ever so long ago. And some people came and signed something."

"They were probably witnesses. And you were not asked to sign? Well then," I argued, rapidly and hopefully, "it is because you are the legatee; she has left all her documents to you!"

"If she has it's with very strict conditions," Miss Tita responded, rising quickly, while the movement gave the words a little character of decision. They seemed to imply that the bequest would be accompanied with a command that the articles bequeathed should remain concealed from every inquisitive eye and that I was very much mistaken if I thought she was the person to depart from an injunction so solemn.

"Oh, of course you will have to abide by the terms," I said; and she uttered nothing to mitigate the severity of this conclusion. None the less, later, just before we disembarked at her own door, on our return, which had taken place almost in silence, she said to me abruptly, "I will do what I can to help you." I was grateful for this—it was very well so far as it went; but it did not keep me from remembering that night in a worried waking hour that I now had her word for it to reinforce my own impression that the old woman was very cunning.

VII

The fear of what this side of her character might have led her to do made me nervous for days afterwards. I waited for an intimation from Miss Tita: I almost figured to myself that it was her duty to keep me informed, to let me know definitely whether or no Miss Bordereau had sacrificed her treasures. But as she gave no sign I lost patience and determined to judge so far as was possible with my own senses. I sent late one afternoon to ask if I might pay the ladies a visit, and my servant came back with surprising news. Miss Bordereau could be approached without the least difficulty; she had been moved out into the sala and was sitting by the window that overlooked the garden. I descended and found this picture correct; the old lady had been wheeled forth into the world and had a certain air, which came mainly perhaps from some brighter element in her dress, of being prepared again to have converse with it. It had not yet, however, begun to flock about her; she was perfectly alone and, though the door leading to her own quarters stood open, I had at first no glimpse of Miss Tita. The window at which she sat had the afternoon shade and, one of the shutters having been pushed back, she could see the pleasant garden, where the summer sun had by this time dried up too many of the plants—she could see the yellow light and the long shadows.

"Have you come to tell me that you will take the rooms for six months more?" she asked, as I approached her, startling me by something coarse in her cupidity almost as much as if she had not already given me a specimen of it. Juliana's desire to make our acquaintance lucrative had been, as I have sufficiently indicated, a false note in my image of the woman who had inspired a great poet with immortal lines; but I may say here definitely that I recognised after all that it behoved me to make a large allowance for her. It was I who had kindled the unholy flame; it was I who had put into her head that she had the means of making money. She appeared never to have thought of that; she had been living wastefully for years, in a house five times too big for her, on a footing that I could explain only by the presumption that, excessive as it was, the space she enjoyed cost her next to nothing and that small as were her revenues they left her, for Venice, an appreciable margin. I had descended on her one day and taught her to calculate, and my almost extravagant comedy on the subject of the garden had presented me irresistibly in the light of a victim. Like all persons who achieve the miracle of changing their point of view when they are old she had been intensely converted; she had seized my hint with a desperate, tremulous clutch.

I invited myself to go and get one of the chairs that stood, at a distance, against the wall (she had given herself no concern as to whether I should sit or stand); and while I placed it near her I began, gaily, "Oh, dear madam, what an imagination you have, what an intellectual sweep! I am a poor devil of a man of letters who lives from day to day. How can I take palaces by the year? My existence is precarious. I don't know whether six months hence I shall have bread to put in my mouth. I have treated myself for once; it has been an immense luxury. But when it comes to going on—!"

"Are your rooms too dear? if they are you can have more for the same money," Juliana responded. "We can arrange, we can *combi-nare*,[9] as they say here."

"Well yes, since you ask me, they are too dear," I said. "Evidently you suppose me richer than I am."

She looked at me in her barricaded way. "If you write books don't you sell them?"

"Do you mean don't people buy them? A little—not so much as I could wish. Writing books, unless one be a great genius—and even then!—is the last road to fortune. I think there is no more money to be made by literature."

"Perhaps you don't choose good subjects. What do you write about?" Miss Bordereau inquired.

"About the books of other people. I'm a critic, an historian, in a small way." I wondered what she was coming to.

"And what other people, now?"

"Oh, better ones than myself: the great writers mainly—the great philosophers and poets of the past; those who are dead and gone and can't speak for themselves."

"And what do you say about them?"

"I say they sometimes attached themselves to very clever women!" I answered, laughing. I spoke with great deliberation, but as my words fell upon the air they struck me as imprudent. However, I risked them and I was not sorry, for perhaps after all the old woman would be willing to treat. It seemed to be tolerably obvious that she knew my secret: why therefore drag the matter out? But she did not take what I had said as a confession; she only asked:

"Do you think it's right to rake up the past?"

"I don't know that I know what you mean by raking it up; but how can we get at it unless we dig a little? The present has such a rough way of treading it down."

"Oh, I like the past, but I don't like critics," the old woman declared, with her fine tranquillity.

"Neither do I, but I like their discoveries."

"Aren't they mostly lies?"

"The lies are what they sometimes discover," I said, smiling at the quiet impertinence of this. "They often lay bare the truth."

"The truth is God's, it isn't man's; we had better leave it alone. Who can judge of it—who can say?"

"We are terribly in the dark, I know," I admitted; "but if we give up trying what becomes of all the fine things? What becomes of the work I just mentioned, that of the great philosophers and poets? It is all vain words if there is nothing to measure it by."

"You talk as if you were a tailor," said Miss Bordereau, whimsically;

9. Arrange things.

and then she added quickly, in a different manner, "This house is very fine; the proportions are magnificent. Today I wanted to look at this place again. I made them bring me out here. When your man came, just now, to learn if I would see you, I was on the point of sending for you, to ask if you didn't mean to go on. I wanted to judge what I'm letting you have. This sala is very grand," she pursued, like an auctioneer, moving a little, as I guessed, her invisible eyes. "I don't believe you often have lived in such a house, eh?"

"I can't often afford to!" I said.

"Well then, how much will you give for six months?"

I was on the point of exclaiming—and the air of excruciation in my face would have denoted a moral fact—"Don't, Juliana; for *his* sake, don't!" But I controlled myself and asked less passionately: "Why should I remain so long as that?"

"I thought you liked it," said Miss Bordereau, with her shrivelled dignity.

"So I thought I should."

For a moment she said nothing more, and I left my own words to suggest to her what they might. I half expected her to say, coldly enough, that if I had been disappointed we need not continue the discussion, and this in spite of the fact that I believed her now to have in her mind (however it had come there), what would have told her that my disappointment was natural. But to my extreme surprise she ended by observing: "If you don't think we have treated you well enough perhaps we can discover some way of treating you better." This speech was somehow so incongruous that it made me laugh again, and I excused myself by saying that she talked as if I were a sulky boy, pouting in the corner, to be "brought round." I had not a grain of complaint to make; and could anything have exceeded Miss Tita's graciousness in accompanying me a few nights before to the Piazza? At this the old woman went on: "Well, you brought it on yourself!" And then in a different tone, "She is a very nice girl." I assented cordially to this proposition, and she expressed the hope that I did so not merely to be obliging, but that I really liked her. Meanwhile I wondered still more what Miss Bordereau was coming to. "Except for me, to-day," she said, "she has not a relation in the world." Did she by describing her niece as amiable and unencumbered wish to represent her as a *parti?*[1]

It was perfectly true that I could not afford to go on with my rooms at a fancy price and that I had already devoted to my undertaking almost all the hard cash I had set apart for it. My patience and my time were by no means exhausted, but I should be able to draw upon them only on a more usual Venetian basis. I was willing to pay the venerable

1. A match, usually said of a woman with money.

woman with whom my pecuniary dealings were such a discord twice as much as any other *padrona di casa*,[2] would have asked, but I was not willing to pay her twenty times as much. I told her so plainly, and my plainness appeared to have some success, for she exclaimed, "Very good; you have done what I asked—you have made an offer!"

"Yes, but not for half a year. Only by the month."

"Oh, I must think of that then." She seemed disappointed that I would not tie myself to a period, and I guessed that she wished both to secure me and to discourage me; to say, severely, "Do you dream that you can get off with less than six months? Do you dream that even by the end of that time you will be appreciably nearer your victory?" What was more in my mind was that she had a fancy to play me the trick of making me engage myself when in fact she had annihilated the papers. There was a moment when my suspense on this point was so acute that I all but broke out with the question, and what kept it back was but a kind of instinctive recoil (lest it should be a mistake), from the last violence of self-exposure. She was such a subtle old witch that one could never tell where one stood with her. You may imagine whether it cleared up the puzzle when, just after she had said she would think of my proposal and without any formal transition, she drew out of her pocket with an embarrassed hand a small object wrapped in crumpled white paper. She held it there a moment and then she asked, "Do you know much about curiosities?"

"About curiosities?"

"About antiquities, the old gimcracks that people pay so much for to-day. Do you know the kind of price they bring?"

I thought I saw what was coming, but I said ingenuously, "Do you want to buy something?"

"No, I want to sell. What would an amateur give me for that?" She unfolded the white paper and made a motion for me to take from her a small oval portrait. I possessed myself of it with a hand of which I could only hope that she did not perceive the tremor, and she added, "I would part with it only for a good price."

At the first glance I recognised Jeffrey Aspern, and I was well aware that I flushed with the act. As she was watching me however I had the consistency to exclaim, "What a striking face! Do tell me who it is."

"It's an old friend of mine, a very distinguished man in his day. He gave it to me himself, but I'm afraid to mention his name, lest you never should have heard of him, critic and historian as you are. I know the world goes fast and one generation forgets another. He was all the fashion when I was young."

She was perhaps amazed at my assurance, but I was surprised at hers; at her having the energy, in her state of health and at her time of

2. Landlady.

life, to wish to sport with me that way simply for her private entertainment—the humour to test me and practise on me. This, at least, was the interpretation that I put upon her production of the portrait, for I could not believe that she really desired to sell it or cared for any information I might give her. What she wished was to dangle it before my eyes and put a prohibitive price on it. "The face comes back to me, it torments me," I said, turning the object this way and that and looking at it very critically. It was a careful but not a supreme work of art, larger than the ordinary miniature and representing a young man with a remarkably handsome face, in a high-collared green coat and a buff waistcoat. I judged the picture to have a valuable quality of resemblance and to have been painted when the model was about twenty-five years old. There are, as all the world knows, three other portraits of the poet in existence, but none of them is of so early a date as this elegant production. "I have never seen the original but I have seen other likenesses," I went on. "You expressed doubt of this generation having heard of the gentleman, but he strikes me for all the world as a celebrity. Now who is he? I can't put my finger on him—I can't give him a label. Wasn't he a writer? Surely he's a poet." I was determined that it should be she, not I, who should first pronounce Jeffrey Aspern's name.

My resolution was taken in ignorance of Miss Bordereau's extremely resolute character, and her lips never formed in my hearing the syllables that meant so much for her. She neglected to answer my question but raised her hand to take back the picture, with a gesture which though ineffectual was in a high degree peremptory. "It's only a person who should know for himself that would give me my price," she said with a certain dryness.

"Oh, then, you have a price?" I did not restore the precious thing; not from any vindictive purpose but because I instinctively clung to it. We looked at each other hard while I retained it.

"I know the least I would take. What it occurred to me to ask you about is the most I shall be able to get."

She made a movement, drawing herself together as if, in a spasm of dread at having lost her treasure, she were going to attempt the immense effort of rising to snatch it from me. I instantly placed it in her hand again, saying as I did so, "I should like to have it myself, but with your ideas I could never afford it."

She turned the small oval plate over in her lap, with its face down, and I thought I saw her catch her breath a little, as if she had had a strain or an escape. This however did not prevent her saying in a moment, "You would buy a likeness of a person you don't know, by an artist who has no reputation?"

"The artist may have no reputation, but that thing is wonderfully well painted," I replied, to give myself a reason.

"It's lucky you thought of saying that, because the painter was my father."

"That makes the picture indeed precious!" I exclaimed, laughing; and I may add that a part of my laughter came from my satisfaction in finding that I had been right in my theory of Miss Bordereau's origin. Aspern had of course met the young lady when he went to her father's studio as a sitter. I observed to Miss Bordereau that if she would entrust me with her property for twenty-four hours I should be happy to take advice upon it; but she made no answer to this save to slip it in silence into her pocket. This convinced me still more that she had no sincere intention of selling it during her lifetime, though she may have desired to satsify herself as to the sum her niece, should she leave it to her, might expect eventually to obtain for it. "Well, at any rate I hope you will not offer it without giving me notice," I said, as she remained irresponsive. "Remember that I am a possible purchaser."

"I should want your money first!" she returned, with unexpected rudeness; and then, as if she bethought herself that I had just cause to complain of such an insinuation and wished to turn the matter off, asked abruptly what I talked about with her niece when I went out with her that way in the evening.

"You speak as if we had set up the habit," I replied. "Certainly I should be very glad if it were to become a habit. But in that case I should feel a still greater scruple at betraying a lady's confidence."

"Her confidence? Has she got confidence?"

"Here she is—she can tell you herself," I said; for Miss Tita now appeared on the threshold of the old woman's parlour. "Have you got confidence, Miss Tita? Your aunt wants very much to know."

"Not in her, not in her!" the younger lady declared, shaking her head with a dolefulness that was neither jocular nor affected. "I don't know what to do with her; she has fits of horrid imprudence. She is so easily tired—and yet she has begun to roam—to drag herself about the house." And she stood looking down at her immemorial companion with a sort of helpless wonder, as if all their years of familiarity had not made her perversities, on occasion, any more easy to follow.

"I know what I'm about. I'm not losing my mind. I daresay you would like to think so," said Miss Bordereau, with a cynical little sigh.

"I don't suppose you came out here yourself. Miss Tita must have had to lend you a hand," I interposed, with a pacifying intention.

"Oh, she insisted that we should push her; and when she insists!" said Miss Tita, in the same tone of apprehension; as if there were no knowing what service that she disapproved of her aunt might force her next to render.

"I have always got most things done I wanted, thank God! The people I have lived with have humoured me," the old woman continued, speaking out of the gray ashes of her vanity.

"I suppose you mean that they have obeyed you."

"Well, whatever it is, when they like you."

"It's just because I like you that I want to resist," said Miss Tita, with a nervous laugh.

"Oh, I suspect you'll bring Miss Bordereau upstairs next, to pay me a visit," I went on; to which the old lady replied:

"Oh no; I can keep an eye on you from here!"

"You are very tired; you will certainly be ill to-night!" cried Miss Tita.

"Nonsense, my dear; I feel better at this moment than I have done for a month. Tomorrow I shall come out again. I want to be where I can see this clever gentleman."

"Shouldn't you perhaps see me better in your sitting-room?" I inquired.

"Don't you mean shouldn't you have a better chance at me?" she returned, fixing me a moment with her green shade.

"Ah, I haven't that anywhere! I look at you but I don't see you."

"You excite her dreadfully—and that is not good," said Miss Tita, giving me a reproachful, appealing look.

"I want to watch you—I want to watch you!" the old lady went on.

"Well then, let us spend as much of our time together as possible—I don't care where—and that will give you every facility."

"Oh, I've seen you enough for to-day. I'm satisfied. Now I'll go home." Miss Tita laid her hands on the back of her aunt's chair and began to push, but I begged her to let me take her place. "Oh yes, you may move me this way—you sha'n't in any other!" Miss Bordereau exclaimed, as she felt herself propelled firmly and easily over the smooth, hard floor. Before we reached the door of her own apartment she commanded me to stop, and she took a long, last look up and down the noble sala. "Oh, it's a magnificent house!" she murmured; after which I pushed her forward. When we had entered the parlour Miss Tita told me that she should now be able to manage, and at the same moment the little red-haired *donna*[3] came to meet her mistress. Miss Tita's idea was evidently to get her aunt immediately back to bed. I confess that in spite of this urgency I was guilty of the indiscretion of lingering; it held me there to think that I was nearer the documents I coveted—that they were probably put away somewhere in the faded, unsociable room. The place had indeed a bareness which did not suggest hidden treasures; there were no dusky nooks nor curtained corners, no massive cabinets nor chests with iron bands. Moreover it was possible, it was perhaps even probable that the old lady had consigned her relics to her bedroom, to some battered box that was shoved under the bed, to the drawer of some lame dressing-table,

3. Housemaid.

where they would be in the range of vision by the dim night-lamp. None the less I scrutinised every article of furniture, every conceivable cover for a hoard, and noticed that there were half a dozen things with drawers, and in particular a tall old secretary, with brass ornaments of the style of the Empire—a receptable somewhat rickety but still capable of keeping a great many secrets. I don't know why this article fascinated me so, inasmuch as I certainly had no definite purpose of breaking into it; but I stared at it so hard that Miss Tita noticed me and changed colour. Her doing this made me think I was right and that wherever they might have been before the Aspern papers at that moment languished behind the peevish little lock of the secretary. It was hard to remove my eyes from the dull mahogany front when I reflected that a simple panel divided me from the goal of my hopes; but I remembered my prudence and with an effort took leave of Miss Bordereau. To make the effort graceful I said to her that I should certainly bring her an opinion about the little picture.

"The little picture?" Miss Tita asked, surprised.

"What do *you* know about it, my dear?" the old woman demanded. "You needn't mind. I have fixed my price."

"And what may that be?"

"A thousand pounds."

"Oh Lord!" cried poor Miss Tita, irrepressibly.

"Is that what she talks to you about?" said Miss Bordereau.

"Imagine your aunt's wanting to know!" I had to separate from Miss Tita with only those words, though I should have liked immensely to add, "For heaven's sake meet me to-night in the garden!"

VIII

As it turned out the precaution had not been needed, for three hours later, just as I had finished my dinner, Miss Bordereau's niece appeared, unannounced, in the open doorway of the room in which my simple repasts were served. I remember well that I felt no surprise at seeing her; which is not a proof that I did not believe in her timidity. It was immense, but in a case in which there was a particular reason for boldness it never would have prevented her from running up to my rooms. I saw that she was now quite full of a particular reason; it threw her forward—made her seize me, as I rose to meet her, by the arm.

"My aunt is very ill; I think she is dying!"

"Never in the world," I answered, bitterly. "Don't you be afraid!"

"Do go for a doctor—do, do! Olimpia is gone for the one we always have, but she doesn't come back; I don't know what has happened to her. I told her that if he was not at home she was to follow him where he had gone; but apparently she is following him all over Venice. I don't know what to do—she looks so as if she were sinking."

"May I see her, may I judge?" I asked. "Of course I shall be delighted to bring some one; but hadn't we better send my man instead, so that I may stay with you?"

Miss Tita assented to this and I despatched my servant for the best doctor in the neighbourhood. I hurried downstairs with her, and on the way she told me that an hour after I quitted them in the afternoon Miss Bordereau had had an attack of "oppression," a terrible difficulty in breathing. This had subsided but had left her so exhausted that she did not come up: she seemed all gone. I repeated that she was not gone, that she would not go yet; whereupon Miss Tita gave me a sharper sidelong glance than she had ever directed at me and said, "Really, what do you mean? I suppose you don't accuse her of making-believe!" I forget what reply I made to this, but I grant that in my heart I thought the old woman capable of any weird manœuvre. Miss Tita wanted to know what I had done to her; her aunt had told her that I had made her so angry. I declared I had done nothing—I had been exceedingly careful; to which my companion rejoined that Miss Bordereau had assured her she had had a scene with me—a scene that had upset her. I answered with some resentment that it was a scene of her own making—that I couldn't think what she was angry with me for unless for not seeing my way to give a thousand pounds for the portrait of Jeffrey Aspern. "And did she show you that? Oh gracious—oh deary me!" groaned Miss Tita, who appeared to feel that the situation was passing out of her control and that the elements of her fate were thickening around her. I said that I would give anything to possess it, yet that I had not a thousand pounds; but I stopped when we came to the door of Miss Bordereau's room. I had an immense curiosity to pass it, but I thought it my duty to represent to Miss Tita that if I made the invalid angry she ought perhaps to be spared the sight of me. "The sight of you? Do you think she can *see*?" my companion demanded, almost with indignation. I did think so but forbore to say it, and I softly followed my conductress.

I remember that what I said to her as I stood for a moment beside the old woman's bed was, "Does she never show you her eyes then? Have you never seen them?" Miss Bordereau had been divested of her green shade, but (it was not my fortune to behold Juliana in her nightcap) the upper half of her face was covered by the fall of a piece of dingy lacelike muslin, a sort of extemporised hood which, wound round her head, descended to the end of her nose, leaving nothing visible but her white withered cheeks and puckered mouth, closed tightly and, as it were, consciously. Miss Tita gave me a glance of surprise, evidently not seeing a reason for my impatience. "You mean that she always wears something? She does it to preserve them."

"Because they are so fine?"

"Oh, to-day, to-day!" And Miss Tita shook her head, speaking very low. "But they used to be magnificent!"

"Yes indeed, we have Aspern's word for that." And as I looked again at the old woman's wrappings I could imagine that she had not wished to allow people a reason to say that the great poet had overdone it. But I did not waste my time in considering Miss Bordereau, in whom the appearance of respiration was so slight as to suggest that no human attention could ever help her more. I turned my eyes all over the room, rummaging with them the closets, the chests of drawers, the tables. Miss Tita met them quickly and read, I think, what was in them; but she did not answer it, turning away restlessly, anxiously, so that I felt rebuked, with reason, for a preoccupation that was almost profane in the presence of our dying companion. All the same I took another look, endeavouring to pick out mentally the place to try first, for a person who should wish to put his hand on Miss Bordereau's papers directly after her death. The room was a dire confusion; it looked like the room of an old actress. There were clothes hanging over chairs, odd-looking, shabby bundles here and there, and various paste-board boxes piled together, battered, bulging and discoloured, which might have been fifty years old. Miss Tita after a moment noticed the direction of my eyes again and, as if she guessed how I judged the air of the place (forgetting I had no business to judge it at all), said, perhaps to defend herself from the imputation of complicity in such untidiness:

"She likes it this way; we can't move things. There are old band-boxes she has had most of her life." Then she added, half taking pity on my real thought, "Those things were *there*." And she pointed to a small, low trunk which stood under a sofa where there was just room for it. It appeared to be a queer, superannuated coffer, or painted wood, with elaborate handles and shrivelled straps and with the colour (it had last been endued with a coat of light green) much rubbed off. It evidently had travelled with Juliana in the olden time—in the days of her adventures, which it had shared. It would have made a strange figure arriving at a modern hotel.

"*Were* there—they aren't now?" I asked, startled by Miss Tita's implication.

She was going to answer, but at that moment the doctor came in— the doctor whom the little maid had been sent to fetch and whom she had at last overtaken. My servant, going on his own errand, had met her with her companion in tow, and in the sociable Venetian spirit, retracing his steps with them, had also come up to the threshold of Miss Bordereau's room, where I saw him peeping over the doctor's shoulder. I motioned him away the more instantly that the sight of his prying face reminded me that I myself had almost as little to do there—an admonition confirmed by the sharp way the little doctor looked at me, appearing to take me for a rival who had the field before him. He was a short, fat, brisk gentleman who wore the tall hat of his profession and seemed to look at everything but his patient. He looked particularly at me, as if it struck him that I should be better for a dose, so that I bowed to him and left him with the women, going down to smoke a cigar in the garden. I was nervous; I could not go further; I could not leave the place. I don't know exactly what I thought might happen, but it seemed to me important to be there. I wandered about in the alleys—the warm night had come on—smoking cigar after cigar and looking at the light in Miss Bordereau's windows. They were open now, I could see; the situation was different. Sometimes the light moved, but not quickly; it did not suggest the hurry of a crisis. Was the old woman dying or was she already dead? Had the doctor said that there was nothing to be done at her tremendous age but to let her quietly pass away; or had he simply announced with a look a little more conventional that the end of the end had come? Were the other two women moving about to perform the offices that follow in such a case? It made me uneasy not to be nearer, as if I thought the doctor himself might carry away the papers with him. I bit my cigar hard as it came over me again that perhaps there were now no papers to carry!

I wandered about for an hour—for an hour and a half. I looked out for Miss Tita at one of the windows, having a vague idea that she might come there to give me some sign. Would she not see the red tip of my cigar moving about in the dark and feel that I wanted eminently to know what the doctor had said? I am afraid it is a proof my anxieties had made me gross that I should have taken in some degree for granted that at such an hour, in the midst of the greatest change that could take place in her life, they were uppermost also in poor Miss Tita's mind. My servant came down and spoke to me; he knew nothing save that the doctor had gone after a visit of half an hour. If he had stayed half an hour then Miss Bordereau was still alive: it could not have taken so much time as that to enunciate the contrary. I sent the man out of the house; there were moments when the sense of his curiosity annoyed me and this was one of them. *He* had been watching my cigar-tip from an upper window, if Miss Tita had not; he could not know what I was after and I could not tell him, though I was conscious he had fantastic private theories about me which he thought fine and which I, had I known them, should have thought offensive.

I went upstairs at last but I ascended no higher than the sala. The door of Miss Bordereau's apartment was open, showing from the parlour the dimness of a poor candle. I went toward it with a light tread and at the same moment Miss Tita appeared and stood looking at me as I approached. "She's better—she's better," she said, even before I had asked. "The doctor has given her something; she woke up, came back to life while he was there. He says there is no immediate danger."

"No immediate danger? Surely he thinks her condition strange!"

"Yes, because she had been excited. That affects her dreadfully."

"It will do so again then, because she excites herself. She did so this afternoon."

"Yes; she mustn't come out any more," said Miss Tita, with one of her lapses into a deeper placidity.

"What is the use of making such a remark as that if you begin to rattle her about again the first time she bids you?"

"I won't—I won't do it any more."

"You must learn to resist her," I went on.

"Oh, yes, I shall; I shall do so better if you tell me its right."

"You mustn't do it for me; you must do it for youself. It all comes back to you, if you are frightened."

"Well, I am not frightened now," said Miss Tita cheerfully. "She is very quiet."

"Is she conscious again—does she speak?"

"No, she doesn't speak, but she takes my hand. She holds it fast."

"Yes," I rejoined, "I can see what force she still has by the way she grabbed that picture this afternoon. But if she holds you fast how comes it that you are here?"

Miss Tita hesitated a moment; though her face was in deep shadow (she had her back to the light in the parlour and I had put down my own candle far off, near the door of the sala), I thought I saw her smile ingenuously. "I came on purpose—I heard your step."

"Why, I came on tiptoe, as inaudibly as possible."

"Well, I heard you," said Miss Tita.

"And is your aunt alone now?"

"Oh no; Olimpia is sitting there."

On my side I hesitated. "Shall we then step in there?" And I nodded at the parlour; I wanted more and more to be on the spot.

"We can't talk there—she will hear us."

I was on the point of replying that in that case we would sit silent, but I was too conscious that this would not do, as there was something I desired immensely to ask her. So I proposed that we should walk a little in the sala, keeping more at the other end, where we should not disturb the old lady. Miss Tita assented unconditionally; the doctor was coming again, she said, and she would be there to meet him at the door. We strolled through the fine superfluous hall, where on the marble floor—particularly as at first we said nothing—our footsteps were more audible than I had expected. When we reached the other end—the wide window, inveterately closed, connecting with the balcony that overhung the canal—I suggested that we should remain there, as she would see the doctor arrive still better. I opened the window and we passed out on the balcony. The air of the canal seemed even heavier, hotter, than that of the sala. The place was hushed and void; the quiet neighbourhood had gone to sleep. A lamp, here and there, over the narrow black water, glimmered in double; the voice of a man going homeward singing, with his jacket on his shoulder and his hat on his ear, came to us from a distance. This did not prevent the scene from being very *comme il faut*, as Miss Bordereau had called it the first time I saw her. Presently a gondola passed along the canal with its slow rhythmical plash, and as we listened we watched it in silence. It did not stop, it did not carry the doctor; and after it had gone on I said to Miss Tita:

"And where are they now—the things that were in the trunk?"

"In the trunk?"

"That green box you pointed out to me in her room. You said her papers had been there; you seemed to imply that she had transferred them."

"Oh, yes; they are not in the trunk," said Miss Tita.

"May I ask if you have looked?"

"Yes, I have looked—for you."

"How for me, dear Miss Tita? Do you mean you would have given them to me if you had found them?" I asked, almost trembling.

She delayed to reply and I waited. Suddenly she broke out, "I don't know what I would do—what I wouldn't!"

"Would you look again—somewhere else?"

She had spoken with a strange, unexpected emotion, and she went on in the same tone: "I can't—I can't—while she lies there. It isn't decent."

"No, it isn't decent," I replied, gravely. "Let the poor lady rest in peace." And the words, on my lips, were not hypocritical, for I felt reprimanded and shamed.

Miss Tita added in a moment, as if she had guessed this and were sorry for me, but at the same time wished to explain that I did drive her on or at least did insist too much: "I can't deceive her that way. I can't deceive her—perhaps on her deathbed."

"Heaven forbid I should ask you, though I have been guilty myself!"

"You have been guilty?"

"I have sailed under false colours." I felt now as if I must tell her that I had given her an invented name, on account of my fear that her aunt would have heard of me and would refuse to take me in. I explained this and also that I had really been a party to the letter written to them by John Cumnor months before.

She listened with great attention, looking at me with parted lips, and when I had made my confession she said, "Then your real name—what is it?" She repeated it over twice when I had told her, accompanying it with the exclamation "Gracious, gracious!" Then she added, "I like your own best."

"So do I," I said, laughing. "Ouf! it's a relief to get rid of the other."

"So it was a regular plot—a kind of conspiracy?"

"Oh, a conspiracy—we were only two," I replied, leaving out Mrs. Prest of course.

She hesitated; I thought she was perhaps going to say that we had been very base. But she remarked after a moment, in a candid, wondering way; "How much you must want them!"

"Oh, I do, passionately!" I conceded, smiling. And this chance made me go on, forgetting my compunction of a moment before. "How can she possibly have changed their place herself? How can she walk? How can she arrive at that sort of muscular exertion? How can she lift and carry things?"

"Oh, when one wants and when one has so much will!" said Miss Tita, as if she had thought over my question already herself and had simply had no choice but that answer—the idea that in the dead of night, or at some moment when the coast was clear, the old woman had been capable of a miraculous effort.

"Have you questioned Olimpia? Hasn't she helped her—hasn't she done it for her?" I asked; to which Miss Tita replied promptly and positively that their servant had had nothing to do with the matter, though without admitting definitely that she had spoken to her. It was as if she were a little shy, a little ashamed now of letting me see how much she had entered into my uneasiness and had me on her mind. Suddenly she said to me, without any immediate relevance:

"I feel as if you were a new person, now that you have got a new name."

"It isn't a new one; it is a very good old one, thank heaven!"

She looked at me a moment. "I do like it better."

"Oh, if you didn't I would almost go on with the other!"

"Would you really?"

I laughed again, but for all answer to this inquiry I said, "Of course if she can rummage about that way she can perfectly have burnt them."

"You must wait—you must wait." Miss Tita moralised mournfully; and her tone ministered little to my patience, for it seemed after all to accept that wretched possibility. I would teach myself to wait; I declared nevertheless; because in the first place I could not do otherwise and in the second I had her promise, given me the other night, that she would help me.

"Of course if the papers are gone that's no use," she said; not as if she wished to recede, but only to be conscientious.

"Naturally. But if you could only find out!" I groaned, quivering again.

"I thought you said you would wait."

"Oh, you mean wait even for that?"

"For what then?"

"Oh, nothing," I replied, rather foolishly, being ashamed to tell her what had been implied in my submission to delay—the idea that she would do more than merely find out. I know not whether she guessed this; at all events she appeared to become aware of the necessity for being a little more rigid.

"I didn't promise to deceive, did I? I don't think I did."

"It doesn't much matter whether you did or not, for you couldn't!"

I don't think Miss Tita would have contested this even had she not been diverted by our seeing the doctor's gondola shoot into the little canal and approach the house. I noted that he came as fast as if he believed that Miss Bordereau was still in danger. We looked down at him while he disembarked and then went back into the sala to meet him. When he came up however I naturally left Miss Tita to go off with him alone, only asking her leave to come back later for news.

I went out of the house and took a long walk, as far as the Piazza, where my restlessness declined to quit me. I was unable to sit down (it was very late now but there were people still at the little tables in front of the cafés); I could only walk round and round, and I did so half a dozen times. I was uncomfortable, but it gave me a certain pleasure to have told Miss Tita who I really was. At last I took my way home again, slowly getting all but inextricably lost, as I did whenever I went out in Venice: so that it was considerably past midnight when I reached my door. The sala, upstairs, was as dark as usual and my lamp as I crossed it found nothing satisfactory to show me. I was disappointed, for I had notified Miss Tita that I would come back for a report, and I thought she might have left a light there as a sign. The door of the ladies' apartment was closed; which seemed an intimation that my faltering friend had gone to bed, tired of waiting for me. I stood in the middle of the place, considering, hoping she would hear me and perhaps peep out, saying to myself too that she would never go to bed with her aunt in a state so critical; she would sit up and watch—she would be in a chair, in her dressing-gown. I went nearer the door; I stopped there and listened. I heard nothing at all and at last I tapped gently. No answer came and after another minute I turned the handle. There was no light in the room; this ought to have prevented me from going in, but it had no such effect. If I have candidly narrated the importunities, the indelicacies, of which my desire to possess myself of Jeffrey Aspern's papers had rendered me capable I need not shrink from confessing this last indiscretion. I think it was the worst thing I did; yet there were extenuating circumstances. I was deeply though doubtless not disinterestedly anxious for more news of the old lady, and Miss Tita had accepted from me, as it were, a rendezvous which it might have been a point of honour with me to keep. It may be said that her leaving the place dark was a positive sign that she released me, and to this I can only reply that I desired not to be released.

The door of Miss Bordereau's room was open and I could see beyond it the faintness of a taper. There was no sound—my footstep caused no one to stir. I came further into the room; I lingered there with my lamp in my hand. I wanted to give Miss Tita a chance to come to me if she were with her aunt, as she must be. I made no noise to call her; I only waited to see if she would not notice my light. She did not, and I explained this (I found afterwards I was right) by the idea that she had fallen asleep. If she had fallen asleep her aunt was not on her mind, and my explanation ought to have led me to go out as I had come. I must repeat again that it did not, for I found myself at the same moment thinking of something else. I had no definite purpose, no bad intention, but I felt myself held to the spot by an acute, though absurd, sense of opportunity. For what I could not have said, inasmuch as it was not in my mind that I might commit a theft. Even if it had been I was confronted with the evident fact that Miss Bordereau did not leave her secretary, her cupboard and the drawers of her tables gaping. I had no keys, no tools and no ambition to smash her furniture. None the less it came to me that I was now, perhaps alone, unmolested, at the hour of temptation and secrecy, nearer to the tormenting treasure than I had ever been. I held up my lamp, let the light play on the different objects as if it could tell me something. Still there came no movement from the other room. If Miss Tita was sleeping she was sleeping sound. Was she doing so—generous creature—on purpose to leave me the field? Did she know I was there and was she just keeping quiet to see what I would do—what I *could* do? But what could I do, when it came to that? She herself knew even better than I how little.

I stopped in front of the secretary, looking at it very idiotically; for what had it to say to me after all? In the first place it was locked, and in the second it almost surely contained nothing in which I was interested. Ten to one the papers had been destroyed; and even if they had not been destroyed the old woman would not have put them in such a place as that after removing them from the green trunk—would not have transferred them, if she had the idea of their safety on her brain, from the better hiding-place to the worse. The secretary was more conspicuous, more accessible in a room in which she could no longer mount guard. It opened with a key, but there was a little brass handle, like a button, as well; I saw this as I played my lamp over it. I did something more than this at that moment: I caught a glimpse of the possibility that Miss Tita wished me really to understand. If she did not wish me to understand, if she wished me to keep away, why had she not locked the door of communication between the sitting-room and the sala? That would have been a definite sign that I was to leave them alone. If I did not leave them alone she meant me to come for a purpose—a purpose now indicated by the quick, fantastic idea that to oblige me she had unlocked the secretary. She had not left the key, but the lid would probably move if I touched the button. This theory fascinated me, and I bent over very close to judge. I did not propose to do anything, not even—not in the least—to let down the lid; I only wanted to test my theory, to see if the cover *would* move. I touched the button with my hand—a mere touch would tell me; and as I did so (it is embarrassing for me to relate it), I looked over my shoulder. It was a chance, an instinct, for I had not heard anything. I almost let my luminary drop and certainly I steped back, straightening myself up at what I saw. Miss Bordereau stood there in her night-dress, in the doorway of her room, watching me; her hands were raised, she had lifted the everlasting curtain that covered half her face, and for the first, the last, the only time I beheld her extraordinary eyes. They glared at me, they made me horribly ashamed. I never shall forget her strange little bent white tottering figure, with its lifted head, her attitude, her expression; neither shall I forget the tone in which as I turned, looking at her, she hissed out passionately, furiously:

"Ah, you publishing scoundrel!"

I know not what I stammered, to excuse myself to explain; but I went towards her, to tell her I meant no harm. She waved me off with her old hands, retreating before me in horror; and the next thing I knew she had fallen back with a quick spasm, as if death had descended on her, into Miss Tita's arms.

IX

I left Venice the next morning, as soon as I learnt that the old lady had not succumbed, as I feared at the moment, to the shock I had given her—the shock I may also say she had given me. How in the world could I have supposed her capable of getting out of bed by herself? I failed to see Miss Tita before going; I only saw the *donna*, whom I entrusted with a note for her younger mistress. In this note I mentioned that I should be absent but for a few days. I went to Treviso, to Bassano, to Castelfranco;[4] I took walks and drives and looked at musty old churches with ill-lighted pictures and spent hours seated smoking at the doors of cafés, where there were flies and yellow curtains, on the shady side of sleepy little squares. In spite of these pastimes, which were mechanical and perfunctory, I scantily enjoyed my journey: there was too strong a taste of the disagreeable in my life. It had been devilish awkward, as the young men say, to be found by Miss Bordereau in the dead of night examining the attachment of her bureau; and it had not been less so to have to believe for a good many hours afterward that it was highly probable I had killed her. In writing

---

4. Treviso and Bassano del Grappa are medieval cities; Castelfranco Veneto is a medieval stronghold, birthplace of the painter Giorgione (1478?–1511), teacher of Titian (ca. 1477–1576). They are all within about forty miles of Venice, on the mainland.

to Miss Tita I attempted to minimise these irregularities; but as she gave me no word of answer I could not know what impression I made upon her. It rankled in my mind that I had been called a publishing scoundrel, for certainly I did publish and certainly I had not been very delicate. There was a moment when I stood convinced that the only way to make up for this latter fault was to take myself away altogether on the instant; to sacrifice my hopes and relieve the two poor women for ever of the oppression of my intercourse. Then I reflected that I had better try a short absence first, for I must already have had a sense (unexpressed and dim) that in disappearing completely it would not be merely my own hopes that I should condemn to extinction. It would perhaps be sufficient if I stayed away long enough to give the elder lady time to think she was rid of me. That she would wish to be rid of me after this (if I was not rid of her) was now not to be doubted: that nocturnal scene would have cured her of the disposition to put up with my company for the sake of my dollars. I said to myself that after all I could not abandon Miss Tita, and I continued to say this even while I observed that she quite failed to comply with my earnest request (I had given her two or three addresses, at little towns, *poste restante*) that she would let me know how she was getting on. I would have made my servant write to me but that he was unable to manage a pen. It struck me there was a kind of scorn in Miss Tita's silence (little disdainful as she had ever been), so that I was uncomfortable and sore. I had scruples about going back and yet I had others about not doing so, for I wanted to put myself on a better footing. The end of it was that I did return to Venice on the twelfth day; and as my gondola gently bumped against Miss Bordereau's steps a certain palpitation of suspense told me that I had done myself a violence in holding off so long.

I had faced about so abruptly that I had not telegraphed to my servant. He was therefore not at the station to meet me, but he poked out his head from an upper window when I reached the house. "They have put her into the earth, *la vecchia*,"[5] he said to me in the lower hall, while he shouldered my valise; and he grinned and almost winked, as if he knew I should be pleased at the news.

"She's dead!" I exclaimed, giving him a very different look.

"So it appears, since they have buried her."

"It's all over? When was the funeral?"

"The other yesterday. But a funeral you could scarcely call it, signore; it was a dull little passeggio of two gondolas. Poveretta!"[6] the man continued, referring apparently to Miss Tita. His conception of funerals was apparently that they were mainly to amuse the living.

I wanted to know about Miss Tita—how she was and where she was—but I asked him no more questions till we had got upstairs. Now

5. The old woman.   6. Poor woman, poor thing.

that the fact had met me I took a bad view of it, especially of the idea that poor Miss Tita had had to manage by herself after the end. What did she know about arrangements, about the steps to take in such a case? Poveretta indeed! I could only hope that the doctor had given her assistance and that she had not been neglected by the old friends of whom she had told me, the little band of the faithful whose fidelity consisted in coming to the house once a year. I elicited from my servant that two old ladies and an old gentleman had in fact rallied round Miss Tita and had supported her (they had come for her in a gondola of their own) during the journey to the cemetery, the little red-walled island of tombs which lies to the north of the town, on the way to Murano. It appeared from these circumstances that the Misses Bordereau were Catholics, a discovery I had never made, as the old woman could not go to church and her niece, so far as I perceived, either did not or went only to early mass in the parish, before I was stirring. Certainly even the priests respected their seclusion; I had never caught the whisk of the curato's skirt. That evening, an hour later, I sent my servant down with five words written on a card, to ask Miss Tita if she would see me for a few moments. She was not in the house, where he had sought her, he told me when he came back, but in the garden walking about to refresh herself and gathering flowers. He had found her there and she would be very happy to see me.

I went down and passed half an hour with poor Miss Tita. She had always had a look of musty mourning (as if she were wearing out old robes of sorrow that would not come to an end), and in this respect there was no appreciable change in her appearance. But she evidently had been crying, crying a great deal—simply, satisfyingly, refreshingly, with a sort of primitive, retarded sense of loneliness and violence. But she had none of the formalism or the self-consciousness of grief, and I was almost surprised to see her standing there in the first dusk with her hands full of flowers, smiling at me with her reddened eyes. Her white face, in the frame of her mantilla, looked longer, leaner than usual. I had had an idea that she would be a good deal disgusted with me—would consider that I ought to have been on the spot to advise her, to help her; and, though I was sure there was no rancour in her composition and no great conviction of the importance of her affairs, I had prepared myself for a difference in her manner, for some little injured look, half familiar, half estranged, which should say to my conscience, "Well, you are a nice person to have professed things!" But historic truth compels me to declare that Tita Bordereau's countenance expressed unqualified pleasure in seeing her late aunt's lodger. That touched him extremely and he thought it simplified his situation until he found it did not. I was as kind to her that evening as I knew how to be, and I walked about the garden with her for half an hour. There was no explanation of any sort between us; I did not ask her why she had not answered my letter. Still less did I repeat what I had said to her in that communication; if she chose to let me suppose that she had forgotten the position in which Miss Bordereau surprised me that night and the effect of the discovery on the old woman I was quite willing to take it that way: I was grateful to her for not treating me as if I had killed her aunt.

We strolled and strolled and really not much passed between us save the recognition of her bereavement, conveyed in my manner and in a visible air that she had of depending on me now, since I let her see that I took an interest in her. Miss Tita had none of the pride that makes a person wish to preserve the look of independence; she did not in the least pretend that she knew at present what would become of her. I forbore to touch particularly on that however, for I certainly was not prepared to say that I would take charge of her. I was cautious; not ignobly, I think, for I felt that her knowledge of life was so small that in her unsophisticated vision there would be no reason why—since I seemed to pity her—I should not look after her. She told me how her aunt had died, very peacefully at the last, and how everything had been done afterwards by the care of her good friends (fortunately, thanks to me, she said, smiling, there was money in the house; and she repeated that when once the Italians like you they are your friends for life); and when we had gone into this she asked me about my *giro*, my impressions, the places I had seen. I told her what I could, making it up partly, I am afraid, as in my depression I had not seen much; and after she had heard me she exclaimed, quite as if she had forgotten her aunt and her sorrow, "Dear, dear, how much I should like to do such things—to take a little journey!" It came over me for the moment that I ought to propose some tour, say I would take her anywhere she liked; and I remarked at any rate that some excursion—to give her a change—might be managed: we would think of it, talk it over. I said never a word to her about the Aspern documents; asked no questions as to what she had ascertained or what had otherwise happened with regard to them before Miss Bordereau's death. It was not that I was not on pins and needles to know, but that I thought it more decent not to betray my anxiety so soon after the catastrophe. I hoped she herself would say something, but she never glanced that way, and I thought this natural at the time. Later however, that night, it occurred to me that her silence was somewhat strange; for if she had talked of my movements, of anything so detached as the Giorgione[7] at Castelfranco, she might have alluded to what she could easily remember was in my mind. It was not to be supposed that the emotion produced by her aunt's death had blotted out the recollection that I was interested

7. The reference is to a particular painting, Giorgione's masterpiece depicting the Madonna and Child between Saint Francis and Saint Liberale in the Duomo (cathedral) at Castelfranco.

in that lady's relics, and I fidgeted afterwards as it came to me that her reticence might very possibly mean simply that nothing had been found. We separated in the garden (it was she who said she must go in); now that she was alone in the rooms I felt that (judged, at any rate, by Venetian ideas) I was on rather a different footing in regard to visiting her there. As I shook hands with her for good-night I asked her if she had any general plan—had thought over what she had better do. "Oh yes, oh yes, but I haven't settled anything yet," she replied, quite cheerfully. Was her cheerfulness explained by the impression that I would settle for her?

I was glad the next morning that we had neglected practical questions, for this gave me a pretext for seeing her again immediately. There was a very practical question to be touched upon. I owed it to her to let her know formally that of course I did not expect her to keep me on as a lodger, and also to show some interest in her own tenure, what she might have on her hands in the way of a lease. But I was not destined, as it happened, to converse with her for more than an instant on either of these points. I sent her no message; I simply went down to the sala and walked to and fro there. I knew she would come out; she would very soon discover I was there. Somehow I preferred not to be shut up with her; gardens and big halls seemed better places to talk. It was a splendid morning, with something in the air that told of the waning of the long Venetian summer; a freshness from the sea which stirred the flowers in the garden and made a pleasant draught in the house, less shuttered, and darkened now than when the old woman was alive. It was the beginning of autumn, of the end of the golden months. With this it was the end of my experiment—or would be in the course of half an hour, when I should really have learned that the papers had been reduced to ashes. After that there would be nothing left for me but to go to the station; for seriously (and as it struck me in the morning light) I could not linger there to act as guardian to a piece of middle-aged female helplessness. If she had not saved the papers wherein should I be indebted to her? I think I winced a little as I asked myself how much, if she *had* saved them, I should have to recognise and, as it were, to reward such a courtesy. Might not that circumstance after all saddle me with a guardianship? If this idea did not make me more uncomfortable as I walked up and down it was because I was convinced I had nothing to look to. If the old woman had not destroyed everything before she pounced upon me in the parlour she had done so afterwards.

It took Miss Tita rather longer than I had expected to guess that I was there; but when at last she came out she looked at me without surprise. I said to her that I had been waiting for her and she asked why I had not let her know. I was glad the next day that I had checked myself before remarking that I had wished to see if a friendly intuition would not tell her: it became a satisfaction to me that I had not indulged in that rather tender joke. What I did say was virtually the truth—that I was too nervous, since I expected her now to settle my fate.

"Your fate?" said Miss Tita, giving me a queer look; and as she spoke I noticed a rare change in her. She was different from what she had been the evening before—less natural, less quiet. She had been crying the day before and she was not crying now, and yet she struck me as less confident. It was as if something had happened to her during the night, or at least as if she had thought of something that troubled her—something in particular that affected her relations with me, made them more embarrassing and complicated. Had she simply perceived that her aunt's not being there now altered my position?

"I mean about our papers. *Are* there any? You must know now."

"Yes, there are a great many; more than I supposed." I was struck with the way her voice trembled as she told me this.

"Do you mean that you have got them in there—and that I may see them?"

"I don't think you can see them," said Miss Tita, with an extraordinary expression of entreaty in her eyes, as if the dearest hope she had in the world now was that I would not take them from her. But how could she expect me to make such a sacrifice as that after all that had passed between us? What had I come back to Venice for but to see them, to take them? My delight at learning they were still in existence was such that if the poor woman had gone down on her knees to beseech me never to mention them again I would have treated the proceeding as a bad joke. "I have got them but I can't show them," she added.

"Not even to me? Ah, Miss Tita!" I groaned, with a voice of infinite remonstrance and reproach.

She coloured and the tears came back to her eyes; I saw that it cost her a kind of anguish to take such a stand but that a dreadful sense of duty had descended upon her. It made me quite sick to find myself confronted with that particular obstacle; all the more that it appeared to me I had been extremely encouraged to leave it out of account. I almost considered that Miss Tita had assured me that if she had no greater hindrance than that—! "You don't mean to say you made her a deathbed promise? It was precisely against your doing anything of that sort that I thought I was safe. Oh, I would rather she had burned the papers outright than that!"

"No, it isn't a promise," said Miss Tita.

"Pray what is it then?"

She hesitated and then she said, "She tried to burn them, but I prevented it. She had hid them in her bed."

"In her bed?"

"Between the mattresses. That's where she put them when she took them out of the trunk. I can't understand how she did it, because Olimpia didn't help her. She tells me so and I believe her. My aunt only told her afterwards so that she shouldn't touch the bed—anything but the sheets. So it was badly made," added Miss Tita, simply.

"I should think so! And how did she try to burn them?"

"She didn't try much; she was too weak, those last days. But she told me—she charged me. Oh, it was terrible! She couldn't speak after that night; she could only make signs."

"And what did you do?"

"I took them away. I locked them up."

"In the secretary?"

"Yes, in the secretary," said Miss Tita, reddening again.

"Did you tell her you would burn them?"

"No, I didn't—on purpose."

"On purpose to gratify me?"

"Yes, only for that."

"And what good will you have done me if after all you won't show them?"

"Oh, none; I know that—I know that."

"And did she believe you had destroyed them?"

"I don't know what she believed at the last. I couldn't tell—she was too far gone."

"Then if there was no promise and no assurance I can't see what ties you."

"Oh, she hated it so—she hated it so! She was so jealous. But here's the portrait—you may have that," Miss Tita announced, taking the little picture, wrapped up in the same manner in which her aunt had wrapped it, out of her pocket.

"I may have it—do you mean you give it to me?" I questioned, staring, as it passed into my hand.

"Oh yes."

"But it's worth money—a large sum."

"Well!" said Miss Tita, still with her strange look.

I did not know what to make of it, for it could scarcely mean that she wanted to bargain like her aunt. She spoke as if she wished to make me a present. "I can't take it from you as a gift," I said, "and yet I can't afford to pay you for it according to the ideas Miss Bordereau had of its value. She rated it at a thousand pounds."

"Couldn't we sell it?" asked Miss Tita.

"God forbid! I prefer the picture to the money."

"Well then keep it."

"You are very generous."

"So are you."

"I don't know why you should think so," I replied; and this was a truthful speech, for the singular creature appeared to have some very fine reference in her mind, which I did not in the least seize.

"Well, you have made a great difference for me," said Miss Tita.

I looked at Jeffrey Aspern's face in the little picture, partly in order not to look at that of my interlocutress, which had begun to trouble me, even to frighten me a little—it was so self-conscious, so unnatural. I made no answer to this last declaration; I only privately consulted Jeffrey Aspern's delightful eyes with my own (they were so young and brilliant, and yet so wise, so full of vision); I asked him what on earth was the matter with Miss Tita. He seemed to smile at me with friendly mockery, as if he were amused at my case. I had got into a pickle for him—as if he needed it! He was unsatisfactory, for the only moment since I had know him. Nevertheless, now that I held the little picture in my hand I felt that it would be a precious possession. "Is this a bribe to make me give up the papers?" I demanded in a moment, perversely. "Much as I value it, if I were to be obliged to choose, the papers are what I should prefer. Ah, but ever so much!"

"How can you choose—how can you choose?" Miss Tita asked, slowly, lamentably.

"I see! Of course there is nothing to be said, if you regard the interdiction that rests upon you as quite insurmountable. In this case it must seem to you that to part with them would be an impiety of the worst kind, a simple sacrilege!"

Miss Tita shook her head, full of her dolefulness. "You would understand if you had known her. I'm afraid," she quavered suddenly—"I'm afraid! She was terrible when she was angry."

"Yes, I saw something of that, that night. She was terrible. Then I saw her eyes. Lord, they were fine!"

"I see them—they stare at me in the dark!" said Miss Tita.

"You are nervous, with all you have been through."

"Oh yes, very—very!"

"You mustn't mind; that will pass away," I said, kindly. Then I added, resignedly, for it really seemed to me that I must accept the situation, "Well, so it is, and it can't be helped. I must renounce." Miss Tita, at this, looking at me, gave a low, soft moan, and I went on: "I only wish to heaven she had destroyed them; then there would be nothing more to say. And I can't understand why, with her ideas, she didn't."

"Oh, she lived on them!" said Miss Tita.

"You can imagine whether that makes me want less to see them," I answered, smiling. "But don't let me stand here as if I had it in my soul to tempt you to do anything base. Naturally you will understand I give up my rooms. I leave Venice immediately." And I took up my hat, which I had placed on a chair. We were still there rather awkwardly, on our feet, in the middle of the sala. She had left the door of the apartments open behind her but she had not led me that way.

A kind of spasm came into her face as she saw me take my hat. "Immediately—do you mean to-day?" The tone of the words was tragical—they were a cry of desolation.

"Oh no; not so long as I can be of the least service to you."

"Well, just a day or two more—just two or three days," she panted. Then controlling herself she added in another manner, "She wanted to say something to me—the last day—something very particular, but she couldn't."

"Something very particular?"

"Something more about the papers."

"And did you guess—have you any idea?"

"No, I have thought—but I don't know. I have thought all kinds of things."

"And for instance?"

"Well, that if you were a relation it would be different."

"If I were a relation?"

"If you were not a stranger. Then it would be the same for you as for me. Anything that is mine—would be yours, and you could do what you like. I couldn't prevent you—and you would have no responsibility."

She brought out this droll explanation with a little nervous rush, as if she were speaking words she had got by heart. They gave me an impression of subtlety and at first I failed to follow. But after a moment her face helped me to see further, and then a light came into my mind. It was embarrassing, and I bent my head over Jeffrey Aspern's portrait. What an odd expression was in his face! "Get out of it as you can, my dear fellow!" I put the picture into the pocket of my coat and said to Miss Tita, "Yes, I'll sell it for you. I sha'n't get a thousand pounds by any means, but I shall get something good."

She looked at me with tears in her eyes, but she seemed to try to smile as she remarked, "We can divide the money."

"No, no, it shall be all yours." Then I went on, "I think I know what your poor aunt wanted to say. She wanted to give directions that her papers should be buried with her."

Miss Tita appeared to consider this suggestion for a moment; after which she declared, with striking decision, "Oh no, she wouldn't have thought that safe!"

"It seems to me nothing could be safer."

"She had an idea that when people want to publish they are capable—" And she paused, blushing.

"Of violating a tomb? Mercy on us, what must she have thought of me!"

"She was not just, she was not generous!" Miss Tita cried with sudden passion.

The light that had come into my mind a moment before increased.

"Ah, don't say that, for we *are* a dreadful race." Then I pursued, "If she left a will, that may give you some idea."

"I have found nothing of the sort—she destroyed it. She was very fond of me," Miss Tita added, incongruously. "She wanted me to be happy. And if any person should be kind to me—she wanted to speak of that."

I was almost awestricken at the astuteness with which the good lady found herself inspired, transparent astuteness as it was and sewn, as the phrase is, with white thread. "Depend upon it she didn't want to make any provision that would be agreeable to me."

"No, not to you but to me. She knew I should like it if you could carry out your idea. Not because she cared for you but because she did think of me," Miss Tita went on, with her unexpected, persuasive volubility. "You could see them—you could use them." She stopped, seeing that I perceived the sense of that conditional—stopped long enough for me to give some sign which I did not give. She must have been conscious however that though my face showed the greatest embarrassment that was ever painted on a human countenance it was not set as a stone, it was also full of compassion. It was a comfort to me a long time afterwards to consider that she could not have seen in me the smallest symptom of disrespect. "I don't know what to do; I'm too tormented, I'm too ashamed!" she continued, with vehemence. Then turning away from me and burying her face in her hands she burst into a flood of tears. If she did not know what to do it may be imagined whether I did any better. I stood there dumb, watching her while her sobs resounded in the great empty hall. In a moment she was facing me again, with her streaming eyes. "I would give you everything—and she would understand, where she is—she would forgive me!"

"Ah, Miss Tita—ah, Miss Tita," I stammered, for all reply. I did not know what to do, as I say, but at a venture I made a wild, vague movement, in consequence of which I found myself at the door. I remember standing there and saying, "It wouldn't do—it wouldn't do!" pensively, awkwardly, grotesquely, while I looked away to the opposite end of the sala as if there were a beautiful view there. The next thing I remember is that I was downstairs and out of the house. My gondola was there and my gondolier, reclining on the cushions, sprang up as soon as he saw me. I jumped in and to his usual "*Dove commanda?*"[8] I replied, in a tone that made him stare, "Anywhere, anywhere; out into the lagoon!"

He rowed me away and I sat there prostrate, groaning softly to myself, with my hat pulled over my face. What in the name of the preposterous did she mean if she did not mean to offer me her hand? That was the price—that was the price! And did she think I wanted it,

8. Where do you wish to go?

poor deluded, infatuated, extravagant lady? My gondolier, behind me, must have seen my ears red as I wondered, sitting there under the fluttering *tenda*,[9] with my hidden face, noticing nothing as we passed—wondered whether her delusion, her infatuation had been my own reckless work. Did she think I had made love to her, even to get the papers? I had not, I had not; I repeated that over to myself for an hour, for two hours, till I was wearied if not convinced. I don't know where my gondolier took me; we floated aimlessly about on the lagoon, with slow, rare strokes. At last I became conscious that we were near the Lido, far up, on the right hand, as you turn your back to Venice, and I made him put me ashore. I wanted to walk, to move, to shed some of my bewilderment. I crossed the narrow strip and got to the sea-beach—I took my way toward Malamocco.[1] But presently I flung myself down again on the warm sand, in the breeze, on the coarse dry grass. It took it out of me to think I had been so much at fault, that I had unwittingly but none the less deplorably trifled. But I had not given her cause—distinctly I had not. I had said to Mrs. Prest that I would make love to her; but it had been a joke without consequences and I had never said it to Tita Bordereau. I had been as kind as possible, because I really liked her; but since when had that become a crime where a woman of such an age and such an appearance was concerned? I am far from remembering clearly the succession of events and feelings during this long day of confusion, which I spent entirely in wandering about, without going home, until late at night; it only comes back to me that there were moments when I pacified my conscience and others when I lashed it into pain. I did not laugh all day—that I do recollect; the case, however it might have struck others, seemed to me so little amusing. It would have been better perhaps for me to feel the comic side of it. At any rate, whether I had given cause or not it went without saying that I could not pay the price. I could not accept. I could not, for a bundle of tattered papers, marry a ridiculous, pathetic, provincial old woman. It was a proof that she did not think the idea would come to me, her having determined to suggest it herself in that practical, argumentative, heroic way, in which the timidity however had been so much more striking than the boldness that her reasons appeared to come first and her feelings afterward.

As the day went on I grew to wish that I had never heard of Aspern's relics, and I cursed the extravagant curiosity that had put John Cumnor on the scent of them. We had more than enough material without them and my predicament was the just punishment of that most fatal of human follies, our not having known when to stop. It was very well to say it was no predicament, that the way out was simple, that I had only to leave Venice by the first train in the morning, after writing a

9. Awning.
1. A fishing village toward the southern end of the Lido.

note to Miss Tita, to be placed in her hand as soon as I got clear of the
house; for it was a strong sign that I was embarrassed that when I tried
to make up the note in my mind in advance (I would put it on paper as
soon as I got home, before going to bed), I could not think of anything
but "How can I thank you for the rare confidence you have placed in
me?" That would never do; it sounded exactly as if an acceptance were
to follow. Of course I might go away without writing a word, but that
would be brutal and my idea was still to exclude brutal solutions. As
my confusion cooled I was lost in wonder at the importance I had
attached to Miss Bordereau's crumpled scraps; the thought of them
became odious to me and I was as vexed with the old witch for the
superstition that had prevented her from destroying them as I was with
myself for having already spent more money than I could afford in
attempting to control their fate. I forget what I did, where I went after
leaving the Lido and at what hour or with what recovery of composure
I made my way back to my boat. I only know that in the afternoon,
when the air was aglow with the sunset, I was standing before the
church of Saints John and Paul and looking up at the small square-
jawed face of Bartolommeo Colleoni, the terrible *condottiere*[2] who sits
so sturdily astride of his huge bronze horse, on the high pedestal on
which Venetian gratitude maintains him. The statue is incomparable,
the finest of all mounted figures, unless that of Marcus Aurelius,[3] who
rides benignant before the Roman Capitol, be finer: but I was not
thinking of that; I only found myself staring at the triumphant captain
as if he had an oracle on his lips. The western light shines into all his
grimness at that hour and makes it wonderfully personal. But he
continued to look far over my head, at the red immersion of another
day—he had seen so many go down into the lagoon through the
centuries—and if he were thinking of battles and stratagems they were
of a different quality from any I had to tell him of. He could not direct
me what to do, gaze up at him as I might. Was it before this or after
that I wandered about for an hour in the small canals, to the continued
stupefaction of my gondolier, who had never seen me so restless and
yet so void of a purpose and could extract from me no order but "Go
anywhere—everywhere—all over the place"? He reminded me that I
had not lunched and expressed therefore respectfully the hope that I
would dine earlier. He had had long periods of leisure during the day,
when I had left the boat and rambled, so that I was not obliged to
consider him, and I told him that that day, for a change, I would touch
no meat. It was an effect of poor Miss Tita's proposal, not altogether
auspicious, that I had quite lost my appetite. I don't know why it

2. The *condottieri* were leaders of mercenary
soldiers in fourteenth- and fifteenth-century
Italy. Here the reference is to the equestrian
statue of one of them, Colleoni (ca. 1400–75),
begun by Verrocchio in 1481 and finished by
Leopardi (1488–96).
3. Roman emperor, stoic philosopher and
writer (121–180).

happened that on this occasion I was more than ever struck with that queer air of sociability, of cousinship and family life, which makes up half the expression of Venice. Without streets and vehicles, the uproar of wheels, the brutality of horses, and with its little winding ways where people crowd together, where voices sound as in the corridors of a house, where the human step circulates as if it skirted the angles of furniture and shoes never wear out, the place has the character of an immense collective apartment, in which Piazza San Marco is the most ornamented corner and palaces and churches, for the rest, play the part of great divans of repose, tables of entertainment, expanses of decoration. And somehow the splendid common domicile, familiar, domestic and resonant, also resembles a theatre, with actors clicking over bridges and, in straggling processions, tripping along fondamen-tas.[4] As you sit in your gondola the footways that in certain parts edge the canals assume to the eye the importance of a stage, meeting it at the same angle, and the Venetian figures, moving to and fro against the battered scenery of their little houses of comedy, strike you as members of an endless dramatic troupe.

I went to bed that night very tired, without being able to compose a letter to Miss Tita. Was this failure the reason why I became conscious the next morning as soon as I awoke of a determination to see the poor lady again the first moment she would receive me? That had something to do with it, but what had still more was the fact that during my sleep a very odd revulsion had taken place in my spirit. I found myself aware of this almost as soon as I opened my eyes; it made me jump out of my bed with the movement of a man who remembers that he has left the house-door ajar or a candle burning under a shelf. Was I still in time to save my goods? That question was in my heart; for what had now come to pass was that in the unconscious cerebration of sleep I had swung back to a passionate appreciation of Miss Bordereau's papers. They were now more precious than ever and a kind of ferocity had come into my desire to possess them. The condition Miss Tita had attached to the possession of them no longer appeared an obstacle worth thinking of, and for an hour, that morning, my repentant imagination brushed it aside. It was absurd that I should be able to invent nothing; absurd to renounce so easily and turn away helpless from the idea that the only way to get hold of the papers was to unite myself to her for life. I would not unite myself and yet I would have them. I must add that by the time I sent down to ask if she would see me I had invented no alternative, though to do so I had had all the time that I was dressing. This failure was humiliating, yet what could

4. The Italian word *fondamento* (foundation) has the masculine plural *fondamenti* and the feminine plural *fondamenta*, referring to abstract and concrete foundations respectively. In Venice *fondamenta* has a specialized meaning: the quays or pathways between canals and buildings. James seems to have added an English plural *s*.

the alternative be? Miss Tita sent back word that I might come; and as I descended the stairs and crossed the sala to her door—this time she received me in her aunt's forlorn parlour—I hoped she would not think my errand was to tell her I accepted her hand. She certainly would have made the day before the reflection that I declined it.

As soon as I came into the room I saw that she had drawn this inference, but I also saw something which had not been in my forecast. Poor Miss Tita's sense of her failure had produced an extraordinary alteration in her, but I had been too full of my literary concupiscence to think of that. Now I perceived it; I can scarcely tell how it startled me. She stood in the middle of the room with a face of mildness bent upon me, and her look of forgiveness, of absolution made her angelic. It beautified her; she was younger; she was not a ridiculous old woman. This optical trick gave her a sort of phantasmagoric brightness, and while I was still the victim of it I heard a whisper somewhere in the depths of my conscience: "Why not, after all—why not?" It seemed to me I was ready to pay the price. Still more distinctly however than the whisper I heard Miss Tita's own voice. I was so struck with the different effect she made upon me that at first I was not clearly aware of what she was saying; then I perceived she had bade me good-bye—she said something about hoping I should be very happy.

"Good-bye—good-bye?" I repeated, with an inflection interrogative and probably foolish.

I saw she did not feel the interrogation, she only heard the words; she had strung herself up to accepting our separation and they fell upon her ear as a proof. "Are you going today?" she asked. "But it doesn't matter, for whenever you go I shall not see you again. I don't want to." And she smiled strangely, with an infinite gentleness. She had never doubted that I had left her the day before in horror. How could she, since I had not come back before night to contradict, even as a simple form, such an idea? And now she had the force of soul—Miss Tita with force of soul was a new conception—to smile at me in her humiliation.

"What shall you do—where shall you go?" I asked.

"Oh, I don't know. I have done the great thing. I have destroyed the papers."

"Destroyed them?" I faltered.

"Yes; what was I to keep them for? I burnt them last night, one by one, in the kitchen."

"One by one?" I repeated, mechanically.

"It took a long time—there were so many." The room seemed to go round me as she said this and a real darkness for a moment descended upon my eyes. When it passed Miss Tita was there still, but the transfiguration was over and she had changed back to a plain, dingy, elderly person. It was in this character she spoke as she said, "I can't stay with you longer, I can't"; and it was in this character that she turned her back upon me, as I had turned mine upon her twenty-four hours before, and moved to the door of her room. Here she did what I had not done when I quitted her—she paused long enough to give me one look. I have never forgotten it and I sometimes still suffer from it, though it was not resentful. No, there was no resentment, nothing hard or vindictive in poor Miss Tita; for when, later, I sent her in exchange for the portrait of Jeffrey Aspern a larger sum of money than I had hoped to be able to gather for her, writing to her that I had sold the picture, she kept it with thanks; she never sent it back. I wrote to her that I had sold the picture, but I admitted to Mrs. Prest, at the time (I met her in London, in the autumn), that it hangs above my writing-table. When I look at it my chagrin at the loss of the letters becomes almost intolerable.

The Pupil

(1891)†

I

The poor young man hesitated and procrastinated: it cost him such an effort to broach the subject of terms, to speak of money to a person who spoke only of feelings and, as it were, of the aristocracy. Yet he was unwilling to take leave, treating his engagement as settled, without some more conventional glance in that direction than he could find an opening for in the manner of the large, affable lady who sat there drawing a pair of soiled *gants de Suède*[1] through a fat, jewelled hand and, at once pressing and gliding, repeated over and over everything but the thing he would have liked to hear. He would have liked to hear the figure of his salary; but just as he was nervously about to sound that note the little boy came back—the little boy Mrs. Moreen had sent out of the room to fetch her fan. He came back without the fan, only with the casual observation that he couldn't find it. As he dropped this cynical confession he looked straight and hard at the candidate for the honour of taking his education in hand. This personage reflected, somewhat grimly, that the first thing he should have to teach his little charge would be to appear to address himself to his mother when he spoke to her—especially not to make her such an improper answer as that.

When Mrs. Moreen bethought herself of this pretext for getting rid of their companion, Pemberton supposed it was precisely to approach the delicate subject of his remuneration. But it had been only to say some things about her son which it was better that a boy of eleven shouldn't catch. They were extravagantly to his advantage, save when she lowered her voice to sigh, tapping her left side familiarly: "And all overclouded by *this*, you know—all at the mercy of a weakness—!" Pemberton gathered that the weakness was in the region of the heart. He had known the poor child was not robust: this was the basis on which he had been invited to treat, through an English lady, an Oxford acquaintance, then at Nice, who happened to know both his needs and those of the amiable American family looking out for something really superior in the way of a resident tutor.

The young man's impression of his prospective pupil, who had first come into the room, as if to see for himself, as soon as Pemberton was

† "The Pupil" was first published in *Longman's Magazine*, March–April 1891. It was reprinted in *The Lesson of the Master* (New York and London: Macmillan and Co., 1892)—the text here used. The American and English issues of this first edition, consisted of the same sheets.
1. Suede gloves.

admitted, was not quite the soft solicitation the visitor had taken for granted. Morgan Moreen was, somehow, sickly without being delicate, and that he looked intelligent (it is true Pemberton wouldn't have enjoyed his being stupid), only added to the suggestion that, as with his big mouth and big ears he really couldn't be called pretty, he might be unpleasant. Pemberton was modest—he was even timid; and the chance that his small scholar might prove cleverer than himself had quite figured, to his nervousness, among the dangers of an untried experiment. He reflected, however, that these were risks one had to run when one accepted a position, as it was called, in a private family; when as yet one's University honours had, pecuniarily speaking, remained barren. At any rate, when Mrs. Moreen got up as if to intimate that, since it was understood he would enter upon his duties within the week she would let him off now, he succeeded, in spite of the presence of the child, in squeezing out a phrase about the rate of payment. It was not the fault of the conscious smile which seemed a reference to the lady's expensive identity, if the allusion did not sound rather vulgar. This was exactly because she became still more gracious to reply: "Oh! I can assure you that all that will be quite regular."

Pemberton only wondered, while he took up his hat, what "all that" was to amount to—people had such different ideas. Mrs. Moreen's words, however, seemed to commit the family to a pledge definite enough to elicit from the child a strange little comment, in the shape of the mocking, foreign ejaculation, "Oh, là-là!"

Pemberton, in some confusion, glanced at him as he walked slowly to the window with his back turned, his hands in his pockets and the air in his elderly shoulders of a boy who didn't play. The young man wondered if he could teach him to play, though his mother had said it would never do and that this was why school was impossible. Mrs. Moreen exhibited no discomfiture; she only continued blandly: "Mr. Moreen will be delighted to meet your wishes. As I told you, he has been called to London for a week. As soon as he comes back you shall have it out with him."

This was so frank and friendly that the young man could only reply, laughing as his hostess laughed: "Oh! I don't imagine we shall have much of a battle."

"They'll give you anything you like," the boy remarked unexpectedly, returning from the window. "We don't mind what anything costs—we live awfully well."

"My darling, you're too quaint!" his mother exclaimed, putting out to caress him a practiced but ineffectual hand. He slipped out of it, but looked with intelligent, innocent eyes at Pemberton, who had already had time to notice that from one moment to the other his small satiric face seemed to change its time of life. At this moment it was infantine; yet it appeared also to be under the influence of curious intuitions and knowledges. Pemberton rather disliked precocity, and he was disappointed to find gleams of it in a disciple not yet in his teens. Nevertheless he divined on the spot that Morgan wouldn't prove a bore. He would prove on the contrary a kind of excitement. This idea held the young man, in spite of a certain repulsion.

"You pompous little person! We're not extravagant!" Mrs. Moreen gayly protested, making another unsuccessful attempt to draw the boy to her side. "You must know what to expect," she went on to Pemberton.

"The less you expect the better!" her companion interposed. "But we *are* people of fashion."

"Only so far as *you* make us so!" Mrs. Moreen mocked, tenderly. "Well, then, on Friday—don't tell me you're superstitious—and mind you don't fail us. Then you'll see us all. I'm so sorry the girls are out. I guess you'll like the girls. And, you know, I've another son, quite different from this one."

"He tries to imitate me," said Morgan to Pemberton.

"He tries? Why, he's twenty years old!" cried Mrs. Moreen.

"You're very witty," Pemberton remarked to the child—a proposition that his mother echoed with enthusiasm, declaring that Morgan's sallies were the delight of the house. The boy paid no heed to this; he only inquired abruptly of the visitor, who was surprised afterwards that he hadn't struck him as offensively forward: "Do you *want* very much to come?"

"Can you doubt it, after such a description of what I shall hear?" Pemberton replied. Yet he didn't want to come at all; he was coming because he had to go somewhere, thanks to the collapse of his fortune at the end of a year abroad, spent on the system of putting his tiny patrimony into a single full wave of experience. He had had his full wave, but he couldn't pay his hotel bill. Moreover, he had caught in the boy's eyes the glimpse of a far-off appeal.

"Well, I'll do the best I can for you," said Morgan; with which he turned away again. He passed out of one of the long windows; Pemberton saw him go and lean on the parapet of the terrace. He remained there while the young man took leave of his mother, who, on Pemberton's looking as if he expected a farewell from him, interposed with: "Leave him, leave him; he's so strange!" Pemberton suspected she was afraid of something he might say. "He's a genius—you'll love him," she added. "He's much the most interesting person in the family." And before he could invent some civility to oppose to this, she wound up with: "But we're all good, you know!"

"He's a genius—you'll love him!" were words that recurred to Pemberton before the Friday, suggesting, among other things that geniuses were not invariably lovable. However, it was all the better if there was an element that would make tutorship absorbing: he had perhaps taken too much for granted that it would be dreary. As he left the villa after his interview, he looked up at the balcony and saw the child leaning over it. "We shall have great larks!" he called up.

Morgan hesitated a moment; then he answered, laughing: "By the time you come back I shall have thought of something witty!"

This made Pemberton say to himself: "After all he's rather nice."

II

On the Friday he saw them all, as Mrs. Moreen had promised, for her husband had come back and the girls and the other son were at home. Mr. Moreen had a white moustache, a confiding manner and, in his buttonhole, the ribbon of a foreign order[2]—bestowed, as Pemberton eventually learned, for services. For what services he never clearly ascertained: this was a point—one of a large number—that Mr. Moreen's manner never confided. What it emphatically did confide was that he was a man of the world. Ulick, the firstborn, was in visible training for the same profession—under the disadvantage as yet, however, of a buttonhole only feebly floral and a moustache with no pretensions to type. The girls had hair and figures and manners and small fat feet, but had never been out alone. As for Mrs. Moreen, Pemberton saw on a nearer view that her elegance was intermittent and her parts didn't always match. Her husband, as she had promised, met with enthusiasm Pemberton's ideas in regard to a salary. The young man had endeavoured to make them modest, and Mr. Moreen confided to him that *he* found them positively meagre. He further assured him that he aspired to be intimate with his children, to be their best friend, and that he was always looking out for them. That was what he went off for, to London and other places—to look out; and this vigilance was the theory of life, as well as the real occupation, of the whole family. They all looked out, for they were very frank on the subject of its being necessary. They desired it to be understood that they were earnest people, and also that their fortune, though quite adequate for earnest people, required the most careful administration. Mr. Moreen, as the parent bird, sought sustenance for the nest. Ulick found sustenance mainly at the club, where Pemberton guessed that it was usually served on green cloth.[3] The girls used to do up their hair and their frocks themselves, and our young man felt appealed to be glad, in regard to Morgan's education, that, though it must naturally be of the best, it didn't cost too much. After a little he *was* glad, forgetting at times his own needs in the interest inspired by the child's

2. In the Middle Ages feudal lords in Europe awarded orders of knighthood to their vassals for bravery in war. In recent, less heroic times membership in an order has been gained by services of various kinds, some less meritorious than others, some even of rather hypothetical merit. The ribbon of Mr. Moreen's order seems to be of that kind. Ulick's buttonhole sports only a flower.

3. Gambling and billiard tables are usually covered in green.

nature and education and the pleasure of making easy terms for him.

During the first weeks of their acquaintance Morgan had been as puzzling as a page in an unknown language—altogether different from the obvious little Anglo-Saxons who had misrepresented childhood to Pemberton. Indeed the whole mystic volume in which the boy had been bound demanded some practice in translation. To-day, after a considerable interval, there is something phantasmagoric, like a prismatic reflection or a serial novel, in Pemberton's memory of the queerness of the Moreens. If it were not for a few tangible tokens—a lock of Morgan's hair, cut by his own hand, and the half-dozen letters he got from him when they were separated—the whole episode and the figures peopling it would seem too inconsequent for anything but dreamland. The queerest thing about them was their success (as it appeared to him for a while at the time), for he had never seen a family so brilliantly equipped for failure. Wasn't it success to have kept him so hatefully long? Wasn't it success to have drawn him in that first morning at *déjeuner*,[4] the Friday he came—it was enough to *make* one superstitious—so that he utterly committed himself, and this not by calculation or a *mot d' ordre*,[5] but by a happy instinct which made them, like a band of gipsies, work so neatly together? They amused him as much as if they had really been a band of gipsies. He was still young and had not seen much of the world—his English years had been intensely usual; therefore the reversed conventions of the Moreens (for they had their standards), struck him as topsyturvy. He had encountered nothing like them at Oxford; still less had any such note been struck to his younger American ear during the four years at Yale in which he had richly supposed himself to be reacting against Puritanism. The reaction of the Moreens, at any rate, went ever so much further. He had thought himself very clever that first day in hitting them all off in his mind with the term "cosmopolite." Later, it seemed feeble and colourless enough—confessedly, helplessly provisional.

However, when he first applied it to them he had a degree of joy—for an instructor he was still empirical—as if from the apprehension that to live with them would really be to see life. Their sociable strangeness was an intimation of that—their chatter of tongues, their gaiety and good humour, their infinite dawdling (they were always getting themselves up, but it took forever, and Pemberton had once found Mr. Moreen shaving in the drawing-room), their French, their Italian and, in the spiced fluency, their cold, tough slices of American. They lived on macaroni and coffee (they had these articles prepared in perfection), but they knew recipes for a hundred other dishes. They overflowed with music and song, were always humming

4. Lunch.   5. Password, secret signal.

and catching each other up, and had a kind of professional acquaintance with continental cities. They talked of "good places" as if they had been strolling players. They had at Nice a villa, a carriage, a piano and a banjo, and they went to official parties. They were a perfect calendar of the "days"[6] of their friends, which Pemberton knew them, when they were indisposed, to get out of bed to go to, and which made the week larger than life when Mrs. Moreen talked of them with Paula and Amy. Their romantic initiations gave their new inmate at first an almost dazzling sense of culture. Mrs. Moreen had translated something, at some former period—an author whom it made Pemberton feel *borné*[7] never to have heard of. They could imitate Venetian and sing Neapolitan, and when they wanted to say something very particular they communicated with each other in an ingenious dialect of their own—a sort of spoken cipher, which Pemberton at first took for Volapuk,[8] but which he learned to understand as he would not have understood Volapuk.

"It's the family language—Ultramoreen," Morgan explained to him drolly enough; but the boy rarely condescended to use it himself, though he attempted colloquial Latin as if he had been a little prelate.

Among all the "days" with which Mrs. Moreen's memory was taxed she managed to squeeze in one of her own, which her friends sometimes forgot. But the house derived a frequented air from the number of fine people who were freely named there and from several mysterious men with foreign titles and English clothes whom Morgan called the princes and who, on sofas with the girls, talked French very loud, as if to show they were saying nothing improper. Pemberton wondered how the princes could ever propose in that tone and so publicly: he took for granted cynically that this was what was desired of them. Then he acknowledged that even for the chance of such an advantage Mrs. Moreen would never allow Paula and Amy to receive alone. These young ladies were not at all timid, but it was just the safeguards that made them so graceful. It was a houseful of Bohemians who wanted tremendously to be Philistines.

In one respect, however, certainly, they achieved no rigour—they were wonderfully amiable and ecstatic about Morgan. It was a genuine tenderness, an artless admiration, equally strong in each. They even praised his beauty, which was small, and were rather afraid of him, as if they recognised that he was of a finer clay. They called him a little angel and a little prodigy and pitied his want of health effusively. Pemberton feared at first that their extravagance would

6. Fixed days of the month or week on which people kept open house.
7. Limited, inexperienced.
8. Volapük was an artificial language invented in 1879 and therefore quite new at the time; it has now been superseded by Esperanto. Morgan, able to use Latin—the international language by which the Catholic clergy and sometimes scholars overcome language barriers—had no taste for his family's private language, although it served him as the subject of a pun: Ultramoreen/ultramarine.

make him hate the boy, but before this happened he had become extravagant himself. Later, when he had grown rather to hate the others, it was a bribe to patience for him that they were at any rate nice about Morgan, going on tiptoe if they fancied he was showing symptoms, and even giving up somebody's "day" to procure him a pleasure. But mixed with this was the oddest wish to make him independent, as if they felt that they were not good enough for him. They passed him over to Pemberton very much as if they wished to force a constructive adoption on the obliging bachelor and shirk altogether a responsibility. They were delighted when they perceived that Morgan liked his preceptor, and could think of no higher praise for the young man. It was strange how they contrived to reconcile the appearance, and indeed the essential fact, of adoring the child with their eagerness to wash their hands of him. Did they want to get rid of him before he should find them out? Pemberton was finding them out month by month. At any rate, the boy's relations turned their backs with exaggerated delicacy, as if to escape the charge of interfering. Seeing in time how little he had in common with them (it was by *them* he first observed it—they proclaimed it with complete humility), his preceptor was moved to speculate on the mysteries of transmission, the far jumps of heredity. Where his detachment from most of the things they represented had come from was more than an observer could say—it certainly had burrowed under two or three generations.

As for Pemberton's own estimate of his pupil, it was a good while before he got the point of view, so little had he been prepared for it by the smug young barbarians to whom the tradition of tutorship, as hitherto revealed to him, had been adjusted. Morgan was scrappy and surprising, deficient in many properties supposed common to the *genus* and abounding in others that were the portion only of the supernaturally clever. One day Pemberton made a great stride: it cleared up the question to perceive that Morgan *was* supernaturally clever and that, though the formula was temporarily meagre, this would be the only assumption on which one could successfully deal with him. He had the general quality of a child for whom life had not been simplified by school, a kind of homebred sensibility which might have been bad for himself but was charming for others, and a whole range of refinement and perception—little musical vibrations as taking as picked-up airs—begotten by wandering about Europe at the tail of his migratory tribe. This might not have been an education to recommend in advance, but its results with Morgan were as palpable as a fine texture. At the same time he had in his composition a sharp spice of stoicism, doubtless the fruit of having had to begin early to bear pain, which produced the impression of pluck and made it of less consequence that he might have been thought at school rather a polyglot little beast. Pemberton indeed quickly found himself rejoicing that school was out of the question: in any million of boys it was probably good for all but one, and Morgan was that millionth. It would have made him comparative and superior—it might have made him priggish. Pemberton would try to be school himself—a bigger seminary than five hundred grazing donkeys; so that, winning no prizes, the boy would remain unconscious and irresponsible and amusing—amusing, because, though life was already intense in his childish nature, freshness still made there a strong draught for jokes. It turned out that even in the still air of Morgan's various disabilities jokes flourished greatly. He was a pale, lean, acute, undeveloped little cosmopolite, who liked intellectual gymnastics and who, also, as regards the behaviour of mankind, had noticed more things than you might suppose, but who nevertheless had his proper playroom of superstitions, where he smashed a dozen toys a day.

III

At Nice once, towards evening, as the pair sat resting in the open air after a walk, looking over the sea at the pink western lights, Morgan said suddenly to his companion: "Do you like it—you know, being with us all in this intimate way?"

"My dear fellow, why should I stay if I didn't?"

"How do I know you will stay? I'm almost sure you won't, very long."

"I hope you don't mean to dismiss me," said Pemberton.

Morgan considered a moment, looking at the sunset. "I think if I did right I ought to."

"Well, I know I'm supposed to instruct you in virtue; but in that case don't do right."

"You're very young—fortunately," Morgan went on, turning to him again.

"Oh yes, compared with you!"

"Therefore, it won't matter so much if you do lose a lot of time."

"That's the way to look at it," said Pemberton accommodatingly.

They were silent a minute; after which the boy asked: "Do you like my father and mother very much?"

"Dear me, yes. They're charming people."

Morgan received this with another silence; then, unexpectedly, familiarly, but at the same time affectionately, he remarked: "You're a jolly old humbug!"

For a particular reason the words made Pemberton change colour. The boy noticed in an instant that he had turned red, whereupon he turned red himself and the pupil and the master exchanged a longish glance in which there was a consciousness of many more things than are usually touched upon, even tacitly, in such a relation. It produced for Pemberton an embarrassment; it raised, in a shadowy form, a question (this was the first glimpse of it), which was destined to play as singular and, as he imagined, owing to the altogether peculiar conditions, an unprecedented part in his intercourse with his little companion. Later, when he found himself talking with this small boy in a way in which few small boys could ever have been talked with, he thought of that clumsy moment on the bench at Nice as the dawn of an understanding that had broadened. What had added to the clumsiness then was that he thought it his duty to declare to Morgan that he might abuse him (Pemberton) as much as he liked, but must never abuse his parents. To this Morgan had the easy reply that he hadn't dreamed of abusing them; which appeared to be true: it put Pemberton in the wrong.

"Then why am I a humbug for saying *I* think them charming?" the young man asked, conscious of a certain rashness.

"Well—they're not *your* parents."

"They love you better than anything in the world—never forget that," said Pemberton.

"Is that why you like them so much?"

"They're very kind to me," Pemberton replied, evasively.

"You *are* a humbug!" laughed Morgan, passing an arm into his tutor's. He leaned against him, looking off at the sea again and swinging his long, thin legs.

"Don't kick my shins," said Pemberton, while he reflected: "Hang it, I can't complain of them to the child!"

"There's another reason, too," Morgan went on, keeping his legs still.

"Another reason for what?"

"Besides their not being your parents."

"I don't understand you," said Pemberton.

"Well, you will before long. All right!"

Pemberton did understand, fully, before long; but he made a fight even with himself before he confessed it. He thought it the oddest thing to have a struggle with the child about. He wondered he didn't detest the child for launching him in such a struggle. But by the time it began the resource of detesting the child was closed to him. Morgan was a special case, but to know him was to accept him on his own odd terms. Pemberton had spent his aversion to special cases before arriving at knowledge. When at last he did arrive he felt that he was in an extreme predicament. Against every interest he had attached himself. They would have to meet things together. Before they went home that evening, at Nice, the boy had said, clinging to his arm:

"Well, at any rate you'll hang on to the last."

"To the last?"

"Till you're fairly beaten."

"*You* ought to be fairly beaten!" cried the young man, drawing him closer.

IV

A year after Pemberton had come to live with them Mr. and Mrs. Moreen suddenly gave up the villa at Nice. Pemberton had got used to suddenness, having seen it practiced on a considerable scale during two jerky little tours—one in Switzerland the first summer, and the other late in the winter, when they all ran down to Florence and then, at the end of ten days, liking it much less than they had intended, straggled back in mysterious depression. They had returned to Nice "for ever," as they said; but this didn't prevent them from squeezing, one rainy, muggy May night, into a second-class railway-carriage— you could never tell by which class they would travel—where Pemberton helped them to stow away a wonderful collection of bundles and bags. The explanation of this manœuvre was that they had determined to spend the summer "in some bracing place;" but in Paris they dropped into a small furnished apartment—a fourth floor in a third-rate avenue, where there was a smell on the staircase and the *portier*[9] was hateful—and passed the next four months in blank indigence.

The better part of this baffled sojourn was for the preceptor and his pupil, who, visiting the Invalides[1] and Notre Dame, the Conciergerie and all the museums, took a hundred remunerative rambles. They learned to know their Paris, which was useful, for they came back another year for a longer stay, the general character of which in Pemberton's memory to-day mixes pitiably and confusedly with that of the first. He sees Morgan's shabby knickerbockers—the everlasting pair that didn't match his blouse and that as he grew longer could only grow faded. He remembers the particular holes in his three or four pair of coloured stockings.

Morgan was dear to his mother, but he never was better dressed than was absolutely necessary—partly, no doubt, by his own fault, for he was as indifferent to his appearance as a German philosopher. "My dear fellow, you *are* coming to pieces," Pemberton would say to him in sceptical remonstrance; to which the child would reply, looking at him serenely up and down: "My dear fellow, so are you! I don't want to cast you in the shade." Pemberton could have no rejoinder for this— the assertion so closely represented the fact. If however the deficiencies of his own wardrobe were a chapter by themselves he didn't like his little charge to look too poor. Later he used to say: "Well, if we are

9. Doorkeeper, janitor.
1. A Paris landmark, originally built to house disabled soldiers, and now a military museum; the tomb of Napoleon I is in an adjoining church. Notre Dame is of course the famous Paris cathedral. The Conciergerie is an ancient prison from which many went to the guillotine during the French Revolution.

poor, why, after all, shouldn't we look it?" and he consoled himself with thinking there was something rather elderly and gentlemanly in Morgan's seediness—it differed from the untidiness of the urchin who plays and spoils his things. He could trace perfectly the degrees by which, in proportion as her little son confined himself to his tutor for society, Mrs. Moreen shrewdly forbore to renew his garments. She did nothing that didn't show, neglected him because he escaped notice, and then, as he illustrated this clever policy, discouraged at home his public appearances. Her position was logical enough—those members of her family who did show had to be showy.

During this period and several others Pemberton was quite aware of how he and his comrade might strike people; wandering languidly through the Jardin des Plantes[2] as if they had nowhere to go, sitting, on the winter days, in the galleries of the Louvre, so splendidly ironical to the homeless, as if for the advantage of the *calorifère*.[3] They joked about it sometimes: it was the sort of joke that was perfectly within the boy's compass. They figured themselves as part of the vast, vague, hand-to-mouth multitude of the enormous city and pretended they were proud of their position in it—it showed them such a lot of life and made them conscious of a sort of democratic brotherhood. If Pemberton could not feel a sympathy in destitution with his small companion (for after all Morgan's fond parents would never have let him really suffer), the boy would at least feel it with him, so it came to the same thing. He used sometimes to wonder what people would think they were—fancy they were looked askance at, as if it might be a suspected case of kidnapping. Morgan wouldn't be taken for a young patrician with a preceptor—he wasn't smart enough; though he might pass for his companion's sickly little brother. Now and then he had a five-franc piece, and except once, when they bought a couple of lovely neckties, one of which he made Pemberton accept, they laid it out scientifically in old books. It was a great day, always spent on the quays, rummaging among the dusty boxes that garnish the parapets.[4] These were occasions that helped them to live, for their books ran low very soon after the beginning of their acquaintance. Pemberton had a good many in England, but he was obliged to write to a friend and ask him kindly to get some fellow to give him something for them.

If the bracing climate was untasted that summer the young man had an idea that at the moment they were about to make a push the cup had been dashed from their lips by a movement of his own. It had been his first blow-out, as he called it, with his patrons; his first successful attempt (though there was little other success about it), to bring them

---

2. The botanical gardens of Paris, founded in the seventeenth century.
3. Heater.
4. In the center of Paris dealers in second-hand books and prints of various kinds still display their wares in large boxes mounted on the parapets along the Seine River.

to a consideration of his impossible position. As the ostensible eve of a costly journey the moment struck him as a good one to put in a signal protest—to present an ultimatum. Ridiculous as it sounded he had never yet been able to compass an uninterrupted private interview with the elder pair or with either of them singly. They were always flanked by their elder children, and poor Pemberton usually had his own little charge at his side. He was conscious of its being a house in which the surface of one's delicacy got rather smudged; nevertheless he had kept the bloom of his scruple against announcing to Mr. and Mrs. Moreen with publicity that he couldn't go on longer without a little money. He was still simple enough to suppose Ulick and Paula and Amy might not know that since his arrival he had only had a hundred and forty francs; and he was magnanimous enough to wish not to compromise their parents in their eyes. Mr. Moreen now listened to him, as he listened to every one and to everything, like a man of the world, and seemed to appeal to him—though not of course too grossly—to try and be a little more of one himself. Pemberton recognised the importance of the character from the advantage it gave Mr. Moreen. He was not even confused, whereas poor Pemberton was more so than there was any reason for. Neither was he surprised—at least any more than a gentleman had to be who freely confessed himself a little shocked, though not, strictly, at Pemberton.

"We must go into this, mustn't we, dear?" he said to his wife. He assured his young friend that the matter should have his very best attention; and he melted into space as elusively as if, at the door, he were taking an inevitable but deprecatory precedence. When, the next moment, Pemberton found himself alone with Mrs. Moreen it was to hear her say: "I see, I see," stroking the roundness of her chin and looking as if she were only hesitating between a dozen easy remedies. If they didn't make their push Mr. Moreen could at least disappear for several days. During his absence his wife took up the subject again spontaneously, but her contribution to it was merely that she had thought all the while they were getting on so beautifully. Pemberton's reply to this revelation was that unless they immediately handed him a substantial sum he would leave them for ever. He knew she would wonder how he would get away, and for a moment expected her to inquire. She didn't, for which he was almost grateful to her, so little was he in a position to tell.

"You won't, you know you won't—you're too interested," she said. "You *are* interested, you know you are, you dear, kind man!" She laughed, with almost condemnatory archness, as if it were a reproach (but she wouldn't insist), while she flirted a soiled pocket-handkerchief at him.

Pemberton's mind was fully made up to quit the house the following week. This would give him time to get an answer to a letter he had despatched to England. If he did nothing of the sort—that is, if he stayed another year and then went away only for three months—it was not merely because before the answer to his letter came (most unsatisfactory when it did arrive), Mr. Moreen generously presented him—again with all the precautions of a man of the world—three hundred francs. He was exasperated to find that Mrs. Moreen was right, that he couldn't bear to leave the child. This stood out clearer for the very reason that, the night of his desperate appeal to his patrons, he had seen fully for the first time where he was. Wasn't it another proof of the success with which those patrons practiced their arts that they had managed to avert for so long the illuminating flash? It descended upon Pemberton with a luridity which perhaps would have struck a spectator as comically excessive, after he had returned to his little servile room, which looked into a close court where a bare, dirty opposite wall took, with the sound of shrill clatter, the reflection of lighted back-windows. He had simply given himself away to a band of adventurers. The idea, the word itself, had a sort of romantic horror for him—he had always lived on such safe lines. Later it assumed a more interesting, almost a soothing, sense: it pointed a moral, and Pemberton could enjoy a moral. The Moreens were adventurers not merely because they didn't pay their debts, because they lived on society, but because their whole view of life, dim and confused and instinctive, like that of clever colour-blind animals, was speculative and rapacious and mean. Oh! they were "respectable," and that only made them more *immondes*. [5] The young man's analysis of them put it at last very simply—they were adventurers because they were abject snobs. That was the completest account of them—it was the law of their being. Even when this truth became vivid to their ingenious inmate he remained unconscious of how much his mind had been prepared for it by the extraordinary little boy who had now become such a complication in his life. Much less could he then calculate on the information he was still to owe to the extraordinary little boy.

V

But it was during the ensuing time that the real problem came up—the problem of how far it was excusable to discuss the turpitude of parents with a child of twelve, of thirteen, of fourteen. Absolutely inexcusable and quite impossible it of course at first appeared; and indeed the question didn't press for a while after Pemberton had received his three hundred francs. They produced a sort of lull, a relief from the sharpest pressure. Pemberton frugally amended his wardrobe and even had a few francs in his pocket. He thought the Moreens looked at him as if he were almost too smart, as if they ought to take

5. Unclean.

care not to spoil him. If Mr. Moreen hadn't been such a man of the
world he would perhaps have said something to him about his
neckties. But Mr. Moreen was always enough a man of the world to let
things pass—he had certainly shown that. It was singular how Pemberton guessed that Morgan, though saying nothing about it, knew
something had happened. But three hundred francs, especially when
one owed money, couldn't last for ever; and when they were gone—
the boy knew when they were gone—Morgan did say something. The
party had returned to Nice at the beginning of the winter, but not to
the charming villa. They went to an hotel, where they stayed three
months, and then they went to another hotel, explaining that they had
left the first because they had waited and waited and couldn't get the
rooms they wanted. These apartments, the rooms they wanted, were
generally very splendid; but fortunately they never *could* get them—
fortunately, I mean, for Pemberton, who reflected always that if they
had got them there would have been still less for educational expenses.
What Morgan said at last was said suddenly, irrelevantly, when the
moment came, in the middle of a lesson, and consisted of the apparently unfeeling words: "You ought to *filer*,[6] you know—you really
ought."

Pemberton stared. He had learnt enough French slang from Morgan to know that to *filer* meant to go away. "Ah, my dear fellow, don't
turn me off!"

Morgan pulled a Greek lexicon toward him (he used a Greek-
German), to look out a word, instead of asking it of Pemberton. "You
can't go on like this, you know."

"Like what, my boy?"

"You know they don't pay you up," said Morgan, blushing and
turning his leaves.

"Don't pay me?" Pemberton stared again and feigned amazement.
"What on earth put that into your head?"

"It has been there a long time," the boy replied, continuing his
search.

Pemberton was silent, then he went on: "I say, what are you
hunting for? They pay me beautifully."

"I'm hunting for the Greek for transparent fiction," Morgan
dropped.

"Find that rather for gross impertinence, and disabuse your mind.
What do I want of money?"

"Oh, that's another question!"

Pemberton hesitated—he was drawn in different ways. The severely
correct thing would have been to tell the boy that such a matter was
none of his business and bid him go on with his lines.[7] But they were

6. Clear out, scram.
7. Go on translating his text, evidently Greek poetry.

really too intimate for that; it was not the way he was in the habit of treating him; there had been no reason it should be. On the other hand Morgan had quite lighted on the truth—he really shouldn't be able to keep it up much longer; therefore why not let him know one's real motive for forsaking him? At the same time it wasn't decent to abuse to one's pupil the family of one's pupil; it was better to misrepresent than to do that. So in reply to Morgan's last exclamation he just declared, to dismiss the subject, that he had received several payments.

"I say—I say!" the boy ejaculated, laughing.

"That's all right," Pemberton insisted. "Give me your written rendering."

Morgan pushed a copybook across the table, and his companion began to read the page, but with something running in his head that made it no sense. Looking up after a minute or two he found the child's eyes fixed on him, and he saw something strange in them. Then Morgan said: "I'm not afraid of the reality."

"I haven't yet seen the thing that you *are* afraid of—I'll do you that justice!"

This came out with a jump (it was perfectly true), and evidently gave Morgan pleasure. "I've thought of it a long time," he presently resumed.

"Well, don't think of it any more."

The child appeared to comply, and they had a comfortable and even an amusing hour. They had a theory that they were very thorough, and yet they seemed always to be in the amusing part of lessons, the intervals between the tunnels, where there were waysides and views. Yet the morning was brought to a violent end by Morgan's suddenly leaning his arms on the table, burying his head in them and bursting into tears. Pemberton would have been startled at any rate; but he was doubly startled because, as it then occurred to him, it was the first time he had ever seen the boy cry. It was rather awful.

The next day, after much thought, he took a decision and, believing it to be just, immediately acted upon it. He cornered Mr. and Mrs. Moreen again and informed them that if, on the spot, they didn't pay him all they owed him, he would not only leave their house, but would tell Morgan exactly what had brought him to it.

"Oh, you *haven't* told him?" cried Mrs. Moreen, with a pacifying hand on her well-dressed bosom.

"Without warning you? For what do you take me?"

Mr. and Mrs. Moreen looked at each other, and Pemberton could see both that they were relieved and that there was a certain alarm in their relief. "My dear fellow," Mr. Moreen demanded, "what use *can* you have, leading the quiet life we all do, for such a lot of money?"— an inquiry to which Pemberton made no answer, occupied as he was in perceiving that what passed in the mind of his patrons was something like: "Oh, then, if we've felt that the child, dear little angel, has judged us and how he regards us, and we haven't been betrayed, he must have guessed—and, in short, it's *general!*" an idea that rather stirred up Mr. and Mrs. Moreen, as Pemberton had desired that it should. At the same time, if he had thought that his threat would do something towards bringing them round, he was disappointed to find they had taken for granted (how little they appreciated his delicacy!) that he had already given them away to his pupil. There was a mystic uneasiness in their parental breasts, and that was the way they had accounted for it. None the less his threat did touch them; for if they had escaped it was only to meet a new danger. Mr. Moreen appealed to Pemberton, as usual, as a man of the world; but his wife had recourse, for the first time since the arrival of their inmate, to a fine *hauteur*, reminding him that a devoted mother, with her child, had arts that protected her against gross misrepresentation.

"I should misrepresent you grossly if I accused you of common honesty!" the young man replied; but as he closed the door behind him sharply, thinking he had not done himself much good, while Mr. Moreen lighted another cigarette, he heard Mrs. Moreen shout after him, more touchingly:

"Oh, you do, you *do*, put the knife to one's throat!"

The next morning, very early, she came to his room. He recognised her knock, but he had no hope that she brought him money; as to which he was wrong, for she had fifty francs in her hand. She squeezed forward in her dressing-gown and he received her in his own, between his bath-tub and his bed. He had been tolerably schooled by this time to the "foreign ways" of his hosts. Mrs. Moreen was zealous, and when she was zealous she didn't care what she did; so she now sat down on his bed, his clothes being on the chairs, and, in her preoccupation, forgot, as she glanced round, to be ashamed of giving him such a nasty room. What Mrs. Moreen was zealous about on this occasion was to persuade him that in the first place she was very good-natured to bring him fifty francs, and, in the second, if he would only see it, he was really too absurd to expect to be *paid*. Wasn't he paid enough, without perpetual money—wasn't he paid by the comfortable, luxurious home that he enjoyed with them all, without a care, an anxiety, a solitary want? Wasn't he sure of his position, and wasn't that everything to a young man like him, quite unknown, with singularly little to show, the ground of whose exorbitant pretensions it was not easy to discover? Wasn't he paid, above all, by the delightful relation he had established with Morgan—quite ideal, as from master to pupil—and by the simple privilege of knowing and living with so amazingly gifted a child, than whom really—she meant literally what she said—there was no better company in Europe? Mrs. Moreen herself took to appealing to him as a man of the world; she said "Voyons, mon cher," and "My dear sir, look here now;" and urged him to be reasonable, putting it before him that it was really a chance for him. She spoke as if, according as he *should* be reasonable, he would prove himself worthy to be her son's tutor and of the extraordinary confidence they had placed in him.

After all, Pemberton reflected, it was only a difference of theory, and the theory didn't matter much. They had hitherto gone on that of remunerated, as now they would go on that of gratuitous, service; but why should they have so many words about it? Mrs. Moreen, however, continued to be convincing; sitting there with her fifty francs she talked and repeated, as women repeat, and bored and irritated him, while he leaned against the wall with his hands in the pockets of his wrapper, drawing it together round his legs and looking over the head of his visitor at the grey negations of his window. She wound up with saying: "You see I bring you a definite proposal."

"A definite proposal?"

"To make our relations regular, as it were—to put them on a comfortable footing."

"I see—it's a system," said Pemberton. "A kind of blackmail."

Mrs. Moreen bounded up, which was what the young man wanted.

"What do you mean by that?"

"You practice on one's fears—one's fears about the child if one should go away."

"And, pray, what would happen to him in that event?" demanded Mrs. Moreen, with majesty.

"Why, he'd be alone with *you*."

"And pray, with whom *should* a child be but with those whom he loves most?"

"If you think that, why don't you dismiss me?"

"Do you pretend that he loves you more than he loves *us*?" cried Mrs. Moreen.

"I think he ought to. I make sacrifices for him. Though I've heard of those *you* make, I don't see them."

Mrs. Moreen stared a moment; then, with emotion, she grasped Pemberton's hand. "*Will* you make it—the sacrifice?"

Pemberton burst out laughing. "I'll see—I'll do what I can—I'll stay a little longer. Your calculation is just—I *do* hate intensely to give him up; I'm fond of him and he interests me deeply, in spite of the inconvenience I suffer. You know my situation perfectly; I haven't a penny in the world, and, occupied as I am with Morgan, I'm unable to earn money."

Mrs. Moreen tapped her undressed arm with her folded bank-note. "Can't you write articles? Can't you translate, as *I* do?"

"I don't know about translating; it's wretchedly paid."

"I am glad to earn what I can," said Mrs. Moreen virtuously, with her head high.

"You ought to tell me who you do it for." Pemberton paused a moment, and she said nothing; so he added: "I've tried to turn off some little sketches, but the magazines won't have them—they're declined with thanks."

"You see then you're not such a phœnix—to have such pretensions," smiled his interlocutress.

"I haven't time to do things properly," Pemberton went on. Then as it came over him that he was almost abjectly good-natured to give these explanations he added: "If I stay on longer it must be on one condition—that Morgan shall know distinctly on what footing I am."

Mrs. Moreen hesitated. "Surely you don't want to show off to a child?"

"To show *you* off, do you mean?"

Again Mrs. Moreen hesitated, but this time it was to produce a still finer flower. "And *you* talk of blackmail!"

"You can easily prevent it," said Pemberton.

"And *you* talk of practicing on fears," Mrs. Moreen continued.

"Yes, there's no doubt I'm a great scoundrel."

His visitor looked at him a moment—it was evident that she was sorely bothered. Then she thrust out her money at him. "Mr. Moreen desired me to give you this on account."

"I'm much obliged to Mr. Moreen; but we have no account."

"You won't take it?"

"That leaves me more free," said Pemberton.

"To poison my darling's mind?" groaned Mrs. Moreen.

"Oh, your darling's mind!" laughed the young man.

She fixed him a moment, and he thought she was going to break out tormentedly, pleadingly. "For God's sake, tell me what *is* in it!" But she checked this impulse—another was stronger. She pocketed the money—the crudity of the alternative was comical—and swept out of the room with the desperate concession: "You may tell him any horror you like!"

VI

A couple of days after this, during which Pemberton had delayed to profit by Mrs. Moreen's permission to tell her son any horror, the two had been for a quarter of an hour walking together in silence when the boy became sociable again with the remark: "I'll tell you how I know it; I know it through Zénobie."

"Zénobie? Who in the world is *she?*"

"A nurse I used to have—ever so many years ago. A charming woman. I liked her awfully, and she liked me."

"There's no accounting for tastes. What is it you know through her?"

"Why, what their idea is. She went away because they didn't pay her. She did like me awfully, and she stayed two years. She told me all about it—that at last she could never get her wages. As soon as they saw how much she liked me they stopped giving her anything. They thought she'd stay for nothing, out of devotion. And she did stay ever so long—as long as she could. She was only a poor girl. She used to send money to her mother. At last she couldn't afford it any longer, and she went away in a fearful rage one night—I mean of course in a rage against *them*. She cried over me tremendously, she hugged me nearly to death. She told me all about it," Morgan repeated. "She told me it was their idea. So I guessed, ever so long ago, that they have had the same idea with you."

"Zénobie was very shrewd," said Pemberton. "And she made you so."

"Oh, that wasn't Zénobie; that was nature. And experience!" Morgan laughed.

"Well, Zénobie was a part of your experience."

"Certainly I was a part of hers, poor dear!" the boy exclaimed. "And I'm a part of yours."

"A very important part. But I don't see how you know that I've been treated like Zénobie."

"Do you take me for an idiot?" Morgan asked. "Haven't I been conscious of what we've been through together?"

"What we've been through?"

"Our privations—our dark days."

"Oh, our days have been bright enough."

Morgan went on in silence for a moment. Then he said: "My dear fellow, you're a hero!"

"Well, you're another!" Pemberton retorted.

"No, I'm not; but I'm not a baby. I won't stand it any longer. You must get some occupation that pays. I'm ashamed, I'm ashamed!" quavered the boy in a little passionate voice that was very touching to Pemberton.

"We ought to go off and live somewhere together," said the young man.

"I'll go like a shot if you'll take me."

"I'd get some work that would keep us both afloat," Pemberton continued.

"So would I. Why shouldn't I work? I ain't such a *crétin!*"[8]

"The difficulty is that your parents wouldn't hear of it," said Pemberton. "They would never part with you; they worship the ground

8. Idiot.

you tread on. Don't you see the proof of it? They don't dislike me; they wish me no harm; they're very amiable people; but they're perfectly ready to treat me badly for your sake."

The silence in which Morgan received this graceful sophistry struck Pemberton somehow as expressive. After a moment Morgan repeated: "You *are* a hero!" Then he added: "They leave me with you altogether. You've all the responsibility. They put me off on you from morning till night. Why, then, should they object to my taking up with you completely? I'd help you."

"They're not particularly keen about my being helped, and they delight in thinking of you as *theirs*. They're tremendously proud of you."

"I'm not proud of them. But you know *that*," Morgan returned.

"Except for the little matter we speak of they're charming people," said Pemberton, not taking up the imputation of lucidity, but wondering greatly at the child's own, and especially at this fresh reminder of something he had been conscious of from the first—the strangest thing in the boy's large little composition, a temper, a sensibility, even a sort of ideal, which made him privately resent the general quality of his kinsfolk. Morgan had in secret a small loftiness which begot an element of reflection, a domestic scorn not imperceptible to his companion (though they never had any talk about it), and absolutely anomalous in a juvenile nature, especially when one noted that it had not made this nature "old-fashioned," as the word is of children— quaint or wizened or offensive. It was as if he had been a little gentleman and had paid the penalty by discovering that he was the only such person in the family. This comparison didn't make him vain; but it could make him melancholy and a trifle austere. When Pemberton guessed at these young dimnesses he saw him serious and gallant, and was partly drawn on and partly checked, as if with a scruple, by the charm of attempting to sound the little cool shallows which were quickly growing deeper. When he tried to figure to himself the morning twilight of childhood, so as to deal with it safely, he perceived that it was never fixed, never arrested, that ignorance, at the instant one touched it, was already flushing faintly into knowledge, that there was nothing that at a given moment you could say a clever child didn't know. It seemed to him that *he* both knew too much to imagine Morgan's simplicity and too little to disembroil his tangle.

The boy paid no heed to his last remark; he only went on: "I should have spoken to them about their idea, as I call it, long ago, if I hadn't been sure what they would say."

"And what would they say?"

"Just what they said about what poor Zénobie told me—that it was a horrid, dreadful story, that they had paid her every penny they owed her."

"Well, perhaps they had," said Pemberton.

"Perhaps they've paid you!"

"Let us pretend they have, and *n'en parlons plus.*"[9]

"They accused her of lying and cheating," Morgan insisted perversely. "That's why I don't want to speak to them."

"Lest they should accuse me, too?"

To this Morgan made no answer, and his companion, looking down at him (the boy turned his eyes, which had filled, away), saw that he couldn't have trusted himself to utter.

"You're right. Don't squeeze them," Pemberton pursued. "Except for that, they *are* charming people."

"Except for *their* lying and *their* cheating?"

"I say—I say!" cried Pemberton, imitating a little tone of the lad's which was itself an imitation.

"We must be frank, at the last; we *must* come to an understanding," said Morgan, with the importance of the small boy who lets himself think he is arranging great affairs—almost playing at shipwreck or at Indians. "I know all about everything," he added.

"I daresay your father has his reasons," Pemberton observed, too vaguely, as he was aware.

"For lying and cheating?"

"For saving and managing and turning his means to the best account. He has plenty to do with his money. You're an expensive family."

"Yes, I'm very expensive," Morgan rejoined, in a manner which made his preceptor burst out laughing.

"He's saving for *you*," said Pemberton. "They think of you in everything they do."

"He might save a little—" The boy paused. Pemberton waited to hear what. Then Morgan brought out oddly: "A little reputation."

"Oh, there's plenty of that. That's all right!"

"Enough of it for the people they know, no doubt. The people they know are awful."

"Do you mean the princes? We mustn't abuse the princes."

"Why not? They haven't married Paula—they haven't married Amy. They only clean out Ulick."

"You *do* know everything!" Pemberton exclaimed.

"No, I don't, after all. I don't know what they live on, or how they live, or *why* they live! What have they got and how did they get it? Are they rich, are they poor, or have they a *modeste aisance?*[1] Why are they always chiveying about—living one year like ambassadors and the next like paupers? Who are they, any way, and what are they? I've thought of all that—I've thought of a lot of things. They're so beastly

9. Let's say no more about it.   1. Are they comfortably off?

worldly. That's what I hate most—oh, I've *seen* it! All they care about is to make an appearance and to pass for something or other. What do they want to pass for? What *do* they, Mr. Pemberton?"

"You pause for a reply," said Pemberton, treating the inquiry as a joke, yet wondering too, and greatly struck with the boy's intense, if imperfect, vision. "I haven't the least idea."

"And what good does it do? Haven't I seen the way people treat them—the 'nice' people, the ones they want to know? They'll take anything from them—they'll lie down and be trampled on. The nice ones hate that—they just sicken them. You're the only really nice person we know."

"Are you sure? They don't lie down for me!"

"Well, you shan't lie down for them. You've got to go—that's what you've got to do." said Morgan.

"And what will become of you?"

"Oh, I'm growing up. I shall get off before long. I'll see you later."

"You had better let me finish you," Pemberton urged, lending himself to the child's extraordinarily competent attitude.

Morgan stopped in their walk, looking up at him. He had to look up much less than a couple of years before—he had grown, in his loose leanness, so long and high. "Finish me?" he echoed.

"There are such a lot of jolly things we can do together yet. I want to turn you out—I want you to do me credit."

Morgan continued to look at him. "To give you credit—do you mean?"

"My dear fellow, you're too clever to live."

"That's just what I'm afraid you think. No, no; it isn't fair—I can't endure it. We'll part next week. The sooner it's over the sooner to sleep."

"If I hear of anything—any other chance, I promise to go," said Pemberton.

Morgan consented to consider this. "But you'll be honest," he demanded; "you won't pretend you haven't heard?"

"I'm much more likely to pretend I have."

"But what can you hear of, this way, stuck in a hole with us? You ought to be on the spot, to go to England—you ought to go to America."

"One would think you were *my* tutor!" said Pemberton.

Morgan walked on, and after a moment he began again: "Well, now that you know that I know and that we look at the facts and keep nothing back—it's much more comfortable, isn't it?"

"My dear boy, it's so amusing, so interesting, that it surely will be quite impossible for me to forego such hours as these."

This made Morgan stop once more. "You *do* keep something back. Oh, you're not straight—I am!"

"Why am I not straight?"

"Oh, you've got your idea!"

"My idea?"

"Why, that I probably sha'n't live, and that you can stick it out till I'm removed."

"You *are* too clever to live!" Pemberton repeated.

"I call it a mean idea," Morgan pursued. "But I shall punish you by the way I hang on."

"Look out or I'll poison you!" Pemberton laughed.

"I'm stronger and better every year. Haven't you noticed that there hasn't been a doctor near me since you came?"

"*I'm* your doctor," said the young man, taking his arm and drawing him on again.

Morgan proceeded, and after a few steps he gave a sigh of mingled weariness and relief. "Ah, now that we look at the facts, it's all right!"

VII

They looked at the facts a good deal after this; and one of the first consequences of their doing so was that Pemberton stuck it out, as it were, for the purpose. Morgan made the facts so vivid and so droll, and at the same time so bald and so ugly, that there was fascination in talking them over with him, just as there would have been heartlessness in leaving him alone with them. Now that they had such a number of perceptions in common it was useless for the pair to pretend that they didn't judge such people; but the very judgment, and the exchange of perceptions, created another tie. Morgan had never been so interesting as now that he himself was made plainer by the sidelight of these confidences. What came out in it most was the soreness of his characteristic pride. He had plenty of that, Pemberton felt—so much that it was perhaps well it should have had to take some early bruises. He would have liked his people to be gallant, and he had waked up too soon to the sense that they were perpetually swallowing humble-pie. His mother would consume any amount, and his father would consume even more than his mother. He had a theory that Ulick had wriggled out of an "affair" at Nice: there had once been a flurry at home, a regular panic, after which they all went to bed and took medicine, not to be accounted for on any other supposition. Morgan had a romantic imagination, fed by poetry and history, and he would have liked those who "bore his name" (as he used to say to Pemberton with the humour that made his sensitiveness manly), to have a proper spirit. But their one idea was to get in with people who didn't want them and to take snubs as if they were honourable scars. Why people didn't want them more he didn't know—that was people's own affair; after all they were not superficially repulsive—they were a hundred times cleverer than most of the dreary grandees, the "poor swells" they rushed about Europe to catch up with. "After all, they *are* amusing—they are!" Morgan used to say, with the wisdom of the ages. To which Pemberton always replied: "Amusing—the great Moreen troupe? Why, they're altogether delightful; and if it were not for the hitch that you and I (feeble performers!) make in the *ensemble*, they would carry everything before them."

What the boy couldn't get over was that this particular blight seemed, in a tradition of self-respect, so undeserved and so arbitrary. No doubt people had a right to take the line they liked; but why should *his* people have liked the line of pushing and toadying and lying and cheating? What had their forefathers—all decent folk, so far as he knew—done to them, or what had *he* done to them? Who had poisoned their blood with the fifth-rate social ideal, the fixed idea of making smart acquaintances and getting into the *monde chic*, [2] especially when it was foredoomed to failure and exposure? They showed so what they were after; that was what made the people they wanted not want *them*. And never a movement of dignity, never a throb of shame at looking each other in the face, never any independence or resentment or disgust. If his father or his brother would only knock some one down once or twice a year! Clever as they were they never guessed how they appeared. They were good-natured, yes—as good-natured as Jews at the doors of clothing-shops! But was that the model one wanted one's family to follow? Morgan had dim memories of an old grandfather, the maternal, in New York, whom he had been taken across the ocean to see, at the age of five: a gentleman with a high neckcloth and a good deal of pronunciation, who wore a dress-coat in the morning, which made one wonder what he wore in the evening, and had, or was supposed to have, "property" and something to do with the Bible Society. [3] It couldn't have been but that *he* was a good type. Pemberton himself remembered Mrs. Clancy, a widowed sister of Mr. Moreen's, who was as irritating as a moral tale and had paid a fortnight's visit to the family at Nice shortly after he came to live with them. She was "pure and refined," as Amy said, over the banjo, and had the air of not knowing what they meant and of keeping something back. Pemberton judged that what she kept back was an approval of many of their ways; therefore it was to be supposed that she too was of a good type, and that Mr. and Mrs. Moreen and Ulick and Paula and Amy might easily have been better if they would.

But that they wouldn't was more and more perceptible from day to day. They continued to "chivey," as Morgan called it, and in due time became aware of a variety of reasons for proceeding to Venice. They

2. Fashionable society, smart set.
3. A society for translating and disseminating Bibles, going back to an organization started in early eighteenth century Germany, from where it spread to England and, in the nineteenth century, to the United States. The Gideons International (founded 1898), which places Bibles in hotel rooms, is an offshoot.

mentioned a great many of them—they were always strikingly frank, and had the brightest friendly chatter, at the late foreign breakfast in especial, before the ladies had made up their faces, when they leaned their arms on the table, had something to follow the *demi-tasse*,[4] and, in the heat of familiar discussion as to what they "really ought" to do, fell inevitably into the languages in which they could *tutoyer*.[5] Even Pemberton liked them, then; he could endure even Ulick when he heard him give his little flat voice for the "sweet sea-city." That was what made him have a sneaking kindness for them—that they were so out of the workaday world and kept him so out of it. The summer had waned when, with cries of ecstasy, they all passed out on the balcony that overhung the Grand Canal; the sunsets were splendid—the Dorringtons had arrived. The Dorringtons were the only reason they had not talked of at breakfast; but the reasons that they didn't talk of at breakfast always came out in the end. The Dorringtons, on the other hand, came out very little; or else, when they did, they stayed—as was natural—for hours, during which periods Mrs. Moreen and the girls sometimes called at their hotel (to see if they had returned) as many as three times running. The gondola was for the ladies; for in Venice too there were "days," which Mrs. Moreen knew in their order an hour after she arrived. She immediately took one herself, to which the Dorringtons never came, though on a certain occasion when Pemberton and his pupil were together at St. Mark's—where, taking the best walks they had ever had and haunting a hundred churches, they spent a great deal of time—they saw the old lord turn up with Mr. Moreen and Ulick, who showed him the dim basilica as if it belonged to them. Pemberton noted how much less, among its curiosities, Lord Dorrington carried himself as a man of the world; wondering too whether, for such services, his companions took a fee from him. The autumn, at any rate, waned, the Dorringtons departed, and Lord Verschoyle, the eldest son, had proposed neither for Amy nor for Paula.

One sad November day, while the wind roared round the old palace and the rain lashed the lagoon, Pemberton, for exercise and even somewhat for warmth (the Moreens were horribly frugal about fires— it was a cause of suffering to their inmate), walked up and down the big bare *sala*[6] with his pupil. The scagliola floor was cold, the high battered casements shook in the storm, and the stately decay of the place was unrelieved by a particle of furniture. Pemberton's spirits were low, and it came over him that the fortune of the Moreens was now even lower. A blast of desolation, a prophecy of disaster and

4. Small cup of coffee, usually after dinner, but here at the end of a late breakfast.
5. Use the informal second-person singular *tu* in French. Here it means that the Moreens fell to talking French or, since they are polyglot, some other language making a similar distinction between formal (polite) and informal (familiar), like German or Italian. The "sweet sea-city," below, refers to Venice.
6. Hallway.

disgrace, seemed to draw through the comfortless hall. Mr. Moreen and Ulick were in the Piazza, looking out for something, strolling drearily, in mackintoshes, under the arcades; but still, in spite of mackintoshes, unmistakable men of the world. Paula and Amy were in bed—it might have been thought they were staying there to keep warm. Pemberton looked askance at the boy at his side, to see to what extent he was conscious of these portents. But Morgan, luckily for him, was now mainly conscious of growing taller and stronger and indeed of being in his fifteenth year. This fact was intensely interesting to him—it was the basis of a private theory (which, however, he had imparted to his tutor) that in a little while he should stand on his own feet. He considered that the situation would change—that, in short, he should be "finished," grown up, producible in the world of affairs and ready to prove himself of sterling ability. Sharply as he was capable, at times, of questioning his circumstances, there were happy hours when he was as superficial as a child; the proof of which was his fundamental assumption that he should presently go to Oxford, to Pemberton's college, and, aided and abetted by Pemberton, do the most wonderful things. It vexed Pemberton to see how little, in such a project, he took account of ways and means: on other matters he was so sceptical about them. Pemberton tried to imagine the Moreens at Oxford, and fortunately failed; yet unless they were to remove there as a family there would be no *modus vivendi* for Morgan. How could he live without an allowance, and where was the allowance to come from? He (Pemberton) might live on Morgan; but how could Morgan live on him? What was to become of him anyhow? Somehow, the fact that he was a big boy now, with better prospects of health, made the question of his future more difficult. So long as he was frail the consideration that he inspired seemed enough of an answer to it. But at the bottom of Pemberton's heart was the recognition of his probably being strong enough to live and not strong enough to thrive. He himself, at any rate, was in a period of natural, boyish rosiness about all this, so that the beating of the tempest seemed to him only the voice of life and the challenge of fate. He had on his shabby little overcoat, with the collar up, but he was enjoying his walk.

It was interrupted at last by the appearance of his mother at the end of the *sala*. She beckoned to Morgan to come to her, and while Pemberton saw him, complacent, pass down the long vista, over the damp false marble, he wondered what was in the air. Mrs. Moreen said a word to the boy and made him go into the room she had quitted. Then, having closed the door after him, she directed her steps swiftly to Pemberton. There *was* something in the air, but his wildest flight of fancy wouldn't have suggested what it proved to be. She signified that she had made a pretext to get Morgan out of the way, and then she inquired—without hesitation—if the young man could lend her sixty francs. While, before bursting into a laugh, he stared at her with surprise, she declared that she was awfully pressed for the money; she was desperate for it—it would save her life.

"Dear lady, *c'est trop fort!*"[7] Pemberton laughed. "Where in the world do you suppose I should get sixty francs, *du train dont vous allez?*"[8]

"I thought you worked—wrote things; don't they pay you?"

"Not a penny."

"Are you such a fool as to work for nothing?"

"You ought surely to know that."

Mrs. Moreen stared an instant, then she coloured a little. Pemberton saw she had quite forgotten the terms—if "terms" they could be called—that he had ended by accepting from herself; they had burdened her memory as little as her conscience. "Oh, yes, I see what you mean—you have been very nice about that; but why go back to it so often?" She had been perfectly urbane with him ever since the rough scene of explanation in his room, the morning he made her accept *his* "terms"—the necessity of his making his case known to Morgan. She had felt no resentment, after seeing that there was no danger of Morgan's taking the matter up with her. Indeed, attributing this immunity to the good taste of his influence with the boy, she had once said to Pemberton: "My dear fellow; it's an immense comfort you're a gentleman." She repeated this, in substance, now. "Of course you're a gentleman—that's a bother the less!" Pemberton reminded her that he had not "gone back" to anything; and she also repeated her prayer that, somewhere and somehow, he would find her sixty francs. He took the liberty of declaring that if he could find them it wouldn't be to lend them to *her*—as to which he consciously did himself injustice, knowing that if he had them he would certainly place them in her hand. He accused himself, at bottom and with some truth, of a fantastic, demoralised sympathy with her. If misery made strange bedfellows it also made strange sentiments. It was moreover a part of the demoralisation and of the general bad effect of living with such people that one had to make rough retorts, quite out of the tradition of good manners. "Morgan, Morgan, to what pass have I come for you?" he privately exclaimed, while Mrs. Moreen floated voluminously down the *sala* again, to liberate the boy; groaning, as she went, that everything was too odious.

Before the boy was liberated there came a thump at the door communicating with the staircase, followed by the apparition of a dripping youth who poked in his head. Pemberton recognised him as the bearer of a telegram and recognised the telegram as addressed to himself. Morgan came back as, after glancing at the signature (that of a

<hr />

7. That's really too much!   8. At the rate you go on.

friend in London), he was reading the words: "Found jolly job for you—engagement to coach opulent youth on own terms. Come immediately." The answer, happily, was paid, and the messenger waited. Morgan, who had drawn near, waited too, and looked hard at Pemberton; and Pemberton, after a moment, having met his look, handed him the telegram. It was really by wise looks (they knew each other so well), that, while the telegraph-boy, in his waterproof cape, made a great puddle on the floor, the thing was settled between them. Pemberton wrote the answer with a pencil against the frescoed wall, and the messenger departed. When he had gone Pemberton said to Morgan:

"I'll make a tremendous charge; I'll earn a lot of money in a short time, and we'll live on it."

"Well, I hope the opulent youth will be stupid—he probably will—" Morgan parenthesised, "and keep you a long time."

"Of course, the longer he keeps me the more we shall have for our old age."

"But suppose *they* don't pay you!" Morgan awfully suggested.

"Oh, there are not two such—!" Pemberton paused, he was on the point of using an invidious term. Instead of this he said "two such chances."

Morgan flushed—the tears came to his eyes. "*Dites toujours,*[9] two such rascally crews!" Then, in a different tone, he added: "Happy opulent youth!"

"Not if he's stupid!"

"Oh, they're happier then. But you can't have everything, can you?" the boy smiled.

Pemberton held him, his hands on his shoulders. "What will become of *you*, what will you do?" He thought of Mrs. Moreen, desperate for sixty francs.

"I shall turn into a man." And then, as if he recognised all the bearings of Pemberton's allusion: "I shall get on with them better when you're not here."

"Ah, don't say that—it sounds as if I set you against them!"

"You do—the sight of you. It's all right; you know what I mean. I shall be beautiful. I'll take their affairs in hand; I'll marry my sisters."[1]

"You'll marry yourself!" joked Pemberton; as high, rather tense pleasantry would evidently be the right, or the safest, tone for their separation.

It was, however, not purely in this strain that Morgan suddenly asked: "But I say—how will you get to your jolly job? You'll have to telegraph to the opulent youth for money to come on."

Pemberton bethought himself. "They won't like that, will they?"

9. Go ahead, say it.   1. Marry them off.

"Oh, look out for them!"

Then Pemberton brought out his remedy. "I'll go to the American Consul; I'll borrow some money of him—just for the few days, on the strength of the telegram."

Morgan was hilarious. "Show him the telegram—then stay and keep the money!"

Pemberton entered into the joke enough to reply that, for Morgan, he was really capable of that; but the boy, growing more serious, and to prove that he hadn't meant what he said, not only hurried him off to the Consulate (since he was to start that evening, as he had wired to his friend), but insisted on going with him. They splashed through the tortuous perforations[2] and over the humpbacked bridges, and they passed through the Piazza, where they saw Mr. Moreen and Ulick go into a jeweller's shop. The Consul proved accommodating (Pemberton said it wasn't the letter, but Morgan's grand air), and on their way back they went into St. Mark's for a hushed ten minutes. Later they took up and kept up the fun of it to the very end; and it seemed to Pemberton a part of that fun that Mrs. Moreen, who was very angry when he had announced to her his intention, should charge him, grotesquely and vulgarly, and in reference to the loan she had vainly endeavoured to effect, with bolting lest they should "get something out" of him. On the other hand he had to do Mr. Moreen and Ulick the justice to recognise that when, on coming in, *they* heard the cruel news, they took it like perfect men of the world.

VIII

When Pemberton got at work with the opulent youth, who was to be taken in hand for Balliol,[3] he found himself unable to say whether he was really an idiot or it was only, on his own part, the long association with an intensely living little mind that made him seem so. From Morgan he heard half-a-dozen times: the boy wrote charming young letters, a patchwork of tongues, with indulgent postscripts in the family Volapuk and, in little squares and rounds and crannies of the text, the drollest illustrations—letters that he was divided between the impulse to show his present disciple, as a kind of wasted incentive, and the sense of something in them that was profanable by publicity. The opulent youth went up,[4] in due course, and failed to pass; but it seemed to add to the presumption that brilliancy was not expected of him all at once that his parents, condoning the lapse, which they good-naturedly treated as little as possible as if it were Pemberton's,

2. Pedestrian traffic between Venetian canals often follows winding footpaths, sometimes cut through walls and buildings.
3. Tutored in preparation for the entrance examination to Balliol College (founded before 1268), probably the most distinguished college in Oxford.
4. Went up to Oxford to take the examination.

should have sounded the rally again, begged the young coach to keep his pupil in hand another year.

The young coach was now in a position to lend Mrs. Moreen sixty francs, and he sent her a post-office order for the amount. In return for his favour he received a frantic, scribbled line from her: "Implore you to come back instantly—Morgan dreadfully ill." They were on the rebound, once more in Paris—often as Pemberton had seen them depressed he had never seen them crushed—and communication was therefore rapid. He wrote to the boy to ascertain the state of his health, but he received no answer to his letter. Accordingly he took an abrupt leave of the opulent youth and, crossing the Channel, alighted at the small hotel, in the quarter of the Champs Elysées, of which Mrs. Moreen had given him the address. A deep if dumb dissatisfaction with this lady and her companions bore him company: they couldn't be vulgarly honest, but they could live at hotels, in velvety *entresols*, amid a smell of burnt pastilles, in the most expensive city in Europe. When he had left them, in Venice, it was with an irrepressible suspicion that something was going to happen; but the only thing that had happened was that they succeeded in getting away. "How is he? where is he?" he asked of Mrs. Moreen; but before she could speak, these questions were answered by the pressure round his neck of a pair of arms, in shrunken sleeves, which were perfectly capable of an effusive young foreign squeeze.

"Dreadfully ill—I don't see it!" the young man cried. And then, to Morgan: "Why on earth didn't you relieve me? Why didn't you answer my letter?"

Mrs. Moreen declared that when she wrote he was very bad, and Pemberton learned at the same time from the boy that he had answered every letter he had received. This led to the demonstration that Pemberton's note had been intercepted. Mrs. Moreen was prepared to see the fact exposed, as Pemberton perceived, the moment he faced her, that she was prepared for a good many other things. She was prepared above all to maintain that she had acted from a sense of duty, that she was enchanted she had got him over, whatever they might say; and that it was useless of him to pretend that he didn't *know*, in all his bones, that his place at such a time was with Morgan. He had taken the boy away from them, and now he had no right to abandon him. He had created for himself the gravest responsibilities; he must at least abide by what he had done.

"Taken him away from you?" Pemberton exclaimed indignantly.

"Do it—do it, for pity's sake; that's just what I want. I can't stand *this*—and such scenes. They're treacherous!" These words broke from Morgan, who had intermitted his embrace, in a key which made Pemberton turn quickly to him, to see that he suddenly seated himself, was breathing with evident difficulty and was very pale.

"Now do you say he's not ill—my precious pet?" shouted his mother, dropping on her knees before him with clasped hands, but touching him no more than if he had been a gilded idol. "It will pass—it's only for an instant; but don't say such dreadful things!"

"I'm all right—all right," Morgan panted to Pemberton, whom he sat looking up at with a strange smile, his hands resting on either side of the sofa.

"Now do you pretend I've been treacherous—that I've deceived?" Mrs. Moreen flashed at Pemberton as she got up.

"It isn't *he* says it, it's I!" the boy returned, apparently easier, but sinking back against the wall; while Pemberton, who had sat down beside him, taking his hand, bent over him.

"Darling child, one does what one can; there are so many things to consider," urged Mrs. Moreen. "It's his *place*—his only place. You see *you* think it is now."

"Take me away—take me away," Morgan went on, smiling to Pemberton from his white face.

"Where shall I take you, and how—oh, *how*, my boy?" the young man stammered, thinking of the rude way in which his friends in London held that, for his convenience, and without a pledge of instantaneous return, he had thrown them over; of the just resentment with which they would already have called in a successor, and of the little help as regarded finding fresh employment that resided for him in the flatness of his having failed to pass his pupil.

"Oh, we'll settle that. You used to talk about it," said Morgan. "If we can only go, all the rest's a detail."

"Talk about it as much as you like, but don't think you can attempt it. Mr. Moreen would never consent—it would be so precarious," Pemberton's hostess explained to him. Then to Morgan she explained: "It would destroy our peace, it would break our hearts. Now that he's back it will be all the same again. You'll have your life, your work and your freedom, and we'll all be happy as we used to be. You'll bloom and grow perfectly well, and we won't have any more silly experiments, will we? They're too absurd. It's Mr. Pemberton's place—every one in his place. You in yours, your papa in his, me in mine—*n'est-ce pas, chéri?*[5] We'll all forget how foolish we've been, and we'll have lovely times."

She continued to talk and to surge vaguely about the little draped, stuffy *salon*, while Pemberton sat with the boy, whose colour gradually came back; and she mixed up her reasons, dropping that there were going to be changes, that the other children might scatter (who knew?—Paula had her ideas), and that then it might be fancied how much the poor old parent-birds would want the little nestling. Morgan

---

5. Isn't that right, darling? Don't you agree?

looked at Pemberton, who wouldn't let him move; and Pemberton knew exactly how he felt at hearing himself called a little nestling. He admitted that he had had one or two bad days, but he protested afresh against the iniquity of his mother's having made them the ground of an appeal to poor Pemberton. Poor Pemberton could laugh now, apart from the comicality of Mrs. Moreen's producing so much philosophy for her defence (she seemed to shake it out of her agitated petticoats, which knocked over the light gilt chairs), so little did the sick boy strike him as qualified to repudiate any advantage.

He himself was in for it, at any rate. He should have Morgan on his hands again indefinitely; though indeed he saw the lad had a private theory to produce which would be intended to smooth this down. He was obliged to him for it in advance; but the suggested amendment didn't keep his heart from sinking a little, any more than it prevented him from accepting the prospect on the spot, with some confidence moreover that he would do so even better if he could have a little supper. Mrs. Moreen threw out more hints about the changes that were to be looked for, but she was such a mixture of smiles and shudders (she confessed she was very nervous), that he couldn't tell whether she were in high feather or only in hysterics. If the family were really at last going to pieces why shouldn't she recognise the necessity of pitching Morgan into some sort of lifeboat? This presumption was fostered by the fact that they were established in luxurious quarters in the capital of pleasure; that was exactly where they naturally *would* be established in view of going to pieces. Moreover didn't she mention that Mr. Moreen and the others were enjoying themselves at the opera with Mr. Granger, and wasn't *that* also precisely where one would look for them on the eve of a smash? Pemberton gathered that Mr. Granger was a rich, vacant American—a big bill with a flourishy heading and no items; so that one of Paula's "ideas" was probably that this time she had really done it, which was indeed an unprecedented blow to the general cohesion. And if the cohesion was to terminate what was to become of poor Pemberton? He felt quite enough bound up with them to figure, to his alarm, as a floating spar in case of a wreck.

It was Morgan who eventually asked if no supper had been ordered for him; sitting with him below, later, at the dim, delayed meal, in the presence of a great deal of corded green plush, a plate of ornamental biscuit and a languor marked on the part of the waiter. Mrs. Moreen had explained that they had been obliged to secure a room for the visitor out of the house; and Morgan's consolation (he offered it while Pemberton reflected on the nastiness of lukewarm sauces), proved to be, largely, that this circumstance would facilitate their escape. He talked of their escape (recurring to it often afterwards), as if they were making up a "boy's book" together. But he likewise expressed his sense that there was something in the air, that the Moreens couldn't keep it up much longer. In point of fact, as Pemberton was to see, they kept it up for five or six months. All the while, however, Morgan's contention was designed to cheer him. Mr. Moreen and Ulick, whom he had met the day after his return, accepted that return like perfect men of the world. If Paula and Amy treated it even with less formality an allowance was to be made for them, inasmuch as Mr. Granger had not come to the opera after all. He had only placed his box at their service, with a bouquet for each of the party; there was even one apiece, embittering the thought of his profusion, for Mr. Moreen and Ulick. "They're all like that," was Morgan's comment; "at the very last, just when we think we've got them fast, we're chucked!"

Morgan's comments, in these days, were more and more free; they even included a large recognition of the extraordinary tenderness with which he had been treated while Pemberton was away. Oh, yes, they couldn't do enough to be nice to him, to show him they had him on their mind and make up for his loss. That was just what made the whole thing so sad, and him so glad, after all, of Pemberton's return—he had to keep thinking of their affection less, had less sense of obligation. Pemberton laughed out at this last reason, and Morgan blushed and said: "You know what I mean." Pemberton knew perfectly what he meant; but there were a good many things it didn't make any clearer. This episode of his second sojourn in Paris stretched itself out wearily, with their resumed readings and wanderings and maunderings, their potterings on the quays, their hauntings of the museums, their occasional lingerings in the Palais Royal,[6] when the first sharp weather came on and there was a comfort in warm emanations, before Chevet's wonderful succulent window. Morgan wanted to hear a great deal about the opulent youth—he took an immense interest in him. Some of the details of his opulence—Pemberton could spare him none of them—evidently intensified the boy's appreciation of all his friend had given up to come back to him; but in addition to the greater reciprocity established by such a renunciation he had always his little brooding theory, in which there was a frivolous gaiety too, that their long probation was drawing to a close. Morgan's conviction that the Moreens couldn't go on much longer kept pace with the unexpended impetus with which, from month to month, they did go on. Three weeks after Pemberton had rejoined them they went on to another hotel, a dingier one than the first; but Morgan rejoiced that his tutor had at least still not sacrificed the advantage of a

6. The Palais Royal, a large complex of buildings and gardens, dates back to the early seventeenth century. In the course of its lively history it has housed kings and nobles, courtesans and gamblers, a theater, and fashionable shops and restaurants. Chevet's was probably a candy or confectioner's store. Today the Palais Royal houses government offices and shops with less succulent wares, like antiques and stamp collections.

room outside. He clung to the romantic utility of this when the day, or rather the night, should arrive for their escape.

For the first time, in this complicated connection, Pemberton felt sore and exasperated. It was, as he had said to Mrs. Moreen in Venice, *trop fort*—everything was *trop fort*. He could neither really throw off his blighting burden nor find in it the benefit of a pacified conscience or of a rewarded affection. He had spent all the money that he had earned in England, and he felt that his youth was going and that he was getting nothing back for it. It was all very well for Morgan to seem to consider that he would make up to him for all inconveniences by settling himself upon him permanently—there was an irritating flaw in such a view. He saw what the boy had in his mind; the conception that as his friend had had the generosity to come back to him he must show his gratitude by giving him his life. But the poor friend didn't desire the gift—what could he do with Morgan's life? Of course at the same time that Pemberton was irritated he remembered the reason, which was very honourable to Morgan and which consisted simply of the fact that he was perpetually making one forget that he was after all only a child. If one dealt with him on a different basis one's misadventures were one's own fault. So Pemberton waited in a queer confusion of yearning and alarm for the catastrophe which was held to hang over the house of Moreen, of which he certainly at moments felt the symptoms brush his cheek and as to which he wondered much in what form it would come.

Perhaps it would take the form of dispersal—a frightened *sauve qui peut*,[7] a scuttling into selfish corners. Certainly they were less elastic than of yore; they were evidently looking for something they didn't find. The Dorringtons hadn't reappeared, the princes had scattered; wasn't that the beginning of the end? Mrs. Moreen had lost her reckoning of the famous "days"; her social calendar was blurred—it had turned its face to the wall. Pemberton suspected that the great, the cruel, discomfiture had been the extraordinary behaviour of Mr. Granger, who seemed not to know what he wanted, or, what was much worse, what *they* wanted. He kept sending flowers, as if to bestrew the path of his retreat, which was never the path of return. Flowers were all very well, but—Pemberton could complete the proposition. It was now positively conspicuous that in the long run the Moreens were a failure; so that the young man was almost grateful the run had not been short. Mr. Moreen, indeed, was still occasionally able to get away on business, and, what was more surprising, he was also able to get back. Ulick had no club, but you could not have discovered it from his appearance, which was as much as ever that of a person looking at life from the window of such an institution; therefore

7. Every man for himself.

Pemberton was doubly astonished at an answer he once heard him make to his mother, in the desperate tone of a man familiar with the worst privations. Her question Pemberton had not quite caught; it appeared to be an appeal for a suggestion as to whom they could get to take Amy. "Let the devil take her!" Ulick snapped; so that Pemberton could see that not only they had lost their amiability, but had ceased to believe in themselves. He could also see that if Mrs. Moreen was trying to get people to take her children she might be regarded as closing the hatches for the storm. But Morgan would be the last she would part with.

One winter afternoon—it was a Sunday—he and the boy walked far together in the Bois de Boulogne.[8] The evening was so splendid, the cold lemon-coloured sunset so clear, the stream of carriages and pedestrians so amusing and the fascination of Paris so great, that they stayed out later than usual and became aware that they would have to hurry home to arrive in time for dinner. They hurried accordingly, arm-in-arm, good-humoured and hungry, agreeing that there was nothing like Paris after all and that after all, too, that had come and gone they were not yet sated with innocent pleasures. When they reached the hotel they found that, though scandalously late, they were in time for all the dinner they were likely to sit down to. Confusion reigned in the apartments of the Moreens (very shabby ones this time, but the best in the house), and before the interrupted service of the table (with objects displaced almost as if there had been a scuffle, and a great wine stain from an overturned bottle), Pemberton could not blink the fact that there had been a scene of proprietary mutiny. The storm had come—they were all seeking refuge. The hatches were down—Paula and Amy were invisible (they had never tried the most casual art upon Pemberton, but he felt that they had enough of an eye to him not to wish to meet him as young ladies whose frocks had been confiscated), and Ulick appeared to have jumped overboard. In a word, the host and his staff had ceased to "go on" at the pace of their guests, and the air of embarrassed detention, thanks to a pile of gaping trunks in the passage, was strangely commingled with the air of indignant withdrawal.

When Morgan took in all this—and he took it in very quickly—he blushed to the roots of his hair. He had walked, from his infancy, among difficulties and dangers, but he had never seen a public exposure. Pemberton noticed, in a second glance at him, that the tears had rushed into his eyes and that they were tears of bitter shame. He wondered for an instant, for the boy's sake, whether he might successfully pretend not to understand. Not successfully, he felt, as Mr. and Mrs. Moreen, dinnerless by their extinguished hearth, rose before

8. A large park in Paris.

him in their little dishonoured *salon,* considering apparently with much intensity what lively capital would be next on their list. They were not prostrate, but they were very pale, and Mrs. Moreen had evidently been crying. Pemberton quickly learned however that her grief was not for the loss of her dinner, much as she usually enjoyed it, but on account of a necessity much more tragic. She lost no time in laying this necessity bare, in telling him how the change had come, the bolt had fallen, and how they would all have to turn themselves about. Therefore cruel as it was to them to part with their darling she must look to him to carry a little further the influence he had so fortunately acquired with the boy—to induce his young charge to follow him into some modest retreat. They depended upon him, in a word, to take their delightful child temporarily under his protection—it would leave Mr. Moreen and herself so much more free to give the proper attention (too little, alas! had been given), to the readjustment of their affairs.

"We trust you— we feel that we can," said Mrs. Moreen, slowly rubbing her plump white hands and looking, with compunction, hard at Morgan, whose chin, not to take liberties, her husband stroked with a tentative paternal forefinger.

"Oh, yes; we feel that we can. We trust Mr. Pemberton fully, Morgan," Mr. Moreen conceded.

Pemberton wondered again if he might pretend not to understand; but the idea was painfully complicated by the immediate perception that Morgan had understood.

"Do you mean that he may take me to live with him—for ever and ever?" cried the boy. "Away, away, anywhere he likes?"

"For ever and ever? *Comme vous-y-allez!*"[9] Mr. Moreen laughed indulgently. "For as long as Mr. Pemberton may be so good."

"We've struggled, we've suffered," his wife went on; "but you've made him so your own that we've already been through the worst of the sacrifice."

Morgan had turned away from his father—he stood looking at Pemberton with a light in his face. His blush had died out, but something had come that was brighter and more vivid. He had a moment of boyish joy, scarcely mitigated by the reflection that, with this unexpected consecration of his hope—too sudden and too violent; the thing was a good deal less like a boy's book—the "escape" was left on their hands. The boyish joy was there for an instant, and Pemberton was almost frightened at the revelation of gratitude and affection that shone through his humiliation. When Morgan stammered "My dear fellow, what do you say to *that?*" he felt that he should say something enthusiastic. But he was still more frightened at something

9. How you do go on!

else that immediately followed and that made the lad sit down quickly on the nearest chair. He had turned very white and had raised his hand to his left side. They were all three looking at him, but Mrs. Moreen was the first to bound forward. "Ah, his darling little heart!" she broke out; and this time, on her knees before him and without respect for the idol, she caught him ardently in her arms. "You walked him too far, you hurried him too fast!" she tossed over her shoulder at Pemberton. The boy made no protest, and the next instant his mother, still holding him, sprang up with her face convulsed and with the terrified cry "Help, help! he's going, he's gone!" Pemberton saw, with equal horror, by Morgan's own stricken face, that he *was* gone. He pulled him half out of his mother's hands, and for a moment, while they held him together, they looked, in their dismay, into each other's eyes. "He couldn't stand it, with his infirmity," said Pemberton—"the shock, the whole scene, the violent emotion."

"But I thought he *wanted* to go to you!" wailed Mrs. Moreen.

"I *told* you he didn't, my dear," argued Mr. Moreen. He was trembling all over, and he was, in his way, as deeply affected as his wife. But, after the first, he took his bereavement like a man of the world.

Brooksmith

(1891)†

We are scattered now, the friends of the late Mr. Oliver Offord; but whenever we chance to meet I think we are conscious of a certain esoteric respect for each other. "Yes, you too have been in Arcadia,"[1] we seem not too grumpily to allow. When I pass the house in Mansfield Street I remember that Arcadia was there. I don't know who has it now, and I don't want to know; it's enough to be so sure that if I should ring the bell there would be no such luck for me as that Brooksmith should open the door. Mr. Offord, the most agreeable, the most lovable of bachelors, was a retired diplomatist, living on his pension, confined by his infirmities to his fireside and delighted to be found there any afternoon in the year by such visitors as Brooksmith allowed to come up. Brooksmith was his butler and his most intimate friend, to whom we all stood, or I should say sat, in the same relation in which the subject of the soverign finds himself to the prime minister. By having been for years, in foreign lands, the most delightful Englishman any one had ever known, Mr. Offord had, in my opinion, rendered signal service to his country. But I suppose he had been too much liked—liked even by those who didn't like *it*—so that as people of that sort never get titles or dotations for the horrid things they have *not* done, his principal reward was simply that we went to see him.

Oh, we went perpetually, and it was not our fault if he was not overwelmed with this particular honour. Any visitor who came once came again—to come merely once was a slight which nobody, I am sure, had ever put upon him. His circle, therefore, was essentially composed of *habitués*, who were *habitués* for each other as well as for him, as those of a happy *salon* should be. I remember vividly every element of the place, down to the intensely Londonish look of the grey opposite houses, in the gap of the white curtains of the high windows,

† "Brooksmith" first appeared in *Harper's Weekly* and simultaneously in *Black and White*, May 2, 1891. It was reprinted in *The Lesson of the Master* (New York and London: Macmillan and Co., 1892); the text here reprinted. The American and English issues of this first edition consisted of the same sheets.

1. Arcadia was a rather barren region of central Greece which poets early turned into a Utopia of rural bliss, an innocent Golden Age, and hence the symbol of an ideal existence. The phrase *"Et in Arcadia ego"* ("I am even in Arcadia") first appeared in a picture by one Giovanni Francesco Guercino painted in the early seventeenth century, which makes the point that death is present even in blissful Arcadia. Perhaps because of the slightly later, more famous French painter Nicolas Poussin, the phrase came to be mistranslated as "I too have been in Arcadia," and since then many authors, including James, have used or alluded to it in this sense. See *"Et in Arcadia Ego: Poussin and the Elegiac Tradition,"* a fascinating essay in *Meaning and the Visual Arts* by Erwin Panofsky.

and the exact spot where, on a particular afternoon, I put down my tea-cup for Brooksmith, lingering an instant, to gather it up as if he were plucking a flower. Mr. Offord's drawing-room was indeed Brooksmith's garden, his pruned and tended human *parterre*,[2] and if we all flourished there and grew well in our places it was largely owing to his supervision.

Many persons have heard much, though most have doubtless seen little, of the famous institution of the *salon*, and many are born to the depression of knowing that this finest flower of social life refuses to bloom where the English tongue is spoken. The explanation is usually that our women have not the skill to cultivate it—the art to direct, between suggestive shores, the course of the stream of talk. My affectionate, my pious memory of Mr. Offord contradicts this induction only, I fear, more insidiously to confirm it. The very sallow and slightly smoked drawing-room in which he spent so large a portion of the last years of his life certainly deserved the distinguished name; but on the other hand it could not be said at all to owe its stamp to the soft pressure of the indispensable sex. The dear man had indeed been capable of one of those sacrifices to which women are deemed peculiarly apt; he had recognised (under the influence, in some degree, it is true, of physical infirmity), that if you wished people to find you at home you must manage not to be out. He had in short accepted the fact which many dabblers in the social art are slow to learn, that you must really, as they say, take a line and that the only way to be at home is to stay at home. Finally his own fireside had become a summary of his habits. Why should he ever have left it?—since this would have been leaving what was notoriously pleasantest in London, the compact charmed cluster (thinning away indeed into casual couples), round the fine old last century chimney-piece which, with the exception of the remarkable collection of miniatures, was the best thing the place contained. Mr. Offord was not rich; he had nothing but his pension and the use for life of the somewhat superannuated house.

When I am reminded by some uncomfortable contrast of to-day how perfectly we were all handled there I ask myself once more what had been the secret of such perfection. One had taken it for granted at the time, for anything that is supremely good produces more acceptance than surprise. I felt we were all happy, but I didn't consider how our happiness was managed. And yet there were questions to be asked, questions that strike me as singularly obvious now that there is nobody to answer them. Mr. Offord had solved the insoluble; he had, without feminine help (save in the sense that ladies were dying to come to him and he saved the lives of several), established a *salon*; but I might have

2. Ornamental flower-bed.

guessed that there was a method in his madness—a law in his success. He had not hit it off by a mere fluke. There was an art in it all, and how was the art so hidden? Who, indeed, if it came to that, was the occult artist? Launching this inquiry the other day, I had already got hold of the tail of my reply. I was helped by the very wonder of some of the conditions that came back to me—those that used to seem as natural as sunshine in a fine climate.

How was it, for instance, that we never were a crowd, never either too many or too few, always the right people *with* the right people (there must really have been no wrong people at all), always coming and going, never sticking fast nor overstaying, yet never popping in or out with an indecorous familiarity? How was it that we all sat where we wanted and moved when we wanted and met whom we wanted and escaped whom we wanted; joining, according to the accident of inclination, the general circle or falling in with a single talker on a convenient sofa? Why were all the sofas so convenient, the accidents so happy, the talkers so ready, the listeners so willing, the subjects presented to you in a rotation as quickly fore-ordained as the courses at dinner? A dearth of topics would have been as unheard of as a lapse in the service. These speculations couldn't fail to lead me to the fundamental truth that Brooksmith had been somehow at the bottom of the mystery. If he had not established the *salon* at least he had carried it on. Brooksmith, in short, was the artist!

We felt this, covertly, at the time, without formulating it, and were conscious, as an ordered and prosperous community, of his evenhanded justice, untainted with flunkeyism. He had none of that vulgarity—his touch was infinitely fine. The delicacy of it was clear to me on the first occasion my eyes rested, as they were so often to rest again, on the domestic revealed, in the turbid light of the street, by the opening of the house-door. I saw on the spot that though he had plenty of school he carried it without arrogance—he had remained articulate and human. *L'Ecole Anglaise*,[3] Mr. Offord used to call him, laughing, when, later, it happened more than once that we had some conversation about him. But I remember accusing Mr. Offord of not doing him quite ideal justice. That he was not one of the giants of the school, however, my old friend, who really understood him perfectly and was devoted to him, as I shall show, quite admitted; which doubtless poor Brooksmith had himself felt, to his cost, when his value in the market was originally determined. The utility of his class in general is estimated by the foot and the inch, and poor Brooksmith had only about five feet two to put into circulation. He acknowledged the inadequacy of this provision, and I am sure was penetrated with the everlasting fitness of the relation between service and stature. If *he* had

3. The English School.

been Mr. Offord he certainly would have found Brooksmith wanting, and indeed the laxity of his employer on this score was one of many things which he had had to condone and to which he had at last indulgently adapted himself.

I remember the old man's saying to me: "Oh, my servants, if they can live with me a fortnight they can live with me for ever. But it's the first fortnight that tries 'em." It was in the first fortnight, for instance, that Brooksmith had had to learn that he was exposed to being addressed as "my dear fellow" and "my poor child." Strange and deep must such a probation have been to him, and he doubtless emerged from it tempered and purified. This was written to a certain extent in his appearance; in his spare, brisk little person, in his cloistered white face and extraordinarily polished hair, which told of responsibility, looked as if it were kept up to the same high standard as the plate; in his small, clear, anxious eyes, even in the permitted, though not exactly encouraged tuft on his chin. "He thinks me rather mad, but I've broken him in, and now he likes the place, he likes the company," said the old man. I embraced this fully after I had become aware that Brooksmith's main characteristic was a deep and shy refinement, though I remember I was rather puzzled when, on another occasion, Mr. Offord remarked: "What he likes is the talk— mingling in the conversation." I was conscious that I had never seen Brooksmith permit himself this freedom, but I guessed in a moment that what Mr. Offord alluded to was a participation more intense than any speech could have represented—that of being perpetually present on a hundred legitimate pretexts, errands, necessities, and breathing the very atmosphere of criticism, the famous criticism of life. "Quite an education, sir, isn't it, sir?" he said to me one day at the foot of the stairs, when he was letting me out; and I have always remembered the words and the tone as the first sign of the quickening drama of poor Brooksmith's fate. It was indeed an education, but to what was this sensitive young man of thirty-five, of the servile class, being educated?

Practically and inevitably, for the time, to companionship, to the perpetual, the even exaggerated reference and appeal of a person brought to dependence by his time of life and his infirmities and always addicted moreover (this was the exaggeration) to the art of giving you pleasure by letting you do things for him. There were certain things Mr. Offord was capable of pretending he liked you to do, even when he didn't, if he thought *you* liked them. If it happened that you didn't either (this was rare, but it might be), of course there were cross-purposes; but Brooksmith was there to prevent their going very far. This was precisely the way he acted as moderator: he averted misunderstandings or cleared them up. He had been capable, strange as it may appear, of acquiring for this purpose an insight into the French tongue, which was often used at Mr. Offord's; for besides being habitual to most of the foreigners, and they were many, who haunted the place or arrived with letters (letters often requiring a little worried consideration, of which Brooksmith always had cognisance), it had really become the primary language of the master of the house. I don't know if all the *malentendus* were in French, but almost all the explanations were, and this didn't a bit prevent Brooksmith from following them. I know Mr. Offord used to read passages to him from Montaigne and Saint-Simon,[4] for he read perpetually when he was alone—when they were alone, I should say—and Brooksmith was always about. Perhaps you'll say no wonder Mr. Offord's butler regarded him as "rather mad." However, if I'm not sure what he thought about Montaigne I'm convinced he admired Saint-Simon. A certain feeling for letters must have rubbed off on him from the mere handling of his master's books, which he was always carrying to and fro and putting back in their places.

I often noticed that if an anecdote or a quotation, much more a lively discussion, was going forward, he would, if busy with the fire or the curtains, the lamp or the tea, find a pretext for remaining in the room till the point should be reached. If his purpose was to catch it you were not discreet to call him off, and I shall never forget a look, a hard, stony stare (I caught it in its passage), which, one day when there were a good many people in the room, he fastened upon the footman who was helping him in the service and who, in an undertone, had asked him some irrelevant question. It was the only manifestation of harshness that I ever observed on Brooksmith's part, and at first I wondered what was the matter. Then I became conscious that Mr. Offord was relating a very curious anecdote, never before perhaps made so public, and imparted to the narrator by an eye-witness of the fact, bearing upon Lord Byron's life in Italy. Nothing would induce me to reproduce it here; but Brooksmith had been in danger of losing it. If I ever should venture to reproduce it I shall feel how much I lose in not having my fellow-auditor to refer to.

The first day Mr. Offord's door was closed was therefore a dark date in contemporary history. It was raining hard and my umbrella was wet, but Brooksmith took it from me exactly as if this were a preliminary for going upstairs. I observed however that instead of putting it away he held it poised and trickling over the rug, and then I became aware that he was looking at me with deep, acknowledging eyes—his air of universal responsibility. I immediately understood; there was scarcely need of the question and the answer that passed between us. When I did understand that the old man had given up, for the first

<hr>

4. Michel Eyquem, Seigneur de Montaigne (1533–92), French essayist. Saint-Simon refers either to Claude Henri, Comte de Saint-Simon (1760–1825), the influential French socialist; or, more likely, to Louis de Rouvroy, Duc de Saint-Simon (1675–1755), French author famous for his memoirs.

time, though only for the occasion, I exclaimed dolefully: "What a difference it will make—and to how many people!"

"I shall be one of them, sir!" said Brooksmith; and that was the beginning of the end.

Mr. Offord came down again, but the spell was broken, and the great sign of it was that the conversation was, for the first time, not directed. It wandered and stumbled, a little frightened, like a lost child—it had let go the nurse's hand. "The worst of it is that now we shall talk about my health—*c'est la fin de tout*,"[5] Mr. Offord said, when he reappeared; and then I recognised what a sign of change that would be—for he had never tolerated anything so provincial. The talk became ours, in a word—not his; and as ours, even when *he* talked, it could only be inferior. In this form it was a distress to Brooksmith, whose attention now wandered from it altogether: he had so much closer a vision of his master's intimate conditions than our superficial-ties represented. There were better hours, and he was more in and out of the room, but I could see that he was conscious that the great institution was falling to pieces. He seemed to wish to take counsel with me about it, to feel responsible for its going on in some form or other. When for the second period—the first had lasted several days—he had to tell me that our old friend didn't receive, I half expected to hear him say after a moment: "Do you think I ought to, sir, in his place?"—as he might have asked me, with the return of autumn, if I thought he had better light the drawing-room fire.

He had a resigned philosophic sense of what his guests—our guests, as I came to regard them in our colloquies—would expect. His feeling was that he wouldn't absolutely have approved of himself as a substi-tute for the host; but he was so saturated with the religion of habit that he would have made, for our friends, the necessary sacrifice to the divinity. He would take them on a little further, till they could look about them. I think I saw him also mentally confronted with the opportunity to deal—for once in his life—with some of his own dumb preferences, his limitations of sympathy, *weeding* a little, in prospect, and returning to a purer tradition. It was not unknown to me that he considered that toward the end of Mr. Offord's career a certain laxity of selection had crept in.

At last it came to be the case that we all found the closed door more often than the open one; but even when it was closed Brooksmith managed a crack for me to squeeze through; so that practically I never turned away without having paid a visit. The difference simply came to be that the visit was to Brooksmith. It took place in the hall, at the familiar foot of the stairs, and we didn't sit down—at least Brooksmith didn't; moreover it was devoted wholly to one topic and always had the

---

5. That's the end of everything.

air of being already over—beginning, as it were, at the end. But it was always interesting—it always gave me something to think about. It is true that the subject of my meditation was ever the same—ever "It's all very well, but what *will* become of Brooksmith?" Even my private answer to this question left me still unsatisfied. No doubt Mr. Offord would provide for him, but *what* would he provide? that was the great point. He couldn't provide society; and society had become a necessity of Brooksmith's nature. I must add that he never showed a symptom of what I may call sordid solicitude—anxiety on his own account. He was rather livid and intensely grave, as befitted a man before whose eyes the "shade of that which once was great"[6] was passing away. He had the solemnity of a person winding up, under depressing circumstances, a long established and celebrated business; he was a kind of social executor or liquidator. But his manner seemed to testify exclusively to the uncertainty of *our* future. I couldn't in those days have afforded it—I lived in two rooms in Jermyn Street and didn't "keep a man"; but even if my income had permitted I shouldn't have ventured to say to Brooksmith (emulating Mr. Offord), "My dear fellow, I'll take you on." The whole tone of our intercourse was so much more an implication that it was *I* who should now want a lift. Indeed there was a tacit assurance in Brooksmith's whole attitude that he would have me on his mind.

One of the most assiduous members of our circle had been Lady Kenyon, and I remember his telling me one day that her ladyship had, in spite of her own infirmities, lately much aggravated, been in person to inquire. In answer to this I remarked that she would feel it more than any one. Brooksmith was silent a moment; at the end of which he said, in a certain tone (there is no reproducing some of his tones), "I'll go and see her." I went to see her myself, and I learned that he had waited upon her; but when I said to her, in the form of a joke but with a core of earnest, that when all was over some of us ought to combine, to club together to set Brooksmith up on his own account, she replied a trifle disappointingly: "Do you mean in a public-house?" I looked at her in a way that I think Brooksmith himself would have approved, and then I answered: "Yes, the Offord Arms." What I had meant, of course, was that, for the love of art itself, we ought to look to it that such a peculiar faculty and so much acquired experience should not be wasted. I really think that if we had caused a few black-edged cards to be struck off and circulated—"Mr. Brooksmith will continue to receive on the old premises from four to seven; business carried on as usual during the alterations"—the majority of us would have rallied.

Several times he took me upstairs—always by his own proposal—

6. A line from Wordsworth's "On the Extinction of the Venetian Republic."

and our dear old friend, in bed, in a curious flowered and brocaded *casaque*[7] which made him, especially as his head was tied up in a handkerchief to match, look, to my imagination, like the dying Voltaire, held for ten minutes a sadly shrunken little *salon*. I felt indeed each time, as if I were attending the last *coucher*[8] of some social sovereign. He was royally whimsical about his sufferings and not at all concerned—quite as if the Constitution provided for the case—about his successor. He glided over *our* sufferings charmingly, and none of his jokes—it was a gallant abstention, some of them would have been so easy—were at our expense. Now and again, I confess, there was one at Brooksmith's, but so pathetically sociable as to make the excellent man look at me in a way that seemed to say: "Do exchange a glance with me, or I sha'n't be able to stand it." What he was not able to stand was not what Mr. Offord said about him, but what he wasn't able to say in return. His notion of conversation, for himself, was giving you the convenience of speaking to him; and when he went to "see" Lady Kenyon, for instance, it was to carry her the tribute of his receptive silence. Where would the speech of his betters have been if proper service had been a manifestation of sound? In that case the fundamental difference would have had to be shown by *their* dumbness, and many of them, poor things, were dumb enough without that provision. Brooksmith took an unfailing interest in the preservation of the fundamental difference; it was the thing he had most on his conscience.

What had become of it, however, when Mr. Offord passed away like any inferior person—was relegated to eternal stillness like a butler upstairs? His aspect for several days after the expected event may be imagined, and the multiplication by funereal observance of the things he didn't say. When everything was over—it was late the same day—I knocked at the door of the house of mourning as I so often had done before. I could never call on Mr. Offord again, but I had come, literally, to call on Brooksmith. I wanted to ask him if there was anything I could do for him, tainted with vagueness as this inquiry could only be. My wild dream of taking him into my own service had died away: my service was not worth his being taken into. My offer to him could only be to help him to find another place, and yet there was an indelicacy, as it were, in taking for granted that his thoughts would immediately be fixed on another. I had a hope that he would be able to give his life a different form—though certainly not the form, the frequent result of such bereavements, of his setting up a little shop. That would have been dreadful; for I should have wished to further any enterprise that he might embark in, yet how could I have brought myself to go and pay him shillings and take back coppers over a counter? My visit then was simply an intended compliment. He took it

7. Jacket with wide sleeves. 8. A reception which precedes the going to bed of a king.

as such, gratefully and with all the tact in the world. He knew I really couldn't help him and that I knew he knew I couldn't, but we discussed the situation—with a good deal of elegant generality—at the foot of the stairs, in the hall already dismantled, where I had so often discussed other situations with him. The executors were in possession, as was still more apparent when he made me pass for a few minutes into the dining-room, where various objects were muffled up for removal.

Two definite facts, however, he had to communicate; one being that he was to leave the house for ever that night (servants, for some mysterious reason, seem always to depart by night), and the other—he mentioned it only at the last, with hesitation—that he had already been informed his late master had left him a legacy of eighty pounds. "I'm very glad," I said, and Brooksmith rejoined: "It was so like him to think of me." This was all that passed between us on the subject, and I know nothing of his judgment of Mr. Offord's memento. Eighty pounds are always eighty pounds, and no one has ever left *me* an equal sum; but, all the same, for Brooksmith, I was disappointed. I don't know what I had expected—in short I was disappointed. Eighty pounds might stock a little shop—a *very* little shop; but, I repeat, I couldn't bear to think of that. I asked my friend if he had been able to save a little, and he replied: "No, sir; I have had to do things." I didn't inquire what things he had had to do; they were his own affair, and I took his word for them as assentingly as if he had had the greatness of an ancient house to keep up; especially as there was something in his manner that seemed to convey a prospect of further sacrifice.

"I shall have to turn round a bit, sir—I shall have to look about me," he said; and then he added, indulgently, magnanimously: "If you should happen to hear of anything for me—"

I couldn't let him finish; this was, in its essence, too much in the really grand manner. It would be a help to my getting him off my mind to be able to pretend I *could* find the right place, and that help he wished to give me, for it was doubtless painful to him to see me in so false a position. I interposed with a few words to the effect that I was well aware that wherever he should go, whatever he should do, he would miss our old friend terribly—miss him even more than I should, having been with him so much more. This led him to make the speech that I have always remembered as the very text of the whole episode.

"Oh, sir, it's sad for *you*, very sad, indeed, and for a great many gentlemen and ladies; that it is, sir. But for me, sir, it is, if I may say so, still graver even than that: it's just the loss of something that was everything. For me, sir," he went on, with rising tears, "he was just *all*, if you know what I mean sir. You have others, sir, I daresay—not that I would have you understand me to speak of them as in any way tantamount. But you have the pleasures of society, sir; if it's only in

talking about him, sir, as I daresay you do freely—for all his blessed
memory has to fear from it—with gentlemen and ladies who have had
the same honour. That's not for me, sir, and I have to keep my
associations to myself. Mr. Offord was *my* society, and now I have no
more. You go back to conversation, sir, after all, and I go back to my
place," Brooksmith stammered, without exaggerated irony or dramatic bitterness, but with a flat, unstudied veracity and his hand on the
knob of the street-door. He turned it to let me out and then he added:
"I just go downstairs, sir, again, and I stay there."

"My poor child," I replied, in my emotion, quite as Mr. Offord
used to speak, "my dear fellow, leave it to me; we'll look after you,
we'll all do something for you."

"Ah, if you could give me some one *like* him! But there ain't two in
the world," said Brooksmith as we parted.

He had given me his address—the place where he would be to be
heard of. For a long time I had no occasion to make use of the
information; for he proved indeed, on trial, a very difficult case. In a
word the people who knew him and had known Mr. Offord, didn't
want to take him, and yet I couldn't bear to try to thrust him among
people who didn't know him. I spoke to many of our old friends about
him, and I found them all governed by the odd mixture of feelings of
which I myself was conscious, and disposed, further, to entertain a
suspicion that he was "spoiled," with which I then would have
nothing to do. In plain terms a certain embarrassment, a sensible
awkwardness, when they thought of it, attached to the idea of using
him as a menial: they had met him so often in society. Many of them
would have asked him, and did ask him, or rather did ask me to ask
him, to come and see them; but a mere visiting-list was not what I
wanted for him. He was too short for people who were very particular;
nevertheless I heard of an opening in a diplomatic household which
led me to write him a note, though I was looking much less for
something grand than for something human. Five days later I heard
from him. The secretary's wife had decided, after keeping him waiting
till then, that she couldn't take a servant out of a house in which there
had not been a lady. The note had a P.S.: "It's a good job there wasn't,
sir, such a lady as some."

A week later he came to see me and told me he was "suited"—
committed to some highly respectable people (they were something
very large in the City), who lived on the Bayswater side of the Park.[9] "I
daresay it will be rather poor, sir," he admitted; "but I've seen the
fireworks, haven't I, sir?—it can't be fireworks *every* night. After
Mansfield Street there ain't much choice." There was a certain
amount, however, it seemed; for the following year, going one day to

9. As a residential district, Bayswater (north of Hyde Park) is socially much inferior to Mans-field Street, where Mr. Offord lived.

call on a country cousin, a lady of a certain age who was spending a fortnight in town with some friends of her own, a family unknown to me and resident in Chester Square, the door of the house was opened, to my surprise and gratification, by Brooksmith in person. When I came out I had some conversation with him, from which I gathered that he had found the large City people too dull for endurance, and I guessed, though he didn't say it, that he had found them vulgar as well. I don't know what judgment he would have passed on his actual patrons if my relative had not been their friend; but under the circumstances he abstained from comment.

None was necessary, however, for before the lady in question brought her visit to a close they honoured me with an invitation to dinner, which I accepted. There was a largeish party on the occasion, but I confess I thought of Brooksmith rather more than of the seated company. They required no depth of attention—they were all referable to usual, irredeemable, inevitable types. It was the world of cheerful commonplace and conscious gentility and prosperous density, a full-fed, material, insular world, a world of hideous florid plate and ponderous order and thin conversation. There was not a word said about Byron. Nothing would have induced me to look at Brooksmith in the course of the repast, and I felt sure that not even my overturning the wine would have induced him to meet my eye. We were in intellectual sympathy—we felt, as regards each other, a kind of social responsibility. In short we had been in Arcadia together, and we had both come to *this!* No wonder we were ashamed to be confronted. When he helped on my overcoat, as I was going away, we parted, for the first time since the earliest days in Mansfield Street, in silence. I thought he looked lean and wasted, and I guessed that his new place was not more "human" than his previous one. There was plenty of beef and beer, but there was no reciprocity. The question for him to have asked before accepting the position would have been not "How many footmen are kept?" but "How much imagination?"

The next time I went to the house—I confess it was not very soon—I encountered his successor, a personage who evidently enjoyed the good fortune of never having quitted his natural level. Could any be higher? he seemed to ask—over the heads of three footmen and even of some visitors. He made me feel as if Brooksmith were dead; but I didn't dare to inquire—I couldn't have borne his "I haven't the least idea, sir." I despatched a note to the address Brooksmith had given me after Mr. Offord's death, but I received no answer. Six months later, however, I was favoured with a visit from an elderly, dreary, dingy person, who introduced herself to me as Mr. Brooksmith's aunt and from whom I learned that he was out of place and out of health and had allowed her to come and say to me that if I could spare half-an-hour to look in at him he would take it as a rare honour.

I went the next day—his messenger had given me a new address—and found my friend lodged in a short sordid street in Marylebone, one of those corners of London that wear the last expression of sickly meanness. The room into which I was shown was above the small establishment of a dyer and cleaner who had inflated kid gloves and discoloured shawls in his shop-front. There was a great deal of grimy infant life up and down the place, and there was a hot, moist smell within, as of the "boiling" of dirty linen. Brooksmith sat with a blanket over his legs at a clean little window, where, from behind stiff bluish-white curtains, he could look across at a huckster's and a tinsmith's and a small greasy public-house. He had passed through an illness and was convalescent, and his mother, as well as his aunt, was in attendance on him. I liked the mother, who was bland and intensely humble, but I didn't much fancy the aunt, whom I connected, perhaps unjustly, with the opposite public-house (she seemed somehow to be greasy with the same grease), and whose furtive eye followed every movement of my hand, as if to see if it were not going into my pocket. It didn't take this direction—I couldn't, unsolicited, put myself at that sort of ease with Brooksmith. Several times the door of the room opened, and mysterious old women peeped in and shuffled back again. I don't know who they were; poor Brooksmith seemed encompassed with vague, prying, beery females.

He was vague himself, and evidently weak, and much embarrassed, and not an allusion was made between us to Mansfield Street. The vision of the *salon* of which he had been an ornament hovered before me, however, by contrast, sufficiently. He assured me that he was really getting better, and his mother remarked that he would come round if he could only get his spirits up. The aunt echoed this opinion, and I became more sure that in her own case she knew where to go for such a purpose. I'm afraid I was rather weak with my old friend, for I neglected the opportunity, so exceptionally good, to rebuke the levity which had led him to throw up honourable positions—fine, stiff, steady berths, with morning prayers, as I knew, attached to one of them—in Bayswater and Belgravia.[1] Very likely his reasons had been profane and sentimental; he didn't want morning prayers, he wanted to be somebody's dear fellow; but I couldn't be the person to rebuke him. He shuffled these episodes out of sight—I saw that he had no wish to discuss them. I perceived further, strangely enough, that it would probably be a questionable pleasure for him to see me again: he doubted now even of my power to condone his aberrations. He didn't wish to have to explain; and his behaviour, in future, was likely to need explanation. When I bade him farewell he looked at me a moment with eyes that said everything: "How can I talk about those exquisite

1. Belgravia is a fashionable section near Buckingham Palace.

years in this place, before these people, with the old women poking their heads in? It was very good of you to come to see me—it wasn't my idea; *she* brought you. We've said everything; it's over; you'll lose all patience with me, and I'd rather you shouldn't see the rest." I sent him some money, in a letter, the next day, but I saw the rest only in the light of a barren sequel.

A whole year after my visit to him I became aware once, in dining out, that Brooksmith was one of the several servants who hovered behind our chairs. He had not opened the door of the house to me, and I had not recognised him in the cluster of retainers in the hall. This time I tried to catch his eye, but he never gave me a chance, and when he handed me a dish I could only be careful to thank him audibly. Indeed I partook of two *entrées* of which I had my doubts, subsequently converted into certainties, in order not to snub him. He looked well enough in health, but much older, and wore, in an exceptionally marked degree, the glazed and expressionless mask of the British domestic *de race*. [2] I saw with dismay that if I had not known him I should have taken him, on the showing of his countenance, for an extravagant illustration of irresponsive servile gloom. I said to myself that he had become a reactionary, gone over to the Philistines, thrown himself into religion, the religion of his "place," like a foreign lady *sur le retour*. [3] I divined moreover that he was only engaged for the evening—he had become a mere waiter, had joined the band of the white-waistcoated who "go out." There was something pathetic in this fact, and it was a terrible vulgarisation of Brooksmith. It was the mercenary prose of butlerhood; he had given up the struggle for the poetry. If reciprocity was what he had missed, where was the reciprocity now? Only in the bottoms of the wine-glasses and five shillings (or whatever they get), clapped into his hand by the permanent man. However, I supposed he had taken up a precarious branch of his profession because after all it sent him less downstairs. His relations with London society were more superficial, but they were of course more various. As I went away, on this occasion, I looked out for him eagerly among the four or five attendants whose perpendicular persons, fluting the walls of London passages, are supposed to lubricate the process of departure; but he was not on duty. I asked one of the others if he were not in the house, and received the prompt answer: "Just left, sir. Anything I can do for you, sir?" I wanted to say "Please give him my kind regards;" but I abstained; I didn't want to compromise him, and I never came across him again.

Often and often, in dining out, I looked for him, sometimes accepting invitations on purpose to multiply the chances of my meeting him. But always in vain; so that as I met many other members of

2. The "thoroughbred" British domestic servant.
3. Past her prime.

the casual class over and over again, I at last adopted the theory that he always procured a list of expected guests beforehand and kept away from the banquets which he thus learned I was to grace. At last I gave up hope, and one day, at the end of three years, I received another visit from his aunt. She was drearier and dingier, almost squalid, and she was in great tribulation and want. Her sister, Mrs. Brooksmith, had been dead a year, and three months later her nephew had disappeared. He had always looked after her a bit—since her troubles; I never knew what her troubles had been—and now she hadn't so much as a petticoat to pawn. She had also a niece, to whom she had been everything, before her troubles, but the niece had treated her most shameful. These were details; the great and romantic fact was Brooksmith's final evasion of his fate. He had gone out to wait one evening, as usual, in a white waistcoat she had done up for him with her own hands, being due at a large party up Kensington way. But he had never come home again, and had never arrived at the large party, or at any party that any one could make out. No trace of him had come to light—no gleam of the white waistcoat had pierced the obscurity of his doom. This news was a sharp shock to me, for I had my ideas about his real destination. His aged relative had promptly, as she said, guessed the worst. Somehow and somewhere he had got out of the way altogether, and now I trust that, with characteristic deliberation, he is changing the plates of the immortal gods. As my depressing visitant also said, he never *had* got his spirits up. I was fortunately able to dismiss her with her own somewhat improved. But the dim ghost of poor Brooksmith is one of those that I see. He had indeed been spoiled.

The Real Thing

(1892)†

I

When the porter's wife (she used to answer the house-bell), announced "A gentleman—with a lady, sir," I had, as I often had in those days, for the wish was father to the thought, an immediate vision of sitters. Sitters my visitors in this case proved to be; but not in the sense I should have preferred. However, there was nothing at first to indicate that they might not have come for a portrait. The gentleman, a man of fifty, very high and very straight, with a moustache slightly grizzled and a dark grey walking-coat admirably fitted, both of which I noted professionally—I don't mean as a barber or yet as a tailor—would have struck me as a celebrity if celebrities often were striking. It was a truth of which I had for some time been conscious that a figure with a good deal of frontage was, as one might say, almost never a public institution. A glance at the lady helped to remind me of this paradoxical law: she also looked too distinguished to be a "personality." Moreover one would scarcely come across two variations together.

Neither of the pair spoke immediately—they only prolonged the preliminary gaze which suggested that each wished to give the other a chance. They were visibly shy; they stood there letting me take them in—which, as I afterwards perceived, was the most practical thing they could have done. In this way their embarrassment served their cause. I had seen people painfully reluctant to mention that they desired anything so gross as to be represented on canvas; but the scruples of my new friends appeared almost insurmountable. Yet the gentleman might have said "I should like a portrait of my wife," and the lady might have said "I should like a portrait of my husband." Perhaps they were not husband and wife—this naturally would make the matter more delicate. Perhaps they wished to be done together—in which case they ought to have brought a third person to break the news.

"We come from Mr. Rivet," the lady said at last, with a dim smile which had the effect of a moist sponge passed over a "sunk"[1] piece of

---

† "The Real Thing" originally appeared in *Black and White*, April 16, 1892. Its first appearance in a book (the text reprinted here) was in *The Real Thing and Other Tales* (New York and London: Macmillan and Co., 1893). The American and English issues, published simultaneously, consisted of the same sheets.

1. In painting certain technical failures, in particular improper preparation of the "ground" (surface), can cause "the 'sinking in' of oil colors" with consequent loss of the original "color effect" (Max Doerner, *The Materials of the Artist and Their Use in Painting with Notes on the Technique of the Old Masters*, translated by Eugen Neuhaus, Ph.D.h.c. (New York: Harcourt, Brace and Company, 1934), pp. 185–86). The application of moisture to such a painting may create a temporary gloss.

painting, as well as of a vague allusion to vanished beauty. She was as tall and straight, in her degree, as her companion, and with ten years less to carry. She looked as sad as a woman could look whose face was not charged with expression; that is her tinted oval mask showed friction as an exposed surface shows it. The hand of time had played over her freely, but only to simplify. She was slim and stiff, and so well-dressed, in dark blue cloth, with lappets and pockets and buttons, that it was clear she employed the same tailor as her husband. The couple had an indefinable air of prosperous thrift—they evidently got a good deal of luxury for their money. If I was to be one of their luxuries it would behove me to consider my terms.

"Ah, Claude Rivet recommended me?" I inquired; and I added that it was very kind of him, though I could reflect that, as he only painted landscape, this was not a sacrifice.

The lady looked very hard at the gentleman, and the gentleman looked round the room. Then staring at the floor a moment and stroking his moustache, he rested his pleasant eyes on me with the remark: "He said you were the right one."

"I try to be, when people want to sit."

"Yes, we should like to," said the lady anxiously.

"Do you mean together?"

My visitors exchanged a glance. "If you could do anything with *me*, I suppose it would be double," the gentleman stammered.

"Oh yes, there's naturally a higher charge for two figures than for one."

"We should like to make it pay," the husband confessed.

"That's very good of you," I returned, appreciating so unwonted a sympathy—for I supposed he meant pay the artist.

A sense of strangeness seemed to dawn on the lady. "We mean for the illustrations—Mr. Rivet said you might put one in."

"Put one in—an illustration?" I was equally confused.

"Sketch her off, you know," said the gentleman, colouring.

It was only then that I understood the service Claude Rivet had rendered me; he had told them that I worked in black and white, for magazines, for story-books, for sketches of contemporary life, and consequently had frequent employment for models. These things were true, but it was not less true (I may confess it now—whether because the aspiration was to lead to everything or to nothing I leave the reader to guess), that I couldn't get the honours, to say nothing of the emoluments, of a great painter of portraits out of my head. My "illustrations" were my pot-boilers; I looked to a different branch of art (far and away the most interesting it had always seemed to me), to perpetuate my fame. There was no shame in looking to it also to make my fortune; but that fortune was by so much further from being made from the moment my visitors wished to be "done" for nothing. I was disappointed; for in the pictorial sense I had immediately *seen* them. I had seized their type—I had already settled what I would do with it. Something that wouldn't absolutely have pleased them, I afterwards reflected.

"Ah, you're—you're—a—?" I began, as soon as I had mastered my surprise. I couldn't bring out the dingy word "models"; it seemed to fit the case so little.

"We haven't had much practice," said the lady.

"We've got to *do* something, and we've thought that an artist in your line might perhaps make something of us," her husband threw off. He further mentioned that they didn't know many artists and that they had gone first, on the off-chance (he painted views of course, but some-times put in figures—perhaps I remembered), to Mr. Rivet, whom they had met a few years before at a place in Norfolk where he was sketching.

"We used to sketch a little ourselves," the lady hinted.

"It's very awkward, but we absolutely *must* do something," her husband went on.

"Of course we're not so *very* young," she admitted, with a wan smile.

With the remark that I might as well know something more about them, the husband had handed me a card extracted from a neat new pocket-book (their appurtenances were all of the freshest) and in-scribed with the words "Major Monarch." Impressive as these words were they didn't carry my knowledge much further; but my visitor presently added: "I've left the army, and we've had the misfortune to lose our money. In fact our means are dreadfully small."

"It's an awful bore," said Mrs. Monarch.

They evidently wished to be discreet—to take care not to swagger because they were gentlefolks. I perceived they would have been willing to recognise this as something of a drawback, at the same time that I guessed at an underlying sense—their consolation in adversity—that they *had* their points. They certainly had; but these advantages struck me as preponderantly social; such for instance as would help to make a drawing-room look well. However, a drawing-room was always, or ought to be, a picture.

In consequence of his wife's allusion to their age Major Monarch observed: "Naturally, it's more for the figure that we thought of going in. We can still hold ourselves up." On the instant I saw that the figure was indeed their strong point. His "naturally" didn't sound vain, but it lighted up the question. "*She* has got the best," he continued, nodding at his wife, with a pleasant after-dinner absence of circumlocution. I could only reply, as if we were in fact sitting over our wine, that this didn't prevent his own from being very good; which led him in turn to rejoin: "We thought that if you ever had to do people like us, we might be something like it. *She,* particularly—for a lady in a book, you know."

I was so amused by them that, to get more of it, I did my best to take their point of view; and though it was an embarrassment to find myself appraising physically, as if they were animals on hire or useful blacks, a pair whom I should have expected to meet only in one of the relations in which criticism is tacit, I looked at Mrs. Monarch judicially enough to be able to exclaim, after a moment, with conviction: "Oh yes, a lady in a book!" She was singularly like a bad illustration.

"We'll stand up, if you like," said the Major; and he raised himself before me with a really grand air.

I could take his measure at a glance—he was six feet two and a perfect gentleman. It would have paid any club in process of formation and in want of a stamp to engage him at a salary to stand in the principal window. What struck me immediately was that in coming to me they had rather missed their vocation; they could surely have been turned to better account for advertising purposes. I couldn't of course see the thing in detail, but I could see them make someone's fortune—I don't mean their own. There was something in them for a waistcoat-maker, an hotel-keeper or a soap-vendor. I could imagine "We always use it" pinned on their bosoms with the greatest effect; I had a vision of the promptitude with which they would launch a table d'hôte.

Mrs. Monarch sat still, not from pride but from shyness, and presently her husband said to her: "Get up my dear and show how smart you are." She obeyed, but she had no need to get up to show it. She walked to the end of the studio, and then she came back blushing, with her fluttered eyes on her husband. I was reminded of an incident I had accidentally had a glimpse of in Paris—being with a friend there, a dramatist about to produce a play—when an actress came to him to ask to be intrusted with a part. She went through her paces before him, walked up and down as Mrs. Monarch was doing. Mrs. Monarch did it quite as well, but I asbstained from applauding. It was very odd to see such people apply for such poor pay. She looked as if she had ten thousand a year. Her husband had used the word that described her: she was, in the London current jargon, essentially and typically "smart." Her figure was, in the same order of ideas, conspicuously and irreproachably "good." For a woman of her age her waist was surprisingly small; her elbow moreover had the orthodox crook. She held her head at the conventional angle; but why did she come to *me?* She ought to have tried on jackets at a big shop. I feared my visitors were not only destitute, but "artistic"—which would be a great complication. When she sat down again I thanked her, observing that what a draughtsman most valued in his model was the faculty of keeping quiet.

"Oh, *she* can keep quiet," said Major Monarch. Then he added, jocosely: "I've always kept her quiet."

"I'm not a nasty fidget, am I?" Mrs. Monarch appealed to her husband.

He addressed his answer to me. "Perhaps it isn't out of place to mention—because we ought to be quite business-like, oughtn't we?—that when I married her she was known as the Beautiful Statue."

"Oh dear!" said Mrs. Monarch, ruefully.

"Of course I should want a certain amount of expression," I rejoined.

"Of *course!*" they both exclaimed.

"And then I suppose you know that you'll get awfully tired."

"Oh, we *never* get tired!" they eagerly cried.

"Have you had any kind of practice?"

They hesitated—they looked at each other. "We've been photographed, *immensely*," said Mrs. Monarch.

"She means the fellows have asked us," added the Major.

"I see—because you're so good-looking."

"I don't know what they thought, but they were always after us."

"We always got our photographs for nothing," smiled Mrs. Monarch.

"We might have brought some, my dear," her husband remarked.

"I'm not sure we have any left. We've given quantities away," she explained to me.

"With our autographs and that sort of thing," said the Major.

"Are they to be got in the shops?" I inquired, as a harmless pleasantry.

"Oh, yes; *hers*—they used to be."

"Not now," said Mrs. Monarch, with her eyes on the floor.

II

I could fancy the "sort of thing" they put on the presentation-copies of their photographs, and I was sure they wrote a beautiful hand. It was odd how quickly I was sure of everything that concerned them. If they were now so poor as to have to earn shillings and pence, they never had had much of a margin. Their good looks had been their capital, and they had good-humouredly made the most of the career that this resource marked out for them. It was in their faces, the blankness, the deep intellectual repose of the twenty years of country-house visiting which had given them pleasant intonations. I could see the sunny drawing-rooms, sprinkled with periodicals she didn't read, in which Mrs. Monarch had continuously sat; I could see the wet shrubberies in which she had walked, equipped to admiration for either exercise. I could see the rich covers the Major had helped to shoot and the wonderful garments in which, late at night, he repaired to the smoking-room to talk about them. I could imagine their leggings and waterproofs, their knowing tweeds and rugs, their rolls of sticks and cases of tackle and neat umbrellas; and I could evoke the exact appearance of their servants and the compact variety of their luggage on the platforms of country stations.

They gave small tips, but they were liked; they didn't do anything themselves, but they were welcome. They looked so well everywhere; they gratified the general relish for stature, complexion and "form." They knew it without fatuity or vulgarity, and they respected themselves in consequence. They were not superficial; they were thorough and kept themselves up—it had been their line. People with such a taste for activity had to have some line. I could feel how, even in a dull house, they could have been counted upon for cheerfulness. At present something had happened—it didn't matter what, their little income had grown less, it had grown least—and they had to do something for pocket-money. Their friends liked them, but didn't like to support them. There was something about them that represented credit—their clothes, their manners, their type; but if credit is a large empty pocket in which an occasional chink reverberates, the chink at least must be audible. What they wanted of me was to help to make it so. Fortunately they had no children—I soon divined that. They would also perhaps wish our relations to be kept secret: this was why it was "for the figure"—the reproduction of the face would betray them.

I liked them—they were so simple; and I had no objection to them if they would suit. But, somehow, with all their perfections I didn't easily believe in them. After all they were amateurs, and the ruling passion of my life was the detestation of the amateur. Combined with this was another perversity—an innate preference for the represented subject over the real one: the defect of the real one was so apt to be a lack of representation. I liked things that appeared; then one was sure. Whether they *were* or not was a subordinate and almost always a profitless question. There were other considerations, the first of which was that I already had two or three people in use, notably a young person with big feet, in alpaca, from Kilburn, who for a couple of years had come to me regularly for my illustrations and with whom I was still—perhaps ignobly—satisfied. I frankly explained to my visitors how the case stood; but they had taken more precautions than I supposed. They had reasoned out their opportunity, for Claude Rivet had told them of the projected *édition de luxe* of one of the writers of our day—the rarest of the novelists—who, long neglected by the multitudinous vulgar and dearly prized by the attentive (need I mention Philip Vincent?) had had the happy fortune of seeing, late in life, the dawn and then the full light of a higher criticism—an estimate in which, on the part of the public, there was something really of expiation. The edition in question, planned by a publisher of taste, was practically an act of high reparation; the wood-cuts with which it was to be enriched were the homage of English art to one of the most independent representatives of English letters. Major and Mrs. Monarch confessed to me that they had hoped I might be able to work *them* into my share of the enterprise. They knew I was to do the first of the books, "Rutland Ramsay," but I had to make clear to them that my participation in the rest of the affair—this first book was to be a test—was to depend on the satisfaction I should give. If this should be limited my employers would drop me without a scruple. It was therefore a crisis for me, and naturally I was making special preparations, looking about for new people, if they should be necessary, and securing the best types. I admitted however that I should like to settle down to two or three good models who would do for everything.

"Should we have often to—a—put on special clothes?" Mrs. Monarch timidly demanded.

"Dear, yes—that's half the business."

"And should we be expected to supply our own costumes?"

"Oh, no; I've got a lot of things. A painter's models put on—or put off—anything he likes."

"And do you mean—a—the same?"

"The same?"

Mrs. Monarch looked at her husband again.

"Oh, she was just wondering," he explained, "if the costumes are in *general* use." I had to confess that they were, and I mentioned further that some of them (I had a lot of genuine, greasy last-century things), had served their time, a hundred years ago, on living, world-stained men and women. "We'll put on anything that *fits*," said the Major.

"Oh, I arrange that—they fit in the pictures."

"I'm afraid I should do better for the modern books. I would come as you like," said Mrs. Monarch.

"She has got a lot of clothes at home: they might do for contemporary life," her husband continued.

"Oh, I can fancy scenes in which you'd be quite natural." And indeed I could see the slipshod rearrangements of stale properties—the stories I tried to produce pictures for without the exasperation of reading them—whose sandy tracts the good lady might help to people. But I had to return to the fact that for this sort of work—the daily mechanical grind—I was already equipped; the people I was working with were fully adequate.

"We only thought we might be more like *some* characters," said Mrs. Monarch mildly, getting up.

Her husband also rose; he stood looking at me with a dim wistfulness that was touching in so fine a man. "Wouldn't it be rather a pull sometimes to have—a—to have—?" He hung fire; he wanted me to help him by phrasing what he meant. But I couldn't—I didn't know. So he brought it out, awkwardly: "The *real* thing; a gentleman, you know, or a lady." I was quite ready to give a general assent—I admitted that there was a great deal in that. This encouraged Major Monarch to say, following up his appeal with an unacted gulp: "It's awfully hard—we've tried everything." The gulp was communicative; it proved too much for his wife. Before I knew it Mrs. Monarch had dropped again upon a divan and burst into tears. Her husband sat down beside her, holding one of her hands; whereupon she quickly dried her eyes with the other, while I felt embarrassed as she looked up at me. "There isn't a confounded job I haven't applied for—waited for—prayed for. You can fancy we'd be pretty bad first. Secretaryships and that sort of thing? You might as well ask for a peerage. I'd be *anything*—I'm strong; a messenger or a coalheaver. I'd put on a gold-laced cap and open carriage-doors in front of the haberdasher's; I'd hang about a station, to carry portmanteaus; I'd be a postman. But they won't *look* at you; there are thousands, as good as yourself, already on the ground. *Gentlemen*, poor beggars, who have drunk their wine, who have kept their hunters!"

I was as reassuring as I knew how to be, and my visitors were presently on their feet again while, for the experiment, we agreed on an hour. We were discussing it when the door opened and Miss Churm came in with a wet umbrella. Miss Churm had to take the omnibus to Maida Vale[2] and then walk half-a-mile. She looked a trifle blowsy and slightly splashed. I scarcely ever saw her come in without thinking afresh how odd it was that, being so little in herself, she should yet be so much in others. She was a meagre little Miss Churm, but she was an ample heroine of romance. She was only a freckled cockney, but she could represent everything, from a fine lady to a shepherdess; she had the faculty, as she might have had a fine voice or long hair. She couldn't spell, and she loved beer, but she had two or three "points," and practice, and a knack, and mother-wit, and a kind of whimsical sensibility, and a love of the theatre, and seven sisters, and not an ounce of respect, especially for the *h*. The first thing my visitors saw was that her umbrella was wet, and in their spotless perfection they visibly winced at it. The rain had come on since their arrival.

"I'm all in a soak; there *was* a mess of people in the 'bus. I wish you lived near a stytion," said Miss Churm. I requested her to get ready as quickly as possible, and she passed into the room in which she always changed her dress. But before going out she asked me what she was to get into this time.

"It's the Russian princess, don't you know?" I answered; "the one

2. A section of London and the closest bus stop to her job.

with the 'golden eyes,' in black velvet, for the long thing in the *Cheapside*."[3]

"Golden eyes? I *say!*" cried Miss Churm, while my companions watched her with intensity as she withdrew. She always arranged herself, when she was late, before I could turn round; and I kept my visitors a little, on purpose, so that they might get an idea, from seeing her, what would be expected of themselves. I mentioned that she was quite my notion of an excellent model—she was really very clever.

"Do you think she looks like a Russian princess?" Major Monarch asked, with lurking alarm.

"When I make her, yes."

"Oh, if you have to *make* her—!" he reasoned, acutely.

"That's the most you can ask. There are so many that are not makeable."

"Well now, *here's* a lady"—and with a persuasive smile he passed his arm into his wife's—"who's already made!"

"Oh, I'm not a Russian princess," Mrs. Monarch protested, a little coldly. I could see that she had known some and didn't like them. There, immediately, was a complication of a kind that I never had to fear with Miss Churm.

This young lady came back in black velvet—the gown was rather rusty and very low on her lean shoulders—and with a Japanese fan in her red hands. I reminded her that in the scene I was doing she had to look over someone's head. "I forget whose it is; but it doesn't matter. Just look over a head."

"I'd rather look over a stove," said Miss Churm; and she took her station near the fire. She fell into position, settled herself into a tall attitude, gave a certain backward inclination to her head and a certain forward droop to her fan, and looked, at least to my prejudiced sense, distinguished and charming, foreign and dangerous. We left her looking so, while I went down-stairs with Major and Mrs. Monarch.

"I think I could come about as near it as that," said Mrs. Monarch.

"Oh, you think she's shabby, but you must allow for the alchemy of art."

However, they went off with an evident increase of comfort, founded on their demonstrable advantage in being the real thing. I could fancy them shuddering over Miss Churm. She was very droll about them when I went back, for I told her what they wanted.

"Well, if *she* can sit I'll tyke to bookkeeping," said my model.

"She's very lady-like," I replied, as an innocent form of aggravation.

"So much the worse for *you*. That means she can't turn round."

"She'll do for the fashionable novels."

3. A magazine publishing fiction.

"Oh yes, she'll *do* for them!" my model humorously declared. "Ain't they bad enough without her?" I had often sociably denounced them to Miss Churm.

It was for the elucidation of a mystery in one of these works that I first tried Mrs. Monarch. Her husband came with her, to be useful if necessary—it was sufficiently clear that as a general thing he would prefer to come with her. At first I wondered if this were for "propriety's" sake—if he were going to be jealous and meddling. The idea was too tiresome, and if it had been confirmed it would speedily have brought our acquaintance to a close. But I soon saw there was nothing in it and that if he accompanied Mrs. Monarch it was (in addition to the chance of being wanted), simply because he had nothing else to do. When she was away from him his occupation was gone—she never *had* been away from him. I judged, rightly, that in their awkward situation their close union was their main comfort and that this union had no weak spot. It was a real marriage, an encouragement to the hesitating, a nut for pessimists to crack. Their address was humble (I remember afterwards thinking it had been the only thing about them that was really professional), and I could fancy the lamentable lodgings in which the Major would have been left alone. He could bear them with his wife—he couldn't bear them without her.

He had too much tact to try and make himself agreeable when he couldn't be useful; so he simply sat and waited, when I was too absorbed in my work to talk. But I liked to make him talk—it made my work, when it didn't interrupt it, less sordid, less special. To listen to him was to combine the excitement of going out with the economy of staying at home. There was only one hindrance: that I seemed not to know any of the people he and his wife had known. I think he wondered extremely, during the term of our intercourse, whom the deuce I *did* know. He hadn't a stray sixpence of an idea to fumble for; so we didn't spin it very fine—we confined ourselves to questions of leather and even of liquor (saddlers and breeches-makers and how to get good claret cheap), and matters like "good trains" and the habits of small game. His lore on these last subjects was astonishing, he managed to interweave the stationmaster with the ornithologist. When he couldn't talk about greater things he could talk cheerfully about smaller, and since I couldn't accompany him into reminiscences of the fashionable world he could lower the conversation without a visible effort to my level.

So earnest a desire to please was touching in a man who could so easily have knocked one down. He looked after the fire and had an opinion on the draught of the stove, without my asking him, and I could see that he thought many of my arrangements not half clever enough. I remember telling him that if I were only rich I would offer him a salary to come and teach me how to live. Sometimes he gave a random sigh, of which the essence was: "Give me even such a bare old barrack as *this*, and I'd do something with it!" When I wanted to use him he came alone; which was an illustration of the superior courage of women. His wife could bear her solitary second floor, and she was in general more discreet; showing by various small reserves that she was alive to the propriety of keeping our relations markedly professional—not letting them slide into sociability. She wished it to remain clear that she and the Major were employed, not cultivated, and if she approved of me as a superior, who could be kept in his place, she never thought me quite good enough for an equal.

She sat with great intensity, giving the whole of her mind to it, and was capable of remaining for an hour almost as motionless as if she were before a photographer's lens. I could see she had been photographed often, but somehow the very habit that made her good for that purpose unfitted her for mine. At first I was extremely pleased with her lady-like air, and it was a satisfaction, on coming to follow her lines, to see how good they were and how far they could lead the pencil. But after a few times I began to find her too insurmountably stiff; do what I would with it my drawing looked like a photograph or a copy of a photograph. Her figure had no variety of expression—she herself had no sense of variety. You may say that this was my business, was only a question of placing her. I placed her in every conceivable position, but she managed to obliterate their differences. She was always a lady certainly, and into the bargain was always the same lady. She was the real thing, but always the same thing. There were moments when I was oppressed by the serenity of her confidence that she *was* the real thing. All her dealings with me and all her husband's were an implication that this was lucky for *me*. Meanwhile I found myself trying to invent types that approached her own, instead of making her own transform itself—in the clever way that was not impossible, for instance, to poor Miss Churm. Arrange as I would and take the precautions I would, she always, in my pictures, came out too tall—landing me in the dilemma of having represented a fascinating woman as seven feet high, which, out of respect perhaps to my own very much scantier inches, was far from my idea of such a personage.

The case was worse with the Major—nothing I could do would keep *him* down, so that he became useful only for the representation of brawny giants. I adored variety and range, I cherished human accidents, the illustrative note; I wanted to characterise closely, and the thing in the world I most hated was the danger of being ridden by a type. I had quarrelled with some of my friends about it—I had parted company with them for maintaining that one *had* to be, and that if the type was beautiful (witness Raphael and Leonardo), the servitude was only a gain. I was neither Leonardo nor Raphael; I might only be a presumptuous young modern searcher, but I held that everything was to be sacrificed sooner than character. When they averred that the haunting type in question could easily *be* character, I retorted, perhaps superficially: "Whose?" It couldn't be everybody's—it might end in being nobody's.

After I had drawn Mrs. Monarch a dozen times I perceived more clearly than before that the value of such a model as Miss Churm resided precisely in the fact that she had no positive stamp, combined of course with the other fact that what she did have was a curious and inexplicable talent for imitation. Her usual appearance was like a curtain which she could draw up at request for a capital performance. This performance was simply suggestive; but it was a word to the wise—it was vivid and pretty. Sometimes, even, I thought it, though she was plain herself, too insipidly pretty; I made it a reproach to her that the figures drawn from her were monotonously (*bêtement*, [4] as we used to say) graceful. Nothing made her more angry: it was so much her pride to feel that she could sit for characters that had nothing in common with each other. She would accuse me at such moments of taking away her "reputytion."

It suffered a certain shrinkage, this queer quantity, from the repeated visits of my new friends. Miss Churm was greatly in demand, never in want of employment, so I had no scruple in putting her off occasionally, to try them more at my ease. It was certainly amusing at first to do the real thing—it was amusing to do Major Monarch's trousers. They *were* the real thing, even if he did come out colossal. It was amusing to do his wife's back hair (it was so mathematically neat,) and the particular "smart" tension of her tight stays. She lent herself especially to positions in which the face was somewhat averted or blurred; she abounded in lady-like back views and *profils perdus*. [5] When she stood erect she took naturally one of the attitudes in which court-painters represent queens and princesses; so that I found myself wondering whether, to draw out this accomplishment, I couldn't get the editor of the *Cheapside* to publish a really royal romance, "A Tale of Buckingham Palace." Sometimes, however, the real thing and the make-believe came into contact; by which I mean that Miss Churm, keeping an appointment or coming to make one on days when I had much work in hand, encountered her invidious rivals. The encounter was not on their part, for they noticed her no more than if she had been the housemaid; not from intentional loftiness, but simply because, as yet, professionally, they didn't know how to fraternise, as I could guess that they would have liked—or at least that the Major would. They couldn't talk about the omnibus—they always

4. Stupidly.
5. Literally, lost profiles; that is, views slightly from the back so that the profile is invisible.

walked; and they didn't know what else to try—she wasn't interested in good trains or cheap claret. Besides, they must have felt—in the air—that she was amused at them, secretly derisive of their ever knowing how. She was not a person to conceal her scepticism if she had had a chance to show it. On the other hand Mrs. Monarch didn't think her tidy; for why else did she take pains to say to me (it was going out of the way, for Mrs. Monarch), that she didn't like dirty women?

One day when my young lady happened to be present with my other sitters (she even dropped in, when it was convenient, for a chat), I asked her to be so good as to lend a hand in getting tea—a service with which she was familiar and which was one of a class that, living as I did in a small way, with slender domestic resources, I often appealed to my models to render. They liked to lay hands on my property, to break the sitting, and sometimes the china—I made them feel Bohemian. The next time I saw Miss Churm after this incident she surprised me greatly by making a scene about it—she accused me of having wished to humiliate her. She had not resented the outrage at the time, but had seemed obliging and amused, enjoying the comedy of asking Mrs. Monarch, who sat vague and silent, whether she would have cream and sugar, and putting an exaggerated simper into the question. She had tried intonations—as if she too wished to pass for the real thing; till I was afraid my other visitors would take offence.

Oh, *they* were determined not to do this; and their touching patience was the measure of their great need. They would sit by the hour, uncomplaining, till I was ready to use them; they would come back on the chance of being wanted and would walk away cheerfully if they were not. I used to go to the door with them to see in what magnificent order they retreated. I tried to find other employment for them—I introduced them to several artists. But they didn't "take," for reasons I could appreciate, and I became conscious, rather anxiously, that after such disappointments they fell back upon me with a heavier weight. They did me the honour to think that it was I who was most *their* form. They were not picturesque enough for the painters, and in those days there were not so many serious workers in black and white. Besides, they had an eye to the great job I had mentioned to them—they had secretly set their hearts on supplying the right essence for my pictorial vindication of our fine novelist. They knew that for this undertaking I should want no costume-effects, none of the frippery of past ages— that it was a case in which everything would be contemporary and satirical and, presumably, genteel. If I could work them into it their future would be assured, for the labour would of course be long and the occupation steady.

One day Mrs. Monarch came without her husband—she explained his absence by his having had to go to the City.[6] While she sat there in

6. The banking and commercial district of London.

her usual anxious stiffness there came, at the door, a knock which I immediately recognised as the subdued appeal of a model out of work. It was followed by the entrance of a young man whom I easily perceived to be a foreigner and who proved in fact an Italian acquainted with no English word but my name, which he uttered in a way that made it seem to include all others. I had not then visited his country, nor was I proficient in his tongue; but as he was not so meanly constituted—what Italian is?—as to depend only on that member for expression he conveyed to me, in familiar but graceful mimicry, that he was in search of exactly the employment in which the lady before me was engaged. I was not struck with him at first, and while I continued to draw I emitted rough sounds of discouragement and dismissal. He stood his ground, however, not importunately, but with a dumb, dog-like fidelity in his eyes which amounted to innocent impudence—the manner of a devoted servant (he might have been in the house for years), unjustly suspected. Suddenly I saw that this very attitude and expression made a picture, whereupon I told him to sit down and wait till I should be free. There was another picture in the way he obeyed me, and I observed as I worked that there were others still in the way he looked wonderingly, with his head thrown back, about the high studio. He might have been crossing himself in St. Peter's. Before I finished I said to myself: "The fellow's a bankrupt orange-monger, but he's a treasure."

When Mrs. Monarch withdrew he passed across the room like a flash to open the door for her, standing there with the rapt, pure gaze of the young Dante spellbound by the young Beatrice.[7] As I never insisted, in such situations, on the blankness of the British domestic, I reflected that he had the making of a servant (and I needed one, but couldn't pay him to be only that), as well as of a model; in short I made up my mind to adopt my bright adventurer if he would agree to officiate in the double capacity. He jumped at my offer, and in the event my rashness (for I had known nothing about him), was not brought home to me. He proved a sympathetic though a desultory ministrant, and had in a wonderful degree the *sentiment de la pose*.[8] It was uncultivated, instinctive; a part of the happy instinct which had guided him to my door and helped him to spell out my name on the card nailed to it. He had had no other introduction to me than a guess, from the shape of my high north window, seen outside, that my place was a studio and that as a studio it would contain an artist. He had wandered to England in search of fortune, like other itinerants, and had embarked, with a partner and a small green handcart, on the sale of penny ices. The ices had melted away and the partner had dissolved

---

7. Dante Alighieri (1265–1321) was the Italian poet of *The Divine Comedy*. Beatrice is a heavenly figure in that poem (as well as in Dante's *Vita Nuova*), inspired by an earthly love.

8. A real feeling for posing.

in their train. My young man wore tight yellow trousers with reddish stripes and his name was Oronte. He was sallow but fair, and when I put him into some old clothes of my own he looked like an Englishman. He was as good as Miss Churm, who could look, when required, like an Italian.

IV

I thought Mrs. Monarch's face slightly convulsed when, on her coming back with her husband, she found Oronte installed. It was strange to have to recognise in a scrap of a lazzarone[9] a competitor to her magnificent Major. It was she who scented danger first, for the Major was anecdotically unconscious. But Oronte gave us tea, with a hundred eager confusions (he had never seen such a queer process), and I think she thought better of me for having at last an "establishment." They saw a couple of drawings that I had made of the establishment, and Mrs. Monarch hinted that it never would have struck her that he had sat for them. "Now the drawings you make from *us*, they look exactly like us," she reminded me, smiling in triumph; and I recognised that this was indeed just their defect. When I drew the Monarchs I couldn't, somehow, get away from them—get into the character I wanted to represent; and I had not the least desire my model should be discoverable in my picture. Miss Churm never was, and Mrs. Monarch thought I hid her, very properly, because she was vulgar; whereas if she was lost it was only as the dead who go to heaven are lost—in the gain of an angel the more.

By this time I had got a certain start with "Rutland Ramsay," the first novel in the great projected series; that is I had produced a dozen drawings, serveral with the help of the Major and his wife, and I had sent them in for approval. My understanding with the publishers, as I have already hinted, had been that I was to be left to do my work, in this particular case, as I liked, with the whole book committed to me; but my connection with the rest of the series was only contingent. There were moments when, frankly, it *was* a comfort to have the real thing under one's hand; for there were characters in "Rutland Ramsay" that were very much like it. There were people presumably as straight as the Major and women of as good a fashion as Mrs. Monarch. There was a great deal of country-house life—treated, it is true, in a fine, fanciful, ironical, generalised way—and there was a considerable implication of knickerbockers and kilts. There were certain things I had to settle at the outset; such things for instance as the exact appearance of the hero, the particular bloom of the heroine. The author of course gave me a lead, but there was a margin for interpretation. I took the Monarchs into my confidence, I told them frankly what I was about, I mentioned my embarrassments and alternatives.

9. Neapolitan rascal.

"Oh, take *him!*" Mrs. Monarch murmured sweetly, looking at her husband; and "What could you want better than my wife?" the Major inquired, with the comfortable candour that now prevailed between us.

I was not obliged to answer these remarks—I was only obliged to place my sitters. I was not easy in mind, and I postponed, a little timidly perhaps, the solution of the question. The book was a large canvas, the other figures were numerous, and I worked off at first some of the episodes in which the hero and the heroine were not concerned. When once I had set *them* up I should have to stick to them—I couldn't make my young man seven feet high in one place and five feet nine in another. I inclined on the whole to the latter measurement, though the Major more than once reminded me that *he* looked about as young as anyone. It was indeed quite possible to arrange him, for the figure, so that it would have been difficult to detect his age. After the spontaneous Oronte had been with me a month, and after I had given him to understand several different times that his native exuberance would presently constitute an insurmountable barrier to our further intercourse, I waked to a sense of his heroic capacity. He was only five feet seven, but the remaining inches were latent. I tried him almost secretly at first, for I was really rather afraid of the judgment my other models would pass on such a choice. If they regarded Miss Churm as little better than a snare, what would they think of the representation by a person so little the real thing as an Italian street-vendor of a protagonist formed by a public school?

If I went a little in fear of them it was not because they bullied me, because they had got an oppressive foothold, but because in their really pathetic decorum and mysteriously permanent newness they counted on me so intensely. I was therefore very glad when Jack Hawley came home: he was always of such good counsel. He painted badly himself, but there was no one like him for putting his finger on the place. He had been absent from England for a year; he had been somewhere—I don't remember where—to get a fresh eye. I was in a good deal of dread of any such organ, but we were old friends; he had been away for months and a sense of emptiness was creeping into my life. I hadn't dodged a missile for a year.

He came back with a fresh eye, but with the same old black velvet blouse, and the first evening he spent in my studio we smoked cigarettes till the small hours. He had done no work himself, he had only got the eye; so the field was clear for the production of my little things. He wanted to see what I had done for the *Cheapside*, but he was disappointed in the exhibition. That at least seemed the meaning of two or three comprehensive groans which, as he lounged on my big divan, on a folded leg, looking at my latest drawings, issued from his lips with the smoke of the cigarette.

"What's the matter with you?" I asked.

"What's the matter with *you?*"

"Nothing save that I'm mystified."

"You are indeed. You're quite off the hinge. What's the meaning of this new fad?" And he tossed me, with visible irreverence, a drawing in which I happened to have depicted both my majestic models. I asked if he didn't think it good, and he replied that it struck him as execrable, given the sort of thing I had always represented myself to him as wishing to arrive at; but I let that pass, I was so anxious to see exactly what he meant. The two figures in the picture looked colossal, but I supposed this was *not* what he meant, inasmuch as, for aught he knew to the contrary, I might have been trying for that. I maintained that I was working exactly in the same way as when he last had done me the honour to commend me. "Well, there's a big hole somewhere," he answered; "wait a bit and I'll discover it." I depended upon him to do so: where else was the fresh eye? But he produced at last nothing more luminous than "I don't know—I don't like your types." This was lame, for a critic who had never consented to discuss with me anything but the question of execution, the direction of strokes and the mystery of values.

"In the drawings you've been looking at I think my types are very handsome."

"Oh, they won't do!"

"I've had a couple of new models."

"I see you have. *They* won't do."

"Are you very sure of that?"

"Absolutely—they're stupid."

"You mean I am—for I ought to get round that."

"You *can't*—with such people. Who are they?"

I told him, as far as was necessary, and he declared, heartlessly: "*Ce sont des gens qu'il faut mettre à la porte.*"[1]

"You've never seen them; they're awfully good," I compassionately objected.

"Not seen them? Why, all this recent work of yours drops to pieces with them. It's all I want to see of them."

"No one else has said anything against it—the *Cheapside* people are pleased."

"Everyone else is an ass, and the *Cheapside* people the biggest asses of all. Come, don't pretend, at this time of day, to have pretty illusions about the public, especially about publishers and editors. It's not for *such* animals you work—it's for those who know, *coloro che sanno*,[2] so

1. They are people one has to put out the door.
2. In Dante's *Inferno* (IV, 131) Aristotle is referred to as "*il maestro di color che sanno,*" that is, as "the master of those who know." James's

coloro is the usual form; Dante with poetic license drops the final *o* for the sake of the rhythm.

keep straight for *me* if you can't keep straight for yourself. There's a certain sort of thing you tried for from the first—and a very good thing it is. But this twaddle isn't *in* it." When I talked with Hawley later about "Rutland Ramsay" and its possible successors he declared that I must get back into my boat again or I would go to the bottom. His voice in short was the voice of warning.

I noted the warning, but I didn't turn my friends out of doors. They bored me a good deal; but the very fact that they bored me admonished me not to sacrifice them—if there was anything to be done with them—simply to irritation. As I look back at this phase they seem to me to have pervaded my life not a little. I have a vision of them as most of the time in my studio, seated, against the wall, on an old velvet bench to be out of the way, and looking like a pair of patient courtiers in a royal ante-chamber. I am convinced that during the coldest weeks of the winter they held their ground because it saved them fire. Their newness was losing its gloss, and it was impossible not to feel that they were objects of charity. Whenever Miss Churm arrived they went away, and after I was fairly launched in "Rutland Ramsay" Miss Churm arrived pretty often. They managed to express to me tacitly that they supposed I wanted her for the low life of the book, and I let them suppose it, since they had attempted to study the work—it was lying about the studio—without discovering that it dealt only with the highest circles. They had dipped into the most brilliant of our novelists without deciphering many passages. I still took an hour from them, now and again, in spite of Jack Hawley's warning: it would be time enough to dismiss them, if dismissal should be necessary, when the rigour of the season was over. Hawley had made their acquaintance—he had met them at my fireside—and thought them a ridiculous pair. Learning that he was a painter they tried to approach him, to show him too that they were the real thing; but he looked at them, across the big room, as if they were miles away: they were a compendium of everything that he most objected to in the social system of his country. Such people as that, all convention and patent-leather, with ejaculations that stopped conversation, had no business in a studio. A studio was a place to learn to see, and how could you see through a pair of feather beds?

The main inconvenience I suffered at their hands was that, at first, I was shy of letting them discover how my artful little servant had begun to sit to me for "Rutland Ramsay." They knew that I had been odd enough (they were prepared by this time to allow oddity to artists,) to pick a foreign vagabond out of the streets, when I might have had a person with whiskers and credentials; but it was some time before they learned how high I rated his accomplishments. They found him in an attitude more than once, but they never doubted I was doing him as an organ-grinder. There were several things they never guessed, and one of them was that for a striking scene in the novel, in which a footman briefly figured, it occurred to me to make use of Major Monarch as the menial. I kept putting this off, I didn't like to ask him to don the livery—besides the difficulty of finding a livery to fit him. At last, one day late in the winter, when I was at work on the despised Oronte (he caught one's idea in an instant), and was in the glow of feeling that I was going very straight, they came in, the Major and his wife, with their society laugh about nothing (there was less and less to laugh at), like country-callers—they always reminded me of that—who have walked across the park after church and are presently persuaded to stay to luncheon. Luncheon was over, but they could stay to tea—I knew they wanted it. The fit was on me, however, and I couldn't let my ardour cool and my work wait, with the fading daylight, while my model prepared it. So I asked Mrs. Monarch if she would mind laying it out—a request which, for an instant, brought all the blood to her face. Her eyes were on her husband's for a second, and some mute telegraphy passed between them. Their folly was over the next instant; his cheerful shrewdness put an end to it. So far from pitying their wounded pride, I must add, I was moved to give it as complete a lesson as I could. They bustled about together and got out the cups and saucers and made the kettle boil. I know they felt as if they were waiting on my servant, and when the tea was prepared I said: "He'll have a cup, please—he's tired." Mrs. Monarch brought him one where he stood, and he took it from her as if he had been a gentleman at a party, squeezing a crush-hat with an elbow.

Then it came over me that she had made a great effort for me—made it with a kind of nobleness—and that I owed her a compensation. Each time I saw her after this I wondered what the compensation could be. I couldn't go on doing the wrong thing to oblige them. Oh, it *was* the wrong thing, the stamp of the work for which they sat—Hawley was not the only person to say it now. I sent in a large number of the drawings I had made for "Rutland Ramsay," and I received a warning that was more to the point than Hawley's. The artistic adviser of the house for which I was working was of opinion that many of my illustrations were not what had been looked for. Most of these illustrations were the subjects in which the Monarchs had figured. Without going into the question of what *had* been looked for, I saw at this rate I shouldn't get the other books to do. I hurled myself in despair upon Miss Churm, I put her through all her paces. I not only adopted Oronte publicly as my hero, but one morning when the Major looked in to see if I didn't require him to finish a figure for the *Cheapside*, for which he had begun to sit the week before, I told him that I had changed my mind—I would do the drawing from my man. At this my visitor turned pale and stood looking at me. "Is *he* your idea of an English gentleman?" he asked.

I was disappointed, I was nervous, I wanted to get on with my work; so I replied with irritation: "Oh, my dear Major—I can't be ruined for *you!*"

He stood another moment; then, without a word, he quitted the studio. I drew a long breath when he was gone, for I said to myself that I shouldn't see him again. I had not told him definitely that I was in danger of having my work rejected, but I was vexed at his not having felt the catastrophe in the air, read with me the moral of our fruitless collaboration, the lesson that, in the deceptive atmosphere of art, even the highest respectability may fail of being plastic.

I didn't owe my friends money, but I did see them again. They re-appeared together, three days later, and under the circumstances there was something tragic in the fact. It was a proof to me that they could find nothing else in life to do. They had threshed the matter out in a dismal conference—they had digested the bad news that they were not in for the series. If they were not useful to me even for the *Cheapside* their function seemed difficult to determine, and I could only judge at first that they had come, forgivingly, decorously, to take a last leave. This made me rejoice in secret that I had little leisure for a scene; for I had placed both my other models in position together and I was pegging away at a drawing from which I hoped to derive glory. It had been suggested by the passage in which Rutland Ramsay, drawing up a chair to Artemisia's piano-stool, says extraordinary things to her while she ostensibly fingers out a difficult piece of music. I had done Miss Churm at the piano before—it was an attitude in which she knew how to take on an absolutely poetic grace. I wished the two figures to "compose" together, intensely, and my little Italian had entered perfectly into my conception. The pair were vividly before me, the piano had been pulled out; it was a charming picture of blended youth and murmured love, which I had only to catch and keep. My visitors stood and looked at it, and I was friendly to them over my shoulder.

They made no response, but I was used to silent company and went on with my work, only a little disconcerted (even though exhilarated by the sense that *this* was at least the ideal thing), at not having got rid of them after all. Presently I heard Mrs. Monarch's sweet voice beside, or rather above me: "I wish her hair was a little better done." I looked up and she was staring with a strange fixedness at Miss Churm, whose back was turned to her. "Do you mind my just touching it?" she went on—a question which made me spring up for an instant, as with the instinctive fear that she might do the young lady a harm. But she quieted me with a glance I shall never forget—I confess I should like to have been able to paint *that*—and went for a moment to my model. She spoke to her softly, laying a hand upon her shoulder and bending over her; and as the girl, understanding, gratefully assented, she disposed her rough curls, with a few quick passes, in such a way as to make Miss Churm's head twice as charming. It was one of the most heroic personal services I have ever seen rendered. Then Mrs. Monarch turned away with a low sigh and, looking about her as if for something to do, stooped to the floor with a noble humility and picked up a dirty rag that had dropped out of my paint-box.

The Major meanwhile had also been looking for something to do and, wandering to the other end of the studio, saw before him my breakfast things, neglected, unremoved. "I say, can't I be useful *here?*" he called out to me with an irrepressible quaver. I assented with a laugh that I fear was awkward and for the next ten minutes, while I worked, I heard the light clatter of china and the tinkle of spoons and glass. Mrs. Monarch assisted her husband—they washed up my crockery, they put it away. They wandered off into my little scullery, and I afterwards found that they had cleaned my knives and that my slender stock of plate had an unprecedented surface. When it came over me, the latent eloquence of what they were doing, I confess that my drawing was blurred for a moment—the picture swam. They had accepted their failure, but they couldn't accept their fate. They had bowed their heads in bewilderment to the perverse and cruel law in virtue of which the real thing could be so much less precious than the unreal; but they didn't want to starve. If my servants were my models, my models might be my servants. They would reverse the parts—the others would sit for the ladies and gentleman, and *they* would do the work. They would still be in the studio—it was an intense dumb appeal to me not to turn them out. "Take us on," they wanted to say—"we'll do *anything.*"

When all this hung before me the *afflatus* vanished—my pencil dropped from my hand. My sitting was spoiled and I got rid of my sitters, who were also evidently rather mystified and awestruck. Then, alone with the Major and his wife, I had a most uncomfortable moment. He put their prayer into a single sentence: "I say, you know—just let *us* do for you, can't you?" I couldn't—it was dreadful to see them emptying my slops; but I pretended I could, to oblige them, for about a week. Then I gave them a sum of money to go away; and I never saw them again. I obtained the remaining books, but my friend Hawley repeats that Major and Mrs. Monarch did me a permanent harm, got me into a second-rate trick. If it be true I am content to have paid the price—for the memory.

The Middle Years

(1893)†

The April day was soft and bright, and poor Dencombe, happy in the conceit of reasserted strength, stood in the garden of the hotel, comparing, with a deliberation in which, however, there was still something of languor, the attractions of easy strolls. He liked the feeling of the south, so far as you could have it in the north, he liked the sandy cliffs and the clustered pines, he liked even the colourless sea. "Bournemouth[1] as a health-resort" had sounded like a mere advertisement, but now he was reconciled to the prosaic. The sociable country postman, passing through the garden, had just given him a small parcel, which he took out with him, leaving the hotel to the right and creeping to a convenient bench that he knew of, a safe recess in the cliff. It looked to the south, to the tinted walls of the Island, and was protected behind by the sloping shoulder of the down. He was tired enough when he reached it, and for a moment he was disappointed; he was better, of course, but better, after all, than what? He should never again, as at one or two great moments of the past, be better than himself. The infinite of life had gone, and what was left of the dose was a small glass engraved like a thermometer by the apothecary. He sat and stared at the sea, which appeared all surface and twinkle, far shallower than the spirit of man. It was the abyss of human illusion that was the real, the tideless deep. He held his packet, which had come by book-post, unopened on his knee, liking, in the lapse of so many joys (his illness had made him feel his age), to know that it was there, but taking for granted there could be no complete renewal of the pleasure, dear to young experience, of seeing one's self "just out."[2] Dencombe, who had a reputation, had come out too often and knew too well in advance how he should look.

His postponement associated itself vaguely, after a little, with a group of three persons, two ladies and a young man, whom, beneath him, straggling and seemingly silent, he could see move slowly together along the sands. The gentleman had his head bent over a book and was occasionally brought to a stop by the charm of this volume, which, as Dencombe could perceive even at a distance, had a cover

†"The Middle Years" appeared in *Scribner's Magazine* in April 1893. Its first publication in a book was in *Terminations* (London: William Heinemann, 1895); this text is here reprinted.
1. On the English Channel coast and famous for its pines and clear air. Though Bourne-mouth is in northern Europe, some of the vegetation in the area resembles that of southern Europe. The island with the tinted walls may be the Isle of Wight, though almost fifteen miles distant and more east than south.
2. Just published.

alluringly red. Then his companions, going a little further, waited for him to come up, poking their parasols into the beach, looking around them at the sea and sky and clearly sensible of the beauty of the day. To these things the young man with the book was still more clearly indifferent; lingering, credulous, absorbed, he was an object of envy to an observer from whose connection with literature all such artlessness had faded. One of the ladies was large and mature; the other had the spareness of comparative youth and of a social situation possibly inferior. The large lady carried back Dencombe's imagination to the age of crinoline; she wore a hat of the shape of a mushroom, decorated with a blue veil, and had the air, in her aggressive amplitude, of clinging to a vanished fashion or even a lost cause. Presently her companion produced from under the folds of a mantle a limp, portable chair which she stiffened out and of which the large lady took possession. This act, and something in the movement of either party, instantly characterised the performers—they performed for Dencombe's recreation—as opulent matron and humble dependent. What, moreover, was the use of being an approved novelist if one couldn't establish a relation between such figures; the clever theory, for instance, that the young man was the son of the opulent matron, and that the humble dependant, the daughter of a clergyman or an officer, nourished a secret passion for him? Was that not visible from the way she stole behind her protectress to look back at him?—back to where he had let himself come to a full stop when his mother sat down to rest. His book was a novel; it had the catchpenny cover, and while the romance of life stood neglected at his side he lost himself in that of the circulating library. He moved mechanically to where the sand was softer, and ended by plumping down in it to finish his chapter at his ease. The humble dependant, discouraged by his remoteness, wandered, with a martyred droop of the head, in another direction, and the exorbitant lady, watching the waves, offered a confused resemblance to a flying-machine that had broken down.

When his drama began to fail Dencombe remembered that he had, after all, another pastime. Though such promptitude on the part of the publisher was rare, he was already able to draw from its wrapper his "latest," perhaps his last. The cover of "The Middle Years" was duly meretricious, the smell of the fresh pages the very odour of sanctity; but for the moment he went no further—he had become conscious of a strange alienation. He had forgotten what his book was about. Had the assault of his old ailment, which he had so fallaciously come to Bournemouth to ward off, interposed utter blankness as to what had preceded it? He had finished the revision of proof before quitting London, but his subsequent fortnight in bed had passed the sponge over colour. He couldn't have chanted to himself a single sentence, couldn't have turned with curiosity or confidence to any particular page. His subject had already gone from him, leaving scarcely a superstition behind. He uttered a low moan as he breathed the chill of this dark void, so desperately it seemed to represent the completion of a sinister process. The tears filled his mild eyes; something precious had passed away. This was the pang that had been sharpest during the last few years—the sense of ebbing time, of shrinking opportunity; and now he felt not so much that his last chance was going as that it was gone indeed. He had done all that he should ever do, and yet he had not done what he wanted. This was the laceration—that practically his career was over: it was as violent as a rough hand at his throat. He rose from his seat nervously, like a creature hunted by a dread; then he fell back in his weakness and nervously opened his book. It was a single volume; he preferred single volumes and aimed at a rare compression.[3] He began to read, and little by little, in this occupation, he was pacified and reassured. Everything came back to him, but came back with a wonder, came back, above all, with a high and magnificent beauty. He read his own prose, he turned his own leaves, and had, as he sat there with the spring sunshine on the page, an emotion peculiar and intense. His career was over, no doubt, but it was over, after all, with *that*.

He had forgotten during his illness the work of the previous year; but what he had chiefly forgotten was that it was extraordinarily good. He lived once more into his story and was drawn down, as by a siren's hand, to where, in the dim underworld of fiction, the great glazed tank of art, strange silent subjects float. He recognised his motive and surrendered to his talent. Never, probably, had that talent, such as it was, been so fine. His difficulties were still there, but what was also there, to his perception, though probably, alas! to nobody's else, was the art that in most cases had surmounted them. In his surprised enjoyment of this ability he had a glimpse of a possible reprieve. Surely its force was not spent—there was life and service in it yet. It had not come to him easily, it had been backward and roundabout. It was the child of time, the nursling of delay; he had struggled and suffered for it, making sacrifices not to be counted, and now that it was really mature was it to cease to yield, to confess itself brutally beaten? There was an infinite charm for Dencombe in feeling as he had never felt before that diligence *vincit omnia*.[4] The result produced in his little book was somehow a result beyond his conscious intention: it was as if he had planted his genius, had trusted his method, and they had grown up and flowered with this sweetness. If the achievement had been real, however, the process had been manful enough. What he saw so intensely to-day, what he felt as a nail driven in, was that only

3. In the nineteenth century long novels were usually published in several volumes—often three. James himself also "aimed" at compression.

4. Diligence "conquers all." Cf. *Amor vincit omnia* ("Love conquers all"), a proverbial phrase found in Virgil's *Eclogues* (X, 69) and inscribed on the brooch of Chaucer's Prioress.

now, at the very last, had he come into possession. His development had been abnormally slow, almost grotesquely gradual. He had been hindered and retarded by experience, and for long periods had only groped his way. It had taken too much of his life to produce too little of his art. The art had come, but it had come after everything else. At such a rate a first existence was too short—long enough only to collect material; so that to fructify, to use the material, one must have a second age, an extension. This extension was what poor Dencombe sighed for. As he turned the last leaves of his volume he murmured: "Ah for another go!—ah for a better chance!"

The three persons he had observed on the sands had vanished and then reappeared; they had now wandered up a path, an artificial and easy ascent, which led to the top of the cliff. Dencombe's bench was half-way down, on a sheltered ledge, and the large lady, a massive, heterogeneous person, with bold black eyes and kind red cheeks, now took a few moments to rest. She wore dirty gauntlets and immense diamond ear-rings; at first she looked vulgar, but she contradicted this announcement in an agreeable off-hand tone. While her companions stood waiting for her she spread her skirts on the end of Dencombe's seat. The young man had gold spectacles, through which, with his finger still in his red-covered book, he glanced at the volume, bound in the same shade of the same colour, lying on the lap of the original occupant of the bench. After an instant Dencombe understood that he was struck with a resemblance, had recognised the gilt stamp on the crimson cloth, was reading "The Middle Years," and now perceived that somebody else had kept pace with him. The stranger was startled, possibly even a little ruffled, to find that he was not the only person who had been favoured with an early copy. The eyes of the two proprietors met for a moment, and Dencombe borrowed amusement from the expression of those of his competitor, those, it might even be inferred, of his admirer. They confessed to some resentment—they seemed to say: "Hang it, has he got it *already?*—Of course he's a brute of a reviewer!" Dencombe shuffled his copy out of sight while the opulent matron, rising from her repose, broke out: "I feel already the good of this air!"

"I can't say I do," said the angular lady. "I find myself quite let down."

"I find myself horribly hungry. At what time did you order luch?" her protectress pursued.

The young person put the question by. "Doctor Hugh always orders it."

"I ordered nothing to-day—I'm going to make you diet," said their comrade.

"Then I shall go home and sleep. *Qui dort dîne!*"[5]

5. Literally, "He who sleeps dines"; i.e., a good sleep is worth a dinner.

"Can I trust you to Miss Vernham?" asked Doctor Hugh of his elder companion.

"Don't I trust *you?*" she archly inquired.

"Not too much!" Miss Vernham, with her eyes on the ground, permitted herself to declare. "You must come with us at least to the house," she went on, while the personage on whom they appeared to be in attendance began to mount higher. She had got a little out of ear-shot; nevertheless Miss Vernham became, so far as Dencombe was concerned, less distinctly audible to murmur to the young man: "I don't think you realise all you owe the Countess!"

Absently, a moment, Doctor Hugh caused his gold-rimmed spectacles to shine at her.

"Is that the way I strike you? I see—I see!"

"She's awfully good to us," continued Miss Vernham, compelled by her interlocutor's immovability to stand there in spite of his discussion of private matters. Of what use would it have been that Dencombe should be sensitive to shades had he not detected in that immovability a strange influence from the quiet old convalescent in the great tweed cape? Miss Vernham appeared suddenly to become aware of some such connection, for she added in a moment: "If you want to sun yourself here you can come back after you've seen us home."

Doctor Hugh, at this, hesitated, and Dencombe, in spite of a desire to pass for unconscious, risked a covert glance at him. What his eyes met this time, as it happened, was on the part of the young lady a queer stare, naturally vitreous, which made her aspect remind him of some figure (he couldn't name it) in a play or a novel, some sinister governess or tragic old maid. She seemed to scrutinise him, to challenge him, to say, from general spite: "What have you got to do with us?" At the same instant the rich humour of the Countess reached them from above: "Come, come, my little lambs, you should follow your old *bergère!*"[6] Miss Vernham turned away at this, pursuing the ascent, and Doctor Hugh, after another mute appeal to Dencombe and a moment's evident demur, deposited his book on the bench, as if to keep his place or even as a sign that he would return, and bounded without difficulty up the rougher part of the cliff.

Equally innocent and infinite are the pleasures of observation and the resources engendered by the habit of analysing life. It amused poor Dencombe, as he dawdled in his tepid air-bath, to think that he was waiting for a revelation of something at the back of a fine young mind. He looked hard at the book on the end of the bench, but he wouldn't have touched it for the world. It served his purpose to have a theory which should not be exposed to refutation. He already felt better of his

6. Shepherdess, guardian.

melancholy; he had, according to his old formula, put his head at the window. A passing Countess could draw off the fancy when, like the elder of the ladies who had just retreated, she was as obvious as the giantess of a caravan. It was indeed general views that were terrible; short ones, contrary to an opinion sometimes expressed, were the refuge, were the remedy. Doctor Hugh couldn't possibly be anything but a reviewer who had understandings for early copies with publishers or with newspapers. He reappeared in a quarter of an hour, with visible relief at finding Dencombe on the spot, and the gleam of white teeth in an embarrassed but generous smile. He was perceptibly disappointed at the eclipse of the other copy of the book; it was a pretext the less for speaking to the stranger. But he spoke notwithstanding; he held up his own copy and broke out pleadingly:

"*Do* say, if you have occasion to speak of it, that it's the best thing he has done yet!"

Dencombe responded with a laugh: "Done yet" was so amusing to him, made such a grand avenue of the future. Better still, the young man took *him* for a reviewer. He pulled out "The Middle Years" from under his cape, but instinctively concealed any tell-tale look of fatherhood. This was partly because a person was always a fool for calling attention to his work. "Is that what you're going to say yourself?" he inquired of his visitor.

"I'm not quite sure I shall write anything. I don't, as a regular thing—I enjoy in peace. But it's awfully fine."

Dencombe debated a moment. If his interlocutor had begun to abuse him he would have confessed on the spot to his identity, but there was no harm in drawing him on a little to praise. He drew him on with such success that in a few moments his new acquaintance, seated by his side, was confessing candidly that Dencombe's novels were the only ones he could read a second time. He had come the day before from London, where a friend of his, a journalist, had lent him his copy of the last—the copy sent to the office of the journal and already the subject of a "notice" which, as was pretended there (but one had to allow for "swagger") it had taken a full quarter of an hour to prepare. He intimated that he was ashamed for his friend, and in the case of a work demanding and repaying study, of such inferior manners; and, with his fresh appreciation and inexplicable wish to express it, he speedily became for poor Dencombe a remarkable, a delightful apparition. Chance had brought the weary man of letters face to face with the greatest admirer in the new generation whom it was supposable he possessed. The admirer, in truth, was mystifying, so rare a case was it to find a bristling young doctor—he looked like a German physiologist—enamoured of literary form. It was an accident, but happier than most accidents, so that Dencombe, exhilarated as well as confounded, spent half an hour in making his visitor talk while he kept himself quiet. He explained his premature possession of "The Middle Years" by an allusion to the friendship of the publisher, who, knowing he was at Bournemouth for his health, had paid him this graceful attention. He admitted that he had been ill, for Doctor Hugh would infallibly have guessed it; he even went so far as to wonder whether he mightn't look for some hygenic "tip" from a personage combining so bright an enthusiasm with a presumable knowledge of the remedies now in vogue. It would shake his faith a little perhaps to have to take a doctor seriously who could take *him* so seriously, but he enjoyed this gushing modern youth and he felt with an acute pang that there would still be work to do in a world in which such odd combinations were presented. It was not true, what he had tried for renunciation's sake to believe, that all the combinations were exhausted. They were not, they were not—they were infinite: the exhaustion was in the miserable artist.

Doctor Hugh was an ardent physiologist, saturated with the spirit of the age—in other words he had just taken his degree; but he was independent and various, he talked like a man who would have preferred to love literature best. He would fain have made fine phrases, but nature had denied him the trick. Some of the finest in "The Middle Years" had struck him inordinately, and he took the liberty of reading them to Dencombe in support of his plea. He grew vivid, in the balmy air, to his companion, for whose deep refreshment he seemed to have been sent; and was particularly ingenuous in describing how recently he had become acquainted, and how instantly infatuated, with the only man who had put flesh between the ribs of an art that was starving on superstitions. He had not yet written to him—he was deterred by a sentiment of respect. Dencombe at this moment felicitated himself more than ever on having never answered the photographers. His visitor's attitude promised him a luxury of intercourse, but he surmised that a certain security in it, for Doctor Hugh, would depend not a little on the Countess. He learned without delay with what variety of Countess they were concerned, as well as the nature of the tie that united the curious trio. The large lady, an Englishwoman by birth and the daughter of a celebrated baritone, whose taste, without his talent, she had inherited, was the widow of a French nobleman and mistress of all that remained of the handsome fortune, the fruit of her father's earnings, that had constituted her dower. Miss Vernham, an odd creature but an accomplished pianist, was attached to her person at a salary. The Countess was generous, independent, eccentric; she travelled with her minstrel and her medical man. Ignorant and passionate, she had nevertheless moments in which she was almost irresistible. Dencombe saw her sit for her portrait in Doctor Hugh's free sketch, and felt the picture of his young friend's relation to her frame itself in his mind. This young friend, for a representative of the new psychology, was himself easily hypnotised, and if he became abnormally communicative it was only a sign of his real subjection. Dencombe did accordingly what he wanted with him, even without being known as Dencombe.

Taken ill on a journey in Switzerland the Countess had picked him up at an hotel, and the accident of his happening to please her had made her offer him, with her imperious liberality, terms that couldn't fail to dazzle a practitioner without patients and whose resources had been drained dry by his studies. It was not the way he would have elected to spend his time, but it was time that would pass quickly, and meanwhile she was wonderfully kind. She exacted perpetual attention, but it was impossible not to like her. He gave details about his queer patient, a "type" if there ever was one, who had in connection with her flushed obesity and in addition to the morbid strain of a violent and aimless will a grave organic disorder; but he came back to his loved novelist, whom he was so good as to pronounce more essentially a poet than many of those who went in for verse, with a zeal excited, as all his indiscretion had been excited, by the happy chance of Dencombe's sympathy and the coincidence of their occupation. Dencombe had confessed to a slight personal acquaintance with the author of "The Middle Years," but had not felt himself as ready as he could have wished when his companion, who had never yet encountered a being so privileged, began to be eager for particulars. He even thought that Doctor Hugh's eye at that moment emitted a glimmer of suspicion. But the young man was too inflamed to be shrewd and repeatedly caught up the book to exclaim: "Did you notice this?" or "Weren't you immensely struck with that?" "There's a beautiful passage toward the end," he broke out; and again he laid his hand upon the volume. As he turned the pages he came upon something else, while Dencombe saw him suddenly change colour. He had taken up, as it lay on the bench, Dencombe's copy instead of his own, and his neighbour immediately guessed the reason of his start. Doctor Hugh looked grave an instant; then he said: "I see you've been altering the text!" Dencombe was a passionate corrector, a fingerer of style; the last thing he ever arrived at was a form final for himself. His ideal would have been to publish secretly, and then, on the published text, treat himself to the terrified revise, sacrificing always a first edition and beginning for posterity and even for the collectors, poor dears, with a second. This morning in "The Middle Years," his pencil had pricked a dozen lights. He was amused at the effect of the young man's reproach; for an instant it made him change colour. He stammered, at any rate, ambiguously; then, through a blur of ebbing consciousness, saw Doctor Hugh's mystified eyes. He only had time to feel he was about to be ill again—that emotion, excitement, fatigue, the heat of the sun, the solicitation of the air, had combined to play him a trick, before, stretching out a hand to his visitor with a plaintive cry, he lost his senses altogether.

Later he knew that he had fainted and that Doctor Hugh had got him home in a bath-chair, the conductor of which, prowling within hail for custom, had happened to remember seeing him in the garden of the hotel. He had recovered his perception in the transit, and had, in bed, that afternoon, a vague recollection of Doctor Hugh's young face, as they went together, bent over him in a comforting laugh and expressive of something more than a suspicion of his identity. That identity was ineffaceable now, and all the more that he was disappointed, disgusted. He had been rash, been stupid, had gone out too soon, stayed out too long. He oughtn't to have exposed himself to strangers, he ought to have taken his servant. He felt as if he had fallen into a hole too deep to descry any little patch of heaven. He was confused about the time that had elapsed—he pieced the fragments together. He had seen his doctor, the real one, the one who had treated him from the first and who had again been very kind. His servant was in and out on tiptoe, looking very wise after the fact. He said more than once something about the sharp young gentleman. The rest was vagueness, in so far as it wasn't despair. The vagueness, however, justified itself by dreams, dozing anxieties from which he finally emerged to the consciousness of a dark room and a shaded candle.

"You'll be all right again—I know all about you now," said a voice near him that he knew to be young. Then his meeting with Doctor Hugh came back. He was too discouraged to joke about it yet, but he was able to perceive, after a little, that the interest of it was intense for his visitor. "Of course I can't attend you professionally—you've got your own man, with whom I've talked and who's excellent," Doctor Hugh went on. "But you must let me come to see you as a good friend. I've just looked in before going to bed. You're doing beautifully, but it's a good job I was with you on the cliff. I shall come in early to-morrow. I want to do something for you. I want to do everything. You've done a tremendous lot for me." The young man held his hand, hanging over him, and poor Dencombe, weakly aware of this living pressure, simply lay there and accepted his devotion. He couldn't do anything less—he needed help too much.

The idea of the help he needed was very present to him that night, which he spent in a lucid stillness, an intensity of thought that constituted a reaction from his hours of stupor. He was lost, he was lost—he was lost if he couldn't be saved. He was not afraid of suffering, of death; he was not even in love with life; but he had had a deep demonstration of desire. It came over him in the long, quiet hours that only with "The Middle Years" had he taken his flight; only on that day, visited by soundless processions, had he recognised his kingdom. He had had a revelation of his range. What he dreaded was the idea that his reputation should stand on the unfinished. It was not with his past but with his future that it should properly be concerned. Illness and age rose before him like spectres with pitiless eyes: how was he to bribe such fates to give him the second chance? He had had the one chance that all men have—he had had the chance of life. He went to sleep again very late, and when he awoke Doctor Hugh was sitting by his head. There was already, by this time, something beautifully familiar in him.

"Don't think I've turned out your physician," he said; "I'm acting with his consent. He has been here and seen you. Somehow he seems to trust me. I told him how we happened to come together yesterday, and he recognises that I've a peculiar right."

Dencombe looked at him with a calculating earnestness. "How have you squared the Countess?"

The young man blushed a little, but he laughed. "Oh, never mind the Countess!"

"You told me she was very exacting."

Doctor Hugh was silent a moment. "So she is."

"And Miss Vernham's an *intrigante*."[7]

"How do you know that?"

"I know everything. One *has* to, to write decently!"

"I think she's mad," said limpid Doctor Hugh.

"Well, don't quarrel with the Countess—she's a present help to you."

"I don't quarrel," Doctor Hugh replied. "But I don't get on with silly women." Presently he added: "You seem very much alone."

"That often happens at my age. I've outlived, I've lost by the way."

Doctor Hugh hesitated; then surmounting a soft scruple: "Whom have you lost?"

"Every one."

"Ah, no," the young man murmured, laying a hand on his arm.

"I once had a wife—I once had a son. My wife died when my child was born, and my boy, at school, was carried off by typhoid."

"I wish I'd been there!" said Doctor Hugh simply.

"Well—if you're here!" Dencombe answered, with a smile that, in spite of dimness, showed how much he liked to be sure of his companion's whereabouts.

"You talk strangely of your age. You're not old."

"Hypocrite—so early!"

"I speak physiologically."

"That's the way I've been speaking for the last five years, and it's exactly what I've been saying to myself. It isn't till we *are* old that we begin to tell ourselves we're not!"

"Yet I know I myself am young," Doctor Hugh declared.

7. Schemer.

"Not so well as I!" laughed his patient, whose visitor indeed would have established the truth in question by the honesty with which he changed the point of view, remarking that it must be one of the charms of age—at any rate in the case of high distinction—to feel that one has laboured and achieved. Doctor Hugh employed the common phrase about earning one's rest, and it made poor Dencombe, for an instant, almost angry. He recovered himself, however, to explain, lucidly enough, that if he, ungraciously, knew nothing of such a balm, it was doubtless because he had wasted inestimable years. He had followed literature from the first, but he had taken a lifetime to get alongside of her. Only to-day, at last, had he begun to *see*, so that what he had hitherto done was a movement without a direction. He had ripened too late and was so clumsily constituted that he had had to teach himself by mistakes.

"I prefer your flowers, then, to other people's fruit, and your mistakes to other people's successes," said gallant Doctor Hugh. "It's for your mistakes I admire you."

"You're happy—you don't know," Dencombe answered.

Looking at his watch the young man had got up; he named the hour of the afternoon at which he would return. Dencombe warned him against committing himself too deeply, and expressed again all his dread of making him neglect the Countess—perhaps incur her displeasure.

"I want to be like you—I want to learn by mistakes!" Doctor Hugh laughed.

"Take care you don't make too grave a one! But do come back," Dencombe added, with the glimmer of a new idea.

"You should have had more vanity!" Doctor Hugh spoke as if he knew the exact amount required to make a man of letters normal.

"No, no—I only should have had more time. I want another go."

"Another go?"

"I want an extension."

"An extension?" Again Doctor Hugh repeated Dencombe's words, with which he seemed to have been struck.

"Don't you know?—I want to what they call 'live.' "

The young man, for good-bye, had taken his hand, which closed with a certain force. They looked at each other hard a moment. "You *will* live," said Doctor Hugh.

"Don't be superficial. It's too serious!"

"You *shall* live!" Dencombe's visitor declared, turning pale.

"Ah, that's better!" And as he retired the invalid, with a troubled laugh, sank gratefully back.

All that day and all the following night he wondered if it mightn't be arranged. His doctor came again, his servant was attentive, but it was to his confident young friend that he found himself mentally appealing. His collapse on the cliff was plausibly explained, and his liberation, on a better basis, promised for the morrow; meanwhile, however, the intensity of his meditations kept him tranquil and made him indifferent. The idea that occupied him was none the less absorbing because it was a morbid fancy. Here was a clever son of the age, ingenious and ardent, who happened to have set him up for connoisseurs to worship. This servant of his altar had all the new learning in science and all the old reverence in faith; wouldn't he therefore put his knowledge at the disposal of his sympathy, his craft at the disposal of his love? Couldn't he be trusted to invent a remedy for a poor artist to whose art he had paid a tribute? If he couldn't, the alternative was hard: Dencombe would have to surrender to silence, unvindicated and undivined. The rest of the day and all the next he toyed in secret with this sweet futility. Who would work the miracle for him but the young man who could combine such lucidity with such passion? He thought of the fairy-tales of science and charmed himself into forgetting that he looked for a magic that was not of this world. Doctor Hugh was an apparition, and that placed him above the law. He came and went while his patient, who sat up, followed him with supplicating eyes. The interest of knowing the great author had made the young man begin "The Middle Years" afresh, and would help him to find a deeper meaning in its pages. Dencombe had told him what he "tried for;" with all his intelligence, on a first perusal, Doctor Hugh had failed to guess it. The baffled celebrity wondered then who in the world *would* guess it: he was amused once more at the fine, full way with which an intention could be missed. Yet he wouldn't rail at the general mind to-day—consoling as that ever had been: the revelation of his own slowness had seemed to make all stupidity sacred.

Doctor Hugh, after a little, was visibly worried, confessing, on inquiry, to a source of embarrassment at home. "Stick to the Countess—don't mind me," Dencombe said, repeatedly; for his companion was frank enough about the large lady's attitude. She was so jealous that she had fallen ill—she resented such a breach of allegiance. She paid so much for his fidelity that she must have it all: she refused him the right to other sympathies, charged him with scheming to make her die alone, for it was needless to point out how little Miss Vernham was a resource in trouble. When Doctor Hugh mentioned that the Countess would already have left Bournemouth if he hadn't kept her in bed, poor Dencombe held his arm tighter and said with decision: "Take her straight away." They had gone out together, walking back to the sheltered nook in which, the other day, they had met. The young man, who had given his companion a personal support, declared with empahsis that his conscience was clear—he could ride two horses at once. Didn't he dream, for his future, of a time when he should have to ride five hundred? Longing equally for virtue, Dencombe replied that in that golden age no patient would pretend to have contracted with him for his whole attention. On the part of the Countess was not such an avidity lawful? Doctor Hugh denied it, said there was no contract but only a free understanding, and that a sordid servitude was impossible to a generous spirit; he liked moreover to talk about art, and that was the subject on which, this time, as they sat together on the sunny bench, he tried most to engage the author of "The Middle Years." Dencombe, soaring again a little on the weak wings of convalescence and still haunted by that happy notion of an organised rescue, found another strain of eloquence to plead the cause of a certain splendid "last manner," the very citadel, as it would prove, of his reputation, the stronghold into which his real treasure would be gathered. While his listener gave up the morning and the great still sea appeared to wait, he had a wonderful explanatory hour. Even for himself he was inspired as he told of what his treasure would consist—the precious metals he would dig from the mine, the jewels rare, strings of pearls, he would hang between the columns of his temple. He was wonderful for himself, so thick his convictions crowded; but he was still more wonderful for Doctor Hugh, who assured him, none the less, that the very pages he had just published were already encrusted with gems. The young man, however, panted for the combinations to come, and, before the face of the beautiful day, renewed to Dencombe his guarantee that his profession would hold itself responsible for such a life. Then he suddenly clapped his hand upon his watch-pocket and asked leave to absent himself for half an hour. Dencombe waited there for his return, but was at last recalled to the actual by the fall of a shadow across the ground. The shadow darkened into that of Miss Vernham, the young lady in attendance on the Countess; whom Dencombe, recognising her, perceived so clearly to have come to speak to him that he rose from his bench to acknowledge the civility. Miss Vernham indeed proved not particularly civil; she looked strangely agitated, and her type was now unmistakable.

"Excuse me if I inquire," she said, "whether it's too much to hope that you may be induced to leave Doctor Hugh alone." Then, before Dencombe, greatly disconcerted, could protest: "You ought to be informed that you stand in his light; that you may do him a terrible injury."

"Do you mean by causing the Countess to dispense with his services?"

"By causing her to disinherit him." Dencombe stared at this, and Miss Vernham pursued, in the gratification of seeing she could produce an impression: "It has depended on himself to come into something very handsome. He has had a magnificent prospect, but I think you've succeeded in spoiling it."

"Not intentionally, I assure you. Is there no hope the accident may be repaired?" Dencombe asked.

"She was ready to do anything for him. She takes great fancies, she lets herself go—it's her way. She has no relations, she's free to dispose of her money, and she's very ill."

"I'm very sorry to hear it," Dencombe stammered.

"Wouldn't it be possible for you to leave Bournemouth? That's what I've come to ask you."

Poor Dencombe sank down on his bench. "I'm very ill myself, but I'll try!"

Miss Vernham still stood there with her colourless eyes and the brutality of her good conscience. "Before it's too late, please!" she said; and with this she turned her back, in order, quickly, as if it had been a business to which she could spare but a precious moment, to pass out of his sight.

Oh, yes, after this Dencombe was certainly very ill. Miss Vernham had upset him with her rough, fierce news; it was the sharpest shock to him to discover what was at stake for a penniless young man of fine parts. He sat trembling on his bench, staring at the waste of waters, feeling sick with the directness of the blow. He was indeed too weak, too unsteady, too alarmed; but he would make the effort to get away, for he couldn't accept the guilt of interference, and his honour was really involved. He would hobble home, at any rate, and then he would think what was to be done. He made his way back to the hotel and, as he went, had a characteristic vision of Miss Verham's great motive. The Countess hated women, of course; Dencombe was lucid about that; so the hungry pianist had no personal hopes and could only console herself with the bold conception of helping Doctor Hugh in order either to marry him after he should get his money or to induce him to recognise her title to compensation and buy her off. If she had befriended him at a fruitful crisis he would really, as a man of delicacy, and she knew what to think of that point, have to reckon with her.

At the hotel Dencombe's servant insisted on his going back to bed. The invalid had talked about catching a train and had begun with orders to pack; after which his humming nerves had yielded to a sense of sickness. He consented to see his physician, who immediately was sent for, but he wished it to be understood that his door was irrevocably closed to Doctor Hugh. He had his plan, which was so fine that he rejoiced in it after getting back to bed. Doctor Hugh, suddenly finding himself snubbed without mercy, would, in natural disgust and to the joy of Miss Vernham, renew his allegiance to the Countess. When his physician arrived Dencombe learned that he was feverish and that this was very wrong: he was to cultivate calmness and try, if possible, not to think. For the rest of the day he wooed stupidity; but there was an ache that kept him sentient, the probable sacrifice of his "extension," the limit of his course. His medical adviser was anything but pleased; his successive relapses were ominous. He charged this personage to put out a strong hand and take Doctor Hugh off his mind—it would contribute so much to his being quiet. The agitating name, in his room, was not mentioned again, but his security was a smothered fear, and it was not confirmed by the receipt, at ten o'clock that evening, of a telegram which his servant opened and read for him and to which, with an address in London, the signature of Miss Vernham was attached. "Beseech you to use all influence to make our friend join us here in the morning. Countess much the worse for dreadful journey, but everything may still be saved." The two ladies had gathered themselves up and had been capable in the afternoon of a spiteful revolution. They had started for the capital, and if the elder one, as Miss Vernham had announced, was very ill, she had wished to make it clear that she was proportionately reckless. Poor Dencombe, who was not reckless and who only desired that everything should indeed be "saved," sent this missive straight off to the young man's lodging and had on the morrow the pleasure of knowing that he had quitted Bournemouth by an early train.

Two days later he pressed in with a copy of a literary journal in his hand. He had returned because he was anxious and for the pleasure of flourishing the great review of "The Middle Years." Here at least was something adequate—it rose to the occasion; it was an acclamation, a reparation, a critical attempt to place the author in the niche he had fairly won. Dencombe accepted and submitted; he made neither objection nor inquiry, for old complications had returned and he had had two atrocious days. He was convinced not only that he should never again leave his bed, so that his young friend might pardonably remain, but that the demand he should make on the patience of beholders would be very moderate indeed. Doctor Hugh had been to town, and he tried to find in his eyes some confession that the Countess was pacified and his legacy clinched; but all he could see there was the light of his juvenile joy in two or three of the phrases of the newspaper. Dencombe couldn't read them, but when his visitor had insisted on repeating them more than once he was able to shake an unintoxicated head. "Ah, no; but they would have been true of what I *could* have done!"

"What people 'could have done' is mainly what they've in fact done," Doctor Hugh contended.

"Mainly, yes; but I've been an idiot!" said Dencombe.

Doctor Hugh did remain; the end was coming fast. Two days later Dencombe observed to him, by way of the feeblest of jokes, that there would now be no question whatever of a second chance. At this the young man stared; then he exclaimed: "Why, it has come to pass—it has come to pass! The second chance has been the public's—the chance to find the point of view, to pick up the pearl!"

"Oh, the pearl!" poor Dencombe uneasily sighed. A smile as cold as a winter sunset flickered on his drawn lips as he added': "The pearl is the unwritten—the pearl is the unalloyed, the *rest*, the lost!

From that moment he was less and less present, heedless to all appearance of what went on around him. His disease was definitely mortal, of an action as relentless, after the short arrest that had enabled him to fall in with Doctor Hugh, as a leak in a great ship. Sinking steadily, though this visitor, a man of rare resources, now cordially approved by his physician, showed endless art in guarding him from pain, poor Dencombe kept no reckoning of favour or neglect, betrayed no symptom of regret or speculation. Yet toward the last he gave a sign of having noticed that for two days Doctor Hugh had not been in his room, a sign that consisted of his suddenly opening his eyes to ask of him if he had spent the interval with the Countess.

"The Countess is dead," said Doctor Hugh. "I knew that in a particular contingency she wouldn't resist. I went to her grave."

Dencombe's eyes opened wider. "She left you 'something handsome'?"

The young man gave a laugh almost too light for a chamber of woe. "Never a penny. She roundly cursed me."

"Cursed you?" Dencombe murmured.

"For giving her up. I gave her up for *you*. I had to choose," his companion explained.

"You chose to let a fortune go?"

"I chose to accept, whatever they might be, the consequences of my infatuation," smiled Doctor Hugh. Then, as a larger pleasantry: "A fortune be hanged! It's your own fault if I can't get your things out of my head."

The immediate tribute to his humour was a long, bewildered moan; after which, for many hours, many days, Dencombe lay motionless and absent. A response so absolute, such a glimpse of a definite result and such a sense of credit worked together in his mind and, producing a strange commotion, slowly altered and transfigured his despair. The sense of cold submersion left him—he seemed to float without an effort. The incident was extraordinary as evidence, and it shed an intenser light. At the last he signed to Doctor Hugh to listen, and, when he was down on his knees by the pillow, brought him very near.

"You've made me think it all a delusion."

"Not your glory, my dear friend," stammered the young man.

"Not my glory—what there is of it! It *is* glory to have been tested, to have had our little quality and cast our little spell. The thing is to have made somebody care. You happen to be crazy, of course, but that doesn't affect the law."

"You're a great success!" said Doctor Hugh, putting into his young voice the ring of a marriage-bell.

Dencombe lay taking this in; then he gathered strength to speak once more. "A second chance—*that's* the delusion. There never was to be but one. We work in the dark—we do what we can—we give what we have. Our doubt is our passion and our passion is our task. The rest is the madness of art."

"If you've doubted, if you've despaired, you've always 'done' it," his visitor subtly argued.

"We've done something or other," Dencombe conceded.

"Something or other is everything. It's the feasible. It's *you!*"

"Comforter!" poor Dencombe ironically sighed.

"But it's true," insisted his friend.

"It's true. It's frustration that doesn't count."

"Frustration's only life," said Doctor Hugh.

"Yes, it's what passes." Poor Dencombe was barely audible, but he had marked with the words the virtual end of his first and only chance.

The Beast in the Jungle

(1903)†

What determined the speech that startled him in the course of their encounter scarcely matters, being probably but some words spoken by himself quite without intention—spoken as they lingered and slowly moved together after their renewal of acquaintance. He had been conveyed by friends, an hour or two before, to the house at which she was staying; the party of visitors at the other house, of whom he was one, and thanks to whom it was his theory, as always, that he was lost in the crowd, had been invited over to luncheon. There had been after luncheon much dispersal, all in the interest of the original motive, a view of Weatherend itself and the fine things, intrinsic features, pictures, heirlooms, treasures of all the arts, that made the place almost famous; and the great rooms were so numerous that guests could wander at their will, hang back from the principal group, and, in cases where they took such matters with the last seriousness, give themselves up to mysterious appreciations and measurements. There were persons to be observed, singly or in couples, bending toward objects in out-of-the-way corners with their hands on their knees and their heads nodding quite as with the emphasis of an excited sense of smell. When they were two they either mingled their sounds of ecstasy or melted into silences of even deeper import, so that there were aspects of the occasion that gave it for Marcher much the air of the "look round," previous to a sale highly advertised, that excites or quenches, as may be, the dream of acquisition. The dream of acquisition at Weatherend would have had to be wild indeed, and John Marcher found himself, among such suggestions, disconcerted almost equally by the presence of those who knew too much and by that of those who knew nothing. The great rooms caused so much poetry and history to press upon him that he needed to wander apart to feel in a proper relation with them, though his doing so was not, as happened, like the gloating of some of his companions, to be compared to the movements of a dog sniffing a cupboard. It had an issue promptly enough in a direction that was not to have been calculated.

It led, in short, in the course of the October afternoon, to his closer meeting with May Bartram, whose face, a reminder, yet not quite a remembrance, as they sat, much separated, at a very long table, had

†"The Beast in the Jungle" had no magazine appearance before it first was published in *The* *Better Sort* (London: Methuen & Co., 1903). This text is here reprinted.

begun merely by troubling him rather pleasantly. It affected him as the sequel of something of which he had lost the beginning. He knew it, and for the time quite welcomed it, as a continuation, but didn't know what it continued, which was an interest, or an amusement, the greater as he was also somehow aware—yet without a direct sign from her—that the young woman herself had not lost the thread. She had not lost it, but she wouldn't give it back to him, he saw, without some putting forth of his hand for it; and he not only saw that, but saw several things more, things odd enough in the light of the fact that at the moment some accident of grouping brought them face to face he was still merely fumbling with the idea that any contact between them in the past would have had no importance. If it had had no importance he scarcely knew why his actual impression of her should so seem to have so much; the answer to which, however, was that in such a life as they all appeared to be leading for the moment one could but take things as they came. He was satisfied, without in the least being able to say why, that this young lady might roughly have ranked in the house as a poor relation; satisfied also that she was not there on a brief visit, but was more or less a part of the establishment—almost a working, a remunerated part. Didn't she enjoy at periods a protection that she paid for by helping, among other services, to show the place and explain it, deal with the tiresome people, answer questions about the dates of the buildings, the styles of the furniture, the authorship of the pictures, the favourite haunts of the ghost? It wasn't that she looked as if you could have given her shillings—it was impossible to look less so. Yet when she finally drifted toward him, distinctly handsome, though ever so much older—older than when he had seen her before—it might have been as an effect of her guessing that he had, within the couple of hours, devoted more imagination to her than to all the others put together, and had thereby penetrated to a kind of truth that the others were too stupid for. She *was* there on harder terms than anyone; she was there as a consequence of things suffered, in one way and another, in the interval of years; and she remembered him very much as she was remembered—only a good deal better.

By the time they at last thus came to speech they were alone in one of the rooms—remarkable for a fine portrait over the chimney-place—out of which their friends had passed, and the charm of it was that even before they had spoken they had practically arranged with each other to stay behind for talk. The charm, happily, was in other things too; it was partly in there being scarce a spot at Weatherend without something to stay behind for. It was in the way the autumn day looked into the high windows as it waned; in the way the red light, breaking at the close from under a low, sombre sky, reached out in a long shaft and played over old wainscots, old tapestry, old gold, old colour. It was most of all perhaps in the way she came to him as if, since she had been turned on to deal with the simpler sort, he might, should he choose to keep the whole thing down, just take her mild attention for a part of her general business. As soon as he heard her voice, however, the gap was filled up and the missing link supplied; the slight irony he divined in her attitude lost its advantage. He almost jumped at it to get there before her. "I met you years and years ago in Rome. I remember all about it." She confessed to disappointment— she had been so sure he didn't; and to prove how well he did he began to pour forth the particular recollections that popped up as he called for them. Her face and her voice, all at his service now, worked the miracle—the impression, operating like the torch of a lamplighter who touches into flame, one by one, a long row of gas jets. Marcher flattered himself that the illumination was brilliant, yet he was really still more pleased on her showing him, with amusement, that in his haste to make everything right he had got most things rather wrong. It hadn't been at Rome—it had been at Naples; and it hadn't been seven years before—it had been more nearly ten. She hadn't been either with her uncle and aunt, but with her mother and her brother; in addition to which it was not with the Pembles that *he* had been, but with the Boyers, coming down in their company from Rome—a point on which she insisted, a little to his confusion, and as to which she had her evidence in hand. The Boyers she had known, but she didn't know the Pembles, though she had heard of them, and it was the people he was with who had made them acquainted. The incident of the thunderstorm that had raged round them with such violence as to drive them for refuge into an excavation—this incident had not occurred at the Palace of the Cæsars, but at Pompeii, on an occasion when they had been present there at an important find.

He accepted her amendments, he enjoyed her corrections, though the moral of them was, she pointed out, that he *really* didn't remember the least thing about her; and he only felt it as a drawback that when all was made conformable to the truth there didn't appear much of anything left. They lingered together still, she neglecting her office—for from the moment he was so clever she had no proper right to him—and both neglecting the house, just waiting as to see if a memory or two more wouldn't again breathe upon them. It had not taken them many minutes, after all, to put down on the table, like the cards of a pack, those that constituted their respective hands; only what came out was that the pack was unfortunately not perfect—that the past, invoked, invited, encouraged, could give them, naturally, no more than it had. It had made them meet—her at twenty, him at twenty-five; but nothing was so strange, they seemed to say to each other, as that, while so occupied, it hadn't done a little more for them. They looked at each other as with the feeling of an occasion missed; the present one would have been so much better if the other, in the far distance, in the foreign land, hadn't been so stupidly meagre. There weren't, apparently, all counted, more than a dozen little old things that had succeeded in coming to pass between them; trivialities of youth, simplicities of freshness, stupidities of ignorance, small possible germs, but too deeply buried—too deeply (didn't it seem?) to sprout after so many years. Marcher said to himself that he ought to have rendered her some service—saved her from a capsized boat in the Bay, or at least recovered her dressing-bag, filched from her cab, in the streets of Naples, by a lazzarone with a stiletto. Or it would have been nice if he could have been taken with fever, alone, at his hotel, and she could have come to look after him, to write to his people, to drive him out in convalescence. *Then* they would be in possession of the something or other that their actual show seemed to lack. It yet somehow presented itself, this show, as too good to be spoiled; so that they were reduced for a few minutes more to wondering a little helplessly why—since they seemed to know a certain number of the same people—their reunion had been so long averted. They didn't use that name for it, but their delay from minute to minute to join the others was a kind of confession that they didn't quite want it to be a failure. Their attempted supposition of reasons for their not having met but showed how little they knew of each other. There came in fact a moment when Marcher felt a positive pang. It was vain to pretend she was an old friend, for all the communities were wanting, in spite of which it was as an old friend that he saw she would have suited him. He had new ones enough—was surrounded with them, for instance, at that hour at the other house; as a new one he probably wouldn't have so much as noticed her. He would have liked to invent something, get her to make-believe with him that some passage of a romantic or critical kind *had* originally occurred. He was really almost reaching out in imagination—as against time—for something that would do, and saying to himself that if it didn't come this new incident would simply and rather awkwardly close. They would separate, and now for no second or for no third chance. They would have tried and not succeeded. Then it was, just at the turn, as he afterwards made it out to himself, that, everything else failing, she herself decided to take up the case and, as it were, save the situation. He felt as soon as she spoke that she had been consciously keeping back what she said and hoping to get on without it; a scruple in her that immensely touched him when, by the end of three or four minutes more, he was able to measure it. What she brought out, at any rate, quite cleared the air and supplied the link—the link it was such a mystery he should frivolously have managed to lose.

"You know you told me something that I've never forgotten and that again and again has made me think of you since; it was that tremendously hot day when we went to Sorrento, across the bay, for the breeze. What I allude to was what you said to me, on the way back, as we sat, under the awning of the boat, enjoying the cool. Have you forgotten?"

He had forgotten, and he was even more surprised than ashamed. But the great thing was that he saw it was no vulgar reminder of any "sweet" speech. The vanity of women had long memories, but she was making no claim on him of a compliment or a mistake. With another woman, a totally different one, he might have feared the recall possibly even some imbecile "offer." So, in having to say that he had indeed forgotten, he was conscious rather of a loss than of a gain; he already saw an interest in the matter of her reference. "I try to think—but I give it up. Yet I remember the Sorrento day."

"I'm not very sure you do," May Bartram after a moment said; "and I'm not very sure I ought to want you to. It's dreadful to bring a person back, at any time, to what he was ten years before. If you've lived away from it," she smiled, "so much the better."

"Ah, if *you* haven't why should I?" he asked.

"Lived away, you mean, from what I myself was?"

"From what *I* was. I was of course an ass," Marcher went on; "but I would rather know from you just the sort of ass I was than—from the moment you have something in your mind—not know anything."

Still, however, she hesitated. "But if you've completely ceased to be that sort—?

"Why, I can then just so all the more bear to know. Besides, perhaps I haven't."

"Perhaps. Yet if you haven't," she added. "I should suppose you would remember. Not indeed that *I* in the least connect with my impression the invidious name you use. If I had only thought you foolish," she explained, "the thing I speak of wouldn't so have remained with me. It was about yourself." She waited, as if it might come to him; but as, only meeting her eyes in wonder, he gave no sign, she burnt her ships. "Has it ever happened?"

Then it was that, while he continued to stare, a light broke for him and the blood slowly came to his face, which began to burn with recognition. "Do you mean I told you—?" But he faltered, lest what came to him shouldn't be right, lest he should only give himself away.

"It was something about yourself that it was natural one shouldn't forget—that is if one remembered you at all. That's why I ask you," she smiled, "if the thing you then spoke of has ever come to pass?"

Oh, then he saw, but he was lost in wonder and found himself embarrassed. This, he also saw, made her sorry for him, as if her allusion had been a mistake. It took him but a moment, however, to feel that it had not been, much as it had been a surprise. After the first little shock of it her knowledge on the contrary began, even if rather strangely, to taste sweet to him. She was the only other person in the world then who would have it, and she had had it all these years, while the fact of his having so breathed his secret had unaccountably faded from him. No wonder they couldn't have met as if nothing had happened. "I judge," he finally said, "that I know what you mean. Only I had strangely enough lost the consciousness of having taken you so far into my confidence."

"Is it because you've taken so many others as well?"

"I've taken nobody. Not a creature since then."

"So that I'm the only person who knows?"

"The only person in the world.

"Well," she quickly replied, "I myself have never spoken. I've never, never repeated of you what you told me." She looked at him so that he perfectly believed her. Their eyes met over it in such a way that he was without a doubt. "And I never will."

She spoke with an earnestness that, as if almost excessive, put him at ease about her possible derision. Somehow the whole question was a new luxury to him—that is, from the moment she was in possession. If she didn't take the ironic view she clearly took the sympathetic, and that was what he had had, in all the long time, from no one whomsoever. What he felt was that he couldn't at present have begun to tell her and yet could profit perhaps exquisitely by the accident of having done so of old. "Please don't then. We're just right as it is."

"Oh, I am," she laughed, "if you are!" To which she added: "Then you do still feel in the same way?"

It was impossible to him not to take to himself that she was really interested, and it all kept coming as a sort of revelation. He had thought of himself so long as abominably alone, and, lo, he wasn't alone a bit. He hadn't been, it appeared, for an hour—since those moments on the Sorrento boat. It was *she* who had been, he seemed to see as he looked at her—she who had been made so by the graceless fact of his lapse of fidelity. To tell her what he had told her—what had it been but to ask something of her? something that she had given, in her charity, without his having, by a remembrance, by a return of the spirit, failing another encounter, so much as thanked her. What he had asked of her had been simply at first not to laugh at him. She had beautifully not done so for ten years, and she was not doing so now. So he had endless gratitude to make up. Only for that he must see just how he had figured to her. "What, exactly, was the account I gave—?"

"Of the way you did feel? Well, it was very simple. You said you had had from your earliest time, as the deepest thing within you, the sense of being kept for something rare and strange, possibly prodigious and terrible, that was sooner or later to happen to you, that you had in your bones the foreboding and the conviction of, and that would perhaps overwhelm you."

"Do you call that very simple?" John Marcher asked.

She thought a moment. "It was perhaps because I seemed, as you spoke, to understand it."

"You do understand it?" he eagerly asked.

Again she kept her kind eyes on him. "You still have the belief?"

"Oh!" he exclaimed helplessly. There was too much to say.

"Whatever it is to be," she clearly made out, "it hasn't yet come."

He shook his head in complete surrender now. "It hasn't yet come. Only, you know, it isn't anything I'm to *do*, to achieve in the world, to be distinguished or admired for. I'm not such an ass as *that*. It would be much better, no doubt, if I were."

"It's to be something you're merely to suffer?"

"Well, say to wait for—to have to meet, to face, to see suddenly break out in my life; possibly destroying all further consciousness, possibly annihilating me; possibly, on the other hand, only altering everything, striking at the root of all my world and leaving me to the consequences, however they shape themselves."

She took this in, but the light in her eyes continued for him not to be that of mockery. "Isn't what you describe perhaps but the expectation—or, at any rate, the sense of danger, familiar to so many people—of falling in love?"

John Marcher thought. "Did you ask me that before?"

"No—I wasn't so free-and-easy then. But it's what strikes me now."

"Of course," he said after a moment, "it strikes you. Of course it strikes *me*. Of course what's in store for me may be no more than that. The only thing is," he went on, "that I think that if it had been that, I should by this time know."

"Do you mean because you've *been* in love?" And then as he but looked at her in silence: "You've been in love, and it hasn't meant such a cataclysm, hasn't proved the great affair?"

"Here I am, you see. It hasn't been overwhelming."

"Then it hasn't been love," said May Bartram.

"Well, I at least thought it was. I took it for that—I've taken it till now. It was agreeable, it was delightful, it was miserable," he explained. "But it wasn't strange. It wasn't what *my* affair's to be."

"You want something all to yourself—something that nobody else knows or *has* known?"

"It isn't a question of what I 'want'—God knows I don't want anything. It's only a question of the apprehension that haunts me—that I live with day by day."

He said this so lucidly and consistently that, visibly, it further imposed itself. If she had not been interested before she would have been interested now. "Is it a sense of coming violence?"

Evidently now too, again, he liked to talk of it. "I don't think of it as—when it does come—necessarily violent. I only think of it as natural and as of course, above all, unmistakeable. I think of it simply as *the* thing. *The* thing will of itself appear natural."

"Then how will it appear strange?"

Marcher bethought himself. "It won't—to *me*."

"To whom then?"

"Well," he replied, smiling at last, "say to you."

"Oh then, I'm to be present?"

"Why, you *are* present—since you know."

"I see." She turned it over. "But I mean at the catastrophe."[1]

At this, for a minute, their lightness gave way to their gravity; it was as if the long look they exchanged held them together. "It will only depend on yourself—if you'll watch with me."

"Are you afraid?" she asked.

"Don't leave me *now*," he went on.

"Are you afraid?" she repeated.

"Do you think me simply out of my mind?" he pursued instead of answering. "Do I merely strike you as a harmless lunatic?"

"No," said May Bartram. "I understand you. I believe you."

"You mean you feel how my obsession—poor old thing!—may correspond to some possible reality?"

"To some possible reality."

"Then you *will* watch with me?"

She hesitated, then for the third time put her question. "Are you afraid?"

"Did I tell you I was—at Naples?"

"No, you said nothing about it."

"Then I don't know. And I should *like* to know," said John Marcher. "You'll tell me yourself whether you think so. If you'll watch with me you'll see."

"Very good then." They had been moving by this time across the room, and at the door, before passing out, they paused as if for the full wind-up of their understanding. "I'll watch with you," said May Bartram.

II

The fact that she "knew"—knew and yet neither chaffed him nor betrayed him—had in a short time begun to constitute between them a sensible bond, which became more marked when, within the year that followed their afternoon at Weatherend, the opportunities for meeting multiplied. The event that thus promoted these occasions was the death of the ancient lady, her great-aunt, under whose wing, since losing her mother, she had to such an extent found shelter, and who, though but the widowed mother of the new successor to the property, had succeeded—thanks to a high tone and a high temper—in not

---

1. The final event, not necessarily disastrous.

forfeiting the supreme position at the great house. The deposition of this personage arrived but with her death, which, followed by many changes, made in particular a difference for the young woman in whom Marcher's expert attention had recognised from the first a dependent with a pride that might ache though it didn't bristle. Nothing for a long time had made him easier than the thought that the aching must have been much soothed by Miss Bartram's now finding herself able to set up a small home in London. She had acquired property, to an amount that made that luxury just possible, under her aunt's extremely complicated will, and when the whole matter began to be straightened out, which indeed took time, she let him know that the happy issue was at last in view. He had seen her again before that day, both because she had more than once accompanied the ancient lady to town and because he had paid another visit to the friends who so conveniently made of Weatherend one of the charms of their own hospitality. These friends had taken him back there; he had achieved there again with Miss Bartram some quiet detachment; and he had in London succeeded in persuading her to more than one brief absence from her aunt. They went together, on these latter occasions to the National Gallery and the South Kensington Museum,[2] where, among vivid reminders, they talked of Italy at large—not now attempting to recover, as at first, the taste of their youth and their ignorance. That recovery, the first day at Weatherend, had served its purpose well, had given them quite enough; so that they were, to Marcher's sense, no longer hovering about the head-waters of their stream, but had felt their boat pushed sharply off and down the current.

They were literally afloat together; for our gentleman this was marked, quite as marked as that the fortunate cause of it was just the buried treasure of her knowledge. He had with his own hands dug up this little hoard, brought to light—that is to within reach of the dim day constituted by their discretions and privacies—the object of value the hiding-place of which he had, after putting it into the ground himself, so strangely, so long forgotten. The exquisite luck of having again just stumbled on the spot made him indifferent to any other question; he would doubtless have devoted more time to the odd accident of his lapse of memory if he had not been moved to devote so much to the sweetness, the comfort, as he felt, for the future, that this accident itself had helped to keep fresh. It had never entered into his plan that anyone should "know," and mainly for the reason that it was not in him to tell anyone. That would have been impossible, since nothing but the amusement of a cold world would have waited on it. Since, however, a mysterious fate had opened his mouth in youth, in

2. The National Gallery is the most famous art museum in London; the South Kensington Museum, now usually called the Victoria and Albert Museum, is another art museum, devoted to architecture and sculpture as well as to painting.

spite of him, he would count that a compensation and profit by it to
the utmost. That the right person *should* know tempered the asperity
of his secret more even than his shyness had permitted him to imagine;
and May Bartram was clearly right, because—well, because there she
was. Her knowledge simply settled it; he would have been sure enough
by this time had she been wrong. There was that in his situation, no
doubt, that disposed him too much to see her as a mere confidant,
taking all her light for him from the fact—the fact only—of her interest
in his predicament, from her mercy, sympathy, seriousness, her
consent not to regard him as the funniest of the funny. Aware, in fine,
that her price for him was just in her giving him this constant sense of
his being admirably spared, he was careful to remember that she had,
after all, also a life of her own, with things that might happen to *her*,
things that in friendship one should likewise take account of. Something fairly remarkable came to pass with him, for that matter, in this
connection—something represented by a certain passage of his consciousness, in the suddenest way, from one extreme to the other.

He had thought himself, so long as nobody knew, the most disinterested person in the world, carrying his concentrated burden, his
perpetual suspense, ever so quietly, holding his tongue about it, giving
others no glimpse of it nor of its effect upon his life, asking of them no
allowance and only making on his side all those that were asked. He
had disturbed nobody with the queerness of having to know a haunted
man, though he had had moments of rather special temptation on
hearing people say that they were "unsettled." If they were as unsettled
as he was—he who had never been settled for an hour in his life—they
would know what it meant. Yet it wasn't, all the same, for him to make
them, and he listened to them civilly enough. This was why he had
such good—though possibly such rather colourless—manners; this
was why, above all, he could regard himself, in a greedy world, as
decently—as, in fact, perhaps even a little sublimely—unselfish. Our
point is accordingly that he valued this character quite sufficiently to
measure his present danger of letting it lapse, against which he
promised himself to be much on his guard. He was quite ready, none
the less, to be selfish just a little, since, surely, no more charming
occasion for it had come to him. "Just a little," in a word, was just as
much as Miss Bartram, taking one day with another, would let him.
He never would be in the least coercive, and he would keep well before
him the lines on which consideration for her—the very highest—
ought to proceed. He would thoroughly establish the heads under
which her affairs, her requirements, her peculiarities—he went so far
as to give them the latitude of that name—would come into their
intercourse. All this naturally was a sign of how much he took the
intercourse itself for granted. There was nothing more to be done
about *that*. It simply existed; had sprung into being with her first

penetrating question to him in the autumn light there at Weatherend. The real form it should have taken on the basis that stood out large was the form of their marrying. But the devil in this was that the very basis itself put marrying out of the question. His conviction, his apprehension, his obsession, in short, was not a condition he could invite a woman to share; and that consequence of it was precisely what was the matter with him. Something or other lay in wait for him, amid the twists and the turns of the months and the years, like a crouching beast in the jungle. It signified little whether the crouching beast were destined to slay him or to be slain. The definite point was the inevitable spring of the creature; and the definite lesson from that was that a man of feeling didn't cause himself to be accompanied by a lady on a tiger-hunt. Such was the image under which he had ended by figuring his life.

They had at first, none the less, in the scattered hours spent together, made no allusion to that view of it; which was a sign he was handsomely ready to give that he didn't expect, that he in fact didn't care always to be talking about it. Such a feature in one's outlook was really like a hump on one's back. The difference it made every minute of the day existed quite independently of discussion. One discussed, of course, *like* a hunchback, for there was always, if nothing else, the hunchback face. That remained, and she was watching him; but people watched best, as a general thing, in silence, so that such would be predominantly the manner of their vigil. Yet he didn't want, at the same time, to be solemn; solemn was what he imagined he too much tended to be with other people. The thing to be, with the one person who knew, was easy and natural—to make the reference rather than be seeming to avoid it, to avoid it rather than be seeming to make it, and to keep it, in any case, familiar, facetious even, rather than pedantic and portentous. Some such consideration as the latter was doubtless in his mind, for instance, when he wrote pleasantly to Miss Bartram that perhaps the great thing he had so long felt as in the lap of the gods was no more than this circumstance, which touched him so nearly, of her acquiring a house in London. It was the first allusion they had yet again made, needing any other hitherto so little; but when she replied, after having given him the news, that she was by no means satisfied with such a trifle, as the climax to so special a suspense, she almost set him wondering if she hadn't even a larger conception of singularity for him than he had for himself. He was at all events destined to become aware little by little, as time went by, that she was all the while looking at his life, judging it, measuring it, in the light of the thing she knew, which grew to be at last, with the consecration of the years, never mentioned between them save as "the real truth" about him. That had always been his own form of reference to it, but she adopted the form so quietly that, looking back at the end of a period, he knew there was no moment at which it was traceable that she had, as he might say, got inside his condition, or exchanged the attitude of beautifully indulging for that of still more beautifully believing him.

It was always open to him to accuse her of seeing him but as the most harmless of maniacs, and this, in the long run—since it covered so much ground—was his easiest description of their friendship. He had a screw loose for her, but she liked him in spite of it, and was practically, against the rest of the world, his kind, wise keeper, unremunerated, but fairly amused and, in the absence of other near ties, not disreputably occupied. The rest of the world of course thought him queer, but she, she only, knew how, and above all why, queer; which was precisely what enabled her to dispose the concealing veil in the right folds. She took his gaiety from him—since it had to pass with them for gaiety—as she took everything else; but she certainly so far justified by her unerring touch his finer sense of the degree to which he had ended by convincing her. *She* at least never spoke of the secret of his life except as "the real truth about you," and she had in fact a wonderful way of making it seem, as such, the secret of her own life too. That was in fine how he so constantly felt her as allowing for him; he couldn't on the whole call it anything else. He allowed for himself, but she, exactly, allowed still more; partly because, better placed for a sight of the matter, she traced his unhappy perversion through portions of its course into which he could scarce follow it. He knew how he felt, but, besides knowing that, she knew how he *looked* as well; he knew each of the things of importance he was insidiously kept from doing, but she could add up the amount they made, understand how much, with a lighter weight on his spirit, he might have done, and thereby establish how, clever as he was, he fell short. Above all she was in the secret of the difference between the forms he went through—those of his little office under Government, those of caring for his modest patrimony, for his library, for his garden in the country, for the people in London whose invitations he accepted and repaid—and the detachment that reigned beneath them and that made of all behaviour, all that could in the least be called behaviour, a long act of dissimulation. What it had come to was that he wore a mask painted with the social simper, out of the eye-holes of which there looked eyes of an expression not in the least matching the other features. This the stupid world, even after years, had never more than half discovered. It was only May Bartram who had, and she achieved, by an art indescribable, the feat of at once—or perhaps it was only alternately—meeting the eyes from in front and mingling her own vision, as from over his shoulder, with their peep through the apertures.

So, while they grew older together, she did watch with him, and so she let this association give shape and colour to her own existence. Beneath *her* forms as well detachment had learned to sit, and behaviour had become for her, in the social sense, a false account of herself. There was but one account of her that would have been true all the while, and that she could give, directly, to nobody, least of all to John Marcher. Her whole attitude was a virtual statement, but the perception of that only seemed destined to take its place for him as one of the many things necessarily crowded out of his consciousness. If she had, moreover, like himself, to make sacrifices to their real truth, it was to be granted that her compensation might have affected her as more prompt and more natural. They had long periods, in this London time, during which, when they were together, a stranger might have listened to them without in the least pricking up his ears; on the other hand, the real truth was equally liable at any moment to rise to the surface, and the auditor would then have wondered indeed what they were talking about. They had from an early time made up their mind that society was, luckily, unintelligent, and the margin that this gave them had fairly become one of their commonplaces. Yet there were still moments when the situation turned almost fresh—usually under the effect of some expression drawn from herself. Her expressions doubtless repeated themselves, but her intervals were generous. "What saves us, you know, is that we answer so completely to so usual an appearance: that of the man and woman whose friendship has become such a daily habit, or almost, as to be at least indispensable." That, for instance, was a remark she had frequently enough had occasion to make, though she had given it at different times different developments. What we are especially concerned with is the turn it happened to take from her one afternoon when he had come to see her in honour of her birthday. This anniversary had fallen on a Sunday, at a season of thick fog and general outward gloom; but he had brought her his customary offering, having known her now long enough to have established a hundred little customs. It was one of his proofs to himself, the present he made her on her birthday, that he had not sunk into real selfishness. It was mostly nothing more than a small trinket, but it was always fine of its kind, and he was regularly careful to pay for it more than he thought he could afford. "Our habit saves you, at least, don't you see? because it makes you, after all, for the vulgar, indistinguishable from other men. What's the most inveterate mark of men in general? Why, the capacity to spend endless time with dull women— to spend it, I won't say without being bored, but without minding that they are, without being driven off at a tangent by it; which comes to the same thing. I'm your dull woman, a part of the daily bread for which you pray at church. That covers your tracks more than anything."

"And what covers yours?" asked Marcher, whom his dull woman could mostly to this extent amuse. "I see of course what you mean by your saving me, in one way and another, so far as other people are concerned—I've seen it all along. Only, what is it that saves *you*? I often think, you know, of that."

She looked as if she sometimes thought of that too, but in rather a different way. "Where other people, you mean, are concerned?"

"Well, you're really so in with me, you know—as a sort of result of my being so in with yourself. I mean of my having such an immense regard for you, being so tremendously grateful for all you've done for me. I sometimes ask myself if it's quite fair. Fair I mean to have so involved and—since one may say it—interested you. I almost feel as if you hadn't really had time to do anything else."

"Anything else but be interested?" she asked. "Ah, what else does one ever want to be? If I've been 'watching' with you, as we long ago agreed that I was to do, watching is always in itself an absorption."

"Oh, certainly," John Marcher said, "if you hadn't had your curiosity—! Only, doesn't it sometimes come to you, as time goes on, that your curiosity is not being particularly repaid?"

May Bartram had a pause. "Do you ask that, by any chance, because you feel at all that yours isn't? I mean because you have to wait so long."

Oh, he understood what she meant. "For the thing to happen that never does happen? For the beast to jump out? No, I'm just where I was about it. It isn't a matter as to which I can *choose*, I can decide for a change. It isn't one as to which there *can* be a change. It's in the lap of the gods. One's in the hands of one's law—there one is. As to the form the law will take, the way it will operate, that's its own affair."

"Yes," Miss Bartram replied; "of course one's fate is coming, of course it *has* come, in its own form and its own way, all the while. Only, you know, the form and the way in your case were to have been—well, something so exceptional and, as one may say, so particularly *your* own."

Something in this made him look at her with suspicion. "You say 'were to *have* been,' as if in your heart you had begun to doubt."

"Oh!" she vaguely protested.

"As if you believed," he went on, "that nothing will now take place."

She shook her head slowly, but rather inscrutably. "You're far from my thought."

He continued to look at her. "What then is the matter with you?"

"Well," she said after another wait, "the matter with me is simply that I'm more sure than ever my curiosity, as you call it, will be but too well repaid."

They were frankly grave now; he had got up from his seat, had turned once more about the little drawing-room to which, year after year, he brought his inevitable topic; in which he had, as he might have said, tasted their intimate community with every sauce, where every object was as familiar to him as the things of his own house and the very carpets were worn with his fitful walk very much as the desks in old counting-houses are worn by the elbows of generations of clerks. The generations of his nervous moods had been at work there, and the place was the written history of his whole middle life. Under the impression of what his friend had just said he knew himself, for some reason, more aware of these things, which made him, after a moment, stop again before her. "Is it, possibly, that you've grown afraid?"

"Afraid?" He thought, as she repeated the word, that his question had made her, a little, change colour; so that, lest he should have touched on a truth, he explained very kindly, "You remember that that was what you asked *me* long ago—that first day at Weatherend."

"Oh yes, and you told me you didn't know—that I was to see for myself. We've said little about it since, even in so long a time."

"Precisely," Marcher interposed—"quite as if it were too delicate a matter for us to make free with. Quite as if we might find, on pressure, that I *am* afraid. For then," he said, "we shouldn't, should we? quite know what to do."

She had for the time no answer to this question. "There have been days when I thought you were. Only, of course," she added, "there have been days when we have thought almost anything."

"Everything. Oh!" Marcher softly groaned as with a gasp, half spent, at the face, more uncovered just then than it had been for a long while, of the imagination always with them. It had always had its incalculable moments of glaring out, quite as with the very eyes of the very Beast, and, used as he was to them, they could still draw from him the tribute of a sigh that rose from the depths of his being. All that they had thought, first and last, rolled over him; the past seemed to have been reduced to mere barren speculation. This in fact was what the place had just struck him as so full of—the simplification of everything but the state of suspense. That remained only by seeming to hang in the void surrounding it. Even his original fear, if fear it had been, had lost itself in the desert. "I judge, however," he continued, "that you see I'm not afraid now."

"What I see is, as I make it out, that you've achieved something almost unprecedented in the way of getting used to danger. Living with it so long and so closely, you've lost your sense of it; you know it's there, but you're indifferent, and you cease even, as of old, to have to whistle in the dark. Considering what the danger is," May Bartram wound up, "I'm bound to say that I don't think your attitude could well be surpassed."

John Marcher faintly smiled. "It's heroic?"

"Certainly—call it that."

He considered. "I *am*, then, a man of courage?"

"That's what you were to show me."

He still, however, wondered. "But doesn't the man of courage know what he's afraid of—or *not* afraid of? I don't know *that*, you see. I don't focus it. I can't name it. I only know I'm exposed.

"Yes, but exposed—how shall I say?—so directly. So intimately. That's surely enough."

"Enough to make you feel, then—at what we may call the end of our watch—that I'm not afraid?"

"You're not afraid. But it isn't," she said, "the end of our watch. That is it isn't the end of yours. You've everything still to see."

"Then why haven't *you*?" he asked. He had had, all along, to-day, the sense of her keeping something back, and he still had it. As this was his first impression of that, it made a kind of date. The case was the more marked as she didn't at first answer; which in turn made him go on. "You know something I don't." Then his voice, for that of a man of courage, trembled a little. "You know what's to happen." Her silence, with the face she showed, was almost a confession—it made him sure. "You know; and you're afraid to tell me. It's so bad that you're afraid I'll find out."

All this might be true, for she did look as if, unexpectedly to her, he had crossed some mystic line that she had secretly drawn round her. Yet she might, after all, not have worried; and the real upshot was that he himself, at all events, needn't. "You'll never find out."

III

It was all to have made, none the less, as I have said, a date; as came out in the fact that again and again, even after long intervals, other things that passed between them wore, in relation to this hour, but the character of recalls and results. Its immediate effect had been indeed rather to lighten insistence—almost to provoke a reaction; as if their topic had dropped by its own weight and as if moreover, for that matter, Marcher had been visited by one of his occasional warnings against egotism. He had kept up, he felt, and very decently on the whole, his consciousness of the importance of not being selfish, and it was true that he had never sinned in that direction without promptly enough trying to press the scales the other way. He often repaired his fault, the season permitting, by inviting his friend to accompany him to the opera; and it not infrequently thus happened that, to show he didn't wish her to have but one sort of food for her mind, he was the cause of her appearing there with him a dozen nights in the month. It even happened that, seeing her home at such times, he occasionally went in with her to finish, as he called it, the evening, and, the better to make his point, sat down to the frugal but always careful little supper that awaited his pleasure. His point was made, he thought, by his not eternally insisting with her on himself; made for instance, at such hours, when it befell that, her piano at hand and each of them familiar with it, they went over passages of the opera together. It chanced to be on one of these occasions, however, that he reminded her of her not having answered a certain question he had put to her during the talk that had taken place between them on her last birthday. "What is it that saves *you?*"—saved her, he meant, from that appearance of variation from the usual human type. If he had practically escaped remark, as she pretended, by doing, in the most important particular, what most men do—find the answer to life in patching up an alliance of a sort with a woman no better than himself—how had she escaped it, and how could the alliance, such as it was, since they must suppose it had been more or less noticed, have failed to make her rather positively talked about?

"I never said," May Bartram replied, "that it hadn't made me talked about."

"Ah well then, you're not 'saved.' "

"It has not been a question for me. If you've had your woman, I've had," she said, "my man."

"And you mean that makes you all right?"

She hesitated. "I don't know why it shouldn't make me—humanly, which is what we're speaking of—as right as it makes you."

"I see," Marcher returned. " 'Humanly,' no doubt, as showing that you're living for something. Not, that is, just for me and my secret."

May Bartram smiled. "I don't pretend it exactly shows that I'm not living for you. It's my intimacy with you that's in question."

He laughed as he saw what she meant. "Yes, but since, as you say, I'm only, so far as people make out, ordinary, you're—aren't you—no more than ordinary either. You help me to pass for a man like another. So if I *am*, as I understand you, you're not compromised. Is that it?"

She had another hesitation, but she spoke clearly enough. "That's it. It's all that concerns me—to help you to pass for a man like another."

He was careful to acknowledge the remark handsomely. "How kind, how beautiful, you are to me! How shall I ever repay you?"

She had her last grave pause, as if there might be a choice of ways. But she chose. "By going on as you are."

It was into this going on as he was that they relapsed, and really for so long a time that the day inevitably came for a further sounding of their depths. It was as if these depths, constantly bridged over by a structure that was firm enough in spite of its lightness and of its occasional oscillation in the somewhat vertiginous air, invited on occasion, in the interest of their nerves, a dropping of the plummet and a measurement of the abyss. A difference had been made moreover, once for all, by the fact that she had, all the while, not appeared to feel the need of rebutting his charge of an idea within her that she didn't dare to express, uttered just before one of the fullest of their later discussions ended. It had come up for him then that she "knew" something and that what she knew was bad—too bad to tell him. When he had spoken of it as visibly so bad that she was afraid he might find it out, her reply had left the matter too equivocal to be let alone and yet, for Marcher's special sensibility, almost too formidable again to touch. He circled about it at a distance that alternately narrowed and widened and that yet was not much affected by the consciousness in him that there was nothing she could "know," after all, better than he did. She had no source of knowledge that he hadn't equally—except of course that she might have finer nerves. That was what women had where they were interested; they made out things, where people were concerned, that the people often couldn't have made out for themseves. Their nerves, their sensibility, their imagination, were conductors and revealers, and the beauty of May Bartram was in particuar that she had given herself so to his case. He felt in these days what, oddly enough, he had never felt before, the growth of a dread of losing her by some catastrophe—some catastrophe that yet wouldn't at all be *the* catastrophe: partly because she had, almost of a sudden, begun to strike him as useful to him as never yet, and partly by reason of an appearance of uncertainty in her health, coincident and equally new. It was characteristic of the inner detachment he had hitherto so successfully cultivated and to which our whole account of him is a reference, it was characteristic that his complications, such as they were, had never yet seemed so as at this crisis to thicken about him, even to the point of making him ask himself if he were, by any chance, of a truth, within sight or sound, within touch or reach, within the immediate jurisdiction of the thing that waited.

When the day came, as come it had to, that his friend confessed to him her fear of a deep disorder in her blood, he felt somehow the shadow of a change and the chill of a shock. He immediately began to imagine aggravations and disasters, and above all to think of her peril as the direct menace for himself of personal privation. This indeed gave him one of those partial recoveries of equanimity that were agreeable to him—it showed him that what was still first in his mind was the loss she herself might suffer. "What if she should have to die before knowing, before seeing—?" It would have been brutal, in the early stages of her trouble, to put that question to her; but it had immediately sounded for him to his own concern, and the possibility was what most made him sorry for her. If she did "know," moreover, in the sense of her having had some—what should he think?— mystical, irresistible light, this would make the matter not better, but worse, inasmuch as her original adoption of his own curiosity had quite become the basis of her life. She had been living to see what would *be* to be seen, and it would be cruel to her to have to give up before the accomplishment of the vision. These reflections, as I say, refreshed his generosity; yet, make them as he might, he saw himself, with the lapse of the period, more and more disconcerted. It lapsed for him with a strange, steady sweep, and the oddest oddity was that it gave him, independently of the threat of much inconvenience, almost the only positive surprise his career, if career it could be called, had yet offered him. She kept the house as she had never done; he had to go to her to see her—she could meet him nowhere now, though there was scarce a corner of their loved old London in which she had not in the past, at one time or another, done so; and he found her always seated by her fire in the deep, old-fashioned chair she was less and less able to leave. He had been struck one day, after an absence exceeding his usual measure, with her suddenly looking much older to him than he had ever thought of her being; then he recognised that the suddenness was all on his side—he had just been suddenly struck. She looked older because inevitably, after so many years, she *was* old, or almost; which was of course true in still greater measure of her companion. If she was old, or almost, John Marcher assuredly was, and yet it was her showing of the lesson, not his own, that brought the truth home to him. His surprises began here; when once they had begun they multiplied; they came rather with a rush: it was as if, in the oddest way in the world, they had all been kept back, sown in a thick cluster, for the late afternoon of life, the time at which, for people in general, the unexpected has died out.

One of them was that he should have caught himself—for he *had* so done—*really* wondering if the great accident would take form now as nothing more than his being condemned to see this charming woman, this admirable friend, pass away from him. He had never so unreservedly qualified her as while confronted in thought with such a possibility; in spite of which there was small doubt for him that as an answer to his long riddle the mere effacement of even so fine a feature of his situation would be an abject anticlimax. It would represent, as connected with his past attitude, a drop of dignity under the shadow of which his existence could only become the most grotesque of failures. He had been far from holding it a failure—long as he had waited for the appearance that was to make it a success. He had waited for a quite other thing, not for such a one as that. The breath of his good faith came short, however, as he recognised how long he had waited, or how long, at least, his companion had. That she, at all events, might be recorded as having waited in vain—this affected him sharply, and all the more because of his at first having done little more than amuse himself with the idea. It grew more grave as the gravity of her condition grew, and the state of mind it produced in him, which he ended by watching, himself, as if it had been some definite disfigurement of his outer person, may pass for another of his surprises. This conjoined itself still with another, the really stupefying consciousness of a question that he would have allowed to shape itself had he dared. What did everything mean—what, that is, did *she* mean, she and her vain waiting and her probable death and the soundless admonition of it all—unless that, at this time of day, it was simply, it was overwhelmingly too late? He had never, at any stage of his queer consciousness, admitted the whisper of such a correction; he had never, till within these last few months, been so false to his conviction as not to hold that what was to come to him had time, whether *he* struck himself as having it or not. That at last, at last, he certainly hadn't it, to speak of, or had it but in the scantiest measure—such, soon enough, as things went with him, became the inference with which his old obsession had to reckon: and this it was not helped to do by the more and more confirmed appearance that the great vagueness casting the long shadow in which he had lived had, to attest itself, almost no margin left. Since it was in Time that he was to have met his fate, so it was in Time that his fate was to have acted; and as he waked up to the sense of no longer being young, which was exactly the sense of being stale, just as that, in turn, was the sense of being weak, he waked up to another matter beside. It all hung together; they were subject, he and the great vagueness, to an equal and indivisible law. When the possibilities themselves had, accordingly, turned stale, when the secret of the gods had grown faint, had perhaps even quite evaporated, that, and that only, was failure. It wouldn't have been failure to be bankrupt, dishonoured, pilloried, hanged; it was failure not to be anything. And so, in the dark valley into which his path had taken its unlooked-for twist, he wondered not a little as he groped. He didn't care what awful crash might overtake him, with what ignominy or what monstrosity he might yet be associated—since he wasn't, after all, too utterly old to suffer—if it would only be decently proportionate to the posture he had kept, all his life, in the promised presence of it. He had but one desire left—that he shouldn't have been "sold."

IV

Then it was that one afternoon, while the spring of the year was young and new, she met, all in her own way, his frankest betrayal of these alarms. He had gone in late to see her, but evening had not settled, and she was presented to him in that long, fresh light of waning April days which affects us often with a sadness sharper than the greyest hours of autumn. The week had been warm, the spring was supposed to have begun early, and May Bartram sat, for the first time in the year, without a fire, a fact that, to Marcher's sense, gave the scene of which she formed part a smooth and ultimate look, an air of knowing, in its immaculate order and its cold, meaningless cheer, that it would never see a fire again. Her own aspect—he could scarce have said why—intensified this note. Almost as white as wax, with the marks and signs in her face as numerous and as fine as if they had been etched by a needle, with soft white draperies relieved by a faded green scarf, the delicate tone of which had been consecrated by the years, she was the picture of a serene, exquisite, but impenetrable sphinx, whose head, or indeed all whose person, might have been powdered with silver. She was a sphinx, yet with her white petals and green fronds she might have been a lily too—only an artificial lily, wonderfully imitated and constantly kept, without dust or stain, though not exempt from a slight droop and a complexity of faint creases, under some clear glass bell. The perfection of household care, of high polish and finish, always reigned in her rooms, but they especially looked to Marcher at present as if everything had been wound up, tucked in, put away, so that she might sit with folded hands and with nothing more to do. She was "out of it," to his vision; her work was over; she communicated with him as across some gulf, or from some island of rest that she had already reached, and it made him feel strangely abandoned. Was it—or, rather, wasn't it—that if for so long she had been watching with him the answer to their question had swum into her ken and taken on its name, so that her occupation was verily gone? He had as much as charged her with this in saying to her, many months before, that she even then knew something she was keeping from him. It was a point he had never since ventured to press, vaguely fearing, as he did, that it might become a difference, perhaps a disagreement, between them. He had in short, in this later time, turned nervous, which was what, in all the other years, he had never been; and the oddity was that his nervousness should have waited till he had begun to doubt, should have held off so long as he was sure. There was something, it seemed to him, that the wrong word would bring down on his head, something that would so at least put an end to his suspense. But he wanted not to speak the wrong word; that would make everything ugly. He wanted the knowledge he lacked to drop on him, if drop it could, by its own august weight. If she was to forsake him it was surely for her to take leave. This was why he didn't ask her again, directly, what she knew; but it was also why, approaching the matter from another side, he said to her in the course of his visit: "What do you regard as the very worst that, at this time of day, *can* happen to me?"

He had asked her that in the past often enough; they had, with the odd, irregular rhythm of their intensities and avoidances, exchanged ideas about it and then had seen the ideas washed away by cool intervals, washed like figures traced in sea-sand. It had ever been the mark of their talk that the oldest allusions in it required but a little dismissal and reaction to come out again, sounding for the hour as new. She could thus at present meet his inquiry quite freshly and patiently. "Oh yes, I've repeatedly thought, only it always seemed to me of old that I couldn't quite make up my mind. I thought of dreadful things, between which it was difficult to choose; and so must you have done."

"Rather! I feel now as if I had scarce done anything else. I appear to myself to have spent my life in thinking of nothing *but* dreadful things. A great many of them I've at different times named to you, but there were others I couldn't name."

"They were too, too dreadful?"

"Too, too dreadful—some of them."

She looked at him a minute, and there came to him as he met it an inconsequent sense that her eyes, when one got their full clearness, were still as beautiful as they had been in youth, only beautiful with a strange, cold light—a light that somehow was a part of the effect, if it wasn't rather a part of the cause, of the pale, hard sweetness of the season and the hour. "And yet," she said at last, "there are horrors we have mentioned."

It deepened the strangeness to see her, as such a figure in such a picture, talk of "horrors," but she was to do, in a few minutes, something stranger yet—though even of this he was to take the full measure but afterwards—and the note of it was already in the air. It was, for the matter of that, one of the signs that her eyes were having again such a high flicker of their prime. He had to admit, however, what she said. "Oh yes, there were times when we did go far." He caught himself in the act of speaking as if it all were over. Well, he wished it were; and the consummation depended, for him, clearly, more and more on his companion.

But she had now a soft smile. "Oh, far—!

It was oddly ironic. "Do you mean you're prepared to go further?"

She was frail and ancient and charming as she continued to look at him, yet it was rather as if she had lost the thread. "Do you consider that we went so far?"

"Why, I thought it the point you were just making—that we *had* looked most things in the face."

"Including each other?" She still smiled. "But you're quite right. We've had together great imaginations, often great fears; but some of them have been unspoken."

"Then the worst—we haven't faced that. I *could* face it, I believe, if I knew what you think it. I feel," he explained, "as if I had lost my power to conceive such things." And he wondered if he looked as blank as he sounded. "It's spent."

"Then why do you assume," she asked, "that mine isn't?"

"Because you've given me signs to the contrary. It isn't a question for you of conceiving, imagining, comparing. It isn't a question now of choosing." At last he came out with it. "You know something that I don't. You've shown me that before."

These last words affected her, he could see in a moment, remarkably, and she spoke with firmness. "I've shown you, my dear, nothing."

He shook his head. "You can't hide it."

"Oh, oh!" May Bartram murmured over what she couldn't hide. It was almost a smothered groan.

"You admitted it months ago, when I spoke of it to you as of something you were afraid I would find out. Your answer was that I couldn't, that I wouldn't, and I don't pretend I have. But you had something therefore in mind, and I see now that it must have been, that it still is, the possibility that, of all possibilities, has settled itself for you as the worst. This," he went on, "is why I appeal to you. I'm only afraid of ignorance now—I'm not afraid of knowledge." And then as for a while she said nothing: "What makes me sure is that I see in your face and feel here, in this air and amid these appearances, that you're out of it. You've done. You've had your experience. You leave me to my fate."

Well, she listened, motionless and white in her chair, as if she had in fact a decision to make, so that her whole manner was a virtual confession, though still with a small, fine, inner stiffness, an imperfect surrender. "It *would* be the worst," she finally let herself say. "I mean the thing that I've never said."

It hushed him a moment. "More monstrous than all the monstrosities we've named?"

"More monstrous. Isn't that what you sufficiently express," she asked, "in calling it the worst?"

Marcher thought. "Assuredly—if you mean, as I do, something that includes all the loss and all the shame that are thinkable."

"It would if it *should* happen," said May Bartram. "What we're speaking of, remember, is only my idea."

"It's your belief," Marcher returned. "That's enough for me. I feel your beliefs are right. Therefore if, having this one, you give me no more light on it, you abandon me."

"No, no!" she repeated. "I'm with you—don't you see?—still." And as if to make it more vivid to him she rose from her chair—a movement she seldom made in these days—and showed herself, all draped and all soft, in her fairness and slimness. "I haven't forsaken you."

It was really, in its effort against weakness, a generous assurance, and had the success of the impulse not, happily, been great, it would have touched him to pain more than to pleasure. But the cold charm in her eyes had spread, as she hovered before him, to all the rest of her person, so that it was, for the minute, almost like a recovery of youth. He couldn't pity her for that; he could only take her as she showed—as capable still of helping him. It was as if, at the same time, her light might at any instant go out; wherefore he must make the most of it.

There passed before him with intensity the three or four things he wanted most to know; but the question that came of itself to his lips really covered the others. "Then tell me if I shall consciously suffer."

She promptly shook her head. "Never!"

It confirmed the authority he imputed to her, and it produced on him an extraordinary effect. "Well, what's better than that? Do you call that the worst?"

"You think nothing is better?" she asked.

She seemed to mean something so special that he again sharply wondered, though still with the dawn of a prospect of relief. "Why not, if one doesn't *know?*" After which, as their eyes, over his question, met in a silence, the dawn deepened and something to his purpose came, prodigiously, out of her very face. His own, as he took it in, suddenly flushed to the forehead, and he gasped with the force of a perception to which, on the instant, everything fitted. The sound of his gasp filled the air; then he became articulate. "I see—if I don't suffer!"

In her own look, however, was doubt. "You see what?"

"Why, what you mean—what you've always meant."

She again shook her head. "What I mean isn't what I've always meant. It's different."

"It's something new?"

She hesitated. "Something new. It's not what you think. I see what you think."

His divination drew breath then; only her correction might be wrong. "It isn't that I *am* a donkey?" he asked between faintness and grimness. "It isn't that it's all a mistake?"

"A mistake?" she pityingly echoed. *That* possibility, for her, he saw, would be monstrous; and if she guaranteed him the immunity from pain it would accordingly not be what she had in mind. "Oh, no," she declared; "it's nothing of that sort. You've been right."

Yet he couldn't help asking himself if she weren't, thus pressed, speaking but to save him. It seemed to him he should be most lost if his history should prove all a platitude. "Are you telling me the truth, so that I sha'n't have been a bigger idiot than I can bear to know? I *haven't* lived with a vain imagination, in the most besotted illusion? I haven't waited but to see the door shut in my face?"

She shook her head again. "However the case stands *that* isn't the truth. Whatever the reality, it *is* a reality. The door isn't shut. The door's open," said May Bartram.

"Then something's to come?"

She waited once again, always with her cold, sweet eyes on him. "It's never too late." She had, with her gliding step, diminished the distance between them, and she stood nearer to him, close to him, a minute, as if still full of the unspoken. Her movement might have been for some finer emphasis of what she was at once hesitating and deciding to say. He had been standing by the chimney-piece, fireless and sparely adorned, a small, perfect old French clock and two morsels of rosy Dresden constituting all its furniture; and her hand grasped the shelf while she kept him waiting, grasped it a little as for support and encouragement. She only kept him waiting, however; that is he only waited. It had become suddenly, from her movement and attitude, beautiful and vivid to him that she had something more to give him; her wasted face delicately shone with it, and it glittered, almost as with the white lustre of silver, in her expression. She was right, incontestably, for what he saw in her face was the truth, and strangely, without consequence, while their talk of it as dreadful was still in the air, she appeared to present it as inordinately soft. This, prompting bewilderment, made him but gape the more gratefully for her revelation, so that they continued for some minutes silent, her face shining at him, her contact imponderably pressing, and his stare all kind, but all expectant. The end, none the less, was that what he had expected failed to sound. Something else took place instead, which seemed to consist at first in the mere closing of her eyes. She gave way at the same instant to a slow, fine shudder, and though he remained staring—though he stared, in fact, but the harder—she turned off and regained her chair. It was the end of what she had been intending, but it left him thinking only of that.

"Well, you don't say—?"

She had touched in her passage a bell near the chimney and had sunk back, strangely pale. "I'm afraid I'm too ill."

"Too ill to tell me?" It sprang up sharp to him, and almost to his lips, the fear that she would die without giving him light. He checked himself in time from so expressing his question, but she answered as if she had heard the words.

"Don't you know—now?"

" 'Now'—?" She had spoken as if something that had made a difference had come up within the moment. But her maid, quickly obedient to her bell, was already with them. "I know nothing." And he was afterwards to say to himself that he must have spoken with odious impatience, such an impatience as to show that, supremely disconcerted, he washed his hands of the whole question.

"Oh!" said May Bartram.

"Are you in pain?" he asked, as the woman went to her.

"No," said May Bartram.

Her maid, who had put an arm round her as if to take her to her room, fixed on him eyes that appealingly contradicted her; in spite of which, however, he showed once more his mystification. "What then has happened?"

She was once more, with her companion's help, on her feet, and, feeling withdrawal imposed on him, he had found, blankly, his hat and gloves and had reached the door. Yet he waited for her answer. "What *was* to," she said.

V

He came back the next day, but she was then unable to see him, and as it was literally the first time this had occurred in the long stretch of their acquaintance he turned away, defeated and sore, almost angry—or feeling at least that such a break in their custom was really the beginning of the end—and wandered alone with his thoughts, especially with one of them that he was unable to keep down. She was dying, and he would lose her; she was dying, and his life would end. He stopped in the park, into which he had passed, and stared before him at his recurrent doubt. Away from her the doubt pressed again; in her presence he had believed her, but as he felt his forlornness he threw himself into the explanation that, nearest at hand, had most of a miserable warmth for him and least of a cold torment. She had deceived him to save him—to put him off with something in which he should be able to rest. What could the thing that was to happen to him be, after all, but just this thing that had begun to happen? Her dying, her death, his consequent solitude—*that* was what he had figured as the beast in the jungle, that was what had been in the lap of the gods. He had had her word for it as he left her; for what else, on earth, could she have meant? It wasn't a thing of a monstrous order; not a fate rare and distinguished; not a stroke of fortune that overwhelmed and immortalized; it had only the stamp of the common doom. But, poor Marcher, at this hour, judged the common doom sufficient. It would serve his turn, and even as the consummation of infinite waiting he would bend his pride to accept it. He sat down on a bench in the twilight. He hadn't been a fool. Something had *been*, as she had said, to come. Before he rose indeed it had quite struck him that the final fact really matched with the long avenue through which he had had to reach it. As sharing his suspense, and as giving herself all, giving her life, to bring it to an end, she had come with him every step of the way. He had lived by her aid, and to leave her behind would be cruelly, damnably to miss her. What could be more overwhelming than that?

Well, he was to know within the week, for though she kept him a while at bay, left him restless and wretched during a series of days on each of which he asked about her only again to have to turn away, she ended his trial by receiving him where she had always received him. Yet she had been brought out at some hazard into the presence of so many of the things that were consciously, vainly, half their past, and there was scant service left in the gentleness of her mere desire, all too visible, to check his obsession and wind up his long trouble. That was clearly what she wanted; the one thing more, for her own peace, while she could still put out her hand. He was so affected by her state that, once seated by her chair, he was moved to let everything go; it was she herself therefore who brought him back, took up again, before she dismissed him, her last word of the other time. She showed how she wished to leave their affair in order. "I'm not sure you understood. You've nothing to wait for more. It *has* come."

Oh, how he looked at her! "Really?"

"Really."

"The thing that, as you said, *was* to?"

"The thing that we began in our youth to watch for."

Face to face with her once more he believed her; it was a claim to which he had so abjectly little to oppose. "You mean that it has come as a positive, definite occurrence, with a name and a date?"

"Positive. Definite. I don't know about the 'name,' but, oh, with a date!"

He found himself again too helplessly at sea. "But come in the night—come and passed me by?"

May Bartram had her strange, faint smile. "Oh no, it hasn't passed you by!"

"But if I haven't been aware of it, and it hasn't touched me—?"

"Ah, your not being aware of it," and she seemed to hesitate an instant to deal with this—"your not being aware of it is the strangeness *in* the strangeness. It's the wonder *of* the wonder." She spoke as with the softness almost of a sick child, yet now at last, at the end of all, with the perfect straightness of a sibyl. She visibly knew that she knew, and the effect on him was of something co-ordinate, in its high character, with the law that had ruled him. It was the true voice of the law; so on her lips would the law itself have sounded. "It *has* touched you," she went on. "It has done its office. It has made you all its own."

"So utterly without my knowing it?"

"So utterly without your knowing it." His hand as he leaned to her, was on the arm of her chair, and, dimly smiling always now, she placed her own on it. "It's enough if *I* know it."

"Oh!" he confusedly sounded, as she herself of late so often had done.

"What I long ago said is true. You'll never know now, and I think you ought to be content. You've *had* it," said May Bartram.

"But had what?"

"Why, what was to have marked you out. The proof of your law. It has acted. I'm too glad," she then bravely added, "to have been able to see what it's *not*."

He continued to attach his eyes to her, and with the sense that it was all beyond him, and that *she* was too, he would still have sharply challenged her, had he not felt it an abuse of her weakness to do more

304 • *Tales of Henry James*

than take devoutly what she gave him, take it as hushed as to a revelation. If he did speak, it was out of the foreknowledge of his loneliness to come. "If you're glad of what it's 'not,' it might then have been worse?"

She turned her eyes away, she looked straight before her with which, after a moment: "Well, you know our fears."

He wondered. "It's something then we never feared?"

On this, slowly, she turned to him. "Did we ever dream, with all our dreams, that we should sit and talk of it thus?"

He tried for a little to make out if they had; but it was as if their dreams, numberless enough, were in solution in some thick, cold mist, in which thought lost itself. "It might have been that we couldn't talk?"

"Well"—she did her best for him—"not from this side. This, you see," she said, "is the *other* side."

"I think," poor Marcher returned, "that all sides are the same to me." Then, however, as she softly shook her head in correction: "We mightn't, as it were, have got across—?"

"To where we are—no. We're *here*"—she made her weak emphasis.

"And much good does it do us!" was her friend's frank comment.

"It does us the good it can. It does us the good that *it* isn't here. It's past. It's behind," said May Bartram. "Before—" but her voice dropped.

He had got up, not to tire her, but it was hard to combat his yearning. She after all told him nothing but that his light had failed—which he knew well enough without her. "Before—?" he blankly echoed.

"Before, you see, it was always to *come*. That kept it present."

"Oh, I don't care what comes now! Besides," Marcher added, "it seems to me I liked it better present, as you say, than I can like it absent with *your* absence."

"Oh, mine!"—and her pale hands made light of it.

"With the absence of everything." He had a dreadful sense of standing there before her for—so far as anything but this proved, this bottomless drop was concerned—the last time of their life. It rested on him with a weight he felt he could scarce bear, and this weight it apparently was that still pressed out what remained in him of speakable protest. "I believe you; but I can't begin to pretend I understand. Nothing, for me, is past; nothing *will* pass until I pass myself, which I pray my stars may be as soon as possible. Say, however," he added, "that I've eaten my cake, as you contend, to the last crumb—how can the thing I've never felt at all be the thing I was marked out to feel?"

She met him, perhaps, less directly, but she met him unperturbed. "You take your 'feelings' for granted. You were to suffer your fate. That was not necessarily to know it."

"How in the world—when what is such knowledge but suffering?"

She looked up at him a while, in silence. "No—you don't understand."

"I suffer,' said John Marcher.

"Don't, don't!"

"How can I help at least *that*?"

"*Don't!*" May Bartram repeated.

She spoke it in a tone so special, in spite of her weakness, that he stared an instant—stared as if some light, hitherto hidden, had shimmered across his vision. Darkness again closed over it, but the gleam had already become for him an idea. "Because I haven't the right—?"

"Don't *know*—when you needn't," she mercifully urged. "You needn't—for we shouldn't."

"Shouldn't?" If he could but know what she meant!

"No—it's too much."

"Too much?" he still asked—but with a mystification that was the next moment, of a sudden, to give way. Her words, if they meant something, affected him in this light—the light also of her wasted face—as meaning *all*, and the sense of what knowledge had been for herself came over him with a rush which broke through into a question. "Is it of that, then, you're dying?"

She but watched him, gravely at first, as if to see, with this, where he was, and she might have seen something, or feared something, that moved her sympathy. "I would live for you still—if I could." Her eyes closed for a little, as if, withdrawn into herself, she were, for a last time, trying. "But I can't!" she said as she raised them again to take leave of him.

She couldn't indeed, as but too promptly and sharply appeared, and he had no vision of her after this that was anything but darkness and doom. They had parted forever in that strange talk; access to her chamber of pain, rigidly guarded, was almost wholly forbidden him; he was feeling now moreover, in the face of doctors, nurses, the two or three relatives attracted doubtless by the presumption of what she had to "leave," how few were the rights, as they were called in such cases, that he had to put forward, and how odd it might even seem that their intimacy shouldn't have given him more of them. The stupidest fourth cousin had more, even though she had been nothing in such a person's life. She had been a feature of features in *his*, for what else was it to have been so indispensable? Strange beyond saying were the ways of existence, baffling for him the anomaly of his lack, as he felt it to be, of producible claim. A woman might have been, as it were, everything to him, and it might yet present him in no connection that anyone appeared obliged to recognise. If this was the case in these closing weeks it was the case more sharply on the occasion of the last offices rendered, in the great grey London cemetery, to what had been mortal, to what had been precious, in his friend. The concourse at her grave was not numerous, but he saw himself treated as scarce more nearly concerned with it than if there had been a thousand others. He was in short from this moment face to face with the fact that he was to profit extraordinarily little by the interest May Bartram had taken in him. He couldn't quite have said what he expected, but he had somehow not expected this approach to a double privation. Not only had her interest failed him, but he seemed to feel himself unattended—and for a reason he couldn't sound—by the distinction, the dignity, the propriety, if nothing else, of the man markedly bereaved. It was as if, in the view of society, he had not *been* markedly bereaved, as if there still failed some sign or proof of it, and as if, none the less, his character could never be affirmed, nor the deficiency ever made up. There were moments, as the weeks went by, when he would have liked, by some almost aggressive act, to take his stand on the intimacy of his loss, in order that it *might* be questioned and his retort, to the relief of his spirit, so recorded; but the moments of an irritation more helpless followed fast on these, the moments during which, turning things over with a good conscience but with a bare horizon, he found himself wondering if he oughtn't to have begun, so to speak, further back.

He found himself wondering indeed at many things, and this last speculation had others to keep it comany. What could he have done, after all, in her lifetime, without giving them both, as it were, away? He couldn't have made it known she was watching him, for that would have published the superstition of the Beast. This was what closed his mouth now—now that the Jungle had been threshed to vacancy and that the Beast had stolen away. It sounded too foolish and too flat; the difference for him in this particular, the extinction in his life of the element of suspense, was such in fact as to surprise him. He could scarce have said what the effect resembled; the abrupt cessation, the positive prohibition, of music perhaps, more than anything else, in some place all adjusted and all accustomed to sonority and to atten-tion. If he could at any rate have conceived lifting the veil from his image at some moment of the past (what had he done, after all, if not lift it to *her?*), so to do this to-day, to talk to people at large of the jungle cleared and confide to them that he now felt it as safe, would have been not only to see them listen as to a goodwife's tale, but really to hear himself tell one. What it presently came to in truth was that poor Marcher waded through his beaten grass, where no life stirred, where no breath sounded, where no evil eye seemed to gleam from a possible lair, very much as if vaguely looking for the Beast, and still more as if missing it. He walked about in an existence that had grown strangely more spacious, and, stopping fitfully in places where the undergrowth of life struck him as closer, asked himself yearningly, wondered secretly and sorely, if it would have lurked here or there. It would have at all events *sprung*; what was at least complete was his belief in the truth itself of the assurance given him. The change from his old sense to his new was absolute and final: what was to happen *had* so absolutely and finally happened that he was as little able to know a fear for his future as to know a hope; so absent in short was any question of anything still to come. He was to live entirely with the other question, that of his unidentified past, that of his having to see his fortune impenetrably muffled and masked.

The torment of this vision became then his occupation; he couldn't perhaps have consented to live but for the possibility of guessing. She had told him, his friend, not to guess; she had forbidden him, so far as he might, to know, and she had even in a sort denied the power in him to learn: which were so many things, precisely, to deprive him of rest. It wasn't that he wanted, he argued for fairness, that anything that had happened to him should happen over again; it was only that he shouldn't, as an anticlimax, have been taken sleeping so sound as not to be able to win back by an effort of thought the lost stuff of consciousness. He declared to himself at moments that he would either win it back or have done with consciousness for ever; he made this idea his one motive, in fine, made it so much his passion that none other, to compare with it, seemed ever to have touched him. The lost stuff of consciousness became thus for him as a strayed or stolen child to an unappeasable father; he hunted it up and down very much as if he were knocking at doors and inquiring of the police. This was the spirit in which, inevitably, he set himself to travel; he started on a journey that was to be as long as he could make it; it danced before him that, as the other side of the globe couldn't possibly have less to say to him, it might, by a possibility of suggestion, have more. Before he quitted London, however, he made a pilgrimmage to May Bartram's grave, took his way to it through the endless avenues of the grim suburban necropolis, sought it out in the wilderness of tombs, and, though he had come but for the renewal of the act of farewell, found himself, when he had at last stood by it, beguiled into long intensities. He stood for an hour, powerless to turn away and yet powerless to penetrate the darkness of death; fixing with his eyes her inscribed name and date, beating his forehead against the fact of the secret they kept, drawing his breath, while he waited as if, in pity of him, some sense would rise from the stones. He kneeled on the stones, however, in vain; they kept what they concealed; and if the face of the tomb did become a face for him it was because her two names were like a pair of eyes that didn't know him. He gave them a last long look, but no palest light broke.

VI

He stayed away, after this, for a year; he visited the depths of Asia, spending himself on scenes of romantic interest, of superlative sanctity; but what was present to him everywhere was that for a man who had known what *he* had known the world was vulgar and vain. The state of mind in which he had lived for so many years shone out to him, in reflection, as a light that coloured and refined, a light beside which the glow of the East was garish, cheap and thin. The terrible truth was that he had lost—with everything else—a distinction as well; the things he saw couldn't help being common when he had become common to look at them. He was simply now one of them himself—he was in the dust, without a peg for the sense of difference; and there were hours when, before the temples of gods and the sepulchres of kings, his spirit turned, for nobleness of association, to the barely discriminated slab in the London suburb. That had become for him, and more intensely with time and distance, his one witness of a past glory. It was all that was left to him for proof or pride, yet the past glories of Pharaohs were nothing to him as he thought of it. Small wonder then that he came back to it on the morrow of his return. He was drawn there this time as irresistibly as the other, yet with a confidence, almost, that was doubtless the effect of the many months that had elapsed. He had lived, in spite of himself, into his change of feeling, and in wandering over the earth had wandered, as might be said, from the circumference to the centre of his desert. He had settled to his safety and accepted perforce his extinction; figuring to himself, with some colour, in the likeness of certain little old men he remembered to have seen, of whom, all meagre and wizened as they might look, it was related that they had in their time fought twenty duels or been loved by ten princesses. They indeed had been wondrous for others, while he was but wondrous for himself; which, however, was exactly the cause of his haste to renew the wonder by getting back, as he might put it, into his own presence. That had quickened his steps and checked his delay. If his visit was prompt it was because he had been separated so long from the part of himself that alone he now valued.

It is accordingly not false to say that he reached his goal with a certain elation and stood there again with a certain assurance. The creature beneath the sod *knew* of his rare experience, so that, strangely now, the place had lost for him its mere blankness of expression. It met him in mildness—not, as before, in mockery; it wore for him the air of conscious greeting that we find, after absence, in things that have closely belonged to us and which seem to confess of themselves to the connection. The plot of ground, the graven tablet, the tended flowers affected him so as belonging to him that he quite felt for the hour like a contented landlord reviewing a piece of property. Whatever had happened—well, had happened. He had not come back this time with the vanity of that question, his former worrying, "What, *what?*" now practically so spent. Yet he would, none the less, never again so cut himself off from the spot; he would come back to it every month, for if

he did nothing else by its aid he at least held up his head. It thus grew
for him, in the oddest way, a positive resource; he carried out his idea
of periodical returns, which took their place at last among the most
inveterate of his habits. What it all amounted to, oddly enough, was
that, in his now so simplified world, this garden of death gave him the
few square feet of earth on which he could still most live. It was as if,
being nothing anywhere else for anyone, nothing even for himself, he
were just everything here, and if not for a crowd of witnesses, or indeed
for any witness but John Marcher, then by clear right of the register
that he could scan like an open page. The open page was the tomb of
his friend, and *there* were the facts of the past, there the truth of his life,
there the backward reaches in which he could lose himself. He did
this, from time to time, with such effect that he seemed to wander
through the old years with his hand in the arm of a companion who
was, in the most extraordinary manner, his other, his younger self; and
to wander, which was more extraordinary yet, round and round a third
presence—not wandering she, but stationary, still, whose eyes, turning with his revolution, never ceased to follow him, and whose seat
was his point, so to speak, of orientation. Thus in short he settled to
live—feeding only on the sense that he once *had* lived, and dependent
on it not only for a support but for an identity.

It sufficed him, in its way, for months, and the year elapsed; it
would doubtless even have carried him further but for an accident,
superficially slight, which moved him, in a quite other direction, with
a force beyond any of his impressions of Egypt or of India. It was a
thing of the merest chance—the turn, as he afterwards felt, of a hair,
though he was indeed to live to believe that if light hadn't come to him
in this particular fashion it would still have come in another. He was to
live to believe this, I say, though he was not to live, I may not less
definitely mention, to do much else. We allow him at any rate the
benefit of the conviction, struggling up for him at the end, that,
whatever might have happened or not happened, he would have come
round of himself to the light. The incident of an autumn day had put
the match to the train laid from of old by his misery. With the light
before him he knew that even of late his ache had only been
smothered. It was strangely drugged, but it throbbed; at the touch it
began to bleed. And the touch, in the event, was the face of a
fellow-mortal. This face, one grey afternoon when the leaves were
thick in the alleys, looked into Marcher's own, at the cemetery, with
an expression like the cut of a blade. He felt it, that is, so deep down
that he winced at the steady thrust. The person who so mutely
assaulted him was a figure he had noticed, on reaching his own goal,
absorbed by a grave a short distance away, a grave apparently fresh, so
that the emotion of the visitor would probably match it for frankness.
This fact alone forbade further attention, though during the time he

stayed he remained vaguely conscious of his neighbour, a middle-aged man apparently, in mourning, whose bowed back, among the clustered monuments and mortuary yews, was constantly presented. Marcher's theory that these were elements in contact with which he himself revived, had suffered, on this occasion, it may be granted, a sensible though inscrutable check. The autumn day was dire for him as none had recently been, and he rested with a heaviness he had not yet known on the low stone table that bore May Bartram's name. He rested without power to move, as if some spring in him, some spell vouchsafed, had suddenly been broken forever. If he could have done that moment as he wanted he would simply have stretched himself on the slab that was ready to take him, treating it as a place prepared to receive his last sleep. What in all the wide world had he now to keep awake for? He stared before him with the question, and it was then that, as one of the cemetery walks passed near him, he caught the shock of the face.

His neighbour at the other grave had withdrawn, as he himself, with force in him to move, would have done by now, and was advancing along the path on his way to one of the gates. This brought him near, and his pace was slow, so that—and all the more as there was a kind of hunger in his look—the two men were for a minute directly con-fronted. Marcher felt him on the spot as one of the deeply stricken—a perception so sharp that nothing else in the picture lived for it, neither his dress, his age, nor his presumable character and class; nothing lived but the deep ravage of the features that he showed. He *showed* them—that was the point; he was moved, as he passed, by some impulse that was either a signal for sympathy or, more possibly, a challenge to another sorrow. He might already have been aware of our friend, might, at some previous hour, have noticed in him the smooth habit of the scene, with which the state of his own senses so scantly consorted, and might thereby have been stirred as by a kind of overt discord. What Marcher was at all events conscious of was, in the first place, that the image of scarred passion presented to him was con-scious too—of something that profaned the air; and, in the second, that, roused, startled, shocked, he was yet the next moment looking after it, as it went, with envy. The most extraordinary thing that had happened to him—though he had given that name to other matters as well—took place, after his immediate vague stare, as a consequence of this impression. The stranger passed, but the raw glare of his grief remained, making our friend wonder in pity what wrong, what wound it expressed, what injury not to be healed. What had the man *had* to make him, by the loss of it, so bleed and yet live?

Something—and this reached him with a pang—that *he*, John Marcher, hadn't; the proof of which was precisely John Marcher's arid end. No passion had ever touched him, for this was what passion meant; he had survived and maundered and pined, but where had been *his* deep ravage? The extraordinary thing we speak of was the sudden rush of the result of this question. The sight that had just met his eyes named to him, as in letters of quick flame, something he had utterly, insanely missed, and what he had missed made these things a train of fire, made them mark themselves in an anguish of inward throbs. He had seen *outside* of his life, not learned it within, the way a woman was mourned when she had been loved for herself; such was the force of his conviction of the meaning of the stranger's face, which still flared for him like a smoky torch. It had not come to him, the knowledge, on the wings of experience; it had brushed him, jostled him, upset him, with the disrespect of chance, the insolence of an accident. Now that the illumination had begun, however, it blazed to the zenith, and what he presently stood there gazing at was the sounded void of his life. He gazed, he drew breath, in pain; he turned in his dismay, and, turning, he had before him in sharper incision than ever the open page of his story. The name on the table smote him as the passage of his neighbour had done, and what it said to him, full in the face, was that *she* was what he had missed. This was the awful thought, the answer to all the past, the vision at the dread clearness of which he turned as cold as the stone beneath him. Everything fell together, confessed, explained, overwhelmed; leaving him most of all stupefied at the blindness he had cherished. The fate he had been marked for he had met with a vengeance—he had emptied the cup to the lees; he had been the man of his time, *the* man, to whom nothing on earth was to have happened. That was the rare stroke—that was his visitation. So he saw it, as we say, in pale horror, while the pieces fitted and fitted. So *she* had seen it, while he didn't, and so she served at this hour to drive the truth home. It was the truth, vivid and monstrous, that all the while he had waited the wait was itself his portion. This the companion of his vigil had at a given moment perceived, and she had then offered him the chance to baffle his doom. One's doom, however, was never baffled, and on the day she had told him that his own had come down she had seen him but stupidly stare at the escape she offered him.

The escape would have been to love her; then, *then* he would have lived. *She* had lived—who could say now with what passion?—since she had loved him for himself; whereas he had never thought of her (ah, how it hugely glared at him!) but in the chill of his egotism and the light of her use. Her spoken words came back to him, and the chain stretched and stretched. The beast had lurked indeed, and the beast, at its hour, had sprung; it had sprung in that twilight of the cold April when, pale, ill, wasted, but all beautiful, and perhaps even then recoverable, she had risen from her chair to stand before him and let him imaginably guess. It had sprung as he didn't guess; it had sprung as she hopelessly turned from him, and the mark, by the time he left her, had fallen where it *was* to fall. He had justified his fear and achieved his fate; he had failed, with the last exactitude, of all he was to fail of; and a moan now rose to his lips as he remembered she had prayed he mightn't know. This horror of waking—*this* was knowledge, knowledge under the breath of which the very tears in his eyes seemed to freeze. Through them, none the less, he tried to fix it and hold it; he kept it there before him so that he might feel the pain. That at least, belated and bitter, had something of the taste of life. But the bitterness suddenly sickened him, and it was as if, horribly, he saw, in the truth, in the cruelty of his image, what had been appointed and done. He saw the Jungle of his life and saw the lurking Beast; then, while he looked, perceived it, as by a stir of the air, rise, huge and hideous, for the leap that was to settle him. His eyes darkened—it was close; and, instinctively turning, in his hallucination, to avoid it, he flung himself, on his face, on the tomb.

The Jolly Corner

(1908)†

I

"Every one asks me what I 'think' of everything," said Spencer
Brydon; "and I make answer as I can—begging or dodging the question, putting them off with any nonsense. It wouldn't matter to any of
them really," he went on, "for, even were it possible to meet in that
stand-and-deliver way so silly a demand on so big a subject, my
'thoughts' would still be almost altogether about something that concerns only myself." He was talking to Miss Staverton, with whom for a
couple of months now he had availed himself of every possible
occasion to talk; this disposition and this resource, this comfort and
support, as the situation in fact presented itself, having promptly
enough taken the first place in the considerable array of rather unattenuated surprises attending his so strangely belated return to
America. Everything was somehow a surprise; and that might be
natural when one had so long and so consistently neglected everything, taken pains to give surprises so much margin for play. He had
given them more than thirty years—thirty-three, to be exact; and they
now seemed to him to have organised their performance quite on the
scale of that licence. He had been twenty-three on leaving New
York—he was fifty-six to-day: unless indeed he were to reckon as he
had sometimes, since his repatriation, found himself feeling; in which
case he would have lived longer than is often allotted to man. It would
have taken a century, he repeatedly said to himself, and said also to
Alice Staverton, it would have taken a longer absence and a more
averted mind than those even of which he had been guilty, to pile up
the differences, the newnesses, the queernesses, above all the big-
nesses, for the better or the worse, that at present assaulted his vision
wherever he looked.

The great fact all the while however had been the incalculability;
since he *had* supposed himself, from decade to decade, to be allowing,
and in the most liberal and intelligent manner, for brilliancy of
change. He actually saw that he had allowed for nothing; he missed
what he would have been sure of finding, he found what he would
never have imagined. Proportions and values were upside-down; the
ugly things he had expected, the ugly things of his far-away youth,

---

†"The Jolly Corner" first appeared in Ford
Madox Ford's *English Review*, December
1908, and had its first appearance in a book in
vol. XVII of *The Novels and Tales of Henry
James* (New York: Charles Scribner's Sons,
1909)—the so-called New York Edition. This
text is here reproduced.

when he had too promptly waked up to a sense of the ugly—these uncanny phenomena placed him rather, as it happened, under the charm; whereas the "swagger" things, the modern, the monstrous, the famous things, those he had more particularly, like thousands of ingenuous enquirers every year, come over to see, were exactly his sources of dismay. They were as so many set traps for displeasure, above all for reaction, of which his restless tread was constantly pressing the spring. It was interesting, doubtless, the whole show, but it would have been too disconcerting hadn't a certain finer truth saved the situation. He had distinctly not, in this steadier light, come over *all* for the monstrosities; he had come, not only in the last analysis but quite on the face of the act, under an impulse with which they had nothing to do. He had come—putting the thing pompously—to look at his "property," which he had thus for a third of a century not been within four thousand miles of; or, expressing it less sordidly, he had yielded to the humour of seeing again his house on the jolly corner, as he usually, and quite fondly, described it—the one in which he had first seen the light, in which various members of his family had lived and had died, in which the holidays of his overschooled boyhood had been passed and the few social flowers of his chilled adolescence gathered, and which, alienated then for so long a period, had, through the successive deaths of his two brothers and the termination of old arrangements, come wholly into his hands. He was the owner of another, not quite so "good"—the jolly corner having been, from far back, superlatively extended and consecrated; and the value of the pair represented his main capital, with an income consisting, in these later years, of their respective rents which (thanks precisely to their original excellent type) had never been depressingly low. He could live in "Europe," as he had been in the habit of living, on the product of these flourishing New York leases, and all the better since, that of the second structure, the mere number in its long row, having within a twelvemonth fallen in, renovation at a high advance had proved beautifully possible.

These were items of property indeed, but he had found himself since his arrival distinguishing more than ever between them. The house within the street, two bristling blocks westward, was already in course of reconstruction as a tall mass of flats; he had acceded, some time before, to overtures for this conversion—in which, now that it was going forward, it had been not the least of his astonishments to find himself able, on the spot, and though without a previous ounce of such experience, to participate with a certain intelligence, almost with a certain authority. He had lived his life with his back so turned to such concerns and his face addressed to those of so different an order that he scarce knew what to make of this lively stir, in a compartment of his mind never yet penetrated, of a capacity for business and a sense for construction. These virtues, so common all round him now, had been dormant in his own organism—where it might be said of them perhaps that they had slept the sleep of the just. At present, in the splendid autumn weather—the autumn at least was a pure boon in the terrible place—he loafed about his "work" undeterred, secretly agitated; not in the least "minding" that the whole proposition, as they said, was vulgar and sordid, and ready to climb ladders, to walk the plank, to handle materials and look wise about them, to ask questions, in fine, and challenge explanations and really "go into" figures.

It amused, it verily quite charmed him; and, by the same stroke, it amused, and even more, Alice Staverton, though perhaps charming her perceptibly less. She wasn't however going to be better-off for it, as *he* was—and so astonishingly much: nothing was now likely, he knew, ever to make her better-off than she found herself, in the afternoon of life, as the delicately frugal possessor and tenant of the small house in Irving Place[1] to which she had subtly managed to cling through her almost unbroken New York career. If he knew the way to it now better than to any other address among the dreadful multiplied numberings which seemed to him to reduce the whole place to some vast ledger-page, overgrown, fantastic, of ruled and criss-crossed lines and figures—if he had formed, for his consolation, that habit, it was really not a little because of the charm of his having encountered and recognised, in the vast wilderness of the wholesale, breaking through the mere gross generalisation of wealth and force and success, a small still scene where items and shades, all delicate things, kept the sharpness of the notes of a high voice perfectly trained, and where economy hung about like the scent of a garden. His old friend lived with one maid and herself dusted her relics and trimmed her lamps and polished her silver; she stood off, in the awful modern crush, when she could, but she sallied forth and did battle when the challenge was really to "spirit," the spirit she after all confessed to, proudly and a little shyly, as to that of the better time, that of *their* common, their quite far-away and antediluvian social period and order. She made use of the street-cars when need be, the terrible things that people scrambled for as the panic-stricken at sea scramble for the boats; she affronted, inscrutably, under stress, all the public concussions and ordeals; and yet, with that slim mystifying grace of her appearance, which defied you to say if she were a fair young woman who looked older through trouble, or a fine smooth older one who looked young through successful indifference; with her precious reference, above

1. A short street between Fourteenth and Twentieth Streets one block east of Union Square and Park Avenue South. The whole action takes place in the general section of New York City where James lived as a child (1847–48 at 11 Fifth Avenue, 1848–55 at 58 West Fourteenth Street). Except for Irving Place the story does not identify streets by name, though the "conservative avenue" mentioned later may be Fifth Avenue.

all, to memories and histories into which he could enter, she was as exquisite for him as some pale pressed flower (a rarity to begin with), and, failing other sweetnesses, she was a sufficient reward of his effort. They had communities of knowledge, "their" knowledge (this discriminating possessive was always on her lips) of presences of the other age, presences all overlaid, in his case, by the experience of a man and the freedom of a wanderer, overlaid by pleasure, by infidelity, by passages of life that were strange and dim to her, just by "Europe" in short, but still unobscured, still exposed and cherished, under that pious visitation of the spirit from which she had never been diverted.

She had come with him one day to see how his "apartment-house" was rising; he had helped her over gaps and explained to her plans, and while they were there had happened to have, before her, a brief but lively discussion with the man in charge, the representative of the building-firm that had undertaken his work. He had found himself quite "standing-up" to this personage over a failure on the latter's part to observe some detail of one of their noted conditions, and had so lucidly argued his case that, besides ever so prettily flushing, at the time, for sympathy in his triumph, she had afterwards said to him (though to a slightly greater effect of irony) that he had clearly for too many years neglected a real gift. If he had but stayed at home he would have anticipated the inventor of the sky-scraper. If he had but stayed at home he would have discovered his genius in time really to start some new variety of awful architectural hare and run it till it burrowed in a gold-mine. He was to remember these words, while the weeks elapsed, for the small silver ring they had sounded over the queerest and deepest of his own lately most disguised and most muffled vibrations.

It had begun to be present to him after the first fortnight, it had broken out with the oddest abruptness, this particular wanton wonderment: it met him there—and this was the image under which he himself judged the matter, or at least, not a little, thrilled and flushed with it—very much as he might have been met by some strange figure, some unexpected occupant, at a turn of one of the dim passages of an empty house. The quaint analogy quite hauntingly remained with him, when he didn't indeed rather improve it by a still intenser form: that of his opening a door behind which he would have made sure of finding nothing, a door into a room shuttered and void, and yet so coming, with a great suppressed start, on some quite erect confronting presence, something planted in the middle of the place and facing him through the dusk. After that visit to the house in construction he walked with his companion to see the other and always so much the better one, which in the eastward direction formed one of the corners, the "jolly" one precisely, of the street now so generally dishonoured and disfigured in its westward reaches, and of the comparatively conservative Avenue. The Avenue still had pretensions, as Miss

Staverton said, to decency; the old people had mostly gone, the old names were unknown, and here and there an old association seemed to stray, all vaguely, like some very aged person, out too late, whom you might meet and feel the impulse to watch or follow, in kindness, for safe restoration to shelter.

They went in together, our friends; he admitted himself with his key, as he kept no one there, he explained, preferring, for his reasons, to leave the place empty, under a simple arrangement with a good woman living in the neighbourhood and who came for a daily hour to open windows and dust and sweep. Spencer Brydon had his reasons and was growingly aware of them; they seemed to him better each time he was there, though he didn't name them all to his companion, any more than he told her as yet how often, how quite absurdly often, he himself came. He only let her see for the present, while they walked through the great blank rooms, that absolute vacancy reigned and that, from top to bottom, there was nothing but Mrs. Muldoon's broomstick, in a corner, to tempt the burglar. Mrs. Muldoon was then on the premises, and she loquaciously attended the visitors, preceding them from room to room and pushing back shutters and throwing up sashes—all to show them, as she remarked, how little there was to see. There was little indeed to see in the great gaunt shell where the main dispositions and the general apportionment of space, the style of an age of ampler allowances, had nevertheless for its master their honest pleading message, affecting him as some good old servant's, some lifelong retainer's appeal for a character,[2] or even for a retiring-pension; yet it was also a remark of Mrs. Muldoon's that, glad as she was to oblige him by her noonday round, there was a request she greatly hoped he would never make of her. If he should wish her for any reason to come in after dark she would just tell him, if he "plased," that he must ask it of somebody else.

The fact that there was nothing to see didn't militate for the worthy woman against what one *might* see, and she put it frankly to Miss Staverton that no lady could be expected to like, could she? "craping up to thim top storeys in the ayvil hours." The gas and the electric light were off the house, and she fairly evoked a gruesome vision of her march through the great grey rooms—so many of them as there were too!—with her glimmering taper. Miss Staverton met her honest glare with a smile and the profession that she herself certainly would recoil from such an adventure. Spencer Brydon meanwhile held his peace—for the moment; the question of the "evil" hours in his old home had already become too grave for him. He had begun some time since to "crape," and he knew just why a packet of candles addressed to that pursuit had been stowed by his own hand, three weeks before, at

2. A character reference.

the back of a drawer of the fine old sideboard that occupied, as a "fixture," the deep recess in the dining-room. Just now he laughed at his companions—quickly however changing the subject; for the reason that, in the first place, his laugh struck him even at that moment as starting the odd echo, the conscious human resonance (he scarce knew how to qualify it) that sounds made while he was there alone sent back to his ear or his fancy; and that, in the second, he imagined Alice Staverton for the instant on the point of asking him, with a divination, if he ever so prowled. There were divinations he was unprepared for, and he had at all events averted enquiry by the time Mrs. Muldoon had left them, passing on to other parts.

There was happily enough to say, on so consecrated a spot, that could be said freely and fairly; so that a whole train of declarations was precipitated by his friend's having herself broken out, after a yearning look round: "But I hope you don't mean they want you to pull *this* to pieces!" His answer came, promptly, with his re-awakened wrath: it was of course exactly what they wanted, and what they were "at" him for, daily, with the iteration of people who couldn't for their life understand a man's liability to decent feelings. He had found the place, just as it stood and beyond what he could express, an interest and a joy. There were values other than the beastly rent-values, and in short, in short—! But it was thus Miss Staverton took him up. "In short you're to make so good a thing of your sky-scraper that, living in luxury on *those* ill-gotten gains, you can afford for a while to be sentimental here!" Her smile had for him, with the words, the particular mild irony with which he found half her talk suffused; an irony without bitterness and that came, exactly, from her having so much imagination—not, like the cheap sarcasms with which one heard most people, about the world of "society," bid for the reputation of cleverness, from nobody's really having any. It was agreeable to him at this very moment to be sure that when he had answered, after a brief demur, "Well yes: so, precisely, you may put it!" her imagination would still do him justice. He explained that even if never a dollar were to come to him from the other house he would nevertheless cherish this one; and he dwelt, further, while they lingered and wandered, on the fact of the stupefaction he was already exciting, the positive mystification he felt himself create.

He spoke of the value of all he read into it, into the mere sight of the walls, mere shapes of the rooms, mere sound of the floors, mere feel, in his hand, of the old silver-plated knobs of the several mahogany doors, which suggested the pressure of the palms of the dead; the seventy years of the past in fine that these things represented, the annals of nearly three generations, counting his grandfather's, the one that had ended there, and the impalpable ashes of his long-extinct youth, afloat in the very air like microscopic motes. She listened to everything; she was a woman who answered intimately but who utterly didn't chatter. She scattered abroad therefore no cloud of words; she could assent, she could agree, above all she could encourage, without doing that. Only at the last she went a little further than he had done himself. "And then how do you know? You may still, after all, want to live here." It rather indeed pulled him up, for it wasn't what he had been thinking, at least in her sense of the words. "You mean I may decide to stay on for the sake of it?"

"Well, *with* such a home—!" But, quite beautifully, she had too much tact to dot so monstrous an *i*, and it was precisely an illustration of the way she didn't rattle. How could any one—of any wit—insist on any one else's "wanting" to live in New York?

"Oh," he said, "I *might* have lived here (since I had my opportunity early in life); I might have put in here all these years. Then everything would have been different enough—and, I dare say, 'funny' enough. But that's another matter. And then the beauty of it—I mean of my perversity, of my refusal to agree to a 'deal'—is just in the total absence of a reason. Don't you see that if I had a reason about the matter at all it would *have* to be the other way, and would then be inevitably a reason of dollars? There are no reasons here *but* of dollars. Let us therefore have none whatever—not the ghost of one."

They were back in the hall then for departure, but from where they stood the vista was large, through an open door, into the great square main saloon, with its almost antique felicity of brave spaces between windows. Her eyes came back from that reach and met his own a moment. "Are you very sure the 'ghost' of one doesn't, much rather, serve—?"

He had a positive sense of turning pale. But it was as near as they were then to come. For he made answer, he believed, between a glare and a grin: "Oh ghosts—of course the place must swarm with them! I should be ashamed of it if it didn't. Poor Mrs. Muldoon's right, and it's why I haven't asked her to do more than look in."

Miss Staverton's gaze again lost itself, and things she didn't utter, it was clear, came and went in her mind. She might even for the minute, off there in the fine room, have imagined some element dimly gathering. Simplified like the death-mask of a handsome face, it perhaps produced for her just then an effect akin to the stir of an expression in the "set" commemorative plaster. Yet whatever her impression may have been she produced instead a vague platitude. "Well, if it were only furnished and lived in—!"

She appeared to imply that in case of its being still furnished he might have been a little less opposed to the idea of a return. But she passed straight into the vestibule, as if to leave her words behind her, and the next moment he had opened the house-door and was standing with her on the steps. He closed the door and, while he re-pocketed his key, looking up and down, they took in the comparatively harsh actuality of the Avenue, which reminded him of the assault of the outer light of the Desert on the traveller emerging from an Egyptian tomb. But he risked before they stepped into the street his gathered answer to her speech. "For me it *is* lived in. For me it *is* furnished." At which it was easy for her to sigh "Ah yes—!" all vaguely and discreetly; since his parents and his favourite sister, to say nothing of other kin, in numbers, had run their course and met their end there. That represented, within the walls, ineffaceable life.

It was a few days after this that, during an hour passed with her again, he had expressed his impatience of the too flattering curiosity—among the people he met—about his appreciation of New York. He had arrived at none at all that was socially producible, and as for that matter of his "thinking" (thinking the better or the worse of anything there) he was wholly taken up with one subject of thought. It was mere vain egoism, and it was moreover, if she liked, a morbid obsession. He found all things come back to the question of what he personally might have been, how he might have led his life and "turned out," if he had not so, at the outset, given it up. And confessing for the first time to the intensity within him of this absurd speculation—which but proved also, no doubt, the habit of too selfishly thinking—he affirmed the impotence there of any other source of interest, any other native appeal. "What would it have made of me, what would it have made of me? I keep for ever wondering, all idiotically; as if I could possibly know! I see what it has made of dozens of others, those I meet, and it positively aches within me, to the point of exasperation, that it would have made something of me as well. Only I can't make out *what*, and the worry of it, the small rage of curiosity never to be satisfied, brings back what I remember to have felt, once or twice, after judging best, for reasons, to burn some important letter unopened. I've been sorry, I've hated it—I've never known what was in the letter. You may of course say it's a trifle—!"

"I don't say it's a trifle," Miss Staverton gravely interrupted.

She was seated by her fire, and before her, on his feet and restless, he turned to and fro between this intensity of his idea and a fitful and unseeing inspection, through his single eye-glass, of the dear little old objects on her chimney-piece. Her interruption made him for an instant look at her harder. "I shouldn't care if you did!" he laughed, however; "and it's only a figure, at any rate, for the way I now feel. *Not* to have followed my perverse young course—and almost in the teeth of my father's curse, as I may say; not to have kept it up, so, 'over there,' from that day to this, without a doubt or a pang; not, above all, to have liked it, to have loved it, so much, loved it, no doubt, with such an abysmal conceit of my own preference: some variation from *that*, I say, must have produced some different effect for my life and for my 'form.' I should have stuck here—if it had been possible; and I was too young, at twenty-three, to judge, *pour deux sous*,[3] whether it *were* possible. If I had waited I might have seen it was, and then I might have been, by staying here, something nearer to one of these types who have been hammered so hard and made so keen by their conditions. It isn't that I admire them so much—the question of any charm in them, or of any charm, beyond that of the rank money-passion, exerted by their conditions *for* them, has nothing to do with the matter: it's only a question of what fantastic, yet perfectly possible, development of my own nature I mayn't have missed. It comes over me that I had then a strange *alter ego* deep down somewhere within me, as the full-blown flower is in the small tight bud, and that I just took the course, I just transferred him to the climate, that blighted him for once and for ever."

"And you wonder about the flower," Miss Staverton said. "So do I, if you want to know; and so I've been wondering these several weeks. I believe in the flower," she continued, "I feel it would have been quite splendid, quite huge and monstrous."

"Monstrous above all!" her visitor echoed; "and I imagine, by the same stroke, quite hideous and offensive."

"You don't believe that," she returned; "if you did you wouldn't wonder. You'd know, and that would be enough for you. What you feel—and what I feel *for* you—is that you'd have had power."

"You'd have liked me that way?" he asked.

She barely hung fire. "How should I not have liked you?"

"I see. You'd have liked me, have preferred me, a billionaire!"

"How should I not have liked you?" she simply again asked.

He stood before her still—her question kept him motionless. He took it in, so much there was of it; and indeed his not otherwise meeting it testified to that. "I know at least what I am," he simply went on; "the other side of the medal's clear enough. I've not been edifying—I believe I'm thought in a hundred quarters, to have been barely decent. I've followed strange paths and worshipped strange gods; it must have come to you again and again—in fact, you've admitted to me as much—that I was leading, at any time these thirty years, a selfish frivolous scandalous life. And you see what it has made of me."

She just waited, smiling at him. "You see what it has made of *me*."

"Oh you're a person whom nothing can have altered. You were born to be what you are, anywhere, anyway: you've the perfection nothing else could have blighted. And don't you see how, without my exile, I shouldn't have been waiting till now—?" But he pulled up for the strange pang.

---

3. "For two cents." I wasn' capable of even the most cursory or hasty judgment.

"The great thing to see," she presently said, "seems to me to be that it has spoiled nothing. It hasn't spoiled your being here at last. It hasn't spoiled this. It hasn't spoiled your speaking—" She also however faltered.

He wondered at everything her controlled emotion might mean. "Do you believe then—too dreadfully!—that I *am* as good as I might ever have been?"

"Oh no! Far from it!" With which she got up from her chair and was nearer to him. "But I don't care," she smiled.

"You mean I'm good enough?"

She considered a little. "Will you believe it if I say so? I mean will you let that settle your question for you?" And then as if making out in his face that he drew back from this, that he had some idea which, however absurd, he couldn't yet bargain away: "Oh you don't care either—but very differently: you don't care for anything but yourself."

Spencer Brydon recognised it—it was in fact what he had absolutely professed. Yet he importantly qualified. "*He* isn't myself. He's the just so totally other person. But I do want to see him," he added. "And I can. And I shall."

Their eyes met for a minute while he guessed from something in hers that she divined his strange sense. But neither of them otherwise expressed it, and her apparent understanding, with no protesting shock, no easy derision, touched him more deeply than anything yet, constituting for his stifled perversity, on the spot, an element that was like breatheable air. What she said however was unexpected. "Well, *I've* seen him."

"You—?"

"I've seen him in a dream."

"Oh a 'dream'—!" It let him down.

"But twice over," she continued. "I saw him as I see you now."

"You've dreamed the same dream—?"

"Twice over," she repeated. "The very same."

This did somehow a little speak to him, as it also gratified him. "You dream about me at that rate?"

"Ah about *him!*" she smiled.

His eyes again sounded her. "Then you know all about him." And as she said nothing more: "What's the wretch like?"

She hesitated, and it was as if he were pressing her so hard that, resisting for reasons of her own, she had to turn away. "I'll tell you some other time!"

II

It was after this that there was most of a virtue for him, most of a cultivated charm, most of a preposterous secret thrill, in the particular form of surrender to his obsession and of address to what he more and more believed to be his privilege. It was what in these weeks he was living for—since he really felt life to begin but after Mrs. Muldoon had retired from the scene and, visiting the ample house from attic to cellar, making sure he was alone, he knew himself in safe possession and, as he tacitly expressed it, let himself go. He sometimes came twice in the twenty-four hours; the moments he liked best were those of gathering dusk, of the short autumn twilight; this was the time of which, again and again, be found himself hoping most. Then he could, as seemed to him, most intimately wander and wait, linger and listen, feel his fine attention, never in his life before so fine, on the pulse of the great vague place: he preferred the lampless hour and only wished he might have prolonged each day the deep crepuscular spell. Later—rarely much before midnight, but then for a considerable vigil—he watched with his glimmering light; moving slowly, holding it high, playing it far, rejoicing above all, as much as he might, in open vistas, reaches of communication between rooms and by passages; the long straight chance or show, as he would have called it, for the revelation he pretended to invite. It was a practice he found he could perfectly "work" without exciting remark; no one was in the least the wiser for it; even Alice Staverton, who was moreover a well of discretion, didn't quite fully imagine.

He let himself in and let himself out with the assurance of calm proprietorship; and accident so far favoured him that, if a fat Avenue "officer" had happened on occasion to see him entering at eleven-thirty, he had never yet, to the best of his belief, been noticed as emerging at two. He walked there on the crisp November nights, arrived regularly at the evening's end; it was as easy to do this after dining out as to take his way to a club or to his hotel. When he left his club, if he hadn't been dining out, it was ostensibly to go to his hotel; and when he left his hotel, if he had spent a part of the evening there, it was ostensibly to go to his club. Everything was easy in fine; everything conspired and promoted: there was truly even in the strain of his experience something that glossed over, something that salved and simplified, all the rest of consciousness. He circulated, talked, renewed, loosely and pleasantly, old relations—met indeed, so far as he could, new expectations and seemed to make out on the whole that in spite of the career, of such different contacts, which he had spoken of to Miss Staverton as ministering so little, for those who might have watched it, to edification, he was positively rather liked than not. He was a dim secondary social success—and all with people who had truly not an idea of him. It was all mere surface sound, this murmur of their welcome, this popping of their corks—just as his gestures of response were the extravagant shadows, emphatic in proportion as they meant little, of some game of *ombres chinoises*. [4] He projected himself all day, in thought, straight over the bristling line of hard unconscious heads

4. Shadow theater.

and into the other, the real, the waiting life; the life that, as soon as he had heard behind him the click of his great house-door, began for him, on the jolly corner, as beguilingly as the slow opening bars of some rich music follow the tap of the conductor's wand.

He always caught the first effect of the steel point of his stick on the old marble of the hall pavement, large black-and-white squares that he remembered as the admiration of his childhood and that had then made in him, as he now saw, for the growth of an early conception of style. This effect was the dim reverberating tinkle as of some far-off bell hung who should say where?—in the depths of the house, of the past, of that mystical other world that might have flourished for him had he not, for weal or woe, abandoned it. On this impression he did ever the same thing; he put his stick noiselessly away in a corner—feeling the place once more in the likeness of some great glass bowl, all precious concave crystal, set delicately humming by the play of a moist finger round its edge. The concave crystal held, as it were, this mystical other world, and the indescribably fine murmur of its rim was the sigh there, the scarce audible pathetic wail to his strained ear, of all the old baffled forsworn possibilities. What he did therefore by this appeal of his hushed presence was to wake them into such measure of ghostly life as they might still enjoy. They were shy, all but unappeasably shy, but they weren't really sinister; at least they weren't as he had hitherto felt them—before they had taken the Form he so yearned to make them take, the Form he at moments saw himself in the light of fairly hunting on tiptoe, the points of his evening-shoes, from room to room and from storey to storey.

That was the essence of his vision—which was all rank folly, if one would, while he was out of the house and otherwise occupied, but which took on the last verisimilitude as soon as he was placed and posted. He knew what he meant and what he wanted; it was as clear as the figure on a cheque presented in demand for cash. His *alter ego* "walked"—that was the note of his image of him, while his image of his motive for his own odd pastime was the desire to waylay him and meet him. He roamed, slowly, warily, but all restlessly, he himself did—Mrs. Muldoon had been right, absolutely, with her figure of their "craping"; and the presence he watched for would roam restlessly too. But it would be as cautious and as shifty; the conviction of its probable, in fact its already quite sensible, quite audible evasion of pursuit grew for him from night to night, laying on him finally a rigour to which nothing in his life had been comparable. It had been the theory of many superficially-judging persons, he knew, that he was wasting that life in a surrender to sensations, but he had tasted of no pleasure so fine as his actual tension, had been introduced to no sport that demanded at once the patience and the nerve of this stalking of a creature more subtle, yet at bay perhaps more formidable, than any beast of the forest. The terms, the comparisons, the very practices of the chase positively came again into play; there were even moments when passages of his occasional experience as a sportsman, stirred memories, from his younger time, of moor and mountain and desert, revived for him—and to the increase of his keenness—by the tremendous force of analogy. He found himself at moments—once he had placed his single light on some mantel-shelf or in some recess—stepping back into shelter or shade, effacing himself behind a door or in an embrasure, as he had sought of old the vantage of rock and tree; he found himself holding his breath and living in the joy of the instant, the supreme suspense created by big game alone.

He wasn't afraid (though putting himself the question as he believed gentlemen on Bengal tiger-shoots or in close quarters with the great bear of the Rockies had been known to confess to having put it); and this indeed—since here at least he might be frank!—because of the impression, so intimate and so strange, that he himself produced as yet a dread, produced certainly a strain, beyond the liveliest he was likely to feel. They fell for him into categories, they fairly became familiar, the signs, for his own perception, of the alarm his presence and his vigilance created; though leaving him always to remark, portentously, on his probably having formed a relation, his probably enjoying a consciousness, unique in the experience of man. People enough, first and last, had been in terror of apparitions, but who had ever before so turned the tables and become himself, in the apparitional world, an incalculable terror? He might have found this sublime had he quite dared to think of it; but he didn't too much insist, truly, on that side of his privilege. With habit and repetition he gained to an extraordinary degree the power to penetrate the dusk of distances and the darkness of corners, to resolve back into their innocence the treacheries of uncertain light, the evil-looking forms taken in the gloom by mere shadows, by accidents of the air, by shifting effects of perspective; putting down his dim luminary he could still wander on without it, pass into other rooms and, only knowing it was there behind him in case of need, see his way about, visually project for his purpose a comparative clearness. It made him feel, this acquired faculty, like some monstrous stealthy cat; he wondered if he would have glared at these moments with large shining yellow eyes, and what it mightn't verily be, for the poor hard-pressed *alter ego*, to be confronted with such a type.

He liked however the open shutters; he opened everywhere those Mrs. Muldoon had closed, closing them as carefully afterwards, so that she shouldn't notice: he liked—oh this he did like, and above all in the upper rooms!—the sense of the hard silver of the autumn stars through the window-panes, and scarcely less the flare of the street-lamps below, the white electric lustre which it would have taken curtains to keep out. This was human actual social; this was of the world he had lived in, and he was more at his ease certainly for the countenance, coldly general and impersonal, that all the while and in spite of his detachment it seemed to give him. He had support of course mostly in the rooms at the wide front and the prolonged side; it failed him considerably in the central shades and the parts at the back. But if he sometimes, on his rounds, was glad of his optical reach, so none the less often the rear of the house affected him as the very jungle of his prey. The place was there more subdivided; a large "extension" in particular, where small rooms for servants had been multiplied, abounded in nooks and corners, in closets and passages, in the ramifications especially of an ample back staircase over which he leaned, many a time, to look far down—not deterred from his gravity even while aware that he might, for a spectator, have figured some solemn simpleton playing at hide-and-seek. Outside in fact he might himself make that ironic *rapprochement*,[5] but within the walls, and in spite of the clear windows, his consistency was proof against the cynical light of New York.

It had belonged to that idea of the exasperated consciousness of his victim to become a real test for him; since he had quite put it to himself from the first that, oh distinctly! he could "cultivate" his whole perception. He had felt it as above all open to cultivation—which indeed was but another name for his manner of spending his time. He was bringing it on, bringing it to perfection, by practice; in consequence of which it had grown so fine that he was now aware of impressions, attestations of his general postulate, that couldn't have broken upon him at once. This was the case more specifically with a phenomenon at last quite frequent for him in the upper rooms, the recognition—absolutely unmistakeable, and by a turn dating from a particular hour, his resumption of his campaign after a diplomatic drop, a calculated absence of three nights—of his being definitely followed, tracked at a distance carefully taken and to the express end that he should the less confidently, less arrogantly, appear to himself merely to pursue. It worried, it finally quite broke him up, for it proved, of all the conceivable impressions, the one least suited to his book. He was kept in sight while remaining himself—as regards the essence of his position—sightless, and his only recourse then was in abrupt turns, rapid recoveries of ground. He wheeled about, retracing his steps, as if he might so catch in his face at least the stirred air of some other quick revolution. It was indeed true that his fully dis-localised thought of these manoeuvres recalled to him Pantaloon, at the Christmas farce, buffeted and tricked from behind by ubiquitous Harlequin;[6] but if left intact the influence of the conditions themselves each time he was re-exposed to them, so that in fact this association, had he suffered it to become constant, would on a certain

5. Comparison.
6. Pantaloon and Harlequin are characters derived from the *Commedia dell' arte*, a popular form of early Italian comedy (sixteenth to eighteenth century), and surviving in the English Pantomime, a theatrical spectacle, traditionally performed during the Christmas season.

side have but ministered to his intenser gravity. He had made, as I have said, to create on the premises the baseless sense of a reprieve, his three absences; and the result of the third was to confirm the after-effect of the second.

On his return, that night—the night succeeding his last intermission—he stood in the hall and looked up the staircase with a certainty more intimate than any he had yet known. "He's *there*, at the top, and waiting—not, as in general, falling back for disappearance. He's holding his ground, and it's the first time—which is a proof, isn't it? that something has happened for him." So Brydon argued with his hand on the banister and his foot on the lowest stair; in which position he felt as never before the air chilled by his logic. He himself turned cold in it, for he seemed of a sudden to know what now was involved. "Harder pressed?—yes, he takes it in, with its thus making clear to him that I've come, as they say, 'to stay.' He finally doesn't like and can't bear it, in the sense, I mean, that his wrath, his menaced interest, now balances with his dread. I've hunted him till he has 'turned': that, up there, is what has happened—he's the fanged or the antlered animal brought at last to bay." There came to him, as I say—but determined by an influence beyond my notation!—the acuteness of this certainty; under which however the next moment he had broken into a sweat that he would as little have consented to attribute to fear as he would have dared immediately to act upon it for enterprise. It marked none the less a prodigious thrill, a thrill that represented sudden dismay, no doubt, but also represented, and with the selfsame throb, the strangest, the most joyous, possibly the next minute almost the proudest, duplication of consciousness.

"He has been dodging, retreating, hiding, but now, worked up to anger, he'll fight!"—this intense impression made a single mouthful, as it were, of terror and applause. But what was wondrous was that the applause, for the felt fact, was so eager, since, if it was his other self he was running to earth, this ineffable identity was thus in the last resort not unworthy of him. It bristled there—somewhere near at hand, however unseen still—as the hunted thing, even as the trodden worm of the adage *must* at last bristle; and Brydon at this instant tasted probably of a sensation more complex than had ever before found itself consistent with sanity. It was as if it would have shamed him that a character so associated with his own should triumphantly succeed in just skulking, should to the end not risk the open; so that the drop of this danger was, on the spot, a great lift of the whole situation. Yet with another rare shift of the same subtlety he was already trying to measure by how much more he himself might now be in peril of fear; so rejoicing that he could, in another form, actively inspire that fear, and simultaneously quaking for the form in which he might passively know it.

The apprehension of knowing it must after a little have grown in him, and the strangest moment of his adventure perhaps, the most memorable or really most interesting, afterwards, of his crisis, was the lapse of certain instants of concentrated conscious *combat*, the sense of a need to hold on to something, even after the manner of a man slipping and slipping on some awful incline; the vivid impulse, above all, to move, to act, to charge, somehow and upon something—to show himself, in a word, that he wasn't afraid. The state of "holding-on" was thus the state to which he was momentarily reduced; if there had been anything, in the great vacancy, to seize, he would presently have been aware of having clutched it as he might under a shock at home have clutched the nearest chair-back. He had been surprised at any rate—of this he *was* aware—into something unprecedented since his original appropriation of the place; he had closed his eyes, held them tight, for a long minute, as with that instinct of dismay and that terror of vision. When he opened them the room, the other contiguous rooms, extraordinarily, seemed lighter—so light, almost, that at first he took the change for day. He stood firm, however that might be, just where he had paused; his resistance had helped him—it was as if there were something he had tided over. He knew after a little what this was—it had been in the imminent danger of flight. He had stiffened his will against going; without this he would have made for the stairs, and it seemed to him that, still with his eyes closed, he would have descended them, would have known how, straight and swiftly, to the bottom.

Well, as he had held out, here he was—still at the top, among the more intricate upper rooms and with the gauntlet of the others, of all the rest of the house, still to run when it should be his time to go. He would go at his time—only at his time: didn't he go every night very much at the same hour? He took out his watch—there was light for that: it was scarcely a quarter past one, and he had never withdrawn so soon. He reached his lodgings for the most part at two—with his walk of a quarter of an hour. He would wait for the last quarter—he wouldn't stir till then; and he kept his watch there with his eyes on it, reflecting while he held it that this deliberate wait, a wait with an effort, which he recognised, would serve perfectly for the attestation he desired to make. It would prove his courage—unless indeed the latter might most be proved by his budging at last from his place. What he mainly felt now was that, since he hadn't originally scuttled, he had his dignities—which had never in his life seemed so many—all to preserve and to carry aloft. This was before him in truth as a physical image, an image almost worthy of an age of greater romance. That remark indeed glimmered for him only to glow the next instant with a finer light; since what age of romance, after all, could have matched either the state of his mind or, "objectively," as they said, the wonder of his situation? The only difference would have been that, brandishing his dignities over his head as in a parchment scroll, he might then —that is in the heroic time—have proceeded downstairs with a drawn sword in his other grasp.

At present, really, the light he had set down on the mantel of the next room would have to figure his sword; which utensil, in the course of a minute, he had taken the requisite number of steps to possess himself of. The door between the rooms was open, and from the second another door opened to a third. These rooms, as he remembered, gave all three upon a common corridor as well, but there was a fourth, beyond them, without issue save through the preceding. To have moved, to have heard his step again, was appreciably a help; though even in recognising this he lingered once more a little by the chimney-piece on which his light had rested. When he next moved, just hesitating where to turn, he found himself considering a circumstance that, after his first and comparatively vague apprehension of it, produced in him the start that often attends some pang of recollection, the violent shock of having ceased happily to forget. He had come into sight of the door in which the brief chain of communication ended and which he now surveyed from the nearer threshold, the one not directly facing it. Placed at some distance to the left of this point, it would have admitted him to the last room of the four, the room without other approach or egress, had it not, to his intimate conviction, been closed *since* his former visitation, the matter probably of a quarter of an hour before. He stared with all his eyes at the wonder of the fact, arrested again where he stood and again holding his breath while he sounded its sense. Surely it had been *subsequently* closed—that is it had been on his previous passage indubitably open!

He took it full in the face that something had happened between— that he couldn't not have noticed before (by which he meant on his original tour of all the rooms that evening) that such a barrier had exceptionally presented itself. He had indeed since that moment undergone an agitation so extraordinary that it might have muddled for him any earlier view; and he tried to convince himself that he might perhaps then have gone into the room and, inadvertently, automatically, on coming out, have drawn the door after him. The difficulty was that this exactly was what he never did; it was against his whole policy, as he might have said, the essence of which was to keep vistas clear. He had them from the first, as he was well aware, quite on the brain: the strange apparition, at the far end of one of them, of his baffled "prey" (which had become by so sharp an irony so little the term now to apply!) was the form of success his imagination had most cherished, projecting into it always a refinement of beauty. He had known fifty times the start of perception that had afterwards dropped; had fifty times gasped to himself 'There!" under some fond brief hallucination. The house, as the case stood, admirably lent itself; he might wonder at the taste, the native architecture of the particular time, which could rejoice so in the multiplication of doors—the opposite extreme to the modern, the actual almost complete proscription of them; but it had fairly contributed to provoke this obsession of the presence encountered telescopically, as he might say, focussed and studied in diminishing perspective and as by a rest for the elbow.

It was with these considerations that his present attention was charged—they perfectly availed to make what he saw portentous. He *couldn't*, by any lapse, have blocked that aperture; and if he hadn't, if it was unthinkable, why what else was clear but that there had been another agent? Another agent?—he had been catching, as he felt, a moment back, the very breath of him; but when had he been so close as in this simple, this logical, this completely personal act? It was so logical, that is, that one might have *taken* it for personal; yet for what did Brydon take it, he asked himself, while, softly panting, he felt his eyes almost leave their sockets. Ah this time at last they *were*, the two, the opposed projections of him, in presence; and this time, as much as one would, the question of danger loomed. With it rose, as not before, the question of courage—for what he knew the blank face of the door to say to him was "Show us how much you have!" It stared, it glared back at him with that challenge; it put to him the two alternatives: should he just push it open or not? Oh to have this consciousness was to *think* —and to think, Brydon knew, as he stood there, was, with the lapsing moments, not to have acted! Not to have acted—that was the misery and the pang—was even still not to act; was in fact *all* to feel the thing in another, in a new and terrible way. How long did he pause and how long did he debate? There was presently nothing to measure it; for his vibration had already changed—as just by the effect of its intensity. Shut up there, at bay, defiant, and with the prodigy of the thing palpably proveably *done*, thus giving notice like some stark signboard—under that accession of accent the situation itself had turned; and Brydon at last remarkably made up his mind on what it had turned to.

It had turned altogether to a different admonition; to a surpeme hint, for him, of the value of Discretion! This slowly dawned, no doubt—for it could take its time; so perfectly, on his threshold, had he been stayed, so little as yet had he either advanced or retreated. It was the strangest of all things that now when, by his taking ten steps and applying his hand to a latch, or even his shoulder and his knee, if necessary, to a panel, all the hunger of his prime need might have been met, his high curiosity crowned, his unrest assuaged—it was amazing, but it was also exquisite and rare, that insistence should have, at a touch, quite dropped from him. Discretion—he jumped at that; and yet not, verily, at such a pitch, because it saved his nerves or his skin, but because, much more valuably, it saved the situation.

When I say he "jumped" at it I feel the consonance of this term with the fact that—at the end indeed of I know not how long—he did move again, he crossed straight to the door. He wouldn't touch it—it seemed now that he might *if* he would: he would only just wait there a little, to show, to prove, that he wouldn't. He had thus another station, close to the thin partition by which revelation was denied him; but with his eyes bent and his hands held off in a mere intensity of stillness. He listened as if there had been something to hear, but this attitude, while it lasted, was his own communication. "If you won't then—good: I spare you and I give up. You affect me as by the appeal positively for pity: you convince me that for reasons rigid and sublime—what do I know?—we both of us should have suffered. I respect them then, and, though moved and privileged as, I believe, it has never been given to man, I retire, I renounce—never, on my honour, to try again. So rest for ever—and let *me!*"

That, for Brydon was the deep sense of this last demonstration—solemn, measured, directed, as he felt it to be. He brought it to a close, he turned away; and now verily he knew how deeply he had been stirred. He retraced his steps, taking up his candle, burnt, he observed, well-nigh to the socket, and marking again, lighten it as he would, the distinctness of his footfall; after which, in a moment, he knew himself at the other side of the house. He did here what he had not yet done at these hours—he opened half a casement, one of those in the front, and let in the air of the night; a thing he would have taken at any time previous for a sharp rupture of his spell. His spell was broken now, and it didn't matter—broken by his concession and his surrender, which made it idle henceforth that he should ever come back. The empty street—its other life so marked even by the great lamplit vacancy—was within call, within touch; he stayed there as to be in it again, high above it though he was still perched; he watched as for some comforting common fact, some vulgar human note, the passage of a scavenger or a thief, some night-bird however base. He would have blessed that sign of life; he would have welcomed positively the slow approach of his friend the policeman, whom he had hitherto only sought to avoid, and was not sure that if the patrol had come into sight he mightn't have felt the impulse to get into relation with it, to hail it, on some pretext, from his fourth floor.

The pretext that wouldn't have been too silly or too compromising, the explanation that would have saved his dignity and kept his name, in such a case, out of the papers, was not definite to him: he was so occupied with the thought of recording his Discretion—as an effect of the vow he had just uttered to his intimate adversary—that the importance of this loomed large and something had overtaken all ironically his sense of proportion. If there had been a ladder applied to the front of the house, even one of the vertiginous perpendiculars employed by painters and roofers and sometimes left standing overnight, he would have managed somehow, astride of the window-sill, to compass by outstretched leg and arm that mode of descent. If there had been some such uncanny thing as he had found in his room at hotels, a workable fire-escape in the form of notched cable or a canvas shoot, he would have availed himself of it as a proof—well, of his present delicacy. He nursed that sentiment, as the question stood, a little in vain, and even—at the end of he scarce knew, once more, how long—found it, as by the action on his mind of the failure of response of the outer world, sinking back to vague anguish. It seemed to him he had waited an age for some stir of the great grim hush; the life of the town was itself under a spell—so unnaturally, up and down the whole prospect of known and rather ugly objects, the blankness and the silence lasted. Had they ever, he asked himself, the hard-faced houses, which had begun to look livid in the dim dawn, had they ever spoken so little to any need of his spirit? Great builded voids, great crowded stillnesses put on, often, in the heart of cities, for the small hours, a sort of sinister mask, and it was of this large collective negation that Brydon presently became conscious—all the more that the break of day was, almost incredibly, now at hand, proving to him what a night he had made of it.

He looked again at his watch, saw what had become of his time-values (he had taken hours for minutes—not, as in other tense situations, minutes for hours) and the strange air of the streets was but the weak, the sullen flush of a dawn in which everthing was still locked up. His choked appeal from his own open window had been the sole note of life, and he could but break off at last as for a worse despair. Yet while so deeply demoralised he was capable again of an impulse denoting—at least by his present measure—extraordinary resolution; of retracing his steps to the spot where he had turned cold with the extinction of his last pulse of doubt as to there being in the place another presence than his own. This required an effort strong enough to sicken him; but he had his reason, which overmastered for the moment everything else. There was the whole of the rest of the house to traverse, and how should he screw himself to that if the door he had seen closed were at present open? He could hold to the idea that the closing had practically been for him an act of mercy, a chance offered him to descend, depart, get off the ground and never again profane it. This conception held together, it worked; but what it meant for him depended now clearly on the amount of forbearance his recent action, or rather his recent inaction, had engendered. The image of the "presence," whatever it was, waiting there for him to go—this image had not yet been so concrete for his nerves as when he stopped short of the point at which certainty would have come to him. For, with all his resolution, or more exactly with all his dread, he did stop short—he hung back from really seeing. The risk was too great and his fear too definite: it took at this moment an awful specific form.

He knew—yes, as he had never known anything—that, *should* he see the door open, it would all too abjectly be the end of him. It would mean that the agent of his shame—for his shame was the deep abjection—was once more at large and in general possession; and what glared him thus in the face was the act that this would determine for him. It would send him straight about to the window he had left open, and by that window, be long ladder and dangling rope as absent as they would, he saw himself uncontrollably insanely fatally take his way to the street. The hideous chance of this he at least could avert; but he could only avert it by recoiling in time from assurance. He had the whole house to deal with, this fact was still there; only he now knew that uncertainty alone could start him. He stole back from where he had checked himself—merely to do so was suddenly like safety—and, making blindly for the greater staircase, left gaping rooms and sounding passages behind. Here was the top of the stairs, with a fine large dim descent and three spacious landings to mark off. His instinct was all for mildness, but his feet were harsh on the floors, and, strangely, when he had in a couple of minutes become aware of this, it counted somehow for help. He couldn't have spoken, the tone of his voice would have scared him, and the common conceit or resource of "whistling in the dark" (whether literally or figuratively) have appeared basely vulgar; yet he liked none the less to hear himself go, and when he had reached his first landing—taking it all with no rush, but quite steadily—that stage of success drew from him a gasp of relief.

The house, withal, seemed immense, the scale of space again inordinate; the open rooms, to no one of which his eyes deflected, gloomed in their shuttered state like mouths of caverns; only the high skylight that formed the crown of the deep well created for him a medium in which he could advance, but which might have been, for queerness of colour, some watery under-world. He tried to think of something noble, as that his property was really grand, a splendid possession; but this nobleness took the form too of the clear delight with which he was finally to sacrifice it. They might come in now, the builders, the destroyers—they might come as soon as they would. At the end of two flights he had dropped to another zone, and from the middle of the third, with only one more left, he recognised the influence of the lower windows, of half-drawn blinds, of the occasional gleam of street-lamps, of the glazed spaces of the vestibule. This was the bottom of the sea, which showed an illumination of its own and which he even saw paved—when at a given moment he drew up to sink a long look over the banisters—with the marble squares of his childhood. By that time indubitably he felt, as he might have said in a commoner cause, better; it had allowed him to stop and draw breath, and the ease increased with the sight of the old black-and-white slabs. But what he most felt was that now surely, with the element of impunity pulling him as by hard firm hands, the case was settled for what he might have seen above had he dared that last look. The closed door, blessedly remote now, was still closed—and he had only in short to reach that of the house.

He came down further, he crossed the passage forming the access to the last flight; and if here again he stopped an instant it was almost for the sharpness of the thrill of assured escape. It made him shut his eyes—which opened again to the straight slope of the remainder of the stairs. Here was impunity still, but impunity almost excessive; inasmuch as the sidelights and the high fan-tracery of the entrance were glimmering straight into the hall; an appearance produced, he the next instant saw, by the fact that the vestibule gaped wide, that the hinged halves of the inner door had been thrown far back. Out of that again the *question* sprang at him, making his eyes, as he felt, half-start from his head, as they had done, at the top of the house, before the sign of the other door. If he had left that one open, hadn't he left this one closed, and wasn't he now in *most* immediate presence of some inconceivable occult activity? It was as sharp, the question, as a knife in his side, but the answer hung fire still and seemed to lose itself in the vague darkness to which the thin admitted dawn, glimmering arch-wise over the whole outer door, made a semicircular margin, a cold silvery nimbus that seemed to play a little as he looked—to shift and expand and contract.

It was as if there had been something within it, protected by indistinctness and corresponding in extent with the opaque surface behind, the painted panels of the last barrier to his escape, of which the key was in his pocket. The indistinctness mocked him even while he stared, affected him as somehow shrouding or challenging certitude, so that after faltering an instant on his step he let himself go with the sense that here *was* at last something to meet, to touch, to take, to know—something all unnatural and dreadful, but to advance upon which was the condition for him either of liberation or of supreme defeat. The penumbra, dense and dark, was the virtual screen of a figure which stood in it as still as some image erect in a niche or as some black-vizored sentinel guarding a treasure. Brydon was to know afterwards, was to recall and make out, the particular thing he had believed during the rest of his descent. He saw, in its great grey glimmering margin, the central vagueness diminish, and he felt it to be taking the very form toward which, for so many days, the passion of his curiosity had yearned. It gloomed, it loomed, it was something, it was somebody, the prodigy of a personal presence.

Rigid and conscious, spectral yet human, a man of his own substance and stature waited there to measure himself with his power to dismay. This only could it be—this only till he recognised, with his advance, that what made the face dim was the pair of raised hands that covered it and in which, so far from being offered in defiance, it was buried as for dark deprecation. So Brydon, before him, took him in; with every fact of him now, in the higher light, hard and acute—his planted stillness, his vivid truth, his grizzled bent head and white masking hands, his queer actuality of evening-dress, of dangling double eye-glass, of gleaming silk lappet and white linen, of pearl button and gold watch-guard and polished shoe. No portrait by a great modern master could have presented him with more intensity, thrust him out of his frame with more art, as if there had been "treatment," of the consummate sort, in his every shade and salience. The revulsion, for our friend, had become, before he knew it, immense—this drop, in the act of apprehension, to the sense of his adversary's inscrutable manœuvre. That meaning at least, while he gaped, it offered him; for he could but gape at his other self in this other anguish, gape as a proof that *he*, standing there for the achieved, the enjoyed, the triumphant life, couldn't be faced in his triumph. Wasn't the proof in the splendid covering hands, strong and completely spread?—so spread and so intentional that, in spite of a special verity that surpassed every other, the fact that one of these hands had lost two fingers, which were reduced to stumps, as if accidentally shot away, the face was effectually guarded and saved.

"Saved," though, *would* it be?—Brydon breathed his wonder till the very impunity of his attitude and the very insistence of his eyes produced, as he felt, a sudden stir which showed the next instant as a deeper portent, while the head raised itself, the betrayal of a braver purpose. The hands, as he looked, began to move, to open; then, as if deciding in a flash, dropped from the face and left it uncovered and presented. Horror, with the sight, had leaped into Brydon's throat, gasping there in a sound he couldn't utter; for the bared identity was too hideous as *his*, and his glare was the passion of his protest. The face, *that* face, Spencer Brydon's?—he searched it still, but looking away from it in dismay and denial, falling straight from his height of sublimity. It was unknown, inconceivable, awful, disconnected from any possibility—! He had been "sold," he inwardly moaned, stalking such game as this: the presence before him was a presence, the horror within him a horror, but the waste of his nights had been only grotesque and the success of his adventure an irony. Such an identity fitted his at *no* point, made its alternative monstrous. A thousand times yes, as it came upon him nearer now—the face was the face of a stranger. It came upon him nearer now, quite as one of those expanding fantastic images projected by the magic lantern of childhood; for the stranger, whoever he might be, evil, odious, blatant, vulgar, had advanced as for aggression, and he knew himself give ground. Then harder pressed still, sick with the force of his shock, and falling back as under the hot breath and the roused passion of a life larger than his own, a rage of personality before which his own collapsed, he felt the whole vision turn to darkness and his very feet give way. His head went round; he was going; he had gone.

III

What had next brought him back, clearly—though after how long?—was Mrs. Muldoon's voice, coming to him from quite near, from so near that he seemed presently to see her as kneeling on the ground before him while he lay looking up at her; himself not wholly on the ground, but half-raised and upheld—conscious, yes, of tenderness of support and, more particularly, of a head pillowed in extraordinary softness and faintly refreshing fragrance. He considered, he wondered, his wit but half at his service; then another face intervened, bending more directly over him, and he finally knew that Alice Staverton had made her lap an ample and perfect cushion to him, and that she had to this end seated herself on the lowest degree of the staircase, the rest of his long person remaining stretched on his old black-and-white slabs. They were cold, these marble squares of his youth; but *he* somehow was not, in this rich return of consciousness— the most wonderful hour, little by little, that he had ever known, leaving him, as it did, so gratefully, so abysmally passive, and yet as with a treasure of intelligence waiting all round him for quiet appropriation; dissolved, he might call it, in the air of the place and producing the golden glow of a late autumn afternoon. He had come back, yes—come back from further away than any man but himself had ever travelled; but it was strange how with this sense of what he had come back *to* seemed really the great thing, and as if his prodigious journey had been all for the sake of it. Slowly but surely his consciousness grew, his vision of his state thus completing itself: he had been miraculously *carried* back—lifted and carefully borne as from where he had been picked up, the uttermost end of an interminable grey passage. Even with this he was suffered to rest, and what had now brought him to knowledge was the break in the long mild motion.

It had brought him to knowledge, to knowledge—yes, this was the beauty of his state; which came to resemble more and more that of a man who has gone to sleep on some news of a great inheritance, and then, after dreaming it away, after profaning it with matters strange to it, has waked up again to serenity of certitude and has only to lie and watch it grow. This was the drift of his patience—that he had only to let it shine on him. He must moreover, with intermissions, still have been lifted and borne; since why and how else should he have known himself, later on, with the afternoon glow intenser, no longer at the foot of his stairs—situated as these now seemed at that dark other end of his tunnel—but on a deep windowbench of his high saloon, over which had been spread, couch-fashion, a mantle of soft stuff lined with grey fur that was familiar to his eyes and that one of his hands kept fondly feeling as for its pledge of truth. Mrs. Muldoon's face had gone, but the other, the second he had recognised, hung over him in a way that showed how he was still propped and pillowed. He took it all in, and the more he took it the more it seemed to suffice: he was as much at peace as if he had had food and drink. It was the two women who had found him, on Mrs. Muldoon's having plied, at her usual hour, her latch-key—and on her having above all arrived while Miss Staverton still lingered near the house. She had been turning away, all anxiety, from worrying the vain bell-handle—her calculation having been of the hour of the good woman's visit; but the latter, blessedly, had come up while she was still there, and they had entered together. He had then lain, beyond the vestibule, very much as he was lying now—quite, that is, as he appeared to have fallen, but all so wondrously without bruise or gash; only in a depth of stupor. What he most took in, however, at present, with the steadier clearance, was that Alice Staverton had for a long unspeakable moment not doubted he was dead.

"It must have been that I *was*." He made it out as she held him. "Yes—I can only have died. You brought me literally to life. Only," he wondered, his eyes rising to her, "only, in the name of all the benedictions, how?"

It took her but an instant to bend her face and kiss him, and something in the manner of it, and in the way her hands clasped and locked his head while he felt the cool charity and virtue of her lips, something in all this beatitude somehow answered everything. "And now I keep you," she said.

"Oh keep me, keep me!" he pleaded while her face still hung over him: in response to which it dropped again and stayed close, clingingly close. It was the seal of their situation—of which he tasted the impress for a long blissful moment in silence. But he came back. "Yet how did you know—?"

"I was uneasy. You were to have come, you remember—and you had sent no word."

"Yes, I remember—I was to have gone to you at one to-day." It caught on to their "old" life and relation—which were so near and so far. "I was still out there in my strange darkness—where was it, what was it? I must have stayed there so long." He could but wonder at the depth and the duration of his swoon.

"Since last night?" she asked with a shade of fear for her possible indiscretion.

"Since this morning—it must have been: the cold dim dawn of to-day. Where have I been," he vaguely wailed, "where have I been?"

He felt her hold him close, and it was as if this helped him now to make in all security his mild moan. "What a long dark day!"

All in her tenderness she had waited a moment. "In the cold dim dawn?" she quavered.

But he had already gone on piecing together the parts of the whole prodigy. "As I didn't turn up you came straight—?"

She barely cast about. "I went first to your hotel—where they told me of your absence. You had dined out last evening and hadn't been back since. But they appeared to know you had been at your club."

"So you had the idea of *this*—?"

"Of what?" she asked in a moment.

"Well—of what has happened."

"I believed at least you'd have been here. I've known, all along," she said, "that you've been coming."

" 'Known' it—?"

"Well, I've believed it. I said nothing to you after that talk we had a month ago—but I felt sure. I knew you *would*," she declared.

"That I'd persist, you mean?"

"That you'd see him."

"Ah but I didn't!" cried Brydon with his long wail. "There's somebody—an awful beast; whom I brought, too horribly, to bay. But it's not me."

At this she bent over him again, and her eyes were in his eyes. "No—it's not you." And it was as if, while her face hovered, he might have made out in it, hadn't it been so near, some particular meaning blurred by a smile. "No, thank heaven," she repeated—"it's not you! Of course it wasn't to have been."

"Ah but it *was*," he gently insisted. And he stared before him now as he had been staring for so many weeks. "I was to have known myself."

"You couldn't!" she returned consolingly. And then reverting, and as if to account further for what she had herself done, "But it wasn't only *that*, that you hadn't been at home," she went on. "I waited till the hour at which we had found Mrs. Muldoon that day of my going with you; and she arrived, as I've told you, while, failing to bring any one to the door, I lingered in my despair on the steps. After a little, if she hadn't come, by such a mercy, I should have found means to hunt her up. But it wasn't," said Alice Staverton, as if once more with her fine intention—"it wasn't only that."

His eyes, as he lay, turned back to her. "What more then?"

She met it, the wonder she had stirred. "In the cold dim dawn, you say? Well, in the cold dim dawn of this morning 'I too saw you."

"Saw *me*—?"

"Saw *him*," said Alice Staverton. "It must have been at the same moment."

He lay an instant taking it in—as if he wished to be quite reasonable.

"At the same moment?"

"Yes—in my dream again, the same one I've named to you. He came back to me. Then I knew it for a sign. He had come to you."

At this Brydon raised himself; he had to see her better. She helped him when she understood his movement, and he sat up, steadying himself beside her there on the window-bench and with his right hand grasping her left. "*He* didn't come to me."

"You came to yourself," she beautifully smiled.

"Ah I've come to myself now—thanks to you, dearest. But this brute, with his awful face—this brute's a black stranger. He's none of *me*, even as I *might* have been," Brydon sturdily declared.

But she kept the clearness that was like the breath of infallibility. "Isn't the whole point that you'd have been different?"

He almost scowled for it. "As different as *that*—?"

Her look again was more beautiful to him than the things of this world. "Haven't you exactly wanted to know *how* different? So this morning," she said, "you appeared to me."

"Like *him?*"

"A black stranger!"

"Then how did you know it was I?"

"Because, as I told you weeks ago, my mind, my imagination, had worked so over what you might, what you mightn't have been—to show you, you see, how I've thought of you. In the midst of that you came to me—that my wonder might be answered. So I knew," she went on; "and believed that, since the question held you too so fast, as you told me that day, you too would see for yourself. And when this morning I again saw I knew it would be because you had—and also then, from the first moment, because you somehow wanted me. *He* seemed to tell me of that. So why," she strangely smiled. "shouldn't I like him?"

It brought Spencer Brydon to his feet. "You 'like' that horror—?"

"I *could* have liked him. And to me," she said, "he was no horror. I had accepted him."

" 'Accepted'—?" Brydon oddly sounded.

"Before, for the interest of his difference—yes. And as *I* didn't disown him, as *I* knew him—which you at last, confronted with him in his difference, so cruelly didn't, my dear—well, he must have been, you see, less dreadful to me. And it may have pleased him that I pitied him."

She was beside him on her feet, but still holding his hand—still with her arm supporting him. But though it all brought for him thus a dim light, "You 'pitied' him?" he grudgingly, resentfully asked.

"He has been unhappy, he has been ravaged," she said.

"And haven't I been unhappy? Am not I—you've only to look at me!—ravaged?"

"Ah I don't say I like him *better*," she granted after a thought. "But he's grim, he's worn—and things have happened to him. He doesn't make shift, for sight, with your charming monocle."

"No"—it struck Brydon: "I couldn't have sported mine 'downtown.' They'd have guyed me there."

"His great convex pince-nez—I saw it, I recognised the kind—is for his poor ruined sight. And his poor right hand—!"

"Ah!" Brydon winced—whether for his proved identity or for his lost fingers. Then, "He has a million a year," he lucidly added. "But he hasn't you."

"And he isn't—no, he isn't—*you!*" she murmured as he drew her to his breast.

The Author on His Craft

Editor's Commentary

James's critical vocabulary derived in part from the criticism of painting, as his seminal essay on "The Art of Fiction" (1884) demonstrates. In childhood he had been exposed to the great monuments of European art, and he studied painting before he took up writing. As a young man he explored the museums and churches of the Old World, reporting the results in a series of articles, and these exercises in the description of visual art in part account for his critical vocabulary. Since the English language lacked an established terminology for the formal criticism of fiction, James was free to draw some of the terms of his literary theory from art critisim. The "analogy between the art of the novelist and the art of the painter," he wrote in "The Art of Fiction," is complete. "They may learn from each other, they may explain and sustain each other." Throughout his life painting terms served him as metaphors for his own art.[1]

One of the traps one must avoid in speaking of James's critical principles is to make him out more consistent than he was. In the essays he wrote over a stretch of decades and even in the prefaces to the New York Edition his esthetic is not very systematic. Some of his terms are informal. The word *story* usually meant narrative to him and might cover anything from a long novel like *The Ambassadors* to a very short piece like "Brooksmith." The new term *short story* (in the *Oxford English Dictionary* first noted for 1898) he used with equal informality when he used it at all. But he did theorize about short fiction, and his theory is reflected in the passages here reprinted from his prefaces. It turns upon two central and related distinctions: of length, between shorter and longer, and of method, between "scenic" and "pictorial."

Length. Editorial rules prevailing in James's time specified that a short story should extend from six to eight thousand words, and James found these limits constricting. His ideal was "the beautiful and blest *nouvelle*,"[2] whose elasticity better fitted his inclinations. It allowed room for growth, for change of character, for interaction between characters, for plot reversal, in a word, for development, as in "Daisy Miller," which he declared "pre-eminently a *nouvelle*" (see p. 369 below). The shorter form he usually termed "anecdote."

Method. The writer of fiction, James maintained, has the choice of treating a subject as picture or as scene.[3] Scene is dramatic, picture is descriptive and internal. Scene shows characters involved in action and speech; picture tells what they experience, what they feel and think, what they remember. If we are surprised to find a character's reflections denoted as picture, the explanation is that their portrayal has affinity with painting, as James's concept of foreshortening or perspective underlines. *Foreshortening* is a key word in his esthetic; it too shows the influence of painting. In painting it refers to the method of achieving depth by shortening the outlines of distant objects. James

1. These and related matters have been treated authoritatively by Viola Hopkins Winner in *Henry James and the Visual Arts* (Charlottes-ville: University Press of Virginia, 1970).

2. *The Art of the Novel* (New York and London: Charles Scribner's Sons, 1948), p. 220.
3. Ibid., p. 300.

knew that the grammar of fiction contains no such exact techniques: "the grammar of painting is . . . much more definite," he says in "The Art of Fiction"(see p. 350 below). Still—as he pointed out some twenty years later in the preface to "Daisy Miller"—in fiction, too, foreshortening achieves perspective. It consists in narrative summary which bridges time and distance and hence is an "economic device." It allows the author to contain the complexities of his subject within a compact treatment.

James's distinction between the scenic method and the pictorial is related to the matter of length and therefore to the distinction between anecdote and *nouvelle*. A picture, an impression, may present a "foreshortened" form of a complex subject which involves progression and development, in other words, the kind of subject James thought appropriate to the *nouvelle*. But in James's own practice the distinction between the scenic and the pictorial method operates in fact everywhere. "The Middle Years," one of his short pieces on a subject "demanding 'developments,' " is poured into the form of the "concise anecdote" (see p. 381 below), though not as concise as he thought, and the nouvelle "Daisy Miller" contains both scenic and pictorial passages. So, we may add, do all of James's short stories. "The Beast in the Jungle," for instance, alternates dramatic scenes with long internalized passages which picture the hero's self-absorbed creation of what he believes to be his fate. The alternation of narrative perspective and dramatic scenes (partly because a memory may include specific scenes) is a hallmark of James's practice from his shortest stories to his longest novels.

James's definition of picture, finally, leads to another formal characteristic of his fiction, his concern with narrative point of view. One of his means of organizing his material was to present characters and action as they are perceived by a participant. The analogy with painting applies to these functional figures—reflectors, registers, central intelligences, centers of consciousness, as James variously called them. Their function is comparable to the painter's frame. What the painter achieves by framing or limiting the field of his vision James achieves by the limited focus of his centers. He explains in his preface to "The Pupil," for instance, that presenting his material, the family of the Moreens, indirectly through the "troubled vision" of their son Morgan and his tutor, was to give it "proportion and perspective" (see p. 379 below). James's formal concerns, in sum, are closely related to his preoccupations as a psychological novelist. He was interested in psychological manifestations of all kinds, and the interest in the varieties of consciousness is reflected in his technical experiments with limited narrative points of view. At first this method of presenting and organizing his subjects served him primarily as a compositional device to achieve focus and thereby clarity and intensity. In time consciousness became his very subject.

HENRY JAMES

The Art of Fiction†

I should not have affixed so comprehensive a title to these few remarks, necessarily wanting in any completeness upon a subject the full consideration of which would carry us far, did I not seem to discover a pretext for my temerity in the interesting pamphlet lately published under this name by Mr. Walter Besant.[1] Mr. Besant's lecture at the Royal Institution—the original form of his pamphlet— appears to indicate that many persons are interested in the art of fiction, and are not indifferent to such remarks, as those who practise it may attempt to make about it. I am therefore anxious not to lose the benefit of this favourable association, and to edge in a few words under cover of the attention which Mr. Besant is sure to have excited. There is something very encouraging in his having put into form certain of his ideas on the mystery of story-telling.

It is a proof of life and curiosity—curiosity on the part of the brotherhood of novelists as well as on the part of their readers. Only a short time ago it might have been supposed that the English novel was not what the French call *discutable*.[2] It had no air of having a theory, a conviction, a consciousness of itself behind it—of being the expression of an artistic faith, the result of choice and comparison. I do not say it was necessarily the worse for that: it would take much more courage than I possess to intimate that the form of the novel as Dickens and Thackeray (for instance) saw it had any taint of incompleteness. It was, however, *naïf*[3] (if I may help myself out with another French word); and evidently if it be destined to suffer in any way for having lost its *naïveté* it has now an idea of making sure of the corresponding advantages. During the period I have alluded to there was a comfortable, good-humoured feeling abroad that a novel is a novel, as a pudding is a pudding, and that our only business with it could be to swallow it. But within a year or two, for some reason or other, there have been signs of returning animation—the era of discussion would appear to have been to a certain extent opened. Art lives upon discussion, upon experiment, upon curiosity, upon variety of attempt,

†From Henry James, *Partial Portraits* (London: Macmillan and Co., Limited, 1905), pp. 375–408. (First edition 1888. Reprinted 1894, 1899, 1905). The essay was originally published in *Longman's Magazine* of September 1884. The text here reprinted was revised by the author. It may bear repeating that although the essay speaks of novels and novelists its subject—as the title indicates—is fiction regardless of length. The footnotes for this selection are by the editor of this Norton Critical Edition.
1. British novelist (1836–1901) On April 25, 1884, Besant had lectured on "The Art of Fiction" at the Royal Institution (founded in 1799 to promote research in connection with the experimental sciences). The lecture was published as a pamphlet and this in turn gave James the impulse and opportunity for his essay.
2. Debatable: a subject for serious discussion.
3. Unsophisticated, unself-conscious.

upon the exchange of views and the comparison of standpoints; and there is a presumption that those times when no one has anything particular to say about it, and has no reason to give for practice or preference, though they may be times of honour, are not times of development—are times, possibly even, a little of dulness. The successful application of any art is a delightful spectacle, but the theory too is interesting; and though there is a great deal of the latter without the former I suspect there has never been a genuine success that has not had a latent core of conviction. Discussion, suggestion, formulation, these things are fertilising when they are frank and sincere. Mr. Besant has set an excellent example in saying what he thinks, for his part, about the way in which fiction should be written, as well as about the way in which it should be published; for his view of the "art," carried on into an appendix, covers that too. Other labourers in the same field will doubtless take up the argument, they will give it the light of their experience, and the effect will surely be to make our interest in the novel a little more what it had for some time threatened to fail to be—a serious, active, inquiring interest, under protection of which this delightful study may, in moments of confidence, venture to say a little more what it thinks of itself.

It must take itself seriously for the public to take it so. The old superstition about fiction being "wicked" has doubtless died out in England; but the spirit of it lingers in a certain oblique regard directed toward any story which does not more or less admit that it is only a joke. Even the most jocular novel feels in some degree the weight of the proscription that was formerly directed against literary levity: the jocularity does not always succeed in passing for orthodoxy. It is still expected, though perhaps people are ashamed to say it, that a production which is after all only a "make-believe" (for what else is a "story"?) shall be in some degree apologetic—shall renounce the pretension of attempting really to represent life. This, of course, any sensible, wide-awake story declines to do, for it quickly perceives that the tolerance granted to it on such a condition is only an attempt to stifle it disguised in the form of generosity. The old evangelical hostility to the novel, which was as explicit as it was narrow, and which regarded it as little less favourable to our immortal part than a stage-play, was in reality far less insulting. The only reason for the existence of a novel is that it does attempt to represent life. When it relinquishes this attempt, the same attempt that we see on the canvas of the painter, it will have arrived at a very strange pass. It is not expected of the picture that it will make itself humble in order to be forgiven; and the analogy between the art of the painter and the art of the novelist is, so far as I am able to see, complete. Their inspiration is the same, their process (allowing for the different quality of the vehicle), is the same, their success is the same. They may learn from each other, they may explain and sustain each other. Their cause is the same, and the honour of one is the honour of another. The Mahometans[4] think a picture an unholy thing, but it is a long time since any Christian did, and it is therefore the more odd that in the Christian mind the traces (dissimulated though they may be) of a suspicion of the sister art should linger to this day. The only effectual way to lay it to rest is to emphasise the analogy to which I just alluded—to insist on the fact that as the picture is reality, so the novel is history. That is the only general description (which does it justice) that we may give of the novel. But history also is allowed to represent life; it is not, any more than painting, expected to apologise. The subject-matter of fiction is stored up likewise in documents and records, and if it will not give itself away, as they say in California, it must speak with assurance, with the tone of the historian. Certain accomplished novelists have a habit of giving themselves away which must often bring tears to the eyes of people who take their fiction seriously. I was lately struck, in reading over many pages of Anthony Trollope,[5] with his want of discretion in this particular. In a digression, a parenthesis or an aside, he concedes to the reader that he and this trusting friend are only "making believe." He admits that the events he narrates have not really happened, and that he can give his narrative any turn the reader may like best. Such a betrayal of a sacred office seems to me, I confess, a terrible crime; it is what I mean by the attitude of apology, and it shocks me every whit as much in Trollope as it would have shocked me in Gibbon or Macaulay.[6] It implies that the novelist is less occupied in looking for the truth (the truth, of course I mean, that he assumes, the premises that we must grant him, whatever they may be), than the historian, and in doing so it deprives him at a stroke of all his standing-room. To represent and illustrate the past, the actions of men, is the task of either writer, and the only difference that I can see is, in proportion as he succeeds, to the honour of the novelist, consisting as it does in his having more difficulty in collecting his evidence, which is so far from being purely literary. It seems to me to give him a great character, the fact that he has at once so much in common with the philosopher and the painter; this double analogy is a magnificent heritage.

It is of all this evidently that Mr. Besant is full when he insists upon the fact that fiction is one of the *fine* arts, deserving in its turn of all the honours and emoluments that have hitherto been reserved for the successful profession of music, poetry, painting, architecture. It is impossible to insist too much on so important a truth, and the place

4. Muhammedans.
5. British novelist (1815–82).
6. Edward Gibbon (1737–94) and Thomas Babington Macaulay (1800–1859) were emi-nent British historians, respectively authors of *The Decline and Fall of the Roman Empire* and *Macaulay's History of England from the Accession of James II*.

that Mr. Besant demands for the work of the novelist may be represented, a trifle less abstractly, by saying that he demands not only that it shall be reputed artistic, but that it shall be reputed very artistic indeed. It is excellent that he should have struck this note, for his doing so indicates that there was need of it, that his proposition may be to many people a novelty. One rubs one's eyes at the thought; but the rest of Mr. Besant's essay confirms the revelation. I suspect in truth that it would be possible to confirm it still further, and that one would not be far wrong in saying that in addition to the people to whom it has never occurred that a novel ought to be artistic, there are a great many others who, if this principle were urged upon them, would be filled with an indefinable mistrust. They would find it difficult to explain their repugnance, but it would operate strongly to put them on their guard. "Art," in our Protestant communities, where so many things have got so strangely twisted about, is supposed in certain circles to have some vaguely injurious effect upon those who make it an important consideration, who let it weigh in the balance. It is assumed to be opposed in some mysterious manner to morality, to amusement, to instruction. When it is embodied in the work of the painter (the sculptor is another affair!) you know what it is: it stands there before you, in the honesty of pink and green and a gilt frame; you can see the worst of it at a glance, and you can be on your guard. But when it is introduced into literature it becomes more insidious—there is danger of its hurting you before you know it. Literature should be either instructive or amusing, and there is in many minds an impression that these artistic preoccupations, the search for form, contribute to neither end, interfere indeed with both. They are too frivolous to be edifying, and too serious to be diverting; and they are moreover priggish and paradoxical and superfluous. That, I think, represents the manner in which the latent thought of many people who read novels as an exercise in skipping would explain itself if it were to become articulate. They would argue, of course, that a novel ought to be "good," but they would interpret this term in a fashion of their own, which indeed would vary considerably from one critic to another. One would say that being good means representing virtuous and aspiring characters, placed in prominent positions; another would say that it depends on a "happy ending," on a distribution at the last of prizes, pensions, husbands, wives, babies, millions, appended paragraphs, and cheerful remarks. Another still would say that it means being full of incident and movement, so that we shall wish to jump ahead, to see who was the mysterious stranger, and if the stolen will was ever found, and shall not be distracted from this pleasure by any tiresome analysis or "description." But they would all agree that the "artistic" idea would spoil some of their fun. One would hold it accountable for all the description, another would see it revealed in the absence of sympathy. Its hostility to a happy ending would be evident, and it might even in some cases render any ending at all impossible. The "ending" of a novel is, for many persons, like that of a good dinner, a course of dessert and ices, and the artist in fiction is regarded as a sort of meddlesome doctor who forbids agreeable aftertastes. It is therefore true that this conception of Mr. Besant's of the novel as a superior form encounters not only a negative but a positive indifference. It matters little that as a work of art it should really be as little or as much of its essence to supply happy endings, sympathetic characters, and an objective tone, as if it were a work of mechanics: the association of ideas, however incongruous, might easily be too much for it if an eloquent voice were not sometimes raised to call attention to the fact that it is at once as free and as serious a branch of literature as any other.

Certainly this might sometimes be doubted in presence of the enormous number of works of fiction that appeal to the credulity of our generation, for it might easily seem that there could be no great character in a commodity so quickly and easily produced. It must be admitted that good novels are much compromised by bad ones, and that the field at large suffers discredit from overcrowding. I think, however, that this injury is only superficial, and that the super-abundance of written fiction proves nothing against the principle itself. It has been vulgarised, like all other kinds of literature, like everything else to-day, and it has proved more than some kinds accessible to vulgarisation. But there is as much difference as there ever was between a good novel and a bad one: the bad is swept with all the daubed canvases and spoiled marble into some unvisited limbo, or infinite rubbish-yard beneath the back-windows of the world, and the good subsists and emits its light and stimulates our desire for perfection. As I shall take the liberty of making but a single criticism of Mr. Besant, whose tone is so full of the love of his art, I may as well have done with it at once. He seems to me to mistake in attempting to say so definitely beforehand what sort of an affair the good novel will be. To indicate the danger of such an error as that has been the purpose of these few pages; to suggest that certain traditions on the subject, applied *a priori*, have already had much to answer for, and that the good health of an art which undertakes so immediately to reproduce life must demand that it be perfectly free. It lives upon exercise, and the very meaning of exercise is freedom. The only obligation to which in advance we may hold a novel, without incurring the accusation of being arbitrary, is that it be interesting. That general responsibility rests upon it, but it is the only one I can think of. The ways in which it is at liberty to accomplish this result (of interesting us) strike me as innumerable, and such as can only suffer from being marked out or fenced in by prescription. They are as various as the temperament of man, and they are successful in proportion as they reveal a particular mind, different from others. A novel is in its broadest definition a personal, a direct impression of life: that, to begin with, constitutes its value, which is greater or less according to the intensity of the impression. But there will be no intensity at all, and therefore no value, unless there is freedom to feel and say. The tracing of a line to be followed, of a tone to be taken, of a form to be filled out, is a limitation of that freedom and a suppression of the very thing that we are most curious about. The form, it seems to me, is to be appreciated after the fact: then the author's choice has been made, his standard has been indicated; then we can follow lines and directions and compare tones and resemblances. Then in a word we can enjoy one of the most charming of pleasures, we can estimate quality, we can apply the test of execution. The execution belongs to the author alone; it is what is most personal to him, and we measure him by that. The advantage, the luxury, as well as the torment and responsibility of the novelist, is that there is no limit to what he may attempt as an executant—no limit to his possible experiments, efforts, discoveries, successes. Here it is especially that he works, step by step, like his brother of the brush, of whom we may always say that he has painted his picture in a manner best known to himself. His manner is his secret, not necessarily a jealous one. He cannot disclose it as a general thing if he would; he would be at a loss to teach it to others. I say this with a due recollection of having insisted on the community of method of the artist who paints a picture and the artist who writes a novel. The painter *is* able to teach the rudiments of his practice, and it is possible, from the study of good work (granted the aptitude), both to learn how to paint and to learn how to write. Yet it remains true, without injury to the *rapprochement*,[7] that the literary artist would be obliged to say to his pupil much more than the other, "Ah, well, you must do it as you can!" It is a question of degree, a matter of delicacy. If there are exact sciences, there are also exact arts, and the grammar of painting is so much more definite that it makes the difference.

I ought to add, however, that if Mr. Besant says at the beginning of his essay that the "laws of fiction may be laid down and taught with as much precision and exactness as the laws of harmony, perspective, and proportion," he mitigates what might appear to be an extravagance by applying his remark to "general" laws, and by expressing most of these rules in a manner with which it would certainly be unaccommodating to disagree. That the novelist must write from his experience, that his "characters must be real and such as might be met with in actual life"; that "a young lady brought up in a quiet country village should avoid descriptions of garrison life," and "a writer whose

7. Comparison.

friends and personal experiences belong to the lower middle-class should carefully avoid introducing his characters into society"; that one should enter one's notes in a common-place book;[8] that one's figures should be clear in outline; that making them clear by some trick of speech or of carriage is a bad method, and "describing them at length" is a worse one; that English Fiction should have a "conscious moral purpose"; that "it is almost impossible to estimate too highly the value of careful workmanship—that is, of style"; that "the most important point of all is the story," that "the story is everything": these are principles with most of which it is surely impossible not to sympathise. That remark about the lower middle-class writer and his knowing his place is perhaps rather chilling; but for the rest I should find it difficult to dissent from any one of these recommendations. At the same time, I should find it difficult positively to assent to them, with the exception, perhaps, of the injunction as to entering one's notes in a common-place book. They scarcely seem to me to have the quality that Mr. Besant attributes to the rules of the novelist—the "precision and exactness" of "the laws of harmony, perspective, and proportion." They are suggestive, they are even inspiring, but they are not exact, though they are doubtless as much so as the case admits of: which is a proof of that liberty of interpretation for which I just contended. For the value of these different injunctions—so beautiful and so vague—is wholly in the meaning one attaches to them. The characters, the situation, which strike one as real will be those that touch and interest one most, but the measure of reality is very difficult to fix. The reality of Don Quixote or of Mr. Micawber[9] is a very delicate shade; it is a reality so coloured by the author's vision that, vivid as it may be, one would hesitate to propose it as a model: one would expose one's self to some very embarrassing questions on the part of a pupil. It goes without saying that you will not write a good novel unless you possess the sense of reality; but it will be difficult to give you a recipe for calling that sense into being. Humanity is immense, and reality has a myriad forms; the most one can affirm is that some of the flowers of fiction have the odour of it, and others have not; as for telling you in advance how your nosegay should be composed, that is another affair. It is equally excellent and inconclusive to say that one must write from experience; to our supposititious aspirant such a declaration might savour of mockery. What kind of experience is intended, and where does it begin and end? Experience is never limited, and it is never complete; it is an immense sensibility, a kind of huge spider-web of the finest silken threads suspended in the chamber of consciousness, and

8. A notebook in which one collects ideas, observations, and noteworthy passages from other writers.

9. Character in *David Copperfield* by Charles Dickens. Don Quixote is of course the title hero of the novel by Miguel de Cervantes (1547–1616).

catching every airborne particle in its tissue. It is the very atmosphere of the mind; and when the mind is imaginative—much more when it happens to be that of a man of genius—it takes to itself the faintest hints of life, it converts the very pulses of the air into revelations. The young lady living in a village has only to be a damsel upon whom nothing is lost to make it quite unfair (as it seems to me) to declare to her that she shall have nothing to say about the military. Greater miracles have been seen than that, imagination assisting, she should speak the truth about some of these gentlemen. I remember an English novelist, a woman of genius, telling me that she was much commended for the impression she had managed to give in one of her tales of the nature and way of life of the French Protestant youth. She had been asked where she learned so much about this recondite being, she had been congratulated on her peculiar opportunities. These opportunities consisted in her having once, in Paris, as she ascended a staircase, passed an open door where, in the household of a *pasteur*,[1] some of the young Protestants were seated at table round a finished meal. The glimpse made a picture; it lasted only a moment, but that moment was experience. She had got her direct personal impression, and she turned out her type. She knew what youth was, and what Protestantism; she also had the advantage of having seen what it was to be French, so that she converted these ideas into a concrete image and produced a reality. Above all, however, she was blessed with the faculty which when you give it an inch takes an ell, and which for the artist is a much greater source of strength then any accident of residence or of place in the social scale. The power to guess the unseen from the seen, to trace the implication of things, to judge the whole piece by the pattern, the condition of feeling life in general so completely that you are well on your way to knowing any particular corner of it—this cluster of gifts may almost be said to constitute experience, and they occur in country and in town, and in the most differing stages of education. If experience consists of impressions, it may be said that impressions *are* experience, just as (have we not seen it?) they are the very air we breathe. Therefore, if I should certainly say to a novice, "Write from experience and experience only," I should feel that this was rather a tantalising monition if I were not careful immediately to add, "Try to be one of the people on whom nothing is lost!"

I am far from intending by this to minimise the importance of exactness—of truth of detail. One can speak best from one's own taste, and I may therefore venture to say that the air of reality (solidity of specification) seems to me to be the supreme virtue of a novel—the merit on which all its other merits (including that conscious moral purpose of which Mr. Besant speaks) helplessly and submissively

1. Clergyman.

depend. If it be not there they are all as nothing, and if these be there, they owe their effect to the success with which the author has produced the illusion of life. The cultivation of this success, the study of this exquisite process, form, to my taste, the beginning and the end of the art of the novelist. They are his inspiration, his despair, his reward, his torment, his delight. It is here in very truth that he competes with life; it is here that he competes with his brother the painter in *his* attempt to render the look of things, the look that conveys their meaning, to catch the colour, the relief, the expression, the surface, the substance of the human spectacle. It is in regard to this that Mr. Besant is well inspired when he bids him take notes. He cannot possibly take too many, he cannot possibly take enough. All life solicits him, and to "render" the simplest surface, to produce the most momentary illusion, is a very complicated business. His case would be easier, and the rule would be more exact, if Mr. Besant had been able to tell him what notes to take. But this, I fear, he can never learn in any manual; it is the business of his life. He has to take a great many in order to select a few, he has to work them up as he can, and even the guides and philosophers who might have most to say to him must leave him alone when it comes to the application of precepts, as we leave the painter in communion with his palette. That his characters "must be clear in outline," as Mr. Besant says—he feels that down to his boots; but how he shall make them so is a secret between his good angel and himself. It would be absurdly simple if he could be taught that a great deal of "description" would make them so, or that on the contrary the absence of description and the cultivation of dialogue, or the absence of dialogue and the multiplication of "incident," would rescue him from his difficulties. Nothing, for instance, is more possible than that he be of a turn of mind for which this odd, literal opposition of description and dialogue, incident and description, has little meaning and light. People often talk of these things as if they had a kind of internecine distinctness, instead of melting into each other at every breath, and being intimately associated parts of one general effort of expression. I cannot imagine composition existing in a series of blocks, nor conceive, in any novel worth discussing at all, of a passage of description that is not in its intention narrative, a passage of dialogue that is not in its intention descriptive, a touch of truth of any sort that does not partake of the nature of incident, or an incident that derives its interest from any other source than the general and only source of the success of a work of art—that of being illustrative. A novel is a living thing, all one and continuous, like any other organism, and in proportion as it lives will it be found, I think, that in each of the parts there is something of each of the other parts. The critic who over the close texture of a finished work shall pretend to trace a geography of items will mark some frontiers as artificial, I fear, as any that have been known to history. There is an old-fashioned distinction between the novel of character and the novel of incident which must have cost many a smile to the intending fabulist who was keen about his work. It appears to me as little to the point as the equally celebrated distinction between the novel and the romance—to answer as little to any reality. There are bad novels and good novels, as there are bad pictures and good pictures; but that is the only distinction in which I see any meaning, and I can as little imagine speaking of a novel of character as I can imagine speaking of a picture of character. When one says picture one says of character, when one says novel one says of incident, and the terms may be transposed at will. What is character but the determination of incident? What is incident but the illustration of character? What is either a picture or a novel that is *not* of character? What else do we seek in it and find in it? It is an incident for a woman to stand up with her hand resting on a table and look out at you in a certain way; or if it be not an incident I think it will be hard to say what it is. At the same time it is an expression of character. If you say you don't see it (character in *that—allons donc!*), [2] this is exactly what the artist who has reasons of his own for thinking he *does* see it undertakes to show you. When a young man makes up his mind that he has not faith enough after all to enter the church as he intended, that is an incident, though you may not hurry to the end of the chapter to see whether perhaps he doesn't change once more. I do not say that these are extraordinary or startling incidents. I do not pretend to estimate the degree of interest proceeding from them, for this will depend upon the skill of the painter. It sounds almost puerile to say that some incidents are intrinsically much more important than others, and I need not take this precaution after having professed my sympathy for the major ones in remarking that the only classification of the novel that I can understand is into that which has life and that which has it not.

The novel and the romance, the novel of incident and that of character—these clumsy separations appear to me to have been made by critics and readers for their own convenience, and to help them out of some of their occasional queer predicaments, but to have little reality or interest for the producer, from whose point of view it is of course that we are attempting to consider the art of fiction. The case is the same with another shadowy category which Mr. Besant apparently is disposed to set up—that of the "modern English novel"; unless indeed it be that in this matter he has fallen into an accidental confusion of standpoints. It is not quite clear whether he intends the remarks in which he alludes to it to be didactic or historical. It is as difficult to suppose a person intending to write a modern English as to suppose him writing an ancient English novel: that is a label which

2. Come on now! Surely not!

begs the question. One writes the novel, one paints the picture, of one's language and of one's time, and calling it modern English will not, alas! make the difficult task any easier. No more, unfortunately, will calling this or that work of one's fellow-artist a romance—unless it be, of course, simply for the pleasantness of the thing, as for instance when Hawthorne gave this heading to his story of *Blithedale*. The French, who have brought the theory of fiction to remarkable completeness, have but one name for the novel, and have not attempted smaller things in it, that I can see, for that. I can think of no obligation to which the "romancer" would not be held equally with the novelist; the standard of execution is equally high for each. Of course it is of execution that we are talking—that being the only point of a novel that is open to contention. This is perhaps too often lost sight of, only to produce interminable confusions and cross-purposes. We must grant the artist his subject, his idea, his *donnée*:[3] our criticism is applied only to what he makes of it. Naturally I do not mean that we are bound to like it or find it interesting: in case we do not our course is perfectly simple—to let it alone. We may believe that of a certain idea even the most sincere novelist can make nothing at all, and the event may perfectly justify our belief; but the failure will have been a failure to execute, and it is in the execution that the fatal weakness is recorded. If we pretend to respect the artist at all, we must allow him his freedom of choice, in the face, in particular cases, of innumerable presumptions that the choice will not fructify. Art derives a considerable part of its beneficial exercise from flying in the face of presumptions, and some of the most interesting experiments of which it is capable are hidden in the bosom of common things. Gustave Flaubert[4] has written a story about the devotion of a servant-girl to a parrot, and the production, highly finished as it is, cannot on the whole be called a success. We are perfectly free to find it flat, but I think it might have been interesting; and I, for my part, am extremely glad he should have written it; it is a contribution to our knowledge of what can be done—or what cannot. Ivan Turgénieff[5] has written a tale about a deaf and dumb serf and a lap-dog, and the thing is touching, loving, a little masterpiece. He struck the note of life where Gustave Flaubert missed it—he flew in the face of a presumption and achieved a victory.

Nothing, of course, will ever take the place of the good old fashion of "liking" a work of art or not liking it: the most improved criticism will not abolish that primitive, that ultimate test. I mention this to guard myself from the accusation of intimating that the idea, the subject, of a novel or a picture, does not matter. It matters, to my sense, in the highest degree, and if I might put up a prayer it would be

---

3. A favorite expression of James's, meaning the starting point, the original notion, the germ from which he develops his narrative.

4. French novelist (1821–80).
5. Russian novelist (1818–83). Also spelled Turgenev.

that artists should select none but the richest. Some, as I have already hastened to admit, are much more remunerative than others, and it would be a world happily arranged in which persons intending to treat them should be exempt from confusions and mistakes. This fortunate condition will arrive only, I fear, on the same day that critics become purged from error. Meanwhile, I repeat, we do not judge the artist with fairness unless we say to him, "Oh, I grant you your starting-point, because if I did not I should seem to prescribe to you, and heaven forbid I should take that responsibility. If I pretend to tell you what you must not take, you will call upon me to tell you then what you must take; in which case I shall be prettily caught. Moreover, it isn't till I have accepted your data that I can begin to measure you. I have the standard, the pitch; I have no right to tamper with your flute and then criticise your music. Of course I may not care for your idea at all; I may think it silly, or stale, or unclean; in which case I wash my hands of you altogether. I may content myself with believing that you will not have succeeded in being interesting, but I shall, of course, not attempt to demonstrate it, and you will be as indifferent to me as I am to you. I needn't remind you that there are all sorts of tastes: who can know it better? Some people, for excellent reasons, don't like to read about carpenters; others, for reasons even better, don't like to read about courtesans. Many object to Americans. Others (I believe they are mainly editors and publishers) won't look at Italians. Some readers don't like quiet subjects; others don't like bustling ones. Some enjoy a complete illusion, others the consciousness of large concessions. They choose their novels accordingly, and if they don't care about your idea they won't, *a fortiori*,[6] care about your treatment."

So that it comes back very quickly, as I have said, to the liking: in spite of M. Zola,[7] who reasons less powerfully than he represents, and who will not reconcile himself to this absoluteness of taste, thinking that there are certain things that people ought to like, and that they can be made to like. I am quite at a loss to imagine anything (at any rate in this matter of fiction) that people *ought* to like or to dislike. Selection will be sure to take care of itself, for it has a constant motive behind it. That motive is simply experience. As people feel life, so they will feel the art that is most closely related to it. This closeness of relation is what we should never forget in talking of the effort of the novel. Many people speak of it as a factitious, artificial form, a product of ingenuity, the business of which is to alter and arrange the things that surround us, to translate them into conventional, traditional moulds. This, however, is a view of the matter which carries us but a very short way, condemns the art to an eternal repetition of a few familiar *clichés*, cuts short its development, and leads us straight up to a dead wall. Catch-

---

6. Even more certainly.   7. Emile Zola (1840–1902), French novelist.

ing the very note and trick, the strange irregular rhythm of life, that is the attempt whose strenuous force keeps Fiction upon her feet. In proportion as in what she offers us we see life *without* rearrangement do we feel that we are touching the truth; in proportion as we see it *with* rearrangement do we feel that we are being put off with a substitute, a compromise and convention. It is not uncommon to hear an extraordinary assurance of remark in regard to this matter of rearranging, which is often spoken of as if it were the last word of art. Mr. Besant seems to me in danger of falling into the great error with his rather unguarded talk about "selection." Art is essentially selection, but it is a selection whose main care is to be typical, to be inclusive. For many people art means rose-coloured window-panes, and selection means picking a bouquet for Mrs. Grundy.[8] They will tell you glibly that artistic considerations have nothing to do with the disagreeable, with the ugly; they will rattle off shallow commonplaces about the province of art and the limits of art till you are moved to some wonder in return as to the province and the limits of ignorance. It appears to me that no one can ever have made a seriously artistic attempt without becoming conscious of an immense increase—a kind of revelation—of freedom. One perceives in that case—by the light of a heavenly ray—that the province of art is all life, all feeling, all observation, all vision. As Mr. Besant so justly intimates, it is all experience. That is a sufficient answer to those who maintain that it must not touch the sad things of life, who stick into its divine unconscious bosom little prohibitory inscriptions on the end of sticks, such as we see in public gardens—"It is forbidden to walk on the grass; it is forbidden to touch the flowers; it is not allowed to introduce dogs or to remain after dark; it is requested to keep to the right." The young aspirant in the line of fiction whom we continue to imagine will do nothing without taste, for in that case his freedom would be of little use to him; but the first advantage of his taste will be to reveal to him the absurdity of the little sticks and tickets. If he have taste, I must add, of course he will have ingenuity, and my disrespectful reference to that quality just now was not meant to imply that it is useless in fiction. But it is only a secondary aid; the first is a capacity for receiving straight impressions.

Mr. Besant has some remarks on the question of "the story" which I shall not attempt to criticise, though they seem to me to contain a singular ambiguity, because I do not think I understand them. I cannot see what is meant by talking as if there were a part of a novel which is the story and part of it which for mystical reasons is not— unless indeed the distinction be made in a sense in which it is difficult to suppose that any one should attempt to convey anything. "The story," if it represents anything, represents the subject, the idea, the

8. A character—and a symbol of conventional propriety—in *Speed the Plough* (1798), a play by   Thomas Morton.

donnée of the novel; and there is surely no "school"—Mr. Besant speaks of a school—which urges that a novel should be all treatment and no subject. There must assuredly be something to treat; every school is intimately conscious of that. This sense of the story being the idea, the starting-point, of the novel, is the only one that I see in which it can be spoken of as something different from its organic whole; and since in proportion as the work is successful the idea permeates and penetrates it, informs and animates it, so that every word and every punctuation-point contribute directly to the expression, in that proportion do we lose our sense of the story being a blade which may be drawn more or less out of its sheath. The story and the novel, the idea and the form, are the needle and thread, and I never heard of a guild of tailors who recommended the use of the thread without the needle, or the needle without the thread. Mr. Besant is not the only critic who may be observed to have spoken as if there were certain things in life which constitute stories, and certain others which do not. I find the same odd implication in an entertaining article in the *Pall Mall Gazette*, devoted, as it happens, to Mr. Besant's lecture. "The story is the thing!" says this graceful writer, as if with a tone of opposition to some other idea. I should think it was, as every painter who, as the time for "sending in" his picture looms in the distance, finds himself still in quest of a subject—as every belated artist not fixed about his theme will heartily agree. There are some subjects which speak to us and others which do not, but he would be a clever man who should undertake to give a rule—an index expurgatorius[9]—by which the story and the no-story should be known apart. It is impossible (to me at least) to imagine any such rule which shall not be altogether arbitrary. The writer in the *Pall Mall* opposes the delightful (as I suppose) novel of *Margot la Balafrée* to certain tales in which "Bostonian nymphs" appear to have "rejected English dukes for psychological reasons."[1] I am not acquainted with the romance just designated, and can scarcely forgive the *Pall Mall* critic for not mentioning the name of the author, but the title appears to refer to a lady who may have received a scar in some heroic adventure. I am inconsolable at not being acquainted with this episode, but am utterly at a loss to see why it is a story when the rejection (or acceptance) of a duke is not, and why a reason, psychological or other, is not a subject when a cicatrix is. They are all particles of the multitudinous life with which the novel deals, and surely no dogma which pretends to make it lawful to touch the one and unlawful to touch the other will stand for a moment on its feet. It is the special picture that must stand or fall, according as it seem

9. The *Index Expurgatorius* is a list of books which the Roman Catholic Church allows its members to read only when expurgated or corrected.

1. This may refer either to James's own *Portrait of a Lady* (1881), in which Isabel Archer rejects an offer of marriage from Lord Warburton, or to his earlier "An International Episode."

to possess truth or to lack it. Mr. Besant does not, to my sense, light up the subject by intimating that a story must, under penalty of not being a story, consist of "adventures." Why of adventures more than of green spectacles? He mentions a category of impossible things, and among them he places "fiction without adventure." Why without adventure, more than without matrimony, or celibacy, or parturition, or cholera, or hydropathy, or Jansenism?[2] This seems to me to bring the novel back to the hapless little *rôle* of being an artificial, ingenious thing— bring it down from its large, free character of an immense and exquisite correspondence with life. And what *is* adventure, when it comes to that, and by what sign is the listening pupil to recognise it? It is an adventure—an immense one—for me to write this little article; and for a Bostonian nymph to reject an English duke is an adventure only less stirring, I should say, than for an English duke to be rejected by a Bostonian nymph. I see dramas within dramas in that, and innumerable points of view. A psychological reason is, to my imagination, an object adorably pictorial; to catch the tint of its complexion—I feel as if that idea might inspire one to Titianesque[3] efforts. There are few things more exciting to me, in short, than a psychological reason, and yet, I protest, the novel seems to me the most magnificent form of art. I have just been reading, at the same time, the delightful story of *Treasure Island*, by Mr. Robert Louis Stevenson[4] and, in a manner less consecutive, the last tale from M. Edmond de Goncourt,[5] which is entitled *Chérie*. One of these works treats of murders, mysteries, islands of dreadful renown, hairbreadth escapes, miraculous coincidences and buried doubloons. The other treats of a little French girl who lived in a fine house in Paris, and died of wounded sensibility because no one would marry her. I call *Treasure Island* delightful, because it appears to me to have succeeded wonderfully in what it attempts; and I venture to bestow no epithet upon *Chérie*, which strikes me as having failed deplorably in what it attempts—that is in tracing the development of the moral consciousness of a child. But one of these productions strikes me as exactly as much of a novel as the other, and as having a "story" quite as much. The moral consciousness of a child is as much a part of life as the islands of the Spanish Main, and the one sort of geography seems to me to have those "surprises" of which Mr. Besant speaks quite as much as the other. For myself (since it comes back in the last resort, as I say, to the preference of the individual), the picture of the child's experience has the advantage that I can at successive steps (an immense luxury, near to the

2. The doctrine of Cornelius Jansen, a seventeenth-century Roman-Catholic bishop in France.
3. In the (grand) manner of Titian (ca. 1477–1576), the Italian painter.
4. British novelist and poet (1850–94). Also,

incidentally, the author of "A Humble Remonstrance," an essay answering James. The result was an exchange of letters and a warm friendship between the two writers.
5. French novelist and critic. (1822–96).

"sensual pleasure" of which Mr. Besant's critic in the *Pall Mall* speaks) say Yes or No, as it may be, to what the artist puts before me. I have been a child in fact, but I have been on a quest for a buried treasure only in supposition, and it is a simple accident that with M. de Goncourt I should have for the most part to say No. With George Eliot,[6] when she painted that country with a far other intelligence, I always said Yes.

The most interesting part of Mr. Besant's lecture is unfortunately the briefest passage—his very cursory allusion to the "conscious moral purpose" of the novel. Here again it is not very clear whether he be recording a fact or laying down a principle; it is a great pity that in the latter case he should not have developed his idea. This branch of the subject is of immense importance, and Mr. Besant's few words point to considerations of the widest reach, not to be lightly disposed of. He will have treated the art of fiction but superficially who is not prepared to go every inch of the way that these considerations will carry him. It is for this reason that at the beginning of these remarks I was careful to notify the reader that my reflections on so large a theme have no pretension to be exhaustive. Like Mr. Besant, I have left the question of the morality of the novel till the last, and at the last I find I have used up my space. It is a question surrounded with difficulties, as witness the very first that meets us, in the form of a definite question, on the threshold. Vagueness, in such a discussion, is fatal, and what is the meaning of your morality and your conscious moral purpose? Will you not define your terms and explain how (a novel being a picture) a picture can be either moral or immoral? You wish to paint a moral picture or carve a moral statue: will you not tell us how you would set about it? We are discussing the Art of Fiction; questions of art are questions (in the widest sense) of execution; questions of morality are quite another affair, and will you not let us see how it is that you find it so easy to mix them up? These things are so clear to Mr. Besant that he has deduced from them a law which he sees embodied in English Fiction, and which is "a truly admirable thing and a great cause for congratulation." It is a great cause for congratulation indeed when such thorny problems become as smooth as silk. I may add that in so far as Mr. Besant perceives that in point of fact English Fiction has addressed itself preponderantly to these delicate questions he will appear to many people to have made a vain discovery. They will have been positively struck, on the contrary, with the moral timidity of the usual English novelist; with his (or with her) aversion to face the difficulties with which on every side the treatment of reality bristles. He is apt to be extremely shy (whereas the picture that Mr. Besant draws is a picture of boldness), and the sign of his work, for the most

6. Pseudonym of Mary Ann Evans (1819–80), British novelist.

part, is a cautious silence on certain subjects. In the English novel (by which of course I mean the American as well), more than in any other, there is a traditional difference between that which people know and that which they agree to admit that they know, that which they see and that which they speak of, that which they feel to be a part of life and that which they allow to enter into literature. There is the great difference, in short, between what they talk of in conversation and what they talk of in print. The essence of moral energy is to survey the whole field, and I should directly reverse Mr. Besant's remark and say not that the English novel has a purpose, but that it has a diffidence. To what degree a purpose in a work of art is a source of corruption I shall not attempt to inquire; the one that seems to me least dangerous is the purpose of making a perfect work. As for our novel, I may say lastly on this score that as we find it in England to-day it strikes me as addressed in a large degree to "young people," and that this in itself constitutes a presumption that it will be rather shy. There are certain things which it is generally agreed not to discuss, not even to mention, before young people. That is very well, but the absence of discussion is not a symptom of the moral passion. The purpose of the English novel—"a truly admirable thing, and a great cause for con-gratulation"—strikes me therefore as rather negative.

There is one point at which the moral sense and the artistic sense lie very near together; that is in the light of the very obvious truth that the deepest quality of a work of art will always be the quality of the mind of the producer. In proportion as that intelligence is fine will the novel, the picture, the statue partake of the substance of beauty and truth. To be constituted of such elements is, to my vision, to have purpose enough. No good novel will ever proceed from a superficial mind; that seems to me an axiom which, for the artist in fiction, will cover all needful moral ground: if the youthful aspirant take it to heart it will illuminate for him many of the mysteries of "purpose." There are many other useful things that might be said to him, but I have come to the end of my article, and can only touch them as I pass. The critic in the *Pall Mall Gazette*, whom I have already quoted, draws attention to the danger, in speaking of the art of fiction, of generalising. The danger that he has in mind is rather, I imagine, that of particularising, for there are some comprehensive remarks which, in addition to those embodied in Mr. Besant's suggestive lecture, might without fear of misleading him be addressed to the ingenuous student. I should remind him first of the magnificence of the form that is open to him, which offers to sight so few restrictions and such innumerable oppor-tunities. The other arts, in comparison, appear confined and ham-pered; the various conditions under which they are exercised are so rigid and definite. But the only condition that I can think of attaching to the composition of the novel is, as I have already said, that it be sincere. This freedom is a splendid privilege, and the first lesson of the young novelist is to learn to be worthy of it. "Enjoy it as it deserves," I should say to him; "take possession of it, explore it to its utmost extent, publish it, rejoice in it. All life belongs to you, and do not listen either to those who would shut you up into corners of it and tell you that it is only here and there that art inhabits, or to those who would persuade you that this heavenly messenger wings her way outside of life altogether, breathing a superfine air, and turning away her head from the truth of things. There is no impression of life, no manner of seeing it and feeling it, to which the plan of the novelist may not offer a place; you have only to remember that talents so dissimilar as those of Alexandre Dumas and Jane Austen,[7] Charles Dickens and Gustave Flaubert have worked in this field with equal glory. Do not think too much about optimism and pessimism; try and catch the colour of life itself. In France to-day we see a prodigious effort (that of Emile Zola, to whose solid and serious work no explorer of the capacity of the novel can allude without respect), we see an extraordinary effort vitiated by a spirit of pessimism on a narrow basis. M. Zola is magnificent, but he strikes an English reader as ignorant; he has an air of working in the dark; if he had as much light as energy, his results would be of the highest value. As for the aberrations of a shallow optimism, the ground (of English fiction especially) is strewn with their brittle particles as with broken glass. If you must indulge in conclusions, let them have the taste of a wide knowledge. Remember that your first duty is to be as complete as possible—to make as perfect a work. Be generous and delicate and pursue the prize."

HENRY JAMES

From His Notebooks†

[*On the origin of* "Brooksmith"]

[LONDON, JUNE 19, 1884]

Another little thing was told me the other day by Mrs. R. about D<uncan> S<tewart>'s little maid (lady's maid), Past, who was with her for years before her death, and whom I often saw there. She

7. Austen (1775–1815), the British novelist, and Dumas (1802–70), the French novelist and dramatist. For the contrast James is less likely to have thought of the son, Alexandre Dumas (1824–95) known as "Dumas *fils*."

†From *The Notebooks of Henry James*, ed.

F. O. Matthiessen and Kenneth Murdock (New York: Oxford University Press, 1947), pp. 64, 71–72, 102–4, 121–22, 311, 367–68. Except as noted, the footnotes for these selections are by the editor of this Norton Critical Edition.

had to find a new place of course, on Mrs. S.'s death, to relapse into ordinary service. Her sorrow, the way she felt the change, and the way she expressed it to Mrs. R. "Ah yes, ma'am, you have lost your mother, and it's a great grief, but what is your loss to mine?" (She was devoted to Mrs. D.S.) "You continue to see good society, to live with clever, cultivated people: but I fall again into my own class, I shall never see such company—hear such talk—again. She was so good to me that I lived *with* her, as it were; and nothing will ever make up to me again for the loss of her conversation. Common, vulgar people now: that's my lot for the future!" Represent this—the refined nature of the little plain, quiet woman—her appreciation—and the way her new conditions sicken her, with a denouement if possible. Represent first, of course, her life with the old lady—figure of old Mrs. D. S. (modified)—her interior—her talk. Mrs. R.'s relations with her servants. "My child—my dear child." (P. 64)

[On the origin of "The Aspern Papers"]

[FLORENCE, JANUARY 12, 1887]

Hamilton (V.L.'s brother) told me a curious thing of Capt. Silsbee—the Boston art-critic and Shelley-worshipper; that is of a curious adventure of his. Miss Claremont,[1] Bryon's *ci-devant* mistress[2] (the mother of Allegra) was living, until lately, here in Florence, at a great age, 80 or thereabouts, and with her lived her niece, a younger Miss Claremont—of about 50. Silsbee knew that they had interesting papers—letters of Shelley's and Byron's—he had known it for a long time and cherished the idea of getting hold of them. To this end he laid the plan of going to lodge with the Misses Claremont—hoping that the old lady in view of her great age and failing condition would die while he was there, so that he might then put his hand upon the documents, which she hugged close in life. He carried out this scheme—and things *se passèrent*[3] as he had expected. The old woman *did* die—and then he approached the younger one—the old maid of 50—on the subject of his desires. Her answer was—'I will give you all the letters if you marry me!' H. says that Silsbee *court encore!*[4] Certainly there is a little subject there: the picture of the two faded, queer, poor and discredited old English women—living on into a strange generation, in their musty corner of a foreign town—with these illustrious letters their most precious possession. Then the plot of

1. [*Note by Matthiessen and Murdock*] Clairmont is the usual form of the name, and the one used by James in his preface to *The Aspern Papers*.

2. Ex-mistress.
3. Happened, took place.
4. Is still running.

the Shelley fanatic—his watchings and waitings—the way he *couvers*[5] the treasure. The denouement needn't be the one related of poor Silsbee; and at any rate the general situation is in itself a subject and a picture. It strikes me much. The interest would be in some price that the man has to pay—that the old woman—or the survivor—sets upon the papers. His hesitations—his struggle—for he really would give almost anything.—The Countess Gamba came in while I was there: her husband is a nephew of the Guiccioli—and it was *à propos* of their having a lot of Byron's letters of which they are rather illiberal and dangerous guardians, that H. told me the above. They won't show them or publish any of them—and the Countess was very angry once on H.'s representing to her that it was her duty—especially to the English public!—to let them at least be seen. *Elle se fiche bien*[6] of the English public. She says the letters—addressed in Italian to the Guiccioli—are discreditable to Byron; and H. elicited from her that she had *burned* one of them! (Pp. 71–72)

[*On the Origin of "The Real Thing"*]

PARIS, HOTEL WESTMINSTER, FEBRUARY 22, 1891

In pursuance of my plan of writing some very short tales—things of from 7000 to 10,000 words, the easiest length to "place," I began yesterday the little story that was suggested to me some time ago by an incident related to me by George du Maurier[7]—the lady and gentleman who called upon him with a word from Frith, an oldish, faded, ruined pair—he an officer in the army—who unable to turn a penny in any other way, were trying to find employment as models. I was struck with the pathos, the oddity and typicalness of the situation—the little tragedy of good-looking gentlefolk, who had been all their life stupid and well-dressed, living, on a fixed income, at country-houses, watering places and clubs, like so many others of their class in England, and were now utterly unable to *do* anything, had no cleverness, no art nor craft to make use of as a *gagne-pain*[8]—could only *show* themselves, clumsily, for the fine, clean, well-groomed animals that they were, only hope to make a little money by—in this manner—just simply *being*. I thought I saw a subject for very brief treatment in this *donnée*[9]—and I think I do still; but to do anything worth while with it I must (as always, great Heavens!) be very clear as to what is in it and what I wish to get out of it. I tried a beginning yesterday, but I instantly became conscious that I must straighten out the little idea. It must be an idea—it can't be a "story" in the vulgar sense of the word. It must be a picture; it must illustrate something.

5. [*Note by Matthiessen and Murdock*] Here James uses the infinitive of a French verb—*couver* ['to brood over"—*Editor*] and adds an English termination.

6. She doesn't give a hoot (She could care less).
7. British novelist and illustrator. (1834–96).
8. Livelihood.
9. Notion, idea.

God knows that's enough—if the thing *does* illustrate. To make little anecdotes of this kind real *morceaux de vie*[1] is a plan quite inspiring enough. *Voyons un peu,*[2] therefore, what one can put into this one—I mean how much of life. One must put a little action—not a stupid, mechanical, arbitrary action, but something that is of the real essence of the subject. I thought of representing the husband as jealous of the wife—that is, jealous of the artist employing her, from the moment that, in point of fact, she begins to sit. But this is vulgar and obvious—worth nothing. What I wish to represent is the baffled, ineffectual, incompetent character of their attempt, and how it illustrates once again the everlasting English amateurishness—the way superficial, untrained, unprofessional effort goes to the wall when confronted with trained, competitive, intelligent, *qualified* art—in whatever line it may be a question of. It is out of *that* element that my little action and movement must come; and now I begin to see just how—as one always *does*—Glory be to the Highest—when one begins to look at a thing hard and straight and seriously—to fix it—as I am so sadly lax and desultory about doing. What subjects I should find—for *everything*—if I could only achieve this more as a habit! Let my contrast and complication here come from the opposition—to my melancholy Major and his wife—of a couple of little vulgar professional people *who know*, with the consequent bewilderment, vagueness, depression of the former—their failure to understand how such people can be better than *they*—their failure, disappointment, disappearance—going forth into the vague again. *Il y a bien quelque chose à tirer de ça.*[3] They have no pictorial sense. They are only clean and stiff and stupid. The others are dirty, even—the melancholy Major and his wife remark on it, wondering. The artist is beginning a big illustrated book, a new edition of a famous novel—say *Tom Jones:* and he is willing to try to work them in—for he takes an interest in their predicament, and feels—sceptically, but, with his flexible artistic sympathy—the appeal of their type. He is willing to give them a trial. Make it out that *he* himself is on trial—he is young and "rising," but he has still his golden spurs to win. He can't afford, *en somme,*[4] to make many mistakes. He has regular work in drawing every week for a serial novel in an illustrated paper; but the great project—that of a big house—of issuing an illustrated Fielding[5] promises him a big lift. He has been intrusted with (say) *Joseph Andrews*, experimentally; he will have to do this brilliantly in order to have the engagement for the rest confirmed. He has already 2 models in his service—the "complication" must come from *them*. One is a common clever, London girl, of the smallest origin and without conventional beauty, but of aptitude, of perceptions—knowing thoroughly *how*. She says "lydy" and

1. Slices of life.
2. Let's see now.
3. Something can certainly be made of this.
4. In short.
5. Henry Fielding (1707–54), British novelist, author of *Tom Jones* and *Joseph Andrews*.

"plice,"[6] but she has the pictorial sense; and can look like anything he wants her to look like. She poses, in short, in perfection. So does her colleague, a professional Italian, a little fellow—ill dressed, smelling of garlic, but admirably serviceable, quite universal. They must be contrasted, confronted, *juxtaposed* with the others; whom they take for people who *pay*, themselves, till they learn the truth when they are overwhelmed with derisive amazement. The denouement simply that the melancholy Major and his wife won't do—they're not "in it." Their surprise—their helpless, proud assent—without other prospects: yet at the same time *their* degree of more silent amazement at the success of the two inferior people—who are so much less nice-looking than themselves. Frankly, however, is this contrast enough of a *story*, by itself? It seems to me Yes—for it's an IDEA—and how the deuce should I get *more* into 7000 words? It must be simply 50 pp. of my manuscript. The little tale of *The Servant (Brooksmith)* which I did the other day for *Black and White* and which I thought of at the same time as this, proved a very tight squeeze into the same tiny number of words, and I probably shall find that there is much more to be done with this than the compass will admit of. Make it tremendously succinct—with a very short pulse or rhythm—and the closest selection of detail—in other words *summarize* intensely and keep down the lateral development. It *should* be a little gem of bright, quick, vivid form. I shall get every grain of "action" that the space admits of if I make something, for the artist, hang in the balance—depend on the way he does this particular work. It's when he finds that he shall lose his great opportunity if he keeps on with them, that he has to tell the gentlemanly couple, that, frankly, they won't serve his turn—and make them wander forth into the cold world again. I must keep them the age I've made them—50 and 40—because it's more touching; but I must bring up the age of the 2 real models to almost the same thing. That increases the incomprehensibility (to the amateurs) of their usefulness. Picture the immanence, in the latter, of the idle, provided-for, country-house habit—the blankness of their *manière d'être*.[7] But in how tremendously few words I must do it. This is a lesson—a *magnificent* lesson—if I'm to do a good many. Something as admirably compact and selected as Maupassant.[8] (Pp. 102–4)

[*On the origin of "The Middle Years"*]

[LONDON, DE VERE GARDENS, MAY 12, 1892]

The idea of the old artist, or man of letters, who, at the end, feels a kind of anguish of desire for a respite, a prolongation—another period

6. Cockney pronunciations of *lady* and *place*.
7. Way of life.
8. Guy de Maupassant (1850–93), French short story writer and novelist.

of life to do the *real* thing that he has in him—the things for which all the others have been but a slow preparation. He is the man who has developed late, obstructedly, with difficulty, has needed all life to learn, to see his way, to collect material, and now feels that if he can only have another life to make use of this clear start, he can show what he is really capable of. Some incident, then, to show that what he *has* done *is* that of which he is capable—that he has done all he can, that he has put into his things the love of perfection and that they will live by that. Or else an incident acting just the other way—showing him what he might do, just when he must give up forever. The 1st idea the best. A young doctor, a young pilgrim who admires him. A deep sleep in which he dreams he *has* had his respite. Then his waking to find that what he has dreamed of is only what he has *done*. (Pp. 121–22)

[*On the origin of "The Beast in the Jungle"*]

[RYE, LAMB HOUSE, AUGUST 27, 1901]

Meanwhile there is something else—a very tiny *fantaisie*[9] probably—in small notion that comes to me of a man haunted by the fear, more and more, throughout life, that *something will happen to him:* he doesn't quite know what. His life *seems* safe and ordered, his liabilities and exposures (as a *result* of the fear) a good deal curtailed and cut down, so that the years go by and the stroke doesn't fall. Yet "It *will* come, it will still come," he finds himself believing—and indeed saying to some one, some second-consciousness in the anecdote. "It will come before death; I shan't die without it." Finally I think it must be *he* who sees—not the 2d consciousness. Mustn't indeed the "2nd consciousness" be some woman, and it be she who *helps* him to see? She has always loved him—yes, *that*, for the story, "pretty," and he, saving, protecting, exempting his life (always, really, with and *for* the fear), has never known it. He likes her, talks to her, confides in her, sees her often—*la côtoie*, as to her hidden passion, but never guesses.[1] She meanwhile, all the time, sees his life as it is. It is to her that he tells his fear—yes, she is the "2nd consciousness." At first she *feels*, herself, for him, his feeling of his fear, and is tender, reassuring, protective. Then she reads, as I say, his real case, and is, though unexpressedly, *lucid*. The years go by and *she sees the thing not happen*. At last one day they are somehow, some day, face to face over it, and then she speaks. "It *has*, the great thing you've always lived in dread of, had the foreboding of—it *has* happened to you." He wonders—when, how, what? "What is it?—why, it is that *nothing* has happened!" Then, later

---

9. Odd fancy.

1. "Keeps coming close" to the question of her secret passion without ever catching on.

on, I think, to keep up the prettiness, it must be that HE sees, that he understands. She has loved him always—and *that* might have happened. But it's too late—she's dead. That, I think, at least, he comes to later on, after an interval, after her death. She is dying, or ill, when she says it. He *then* DOESN'T understand, doesn't see—or so far, only as to agree with her, ruefully, that that very well *may* be it: that nothing has happened. He goes back; she is gone; she is dead. *What* she has said to him has in a way, by its truth, created the need for her, made him want her, *positively* want her, more. But she is gone, he has lost her, and *then* he sees all she has meant. She has loved him. *(It must come for the* READER *thus, at this moment.)* With his base safety and shrinkage he never knew. *That* was what might have happened, and what *has* happened is that it didn't. (P. 311)

[*Regarding "The Jolly Corner" in retrospect*]

[LONDON, 1914]

The most intimate idea of *that*[2] is that my hero's adventure there takes the form so to speak of his turning the tables, as I think I called it, on a "ghost" or whatever, a visiting or haunting apparition otherwise qualified to appal *him;* and thereby winning a sort of victory by the appearance, and the evidence, that this personage or presence was more overwhelmingly affected by him than he by *it.* (Pp. 367–68)

HENRY JAMES

From His Prefaces

[*On "Daisy Miller"*]†

It was in Rome during the autumn of 1877; a friend then living there but settled now in a South less weighted with appeals and memories happened to mention . . . some simple and uninformed American lady of the previous winter, whose young daughter, a child of nature and of freedom, accompanying her from hotel to hotel, had "picked up" by the wayside, with the best conscience in the world, a good-looking Roman, of vague identity, astonished at his luck, yet . . . all innocently, all serenely exhibited and introduced: this at least till the occurrence of some small social check, some interrupting incident, of no great gravity or dignity, and which I forget. I had never

2. "The Jolly Corner."
†From *The Novels and Tales of Henry James,*

vol. XVIII (New York: Charles Scribner's Sons, 1909), pp. v–viii.

heard, save on this showing, of the amiable but not otherwise eminent ladies, who weren't in fact named, I think, and whose case had merely served to point a familiar moral; and it must have been just their want of salience that left a margin for the small pencil-mark inveterately signifying, in such connexions, "Dramatise, dramatise!" The result of my recognising a few months later the sense of my pencil-mark was the short chronicle of "Daisy Miller," which I indited in London the following spring and then addressed, with no conditions attached, as I remember, to the editor of a magazine[1] that had its seat of publication at Philadelphia and had lately appeared to appreciate my contributions. That gentleman however (an historian of some repute) promptly returned me my missive, and with an absence of comment that struck me at the time as rather grim—as, given the circumstances, requiring indeed some explanation: till a friend to whom I appealed for light, giving him the thing to read, declared it could only have passed with the Philadelphian critic for "an outrage on American girlhood." This was verily a light, and of bewildering intensity; though I was presently to read into the matter a further helpful inference. To the fault of being outrageous this little composition added that of being essentially and pre-eminently a *nouvelle*; a signal example in fact of that type, foredoomed at the best, in more cases than not, to editorial disfavour. If accordingly I was afterwards to be cradled, almost blissfully, in the conception that "Daisy" at least, among my productions, might approach "success," such success for example, on her eventual appearance, as the state of being promptly pirated in Boston—a sweet tribute I hadn't yet received and was never again to know—the irony of things yet claimed its rights, I couldn't but long continue to feel, in the circumstance that quite a special reprobation had waited on the first appearance in the world of the ultimately most prosperous child of my invention. So doubly discredited, at all events, this bantling met indulgence, with no great delay, in the eyes of my admirable friend the late Leslie Stephen[2] and was published in two numbers of *The Cornhill Magazine (1878)*.

It qualified itself in that publication and afterwards as "a Study"; for reasons which I confess I fail to recapture unless they may have taken account simply of a certain flatness in my poor little heroine's literal denomination. Flatness indeed, one must have felt, was the very sum of her story; so that perhaps after all the attached epithet was meant but as a deprecation, addressed to the reader, of any great critical hope of stirring scenes. It provided for mere concentration, and on an object scant and superficially vulgar—from which, however, a sufficiently brooding tenderness might eventually extract a shy incongruous

1. *Lippincott's Magazine.* [*Editor.*]
2. British man of letters (1832–1904)—philosopher, critic, biographer, editor of the

Dictionary of National Biography, father of Virginia Woolf. [*Editor.*]

charm. I suppress at all events here the appended qualification—in view of the simple truth, which ought from the first to have been apparent to me, that my little exhibition is made to no degree whatever in critical but, quite inordinately and extravagantly, in poetical terms. It comes back to me that I was at a certain hour long afterwards to have reflected, in this connexion, on the characteristic free play of the whirligig of time. It was in Italy again—in Venice and in the prized society of an interesting friend, now dead, with whom I happened to wait, on the Grand Canal, at the animated water-steps of one of the hotels. The considerable little terrace there was so disposed as to make a salient stage for certain demonstrations on the part of two young girls, children *they*, if ever, of nature and of freedom, whose use of those resources, in the general public eye, and under our own as we sat in the gondola, drew from the lips of a second companion, sociably afloat with us, the remark that there before us, with no sign absent, were a couple of attesting Daisy Millers. Then it was that, in my charming hostess's prompt protest, the whirligig, as I have called it, at once betrayed itself. "How can you liken *those* creatures to a figure of which the only fault is touchingly to have transmuted so sorry a type and to have, by a poetic artifice, not only led our judgement of it astray, but made *any* judgement quite impossible?" With which this gentle lady and admirable critic turned on the author himself. "You *know* you quite falsified, by the turn you gave it, the thing you had begun with having in mind, the thing you had had, to satiety, the chance of 'observing': your pretty perversion of it, or your unprincipled mystification of our sense of it, does it really too much honour—in spite of which, none the less, as anything charming or touching always to that extent justifies itself, we after a fashion forgive and understand you. But why *waste* your romance? There are cases, too many, in which you've done it again; in which, provoked by a spirit of observation at first no doubt sufficiently sincere, and with the measured and felt truth fairly twitching your sleeve, you have yielded to your incurable prejudice in favour of grace—to whatever it is in you that makes so inordinately for form and prettiness and pathos; not to say sometimes for misplaced drolling. Is it that you've after all too much imagination? Those awful young women capering at the hotel-door, *they* are the real little Daisy Millers that were; whereas yours in the tale is such a one, more's the pity, as—for pitch of the ingenuous, for quality of the artless—couldn't possibly have been at all." My answer to all which bristled of course with more professions than I can or need report here; the chief of them inevitably to the effect that my supposedly typical little figure was of course pure poetry, and had never been anything else; since this is what helpful imagination, in however slight a dose, ever directly makes for.

[*On "The Aspern Papers"*]†

I not only recover with ease, but I delight to recall, the first impulse given to the idea of "The Aspern Papers." It is at the same time true that my present mention of it may perhaps too effectually dispose of any complacent claim to my having "found" the situation. Not that I quite know indeed what situations the seeking fabulist does "find"; he seeks them enough assuredly, but his discoveries are, like those of the navigator, the chemist, the biologist, scarce more than alert recognitions. He *comes upon* the interesting thing as Columbus came upon the isle of San Salvador, because he had moved in the right direction for it—also because he knew, with the encounter, what "making land" then and there represented. Nature had so placed it, to profit—if as profit we may measure the matter!—by his fine unrest, just as history, "literary history" we in this connexion call it, had in an out-of-the-way corner of the great garden of life thrown off a curious flower that I was to feel worth gathering as soon as I saw it. I got wind of my positive fact, I followed the scent. It was in Florence years ago; which is precisely, of the whole matter, what I like most to remember. The air of the old-time Italy invests it, a mixture that on the faintest invitation I rejoice again to inhale—and this in spite of the mere cold renewal, ever, of the infirm side of that felicity, the sense, in the whole element, of things too numerous, too deep, too obscure, too strange, or even simply too beautiful, for any ease of intellectual relation. One must pay one's self largely with words, I think, one must induce almost any "Italian subject" *to make believe* it gives up its secret, in order to keep at all on working—or call them perhaps rather playing—terms with the general impression. We entertain it thus, the impression, by the aid a merciful convention which resembles the fashion of our intercourse with Iberians or Orientals whose form of courtesy places everything they have at our disposal. We thank them and call upon them, but without acting on their professions. The offer has been too large and our assurance is too small; we peep at most into two or three of the chambers of their hospitality, with the rest of the case stretching beyond our ken and escaping our penetration. The pious fiction suffices; we have entered, we have seen, we are charmed. So, right and left, in Italy—before the great historic complexity at least—penetration fails; we scratch at the extensive surface, we meet the perfunctory smile, we hang about in the golden air. But we exaggerate our gathered values only if we are eminently witless. It is fortunately the exhibition in all the world before which, as admirers, we can most remain superficial without feeling silly.

All of which I note, however, perhaps with too scant relevance to

†From *The Novels and Tales of Henry James,*   1908), pp. v–xiv.
vol. XII (New York: Charles Scribner's Sons,

the inexhaustible charm of Roman and Florentine memories. Off the ground, at a distance, our fond indifference to being "silly" grows fonder still; the working convention, as I have called it—the convention of the real revelations and surrenders on one side and the real immersions and appreciations on the other—has not only nothing to keep it down, but every glimpse of contrast, every pang of exile and every nostalgic twinge to keep it up. These latter haunting presences in fact, let me note, almost reduce at first to a mere blurred, sad, scarcely consolable vision this present revisiting, re-appropriating impulse. There are parts of one's past, evidently, that bask consentingly and serenely enough in the light of other days—which is but the intensity of thought; and there are other parts that take it as with agitation and pain, a troubled consciousness that heaves as with the disorder of drinking it deeply in. So it is at any rate, fairly in too thick and rich a retrospect, that I see my old Venice of "The Aspern Papers," that I see the still earlier one of Jeffrey Aspern himself, and that I see even the comparatively recent Florence that was to drop into my ear the solicitation of these things. I would fain "lay it on" thick for the very love of them—that at least I may profess; and, with the ground of this desire frankly admitted, something that somehow makes, in the whole story, for a romantic harmony. * * * I shall presently say why this small case so ranges itself, but must first refer more exactly to the thrill of appreciation it was immediately to excite in me. I saw it somehow at the very first blush as romantic—for the use, of course I mean, I should certainly have had to make of it—that Jane Clairmont, the half-sister of Mary Godwin, Shelley's second wife and for a while the intimate friend of Byron and the mother of his daughter Allegra, should have been living on in Florence, where she had long lived, up to our own day, and that in fact, had I happened to hear of her but a little sooner, I might have seen her in the flesh. The question of whether I should have wished to do so was another matter—the question of whether I shouldn't have preferred to keep her preciously unseen, to run no risk, in other words, by too rude a choice, of depreciating that romance-value which, as I say, it was instantly inevitable to attach (through association above all, with another signal circumstance) to her long survival.

I had luckily not had to deal with the difficult option; difficult in such a case by reason of that odd law which somehow always makes the minimum of valid suggestion serve the man of imagination better than the maximum. The historian, essentially, wants more documents than he can really use; the dramatist only wants more liberties than he can really take. Nothing, fortunately, however, had, as the case stood, depended on my delicacy; I might have "looked up" Miss Clairmont in previous years had I been earlier informed—the silence about her seemed full of the "irony of fate"; but I felt myself more concerned with the mere strong fact of her having testified for the reality and the closeness of our relation to the past than with any question of the particular sort of person I might have flattered myself I "found." I had certainly at the very least been saved the undue simplicity of pretending to read meanings into things absolutely sealed and beyond test or proof—to tap a fount of waters that couldn't possibly not have run dry. The thrill of learning that she had "overlapped," and by so much, and the wonder of my having doubtless at several earlier seasons passed again and again, all unknowing, the door of her house, where she sat above, within call and in her habit as she lived, these things gave me all I wanted; I seem to remember in fact that my more or less immediately recognising that I positively oughtn't—"for anything to come of it"—to have wanted more. I saw, quickly, how something might come of it *thus:* whereas a fine instinct told me that the effect of a nearer view of the case (the case of the overlapping) would probably have had to be quite differently calculable. It was really with another item of knowledge, however, that I measured the mistake I should have made in waking up sooner to the question of opportunity. That item consisted of the action taken on the premises by a person who *had* waked up in time, and the legend of whose consequent adventure, as a few spoken words put it before me, at once kindled a flame. This gentleman, an American of long ago, an ardent Shelleyite, a singularly marked figure and himself in the highest degree a subject for a free sketch—I had known him a little, but there is not a reflected glint of him in "The Aspern Papers"—was named to me as having made interest with Miss Clairmont to be accepted as a lodger on the calculation that she would have Shelley documents for which, in the possibly not remote event of her death, he would thus enjoy priority of chance to treat with her representatives. He had at any rate, according to the legend, become, on earnest Shelley grounds, her yearning, though also her highly diplomatic, *pensionnaire*[3]—but without gathering, as was to befall, the fruit of his design.

Legend here dropped to another key; it remained in a manner interesting, but became to my ear a trifle coarse, or at least rather vague and obscure. It mentioned a younger female relative of the ancient woman as a person who, for a queer climax, had had to be dealt with; it flickered so for a moment and then, as a light, to my great relief, quite went out. It had flickered indeed but at the best—yet had flickered enough to give me my "facts," bare facts of intimation; which, scant handful though they were, were more distinct and more numerous than I mostly *like* facts: like them, that is, as we say of an etcher's progressive subject, in an early "state." Nine tenths of the artist's interest in them is that of what he shall add to them and how he shall turn them. Mine, however, in the connexion I speak of, had

---

3. Lodger, boarder. [*Editor.*]

374 • *Henry James*

fortunately got away from me, and quite of their own movement, in time not to crush me. So it was, at all events, that my imagination preserved power to react under the mere essential charm—that, I mean, of a final scene of the rich dim Shelley drama played out in the very theatre of our own "modernity." This was the beauty that appealed to me; there had been, so to speak, a forward continuity, from the actual man, the divine poet, on; and the curious, the ingenious, the admirable thing would be to throw it backward again, to compress—squeezing it hard!—the connexion that had drawn itself out, and convert so the stretched relation into a value of nearness on our own part. In short I saw my chance as admirable, and one reason, when the direction is right, may serve as well as fifty; but if I "took over," as I say, everything that was of the essence, I stayed my hand for the rest. The Italian side of the legend closely clung; if only because the so possible terms of my Juliana's life in the Italy of other days could make conceivable for her the fortunate privacy, the long uninvaded and uninterviewed state on which I represent her situation as founded. Yes, a surviving unexploited unparagraphed Juliana was up to a quarter of a century since still supposeable—as much so as any such buried treasure, any such grave unprofaned, would defy probability now. And then the case had the air of the past just in the degree in which that air, I confess, most appeals to me—when the region over which it hangs is far enough away without being too far.

I delight in a palpable imaginable *visitable* past—in the nearer distances and the clearer mysteries, the marks and signs of a world we may reach over to as by making a long arm we grasp an object at the other end of our own table. The table is the one, the common expanse, and where we lean, so stretching, we find it firm and continuous. That, to my imagination, is the past fragrant of all, or of almost all, the poetry of the thing outlived and lost and gone, and yet in which the precious element of closeness, telling so of connexions but tasting so of differences, remains appreciable. * * * We are divided of course between liking to feel the past strange and liking to feel it familiar; the difficulty is, for intensity, to catch it at the moment when the scales of the balance hang with the right evenness. I say for intensity, for we may profit by them in other aspects enough if we are content to measure or to feel loosely. It would take me too far, however, to tell why the particular afternoon light that I thus call intense rests clearer to my sense on the Byronic age, as I conveniently name it, than on periods more protected by the "dignity" of history. With the times beyond, intrinsically more "strange," the tender grace, for the backward vision, has faded, the afternoon darkened; for any time nearer to us the special effect hasn't begun. So there, to put the matter crudely, is the appeal I fondly recognise, an appeal residing doubtless more in the "special effect," in some deep associational force, than in a virtue more intrinsic. I am afraid I must add, since I allow myself so much to fantasticate, that the impulse had more than once taken me to project the Byronic age and the afternoon light across the great sea, to see in short whether association would carry so far and what the young century might pass for on that side of the modern world where it was not only itself so irremediably youngest, but was bound up with youth in everything else. There was a refinement of curiosity in this imputation of a golden strangeness to American social facts—though I cannot pretend, I fear, that there was any greater wisdom.

Since what it had come to then was, harmlessly enough, cultivating a sense of the past under that close protection, it was natural, it was fond and filial, to wonder if a few of the distilled drops mightn't be gathered from some vision of, say, "old" New York. Would that human congeries, to aid obligingly in the production of a fable, be conceivable as "taking" the afternoon light with the right happy slant?—or could a recogniseable reflexion of the Byronic age, in other words, be picked up on the banks of the Hudson? (Only just there, beyond the great sea, if anywhere: in no other connexion would the question so much as raise its head. I admit that Jeffrey Aspern isn't even feebly localised, but I *thought* New York as I projected him.) It was "amusing," in any case, always, to try experiments; and the experiment for the right *transposition* of my Juliana would be to fit her out with an immortalising poet as transposed as herself. Delicacy had demanded, I felt, that my appropriation of the Florentine legend should purge it, first of all, of references too obvious; so that, to begin with, I shifted the scene of the adventure. Juliana, as I saw her, was thinkable only in Byronic and more or less immediately post-Byronic Italy; but there were conditions in which she was ideally arrangeable, as happened, especially in respect to the later time and the long undetected survival; there being absolutely no refinement of the mouldy rococo, in human or whatever other form, that you may not disembark at the dislocated water-steps of almost any decayed monument of Venetian greatness in auspicious quest of. It was a question, in fine, of covering one's tracks—though with no great elaboration I am bound to admit; and I felt I couldn't cover mine more than in postulating a comparative American Byron to match an American Miss Clairmont—she as absolute as she would. I scarce know whether best to say for this device to-day that it cost me little or that it cost me much; it was "cheap" or expensive according to the degree of verisimilitude artfully obtained. If that degree appears *nil* the "art," such as it was, is wasted, and my rememberance of the contention, on the part of a highly critical friend who at that time and later on often had my ear, that it had been simply foredoomed to be wasted, puts before me the passage in the private history of "The Aspern Papers," that I now find, I confess, most interesting. * * *

My friend's argument bore then—at the time and afterward—on my vicious practice, as he maintained, of postulating for the purpose of my fable celebrities who not only *hadn't* existed in the conditions I imputed to them, but who for the most part (and in no case more markedly than in that of Jeffrey Aspern) couldn't possibly have done so. * * *

The charge being that I foist upon our early American annals a distinguished presence for which they yield me absolutely no warrant—"Where, within them, gracious heaven, were we to look for so much as an approach to the social elements of habitat and climate of birds of that note and plumage?"—I find his link with reality then just in the tone of the picture wrought round him. What was that tone but exactly, but exquisitely, calculated, the harmless hocus-pocus under cover of which we might suppose him to have existed? This tone is the tone, artistically speaking of "amusement," the current floating that precious influence home quite as one of those high tides watched by the smugglers of old might, in case of their boat's being boarded, be trusted to wash far up the strand the cask of foreign liquor expertly committed to it. If through our lean prime Western period no dim and charming ghost of an adventurous lyric genius might by a stretch of fancy flit, if the time was really too hard to "take," in the light form proposed, the elegant reflexion, then so much the worse for the time—it was all one could say! The retort to that of course was that such a plea represented no "link" with reality—which was what was under discussion—but only a link, and flimsy enough too, with the deepest depths of the artificial: the restrictive truth exactly contended for, which may embody my critic's last word rather of course than my own. My own, so far as I shall pretend in that especial connexion to report it, was that one's warrant, in such a case, hangs essentially on the question of whether or no the false element imputed would have borne that test of further development which so exposes the wrong and so consecrates the right. My last word was, heaven forgive me, that, occasion favouring, I could have perfectly "worked out" Jeffrey Aspern.

[On "The Pupil"]†

My urchin of "The Pupil" (1891) has sensibility in abundance, it would seem—and yet preserves in spite of it, I judge, his strong little male quality. But there are fifty things to say here; which indeed rush upon me within my present close limits in such a cloud as to demand much clearance. This is perhaps indeed but the aftersense of the

†From *The Novels and Tales of Henry James,* 1908), pp. xiv–xviii. vol. XI (New York: Charles Scribner's Sons,

assault made on my mind, as I perfectly recall, by every aspect of the original vision, which struck me as abounding in aspects. It lives again for me, this vision, as it first alighted; though the inimitable prime flutter, the air as of an ineffable sign made by the immediate beat of the wings of the poised figure of fancy that has just settled, is one of those guarantees of value that can never be recaptured. The sign has been made to the seer only—it is *his* queer affair; of which any report to others, not as yet involved, has but the same effect of flatness as attends, amid a group gathered under the canopy of night, any stray allusion to a shooting star. The miracle, since miracle it seems, is all for the candid exclaimer. The miracle for the author of "The Pupil," at any rate, was when, years ago, one summer day, in a very hot Italian railway-carriage, which stopped and dawdled everywhere, favouring conversation, a friend with whom I shared it, a doctor of medicine who had come from a far country to settle in Florence, happened to speak to me of a wonderful American family, an odd adventurous, extravagant band, of high but rather unauthenticated pretensions, the most interesting member of which was a small boy, acute and preco-cious, afflicted with a heart of weak action, but beautifully intelligent, who saw their prowling precarious life exactly as it was, and measured and judged it, and measured and judged *them*, all round, ever so quaintly; presenting himself in short as an extraordinary little person. Here was more than enough for a summer's day even in old Italy— here was a thumping windfall. No process and no steps intervened: I *saw* on the spot, little Morgan Moreen, I saw all the rest of the Moreens; I felt, to the last delicacy, the nature of my young friend's relation with them (he had become at once my young friend) and, by the same stroke, to its uttermost fine throb, the subjection to *him* of the beguiled, bewildered, defrauded, unremunerated, yet after all richly repaid youth who would to a certainty, under stress of compassion, embark with the tribe on tutorship, and whose edifying connexion with it would be my leading document.

This must serve as my account of the origin of "The Pupil": it will commend itself, I feel, to all imaginative and projective persons who have had—and what imaginative and projective person hasn't?—any like experience of the suddenly-determined *absolute* of perception. The whole cluster of items forming the image is on these occasions born at once; the parts are not pieced together, they conspire and interdepend; but what it really comes to, no doubt, is that at a simple touch an old latent and dormant impression, a buried germ, im-planted by experience and then forgotten, flashes to the surface as a fish, with a single "squirm," rises to the baited hook, and there meets instantly the vivifying ray. I remember at all events having no doubt of anything or anyone here; the vision kept to the end its case and its charm; it worked itself out with confidence. These are minor matters when the question is of minor results; yet almost any assured and downright imaginative act is—granted the sort of record in which I here indulge—worth fondly commemorating. One cherishes, after the fact, any proved case of the independent life of the imagination; above all if by that faculty one has been appointed mainly to live. We are then *never* detached from the question of what it may out of simple charity do for us. Besides which, in relation to the poor Moreens, innumerable notes, as I have intimated, all equally urging their relevance, press here to the front. The general adventure of the little composition itself—for singular things were to happen to it, though among such importunities not the most worth noting now—would be, occasion favouring, a thing to live over; moving as one did, round-about it, in I scarce know what thick and coloured air of slightly tarnished anecdote, of dim association, of casual confused romance; a compound defying analysis, but truly, for the social chronicler, any student in especial of the copious "cosmopolite" legend, a boundless and tangled, but highly explorable, garden. Why, somehow—these were the intensifying questions—did one see the Moreens, whom I place at Nice, at Venice, in Paris, as of the special essence of the little old miscellaneous cosmopolite Florence, the Florence of other, of irrecoverable years, the restless yet withal so convenient scene of a society that has passed away for ever with all its faded ghosts and fragile relics; immaterial presences that have quite ceased to revisit (trust an old romancer's, an old pious observer's fine sense to have made sure of it!) walks and prospects once sacred and shaded, but now laid bare, gaping wide, despoiled of their past and unfriendly to any appreciation of it?—through which the unconscious Barbarians troop with the regularity and passivity of "supplies," or other promiscuous goods, prepaid and forwarded.

They had nothing to do, the dear Moreens, with this dreadful period, any more than I, as occupied and charmed with them, was humiliatingly subject to it; we were, all together, of a better romantic age and faith; we referred ourselves, with our highest complacency, to the classic years of the great Americano-European legend; the years of limited communication, of monstrous and unattenuated contrast, of prodigious and unrecorded adventure. The comparatively brief but infinitely rich "cycle" of romance embedded in the earlier, the very early American reactions and returns (mediaeval in the sense of being, at most, of the mid-century), what does it resemble today but a gold-mine overgrown and smothered, dislocated, and no longer workable?—all for want of the right indications for sounding, the right implements for digging, doubtless even of the right workmen, those with the right tradition and "feeling" for the job. The most extraordinary things appear to have happened, during that golden age, in the "old" countries—in Asia and Africa as well as in Europe—to the candid children of the West, things admirably incongruous and incredible; but no story of all the list was to find its just interpreter, and nothing is now more probable than that every key to interpretation has been lost. The modern reporter's big brushes, attached to broom-handles that match the height of his sky-scrapers, would sadly besmear the fine parchment of our missing record. We were to lose, clearly, at any rate, a vast body of precious anecdotes, a long gallery of wonderful portraits, an array of the oddest possible figures in the oddest possible attitudes. The Moreens were of the family then of the great unstudied precursors—poor and shabby members, no doubt; dim and super-seded types. I must add indeed that, such as they were, or as they may at present incoherently appear, I don't pretend really to have "done" them; all I have given in "The Pupil" is little Morgan's troubled vision of them as reflected in the vision, also troubled enough, of his devoted friend. The manner of the thing may thus illustrate the author's incorrigible taste for gradations and superpositions of effect; his love, when it is a question of a picture, of anything that makes for proportion and perspective, that contributes to a view of *all* the dimensions. Addicted to seeing "through"—one thing through another, accord-ingly, and still other things through *that*—he takes, too greedily perhaps, on any errand, as many things as possible by the way. It is after this fashion that he incurs the stigma of labouring uncannily for a certain fulness of truth—truth diffused, distributed and, as it were, atmospheric.

[On "Brooksmith" and "The Real Thing"]†

As to the "The Real Thing" (1890) and "Brooksmith" (1891) my recollection is sharp; the subject of each of these tales was suggested to me by a briefly-reported case. To begin with the second-named of them, the appreciative daughter of a friend some time dead had mentioned to me a visit received by her from a servant of the late distinguished lady, a devoted maid whom I remembered well to have repeatedly seen at the latter's side and who had come to discharge herself so far as she might of a sorry burden. She had lived in her mistress's delightful society and in that of the many so interesting friends of the house; she had been formed by nature, as unluckily happened, to enjoy this privilege to the utmost, and the deprivation of everything was now bitterness in her cup. She had had her choice, and had made her trial, of common situations or of a return to her own people, and had found these ordeals alike too cruel. She had in her years of service tasted of conversation and been spoiled for life; she had, in recall of Stendhal's[4] inveterate motto, caught at glimpse, all untimely, of "la beauté parfaite," and should never find again what

† From *The Novels and Tales of Henry James*, vol. XVIII (New York: Charles Scribner's Sons, 1909), pp. xix–xxi.
4. Stendhal is the pseudonym of the French novelist Marie Henri Beyle (1783–1842); his motto *"la beauté parfaite,"* means "perfect (or absolute) beauty." [*Editor.*]

she had lost—so that nothing was left her but to languish to her end. *There* was a touched spring, of course, to make "Dramatise, dramatise!" ring out; only my little derived drama, in the event, seemed to require, to be ample enough, a hero rather than a heroine. I desired for my poor lost spirit the measured maximum of the fatal experience: the thing became, in a word, to my imagination, the obscure tragedy of the "intelligent" butler present at rare table-talk, rather than that of the more effaced tirewoman,[5] with which of course was involved a corresponding change from mistress to master.

In like manner my much-loved friend George du Maurier[6] had spoken to me of a call from a strange and striking couple desirous to propose themselves as artist's models for his weekly "social" illustrations to *Punch*,[7] and the acceptance of whose services would have entailed the dismissal of an undistinguished but highly expert pair, also husband and wife, who had come to him from far back on the irregular day and whom, thanks to a happy, and to that extent lucrative, appearance of "type" on the part of each, he had reproduced, to the best effect, in a thousand drawing-room attitudes and combinations. Exceedingly modest members of society, they earned their bread by looking and, with the aid of supplied toggery, dressing, greater favourites of fortune to the life; or, otherwise expressed, by skilfully feigning a virtue not in the least native to them. Here meanwhile were their so handsome proposed, so anxious, so almost haggard competitors, originally, by every sign, of the best condition and estate, but overtaken by reverses even while conforming impeccably to the standard of superficial "smartness" and pleading with well-bred ease and the right light tone, not to say with feverish gaiety, that (as in the interest of art itself) *they* at least shouldn't have to "make believe." The question thus thrown up by the two friendly critics of the rather lurid little passage was of whether their not having to make believe *would* in fact serve them, and above all serve their interpreter as well as the borrowed graces of the comparatively sordid professionals who had had, for dear life, to *know how* (which was to have learnt how) to do something. The question, I recall, struck me as exquisite, and out of a momentary fond consideration of it "The Real Thing" sprang at a bound.

[On "The Middle Years"]†

What I had lately and most particularly to say of "The Coxon Fund" is no less true of "The Middle Years," first published in *Scribner's*

---

5. Lady's maid (who "attires" her mistress). [*Editor.*]
6. British illustrator and novelist (1834–96) [*Editor.*]
7. Illustrated comic weekly, founded in 1841

and still going strong. [*Editor.*]
†From *The Novels and Tales of Henry James*, vol. XVI (New York: Charles Scribner's Sons, 1909), pp. v–vi.

Magazine (1893)—that recollection mainly and most promptly associates with it the number of times I had to do it over to make sure of it. To get it right was to squeeze my subject into the five or six thousand words I had been invited to make it consist of—it consists, in fact, should the curious care to know, of some 5550[8]—and I scarce perhaps recall another case, with the exception I shall presently name, in which my struggle to keep compression rich, if not, better still, to keep accretions compressed, betrayed for me such community with the anxious effort of some warden of the insane engaged at a critical moment in making fast a victim's straitjacket. The form of "The Middle Years" is not that of the *nouvelle,* but that of the concise anecdote; whereas the subject treated would perhaps seem one comparatively demanding "developments"—if indeed, amid these mysteries, distinctions were so absolute. (There is of course neither close nor fixed measure of the reach of a development, which in some connexions seems almost superfluous and then in others to represent the whole sense of the matter; and we should doubtless speak more thoroughly by book had we some secret for exactly tracing deflexions and returns.) However this may be, it was as an anecdote, an anecdote only, that I was determined my little situation here should figure; to which end my effort was of course to follow it as much as possible from its outer edge in, rather than from its centre outward. That fond formula, I had alas already discovered, may set as many traps in the garden as its opposite may set in the wood; so that after boilings and reboilings of the contents of my small cauldron, after added pounds of salutary sugar, as numerous as those prescribed in the choicest recipe for the thickest jam, I well remember finding the whole process and act (which, to the exclusion of everything else, dragged itself out for a month) one of the most expensive of its sort in which I had ever engaged.

But I recall, by good luck, no less vividly how much finer a sweetness than any mere spooned-out saccharine dwelt in the fascination of the questions involved. Treating a theme that "gave" much in a form that, at the best, would give little, might indeed represent a peck of troubles; yet who, none the less, beforehand, was to pronounce with authority such and such an idea anecdotic and such and such another developmental?

[*On "The Beast in the Jungle"*][†]

* * * The subject of this elaborated fantasy—which, I must add, I hold a successful thing only as its motive may seem to the reader to

---

8. If the curious care enough to count they find that it is almost 8,000. [*Editor.*]

† From *The Novels and Tales of Henry James,*

vol. XVII (New York: Charles Scribner's Sons, 1909), pp. ix–xi.

stand out sharp—can't quite have belonged to the immemorial company of such solicitations; though in spite of this I meet it, in ten lines of an old note-book, but as a recorded conceit and an accomplished fact. Another poor sensitive gentleman, fit indeed to mate with Stransom of "The Altar"—my attested predilection for poor sensitive gentlemen almost embarrasses me as I march!—was to have been, after a strange fashion and from the threshold of his career, condemned to keep counting with the unreasoned prevision of some extraordinary fate; the conviction, lodged in his brain, part and parcel of his imagination from far back, that experience would be marked for him, and whether for good or for ill, by some rare distinction, some incalculable violence or unprecedented stroke. So I seemed to see him start in life—under the so mixed star of the extreme of apprehension and the extreme of confidence; all to the logical, the quite inevitable effect of the complication aforesaid: his having to wait and wait for the right recognition; none of the mere usual and normal human adventures, whether delights or disconcertments, appearing to conform to the great type of his fortune. So it is that he's depicted. No gathering appearance, no descried or interpreted promise or portent, affects his superstitious soul either as a damnation deep enough (if damnation be in question) for his appointed *quality* of consciousness, or as a translation into bliss sublime enough (on *that* hypothesis) to fill, in vulgar parlance, the bill. Therefore as each item of experience comes, with its possibilities, into view, he can but dismiss it under this sterilising habit of the failure to find it good enough and thence to appropriate it.

His one desire remains of course to meet his fate, or at least to divine it, to see it as intelligible, to learn it, in a word; but none of its harbingers, pretended or supposed, speak his ear in the true voice; they wait their moment at his door only to pass on unheeded, and the years ebb while he holds his breath and stays his hand and—from the dread not less of imputed pride than of imputed pusillanimity—stifles his distinguished secret. He perforce lets everything go—leaving all the while his general presumption disguised and his general abstention unexplained; since he's ridden by the idea of what things may lead to, since they mostly always lead to human communities, wider or intenser, of experience, and since, above all, in his uncertainty, he mustn't compromise others. Like the blinded seeker in the old-fashioned game he "burns," on occasion, as with the sense of the hidden thing near—only to deviate again however into the chill; the chill that indeed settles on him as the striking of his hour is deferred. His career thus resolves itself into a great negative adventure, my report of which presents, for its centre, the fine case that has caused him most tormentedly to "burn," and then most unprofitably to stray. He is afraid to recognise what he incidentally misses, since what his high belief amounts to is not that he shall have felt and vibrated less than any one else, but that he shall have felt and vibrated more; which no acknowledgement of the minor loss must conflict with. Such a course of existence naturally involves a climax—the final flash of the light under which he reads his lifelong riddle and sees his conviction proved. He has indeed been marked and indeed suffered his fortune—which is precisely to have been the man in the world to whom nothing whatever was to happen. My picture leaves him overwhelmed—at last he has understood; though in thus disengaging my treated theme for the reader's benefit I seem to acknowledge that this more detached witness may not successfully have done so. I certainly grant that any felt merit in the thing must all depend on the clearness and charm with which the subject just noted expresses itself.

[On "The Jolly Corner"]†

* * * odd though it may sound to pretend that one feels on safer ground in tracing such an adventure as that of the hero of "The Jolly Corner" than in pursuing a bright career among pirates or detectives, I allow that composition to pass as the measure or limit, on my own part, of any achievable comfort in the "adventure-story"; and this not because I may "render"—well, what my poor gentleman attempted and suffered in the New York house—better than I may render detectives or pirates or other splendid desperadoes, though even here too there would be something to say; but because the spirit engaged with the forces of violence interests me most when I can think of it as engaged most deeply, most finely and most "subtly" (precious term!). For then it is that, as with the longest and firmest prongs of consciousness, I grasp and hold the throbbing subject; *there* it is above all that I find the steady light of the picture.

HENRY JAMES

From His Letters††

To Eliza Lynn Linton

[ca. August 1880]

My dear Mrs. Linton,—I will answer you as concisely as possible—and with great pleasure—premising that I feel very guilty at having excited such ire in celestial minds, and painfully responsible at the present moment.

†From *The Novels and Tales of Henry James*, vol. XVII (New York: Charles Scribner's Sons, 1909), pp. xx–xxi. ††From *The Selected Letters of Henry James*, ed. Leon Edel (New York: Farrar, Straus and Cudahy, 1955), pp. 138–40, 73–78.

Poor little Daisy Miller was, as I understand her, above all things *innocent*. It was not to make a scandal, or because she took pleasure in scandal, that she "went on" with Giovanelli. She never took the measure really of the scandal she produced, and had no means of doing so: she was too ignorant, too irreflective, too little versed in the proportions of things. She intended infinitely less with G. than she appeared to intend—and he himself was quite at sea as to how far she was going. She was a flirt, a perfectly superficial and unmalicious one, and she was very fond, as she announced at the outset, of "gentlemen's society." In Giovanelli she got a gentleman—who, to her uncultivated perception, was a very brilliant one—all to herself, and she enjoyed his society in the largest possible measure. When she found that this measure was thought too large by other people—especially by Winterbourne—she was wounded; she became conscious that she was accused of something of which her very comprehension was vague. This consciousness she endeavoured to throw off; she tried not to think of what people meant, and easily succeeded in doing so; but to my perception she never really tried to take her revenge upon public opinion—to outrage it and irritate it. In this sense I fear I must declare that she was not *defiant*, in the sense you mean. If I recollect rightly, the word "defiant" is used in the text—but it is not intended in that large sense; it is descriptive of the state of her poor little heart, which felt that a fuss was being made about her and didn't wish to hear anything more about it. She only wished to be left alone—being herself quite unaggressive. The keynote of her *character* is her innocence—that of her *conduct* is, of course, that she has a little sentiment about Winterbourne, that she believes to be quite unreciprocated—conscious as she was only of his protesting attitude. But, even here, I did not mean to suggest that she was playing off Giovanelli against Winterbourne—for she was too innocent even for that. She didn't try to provoke and stimulate W. by flirting overtly with G.—she never believed that Winterbourne was provokable. She would have liked him to think well of her—but had an idea from the first that he cared only for higher game, so she smothered this feeling to the best of her ability (though at the end a glimpse of it is given), and tried to help herself to do so by a good deal of lively movement with Giovanelli. The whole idea of the story is the little tragedy of a light, thin, natural, unsuspecting creature being sacrificed as it were to a social rumpus that went on quite over her head and to which she stood in no measurable relation. To deepen the effect, I have made it go over her mother's head as well. She never had a thought of scandalising anybody—the most she ever had was a regret for Winterbourne.

This is the only witchcraft I have used—and I must leave you to extract what satisfaction you can from it. Again I must say that I feel "real badly," as D. M. would have said, at having supplied the

occasion for a breach of cordiality. May the breach be healed
herewith! . . . Believe in the very good will of yours faithfully,

H. James

To Mrs. F. H. Hill

3 Bolton Street,
March 21st [1879]

My dear Mrs. Hill[1]—

I must thank you without delay for the little notice of *Daisy Miller*
and the "Three Meetings,"[2] in the morning's D[aily] N[ews], in
which you say so many kind things so gracefully. You possess in great
perfection that amiable art. But, shall I confess it? (you will perhaps
guess it,) my eagerness to thank you for your civilities to two of my
tales, is slightly increased by my impatience to deprecate your strictures with regard to the third. I am distressed by the evident disfavour
with which you view the "International Episode;" and meditating on
the matter as humbly as I can, I really think you have been unjust to it.
No, my dear Mrs. Hill, *bien non*,[3] my two Englishmen are not
represented as "Arries";[4] it was perhaps the fond weakness of a creator,
but I even took to myself some credit for the portrait of Lord Lambeth,
who was intended to be the image of a loveable, sympathetic,
excellent-natured young personage, full of good feelings and of all
possible delicacies of conduct. That he says "I say" rather too many
times is very probable (I thought so, quite, myself, in reading over the
thing as a book:) but that strikes me as a rather venial flaw. I differ from
you in thinking that he would, in fact, have been likely to say it with

1. This letter, generously furnished by Mr.
Robert H. Taylor, is unique among the thousands extant: it is the only one found so far
written to a reviewer of one of Henry James's
works. James, however, had met Mrs. Hill, wife
of the editor of the *Daily News* in London
drawing-rooms and seems to have felt acutely
that he could not allow her strictures to go
unanswered. His usual rule was to ignore re-
views and reviewers and there exist letters to
various publishers instructing them not to send
him any cuttings about himself from the press.
This letter was written at a moment when James
was being sharply criticized in the United States
for having committed an "outrage" upon
American girlhood in his portrait of Daisy Miller, and he now found himself under English
fire for his social satire of certain English types.
On Jan. 18th, 1879 he had written to his mother
about "An International Episode": "It is an entirely new sensation for them (the people here)
to be (at all delicately) *ironized* and satirized,
from the American point of view, and they don't
at all relish it. Their conception of the normal

in such a relation is that the satire should be all
on their side against the Americans; and I suspect that if we were to push this a little further
we would find that they are extremely sensitive.
But I like them too much and feel too kindly to
them to go into the satire-business or even the
light-ironical in any case in which it would
wound them—even if in such a case I should
see my way to it very clearly."
2. The volume reviewed was *Daisy Miller and
Other Stories*, issued in two volumes by Macmillan on Feb. 15, 1879. James makes an interesting slip of the pen here in speaking of
"Three Meetings" although the title of his story
was "Four Meetings," which suggests that
perhaps his title was inspired by one of
Turgenev's tales which did bear the title "Three
Meetings."
3. Absolutely no. [*Editor.*]
4. " 'Arry' is used humorously for a low-bred
fellow (who 'drops his *h's*') of lively temper and
manners. It derives from the name *Harry* vulgarly pronounced without the aspirate" (Oxford
English Dictionary). [*Editor.*]

considerable frequency. I used the words because I remembered that when I was fresh to England and first began to "go out," I was struck with the way in which they flourished among the younger generation, especially when the younger generation was of the idle and opulent and pleasure-loving type. Depend upon it, it is not only "Arry" who says "I say." There are gentlemen and gentlemen—those who are constantly particular about what they say, and those who go in greatly for amusement and who say anything, almost, that comes into their heads. It has always seemed to me that in this latter racketing, pleasure-loving "golden-youth" section of English society, the very atmosphere was impregnated with slang. A year ago I went for six months to the St. James's Club, where (to my small contentment personally,) the golden youth of every description used largely to congregate, and during this period, being the rapacious and shameless observer that you know, I really made studies in London colloquialisms. I certainly heard more "I says" than I had ever done before; and I suppose that 19 out of 20 of the young men in the place had been to a public school. However, this detail is not of much importance; what I meant to indicate is the (I think) incontestable fact that certain people in English society talk in a very offhand, informal, irregular manner, and use a great many roughnesses and crudities. It didn't seem to me that one was bound to handle their idiosyncrasies of speech so very tenderly as to weigh one idiom very long against another. In a word the Lord Lambeths of the English world are, I think, distinctly liable, in the turn of their phrases, just as they are in the gratification of their tastes—or of some of them—to strike quiet conservative people like your humble servant as vulgar. I meant to do no more than just rapidly indicate this liability—I meant it to be by no means the last impression that he would leave. It doesn't in the least seem to have been so, with most people, and if it didn't sound fatuous I should say that I had been congratulated by several people whom I supposed to be of an observing turn upon the verisimilitude of his conversation.—If it didn't seem fatuous, too, or unmannerly, to inflict upon you so very bulky a bundle of exposition as this letter has grown into, I should go on to say that I don't think you have been liberal to the poor little women-folk of my narrative. (That liberal, by the way, is but a conciliatory substitute for some more rigid epithet— say *fair*, or *just*.) I want at any rate to remonstrate with you for your apparent assumption that in the two English ladies, I meant to make a resumé of my view of English manners. My dear Mrs. Hill—the idea is fantastic! The two ladies are a picture of a special case, and they are certainly not an over-charged one. They were very determined their manners should not be nicer; it would have quite defeated the point they wished to make, which was that it didn't at all suit them that a little unknown American girl should marry their coveted kinsman.

Such a consummation certainly does not suit English duchesses and countesses in general—it would be quite legitimate to draw from the story an induction as to my conviction on that point. The story was among other things an attempt at a sketch of this state of mind, and, given what I wished to represent, I thought the touches by which the attitude of the duchess and her daughter is set forth, were rather light and discreet than otherwise. A man in my position, and writing the sort of things I do, feels the need of protesting against this extension of his idea in which in many cases, many readers are certain to indulge. One may make figures and figures without intending generalizations—generalizations of which I have a horror. I make a couple of English ladies doing a disagreeable thing—*cela s'est vu:*[5] excuse me!—and forthwith I find myself responsible for a representation of English manners! Nothing is my *last word* about anything—I am interminably super-subtle and analytic—and with the blessing of heaven, I shall live to make all sorts of representations of all sorts of things. It will take a much cleverer person than myself to discover my last impression—among all these things—of anything. And then, in such a matter, the bother of being an American! Trollope, Thackeray, Dickens,[6] even [sic] with their big authoritative talents, were free to draw all sorts of unflattering English pictures, by the thousand. But if I make a single one, I am forthwith in danger of being confronted with a criminal conclusion—and sinister rumours reach me as to what I think of English society. I think more things than I can undertake to tell in 40 pages of the Cornhill. Perhaps some day I shall take more pages, and attempt to tell some of these things; in that case, I hope, there will be a little, of every sort, for every one! Meanwhile I shall draw plenty of pictures of disagreeable Americans, as I have done already, and the friendly Briton will see no harm in that!—it will seem to him a part of the natural fitness!—Since I am in for it—with this hideously egotistic document—I do just want to add that I am sorry you didn't find a little word of appreciation for the two other women's figures in the *I. E.*, which I really think a success. (You will smile at the artless crudity of my vanity!) The thing was the study—a very sincere, careful, intendedly minute one—of the state of mind of a couple of American women pressed upon by English circumstances—and I had a faith that the picture would seem life-like and comprehensible. In the case of the heroine I had a fancy it would even seem charming. In that of the elder sister, no, I hadn't such a faith: she is too garrulous, and, on the whole, too silly;—it is for a silly woman that she is offered. But I should have said it was obvious that her portrait is purely objective—she is not in the least intended to throw light upon the objects she criticizes, (English life and manners

---

5. One has seen that kind of thing. [*Editor.*]
6. Anthony Trollope (1815–82), William Makepeace Thackeray (1811–63), Charles Dickens (1812–70)—British novelists. [*Editor.*]

&c;) she is intended to throw light on the American mind alone, and its way of taking things. When I attempt to deal with English manners, I shall approach them through a very different portal than that of Mrs. Westgate's intelligence. I was at particular pains to mark the limitations of this organ—by some of the speeches I have put into her mouth—such as the grotesque story about the Duke who cuts the Butterworths. In a word she is, throughout, an ironical creation!—Forgive this inordinate and abominable scrawl—I certainly didn't mean to reward you for your friendly zeal in reading so many of my volumes by despatching you another in the innocent guise of a note. But your own frankness has made me expansive—and there goes with this only a grain of protest to a hundredweight of gratitude. Believe me, dear Mrs. Hill, very faithfully yours

H. James jr.

Background

KATHERINE ANNE PORTER

The Days Before†

Really, universally, relations stop nowhere, and the exquisite problem of the
artist is eternally but to draw, by a geometry of his own, the circle within
which they shall happily *appear* to do so.

H.J.: Preface to Roderick Hudson.

We have, it would seem, at last reluctantly decided to claim Henry
James as our own, in spite of his having renounced, two years before
his death, so serious an obligation as his citizenship, but with a
disturbing tendency among his critics and admirers of certain schools
to go a step further and claim him for the New England, or Puritan,
tradition.

This is merely the revival and extension of an old error first made by
Carlyle[1] in regard to Henry James the elder: "Mr. James, your New-
England friend," wrote Carlyle in a letter, "I saw him several times
and liked him." This baseless remark set up, years later, a train of
reverberations in the mind of Mr. James's son Henry, who took pains
to correct the "odd legend" that the James family were a New England
product, mentioning that Carlyle's mistake was a common one among
the English, who seemed to have no faintest care or notion about our
regional differences. With his intense feeling for place and family
relations and family history, Henry James the younger could not allow
this important error to pass uncorrected. With his very special eyes,
whose threads were tangled in every vital center of his being, he looked
long through "a thin golden haze" into his past, and recreated for our
charmed view an almost numberless family connection, all pure
Scotch-Irish so far back as the records run, unaltered to the third
generation in his branch of the family; and except for the potent
name-grandfather himself—a Presbyterian of rather the blue-nosed
caste, who brought up his eleven or was it thirteen children of three
happy marriages in the fear of a quite improbable God—almost
nothing could be less Puritanic, less New England, than their careers,
even if they were all of Protestant descent. The earliest branch came
late to this country (1764) according to Virginia or New England
standards, and they settled in the comparatively newly opened country
of upstate New York—new for the English and Scotch-Irish, that is,
for the Dutch and the French had been there a good while before, and
they married like with like among the substantial families settled along

---

†From *The Collected Essays and Occasional
Writings of Katherine Anne Porter* (New York:
Delacorte Press, 1970), pp. 233–48. Originally
published in *Kenyon Review* V (Autumn 1943)
and first reprinted with revisions in *The Days*
Before (New York: Harcourt, Brace and Company, 1952). The footnotes for this selection are
by the editor of this Norton Critical Edition.
1. Thomas Carlyle (1795–1881), British historian and essayist.

the Hudson River. Thus the whole connection in its earlier days was spared the touch of the specifically New England spirit, which even then was spreading like a slow blight into every part of the country.

(But the young Henry James feared it from the first, distrusted it in his bones. Even though his introduction to New England was by way of "the proud episcopal heart of Newport," when he was about fifteen years old, and though he knew there at least one artist, and one young boy of European connection and experience, still, Boston was not far away, and he felt a tang of wintry privation in the air, a threat of "assault and death." By way of stores against the hovering famine and siege, he collected a whole closet full of the beloved *Revue des Deux Mondes*, in its reassuring salmon-pink cover.)

Henry James's grandfather, the first William James, arrived in America from Ireland, County Cavan, an emigrant boy of seventeen, and settled in Albany in 1789. He was of good solid middle-class stock, he possessed that active imagination and boundless energy of the practical sort so useful in ancestors; in about forty years of the most blameless, respected use of every opportunity to turn an honest penny, on a very handsome scale of operations, he accumulated a fortune of three million dollars, in a style that was to become the very pattern of American enterprise. The city of Albany was credited to him, it was the work of his hands, it prospered with him. His industries and projects kept hundreds of worthy folk gainfully employed the year round, in the grateful language of contemporary eulogy; in his time only John Jacob Astor[2] gathered a larger fortune in New York state. We may as well note here an obvious irony, and dismiss it: James's grandfather's career was a perfect example of the sort of thing that was to become "typically American," and still is, it happens regularly even now; and Henry James the younger had great good of it, yet it did create the very atmosphere which later on he found so hard to breathe that he deserted it altogether for years, for life.

The three millions were divided at last among the widow and eleven surviving children, the first Henry James, then a young man, being one of them. These twelve heirs none of them inherited the Midas touch,[3] and all had a taste for the higher things of life enjoyed in easy, ample surroundings. Henry the younger lived to wonder, with a touch of charming though acute dismay, just what had become of all that delightful money. Henry the elder, whose youth had been gilded to the ears, considered money a topic beneath civilized discussion, business a grimy affair they all agreed to know nothing about, and neglected completely to mention what he had done with his share. He

2. John Jacob Astor (1763–1848), immigrant from Germany, fur merchant, capitalist, war profiteer, and, after the war of 1812, the wealthiest man in the United States.

3. Midas, the legendary Phrygian king, turned everything he touched to gold until desperate with hunger (since gold is indigestible) he washed himself clean in a river.

fostered a legend among his children that he had been "wild" and appeared, according to his fascinating stories, to have been almost the only young man of his generation who had not come to a bad end. His son Henry almost in infancy had got the notion that the words "wild" and "dissipated" were synonymous with "tipsy." Be that as it may, Henry the first in his wild days had a serious if temporary falling out with his father, whom he described as the tenderest and most sympathetic of parents; but he also wrote in his fragment of autobiography, "I should think indeed that our domestic intercourse had been on the whole most innocent as well as happy, were it not for a certain lack of oxygen which is indeed incidental to the family atmosphere and which I may characterize as the lack of any ideal of action except that of self-preservation." Indeed, yes. Seeking fresh air, he fled into the foreign land of Massachusetts: Boston, precisely: until better days should come. "It was an age," wrote his son Henry, "in which a flight from Albany to Boston . . . counted as a far flight." It still does. The point of this episode for our purposes was, that Henry the first mildewed in exile for three long months, left Boston and did not again set foot there until he was past thirty-five. His wife never went there at all until her two elder sons were in Harvard, a seat of learning chosen *faute de mieux,*[4] for Europe, Europe was where they fain all would be; except that a strange, uneasy, even artificially induced nationalism, due to the gathering war between the states, had laid cold doubts on their minds—just where did they belong, where was their native land? The two young brothers, William and Henry, especially then began, after their shuttlings to and from Europe, to make unending efforts to "find America" and to place themselves once for all either in it or out of it. But this was later.

It is true that the elder Jameses settled in Boston, so far as a James of that branch could ever be said to settle, for the good reason that they wished to be near their sons; but they never became, by any stretch of the word, New Englanders, any more than did their son William, after all those years at Harvard; any more than did their son Henry become an Englishman, after all those years in England. He realized this himself, even after he became a British subject in 1914; and the British agree with him to this day. He was to the end an amiable, distinguished stranger living among them. Yet two generations born in this country did not make them Americans, either, and in the whole great branching family connection, with its "habits of ease" founded on the diminishing backlog of the new fortune, the restless blood of the emigrant grandparents ran high. Europe was not so far away as it is now, and though Albany and "the small, warm dusky homogeneous New York world of the mid-century" were dear to

4. For want of something better.

them, they could not deny, indeed no one even thought of denying, that all things desirable in the arts, architecture, education, ways of living, history, the future, the very shape of the landscape and the color of the air, lay like an inheritance they had abandoned, in Europe.

"This question of Europe" which never ceased to agitate his parents from his earliest memory was paradoxically the only permanent element in the Jameses' family life. All their movements, plans, interests were based, you might say, on that perpetually unresolved problem. It was kept simmering by letters from friends and relatives traveling or living there; cousins living handsomely at Geneva, enjoying the widest possible range of desirable social amenities; other cousins living agreeably at Tours, or Trouville; the handsomest of the Albany aunts married advantageously and living all over Europe, urging the Henry Jameses to come with their young and do likewise for the greater good of all. There was an older cousin who even lived in China, came back to fill a flat in Gramercy Square with "dim Chinoiseries"[5] and went on to old age in Surrey and her last days in Versailles. There was besides the constant delicious flurry of younger cousins and aunts with strange wonderful clothes and luggage who had always just been there, or who were just going there, "there" meaning always Europe, and oddly enough, specifically Paris, instead of London. The infant Henry, at the age of five, received his "positive initiation into History" when Uncle Gus returned bringing the news of the flight of Louis Philippe[6] to England. To the child, *flight* had been a word with a certain meaning; *king* another. "Flight of kings" was a new, portentous, almost poetic image of strange disasters, it early gave to political questions across the sea a sense of magnificence they altogether lacked at home, where society outside the enthralling family circle and the shimmering corona of friends seemed altogether to consist of "the busy, the tipsy, and Daniel Webster."

Within that circle, however, nothing could exceed the freedom and ease with which artists of all sorts, some of them forgotten now, seemed to make the James fireside, wherever it happened to be, their own. The known and acclaimed were also household guests and dear friends.

Mr. Emerson,[7] "the divinely pompous rose of the philosophical garden," as Henry James the elder described him, or, in other lights and views, the "man without a handle"—one simply couldn't get hold of him at all—had been taken upstairs in the fashionable Astor Hotel

5. Chinese curios. Gramercy Square is in New York City, Surrey is in the south of England, and Versailles near Paris.
6. French king from 1830–48.
7. Ralph Waldo Emerson (1803–82), U.S. essayist and poet. Others mentioned in this paragraph, besides Poe and Dickens, are U.S. General Winfield Scott (1786–1866); Washington Irving (1783–1859), American essayist, historian, and author (of "Rip Van Winkle," "The Legend of Sleepy Hollow," etc.); Margaret Fuller (1810–50), U.S. author and critic.

to admire the newly born William; and in later times, seated in the firelit dusk of the back parlor in the James house, had dazzled the young Henry, who knew he was great. General Winfield Scott in military splendor had borne down upon him and his father at a street corner for a greeting; and on a boat between Fort Hamilton and New York Mr. Washington Irving had apprised Mr. James of the shipwreck of Margaret Fuller, off Fire Island, only a day or so before. Edgar Allan Poe was one of the "acclaimed," the idolized, most read and recited of poets; his works were on every drawing room or library table that Henry James knew, and he never outgrew his wonder at the legend that Poe was neglected in his own time.

Still it was Dickens who ruled and pervaded the literary world from afar; the books in the house, except for a few French novels, were nearly all English; the favorite bookstore was English, where the James children went to browse, sniffing the pages for the strong smell of paper and printer's ink, which they called "the English smell." The rule of the admired, revered *Revue des Deux Mondes* was to set in shortly; France and French for Henry James, Germany and German for William James, were to have their great day, and stamp their images to such a degree that ever after the English of the one, and of the other, were to be "larded" and tagged and stuffed with French and German. In the days before, however, the general deliciousness and desirability of all things English was in the domestic air Henry James breathed; his mother and father talked about it so much at the breakfast table that, remembering, he asked himself if he had ever heard anything else talked about over the morning coffee cups. They could not relive enough their happy summer in England with their two babies, and he traveled again and again with them, by way of "Windsor and Sudbrook and Ham Common",[8] an earthly Paradise, they believed, and he believed with them. A young aunt, his mother's sister, shared these memories and added her own: an incurable home-sickness for England possessed her. Henry, asking for stories, listened and "took in" everything: taking in was to be his life's main occupation: as if, he said, his "infant divination proceeded by the light of nature," and he had learned already the importance of knowing in advance of any experience of his own, just what life in England might be like. A small yellow-covered English magazine called *Charm* also "shed on the question the softest lustre" and caused deep pangs of disappointment when it failed to show up regularly at the bookstore.

Henry James refers to all these early impressions as an "infection," as a sip of "poison," as a "twist"—perhaps of some psychological thumbscrew—but the twinges and pangs were all exciting, joyful, mysterious, thrilling, sensations he enjoyed and sought eagerly, half

8. Windsor Castle is the royal residence near London. Richmond, Sudbrook, and Ham Common are also in the vicinity of London.

their force at least consisting of his imaginative projection of his own future in the most brilliant possible of great worlds. He saw his parents and his aunt perpetually homesick for something infinitely lovable and splendid they had known, and he longed to know it too. "Homesickness was a luxury I remember craving from the tenderest age," he confessed, because he had at once perhaps too many homes and therefore no home at all. If his parents did not feel at home anywhere, he could not possibly, either. He did not know what to be homesick for, unless it were England, which he had seen but could not remember.

This was, then, vicarious, a mere sharing at second-hand; he needed something of his own. When it came, it was rather dismaying; but it was an important episode and confirmed in him the deep feeling that England had something formidable in its desirability, something to be lived up to: in contrast to France as he discovered later, where one "got life," as he expressed it; or Germany, where the very trees of the great solemn forests murmured in his charmed ear of their mystical "culture." What happened was this: the celebrated Mr. Thackeray, fresh from England, seated as an honored much-at-ease guest in the James library, committed an act which somehow explains everything that is wrong with his novels.

"Come here, little boy," he said to Henry, "and show me your extraordinary jacket." With privileged bad manners he placed his hand on the child's shoulder and asked him if his garments were the uniform of his "age and class," adding with brilliant humor that if he should wear it in England he would be addressed as "Buttons." No matter what Mr. Thackeray thought he was saying—very likely he was not thinking at all—he conveyed to the overwhelmed admirer of England that the English, as so authoritatively represented by Mr. Thackeray, thought Americans "queer." It was a disabling blow, recalled in every circumstance fifty years later, with a photograph, of all things, to illustrate and prove its immediate effect.

Henry was wearing that jacket, buttoned to the chin with a small white collar, on the hot dusty summer day when his companionable father, who never went anywhere without one or the other of his two elder sons, brought him up from Staten Island, where the family were summering, to New York, and as a gay surprise for everybody, took him to Mr. Brady's[9] for their photograph together. A heavy surprise indeed for Henry, who forever remembered the weather, the smells and sights of the wharf, the blowzy summer lassitude of the streets, and his own dismay that by his father's merry whim he was to be immortalized by Mr. Brady in his native costume which would appear so

9. Presumably Mathew B. Brady (1823–96), U.S. photographer, especially of the Civil War.

absurd in England. Mr. Brady that day made one of the most expressive child pictures I know. The small straight figure has a good deal of grace and dignity in its unworthy (as he feared) clothes; the long hands are holding with what composure they can to things they know; his father's shoulder, his large and, according to the fashion plates of the day, stylish straw hat. All the life of the child is in the eyes, rueful, disturbed, contemplative, with enormous intelligence and perception, much older than the face, much deeper and graver than his father's. His father and mother bore a certain family resemblance to each other, such as closely interbred peoples of any nation are apt to develop; Henry resembled them both, but his father more nearly, and judging by later photographs, the resemblance became almost identical, except for the expression of the eyes—the unmistakable look of one who was to live intuitively and naturally a long life in "the air of the passions of the intelligence."

In Mr. Brady's daguerreotype, he is still a child, a stranger everywhere, and he is unutterably conscious of the bright untimeliness of the whole thing, the lack of proper ceremony, ignored as ever by the father; the slack, unflattering pose. His father is benevolent and cheerful and self-possessed and altogether pleased for them both. He had won his right to gaiety of heart in his love; after many a victorious engagement with the powers of darkness, he had Swedenborg[1] and all his angels round about, bearing him up, which his son was never to have; and he had not been lately ridiculed by Mr. Thackeray, at least not to his face. Really it was not just the jacket that troubled him—that idle remark upon it was only one of the smallest of the innumerable flashes which lighted for him, blindingly, whole territories of mystery in which a long lifetime could not suffice to make him feel at home. "I lose myself in wonder," he wrote in his later years, "at the loose ways, the strange process of waste, through which nature and fortune may deal on occasion with those whose faculty for application is all and only in their imagination and sensibility."

By then he must have known that in his special case, nothing at all had been wasted. He was in fact a most glorious example in proof of his father's favorite theories of the uses and virtues of waste as education, and at the end felt he had "mastered the particular history of just that waste." His father was not considered a good Swedenborgian by those followers of Swedenborg who had, against his expressed principles, organized themselves into a church. Mr. James could not be organized in the faintest degree by anyone or anything. His daughter Alice wrote of him years later: ". . . Father, the delicious infant, couldn't submit even to the thralldom of his own whim." That

1. Emanuel Swedenborg (1688–1772), the Swedish scientist and religious philosopher whose system the elder Henry James adopted and adapted to his own needs.

smothering air of his childhood family life had given him a permanent longing for freedom and fresh air; the atmosphere he generated crackled with oxygen; his children lived in such a state of mental and emotional stimulation that no society ever again could overstimulate them. Life, as he saw it—was nobly resolved to see it, and to teach his beloved young ones to see it—was so much a matter of living happily and freely by spiritual, ethical, and intellectual values, based soundly on sensuous richness, and inexhaustible faith in the goodness of God; a firm belief in the divinity in human nature, God's self in it; a boundlessly energetic aspiration toward the higher life, the purest humanities, the most spontaneous expression of feeling and thought.

Despair was for the elder James a word of contempt. He declared "that never for a moment had he known a skeptical state." Yet, "having learned the nature of evil, and admitted its power, he turned towards the sun of goodness." He believed that "true worship is always spontaneous, the offspring of delight, not duty." Thus his son Henry: "The case was really of his feeling so vast a rightness close at hand or lurking immediately behind actual arrangements that a single turn of the inward wheel, one real response to the pressure of the spiritual spring, would bridge the chasms, straighten the distortions, rectify the relations, and in a word redeem and vivify the whole mass." With all his considerable powers of devotion translated into immediate action, the father demonstrated his faith in the family circle; the children responded to the love, but were mystified and respectful before the theory: they perceived it was something very subtle, as were most of "father's ideas." But they also knew early that their father did not live in a fool's paradise. "It was of course the old story that we had only to *be* with more intelligence and faith—an immense deal more, certainly, in order to work off, in the happiest manner, the many-sided ugliness of life; which was a process that might go on, blessedly, in the quietest of all quiet ways. *That* wouldn't be blood and fire and tears, or would be none of these things stupidly precipitated; it would simply take place by *enjoyed* communication and contact, enjoyed concussion or convulsion even—since pangs and agitations, the very agitations of perception itself, are the highest privilege of the soul, and there is always, thank goodness, a saving sharpness of play or complexity of consequence in the intelligence completely alive."

Blood and fire and tears each in his own time and way each of them suffered, sooner or later. Alice, whose life was a mysterious long willful dying, tragic and ironic, once asked her father's permission to kill herself. He gave it, and she understood his love in it, and refrained: he wrote to Henry that he did not much fear any further thoughts of suicide on her part. William took the search for truth as hard as his father had, but by way of philosophy, not religion; the brave psychologist and philosopher was very sick in his soul for many years. Henry was maimed for life in an accident,[2] as his father had been before him, but he of them all never broke, never gave way, sought for truth not in philosophy nor in religion, but in art, and found his own; showed just what the others had learned and taught, and spoke for them better than they could for themselves, thus very simply and grandly fulfilling his destiny as artist; for it was destiny and he knew it and never resisted a moment, but went with it as unskeptically as his father had gone with religion.

The James family, as we have seen, were materially in quite comfortable circumstances. True the fine fortune had misted away somewhat, but they had enough. If people are superior to begin with, as they were, the freedom of money is an added freedom of grace and the power of choice in many desirable ways. This accounts somewhat then for the extraordinary ability, ease of manners, and artless, innocent unselfconsciousness of the whole family in which Henry James was brought up, which he has analyzed so acutely, though with such hovering tenderness. It was merely a fact that they could afford to be beyond material considerations because in that way they were well provided. Their personal virtues, no matter on what grounds, were real, their kindness and frankness were unfeigned. "The cousinship," he wrote, "all unalarmed and unsuspecting and unembarrassed, lived by pure serenity, sociability, and loquacity." Then with the edge of severity his own sense of truth drew finally upon any subject, he added: "The special shade of its identity was thus that it was not conscious—really not conscious of anything in the world; or was conscious of so few possibilities at least, and these so immediate, and so a matter of course, that it came to the same thing." There he summed up a whole society, limited in number but of acute importance in its place; and having summed up, he cannot help returning to the exceptions, those he loved and remembered best.

There were enough intellectual interests and consciousness of every kind in his father's house to furnish forth the whole connection, and it was the center. Education, all unregulated, to be drawn in with the breath, and absorbed like food, proceeded at top speed day and night. Though William, of all the children, seemed to be the only one who managed to acquire a real, formal university training of the kind recognized by academicians, Henry got his, in spite of the dozen schools in three countries, in his own time and his own way; in the

2. In 1861, while helping to put out a fire, James damaged his back and, neglecting to take proper care of the injury at the time, suffered from it through much of his life. But in his autobiography and elsewhere he refers to the "obscure hurt" in mystifying terms, which set critics and biographers speculating wildly about its nature and its possible relation to his lifelong celibacy. Leon Edel in the first volume of his biography of James finally calmed the waters with his conclusion that "the evidence points clearly to a back injury—a slipped disk, a sacroiliac or muscular strain—obscure but clearly painful."

streets, in theaters (how early grew in him that long, unrequited passion for the theater!), at picture galleries, at parties, on boats, in hotels, beaches, at family reunions; by listening, by gazing, dawdling, gaping, wondering, and soaking in impressions and sensations at every pore, through every hair. Though at moments he longed to be an orphan when he saw the exciting life of change and improvisation led by his cheerful orphaned cousins, "so little sunk in the short range," it is clear that his own life, from minute to minute, was as much as he could endure; he had the only family he could have done with at all, and the only education he was capable of receiving. His intuitions were very keen and pure from the beginning, and foreknowledge of his ineducability in any practical sense caused him very rightly to kick and shriek as they hauled him however fondly to his first day of school. There he found, as he was to find in every situation for years and years, elder brother William, the vivid, the hardy, the quick-learning, the outlooking one, seated already: accustomed, master of his environment, lord of his playfellows. For so Henry saw him; William was a tremendous part of his education. William was beyond either envy or imitation: the younger brother could only follow and adore at the right distance.

So was his mother his education. Her children so possessed her they did not like her even to praise them or be proud of them because that seemed to imply that she was separate from them. After her death, the younger Henry wrote of her out of depths hardly to be stirred again in him, "she was our life, she was the house, she was the keystone of the arch"—suddenly his language took on symbols of the oldest poetry. Her husband, who found he could not live without her, wrote in effect to a friend that very early in their marriage she had awakened his torpid heart, and helped him to become a man.

The father desired many things for the children, but two things first: spiritual decency, as Henry James says it, and "a sensuous education." If Henry remembered his share in the civilizing atmosphere of Mr. Jenks's school as "merely contemplative," totally detached from any fact of learning, at home things were more positive. Their father taught them a horror of priggishness, and of conscious virtue; guarded them, by precept and example, from that vulgarity he described as "flagrant morality"; and quite preached, if his boundless and changing conversation could be called that, against success in its tangible popular meaning. "We were to convert and convert, success—in the sense that was in the general air—or no success; and simply everything that happened to us, every contact, every impression and every experience we should know, were to form our soluble stuff; with only ourselves to thank should we remain unaware, by the time our perceptions were decently developed, of the substance finally projected and most desirable. That substance might be just consummately Virtue, as a social grace and value . . . the moral of all of which was that we need never fear not to be good enough if only we were social enough. . . ."

Again he told them that the truth—the one truth as distinguished from the multiple fact—"was never ugly and dreadful, and (we) might therefore depend upon it for due abundance, even of meat and drink and raiment, even of wisdom and wit and honor."

No child ever "took in" his father's precepts more exactly and more literally than did Henry James, nor worked them more subtly and profoundly to his own needs. He was at last, looking back, "struck . . . with the rare fashion after which, in any small victim of life, the inward perversity may work. It works by converting to its uses things vain and unintended, to the great discomposure of their prepared opposites, which it by the same stroke so often reduces to naught; with the result indeed that one may most of all see it—so at least have I quite exclusively seen it, the little life out for its chance—as proceeding by the inveterate process of conversion."

The little life out for its chance was oh how deeply intent on the chance it *chose* to take; and all this affected and helped to form a most important phase of his interests: money, exactly, and success, both of which he desired most deeply, but with the saving justifying clause that he was able only to imagine working for and earning them honestly—and though money was only just that, once earned, his notion of success was really his father's, and on nothing less than the highest ground did it deserve that name. In the meantime, as children, they were never to be preoccupied with money. But how to live? "The effect of his attitude, so little thought out as shrewd or vulgarly providential, but . . . so socially and affectionately founded, could only be to make life interesting to us at worst, in default of making it extraordinarily paying." His father wanted all sorts of things for them without quite knowing what they needed, but Henry the younger began peering through, and around the corners of, the doctrine. "With subtle indirectness," the children, perhaps most of all Henry, got the idea that the inward and higher life, well rounded, *must* somehow be lived in good company, with good manners and surroundings fitting to virtue and sociability, good, you might say, attracting good on all planes: of course. But one of the goods, a main good, without which the others might wear a little thin, was material ease. Henry James understood and anatomized thoroughly and acutely the sinister role of money in society, the force of its corrosive powers on the individual; the main concern of nearly all his chief characters is that life shall be, one way or another, and by whatever means, a paying affair . . . and the theme is the consequences of their choice of means, and their notion of what shall pay them.

This worldly knowledge, then, was the end-product of that unworldly education which began with the inward life, the early inculcated love of virtue for its own sake, a belief in human affections and natural goodness, a childhood of extraordinary freedom and privilege, passed in a small warm world of fostering love. This world for him was never a landscape with figures, but a succession of rather small groups of persons intensely near to him, for whom the landscape was a setting, the houses they lived in the appropriate background. The whole scene of his childhood existed in his memory in terms of the lives lived in it, with his own growing mind working away at it, storing it, transmuting it, reclaiming it. Through his extreme sense of the appearance of things, manners, dress, social customs, the lightest gesture, he could convey mysterious but deep impressions of individual character. In crises of personal events, he could still note the look of tree-shaded streets, family gardens, the flash of a grandmother's scissors cutting grapes or flowers, fan-shaped lights, pink marble steps; the taste of peaches, baked apples, custards, ice creams, melons, food indeed by the bushel and the barrel; the colors and shapes of garments, the headdresses of ladies, their voices, the way they lifted their hands. If these were all, they would have been next to nothing, but the breathing lives are somewhere in them.

The many schools he attended, if that is the word, the children he knew there, are perfectly shown in terms of their looks and habits. He was terrorized by the superior talents of those boys who could learn arithmetic, apparently without effort, a branch of learning forever closed to him, as by decree of nature. A boy of his own age, who lived in Geneva, "opened vistas" to him by pronouncing Ohio and Iowa in the French manner: an act of courage as well as correctness which was impressive, surrounded as he was by tough little glaring New Yorkers with stout boots and fists, who were not prepared to be patronized in any such way. Was there anybody he ever thought stupid, he asked himself, if only they displayed some trick of information, some worldly sleight of hand of which he had hitherto been ignorant? On a sightseeing tour at Sing Sing he envied a famous criminal his self-possession, inhabiting as he did a world so perilous and so removed from daily experience. His sense of social distinctions was early in the bud: he recognized a Dowager on sight, at a very tender age. An elegant image of a "great Greek Temple shining over blue waters"—which seems to have been a hotel at New Brighton called the Pavilion—filled him with joy when he was still in his nurse's arms. He had thought it a finer thing than he discovered it to be, and this habit of thought was to lead him far afield for a good number of years.

For his freedoms were so many, his instructions so splendid, and yet his father's admirable, even blessed teachings failed to cover so many daily crises of the visible world. The visible world was the one he would have, all his being strained and struggled outward to meet it, to absorb it, to understand it, to be a part of it. The other children asked him to what church he belonged, and he had no answer; for the even more important question, "What does your father *do?*" or "What business is he in?" no reply had been furnished him for the terrible occasion. His father was no help there, though he tried to be. How could a son explain to his father that it did no good to reply that one had the freedom of all religion, being God's child; or that one's father was an author of books and a truth-seeker?

So his education went forward in all directions and on all surfaces and depths. He longed "to be somewhere—almost anywhere would do—and somehow to receive an impression or an accession, feel a relation or a vibration"; while all the time a performance of *Uncle Tom's Cabin*, which gave him his first lesson in ironic appreciation of the dowdy, the overwrought and underdone; or Mrs. Cannon's mystifyingly polite establishment full of scarfs, handkerchiefs, and colognes for gentlemen, with an impalpable something in the air which hinted at mysteries, and which turned out to be only that gentlemen, some of them cousins, from out of town took rooms there; or the gloomy show of Italian Primitives, all frauds, which was to give him a bad start with painting—such events were sinking into him as pure sensation to emerge from a thousand points in his memory as knowledge.

Knowledge—knowledge at the price of finally, utterly "seeing through" everything—even the fortunate, happy childhood; yet there remained to him, to the very end, a belief in that good which had been shown to him as good in his infancy, embodied in his father and mother. There was a great deal of physical beauty in his family, and it remained the kind that meant beauty to him: the memory of his cousin Minnie Temple, the face of his sister Alice in her last photograph, these were the living images of his best-loved heroines; the love he early understood as love never betrayed him and was love at the latest day; the extraordinarily sensitive, imaginative excitements of first admirations and friendships turned out to be not perhaps so much irreplaceable as incomparable. What I am trying to say is that so far as we are able to learn, nothing came to supplant or dislocate in any way those early affections and attachments and admirations.

This is not to say he never grew up with them, for they expanded with his growth, and as he grew his understanding gave fresh life to them; nor that he did not live to question them acutely, to inquire as to their nature and their meaning, for he did; but surely no one ever projected more lovingly and exactly the climate of youth, of budding imagination, the growth of the tender, perceptive mind, the particular freshness and keenness of feeling, the unconscious generosity and warmth of heart of the young brought up in the innocence which is their due, and the sweet illusion of safety, dangerous because it must be broken at great risk. He survived all, and made it his own, and used it with that fullness and boldness and tenderness and intent reverence which is the sum of his human qualities, indivisible from his sum as artist. For though no writer ever "grew up" more completely than Henry James, and "saw through" his own illusions with more sobriety and pure intelligence, still there lay in the depths of his being the memory of a lost paradise; it was in the long run the standard by which he measured the world he learned so thoroughly, accepted in certain ways—the ways of a civilized man with his own work to do—after such infinite pains: or pangs, as he would have called them, that delight in deep experience which at a certain point is excruciating, and by the uninstructed might be taken for pain itself. But the origin is different, it is not inflicted, not even invited, it comes under its own power and the end is different; and the pang is *not* suffering, it is delight.

Henry James knew about this, almost from the beginning. Here is his testimony: "I foresee moreover how little I shall be able to resist, throughout these notes, the force of persuasion expressed in the individual *vivid* image of the past wherever encountered, these images having always such terms of their own, such subtle secrets and insidious arts for keeping us in relation with them, for bribing us by the beauty, the authority, the wonder of their saved intensity. They have saved it, they seem to say to us, from such a welter of death and darkness and ruin that this alone makes a value and a light and a dignity for them. . . . Not to be denied also, over and above this, is the downright pleasure of the illusion yet again created, the *apparent* transfer from the past to the present of the particular combination of things that did at its hour ever so directly operate and that isn't after all then drained of virtue, wholly wasted and lost, for sensation, for participation in the act of life, in the attesting sights, sounds, smells, the illusion, as I say, of the recording senses."

Brother William remained Big Brother to the end, though Henry learned to stand up to him manfully when the philosopher invaded the artist's territory. But William could not help being impatient with all this reminiscence, and tried to discourage Henry when he began rummaging through his precious scrapbags of bright fragments, patching them into the patterns before his mind's eye. William James was fond of a phrase of his philosopher friend Benjamin Paul Blood: "There is no conclusion. What has concluded, that we might conclude in regard to it?"

That is all very well for philosophy, and it has within finite limits the sound of truth as well as simple fact—no man has ever seen any relations concluded. Maybe that is why art is so endlessly satisfactory: the artist can choose his relations, and "draw, by a geometry of his own, the circle within which they shall happily *appear* to do so." While accomplishing this, one has the illusion that destiny is not absolute, it can be arranged, temporized with, persuaded, a little here and there. And once the circle is truly drawn around its contents, it too becomes truth.

> *First version: July, 1943*
> *Revised: 27 February 1952*

LEON EDEL

Henry James:
The Americano-European Legend†

To speak of "the Americano-European legend" and Henry James's cosmopolitan spirit is to refer to an earlier and more leisurely time when travellers crossed the ocean with the unhurried throb of the steamer, slowly enough to accommodate themselves to the changing and visible environment; when they moved from city to city in small inconvenient trains that seemed the height of luxury and took side-trips into little towns and villages in the rambling horse and buggy or even in the lingering diligence.[1] Travel then still had some relation, however remote, to the faring forth of Columbus or the Pilgrim Fathers; it was active, observant, at times even heroic, filled with the risks of storms at sea and plagues abroad. Today it has become more commonplace; we travel anywhere on the instalment plan, in a world of comparative antibiotic security, passively, with our seat-belts fastened. The jets in their hundreds deposit the Jamesian heroines, in their thousands, in Venice or Rome, London or Paris. The "international" of Henry James has yielded to the intercontinental; the intercontinental will yield to the interstellar. Odysseus[2] wanders, in electronic garb, in outer space.

The myth of travel embodied in Henry James represented a still finite world; one spoke with respect in those days of going around the world in eighty days. City and nation, province and the world remained distinct; time had not yet devoured space. The young man from the provinces, in a Balzac[3] novel, embarked upon a hazardous picaresque journey that put him on his way to Paris, at a greater

†From Leon Edel, "Henry James: The Americano-European Legend," *University of Toronto Quarterly* IV (July 1967), pp. 321–34. The footnotes for this selection are by the editor.
1. A public stagecoach.
2. The hero of Homer's *Odyssey*, who spent ten years traveling from the war in Troy back to his home on the Greek island of Ithaca, has become a symbol of man's restless desire for new experience.
3. Honoré de Balzac (1799–1850), the French novelist whom James admired more than any other. *Picaresque* usually refers to a narrative dealing with a rogue's adventures, but here means simply "adventurous."

time-distance from his home than the distance which separates two sides of the globe today. We must recognize thus that it required an even wider imagination to have, in such an era, an international point of view. The Church[4] to be sure has always aspired to be universal; the philosophers of the Enlightenment had regarded themselves as citizens of the world—the world of ideas. But the vision of golden threads binding America to Europe and Europe to America, as Henry James precociously acquired it, was distinctly rare, more so than we are likely to recognize now. We have only to remember how widely the term "American isolation" was used in the era before the Second World War to understand the powerful nationalism and sense of self-sufficiency which had developed in the United States. Thus when Henry James spoke of "the real cosmopolitan spirit, the easy imagination of differences and hindrances surmounted," he invoked an idea peculiarly repugnant to his fellow-Americans.

* * *

I

We could go very far back indeed if we wanted to look into the history of parochialism and provincialism and the concepts of internationalism, from the tight self-sufficient warring city states of ancient times to the humane ideal of *urbi et orbi*[5] embodied in the Papal blessing; the struggle of the cities in renaissance Italy; the wars and blood-letting of European conquests and unifications. Our ground at the moment, however, is literary; and the example of Henry James is unusual: he was at once the most nationally conscious and least national of novelists. Within his work we find not merely a superficial chronicle of comedies of tourism, but great cosmopolitan feeling, that act of life that resides in observation and notation, in sympathetic comprehension and acceptance of international differences—manners, customs, traditions, the fabric of social history which is the fabric of the art of fiction.

There is an anecdote that when Henry James met Oscar Wilde in Washington in 1882, during the aesthete's triumphant American tour, James spoke with nostalgia of London. "Really?" Oscar said, "you care for *places?* The world is my home." This was Oscar's way of calling Henry James a provincial and assuming a cosmopolitan pose; but it was precisely because Henry James cared for places that he was able to call the world his country. His first book was *Transatlantic Sketches*; and to reread his travel writing—*Portraits of Places, A Little Tour in France, English Hours* and *Italian Hours,* not to speak of the remarkable late volume of travel, *The American Scene*—is to journey

---

4. The Roman Catholic church.
5. Latin for "to the city (i.e. Rome) and to the world." The Pope thus addresses his blessings to indicate that they cover the universe.

with a civilized appreciator, a man who, because he learned the parish, came to know the world.

Yet there is a paradox; for Henry James, of all the novelists, was the one who became a cosmopolitan without ever having been a provincial. It was a little like skipping grades in school. He was born in 1843, some sixty and more years after the Declaration of Independence. Ben Franklin was fifty years dead. Thomas Jefferson seventeen. Toqueville[6] had performed his cosmopolitan act of appraising the U.S. democracy, which had already taken its modern shape. James was born at a moment when the ideals of the men of Philadelphia, who had read the world's constitutions to write America's, were being narrowed into the nationalism of a spreading continent. The Americans had their backs turned to Europe; they were looking to the Far West; their thoughts were continental, not international. But the American aristocracy of intellect and those who had made fortunes in the trade along the eastern seaboard travelled strenuously in the Old World; and parents took their daughters to Paris to learn French.

James was born at No. 21 Washington Place, a little street that runs between Washington Square and Broadway in New York. He was a child of a then modest metropolis—modest by comparison with London or Paris, though large by American standards. Uptown New York ended at the Square; farmland lay beyond; and the reservoir was located where the New York Public Library today stands at 5th Avenue and 42nd Street. Henry was still in his cradle when Thoreau of Concord came to call on the elder Henry James. We might say that the man of Walden, if he gazed at the infant, was one of the few to see little Harry James in his original state of national innocence. The future novelist's innocence ended when he was six months old. He was carried aboard a steamer in New York harbour and conveyed, with his elder brother, his parents and appropriate servants, to England. When Henry James began to toddle about and look at the world, the first scene that met his eyes was Windsor Park: a royal perspective. After that there was a glimpse of the column in the Place Vendôme,[7] his first tangible memory, with its suggestion of power, of conquest, of *gloire*. In his later years, James was to speak of having eaten prematurely of the forbidden fruit of the Tree of Knowledge, or in another image, of having drunk too deeply of the nostalgic cup. "I had been hurried off to London and to Paris immediately after my birth and then and there, I was ever afterwards to feel, that poison had entered

6. Alexis Comte de Tocqueville (1805–59), French liberal politician and writer, who published a famous study of American democracy.
7. A monumental square in Paris, graced by a tall central column covered by a spiral band of bronze, representing military scenes, made from the 1,200 cannons which Napoleon's army captured at Austerlitz in 1805. The statue at the top of the column has changed occasionally according to who has been thought most worthy of representing the national honor (*gloire*) though Napoleon I has been the most steady tenant of the spot. He is now the tenant, and he was when baby James first saw the statue that became his earliest memory.

my veins." The poison was cosmopolitanism, a vision of far horizons not visible in domestic Manhattan. By the time he was three he was, however, trudging behind a nursemaid in Washington Square, sniffing at the peculiar odor of the ailanthus trees—a Square as yet archless,[8] but celebrating American *gloire*—the deeds of the citizen and soldier, George Washington.

Thus from the first, the future novelist's world was a world of contrasts, American and European, a legend fostered in his childhood and sustained by the observant eyes of genius. The trans-Atlantic experiences were oft repeated. At twelve Henry was in Paris seeing the eagles and hearing the trumpets of the Second Empire.[9] By this time French was his second language. He had a period at school in Switzerland, and a summer at Bonn. He had been tutored in England; and in late adolescence he returned again to the United States, this time—and for the first time—to that England which was called New—at Newport. The word "new" was heavily underlined in James's memory: New York, New England, Newport; and by the time he began to write he had an abiding sense of old and new. His American roots were strong: fourteen of his formative years were spent in his homeland out of the first 21; seven were spent abroad; and there were seven more years in Cambridge and New York before he finally became an expatriate at 33. The tug between America and Europe in Henry James was to be constant for many years.

The covered wagons were still moving westward during all this time; and critics later would ask why James "turned his back" on the spectacle of a nation engaged in hard domestic tasks—the drama of the West, the founding of cities, the building of railroads, the courage and industry of his fellow-citizens, while he looked eastward to "our old home."[1] Genius, however, creates as it must, not as critics prescribe; and criticism must concern itself with what is achieved, not with what might have been. James's subject was, from the first, America and Europe, as Mark Twain's was the Mississippi and the humour of the frontier. The cosmopolitan subject was James's natural subject. His first hero was named Hudson,[2] after the explorer who gave his name both to a river and a bay in the New World. James's second hero bore the name Christopher, and his last name was Newman. Again we hear the word new, New*man* the *novus homo* of the new world. Like Columbus, Christopher Newman crosses an ocean bent on explora-

8. Washington Arch in Washington Square, erected to commemorate George Washington's inauguration as the first president of the United States, was designed by Stanford White in 1889 and finished in 1892.
9. The reign of Napoleon III, from 1852 to 1870.
1. Nathaniel Hawthorne used this phrase as the title of a volume of essays and sketches of Great Britain.
2. James's *Roderick Hudson* (1876) and *The American* (1877), the novel dealing with Christopher Newman, had been preceded by the serial publication of a minor novel entitled *Watch and Ward*. *Novus homo* is Latin for "new man."

tion. But he travels in the opposite direction, as James himself had done. The Jamesian voyage is thus a voyage of rediscovery, of renewal. And the noble Italian, in James's late novel *The Golden Bowl*, bears the name of the explorer who gave us the name America. That Prince Amerigo should marry the daughter of an American tycoon named Adam seems logical enough. Amerigo and Adam, Hudson, Columbus, Vespucci: James's heroes are "first men." They sail for worlds unknown, and in the Jamesian mythology, young Americans, young girls as well as young men, Daisies and Pandoras, Francies and Isabels, put out to sea for the unknown of Europe. Some of the pilgrims are passionate and filled with beautiful if false romanticism, that superstitious valuation of Europe against which James warned. Some are passionless, and are untouched by all they see abroad. For half a century, in novel and tale, with constant subtle variations, Henry James devoted his attention to the cosmopolite subject. He dramatized the American businessman abroad, the untutored artist, the ambitious girl, the self-made American young woman, and a generation of naïve innocents. He was prophetic too. He seems to have suspected in his chronicles of the chase for a husband abroad that a movie actress would one day occupy a minor throne,[3] or that an American divorcée might make high conquest in England. The little comedy of "The Siege of London" has a heroine named Nancy Headway. She makes considerable headway, given her western past, to marry the simple-minded Sir Arthur Demesne: indeed her conquest is so easy she wonders whether she shouldn't have set her cap for a Lord. James saw both the comedy and the tragedy, the irony and the pathos, of the provincials who would be cosmopolitan—and of the cosmopolitans who visit among the provincials.

The ground of his writings is described in his late prefaces. He had dealt, he said, with "the bewilderment of the good American of either sex, and of almost any age, in the presence of the 'European' order" and this was, James wryly observed, a confrontation of "the fruits of a constituted order with the fruit of no order at all." * * * He had created a vivid series of pictures, recorded the conflict of manners, shown Americans in their confusion in Piccadilly, Englishmen in their confusion on Broadway. The Americans resented his stories about themselves abroad, and laughed at stories about the English. The English laughed at his Americans, and took umbrage at his picture of young British peers behaving like tourists in Newport. The American novelist created a large international gallery filled with his acute observation of national behavior and national idiosyncrasy. Sometimes, to be sure, he lapsed into stereotypes—Italians, French-

3. Grace Kelly (1929–82), who married Prince Rainier of Monaco. The American divorcee: Wallis Warfield Simpson (1896–   ) for whom Edward VIII abdicated in 1936; thereafter the couple were known as the Duke and Duchess of Windsor.

men, Jews, even sometimes stereotype English and Americans; he was sometimes superficial, but there was never malice or hate in his treatment of national types. James did not even hate the philistines; they were all-too-easy to satirize. On the whole, he took the world as he found it: it provided an endless and fascinating spectacle for a curious imaginative artist. There was no end to what could be done.

II

If Henry James dealt so much in the lighter stuff of international manners, in observation of changing habits and customs and made comparison of national types and societies in constant flux—if he had such quaint, frivolous, charming tales to tell—why, we may ask, has he not been relegated to the ranks of minor writers, ephemeral *raconteurs*, few of whose observations and jests are remembered once they themselves are no longer upon the scene? The answer to this question is to be found in what James did with his cosmopolitan legend: in the fact that he grasped its tragic irony as well as its delicate comedy. He was a determined moralist. His cosmopolitan legend was above all a moral legend. Within the tales he told, there is present the eternal drama of good and of evil, the eternal battle of the life-enhancing and the life-destroying. His passionate and passionless pilgrims, many of them, are still the children of Eden; they possess its insulated innocence; they have not eaten of the fruit of the tree. So James saw one part of his American generation. Hawthorne, to be sure, writing in Concord, had a constant vision of evil, even in his lightest romances. James, however, remarked that at the other end of the avenue of elms, there lived the transcendental Mr. Emerson, thinking high thoughts, observing the changing seasons, untouched by violence or cruelty, seeing only the higher philosophy. James in the early 1870s, had encountered Emerson in Rome and taken him to see the sculptures at the Vatican; meeting him later in Paris, Emerson had asked James to conduct him through the Louvre. The novelist was to say how he had been struck by "the anomaly of a man so refined and intelligent, being so little spoken to by works of art." And in a memorable essay he set down these words about the "exquisite provincial" of Concord:

> Emerson's personal history is condensed into a single word, Concord, and all the condensation in the world will not make it look rich . . . The plain, God-fearing, practical society which surrounded him was not fertile in variations; it had great intelligence and energy, but it moved altogether in the straightforward direction. On three occasions later—three journeys to Europe—he was introduced to a more complicated world; but his spirit, his moral taste, as it were, abode always within the undecorated walls of his youth.

Evil "was a side of life," said James, "as to which Emerson's eyes were thickly bandaged."

In a word, many Americans looked upon Europe unaware, in naïve and child-like wonder, or bewilderment, or with patriotic contempt. They saw picturesque and beautiful things, and sometimes did not guess that these had emerged from the barbarism of history, the nightmare and bloodshed of the ages. On its side, Europe, old, worldly-wise, possessing the shrewdness and the wisdom of these ages, looked upon the American innocents with a knowing and often corrupt eye. James's drama reposed thus upon the eternal drama of evil and innocence—an innocence devoid of the sense of the past. The Americans were the children of the present and perhaps of the future. Europe distinctly was of the past. James himself argued that this gave the Americans an advantage. The old world had, as it were, lived; Americans could encounter uncharted experience. "We have exquisite qualities as a race,"[4] James wrote when he was twenty-four, "and it seems to me that we are ahead of the European races in the fact that . . . we can deal freely with forms of civilization not our own, can pick and choose and assimilate and in short (aesthetically etc.) claim our property wherever we find it." Henry James was ready "to let all the breezes of the west blow through me at their will." We hear the voice of the cosmopolite as he continues:

> To have no national stamp has hitherto been a regret and a draw-back, but I think it not unlikely that American writers may yet indicate that a vast intellectual fusion and synthesis of the various National tendencies of the world is the condition of more important achievements than any we have seen. We must of course have something of our own—something distinctive and homogenous —and I take it that we shall find it in our moral consciousness, our unprecedented spiritual lightness and vigour. In this sense at least we shall have a national *cachet.*—I expect nothing great during your lifetime or mine perhaps [he wrote his friend]; but my instincts quite agree with yours in looking to see something original and beautiful disengage itself from our ceaseless fermentation and tur-moil. You see I am willing to leave it a matter of instinct. God Speed the day!

This enlightened vision of his young manhood was to be reinforced by a long sojourn in the Rome of the Risorgimento.[5] Henry James watched with fascination a series of excavations in the Holy City. Out of the Roman earth came the artifacts of the past, fragments of statues, the overlays and accretions of pagan and Christian, ancient and

---

4. As a nation or cultural group.
5. The word is Italian for *resurgence* and refers to a period of cultural nationalism and political activism beginning in the Napoleonic era,

when Italy struggled for independence and uni-fication. The period culminated in 1870, when the Kingdom of Italy (proclaimed in 1861) seized the last papal territories.

mediaeval, sometimes surmounted and gilded by the renaissance, a mocking pastiche of the centuries. History was being turned up with a spade. Riding on horseback across the Campagna[6] during these years James experienced, on that rolling terrain and in the exquisite play of light, the stir of ancient things. He had Shelley's vision of Ozymandias. Empires seemed to lie under his horse's feet as he galloped across the daisy-covered countryside. Unlike the romantic poets, however, who wept for an evanescent and vanished past, James marvelled that so much had survived. And yet he was uneasy. He read his Byron and Stendhal, his President de Brosses or Gregorovius;[7] the ruins were sad and picturesque; like Hawthorne he experienced a sense of terror as well as of beauty or sadness, "a dark efflorescence of the evil germs which history had implanted." He wrote a tale at that time of a young American girl who marries a handsome Roman prince. The story has in it the bright surface of sun and Rome, but it harbours within it also strange uneasy things. A splendid Juno is dug up in the grounds of the young couple's villa and it becomes a threat to the marriage. The Italian Count forgets his wife—he loses himself in contemplation and worship of the ancient statue. The pagan reconquers the Christian. The daughter of the new world must find a solution; with quiet American efficiency she does the American thing: the past is reinterred. The statue is returned to the mouldy earth.[8] So in another tale an imperial topaz, symbol of the evil of Tiberias, must be restored to the muddy slime of the Tiber, if the moderns are to be free of history's nightmares. James gives us the feeling of a beautiful, yet mouldering antiquity; and he warns against a blind worship of the past. There is a deeper implication: it is dangerous to exhume dormant primeval things of the spirit; they contain within them the evil that man has eternally sought to control and master.

III

The cosmopolitan imagination of Henry James thus involved the recognition of an historical process; and within this process James never lost sight of the forces that have guided man to the conquest of ignorance, fear, and strife among nations. His work contains within it an ideal of tolerance, an acceptance of differences, a recognition of similarities, a code of non-violence, a feeling for a world made rich and disprovincialized by the knowledge of the multitude of peoples

6. A desolate plain surrounding Rome.
7. Charles de Brosses (1709–77), French magistrate and scholar, wrote the first work on the ruins of Herculaneum, a famous series of familiar letters from Italy, and finally a history of the Roman republic. Ferdinand Gregorovius (1821–91), a German historian, was the author of A *History of the City of Rome in the Middle Ages*, in eight volumes. Stendhal, the French novelist, and the English poet Byron also wrote about Italy, the latter for instance in the fourth canto of his *Childe Harold's Pilgrimage*.
8. "The Last of the Valerii" (1874). The tale about the imperial topaz is entitled "Adina" (1874).

and types and customs. To read James's travel writings shows him a consistently sophisticated and sentient observer; he watches the people in the streets, he sees riches and poverty, he dresses before his American readers images of the daily life, the charm or oddity of the architecture and of out-of-the-way corners. He makes his readers aware always of his angle of vision. He calls himself "the sentimental traveller," but he can also be the "observant stranger." He is always careful that his readers in the provinces be told of his cosmopolitan view. There is a capital passage in a sketch of Paris which offers a very clear statement of his ground. He has just left England after a year's residence; and he describes the pleasure of setting foot on French soil; he is grateful for the fresh white napkin at the *restaurant de la gare*,[9] he enjoys the fragrant bowl of soup; he sees the French types around him and sketches them with an easy hand. In Paris he returns to his favorite café and is greeted as if he had never been away; in all this one gets the feeling that James is expressing relief to be out of stuffy Victorian London and to be enjoying the relaxed independence and easy anarchy of the French. But he looks behind the lively surface of the Parisian scene; he recognizes the presence of penury and toil and he keeps before us also a vision of the ordered, conventional, philistine world he has just quitted. We catch his tone and see his gift of style in the opening passage:

> To be a cosmopolite is not, I think, an ideal: the ideal should be to be a concentrated patriot. Being a cosmopolite is an accident, but one must make the best of it. If you have lived about, as the phrase is, you have lost that sense of the absoluteness and the sanctity of the habits of your fellow-patriots which once made you so happy in the midst of them. You have seen that there are a great many *patriae*[1] in the world, and that each of these is filled with excellent people for whom the local idiosyncrasies are the only thing that is not rather barbarous. There comes a time when one set of customs, wherever it may be found, grows to seem to you about as provincial as another; and then I suppose it may be said of you that you have become a cosmopolite. You have formed the habit of comparing, of looking for points of difference and of resemblance, for present and absent advantages, for the virtues that go with certain defects, and the defects that go with certain virtues. If this is poor work compared with the active practice, in the sphere to which a discriminating Providence has assigned you, of the duties of a tax-payer, an elector, a juryman or a diner-out, there is nevertheless something to be said for it. It is good to think well of mankind, and this, on the whole, a cosmopolite does. . . . The consequence of the cosmopolite spirit is to initiate you into the merits of all peoples; to convince you that national virtues are numerous, though they may be very different, and to make downright preference really very hard.

9. Train-station restaurant. In Europe train depots in many cities contain restaurants, some quite elegant.

1. Native country, homeland.

He had, he said, his own preferences. He had every "disposition to think better of the English race than of any other except my own." But to do this was like sitting in a room with the window shut. Henry James preferred to keep his window on the world open.

IV

In the provinces, unfortunately, in the very nature of local needs and local horizons, windows on the world tend to be shut. So long as Henry James showed Daisy Miller reproving the American snobs in Rome and asserting the superiority of life in Schenectady, N.Y., American readers applauded. So long as a Jamesian character quipped that as for manners, there are bad manners everywhere, but an aristocracy "is bad manners organized," James spoke with a voice pleasing to the American provincials. However, there are two moments in the history of the novelist's relation to his land in which his cosmopolitanism caused an uproar. The first occurred when he published his little book on Hawthorne. The second was a large critical manifestation, in the 1920s. James's book on Hawthorne, written in 1879, even today is not received with equanimity among American critics, who find a tone of condescension in it. There may be in its pages that note of superiority which the present often adopts toward the simpler life of the past. The condescension may also be in the eye of the critic. However, James did use the word "provincial" rather often, and there was a passage, a series of variations on a theme by Hawthorne, which offended. Hawthorne had complained that the daylight prosperity of America deprived the novelist of the picturesque to be found in Europe. James took this as ground for pointing out that the realistic novelist in America, no less than the romantic, confronted a less complex social fabric than his English confreres. The list of thing absent from American life which James drew up clearly wounded the complacent and touched the patriotic. No Eton, no Harrow,[2] no House of Lords, no pomp and ritual, no national religion and so on. These were institutions available to the English novelist whereas American novelists had merely a society living in frame houses and much sunlight, indulging in moral thinking, and simple Puritanical habits; or, if the novelist were a Fenimore Cooper, he had a particular subject, the Plains and the Indians. What James said was obvious enough. But his list was long and it depended on what tone the reader imparted to it. James was not advocating an American monarchy or a House of Lords, but certain editors read him as if he were. * * *

* * *

2. Eton College (founded in 1440) and Harrow (founded 1571) are famous English boys' schools, i.e., prep schools.

This little debate, in which the press fiercely attacked James and permanently fixed his image in the American mind as an absentee writer who abused his own land, was of 1880. And it was but a tempest in a teapot compared with the outcry James caused in 1915 when he threw in his lot with "this decent and dauntless people" (a phrase Churchill was to borrow with fine effect in the later war). James had kept his American citizenship for 40 years while abroad in the belief that one could be a national and be a cosmopolitan as well. He became a British subject because he could not think of himself as alien in an England at war, particularly in the face of American neutrality. The denunciation in the American press was violent and James could only shrug his shoulders; he could not understand a logic in which his countrymen demanded that foreigners settled in the U.S. become American citizens but would not allow Americans the same privilege, that is to become nationals of other countries in which they happened to live.

All his life James had weighed his relation to his homeland. He was recurrently haunted by the thought of the life he might have led had he remained in the United States. He had tried in 1875 to earn his living as a writer in New York, but had discovered he could write more and sell more if he lived abroad. Thus eminently practical reasons had conspired to reinforce his constitutional cosmopolitanism. He had always argued, as we have seen, that the ideal was to have native roots; and he urged that Edith Wharton[3] remain "tethered in native pastures, even if it confines her to a backyard in New York." There is a late tale written after his 1904 visit to America called "The Jolly Corner" which is richly autobiographical. In it a repatriated American, in the old family house in Greenwich Village, stalks a ghost and finally confronts it in the belief that it is the ghost of himself as he would have been had he stayed at home. When he sees the apparition, it has its face covered with its hands, and one of the hands has lost two fingers which are reduced to stumps, as if accidentally shot away. The face which the phantom finally reveals is a face of horror. The repatriated gentleman recognizes that this is indeed his other self—in evening dress, with dangling pince-nez, pearl buttons and gold watch-guard, an individual in Wall Street with perhaps a million a year.

We may judge from the missing fingers that James was telling himself that to have remained in America would have indeed maimed him, maimed his art. * * *

* * *

3. Edith Newbold Jones Wharton (1862– 1937), U.S. novelist and friend of Henry James, who lived the better part of her adult life near Paris.

* * * "The Jolly Corner" admirably suggests to us that James found fulfilment in the one world for which his childhood and youth had prepared him. And his cosmopolitanism must be related to an earlier stage in American history. The great task of men like Franklin and Jefferson, after the Revolution, had been to overcome America's alienation from the world; the Revolution was feared abroad as new revolutions are feared today. The early Americans, many of them men of the Enlightenment, set out to read America into the world. Henry James, coming fifty years later, sought to read the cultivated American—someone like himself—into this same world, that is into the Western World. By the time Henry James took up in letters what Franklin and Jefferson had sought to accomplish as Americano-Europeans in diplomacy and international relations, the United States had turned away from the international ideals of its founders. It had not only to build the nation but to heal the wounds of a disastrous Civil War. An intense and fervent nationalism had supplanted the wider views of the writers of the Constitution. In this sense Henry James was distinctly out of step with his time—yet he was very much in step with his country's original purpose. If his experiments in form, his grandeur of style, and the peculiar force of his personal aestheticism have ultimately been recognized, there still remains to be fully learned the lesson and the vision of his cosmopolitanism—of "differences and hindrances surmounted" among the nations, *urbi et orbi.*

Criticism

DAVID DAICHES

Sensibility and Technique
(Preface to a Critique)†

"There is, I think, no more nutritive or suggestive truth . . . than that of the perfect dependence of the 'moral' sense of a work of art on the amount of felt life concerned in producing it. The question comes back thus, obviously, to the kind and the degree of the artist's prime sensibility, which is the soil out of which his subject springs. The quality and capacity of that soil, its ability to 'grow' with due freshness and straightness any vision of life, represents, strongly or weakly, the projected morality. That element is but another name for the more or less close connexion of the subject with some mark made on the intelligence, with some sincere experience." Preface to *The Portrait of a Lady*.

"A novel is in its broadest definition a personal, a direct impression of life: that, to begin with, constitutes its value, which is greater or less according to the intensity of the impression." *The Art of Fiction*.

If the literary historian is justified at all in making a distinction between a "modern" school of novelists—a school only in the loosest sense, which would include such diverse writers as Henry James, Proust, and Virginia Woolf—and an earlier species of fiction, equally diverse, practised by both Scott and Dickens, Fielding and Jane Austen, this distinction would lie in the fact that the "modern" novelist is concerned to portray a quality of experience filtered through an individual sensibility, while his predecessor's concern was to provide a highly finished literary *exemplum* of a public truth, or at least of a kind of experience which writer and reader looked at from the same vantage point and through the same kind of glasses. The distinction between these two ways of writing is not, of course, essentially chronological, though certain accidents of history have conspired to make it appear so; or at least it is chronological only in the sense that the "modern" novel would seem to be the natural phenomenon to emerge at a certain point in the development of the craft of fiction. There comes a point in the technical development of any art at which that art is equipped to express, not the "ideal truth" of the older practitioners and critics, but the "sensibility" of the newer ones. That is, the later artist uses a purely personal sensitivity to the quality of events as a guide to tell him what ideal truth is, while his predecessor was less concerned to discover what ideal truth was—did not everybody know what it was?—than how to express it in the most effective literary form.

For it is a monstrous, though popular, misconception that modern art is concerned with form, with the technique of expression merely, while artists of an earlier generation were more interested in the *what*

†From *Kenyon Review* V (Autumn 1943), pp. 569–73, 575–79.

than in the *how*. Shakespeare took any well-known story that he could find, and by his method of telling it changed its significance. That was the way of all the artists of his age, in the plastic arts as well as in drama and fiction. The characteristic "modern," however, is not the writer who re-writes *Hamlet* in terms of contemporary ideas and idioms, but the one who struggles to invent a story capable of bearing the construction that his personal insights demand. This is not to say that in modern fiction the plot has become all-important while in older writing invention was less important than style. "People often talk of these things," remarked James in *The Art of Fiction*, "as if they had a kind of internecine distinctness, instead of melting into each other at every breath, and being intimately associated parts of one general effort of expression." Art begins as an endeavor on the artist's part to show the public what the public is assumed to know (that is why its subject in the early stages is so often religious, for religion represented the great body of common knowledge shared by all), and later, when a certain sophistication of technique has been achieved and when certain historical circumstances have altered the artist's function somewhat (the two steps nearly always come together) it ceases to be an endeavor to illustrate magnificently for the public what the public knows or thinks it knows, and becomes an endeavor to persuade the public of the validity of the unique insight of the artist.

I have said "when a certain sophistication of technique has been achieved," and that sounds rather patronizing to Shakespeare and Scott. But sophistication is not the same thing as technical brilliance: it is a special use of technical apparatus, namely, the use of technique to change the meaning (or perhaps to create it) rather than to reinforce it. An article in the *Pall Mall Gazette* which both amused and annoyed James referred to his novels as "tales in which Bostonian nymphs rejected English dukes for psychological reasons." The writer assumed that "psychological reasons" were in fact insignificant in such a connection. To James, of course, these reasons were significant and important. His duty as a novelist was to present the situation and the episode referred to so that this significance and this importance became clear to the reader. The meaning of a series of episodes was altered in the light of its method of presentation: it meant something different when told *just that way* than when told in any other way. Now a novel of Jane Austen or of Trollope would not have meant something *different* if narrated in another style—only something *less*. The meaning would have been less effectively put across, the full significance would not have been communicated—the novel, in fact, would have been tremendously impoverished, its meaning would have been thinned, it would have contained but a small proportion of the full meaning which the novel as we have it is able to communicate, yet it would not have been utterly changed. But any story by

James—*The Ambassadors* or *The Turn of the Screw, Daisy Miller* or *The Golden Bowl*—would be utterly changed, its meaning would be wholly altered, if it were told in any other way.

It might be countered that this distinction is a false one, that every work of art will lose tremendously if done over or re-expressed in a different style. This is perfectly true, but the question is not *whether* it would lose but *what* it would lose. Some fraction of the power and significance of *Hamlet* could be got across in a paraphrase—there would be a tremendous qualitative and quantitative loss, but the resulting story would not become unrecognizable—while a paraphrase of a novel of James or of Virginia Woolf or of a story of Katherine Mansfield would be something totally different from the original both in nature and meaning.

All this is perhaps a roundabout way of saying that James is in the tradition of the modern novel of sensibility and that his technique is dependent on his sensibility. But the matter must be put in a roundabout way because it is a far less simple fact than it appears, and unless the critic takes every precaution to avoid misunderstanding he will be accused of perpetrating some monstrous piece of critical naiveté. Sensibility is an ambiguous term, and, however defined, it is certainly not a modern prerogative. Some sense of what it is—at least, as the term is being employed here—and what it means to modern fiction can be got from a study of James's practice of the art of fiction.

That James's sensibility was essentially moral is made clear at once if we set his work beside that of, say, Proust. James was concerned with moral issues as they emerged in social behavior, while Proust's interest was in social behavior as such, a purely psychological interest in social mannerisms. Both writers, however, were novelists of sensibility: what interested them in human affairs was determined not by any public standard but by a sense of values peculiar to themselves for the communication of which they depended on technique—on style, on pattern, on the way emphasis was distributed throughout the narrative. And the "story" did not in any real sense exist apart from the technique.

One can see in James's early writing a certain confusion which arises from his not yet having fully developed a consistent technique appropriate to a novelist of sensibility. The death of Roderick Hudson, for example, at the end of the novel of that name, represents a completion in the simple realm of physical action (of separable and summarizable "plot") of a pattern which does not really belong to that realm. *Roderick Hudson* is the study of a moral problem and the climax should have been a moral one—a decision, or the failure to take a decision at a certain point—whereas James has instead tried to symbolize the climax of his hero's moral history by simply killing him off, in a manner unprepared for and unrelated to anything that has gone before. This same inorganic use of death is found in several of James's early short stories—in "A Most Extraordinary Case" and "The Madonna of the Future"—where he had not yet adequately developed a technique for the kind of fiction he was trying to write. The death of Daisy Miller is rather different, and marks an important advance: it serves to move the story as a whole into a suitable retrospect, to give it a unity and a completeness, so that the story, in virtue of its conclusion, becomes a total work of art instead of an incident in a society novel.

* * *

But what do we mean by James's "moral sensibility"? Simply his sense that in the decisions and emotions that arise out of the personality of individuals placed in certain testing circumstances lie some of the most significant truths about human character. These truths are "moral" truths in that they concern, in the last analysis, the success or failure of the personality to whom they relate, and this success or failure is measured, not on worldly standards or on any other public standard, but on a standard personal to James and made convincing to the reader by devices of style and pattern. James is the antithesis of both John Bunyan and Horatio Alger, of Defoe and of Hemingway. For his moral sense is not religious (the most public kind of moral sense) nor in any way communal: it is wholly dependent on his sense of aesthetic significance.

For to James, as to so many "modern" novelists who avoid both the terms "moral" and "aesthetic," what has aesthetic significance possesses moral significance automatically. He talks of "the perfect dependence of the 'moral' sense of a work of art on the amount of felt life concerned in producing it." The novelist's prime concern, that is, lies with his own sensibility, with life "felt" in his own terms, and this automatically produces a moral significance. Thus any attempt to separate out a moral purpose in, say, *The Turn of the Screw* is wholly to miss the point of the work. Once the sense of evil is specified, is translated into concrete sexual or psychological terms, the whole close-knit fabric in virtue of which significance automatically becomes moral significance is destroyed, and we find a 'meaning' in the work at the expense of losing the art.

And is not this equally true of writers like Proust and Virginia Woolf, different though they are in so many respects from James and from each other? And is it not untrue of *Hamlet* and *Adam Bede*, of *Clarissa* and *Great Expectations?* We read *What Happens in Hamlet* and return to the play with added enjoyment and understanding, whether or not we agree with Dover Wilson. Wilson's interpretation finds its place among an infinite number of other possible or probable interpretations, and the richness of the work becomes more than ever apparent to us. But Edmund Wilson's interpretation of *The Turn of* *the Screw*, brilliant though it is, spoils the curious and individual unity of the work, for it imposes a specific, overt morality on a work whose very essence depends on the fact that its morality is neither specific nor overt. * * *

The difference between a novelist or dramatist in the older tradition and one in the tradition in which James writes is that in the former there is a great number—perhaps an infinite number—of specific moral meanings echoing into each other, and the explicit discovery of any one, while an inadequate explanation of the work in its entirety, is often helpful to the reader; while in the latter no separate moral meaning can be taken out at all: meaning is itself moral, and significance and moral illumination are co-existent.

Does this mean that the critic must give up any attempt to interpret the work of James? Not at all; but it does mean that in dealing with the work of a writer like James the critic, if he wishes to treat in any detail of individual works, can be best assured of producing profitable insights with an examination of technique. For technique, in this kind of writing, is the filter that distinguishes "life" from "felt life," and by an examination of it we can hope to come to some fuller understanding of the real meaning of a James novel—of the nature of James's sensibility, in fact, for that is the key to the meaning. When James himself writes of his novels, he nearly always does so autobiographically—he explains *how he came to write that way*: that is, he explains the operation of his sensibility. But the critic, who can only look at the work from the outside, must take the only alternative method; he must examine the technique, deal carefully with matters of style, structure and organization. By doing so he will be led to an understanding of what it was that James, in his novels, was trying to do with the fact about human behavior that he observed so carefully.

All the talk about James's relation to Europe and America, the diagnosis of his character based on the idea that he fell between the European and the American stools, is really beside the point. James chose the vantage point from which his sensibility could operate most successfully, and the tradition of American life and letters was in his day so firmly opposed to any art based on individual sensibility that he was bound to migrate to an atmosphere in which the preoccupation of the arts with *fable* rather than with *vision* had, in the mellowness of time, given way to a sophistication of thought and of living which, however uncongenial to James in many respects, was nevertheless a possible atmosphere for his kind of writing. One might say, perhaps, that James as a man preferred America but as an artist required Europe, though such a statement is open to much misunderstanding. James's approval of Flaubert was qualified, but his condemnation of Whitman was absolute. Yet it is not true that James as critic reserves his praise for novelists working in the same tradition as himself: his great admiration for George Eliot is sufficient evidence to the contrary. He often demands a more explicit morality in the work of others than is consistent with his own method. Nevertheless, his prefaces to his own novels and certain passages in his discussion of writers whom he admired most—such as Turgenev—amply reinforce the conclusions to which a study of James's novels lead us. "Imagination guides his hand and modulates his touch, and makes the artist worthy of the observer. In a word, he is universally sensitive." This praise of Turgenev, making clear that the function of art is to serve faithfully the artist's sensibility—for what do imagination and sensitivity add up to but sensibility, in the sense in which the term has been used here?—can be paralleled by many other revealing remarks in his critical writing.

In the case of some artists, the critic can study the subtlety of ideas and the complex of meanings, and that study will throw light on the technique the artist employs. With others, a study of the technique will reveal the meaning and significance of the work as a whole. With a novelist of moral sensibility, of the kind that James is, unless one begins a study of any individual work with an examination of the technique—and I use the term in its broadest sense—one will run the danger either of interpreting the novel in too limited and specific a manner, or of misinterpreting it completely and seeing only rather dull and needlessly involved elaborations, like the writer who saw *The Portrait of a Lady* as a silly tale in which a Bostonian nymph rejected an English duke for psychological reasons. James has been unfortunate in that few critics have discovered how to read him. But by now we have had enough experience of the tradition in which, broadly speaking, James was writing, to make a re-estimate of his work both desirable and possible. For full justice has not yet been done to James as a writer whose technical skill enabled him to make convincing and inevitable a personal moral interpretation of human behavior—in other words, as a novelist of sensibility.

JACQUES BARZUN

James the Melodramatist†

In a foolish essay entitled "Books and You," Mr. Somerset Maugham,[1] while scorning James's work as trivial and superficial, is nevertheless forced to admit that it somehow "keeps the reader going

† From *Kenyon Review* V (Autumn 1943), pp. 508–15, 517–21. The footnotes for this selection are by the editor.

1. William Somerset Maugham (1874–1965), a widely read English writer of fiction and plays.

from page to page." The opinion that James's novels deal only with the amenities of high life is of course not confined to those who agree with Mr. Maugham and who would be content, like a famous American critic, to dismiss James as a "social twitterer." For certain of James's admirers, the pleasure he affords is in direct proportion to the elegance of his atmosphere and the rarefaction of his meaning. These readers are never so sure of his artistry as when he entrusts to a lordling some stammering speech, heavy with adverbs and precious with col-loquialisms, which together suggest one of Ollendorf's[2] conversation manuals. Whether scornful or admiring, this attitude toward James only proves how often critical generalities are based not on what is plainly there to be generalized about, but solely on what is strange or striking. For the high life, the fine-spun surface, the Old Pretender[3] style, would not of themselves account for the truth which Mr. Maugham grants but does not explain: we still ask what it is that keeps the reader going.

The first step towards a right answer is to recognize that James does not deal with etiquette detached from deep feeling; that his characters are not exclusively, or even mainly, drawn from a class which is beyond the reach of gross circumstance or vulgar appetites. On the contrary, most of his novels and tales deal with middling people pursuing the two simplest objects of human concern—love and money. When I say "simplest," I mean of course that abstractly considered they are elemental and have kept their primacy in life and literature ever since the war that was fought for "Helen and all her wealth."[4] It is true that James's mind is engrossed by the complexities and refinements to which passion and greed give rise in a world of elaborate laws and subtle modes of communication. But even in the course of inventing and unmasking the numberless disguises which these basic passions can assume, James holds to a simple view of their meaning; in acting out their feelings, people turn out either good or evil—a moral attitude which, taken with James's addiction to violent

2. Heinrich Gottfried Ollendorf (1803–65) published *A New Method of Learning to Read, Write, and Speak a Language in Six Months . . . for the Use of Schools and Private Teach-ers.* He and his assistants adapted these manuals to teaching each of the major European lan-guages, including Russian, to the speakers of the others, e.g., French to the English and Germans as well as English and German to the French. His publications ran into the hundreds (their listings in the National Union Catalogue take up fifteen pages)—a commercial exploita-tion of pedagogical method in which the subtle nuances of language may well have lost their edge on occasion. Barzun's point seems to be the artificiality which can result from the con-scious use of colloquial idioms by speakers or authors who have observed and learned them but to whom they are not native, as a German, for instance, learns English and as James ob-served the occasional stammering colloqui-alisms of upper-class British speech.

3. In 1919 the British critic Philip Guedalla divided James's career into three periods, metaphorically into the three reigns of James I, James II, and the Old Pretender—a humorous declaration of his preference for the work of James's middle period. See *The New Statesman* XII, 306 (February 15, 1919), p. 422.

4. Ever since the Trojan War which supplied the subjects of Homer's *Iliad* and *Odyssey* as well as other early Greek masterworks. Barzun is quoting the *Iliad*, Book III, line 91.

plots, leads me to say that he is a writer of melodrama.

No doubt the word needs to be enlarged upon in order to convey the sense I intend. We generally think of melodrama as a form of stage play which flourished "in the nineties"—we are no longer quite sure of the century—and which had to do with mothers and mortgages, destitution and drink. The villain was a deliberate evil-doer, identifiable by his clothes, coloring, and intonation, and providentially created to bring out the finest exertions on the part of the hero. In short, melodrama, even at its crudest, depicts the endless battle of God and Satan. For although the villain in these conventional pieces usually came to grief before the final curtain, it was clear in retrospect that his aims were precisely the same as the hero's: he wanted the girl and the money. The difference which marked him off as evil was evidently a matter of style. He was simply not fastidious enough in the means he employed to gratify his otherwise natural desires. Hence if we disregard the particular symbols employed to move the theatrical audience of a given period, and consider only the beliefs leading to the use of those symbols, the essence of melodrama appears as a deep conviction that certain deformed expressions of human feeling are evil and that this evil is positive and must be resisted.

This definition would of course put many great works of the past, hitherto called tragedies, into the class of melodrama. Much of Shakespeare and Euripides is melodrama in this sense. If it is asked why we need to reclassify or re-label these works, the answer is that criticism ought to bring together under one name those fictions that record man's horror in the face of evil. Tragedy is not a sufficiently wide name, for it traditionally implies a *heroic* fall under the blow of a *fated* evil. What do we make of the plays, and of the even more numerous novels and tales, which lack a magnanimous hero as well as a sense of overriding fate? Tragedy can only be a sub-class under melodrama—the highest, just as the plays of the nineties were the lowest and cheapest.

Considered from the point of view of substance, the difference between them is that tragedy respects the limits I have named; considered from the point of view of artistic pleasure, the only difference between them is one of skill. In cheap melodrama, the words, symbols, and plots are hackneyed. They are loosely put together to bring out an automatic response. In the highest tragedy these artistic elements satisfy more exacting demands by their uniqueness and close articulation: they make poetry. In between the two groups stands the bulk of modern prose fiction, from Richardson to Balzac[5]—"aesthetic

---

5. Samuel Richardson (1689–1761), English novelist, and Honoré de Balzac (1799–1850), the French novelist whom James admired more than any other. Molière, below, is the pseudonym of Jean-Baptiste Poquelin (1622–73), French dramatist.

melodrama," if you will—and it is to this class that James's work belongs.

In this nomenclature, melodrama is distinguished by its feeling and intention from the parallel and contrasting category of comedy. Comedy likewise has its common and rare forms, ranging as it does from burlesque and farce to the "high" or serious comedies of Molière and Shakespeare. All story-telling falls into one or the other of these two great realms, and there is, I think, some virtue in being aware of their mutual exclusiveness. I have long puzzled over the undoubted fact that relatively few persons are admirers of both Henry James and Meredith.[6] Superficially, it should seem as if the same kind of social, intellectual, and even verbal art were displayed by the two men. But deep down they are antithetical. Meredith takes the comic point of view, not only in his own special sense, but also in the sense I contrast here with melodrama. He creates no superstitious dread of man's passions. He believes in faults, errors, follies, but not in terrifying evil. * * * There is nothing dark or inhuman about * * * Meredith's villains * * * They cause deep unhappiness * * * but this yields tragicomedy, not melodrama.

* * * the freezing fear, the mysteriousness of the force[7] at work, are entirely absent from Meredith's treatment and overwhelmingly present in James. Perhaps the point needs illustration and refining rather than amplification. If we extract what might be called the prose meaning of *The Golden Bowl* or *The Wings of the Dove*, that is, if we make a synopsis of their plots, what do we find? Both novels revolve about the possession of human beings or of money for the love of either or both. Accordingly we find two stage moralities—the one, a story of supreme goodness overcoming surreptitious evil; the other, a story of greed allied to weakness destroying pure affection. * * *

It is perfectly true that Charlotte Stant and Kate Croy[8] are not villainesses according to the crude pattern of the green-eyed siren, but this is the difference of texture and surface and skill that I spoke of as establishing gradations in melodrama. James obviously works in a spirit and in a social milieu that exclude stagey expression; sometimes they even exclude direct expression of any kind. The ramification of self-contained thought seeking to convey a hint or to redirect its own passion is what deceives Mr. Maugham and delights the professional Jamesian. But neither should remain blind to the fire and force beneath the surface. There is only one kiss in *The Golden Bowl*, but it is as fully expressive and adulterous as would be a juridical account of the lovers' every assignation. Melodrama does not require a set form of

6. George Meredith (1820–1909), English novelist and poet.
7. Of evil.

8. Characters in James's *The Golden Bowl* and *The Wings of the Dove*.

words or choice of instances. Aeschylus and Shakespeare find other words for Clytemnestra and Gertrude[9] rebuking their sons than "How can you treat your poor mother so?" Yet that is surely what the two women are feeling; or rather, like James's characters, they are feeling this common core of emotion *plus* the fringes of other feelings that belong to themselves alone and give rise to the precise words they use. To the ear trained to catch the nuances of a subdued rhetoric, the impact is no less great; it is in fact reinforced by the minute particulars, by the complete personification of the more general melodramatic truth that is being portrayed.

Recall how often, especially in his short stories, James wants simply to administer a moral shock: "Look! It is not as you think!" Then observe how often this shocking effect is achieved either by carefully maintained mystery—by hinting everything and thus drawing on the reader's own supply of "melodramatic truth"; or more simply still by making much of little, raising expectancy by defeating it. * * *

* * *

The paradox of James's way with melodramatic material is that he seems to conceive with all the exaggeration necessary for "straight" effects and then to submerge the felt enormity under a flood of details relevant to be sure, and illuminating as well, but above all lifelike in their haphazard discovery and disconnected sequence. At times the dimming effect of detail is purposely left incomplete, and soft and harsh are given us side by side, as it were, to show us that the beast is not in the jungle but in the drawing room. Think for instance of *The Bench of Desolation*, which has to do with a breach of promise. It begins: "She had practically, he believed, conveyed the intimation"—so far this is Jamesian haze but now comes, without a break, the Jamesian "riot of the raw"—"the horrid, brutal, vulgar menace in their last dreadful conversation. . . ." This juxtaposition of effects is repeated a few lines below: "There was no question of not understanding—the ugly, the awful words ruthlessly formed by her lips. . . ." And finally, after another cushion of comment comes her "I'll sue, unless. . . ."

At other times, the horror is less certain. We feel it but know neither where to find it, nor how to confound the evil doers. * * * All we can do is to say with James that "they go too far." For James is free enough from the preconceptions of uniformity in wickedness to recognize that the commonest social form of human evil is not the palpable villain but the shady character. His gallery illustrating the type is very rich, from Madame Merle and the young Bostonian

9. Clytemnestra murders her husband and in turn is murdered by their son in the *Orestia*, by Aeschylus. Gertrude betrays her husband and in return is harrowed by their son in Shakespeare's *Hamlet*.

aboard the S. S. Patagonia[1] to the satanic families in which Newman, the American, and the English tutor of *The Pupil* find themselves. Again in these more shaded performances, the management of the plot is by mystery or the accumulation of trivialities—little lies, easy-going indifference to small duties, failures to act or respond in time. Time is important, for under the laws of society as well as under those of melodrama, technicalities are the very abettors of evil.

It is simply because life in society makes multitudinous occasions for pain that James's studies report evil as nearly always triumphant. The possible complications of life—and none are impossible—translate themselves into plots for stories, in which it is remarkable with what disregard of their intelligence or merit the guileless are undone. Lovers—on whom James lavishes his manly tenderness—are separated by money or the lack of it; by misunderstanding or excessive insight; by secrets or revelations; by pride or humility. Free will makes the wrong choice in either case simply because it is will. It seemed so to James from the very beginning, * * * and this may be why even when he works in his most delicate impressionist manner, James is not afraid of crashing cymbals for the denouement. Daisy Miller dies; * * * the Pupil wastes away. * * * Strictly considered, all these deaths are unnecessary, implausible; but they are indispensable as a relief from and as sanctions for James's moral judgment, which is that the world is too full of desires and not sufficiently full of people in whom desire is purified by grace.

* * *

* * * James felt—and said—that he was basically and always a dramatist. He was twice lured into writing for the stage not simply for its rewards in money but because he sought the intensified effect of the play form—the short sharp conflict which must be made plain as it progresses and which must nonetheless be kept half-hidden to hold the feelings of wonder or horror in suspense. On these topics, both before and after his failure with the London managers and the London audience, James wrote much, in his letters as well as in his stories and prefaces. And this concern left a significant mark on all his later work. The observance of the "point of view" which he made into a dogma for the novelist, the building up of his novels and tales by scenes, the division of his characters into actors and narrators—all imply an adaptation of stage effects to printed fiction. Even the expansion of dialogue into something gigantic, searching, omniscient, does not contradict this tendency; Jamesian dialogue only expresses the conflict of wills more precisely than the crude traditional words associated with stock situations. The proof of this effectiveness is that such a reader as

1. Characters in James's *The Portrait of a Lady* and "The Patagonia." Newman is the hero of James's *The American*.

Mr. Maugham, even while he complains of James's "involuted style," feels himself pulled along by the strong current beneath.

Besides, in all the fiction of the later years, James made use of physical images and of vulgar colloquialisms for the special purpose of maintaining the intensity of his scenes at the requisite pitch. Only think how often his dialogue is buttressed by endless variants of the one metaphor: "she gave it to him full in the face"—"he braced himself to meet it"—and so down to the very nearly "pulp" level of "she let him have it." And action follows metaphor. How many readers, if asked to identify this bit of fiction would give James as its author:

> "Listen to me before you go. I will give you a life's devotion," the young man pleaded. He barred her way.
> "I shall never think of you—let me go!" she cried with passion.

This propensity toward violence, and even more this sense that violence is to be found even in casual utterance and gesture is of course by now good Freudian analysis. The "civilized" being, if he is also human, can always be caught off guard, and the conflicts that interest a dramatist are nothing but a succession of these moments. It is not necessary to add that James's "psychology" was not a doctrine learned and applied; it came out of his temperament and self-education. His readers have perhaps not sufficiently noticed how native to his character is the love of exaggeration. His reported speech is always a magnification of feeling—" 'COME!' " Henry James cried, raising his hands to Heaven. " 'I would walk across London with bare feet on the snow to meet George Santayana.[2] At what time? One thirty! I will come. At one thirty I shall inevitably, inexorably make my appearance!' " This was no isolated outburst. Most anecdotes of his apprehensions or predicaments, like his comments upon the feelings of his fictional heroes, are filled with "big," "dreadful," "hideous" or conversely, with "beautifully," "so admirably," "all too wonderfully."

With the exquisiteness of a Lilliputian, his sensorium yields Brobdingnagian[3] images. Occasionally one of these will rise to the height of genius, as when he greeted the recital of a friend's morning activities with the exclamation, "What a princely expenditure of time!"[4] But it also accounts for the appearance of pusillanimity for which he has been rather too easily ridiculed. He has been called snob and weakling because he seemed afraid of doing the wrong thing and of not having enough money; and his brother William has been shown off in contrast as a man who courageously breasted every adverse tide. This

2. U.S. poet, philosopher, and essayist (1863–1952), born in Spain.
3. The Lilliputians are the tiny human beings, the Brobdingnagians the giants in Swift's *Gulliver's Travels*.
4. The morning activities took place on the golf course and golfers will appreciate James's expert description of the scene: "Some beflagged jam pots . . . let into the soil at long but varying distances. A swoop, a swing, a flourish of steel, a dormy" (quoted in Simon Nowell-Smith, *The Legend of the Master*, p. 159).

is true of William, and Henry's apprehensions no doubt make rather unsatisfactory biographical matter. Yet I think the sense of threatening evil was not at bottom very different in the two brothers. William was a Manichean[5] whose courage, though real, was born of deep inner uncertainty—an irrepressible doubt which in its philosophic guise made him the critic of all dogmatic and optimistic certainties: nothing for him was ever finally won or held safe.

Henry, one feels, shared the same conviction, but was too intent on expressing it in fiction to devise a fighting strategy for his own personal use. This in itself was a form of courage. He spoke his fears and unlike some of his deeply mistaken devotees, never wished life secure. "Life," he said, "is far more interesting than its regularization," and he thought so well of it that he had the strength, at the age of seventy-two, to go, Whitman-like, among the wounded of the World War and reanimate their wish to live. One desperately mutilated man, it is recorded, he brought back when everyone else had failed.

This feat alone should help to correct the overwritten portrait which we owe to Edith Wharton and her kind, of a helpless, complicated, timorous great man. A better image—if we must put a pinch of derision into our mixture—is that of James coping with fire at Lamb House[6] in Rye. His own account is symbolic of the Manichean fight: he personifies the burning rafter: "We put him out, we made him stop, with soaked sponges—and then the relief: even while gazing at the hacked and smashed and disfigured floors." James goes to bed, well-pleased with his heroism, but the fire breaks out again, the professionals come and act, fortunately "without too much zeal," and after a sleepless night James signs himself to his correspondent "your startled but re-quieted and fully insured H. J."

To describe what personal influences played upon and shaped his sense of ever-present evil would be a study in itself. The "Small Boy" and other notes,[7] which give us, like William's earlier letters, glimpses of a retiring, impressionable youth overwhelmed by exceedingly bright and articulate relatives; the four years of war, experienced from afar but at the formative close of adolescence; the death of the fair cousin,[8] the peculiar patent ugliness of the American catch-as-catch-can, comparable to the more concealed cut-throat rivalries of literary Paris—these things among others seen by James before his thirtieth year must have corroborated his sense of the rawness of human passion and concentrated his mind on the problem, How to keep passion

5. Manichaeism is an ancient doctrine which asserts the independent existence of evil as well as good in the world.

6. From 1898 to his death James's principal residence, in the old village of Rye on the coast of Sussex.

7. The first volume of James's autobiography is entitled A *Small Boy and Others* (1913), the second volume *Notes of a Son and Brother* (1914).

8. Mary (Minny) Temple, who died at the age of twenty-five. James greatly admired her "divinely restless spirit," which is reflected in some of his young heroines.

natural and yet extinguish its harvest of evil.

For James is no ascetic, no admirer of tepid feeling, systematic constraint or dilettante refinements. He pillories Gilbert Osmond[9] for being such a dilettante and makes us love Isabel Archer for her moral spontaneity. We are made to share the zest with which she wants to taste life and even to admire Caspar Goodwood for the robustness of his desires, which embrace equally the possession of Isabel and of worldly goods. M. A. de Wolfe Howe[1] has also told us how on one occasion James passed judgment on the brownstone fronts of Boston by exclaiming, "Do you feel that Marlborough Street is—precisely— *passionate?*"

This acceptance of life *quand même*,[2] or even because of encompassing evil, James held to from the first. In a review of Dickens' *Our Mutual Friend*, written when he was twenty-two, James complains that "the friction of two *men*, of two characters, of two passions, produces stronger sparks than Wrayburn's boyish repartees and Headstone's melodramatic commonplaces." The review as a whole is less a balanced judgment on Dickens' masterpiece than a program for James's future fiction. The keynote, from the partial point of view I have adopted in these pages, is of course "melodramatic commonplaces." Finding new artistic forms to kindle into life by means of the sparks that conflicting passions strike was to be James's problem, and having succeeded in making them is his title to greatness.

In so doing he was not only expressing his own personal awareness of the vast dominions of human evil but performing a task assigned him by the literature of the 19th Century. He must criticize the melodrama that had become commonplace—in Dickens, in Balzac, in George Sand, in Victor Hugo. But contrary to a usual belief, James was not turning his back on their view of life, on their "exaggeration," on their "romanticism." James was not a "realist" in the meaning that Flaubert gave to the term: realism had been the first reaction to 19th Century romanticism. James came a full generation after Flaubert, whose artistic passion he admired more than its product, for the product was tame and, in the end, life-denying. Rather James went back, over the realists' heads, to the romanticists whom he wished to purge and renovate. His published criticism of that earlier generation is fundamentally sympathetic; and his opinion remarkably appreciative when it has to deal with a neo-romantic calling himself a naturalist in the person of Zola,[3] and even with a pastiche-romantic in the person of Robert Louis Stevenson. James's allegiance in fact never swerved from the master of them all, Balzac, in whom melodrama can be found at its most conscious, forthright, and moralistic; put there for

---

9. Gilbert Osmond, Isabel Archer, and Caspar Goodwood are characters in James's *The Portrait of a Lady.*
1. New England editor, poet, scholar (1864–

1960).
2. All the same, in spite of everything.
3. Émile Zola (1840–1902), French novelist.

the double purpose of nerving men to face life and of keeping the reader going.

F. O. MATTHIESSEN and KENNETH B. MURDOCK

[How His Ideas Came to Him]†

His ideas often came to him in the fashion described in his preface to *The Spoils of Poynton*, through a chance anecdote communicated by the lady to whom he sat next at some dinner. That would hardly seem a promising source for anything but the most superficial society fiction, and yet as we know, and as the notebooks reaffirm, James always stressed the importance of subject. When he felt some misgivings even about *The Altar of the Dead*, he reminded himself that "solidity of subject, importance, emotional capacity of subject, is the only thing on which, henceforth, it is of the slightest use for me to expend myself. Everything else breaks down, collapses, turns thin, turns poor, turns wretched—betrays one miserably. Only the fine, the large, the human, the natural, the fundamental, the passionate things." How he found such things while dining out may be attributed in part to some of the ladies whose names occur most often in his notes: to Thackeray's daughter, Mrs. Richmond Ritchie, and especially to Fanny Kemble,[1] who, thirty-five years James's senior, brought him into connection "with a thousand vanished and present things," and whose warm and eloquent talk, as he celebrated it in a memorial essay, "swarmed with people and with criticism of people, with the ghosts of a dead society. She had, in two hemispheres, seen everyone and known everyone, had assisted at the social comedy of her age."

But mainly, like all greatly perceptive artists, James took from these interlocutresses what he brought himself, as the opening of his preface to *The Spoils of Poynton* declares:

> It was years ago, I remember, one Christmas Eve when I was dining with friends: a lady beside me made in the course of talk one of those allusions that I have always found myself recognizing on the spot as "germs." The germ, wherever gathered, has ever been for me the germ of a "story," and most of the stories straining to shape under my hand have sprung from a single small seed, a seed as minute and wind-blown as that casual hint for *The Spoils of Poynton* dropped

† From *The Notebooks of Henry James*, edited by F. O. Matthiessen and Kenneth B. Murdock (New York: Oxford University Press, 1947), pp. xii–xiv.

1. Frances Anne Kemble (1809–93), a prominent British actress. James's essay on her is included in his *Essays in London and Elsewhere* (1893). [*Editor.*]

unwittingly by my neighbour, a mere floating particle in the stream of talk. What above all comes back to me with this reminiscence is the sense of the inveterate minuteness, on such happy occasions, of the precious particle—reduced, that is, to its mere fruitful essence. Such is the interesting truth about the stray suggestion, the wandering word, the vague echo, at touch of which the novelist's imagination winces as at the prick of some sharp point: its virtue is all in its needlelike quality, the power to penetrate as finely as possible. This fineness it is that communicates the virus of suggestion, anything more than the minimum of which spoils the operation. If one is given a hint at all designedly one is sure to be given too much; one's subject is in the merest grain, the speck of truth, of beauty, of reality, scarce visible to the common eye—since, I firmly hold, a good eye for a subject is anything but usual. Strange and attaching, certainly, the consistency with which the first thing to be done for the communicated and seized idea is to reduce almost to nought the form, the air as of a mere disjoined and lacerated lump of life, in which we may have happened to meet it. Life being all inclusion and confusion, and art being all discrimination and selection, the latter, in search of the hard latent *value* with which alone it is concerned, sniffs round the mass as instinctively and unerringly as a dog suspicious of some buried bone. The difference here, however, is that, while the dog desires his bone but to destroy it, the artist finds in *his* tiny nugget, washed free of awkward accretions and hammered into a sacred hardness, the very stuff for a clear affirmation, the happiest chance for the indestructible.

In a few cases James proceeded in the way habitual to Hawthorne, that is to say he started with an abstraction and sought an embodiment for it. "What is there," he asked himself, "in the idea of *Too late*—of some friendship or passion or bond—some affection long desired and waited for?" Meditation on this theme yielded both *The Friends of the Friends* and *The Beast in the Jungle*. Or, again, he began with "the notion of a young man (young, presumably) who has something—some secret sorrow, trouble, fault—to *tell* and can't find the *recipient*." Further reflection persuaded him that "there is probably something worth thinking of in the idea," but that "the thing needs working out—maturing." Not until fifteen years after his first entry on this theme did he devise the right chain of events for *A Round of Visits*.

In his more usual procedure some concrete incident appealed to him by the possibilities it offered for development. Sometimes he seems to have been attracted first by the formal neatness of a subject, by the chance it gave for an "intensely structural, intensely hinged and jointed preliminary frame," but as he worked he almost always clothed the bare bones of structure so that the final effect of the tale depended not on symmetrical construction but on the depiction of relations between characters or on the full presentation of an individual. * * * "Form," in the sense of ordered construction, was essential, but as a means not as an end. The end was the revelation of character.

Accordingly, most of the incidents that suggested stories to him did so because they offered material for portraits.

CHRISTOF WEGELIN

Revision and Style

In 1904 James visited the United States for the first time in some twenty years, and one of the results of that visit was an invitation from Scribner's to prepare a collected edition of his works. The so-called New York Edition—he named it in homage to his native city— appeared from 1907 to 1917, the last two volumes posthumously.[1] It contains about half of his fiction, laboriously revised and supplied with a set of prefaces. All through his career James revised a great deal, many of his stories several times. Most of them first appeared in magazines in America and England and were revised slightly when first incorporated in a book. When a story was reprinted in a subsequent collection James repeated the process. But in the New York Edition he made a great many changes, particularly in his early stories.

"The Madonna of the Future," for instance, supplies the following statistics: Between its first appearance in the *Atlantic Monthly* in 1873 and its inclusion in James's first collection in 1875, the first eight paragraphs contained five minor changes of diction or grammar, but between the *Atlantic* and the New York Edition fifty-one, that is, ten times as many, and several of greater substance. (If the count includes changes in punctuation and spelling, contractions and italics, the respective figures are thirteen and ninety-nine.)

James intended the New York Edition to represent his life's work in a carefully reasoned selection and arrangement, distantly modelled on the *Comédie Humaine* of Balzac, the French novelist whom he admired more than any other. He therefore included only what he could still approve or make acceptable, and revising now meant not just mending and polishing but re-imagining, re-seeing his material. This is no doubt why the prefaces so often recall the first germs of the stories and the occasions which supplied them. He was returning to the source, remembering the places—cities, houses, streetcars,

1. *The Novels and Tales of Henry James*, 26 vols. (New York: Scribner's, 1907–17). The last two volumes, published posthumously, contain two novels (*The Ivory Tower* and *The Sense of the Past*) unfinished when James died in 1916. The prefaces were later collected in one volume and supplied with an analytical introduction by Richard P. Blackmur (New York and London: Scribner's, 1934). This volume has been reissued frequently.

436 • Christof Wegelin

trains—where he first observed a human situation, conceived an idea, or heard an anecdote later explored and developed, and sometimes discarded. In the preface to *The Golden Bowl* he speaks at some length of the process of revision. As he reread his *later* stories, he says, he found that his sensibility as a reader fitted the sensibility of the author without effort. But in rereading his *early* stories he realized that intervening years and decades had made a different man of him, had modified his sensibility profoundly. Revising his early work, therefore, became a process of reassessing the old "matter" and of registering the result of these "renewals of vision." And that meant changes much more extensive than those he made in his later works.

It is only in recent years that James's revisions have attracted much critical attention. The publication of the New York Edition had produced some protests against his "late manner," but up to the centennial of his birth in 1943 his revisions had remained largely unexplored. In 1944 F. O. Matthiessen published a detailed study of those of *The Portrait of a Lady*, and since then more such studies have appeared, including a number of doctoral dissertations. The most thoroughly revised piece in the New York Edition is the early novel *The American*; its revisions have also been among those most studied. In recent years the analysis of James's late style has profited from the comparison of early and revised texts. Not everyone approves of James's late manner; some prefer the greater simplicity of the early works, their sharp images of men and manners, to the internalized "impressionism" of the late. The novelist's brother William, for one, took this view.

One may well ask what caused the remarkable change in James's style. No doubt his new manner of composing by dictation instead of in longhand had something to do with it, as Theodora Bosanquet, who was his secretary during the years of the New York Edition, suggested in *Henry James at Work*. The novelist Robert Herrick once reported that when he told James that he must have started to dictate in the middle of *The Princess Casamassima*, James confirmed the truth of the guess by his startled question, "How did you know that?" Because, Herrick answered, "that is when your style began to change." Dictating may have helped to form James's late style because it involved repeated revisions of a series of typescripts. Edel has called it a "revised" style, shaped by a "process of accretion" which opened the door to elaboration and mannerisms. But if its sentences appear more complicated, if they seem to be made diffuse by an invasion of parenthetical clauses and phrases, for instance, upon examination they often turn out to be like "free, involved, unanswered talk." This is how Theodora Bosanquet described them, who remembered the dictating voice. Indeed, the oral cadences of the late style often appear in being read aloud. But it must of course be remembered that if James wrote as he talked, his talk was Jamesian.

A number of the routine changes in the New York Edition are in harmony with the oral quality, among them the simplified punctuation (James deletes many commas and semicolons, for instance) and the contractions ("I've" for "I have," "thing's" for "thing is," "wasn't" for "was not," etc.). Other changes, like the anglicized spelling, are part of James's late linguistic habits. Many changes in diction achieve greater precision or eliminate dead wood; some (perhaps to help monolingual Anglo-Saxons) eliminate foreign, especially French, expressions although, at the same time, the late style contains a sprinkling of gallicisms. Indeed, some changes are simply mannerisms. Most notorious among them is the combination of elegant variations on verbs of saying with the inversion of the customary order of adverb following verb. "Daisy Miller" supplies the following examples: "said her mother" is changed into "she then quite colorlessly remarked"—a needless elaboration since the tone of Mrs. Miller's speech is self-evident; similarly the original "said Miss Miller" turns into "she beautifully answered"—and again the revision adds nothing except what may be called the narrator's approval, which is neither functional nor appropriate. Such examples of James's ingenuity in inventing substitutes for the simple "she said," "he replied" could be multiplied many times. The inversion of the word order is the more striking since it draws the emphasis away from the strenuous adverbs and places it on the often quite colorless verbs. These and other changes in diction which appear in the New York Edition are difficult to account for except as what may be called James's stylistic signature—his "verbal tics," as one critic called them.

Many routine changes in the New York Edition are syntactical and achieve a logical tightening of the sentence structure through increased subordination. In contrast to the simplified punctuation, to the contractions, and to the occasional introduction of colloquialisms, the changes in syntax often go in the direction of greater formality, as when "he stopped short, and eyed me" turns into "he stopped short, eyeing me." This is from "The Madonna of the Future," an early story,[2] where James seems to have made such changes systematically, they are so frequent. When he made them in passages of conversation, the original version may be more appropriate just *because* it is more colloquial. The grammatical subordination in the revised "I've known a poor fellow who painted his one masterpiece,

2. First published in *The Atlantic Monthly* of March 1873. A letter of February 1, 1873, from James in Rome to his father reveals that William Dean Howells, the *Atlantic* editor, requested revisions of certain "immoral" episodes. James thought that "such a standard of propriety" made "a bad outlook ahead for imaginative writing"; but he was "much obliged to [Howells] for performing the excision personally, for of course he will have done it neatly." This was probably the first, though not the last, time moral objections were made to James's fiction; but it may have been the only time he was actually censored.

and who didn't even paint that" is perhaps logically tighter, but the original coordination in "I've known a poor fellow who painted his one masterpiece, and he didn't even paint that" is more in keeping with the tone of conversational narrative as well as being more emphatic.

Other changes seem to owe something to James's re-exposure to the American scene late in his life. Occasionally he introduced into the speech of American characters idioms which struck him as typical of American lingo ("kind of," "cute," etc.) or added details which reflect his critical detachment from certain American social phenomena. In "An International Episode," for instance, the boat between New York and Newport is originally described as "an extrodinary mixture of a ship and an hotel," but in the New York Edition it has become "a semi-submerged Kindergarten." Here James seems to be alluding to the democratic homogeneity of American society which admits children everywhere. When he first wrote the story he still took such things too much for granted to mention them. Several late stories, like "The Jolly Corner," suggest ruthlessness in business; and the "awful game of grab," as he came to call it, seems to have thrown its shadow over some earlier portrayals of the scene when he came to revise them. The American Mr. Westgate of "An International Episode" originally speaks in a "slow, humorous voice, with a distinctness of utterance which appeared to his visitors to be part of a humorous intention—a strangely leisurely, speculative voice for a man evidently so busy and, as they felt, so professional." In revision all of this is replaced by "with his face of toil, his voice of leisure and his general intention, apparently, of everything." An individualized sketch, the positive impression two characters have of a third, here becomes less detailed, less concrete, and more vaguely suggestive of a national type, the energetic American entrepreneur of the 1870s now faintly tinged by the ominous implications of the Gilded Age.

Other revisions sharpen original thematic elements rather than qualifying or modifying them. Striking examples occur in *The American*, a novel almost contemporary with "An International Episode." Christopher Newman, its hero, may be the same general type as the original Westgate, but not as the revised. Newman started out as a representative American idealized, and in revision James reenforced his idealization. Originally described as "a *noble* fellow," he turns into "one of nature's noblemen"—the phrase is a cliché of nineteenth-century American social thought; originally calling himself "highly civilized," in the New York Edition he orates, "I have the instincts— have them deeply—if I haven't the forms of a high old civilization." This may be pompous, but it puts a kind of official seal on his representative role: his nobility is a matter of character, not of social rank; what is "civilized" about him are his innate impulses, not his acquired social forms. Some thirty years after the original conception James recognized and emphasized the traditional American idea underlying Newman's character and related it to the more general contrast between American nature and European civilization.

Some of the revisions of "Daisy Miller" strive for the same effect. James adds in the New York Edition, for instance, that Daisy's manner of conversing was "the result of her having no idea whatever of form (with such a telltale appendage as Randolph where in the world would she have got it?)" A little later, when Daisy tells Winterbourne that Randolph doesn't like Europe, James adds in revision a reference to her "artless instinct for truth," while Winterbourne himself has just been made to proceed "artfully." In revision Daisy becomes "the child of nature," and every now and then James introduces nature images into her presentation, as when her expression is said to be "as decidedly limpid as the very cleanest water." This makes her perhaps more attractive but certainly more representative of the socially unsophisticated New World. In another revealing change she has no longer "the *tournure* of a princess" but simply "natural elegance." The original wording associated her with nature's nobility, but in James's later view, as the preface bears out, her character is less exalted. Still, her newly emphasized association with nature's ways reinforces the ethical implications of the satire. Another change bears on the theme of American snobbery abroad. In the passage beginning originally "Winterbourne perceived at some distance a little man . . ." (see p. 31 above), the New York Edition turns the little man Giovanelli first into a *figure* and then into a *thing*, and the personal pronouns referring to him from *he* into *it*. Here is the revised version:

> Winterbourne descried hereupon at some distance a little figure that stood with folded arms and nursing its cane. It had a handsome face, a hat artfully poised, a glass in one eye and a nosegay in its button-hole. Daisy's friend looked at it a moment and then said: "Do you mean to speak to that thing?"

The point of the revision is not so much to strip the Italian of his dignity, as one critic believed, as it is to emphasize Winterbourne's muddlement. It is Winterbourne who sees Giovanelli as a thing; to us James finally reveals the Italian as the only one, ironically, who has recognized Daisy's American innocence. These particular changes thus not only underline a commonplace of his international subject but also promote what perhaps most distinguishes his late fiction: the focus on consciousness and its role in human relationships.

Human consciousness, first as a technical device, then as a subject, absorbed James more and more as time went on. He had begun as a chronicler of manners; he had observed and recorded how men and women behaved in society, in various societies; but in his later years he

was concerned increasingly with inner drama, with "spiritual manners," as an early critic put it, with states of feeling and the general
nature of existence rather than with specific problems of conduct. The
realist turned symbolist, almost romancer in Hawthorne's sense of the
term, concerned not with reporting everyday externals accurately but
with the "truth of the human heart." Even his titles occasionally
suggest this change: "Daisy Miller," "An International Episode,"
"The Madonna of the Future," announce flesh-and-blood characters
or specific external circumstances, even material objects: "The Beast
in the Jungle" refers to a central symbol (as do *The Wings of the Dove*
and the *The Golden Bowl*). Dorothea Krook has summarized certain
principles which underlie these late stories:

> That art concerns itself to render the world of appearances; that
> these appearances exist only in the consciousness, indeed are the
> content of the consciousness, of human observers; that the world of
> art therefore is a beautiful representation of the appearances present
> to a particular consciousness under particular conditions, and the
> artist's overriding task is accordingly to exhibit in the concrete, with
> the greatest possible completeness and consistency, as well as vivid-
> ness and intensity, the particular world of appearances accessible to
> a particular consciousness under the specific conditions created for
> it by the artist: these are the elements of James's theory of art.

These principles account for what has been called the abstraction or
the intangibility of James's late style. In recent years this style has
undergone a number of linguistic analyses, which have discovered the
grammatical means by which the focus on feeling is sharpened. In his
pioneering examination of the first paragraph of *The Ambassadors* Ian
Watt has shown that physical events tend to be subordinated grammat-
ically, that grammatical subjects "are often nouns referring to mental
ideas" and that verbs "tend to express states of being rather than
particular finite actions affecting objects." More recently Seymour
Chatman has enlarged the linguistic analysis of James's late style and
compared certain aspects statistically to the styles of writers contemporary with him (Gissing, Butler, Conrad, Forster).[3] He concludes
that in late James many more grammatical subjects are intangible or
abstract nouns than in the others, that in late James intangible grammatical subjects in fact outnumber tangible ones while in the other
authors "the reverse is true." Words for "thing-perceived" like *indications, sign, view*, dot James's pages and "the human perceiver is
regularly object rather than subject" since "James is less concerned
with the things of the world than with the view of those things that

3. George Robert Gissing (1857–1902), (1857–1924), Edward Morgan Forster (1879–
Samuel Butler (1835–1902), Joseph Conrad 1970) are all British novelists.

characters have and the meanings that are thus registered in their minds."[4]

This "growing preference for abstract over human subjects" also enters James's revisions, which often replace personal grammatical subjects with abstract ones. Chatman gives a number of examples from *Roderick Hudson*. Here are some illustrations from the early "Madonna of the Future" and from two stories in this collection, "Daisy Miller," and "An International Episode," in that order. The original versions were published in the 1870s, the revised in 1909:

First Version	*New York Edition*
I had been afraid that . . .	My fear had been that . . .
Daisy had entered upon a lively conversation with her hostess . . .	As Daisy's conversation with her hostess still occupied her . . .
He was a man of conscience . . .	His conception of certain special duties and decencies . . . was strong . . .

In these examples personal subjects (I, Daisy, He) are replaced with intangible ones (fear, conversation, conception) and similar changes occur in other grammatical functions:

First Version	*New York Edition*
. . . tapping her forehead with the gesture she had used a minute before . . .	. . . repeating the vivid reference to the contents of our poor friend's head . . .
. . . looking with a pale grave face . . .	. . . looking with a small white prettiness . . .
What she said aloud was . . .	. . . the form she gave her doubt was . . .

The cumulative effect of such changes is to internalize the presentation, to replace the reality of things with their appearances.

Like his later works, the revisions of the early ones tended to increase the emphasis on the inner life of his characters though sometimes at some cost to consistency. Here and there, the taste of the reviser or his "active sense of life" seems to have interfered with the original conception. But it would be foolish to deny that whether in

---

4. Opening sentences of novels may be revealing too, Chatman points out. James's *The Ambassadors*, for instance, begins with "Strether's question" (not with "Strether"); Gissing's *Veranilda* begins with "armies," Butler's *The Way of All Flesh* with "I," Conrad's *Typhoon* with "Captain MacWhirr," Forster's *Where Angels Fear to Tread* with a human "they."

general we approve or disapprove of James's revisions is partly a matter of our taste, like the preference for early James or late.

PHILIP RAHV

Daisy Miller†

Daisy Miller, the pretty girl from Schenectady who defies European conventions and dies of the Roman fever and a broken heart, is the only one of Henry James's characters to have achieved national renown. For that there is reason enough. Daisy embodies the spirit of her country in a more direct and simple manner than any of her sisters in the Jamesian gallery of native types. And no one has ever offered a better explanation of her great popularity than Edmund Wilson when he said that it is due to the impression somehow conveyed by her creator that "her spirit went marching on."[1]

It should be recalled that originally the story of Daisy Miller was considered by a good many patriots to be a disloyal criticism of American manners and an outrage on American girlhood. Rejected on some such grounds by an editor in Philadelphia, it was first published in England, in *The Cornhill Magazine* (1878). But before long America reclaimed its own, for Daisy was destined to be enshrined in the national pantheon. Not long after her author's death, William Dean Howells wrote in a preface to a new edition of the story that "never was any civilization offered a more precious tribute than that which a great artist paid ours in the character of Daisy Miller." Thus through her phenomenal rise in public favor she finally received what amounted to almost official recognition.

The principal quality of this famous heroine is her spontaneity—a quality retained by her successors in James's novels and stories and invariably rendered as beautifully illustrative of the vigor and innocence of life in the western world. In picturing Daisy, James was mostly concerned with exhibiting her "inscrutable combination of audacity and innocence," for that was the essential characteristic making possible her entry into literature as an altogether new type. Before James no such light had ever been thrown on the character of the American young lady; in Hawthorne, for instance, boldness in the feminine nature is simply the equivalent of badness, and his "good" young ladies (e.g. Priscilla in *The Blithedale Romance* and Hilda in *The Marble Faun*) have literally nothing but their innocence to

---

†From *The Great Short Novels of Henry James*, ed. Philip Rahv (New York: Dial Press, 1944), pp. 87–88.

1. Edmund Wilson, "The Ambiguity of Henry James," in *The Triple Thinkers* (New York, 1938), reprinted in *The Question of Henry James*, ed. F.W. Dupee (New York, 1945), p. 176. [Editor.]

recommend them. In the observation of his compatriots at home and abroad, James, however, was able to bring to bear the new method of realism absorbed in his study of writers like Balzac, Thackeray, Turgenev and Flaubert. As character creation Daisy is a triumph of the novelist's faculty at work on materials drawn directly from experience. It is interesting, too, to trace the lines of force that radiate from this early Jamesian heroine to later heroines of American fiction. One example that may be cited is Scott Fitzgerald's Daisy in *The Great Gatsby*, who has quite a few features in common with her namesake. And the continuity is primarily of the national experience rather than of literary influence.

One cannot say, however, that in the main it is the quantity of "real life" in Daisy Miller which accounts for her vitality. The mere imitation of life has seldom produced great results in a work of art. The truth is that Daisy—as her author once observed—is at one and the same time a typical little figure and a piece of pure poetry. That is the real secret of her lasting charm—the charm of "a child of nature and of freedom."

CAROL OHMANN

Daisy Miller: A Study of Changing Intentions†

Henry James's most popular nouvelle seems to have owed its initial prominence as much to the controversy it provoked as to the artistry it displayed. *Daisy Miller* caused a bitter dispute in the customarily urbane dining room of Mrs. Lynn Linton;[1] it gave American writers of etiquette a satisfying opportunity to chastise native mothers and daughters (Daisy should have had a chaperone; dear reader, take heed);[2] it brought Henry James himself, while he sat in the confines of a Venetial gondola, a round scolding from a highly articulate woman of the cosmopolitan world. The causes of argument, of course, were the character of James's heroine and the judgment her creator made of her. In late Victorian eyes, Daisy was likely to be either wholly innocent or guilty; James, either all for her or against her.

Today, Daisy's notoriety attends her only in her fictional world. We take her now as one of our familiars; we invoke her, in the assurance that she will come and be recognized, as an American figure both vital and prototypical. Thus Ihab Hassan, for example, joins her in his

†From *American Literature* XXXVI (March 1964), pp. 1–11.

1. B. R. McElderry, Jr., "The 'Shy Incongruous Charm' of 'Daisy Miller,'" *Nineteenth-Century Fiction*, X, 163–164 (Sept., 1955).

[Cf. pp. 383–385 above—*Editor.*]
2. Elizabeth F. Hoxie discusses the use writers of etiquette made of James's nouvelle in "Mrs. Grundy Adopts Daisy Miller," *New England Quarterly*, XIX, 474–484 (Dec., 1946).

444 • Carol Ohmann

Radical Innocence with Twain's Huck Finn and Crane's Henry Fleming, and notes that all three are young protagonists faced with "the first existential ordeal, crisis, or encounter with experience."[3] Taking Daisy with appreciation and without alarm, we also re-read her character and re-evaluate her moral status. We seem to meet James's sophistication with our own, by agreeing on a mixed interpretation of Daisy: she is literally innocent, but she is also ignorant and incautious. Or, as F. W. Dupee writes, and his view meets with considerable agreement elsewhere in our criticism, "[Daisy] does what she likes because she hardly knows what else to do. Her will is at once strong and weak by reason of the very indistinctness of her general aims."[4]

Our near consensus of opinion on *Daisy Miller* seems to me largely correct. I certainly do not want to dismiss it, although I do wish to elaborate upon it and ground it in Jamesian text and method. At the same time, however, I wish to suggest that our very judiciousness is supported by only part of James's nouvelle and that other parts, certain scenes in Rome, really call for franker and more intense alignments of both sympathy and judgment. In a sense, the early and extreme reactions to Daisy were adequate responses to James's creation. Whether black or white, these responses did at least perceive that the final issue of the nouvelle was a matter of total commitment. In short, I think James began writing with one attitude toward his heroine and concluded with a second and different attitude toward her.

I

James begins his nouvelle by building a dramatic, and largely comic, contrast between two ways of responding to experience—a contrast at once suggested by the first-person narrator in the opening paragraph:

in the month of June, American travellers are extremely numerous; it may be said, indeed, that Vevey assumes at this period some of the characteristics of an American watering-place. There are sights and sounds which evoke a vision, an echo, of Newport and Saratoga. There is a flitting hither and thither of "stylish" young girls, a rustling of muslin flounces, a rattle of dance-music in the morning hours, a sound of high-pitched voices at all times. You receive an impression of these things at the excellent inn of the "Trois Couronnes," and are transported in fancy to the Ocean House or to Congress Hall. But at the "Trois Couronnes," it must be added,

3. Princeton, 1961, p. 41.

4. *Henry James: His Life and Writings* (New York, 1956), p. 95. References to James's qualified approval of his heroine also appear in the following studies: Osborn Andreas, *Henry James and the Expanding Horizon* (Seattle, 1948); Peter Buitenhuis, "From *Daisy Miller* to *Julia Bride*: 'A Whole Passage of Intellectual History,'" *American Quarterly*, XI, 136–146 (Summer, 1959); Leon Edel, *Henry James*, Vol. II: *The Conquest of London, 1870–1881* (Philadelphia and New York, 1962); Charles G. Hoffman, *The Short Novels of Henry James* (New York, 1957); Joseph A. Ward, *The Imagination of Disaster: Evil in the Fiction of Henry James* (Lincoln, Neb., 1961).

there are other features that are much at variance with these suggestions: neat German waiters, who look like secretaries of legation; Russian princesses sitting in the garden; little Polish boys walking about, held by the hand, with their governors. . . .[5]

The carefree exuberance, the noisy frivolity, of the American visitors is set against the quiet formality and restraint of the Europeans, who hold even their little boys in check.

James repeats his opening contrast in virtually every piece of dialogue that follows. While the hero Frederick Winterbourne is an American by birth, he has lived "a long time" in Geneva, the "little metropolis of Calvinism," the "dark old city at the other end of the lake." And Winterbourne's mode of speech suggests the extent to which he has become Europeanized. In Vevey, he finds himself "at liberty," on a little holiday from Geneva. He takes a daring plunge into experience; with no more than a very casual introduction from her little brother Randolph, he speaks to Daisy Miller.[6] "This little boy and I have made acquaintance," he says. Daisy glances at him and turns away. In a moment, Winterbourne tries again. "Are you going to Italy?" he asks. Daisy says, "Yes, sir," and no more. "Are you—a—going over the Simplon?" Winterbourne continues. Shortly afterwards, as Daisy continues to ignore him, Winterbourne "risk[s] an observation upon the beauty of the view." Winterbourne's feelings of "liberty" and of "risk" and, later, of "audacity" become ironic in conjunction with his speech. For all his holiday spirit, his language is studiously formal, his opening conversational bits, unimaginative and conventional.

In opposition to Winterbourne, Daisy often speaks in the language of extravagant, if unoriginal, enthusiasm. In her opinion, Europe is "perfectly sweet. . . . She had ever so many intimate friends that had been there ever so many times. . . . she had had ever so many dresses and things from Paris." She wants to go to the Castle of Chillon "dreadfully." Or, unlike Winterbourne again, Daisy speaks in an idiom that is homely and matter-of-fact. When Winterbourne asks, "Your brother is not interested in ancient monuments?" she rejects his formal phrasing and says simply, '[Randolph] says he don't care much about old castles."

For all their differences, Winterbourne and Daisy may still be capable of *rapprochement*. Toward the end of Part I, Daisy teases Winterbourne out of his formality and makes him, for a moment, speak her language—makes him, for a moment, express himself

---

5. This quotation, and unless otherwise noted every one subsequent, appears in the original version, "Daisy Miller: A Study," *Cornhill Magazine*, XXXVII, 678–698 (June, 1878) and XXXVIII, 44–67 (July, 1878).

6. James W. Gargano ("*Daisy Miller*: An Abortive Quest for Innocence," *South Atlantic Quarterly*, LIX, 114–120, Winter, 1960) also notes that Winterbourne's association with Daisy represents an adventure, a departure from convention, for him.

enthusiastically. "Do, then, let me give you a row," Winterbourne says. Daisy replies, "It's quite lovely, the way you say that!" And Winterbourne answers, "It will be still more lovely to do it." Winterbourne is, and Daisy notices this, a "mixture." He is not quite, or at least not yet, thoroughly Europeanized.

Winterbourne may be influenced by Daisy, but he is also subject to the sway of his aunt. Mrs. Costello is a woman of few words. When Winterbourne asks her, in Vevey, if she has observed Mrs. Miller, Daisy, and Randolph, she raps out the reply: "Oh, yes, I have observed them. Seen them—heard them—and kept out of their way." Epigram is Mrs. Costello's favorite way of speaking and perfectly expresses the inflexibility of her approach to experience. Her principles of value have long been set—she need only apply them. Whatever is vulgar, whatever is improper, she condemns out of hand, and shuns. Sage and spokesman of the American set abroad, she guards a *style* of life and reveals its furthest limit of permissible emotion by exclaiming, "I am an old woman, but I am not too old—thank Heaven—to be shocked!"

The opening, then, and indeed the chief focus of *Daisy Miller* is a comic portrayal of different ways of living, different manners. In the social settings with which they are identified, in the ways they speak, as well as in what they say, the various characters range themselves along an axis that runs from the natural to the cultivated, from the exuberant to the restrained.

In the conflict between Geneva and Schenectady, there is, I think, little doubt of the direction James gives our sympathies. Presented with the collision between the artificial and the natural, the restrained and the free, we side emotionally with Daisy. We sympathize with Winterbourne, too, to the extent that he seems capable of coming "alive" and to the extent that he speaks up in favor of Daisy to Mrs. Costello in Vevey and, later, in Rome, to Mrs. Costello and also to Mrs. Walker, another American who has lived in Geneva. For the rest, however, our emotional alliance with Winterbourne is disturbed or interrupted by his Genevan penchant for criticism.[7] At his first meeting with Daisy in Vevey, Winterbourne mentally accuses her— "very forgivingly—of a want of finish." But when Daisy blithely announces that she has always had "a great deal of gentlemen's society," Winterbourne is more alarmed. He wonders if he must accuse her of "actual or potential *inconduite*, as they said at Geneva."

In Rome, although Winterbourne defends Daisy to the American colony publicly, he is, privately, increasingly shocked by her friend-

7. For the most part, of course, we see the action through Winterbourne's eyes. This is not to say, though, that we see no more than Winterbourne sees. He is a central intelligence who is less or more trustworthy—according to the judgments he makes at each particular moment.

ship with the "third-rate" Italian Giovanelli. Her walks with Giovanelli, her rides with Giovanelli, her tête-à-têtes in her own drawing
room with Giovanelli—all worry Winterbourne. He imitates Mrs.
Walker in scolding Daisy. And so he removes himself farther and
father from her. When he finally comes upon her with Giovanelli in
the colosseum at night, he thinks that she has certainly compromised
herself. And he is relieved. For his personal feelings for Daisy have
gradually been overwhelmed by his intellectual involvement in the
problem of Daisy. He is relieved and "exhilarated" that the "riddle"
has suddenly become "easy to read." He promptly judges Daisy by her
manners—as Mrs. Costello and Mrs. Walker have already done—and
condemns her. "What a clever little reprobate she was," he thinks,
"and how smartly she played at injured innocence!"

He learns otherwise too late. He knows, for a moment at the end of
the nouvelle, that he has made a mistake; he knows he has wronged
Daisy because he has stayed too long abroad, has become too rigid in
his values. Yet his knowledge does not change him. The authorial
voice concludes the tale by mocking Winterbourne's return to the
narrow social code of restraint and prejudice:

> Nevertheless, he went back to live at Geneva, whence there
> continue to come the most contradictory accounts of his motives
> of sojourn: a report that he is "studying" hard—an intimation
> that he is much interested in a very clever foreign lady.

Like so many Jamesian heroes, Winterbourne has lost the capacity for
love, and he has lost the opportunity to come to life.

As Winterbourne judges Daisy, judges her unfairly, and completes
her expulsion from the American set in Rome, our sympathy for her
naturally increases. But I think James does not—save through a
certain pattern of symbolic imagery to which I wish to return in a
moment—guide us to any such simple intellectual alignment with his
American heroine.

Daisy's sensibility has very obvious limitations, limitations we hear
very clearly in the statement that Europe is "perfectly sweet." Daisy is
more intensely alive than anyone else we meet in Vevey or Rome. But
James hints from time to time at a possible richness of aesthetic
experience that is beyond Daisy's capabilities—a richness that would
include an appreciation of the artificial, or the cultivated, not as it is
represented by the mores of Geneva but by the "splendid chants and
organ-tones" of St. Peter's and by the "superb portrait of Innocent X.
by Velasquez."

And Daisy has other limitations. The members of the American
community abroad are very much aware of one another's existence.
True, they use their mutual awareness to no good purpose—they are
watchbirds watching one another for vulgarity, for any possible lapse

from propriety. But Daisy's social awareness is so primitive as scarcely to exist. At Rome, in the Colosseum, Winterbourne's imagination cannot stretch to include the notion of unsophisticated innocence. But neither can Daisy's imagination stretch to include the idea that manners really matter to those who practice them. She never realizes the consternation she causes in Rome. "I don't believe it," she says to Winterbourne. "They are only pretending to be shocked." Her blindness to the nature of the American colony is equalled by her blindness to Winterbourne and Giovanelli as individuals. While Winterbourne fails to "read" her "riddle" rightly, she fails to "read" his. She feels his disapproval in Rome, but she is not aware of his affection for her. Neither does she reveal any adequate perception of her impact on Giovanelli. To Daisy, going about with Mr. Giovanelli is very good fun. Giovanelli's feelings, we learn at the end, have been much more seriously involved.

James therefore hands a really favorable intellectual judgment to neither Geneva nor Schenectady. He gives his full approval neither to the manners of restraint nor to those of freedom. His irony touches Daisy as well as the Europeanized Americans. And the accumulation of his specific ironies hints at an ideal of freedom and of vitality and also of aesthetic and social awareness that is nowhere fully exemplified in the nouvelle. To be from Schenectady, to be from the new world, is to be free from the restrictions of Geneva. But merely to be free is not enough.

II

Such, then, in some detail are the Jamesian dynamics of social contrast that give us our prudent estimate of Daisy—a heroine innocent and exuberant and free, but also unreflective and insensible of the world around her. But, as I have already suggested, this estimate does not receive support from the whole of the story. To begin with, prudence leads straight to the conclusion that Daisy dies as a result of social indiscretion. What began as a comedy of manners, ends in the pathos, if not the tragedy, of a lonely Roman deathbed and burial. And there is, it seems to me, in this progress from the Trois Couronnes to the Protestant cemetery a change in tone so pronounced, a breach in cause and appropriate effect so wide, as to amount to a puzzling disruption of James's artistry.

To be sure, James tries to make Daisy's death inevitable, and to make it so within, as it were, the boundaries of his comedy of manners. Early in Part II, at Mrs. Walker's late one afternoon, Daisy remarks that she is going to take a walk on the Pincian Hill with Giovanelli. Mrs. Walker tries to dissuade her from the impropriety—a walk at such a time in such a place with such a dubious companion. It isn't "safe," Mrs. Walker says, while Mrs. Miller adds, "You'll get the fever as sure as you live." And Daisy herself, as she walks towards the Pincian Hill with Winterbourne, alludes to the fever: "We are going to stay [in Rome] all winter—if we don't die of the fever; and I guess we'll stay then."

With these remarks, James foreshadows Daisy's death, and links her fate with her carelessness of the manners of restraint. But these preparations do not successfully solve his difficulties either of tone or of cause and effect. They croak disaster far too loudly, far too obviously, and, still, the punishment no more fits the crime than it does in a typical cautionary tale.

In Part I, James has already used the words "natural," "uncultivated," and "fresh" to describe his heroine. And in the choice of the name, Daisy, he may have suggested her simplicity and her spontaneous beauty. In Part II, just after the opening scene at Mrs. Walker's, James follows up the implications of these epithets—"natural," "uncultivated," "fresh"—and of the name Daisy and gives them a somewhat different significance.

In Rome, after Winterbourne has been taken up in Mrs. Walker's carriage and set down again, he sees Daisy with Giovanelli in a natural setting—a setting that James describes in brilliant and expansive terms. Daisy and Giovanelli are in the Pincian Garden overlooking the Villa Borghese:

> They evidently saw no one; they were too deeply occupied with each other. When they reached the low garden-wall they stood a moment looking off at the great flat-topped pine-clusters of the Villa Borghese; then Giovanelli seated himself, familiarly, upon the broad ledge of the wall. The western sun in the opposite sky sent out a brilliant shaft through a couple of cloud-bars, whereupon Daisy's companion took her parasol out of her hands and opened it. She came a little nearer and he held the parasol over her; then, still holding it, he let it rest upon her shoulder, so that both of their heads were hidden from Winterbourne. This young man lingered a moment, then he began to walk. But he walked—not towards the couple with the parasol; towards the residence of his aunt, Mrs. Costello.

This scene links Daisy with the natural world, and links her with that world more closely than any other scene James has so far given us. And it suggests that the distance between Winterbourne and Daisy is greater even than the distance that separates artificial from natural manners, greater than the distance that separates restraint from free self-expression.

That suggestion becomes a certainty on the Palatine Hill:

> A few days after his brief interview with her mother, [Winterbourne] encountered her in that beautiful abode of flowering desolation known as the Palace of the Cæsars. The early Roman

spring had filled the air with bloom and perfume, and the rugged surface of the Palatine was muffled with tender verdure. Daisy was strolling along the top of one of those great mounds of ruin that are embanked with mossy marble and paved with monumental inscriptions. It seemed to him that Rome had never been so lovely as just then. He stood looking off at the enchanting harmony of line and colour that remotely encircles the city, inhaling the softly humid odours and feeling the freshness of the year and the antiquity of the place reaffirm themselves in mysterious interfusion. It seemed to him also that Daisy had never looked so pretty; but this had been an observation of his whenever he met her. Giovanelli was at her side, and Giovanelli, too, wore an aspect of even unwonted brilliancy.

Here Daisy is not identified with a particular society, as she was with the gay American visitors by the lakeside and in the garden of Vevey, but simply and wholly with the natural world, which has its own eternal and beautiful rhythms. Birth is followed by death, and death is followed again by birth. And the beauty of the natural world—the world to which Daisy belongs—is supreme. Rome has never been so lovely as when its relics are "muffled with tender verdure." The monuments of men, the achievements of civilization, are most beautiful when they are swept again into the round of natural process. At the moment, Daisy seems to share the natural world, as she did in the Pincian Garden, with Giovanelli. But at the end of the nouvelle that "subtle Roman" is quite aware of Daisy's distance even from himself. He knew, beforehand, that the Colosseum would not be for him, as it was for Daisy, a "fatal place." "For myself," he says to Winterbourne, "I had no fear."

Once Daisy is identified with the world of nature, we see that she is subject to its laws of process. Her very beauty becomes a reminder of her mortality. So the scene on the Palatine (unlike the scenes at Mrs. Walker's and on the way to the Pincian Hill) does prepare us effectively for Daisy's burial in the Protestant cemetery; it does convince us that her death is inevitable.

III

Yet James's use of his symbolic natural imagery is at once a gain and a loss. If it solves, almost at the eleventh hour, certain difficulties of tone and of cause and effect regarding Daisy's death, it also leaves us with some permanent breaks in the nouvelle's unity of structure. If Daisy is translated or transfigured in the end into a purely natural ideal of beauty and vitality and innocence, then what relevance has that ideal to Schenectady, or to Geneva? If Daisy's death is "fated," does it matter at all what Winterbourne does? And what sort of agent is Giovanelli? Or can we even call him an agent? Hasn't James made inconsequent by the end of his tale, the dramatic conflict—the conflict between two kinds of manners—that he set up in the beginning?

The contrast in manners seems to suggest, to hold up as an ideal, a certain way of responding to life. This ideal would combine freedom and vitality with a sophisticated awareness of culture and society. Yet the symbolic imagery of the Palatine Hill seems to elevate natural freedom and vitality and innocence into an ideal so moving, so compelling, that all other considerations pale beside it. Or, if I rephrase my questions about Schenectady and Geneva, Winterbourne and Giovanelli, and answer them in terms of James's creative experience, they come to this: James began writing *Daisy Miller* as a comedy of manners and finished it as a symbolic presentation of a metaphysical ideal. He began by criticizing Daisy in certain ways and ended simply by praising her.

James's friend in the Venetial gondola was, at least in a general way, aware of his transfiguration of Daisy. And James records her opinion—in effect her scolding—in his preface to the New York edition of his nouvelle:

> "[Daisy's] only fault is touchingly to have transmuted so sorry a type [as the uncultivated American girl] and to have, by a poetic artifice, not only led our judgement of it astray, but made *any* judgement quite impossible. . . . You *know* you quite falsified, by the turn you gave it, the thing you had begun with having in mind, the thing you had had, to satiety, the chance of 'observing': your pretty perversion of it, or your unprincipled mystification of our sense of it, does it really too much honour. . . ."[8]

James virtually accepts his friend's criticism. Elsewhere in the preface, speaking in his own voice, he says that, when his nouvelle was first published, the full title ran: *Daisy Miller: A Study*. Now, for the New York edition, he subtracts the apposition "in view of the simple truth, which ought from the first to have been apparent to me, that my little exhibition is made to no degree whatever in critical but, quite inordinately and extravagantly, in poetical terms." It appears, then, that James's natural symbolic imagery and his translation of his heroine into a metaphysical figure were unconscious developments. Only after he wrote his nouvelle did James himself discover and acknowledge his own "poetical terms."

Once he had discovered those "terms," he chose to emphasize them, not only in his preface, but also in his text for the New York edition. Viola R. Dunbar has already noted that in a number of places in the final version of *Daisy Miller* James eases his criticism of Daisy and bears down more heavily on the Europeanized Americans.[9] Briefly, he places more stress on Daisy's beauty and innocence, and he associates her more frequently with nature, and more pointedly. At

8. *The Novels and Tales of Henry James* (New York, 1922), XVIII, vii.

9. *"The Revision of Daisy Miller,"* *Modern Language Notes*, LXV, 311–317 (May, 1950).

the same time, he gives more asperity to the judgments of Winter-bourne and Mrs. Costello and Mrs. Walker. And it is interesting to note as well that James inserts very early in Part I at least two sugges-tions of Daisy's final transfiguration. She looks at Winterbourne "with lovely remoteness";[1] she strikes him as a "charming apparition."[2]

These revisions, though, are occasional and do not essentially change *Daisy Miller*. In the New York edition, as well as in the original version, it remains a narrative of imperfect unity, a work that shows unmistakable signs of shifting authorial intention and attitude. And yet, as I have already suggested, James's idealization of his heroine is a matter of gain as well as loss. It resolves certain problems about Daisy's death. More importantly, it adds to the emotional appeal of the second part of the nouvelle. In other words, even if James may have lost something in intellectual consistency by introducing the poetry of Daisy, even if he does to some extent throw away his original comedy of manners, his symbolic natural imagery nonethe-less intensifies our response to his story. Again, I return to the articu-late lady in the gondola: "As anything charming or touching always to that extent justifies itself, we after a fashion forgive and understand you."

The ideal of a purely natural vitality and freedom and innocence is a strongly, and persistently, attractive ideal. It is attractive, especially, to American writers, and in one variation or another we have, of course, met it before—in Melville, for example, in Hawthorne, in Fitzgerald, in Faulkner. We take James's Daisy Miller, rightly, as prototypical. My purpose here has been to suggest that her relationship to certain major areas of our American experience is even more various than we may previously have thought.

CHRISTOF WEGELIN

[An International Episode] †

"An International Episode" (1878–79) is the classic example of James's dramatization of the mutual misunderstanding of Americans and Europeans. It still reflects some of the traditional American views of the differences between a democratic and an aristocratic society, but these differences are here not his major subject. The story is based on a conflict of visions: between two American visions of England—a romantic and a skeptical one—and between two English visions of

1. *The Novels and Tales of Henry James,* XVIII, 9.
2. *Ibid.,* p. 17.
† From Christof Wegelin, *The Image of Europe*

in *Henry James* (Dallas: Southern Methodist University Press, 1958), pp. 48–51. Editor's notes have been added for the present edition.

America, similarly differentiated. It would be a tragedy of innocence if it were not a comedy of the errors of pseudo sophistication. It is a story specifically of the period after the Civil War, which James later recalled ironically as a time when "introductions, photographs, travellers' tales and other aids to knowingness" were the mark of the American traveler in Europe.[1] The contrast between the folly of this "knowingness" and the wisdom of an earlier romantic innocence is implicit in "An International Episode"—only, we must add, with the ironic barbs cutting East as well as West.

James's impartiality is reflected in the symmetrical structure of the story. It begins in America, where Bessie Alden, a young American girl, and Lord Lambeth, a young English nobleman, meet and, immediately interested in each other, plan to meet again in England. Bessie's older sister, Mrs. Westgate, however, whose representative type James establishes from the start by filling her social patter—pages of it!—with all the American clichés about the differences between the two countries, does what she can to protect Bessie from disappointment. Upon their arrival in London, where the second half of the story takes place, she tells her a lurid "travellers tale" to prove what every up-to-date American knows: that English noblemen repay American hospitality habitually by snubs and outright insult. And when Bessie refuses to believe her, all she can do is commiserate with the "poor, sweet child," as she keeps calling her. For Mrs. Westgate is past that "primitive stage" of culture when Americans expressed their romantic sense of England's greatness by pilgrimages to historical monuments; she has graduated to the higher sophistication of those Americans who, fully alive to the importance of social matters, will neither forget their democratic dignity nor let anybody suspect the slightest gap in their familiarity with aristocratic etiquette. Hence, "following the fashion of many of her compatriots," she conforms minutely with all its requirements while at the same time, thanks to her vigilant watch for signs of English condescension, forgetting not infrequently her own good manners. Always on the defense, she can be discourteously aggressive—a fact which, typically, Englishmen note in her as typical of American women. Above all, however, she harasses Bessie with a protectiveness no less ungenerous than unnecessary since Lord Lambeth, with not a speck of snobbery or guile, ends quite simply by proposing.

Bessie's refusal of him knocks the last nail in the coffin of Mrs. Westgate's sophistication, for now she is driven to admit that, despite her democratic pretensions to the contrary, not to become allied to the English aristocracy is disappointing. It also cuts, however, with sharp irony through the fog of English notions. Just as Bessie is chaperoned

1. Henry James, *William Wetmore Story and His Friends* (Edinburgh and London, 1903), I, 10–11.

by her sister, so Lord Lambeth by his cousin, Percy Beaumont, thereto appointed by Lambeth's mamma. Like Mrs. Westgate, Beaumont is the knowing one of the pair, "the man of talent," "the clever man," as James keeps ironically calling him. *He* is highly conscious of what is common *English* knowledge: that naturally American girls are out to hook an English lord. We are not there to see his face when he hears of Bessie's refusal, but we may assume that his reaction is not unlike that of the British reviewer who was indignant at the impudence of James's imagining the situation.

That the English should have taken this story amiss surprised James. He felt that he had been "very delicate,"[2] and indeed this tragicomedy of innocence ground in the mill of convention is more subtly ironic than may appear at first glance. But if it plays with equal irony over the foibles of the two nations, it is almost as impartial in its praise. For if Bessie is a compliment to American women, Lambeth is no mean portrait of an English lord. Perhaps it is not saying very much for him that he appreciates Bessie, though it is significant that he likes her for the very self-reliance which we, too, admire and—more important—of which he has his own share. But what James means to emphasize are of course the qualities by which he is distinguished from his hidebound foil—his modesty, his gaiety, and above all his openness to the world. Always ready for adventure and experiment, though typically he speaks of them as mere "larks," he is the opposite of the stereotype of the stuffy lord. And yet, he does not come up to Bessie's expectations. In part, her refusal is motivated by democratic pride, but it has a deeper cause than that.

For likable as the young man is, he has the misfortune of being a "hereditary legislator," as much to his embarrassment she keeps telling him, and therefore, *properly* should be "a great mind—a great character." This he is not, and nobody knows it better than himself. He is on the contrary simply a very nice young man, which is what after all attracts her to him, but of a modesty which, while commending him to the reader, is fatal to his chances with Bessie. For Bessie, good American romantic that she is, has formed her own image of England, so that what she expects in going there—and James means us to note the Irvingesque[3] vocabulary of this key passage—are charming "associations," the pleasure of resting her eyes on "the things she had read about in the poets and historians," mementos of the past and

2. *The Letters of Henry James*, edited by Percy Lubbock (New York, 1920), I, 67–68.
3. In the manner of Washington Irving (1783–1859), the first American author widely read in England as well as the United States. In the early decades of the nineteenth century a voyage across the Atlantic was long, uncomfortable, and expensive, and few Americans knew England at first hand. But they read the English classics, the "poets and historians," and were eager for actual travellers' reports of the scenes they knew from books. Irving's romantic *Sketch Book* (1819–20), *Bracebridge Hall* (1822), and other only slightly less popular volumes catered to this appetite and created a literary fashion. [*Editor.*]

"reverberations of greatness." What she unfortunately expects of Lord Lambeth in particular is that "he would be an unconscious part of the antiquity, the impressiveness" of England and, over and above this, an authority on English history—imputations, all of these, which now amuse him, now bore him, now embarrass him, but which above all he denies by deed and word with disarming candor. Alas, he is only too unconscious; he refuses to reverberate.

Whether James's irony points more at Lambeth's simplicity or Bessie's unreasonable expectations is perhaps an academic question. But remembering *Vanity Fair* and the great Lord Steyne,[4] we cannot help suspecting a motive behind James's repeated references to Thackeray as the particular source of Bessie's exalted notions of nobility. And when he tells us that for a young man in Lambeth's position—though the young man dislikes talking about *that* and usually changes the subject—she has conceived an "ideal of conduct," the striking verbal echo reminds us of Euphemia de Mauves,[5] another victim of romantic illusions about nobility. The difference between that story and this is of course that there is no doubt whatever about James's sympathy with Bessie. Nor, for that matter, with Lord Lambeth. For while he is the victim of her illusions, they are both victims of a world so deeply entangled in international prejudice as to make a simple human relationship impossible, a world whose ignorance differs from theirs only by being snobbish instead of gracious, suspicious instead of trusting, small and fatuous instead of generous.

But such a summary overstates the moral tone of this story. For it is essentially a comedy of the international conflict of manners, and whatever moral discriminations it suggests are not * * * between a democratic and an aristocratic society, but between types common to both.

WAYNE C. BOOTH

"The Purloining of the Aspern Papers" or "The Evocation of Venice"?†

The effect of an incompletely resolved double focus gives us even more difficulty in a better-known story, "The Aspern Papers," * * * [which] seems to have been conceived from the beginning as a story about the narrator. Though James's original notation of the

---

4. A vicious nobleman in William Makepeace Thackeray's novel *Vanity Fair* (1847–48). [*Editor.*]
5. The heroine of James's "Madame de Mauves" (1874). [*Editor.*]

†From Wayne C. Booth, *The Rhetoric of Fiction* (Chicago and London: The University of Chicago Press, 1961), pp. 354–64. One of Booth's footnotes, unnecessary in the present context, has been omitted.

possibilities of a story about his "publishing scoundrel" did not picture the full "immorality" which he finally portrays, from the beginning James clearly had in mind the comic and ironic excitement of the antiquarian's quest. "The interest would be in some price that the man has to pay—that the old woman—or the survivor—sets upon the papers. His hesitations—his struggle—for he really would give almost anything"—this is clearly moving in the direction of the narrator's statement in the finished story, "I'm sorry for it, but there's no baseness I wouldn't commit for Jeffrey Aspern's sake."

The astonishing thing is that in this first notebook entry there is only the barest suggestion of the "picture" of the romantic past that James described many years later as so important to the story. The closest James comes to it here is "the picture of the two faded, queer, poor and discredited old English women—living on into a strange generation, in their musty corner of a foreign town—with these illustrious letters their most precious possession." The primary interest is in the plotting "of the Shelley fanatic" against these two romantic figures.

When in the Preface he comes to remember his idea years later, however, the plot of the Shelley fanatic is passed over completely in favor of a discussion of his own effort to realize the "palpable imaginable *visitable* past." It is all talk about atmosphere and atmospheric contrasts, the delight in rendering "my old Venice" and "the still earlier one of Jeffrey Aspern"; it is all about the "romance" of his effort to evoke "a final scene of the rich dim Shelley drama played out in the very theatre of our own 'modernity.' " Except to indicate that the original "Shelleyite" whose adventure suggested the story is not to the slightest extent reflected in the finished story, James does not even mention the protagonist.

We have here, then, two neatly distinct subjects. There is a plot, the narrator's unscrupulous quest for the papers and his ultimate frustration; it is a plot that requires an agent of a particularly insensitive kind. There is, secondly, a "picture," an air or an atmosphere, a past to be visited and recorded with all the poetic artistry at James's command. So far so good; there is nothing inherently incompatible about these two subjects. On the contrary, the notion of a "visitable past" being in effect violated by a modern antiquarian who hasn't the slightest idea of how the past can be effectively visited seems on the face of it a good one. But unfortunately there is a general principle in accordance with which James feels constrained to write his stories. "Picture" must not come from the author in his own voice. It should be pushed back into the consciousness of a large, *lucid* reflector. And who should that reflector be—who can it be in this case but the antiquarian himself? * * * He it is who must visit and evoke the past. And yet he must "pounce on" the possessions of the poet's aging mistress and violate the naïve spirit of the dying woman's niece.

The completed story is a good one, but to me it has paid a price for the mode of narration. Foolhardy as it may seem to tamper with the procedures of the great master, one cannot help concluding that the narrator as realized, though well-suited for the jilting of Tina Bordereau,[1] was not adequate to the task of evoking the poetry of the visitable past.

All of the motive power, all of the sense of direction in the plot is concentrated on the narrator's efforts to get the Aspern papers, and particularly on the use he makes of Tina's affection. In his immorality, though not in the precise details of his quest, he is half-brother to other "publishing scoundrels" in James's fiction. * * * We have passed through a time when fidelity and honor have meant so little, in terms of literary convention, that it is easy to overlook what it meant still to James. But * * * if one judges the narrator * * * by the standards of any one of James's really *lucid* reflectors, the antiquarian's immorality can only be seen as central to the effect. Our attention from first to last cannot help being centered on the comedy of the biter bit, the man of light character who manipulates others so cleverly that he "destroys" himself.

* * * the New York revision moves in the direction of our sharper awareness of the narrator's immorality. Anyone who doubts that James's final attention was primarily on the narrator should re-read the tale in the New York revision, checking against the original those passages that show him cheating, stealing, lying, or admitting to shame. * * * The following examples are only some of the more extreme instances of James's efforts to prevent, in revision, the kind of identification with the narrator which, even in this "obvious" story, might easily result from the narrator's position of command. The italics have been added.

Original	Revised
I'm sorry for it, but for Jeffrey Aspern's sake I would do *worse still*.	I'm sorry for it, but there's no *baseness* I wouldn't commit for Jeffrey Aspern's sake.
"You are very extravagant . . .," said my companion. "Certainly you are prepared to go *far!*"	"You're very extravagant—it adds to your *immorality*."
She would die next week, she would die tomorrow—then I could *seize her papers*.	. . . then I could *pounce on her possessions and ransack her drawers*.

1. When James revised the story for the New York Edition, he changed *Tita* (as she is called in our version) into *Tina*. [*Editor.*]

. . . for the first, the last, the only time I beheld her extra-ordinary eyes. They glared at me, they made me horribly ashamed.

. . . They glared at me; *they were like the sudden drench, for a caught burglar, of a flood of gaslight;* they made me horribly ashamed.

I had said to Mrs. Prest that I would make love to her [the daughter]; but it had been a joke without consequence and I had never said it to *Tita Bordereau* [note that "Tita" is revised to the more attarctive "Tina"].

. . . I had never said it to *my victim.*

How could she, since I had not come back before night to con-tradict, even as a simple form, such an idea [Miss Tina's idea that he has recoiled in horror from her offer of love]?

. . . to contradict, even as a simple form, *even as an act of common humanity,* such an idea?

These isolated quotations give, of course, only a fraction of the emphasis one finds, in both versions, on the moral deterioration and ultimate baseness of James's narrator.[2] The effect of these and the other changes is in no case to make him worse *in fact;* his actions remain objectively the same in both versions. Rather they worsen only his picture of himself and thus increase our awareness that the drama is that of his unprincipled relationship with Miss Tina. They thus lessen the burden on the reader by making this aspect of the story less subtle and ambiguous than it originally was.

The story, then, consists simply of this unscrupulous man's quest for the Aspern papers, his discovery that his best way to get to them is to make love to the owner's unattractive niece, Tina, his further discov-ery that marriage is to be the price of full possession, his temporary withdrawal in the face of such a conflict and—but he should tell the climax in his own words. Observe how he betrays himself when he next encounters the undesirable woman he must learn to accept if he wants the papers. As he comes into the room, he recognizes that she

---

2. For a clear-headed reading of the narrator's wide-ranging perfidies, see Sam S. Baskett, "The Sense of the Present in *The Aspern Papers,*" *Papers of the Michigan Academy of Science, Arts, and Letters,* XLIV (1959), 381–88. Baskett recognizes that the narrator's vision of the past is far from a reliable one and that in fact the ironies of the story are based on an implied contrast between his "sense of the past" and the reader's and author's sense. He is wil-ling to make use of the past for his present "base"

ends. The past he evokes is tainted—though Baskett does not stress this point—by his mode of evocation. Another prosecution of the nar-rator is conducted by William Bysshe Stein in "*The Aspern Papers*: A Comedy of Masks," *Nineteenth-Century Fiction.* XIV (September, 1959), 172–78. Stein deals more fully with the narrator's aesthetic deficiencies; his view of the past is tainted, and the past he evokes is largely an absurd one—as we see in the absurdities of Juliana, the last living remnant of that past.

has understood his involuntary recoil when she offered herself in exchange for the papers the day before.

> . . . I also saw something which had not been in my forecast. Poor Miss Tina's sense of her failure had produced a rare alteration in her, but I had been too full of stratagems and spoils to think of that. Now I took it in; I can scarcely tell how it startled me. She stood in the middle of the room with a face of mildness bent upon me, and her look of forgiveness, of absolution, made her angelic. It beautified her; she was younger; she was not a ridiculous old woman. This trick of her expression, this magic of her spirit, transfigured her, and while I still noted it I heard a whisper somewhere in the depths of my conscience: "Why not, after all—why not?" It seemed to me I *could* pay the price.

This is *his* idea of the voice of *conscience*. If he is so unreliable about that, what of his notion that her countenance has actually changed? Is the change simply his subjective interpretation? James increases our suspicions at once: "Still more distinctly however than the whisper I heard Miss Tina's own voice" saying that the papers have been destroyed and with them, of course, all reason for "paying the price."

"The room seemed to go round me as she said this and a real darkness for a moment descended on my eyes. When it passed, Miss Tina was there still, but the transfiguration was over and she had changed back to a plain dingy elderly person." Because of the narrative method, we are forever barred from knowing whether Miss Tina was, in fact, capable of forgiveness, whether she was, in fact, transformed, whether she was, in fact, a dingy elderly person in the first place. We are confined to the drama of the narrator's own scheming, and when he concludes by regretting his loss—"I mean of the precious papers"[3]—we are left permanently in doubt as to whether he has any suspicion of suffering a more serious loss, whether we think of that loss as of his honor or as of Miss Tina herself. What we do know is, however, sufficient to make this aspect of the story highly successful: the schemer has shown himself as the chief victim of his own elaborate scheming.

But where has that other subject, as described in the Preface, been all this while? What has happened to the "visitable past"? Well, the poor blind narrator has been periodically struggling to bring himself back up to the level of sensitivity necessary to record, with the reader's unequivocal concurrence, the romantic atmosphere of Venice and particularly of this one corner of the past, the Bordereaus' villa. Here is the comic schemer in his other role, as poetic celebrant: "There could be no Venetian business without patience, and since I adored the

3. This clause is added in the New York Edition. See the conclusion of Booth's treatment, p. 462 below. [*Editor.*]

place I was much more in the spirit of it for having laid in a large provision. That spirit kept me perpetual company and seemed to look out at me from the revived immortal face—in which all his genius shone—of the great poet who was my prompter. I had invoked him and he had come." Surely this is no ridiculous schemer; this is the worthy disciple of the great poet, speaking in the voice that James himself uses in describing *his* feelings about Venice and his imagined Aspern. and the narrator carries on in this voice at some length. In the long passage concluding section four, which contains the narrator's opinions about Aspern, about America, and about American art, surely he is intended to be reliable as a spokesman for James's theme: "That was originally what I had prized him for: that at a period when our native land was nude and crude and provincial, when the famous 'atmosphere' it is supposed to lack was not even missed, when literature was lonely there and art and form almost impossible, he had found means to live and write like one of the first; to be free and general and not at all afraid; to feel, understand and express everything."

This can scarcely be considered as the same person at all. And there is a third tone of voice when the first two openly conflict.

> It was as if his [Aspern's] bright ghost had returned to earth to assure me he regarded the affair as his own no less than as mine and that we should see it fraternally and fondly to a conclusion. . . . My eccentric private errand became a part of the general romance and the general glory—I felt even a mystic companionship, a moral fraternity with all those who in the past had been in the service of art. They had worked for beauty, for a devotion; and what else was I doing? That element was in everything that Jeffrey Aspern had written, and I was only bringing it to light.

There can be little doubt that James has deliberately planted clues here to make us see that the narrator is rationalizing his conduct. In the service of art? *Only* bringing beauty to light? And what of Aspern's own conduct? "We were glad to think at least that in all our promulgations acquitting Aspern conscientiously of any grossness—some people now consider I believe that we have overdone them—we had only touched in passing and in the most discreet manner on Miss Bordereau's connexion. Oddly enough, even if we had had the material . . . this would have been the most difficult episode to handle." Aspern is, then, also tainted with the immorality shown by the narrator? Again, debating whether Aspern had "betrayed" Juliana in his works, "had given her away, as we say nowadays, to posterity," the antiquarian exonerates Aspern, in what must be another instance of his "overdone promulgations": "Moreover was not any frame fair enough that was so sure of duration and was associated with works immortal through their beauty?" Was James so naïve as to allow his narrator to get away with blurring the distinction between this kind of betrayal, without which romantic poetry could not exist at all, and the personal betrayals of the narrator in his antiquarian quest? Again and again in the story one is forced to throw up his hands and decide that James simply has provided insufficient clues for the judgments which he still quite clearly expects us to be able to make.

We have, then, three distinct narrative voices in this story: the narrator's self-betrayals, evident to any careful reader; his efforts at straightforward evocation of the past, which taken out of context might be indistinguishable from James's own voice; and the passages of mumbling, as it were, that lie between. There are so many good things in the story that it seems almost ungrateful of us to ask whether the three narrative voices are ever really harmonized. Critics have generally followed James himself in steering clear of such questions. It is so much easier to "dislike James" for his obscurities—without troubling very much to say what we mean—or to idolize him for his subtle ambiguities. Both positions are wholly safe, backed by troops in rank on rank, with traditions of honorable battle going back many decades. What is hard is to look squarely at the master and decide—without idolatry or iconoclasm—whether he has done, after all, as well as he might have.

It is time, then, to ask that final hard question about this story, even if we feel no great confidence about being able to answer it: Was James wrong to "give" the story to a single narrator, a narrator used on the one hand to reveal his own deficiencies with unconscious irony and on the other to praise praiseworthy things? * * *

* * *

It seems clear that James always thought of this story as an effort to realize both of the elements he himself describes: the ironic comedy and the romantic evocation as background and contrast. He cannot have thought of either the publishing scoundrel or the evoked past as independent subjects with independent effects; the stronger the evocation of the true romance of Venice and its past, the greater the ironic comedy of the misled antiquarian who violates that past. And on the contrary, the more clearly his modern baseness is made to stand out, the more effective should be the contrasting genuine passion for beauty of the romantics. Far from being truly contradictory, the two effects could easily be seen as complementary; the deeper the ironic bite the sharper the contrast with what is not treated ironically. But it is evident from the published criticism of this story that most readers have fallen to one side or the other of this true complexity—not mere haze and muddlement—that the story implicitly seems to be striving for.

* * *

We might, of course, imagine a reader so flexible and so thoroughly attuned to James's own values that he could shift nimbly from stance to stance, allowing the narrator to shift his character from moment to moment. But James has surrendered the very conventions which, in earlier fiction and drama, made such shifts easily acceptable. One has no difficulty when Shakespeare forces some of his characters, particularly in soliloquy, into narrative and evaluative statements that go far beyond any realistic assessment of their true capabilities within the world of the action. Shakespeare has made no claim that his *manner* will be realistically consistent. But James reminds us constantly, page by page, that he is attempting a new realistic intensity of narrative manner. How can I, then, excuse him when I find his narrator to be one kind of man in one paragraph and another kind of man in the next? Only by surrendering my responsibilities as a reader and saying that just because it is by James it is perfect. Good as it is, "The Aspern Papers" is not as good as James might have made it if he had preserved for a reliable voice the right to evoke the true visitable past and used the present narrator only on jobs for which he is qualified.

The attenuation of effect that must result for any reader who takes the work seriously as a whole can be seen by looking at any passage in which the narrator must do both of his jobs simultaneously. A good example is the concluding sentence: "When I look at it"—the portrait of Jeffrey Aspern—"I can scarcely bear my loss—I mean of the precious papers." In the original this read simply, "When I look at it my chagrin at the loss of the letters becomes almost intolerable." But it is not, as James well knew, really the letters that the narrator has lost, and he quite appropriately revised to introduce a shadow of doubt, a shadow of self-awareness of the price he has paid, in loss of human decency. But what happens, through this revision, to the evocation of the visitable past? Are the papers precious? Of course, one would say, of course they are precious. But they have been made to seem less so—indeed they become almost contemptible—as the result of a revision which beautifully reminds us of what the narrator has really lost.

In discussing what happens when Shakespeare's moral maxims come to us through an "unreliable spokesman," Alfred Harbage says that the effect is to "throw the maxims a little out of focus, to blur them somewhat, to rob them of finality."[4] The effect in James is similar: some—though by no means all—of the narrator's usefulness in evoking the romance of Shelley's Italy has been blurred and robbed of finality.

* * *

4. "The Unreliable Spokesman," *As They Liked It: An Essay on Shakespeare and Morality* (New York, 1947), p. 106.

MILDRED HARTSOCK

Unweeded Garden: A View of *The Aspern Papers*†

Recent criticism has explored many aspects of the art of Henry James: his ethical concerns, his "method," his "phases," his themes, his symbolic imagery, his tragic vision, his humor, his cult of consciousness, his Americanism or lack of it—in short, his clear claim to the variety of explication that we accord to true genius. One fact of the fiction of James, however, has not been sufficiently acknowledged: at its best, it strikes the resonances of the heart. The chief lesson of the master in *The Art of Fiction* is his insistence that the novelist must take to himself the "faintest hints of life"; must "convert the very pulses of the air into revelations."[1] Indeed, he says that the "only reason for the existence of a novel is that it does attempt to represent life."[2] And yet, even among critics devoted to James, the view persists that André Gide's judgment is right:

> The skillfully made network spun out by his intelligence capitvates only the intelligence: the intelligence of the reader, the intelligence of the heroes of his books. The latter seem never to exist except in the functioning of their intellects . . . all the weight of the flesh is absent, and all the shaggy, tangled undergrowth, all the wild darkness.[3]

Joseph Warren Beach, too, confesses that ". . . for most readers, James carries too far this sterilizing or deodorizing process. Even his fondest admirers have moments of irritation with him for what must seem his . . . almost spinsterly fear of any note too loud, any scent too strong."[4] And Beach regrets the absence of "straggling weeds" in the novelist's "pruned and weeded garden."[5] Pelham Edgar, with all his perceptive defenses of James, is sorry that he did not have "a richer sense of life."[6] Geismar and Edmund Wilson are in agreement that James "tended to hold life at arm's length":[7] that emotional deficiencies within himself somehow damaged the artist's power to portray raw

†From *Studies in Short Fiction* V (1967), pp. 60–68. Hartsock's page references are to the New York Edition, which differs from our version in some details. See Booth (above) for examples of the differences. The footnotes have been renumbered.

1. Henry James, *Selected Fiction*. Leon Edel, ed. (New York, 1953), p. 594. [see p. 352 above—*Editor.*]
2. Ibid., p. 587. [See p. 346 above—*Editor.*]
3. André Gide, "Henry James" (from an unsent letter) in F. W. Dupee, ed., *The Question of Henry James* (New York, 1945), p. 251.

4. Joseph Warren Beach, *The Method of Henry James* (Philadelphia, 1954), pp. 115–116.
5. Ibid.
6. Pelham Edgar, "The Essential Novelist?", from *The Art of the Novel* (New York, 1933). Reprinted in Leon Edel, ed., *Henry James* (Englewood Cliffs, 1963), p. 98.
7. Edmund Wilson, "The Ambiguity of Henry James," *Hound and Horn*, VII (1934), 385–406. Reprinted in Dupee *The Question of Henry James*, p. 189. See also Maxwell Geismar, *Henry James and the Jacobites* (Boston, 1963), Ch. 3, pp. 48–92.

feeling.

The implication of artistic and emotional timidity seems incomprehensible, however, when themes and scenes are recalled from major long and short works. If Hardy's *Jude* shocked the nineties and foreshadowed the modern novel, what are we to say of James's candid explorations of marital infidelity, the effects of divorce upon children, suicide, homosexuality, the class-struggle, social mores that parallel our own? Indeed, the contemporaneity of James's themes is astounding as we remember when his fiction was written. But, then, the question remains: does James deal obliquely or timidly or "voyeuristically" with these themes? The answer is emphatically "NO!" and that answer may be found in countless places. The agony of John Marcher at the grave of May Bartram; the death of Morgan Moreen; the final encounter of Strether and Madame de Vionnet; the epiphany before the candles in "The Altar of the Dead"; the revelation to Milly Theale and her turning to death; the last communion of Mitchie and Nanda; the travails of Maisie; the dim, dumb uncomprehending wrack of Olive Chancellor[8]—these, to mention a few, are scenes that speak to heart, not mind. These gardens are "shaggy" enough: they are not walked in timidly; they capture the feeling of the life to which James dedicated his art.

* * *

In no story are feelings more the heart of the matter than in *The Aspern Papers*. The emphasis in discussions of this nouvelle of 1888, however, has commonly been put upon the ethical question personified in the narrator: does he have the right to invade the privacy of a famous man of letters, a romantic poet long dead? Charles G. Hoffmann, for example, says that the novel "portrays with complete candor . . . the crassness and duplicity of the snooping journalist * * * dedicated to the principle of the profession that all private affairs are public property."[9] Walter F. Wright shares this opinion that the narrator is as evil as journalists always are in James's stories. His motivation, according to Wright, is an "egotistic concern for the fame that will come to him."[1] Osborn Andreas flatly describes the theme wholly in terms of two opposing attitudes toward privacy: "The story tells of a deep duel between a modern democratic violator of the private lives of famous folk and a late surviving representative of the traditional aristocratic thesis that constituted privacy is a defensible and an inalienable luxury—and the winner of the duel is the aged

8. John Marcher and May Bartram are in "The Beast in the Jungle," Morgan Moreen in "The Pupil," Strether and Madame de Vionnet in *The Ambassadors*, Milly Theale in *The Wings of the Dove*, Mitchie and Nanda in *The Awkward Age*, Maisie in *What Maisie Knew*, and Olive Chancellor in *The Bostonians* [*Editor.*]
9. Charles G. Hoffmann, *The Short Novels of Henry James* (New York, 1957), p. 45.
1. Walter F. Wright, *The Madness of Art* (Lincoln, Nebraska, 1962), p. 103.

lady."[2] Edmund Wilson agrees that the narrator is "an annoying fellow who is finally foiled and put to rout by the old lady. . . ."[3]

Those who see *The Aspern Papers* as an intellectual protest against invasion of privacy point to two evidences: James's well known aversion to any intrusion upon his own privacy and his several stories that clearly do deal with this theme. One of them, *The Reverberator*, belongs to the same year as *The Aspern Papers*; others are "The Lesson of the Master" and "The Figure in the Carpet." *The Aspern Papers*, however, has kinship, not with these defenses of privacy or claims for the irrelevancy of the biographical, but with works that treat of the "sense of the past" and the primacy of the present: "The Altar of the Dead," "The Beast in the Jungle," *The Sense of the Past*, and "The Jolly Corner." The theme of *The Aspern Papers* could be Lambert Strether's advice to little Bilham: "Live while you can; it's a mistake not to."[4] It is, in fact, a sentence spoken from the eye-shaded skull of the "divine Juliana" that covertly and rather incongruously states the theme: when the narrator asked after her health, she replied that "it was good enough—good enough; that it was a great thing to be alive."[5] And in support of that proposition learned in the love of Jeffrey Aspern, the aged woman directs all her wily perceptions to the final goal of her ebbing years: the salvaging of life for Tina, "that high tremulous spinster" who proves capable of being transfigured into beauty by the "magic of her spirit" (p. 141). Roses for Tina infuse in her the same insistency for life that Emily ("A Rose for Emily") brought to her second-floor room. And no one has ever accused Faulkner of timidity about the Gothic horrors of the inner life! Unimaginable courage and imaginable thirsting for love bring the shyness of a wholly unworldly middle-aged innocent to the plea for a marriage that could restore the life for which she is abundantly ready. This is the crisis, and this is the story.

The problem of the papers is—to use James's overworked word— the *donnée*: the scale on which a Liebestod is played. And one must grasp certain facts before the story is really accessible. The first is that the narrator is not a "journalist" in the pejorative sense in which the critics quoted above use the word.[6] He is a scholar and a romantic, in love with the past and devoted to the poet about whose work he has written. A gossip-columnist would not say of the poet: "he's a part of the light by which we walk" or regard himself as a "minister" to Aspern's "temple" (p. 6). He, indeed, believes it inconceivable that anything derogatory could be discovered about his "god." He admires

2. Osborn Andreas, *Henry James and the Expanding Horizon* (Seattle, 1948), p. 147.
3. Edmund Wilson, p. 170.
4. Henry James, *The Ambassadors* (New York, 1908), I, 217.
5. Henry James, *The Aspern Papers*, The New York Edition (New York, 1908), p. 69. All references will be to this edition.
6. Dupee recognizes, as Wright, Andreas, Blackmur, and others do not, that the narrator is a scholar and aesthete, not a "journalist."

Aspern because he "had found means to live and write like one of the first; to be free and general and not at all afraid; to feel, understand, and express everything" (p. 7). * * *

A better proof of the character of the narrator lies in Juliana's acceptance of him into her home and into her plans for Tina. In the first encounter, the narrator, unable to pierce the green eye-shade, says, "I felt her look at me with great penetration. . . ." and a moment later, ". . . her attitude worried me by suggesting that she had a fuller vision of me than I had of her" (pp. 26–27). It is clear that she identifies his purposes and the nature of his interest at once. She measures his fidelity to Aspern by his willingness to meet exhorbitant demands for money as the price for admission to their "garden." And with all her acerbity and withdrawal, she decides that he *is* suitable for her purposes: one "who lives on flowers," who has romance in his soul, may "do" for Tina. If it proves otherwise, Tina will, at least, have the money.

And so, the two counter-plotters prepare the garden for the re-enactment of romance: the man for the romance of living for a brief time with his pulse beating to the felt presence of the "bright ghost" of Jeffrey Aspern; Juliana for the last hope that the meanings of her own lost life may be recreated for Tina in the Now. For a time, the garden of the dim old palace becomes a found Eden. It is an Eden for the man because he is insulated there in the romance of the past, which he now really *lives into*: "Meanwhile aren't we in Venice together, and what better place is there for the meeting of dear friends? See how it glows with the advancing summer; how the sky and the sea and the rosy air and the marble of the palaces all shimmer and melt together" (p. 43). He continues: "My eccentric private errand became a part of the general romance and the general glory—I felt even a mystic compan-ionship, a moral fraternity with all those who in the past had been in the service of art" (p. 43). These summer days were to seem "almost the happiest" of his life. (p. 45)

Meanwhile, Tina begins to breathe an air as "delicious" as "must have trembled with Romeo's vows when he stood among the thick flowers and raised his arms to his mistress's balcony" (p. 52). She tells her new-found friend that Juliana has sent her to the garden and has urged her often to go there. It is Juliana who adjures her to go to the Piazza: "You're old enough, my dear, and this gentleman won't hurt you. He'll show you the famous sunsets, if they still go on—do they go on? The sun set for me so long ago." (p. 73)

Both the narrator and certain critics comment upon the "crass" concern of Juliana with the "pecuniary question." It offends the man to think that the mistress of Aspern could care about money. F. W. Dupee describes Juliana as a "diabolical incarnation of the past, greedy of its power to bargain with the present."[7] And Robert L. Gale says that Juliana might be called an "embattled Shylock."[8] When the real core of the meaning of the story is located, however, it is clear that the money-demands and the bait of Aspern's portrait are Juliana's means, first of testing, then of holding the man whom she literally thrusts toward Tina. Waiting in her shadows for her "very dark shade" to come, she makes her most candid bid for the life of Tina when she dangles the portrait before the man. Her terms are unmistakably clear: "She's a very fine girl. . . . Except for me, today . . . she hasn't a relation in the world" (p. 92). Juliana's hope dies when the narrator, led by his passion for the papers, comes skulking to her bedroom. Unlike Aspern, he does not see all, understand all. Her plan, she sees, has failed—and she cries out: "You publishing scoundrel" (p. 118)

The special note of Miss Tina is struck in early dialogue. When the narrator is admitted to the palace, he asks, artfully, "The garden, the garden—do me the pleasure to tell me if it's yours!" (p. 17). Miss Tina remarks sadly that nothing there is hers. She shows a disconcerting tendency to repeat his phrases "almost as for the rich unwonted joy to her of spoken words" (p. 20). Later, when the narrator asks her whether Juliana does have the papers, she indicates that she understands the privations of her own life: " 'Oh, she has everything!' sighed Miss Tina with a curious weariness, a sudden lapse into gloom." (p. 78)

With the greatest possible economy of means, James evokes the character and condition of Miss Tina. The startling and uninhibited warmth of her greeting of her new friend when he returns to the garden unexpectedly; the ingenuousness of her reply to his wonder that she had never before enjoyed the "fragrant alleys, blooming here under your nose": "Ah . . . they were never nice till now!"; the pathos in the hoarded memory of the long-ago picnic on the Lido—these are touching insights into her feelings. Her lover-like curiosity about what he will do when he leaves her ["Shall you study—shall you read and write—when you go up to your rooms?" (p. 62)] is reminiscen. strangely, of Cleopatra: "Stands he, or sits he?"[9]

Then comes the *coup de grâce*:[1] the night in the gondola, the "return to society." On Tina's face is the "flush of a wounded surprise . . ." (p. 79). She did not speak, "sunk in the sense of opportunities forever lost. . . ." In all Miss Tina says and does, there is utter candor, utter simplicity, utter incomprehension of the motives of the man, even after he has confessed them to her. Yet, about her is a curious dignity that prepares, in a way, for the superb control of the

7. F. W. Dupee, *Henry James: His Life and Writing* (New York, 1951), p. 83.
8. Robert Gale, *The Caught Image* (Chapel Hill, 1964), p. 130.
9. *Antony and Cleopatra.* I, v., ll. 19 ff.
1. Finishing stroke. [*Editor.*]

468 • *Mildred Hartsock*

woman in the final tragic confrontation. This scene, however, is preceded by the emotional crisis of the story: the meeting at which Miss Tina, with shameless, pride-less courage, offers the Aspern papers[2] in return for love. She understands, finally, the ends to which Juliana had intended the papers; she even knows now what her aunt had known when she tried to burn the treasures: that they cannot serve these ends. But—she must try. And try she does: "I'd give you everything, and she'd understand. . . ." (p. 135)

Every reader has felt the ironies that inhere in the twists of this tragedy of middle-aged loneliness and frustration. The narrator, looking into the eyes of Jeffrey Aspern, asked him "What on earth was the matter with Miss Tina. And he, in the portrait, seemed to smile at me with mild mockery" (p. 131). Indeed, he might smile at the ironic blindness of this devotée of the romantic arts who, in real life, cannot see Juliet on the balcony. Then there is the irony of the schemer out-schemed and both, finally, outwitted by the simple human need of one who can share neither the romantic past of the one nor the aesthetic present of the other. The "love-affair" of Miss Tina and the narrator cannot be called a parody of the Juliana–Aspern relationship as Laurence Holland seems to imply.[3] Tina is not a ridiculous maenad pursuing an unworthy Orpheus.[4] She is a pathetic spinster whose pathos becomes true tragedy as she sees what her choice must be—and makes it with dignity.

There are not "villains" in this piece in any usual sense of the word. One cannot condone the duplicities of the narrator—no! But his motives are understandable, and he really intends no harm to the two women. He is sensitive; he is imaginative; he suffers pangs of conscience when he sees the outcome of his zeal. In the special James sense, however, he *is* culpable. His trouble is that, to borrow a phrase from Wallace Stevens, he is "the lunatic of one idea."[5] An *idée fixe* keeps him from seeing what he needs to see: he is a Lambert Strether on the streets of Chester, who never quite reaches the river bank of the ultimate insight. The final irony attests this estimate of the narrator. As he looks at Aspern's portrait, he laments, "I can scarcely bear my loss—I mean of the precious papers" (p. 143). He comes close to a knowledge of what he has really lost when he senses the true quality of Miss Tina:

2. The argument of Jacob Korg that there are no papers seems unconvincing. To deny their existence would be to suggest a wholly untenable conception of Tina's character. One does not associate her innocence with deliberate lying. Cf. Jacob Korg, "What Aspern Papers? A Hypothesis," *College English*, XXIII (February, 1962).
3. Laurence Bedwell Holland, *The Expense of*

Vision (Princeton, 1964), pp. 139–154.
4. In Greek mythology the marvelous singer Orpheus, whose music charmed even the gods of the underworld, was torn to pieces by a band of raging female worshippers of Dionysus (Bacchus) called Maenads. Authorities cannot agree about their motive. [*Editor.*]
5. Wallace Stevens, *Collected Poems* (New York, 1954), p. 325.

She stood in the middle of the room with a face of mildness bent upon me, and her look of forgiveness, of absolution, made her angelic. It beautified her; she was younger; she was not a ridiculous old woman. This trick of her expression, this magic of her spirit, transfigured her, and while I still noted it I heard a whisper some-where in the depths of my conscience: "Why not, after all—why not?" It seemed to me I *could* pay the price! (pp. 141–142)

But Tina's "Goodbye" impinges upon his recognition; and when he has gone, it is again of the lost papers that he thinks. The "evil" in the narrator is the evil that Lambert Strether is finally able to excise: the failure to be fully conscious. In an interesting study of the influence of pragmatism upon Henry James, Edward Rich Levy describes the role of perception in James: "Meaning in life comes through the full sense of all there is to know. . . . This view of the double burden of intelligent sensibility, in the pleasure and pain of conscious aware-ness, becomes the sign of the gift of enlarged perspective to the fine intelligence open to possibilities."[6] The narrator is deficient in this "full sense of all there is to know."

When the germ of the story first came to James from a conversation about Jane Clairmont's living on into the 1880's, attended by her niece, he had expected to make the tale relatively short.[7] But, like so many others, it developed its own special need for length. The method of *The Aspern Papers* involves what Marianne Moore, in another context, called "The interiorized climax."[8] It is one of James's early experiments with the singly focussed point of view, so signally success-ful in *What Maisie Knew* and *The Ambassadors*. The method is useful to this story for several obvious reasons. By projecting the events through the eyes of the centrally involved narrator, James makes possible the ironies that flow from the limited consciousness of the man and at the same time delays the reader's perception that the heart of the matter is not the papers but the tragedy of a woman. This indirection allows, too, for the necessarily slow emergence of the character of Tina. A frontal approach to the portrayal of Tina would have raised the problem Faulkner might have had with a direct approach to Emily. In both stories, the shock and the anguish gain both credibility and emotional impact by being filtered through the incomprehension of others. Percy Lubbock could have been thinking of *The Aspern Papers* when he wrote of James: "It is not through any shy timidity that so often in his books he requires us to infer the presence of naked emotion from the faintest stirrings of an all but

6. Edward Rich Levy, *Henry James and the Pragmatic Assumption: The Conditions of Per-ception* (doctoral dissertation, University of Il-linois, 1964), p. 145.
7. F. O. Matthiessen and Kenneth B. Mur-dock, eds., *The Notebooks of Henry James* (New York, 1961), pp. 71–75.
8. Marianne Moore, *Predilections* (New York, 1955), p. 8. Miss Moore's comment upon James is worthy of note: "In every photograph of Henry James that we have, the thing that arrests one is a kind of terrible truthfulness," p. 28.

unruffled surface; it is because these monitory signals . . . tell a story that would be weakened by a directer method."[9]

The nouvelle provides another ironic instance of the ease with which the best James stories lend themselves to dramatization. Notwithstanding James's failures in the theatre, the essentially dramatic character of many of the stories and the realism of dialogue make for successful adaptation. In 1959 Michael Redgrave's dramatic version of *The Aspern Papers* in Queen's Theatre, London, earned the praise of critics. Mollie Panter–Downes described it as "handsomely redone," but regretted that Redgrave's narrator, whom she insists on identifying with James himself, "seems merely an intrusive bounder when deprived of the intellectual reasoning that James works out in the story."[1]

The Aspern Papers is one of the most evocative and subtle of James's fictions. It is hard to name another story that so perfectly does what it sets out to do. In the interesting *Preface*, written in 1908, James speaks of his delight in the "visitable past," with its "haunting presences," the "poetry of the thing outlived and lost and gone"—and all "played out in the very theater of our own modernity."[2] This sense of the past he does, indeed, evoke: through the great age of the divine Juliana who possesses now only the magnificent eyes in a "grinning skull"; through the dim, forgotten old palace where the two women live "like hunted creatures feigning death"; through the enchantment of the rose-filled garden; through the whole romantic aura of the Venetian summer. With the narrator, one falls in love with this past, anachronistically present. For Juliana, the past is dead, and she will veritably sell the remnants of it so that Tina may have a life. But the man, unlike Ralph Pendrel, in *The Sense of the Past*, though he is shaken by the collision of past and present, chooses not to "come back." If one must single out a thesis for *The Aspern Papers*, it is that the past has a continuity and a beauty to which the imaginative man must be sensitive; but he cannot light all his candles for the dead. * * * The greatness of the story, however, does not reside in the theme but in the "caught image" of a felt human life.

MILDRED HARTSOCK

[The Pupil] †

* * * Henry James wrote with courage and understanding and uncompromised honesty about themes that were rarely explored in

9. Percy Lubbock, ed., Introduction, *The Letters of Henry James* (New York, 1920), p. xxiv.
1. Mollie Panter-Downes, "Letter from London," *The New Yorker*, XXXIV (Sept. 12, 1959), 154.
2. Henry James, Preface, *The Aspern Papers*.

New York Edition, XII, x.
†From Mildred Hartsock, "Henry James and the Cities of the Plain," *Modern Language Quarterly*, XXIX (1968), pp. 298, 299, 305–6. Footnotes for this selection are by the editor.

the nineteenth century, but have become the common literary coin of
our day.

One of these is the theme of homosexuality. Today, confronted
with this subject *ad nauseam*, we might well demur at an emphasis
upon it in the work of James. The theme, long since identified in his
fiction, has been mentioned by various critics in various connections.
It is still a matter of debate, however, even in those works in which it is
most obvious; and many scholars have tended to believe that, even if it
is present, it was an element that James himself did not consciously
recognize.

It is a strange fact that putting a term from psychology to characters
somehow causes readers immediately to take a case-history approach
to a literary work. Such a response would be regrettable if it marred the
beauty of James's story "The Pupil" (1891), at the heart of which lies
the deep emotional relationship between Morgan and Pemberton.
When the two meet, Morgan is a child—but a pathetically aged and
cynical child in the midst of his irresponsible and dishonest family;
the years pass until he is fifteen—and older than Pemberton both in
suffering and understanding. The two want, somehow, to make a life
together. Frail though he is physically, Morgan is manly and never
surrenders to self-pity. Pemberton, leaving him to tutor "the opulent
youth," says, "I'll make a tremendous charge; I'll earn a lot of money
in a short time, and we'll live on it." The boy, trying to keep a tone of
jest, exclaims: "Happy opulent youth!" Pemberton replies, "Not if
he's a dismal dunce"; and Morgan, with a kind of fatalism, answers:
"Oh they're happier then. But you can't have everything, can you?"
and James tells us: "Pemberton held him fast, hands on his
shoulders—he had never loved him so. 'What will become of *you*,
what will you do?' Pemberton rushes back to Morgan, at the ruse of
Mrs. Moreen. There is a depth of feeling involved which makes
irrelevant the mere matter of money.

Despite all the critical emphasis upon the evil in the Moreens, they
really love Morgan. They had for him, James tells us, "a genuine
tenderness, an artless admiration" and "the oddest wish to make him
independent, as if they had felt themselves not good enough for him."
This concern is the one virtue in their otherwise sordid lives. At the
end, when they offer Morgan to Pemberton, they are doing the one
thing that might have saved him. Morgan's joy at the prospect of living
always with Pemberton is, in effect, what kills him. (One remembers
the association of joy and death in Gide's[1] portrayal of Edward in *The
Counterfeiters*.) From the first moment of shamed humiliation, Morgan turned to "boyish joy." He looked at Pemberton "with a light in
his face" at this "unexpected consecration of his hope." Readers who
feel that Pemberton somehow fails him here do not take into account

1. André Gide (1869–1951), French novelist,   novels.
critic, essayist. *The Counterfeiters* is one of his

the time element or the fact that Pemberton *does* respond. They forget, too, the clear indications earlier in the story that, if only the financial problems could be solved, Pemberton would accept "the prospect on the spot" of Morgan's giving him his life. No, Morgan dies of joy. Pemberton pulls the dying boy "half out of his mother's hands"—and then comes the sharp irony of Mrs. Moreen's cry: "But I thought he *wanted* to go to you!"

The most sensitive account of "The Pupil," and a clear recognition, too, of the theme under discussion, is Clifton Fadiman's:

> The relation between them [Pemberton and Morgan] goes beyond mutual respect and affection. Its roots reach deep into the dark soil of their emotional under-lives. The conventions of his day (which James, through his subtle magic, both obeyed and evaded) prevented him from making any more explicit the perfectly unconscious homosexual love—of a type that could never ripen into overt action—binding Morgan and Pemberton. Yet we feel it, and perhaps with added force just because it is touched upon with such delicate restraint. It adds still another dimension to this rich narrative, endowing it with a troubling beauty whose parallel is perhaps to be found nowhere else save in Thomas Mann's "Death in Venice."[2]

The degree of "explicitness" is not merely a question of nineteenth-century taboos, but of artistry. * * *

EARLE LABOR

James's "The Real Thing": Three Levels of Meaning†

Despite its popularity in the classroom (it is perhaps the most anthologized of all Henry James's stories), "The Real Thing" continues to be read as a little masterpiece which, according to Clifton Fadiman, "expresses amusingly (and no more than that) the old truth that art is a *transformation* of reality, not a mere reflection of the thing itself."[1] Without commenting upon Mr. Fadiman's curious sense of

2. Hartsock quotes Clifton Fadiman from his edition of *The Short Stories of Henry James* (New York: Random House, 1945), p. 272.

† From *College English* XXIII (February 1962), pp. 376–78.

1. "A Note on The Real Thing," *The Short Stories of Henry James* (New York, 1945), p. 217. Several critics have gone beyond Fadiman's superficial reading of this story; especially noteworthy are the following: William F. Marquardt, "A Practical Approach to *The Real Thing* by Henry James," *English "A" Analyst* (Northwestern University), No. 14 (June 13, 1949); Quentin Anderson, ed., *Henry James: Selected Short Stories* (New York, 1957), pp. vii–ix; and Walter F. Wright, "The Real Thing," *Research Studies of the State College of Washington*, XXV (March, 1957), 85–90. Also, see Edward Stone, ed., *Henry James: Seven Stories and Studies* (New York, 1961), pp. 131–141, 309; and Maurice Beebe and William T. Stafford, "Criticism of Henry James: A Selected Checklist with an Index to Studies of Separate Works," *Modern Fiction Studies*, III (Spring, 1957), 91.

humor, I should like to demonstrate that James's theme—an "exquisite" question, as he put it—includes considerably "more than that."

It should be evident that, were the central meaning of "The Real Thing" no more than an esthetic cliché, the question that struck James's sensibility could hardly have been an exquisite one. An intelligence so fine seldom concerned itself with platitudes. It is of course James's remarkable fusion of the simple and the complex, the explicit and the subtle, that makes "The Real Thing" so admirably suited to the literary and critical initiation of the college student. Not only does James provide a commentary upon the nature of art (his theme obviously applies to writing as well as to painting); his story is also an excellent illustration of the thing itself. Like his painter-narrator, the author has, through "the alchemy of art," transformed a rather trivial episode involving two dull social has-beens, the Monarchs, and a couple of grubby nobodies, Miss Churm and Oronte, into a work of art that is rich with universality and "felt life." From this standpoint, the story is itself "the real thing," though I doubt that James intended to be so "clever" about his title.

From a more serious point of view, there are three major thematic levels in "The Real Thing": (1) the social, (2) the esthetic, and (3) the moral. About (1) James is quite explicit: socially speaking, Major and Mrs. Monarch have been and still are the real thing; they are, as the porter's wife immediately informs us, "a gentleman and a lady." They are neither "celebrities" nor "personalities," and they have lost their money; but they have retained the essential quality that makes them what they are: their manners. Furthermore, "They weren't superficial." And their marriage (*the* social institution) "had no weak spot. It was a real marriage . . . a nut for pessimists to crack."

Unhappily, as the narrator complains, the real thing for society is "the wrong thing" for art. In the "deceptive atmosphere of art even the highest respectability may fail of being plastic." In other words, the real thing for the artist must be "the ideal thing." On a second and higher level of meaning, then, the real thing—esthetically—is the creative imagination of the artist himself. (1) cannot accommodate itself to (2), nor vice versa. It is from the conflict between these two levels of meaning that the tension within the story partially derives. The Monarchs prove to be utterly intractable for the artist's purposes. The painter's foolish attempt to amalgamate these incompatible elements almost ruins his project and, worse, perhaps irreparably mars his creative talent, if we are to accept the word of his esthetic conscience, Jack Hawley.

But are we to accept Hawley's judgment? I think we must—at least from the purely esthetic viewpoint. Our narrator makes it fairly clear that his friend's critical insights are trustworthy: ". . . he was always of such good counsel. He painted badly himself, but there was no one like him for putting his finger on the place." Hawley perceives almost immediately that if the painter is to preserve his artistic integrity the Monarchs must be got rid of: " 'Ce sont des gens qu'il faut mettre à la porte.' " Notwithstanding his critical incisiveness, however, Jack Hawley is heartless. And this is the key to the third level of meaning in the story, a meaning that James skillfully withholds until his concluding sentence—a meaning so deftly manipulated that it has apparently been overlooked by most of James's critics.

Following his friend's sound advice, the painter dismisses the pathetically inept Monarchs, who, according to Hawley, "did me a permanent harm, got me into false ways." Then he concludes with this enigmatic qualification: "If it be true I'm content to have paid the price—for the memory." An astounding concession for any artist to make! In essence, the narrator admits that he has been willing to sacrifice something of the artist's most precious gift, his creative talent, for something else termed vaguely as "the memory."

In order to determine exactly what the painter (and James) means by this, we must carefully re-examine the story. That the narrator, not the Monarchs, is James's central character is patent. It is he who undergoes the most subtle and dynamic inner change during the course of the narrative. The change is manifested primarily in his attitude toward the Monarchs. At first he views them from the commercial perspective: "Sitters my visitors in this case proved to be; but not in the sense I should have preferred"—*i.e.*, the *commercial* sense. When Major Monarch confesses, "We should like to make it pay," the painter immediately supposes that he means "pay the artist." Significantly, the narrator also looks at his art chiefly as a means "to perpetuate my fame" and "to make my fortune." Upon discovering that the Monarchs have no useful purpose in this scheme, he regards them with detached, even slightly cruel, amusement: "I had seized their type—I had already settled what I would do with it. Something that wouldn't absolutely have pleased them, I afterwards reflected." When he good-naturedly attempts to take their point of view, he cannot help "appraising physically, as if they were animals on hire. . . ." The metaphor recurs when Mrs. Monarch is put "through her paces before him," like a prize mare. The extent of the painter's sympathy for her humiliating gesture is that he abstains from applauding. And, when she bursts into tears, he merely reassures her politely.

Compare this opening scene with the final one in which the Monarchs, stripped of everything but the wistful desire not to starve, voluntarily assume the services of menials. Here, the tears are those, not of Mrs. Monarch, but of the painter himself: "When it came over me, the latent eloquence of what they were doing, I confess that my drawing was blurred for a moment—the picture swam." His attitude has changed radically from what it was at the beginning of the story.

He is now involved with mankind. Though such involvement may have blurred his esthetic perspective, it has sharpened his moral insight; if he has lost something as an artist, he has gained infinitely more as a man. From his painful experience with the Monarchs James's narrator emerges with a finer understanding of the human situation and with a new awareness of what constitutes "the real thing" in human relationships: compassion.

This is the third and highest level of meaning in James's title, and it is this alone that justifies the artist's willingness to renounce his talent. Paradoxically, Henry James implies that only through such an attitude may the artist achieve true greatness. As he says in his preface to *The Portrait of a Lady*, it is, after all, the "enveloping air of the artist's humanity—which gives the last touch to the worth of the work. . . ." And it is the latent moral value of the painter's "memory" which gives the last exquisite touch to the worth of "The Real Thing."

KRISHNA BALDEV VAID

The Beast in the Jungle†

* * *

The wider thematic context of "The Beast" is perhaps too obvious to merit more than a bare mention: it is a "fantastic" embodiment of the central Jamesian theme of the unlived life, dealt with most amply in *The Ambassadors*. What gives "The Beast" its distinctive place among James's shorter masterpieces, however, is its spell-binding power. Without this special quality, even with all its thematic meaningfulness, it might have been as ordinary a tale as, for instance, "The Friends of the Friends" or "Maud-Evelyn," the two tales written during the same phase and around a similar idea. We need not dwell any longer on the theme, then, for James has clearly disengaged in his preface the "treated theme for the reader's benefit."[1] As he goes on to say, "any felt merit in the thing must all depend on the clearness and charm with which the subject just noted expresses itself."[2] In what follows I shall be almost exclusively concerned with evaluating this "clearness and charm."

Each of the six sections contains at least one dramatized scene that

†From Krishna Baldev Vaid, *Technique in the Tales of Henry James* (Cambridge: Harvard University Press, 1964), pp. 224–32. Vaid's parenthetical page references are to the New York Edition, vol. XVII (1909), whose wording occasionally differs from the version reprinted here. Vaid's footnotes have been renumbered.
1. *The Art of the Novel*, p. 247.
2. Ibid., p. 248. See pp. 245–247 for James's comments on the theme of the tale.

is embedded in an analytical summary. The summary is a heavily foreshortened account of the long intervals separating one scene from another and an analysis of the progressive stages of Marcher's obsession. The scenes dramatize these stages through increasingly tense conversations between Marcher and May, except in the last scene where Marcher faces the Beast alone. Thus in the first section, the summary is used to provide the background for the scene in which Marcher and May reminisce about their meeting of ten years ago. The less essential part of this conversation is also given through indirect narration, editorially compressed, with the accent on Marcher's response to this unexpected renewal of an old acquaintance. The scenic half of the section begins with May's speech, mentioned in the opening sentence of the tale. By the close of the scene, the nature of Marcher's obsession has been dramatically defined and the partnership he offers May clearly established.

In the second section, the summary is employed to give us the idea of their growing "older together" (XVII, 82) * * * Marcher does not have the ghost of a perception that May is in love with him; he himself does not love her. He satisfies his conscience by trying not to appropriate her entirely for his own selfish purpose—but this is a veneer beneath which his egotism still lives. Marcher himself is not quite conscious of the veneer, but the reader is left in very little doubt. As L. C. Knights has pointed out, everything is " 'seen' largely through the eyes of Marcher, but the seeing is flecked with unobtrusive irony so that we are aware of two views—Marcher's and that of James himself—existing simultaneously."[3] The simultaneity of views can be seen, for instance, in the tone of the passages that show Marcher grappling with the question of his selfishness: "This was why [the fact that he "had thought himself, so long as nobody knew, the most disinterested person in the world" and "hadn't disturbed people with the queerness of their having to know a haunted man" (XVII, 77–78)] he had such good—though possibly such rather colourless—manners; this was why, above all, he could regard himself, in a greedy world, as decently—as in fact perhaps even a little sublimely—unselfish" (XVII, 78). Or later, when he knows of "a deep disorder in her blood," his reactions are given in these words: "This indeed gave him one of those partial recoveries of equanimity that were agreeable to him—it showed him that what was still first in his mind was the loss she herself might suffer. 'What if she should have to die before knowing, before seeing—?' " (XVII, 94). Even when he thinks he is being least selfish, the reader is made subtly aware of the telltale error in his thought. Many more illustrations can be adduced to refute the notion that "the point of view is consistently that of

3. Knights, "Henry James and the Trapped Spectator," *Southern Review*, IV (Winter 1938), 612.

Marcher."[4] In addition to the ironic interplay of the author's and Marcher's point of view, we also have a brief glimpse of May's—for instance in the passage that begins, "So while they grew older together she did watch with him, and so she let this association give shape and colour to her own existence. Beneath *her* forms as well detachment had learned to sit, and behaviour had become for her, in a social sense, a false account of herself" (XVII, 82).

The summary gives way to the scene in the second half of the section: "What we are especially concerned with is the turn it happened to take from her one afternoon when he had come to see her in honour of her birthday" (XVII, 83). A good deal has happened, and time has elapsed, since the scene in the first section. The vigil May had agreed to keep with Marcher has not yet been rewarded by any sign of the long-awaited Beast. But what this scene establishes most trenchantly is Marcher's disconcerting suspicion that May has perhaps already seen the Beast. This suspicion is shared by the reader, who is free to read something more into May's speeches and silences and guarded hints—for instance, he knows without being explicitly told that she is in love with Marcher and can almost predict what the dreadful Beast will turn out to be, although he has no idea of how and when it will spring.

The third section opens with the summary, giving the effect on Marcher of their last important conversation, passes on to a brief scene, dramatizing his slight uneasiness about what she has "got" out of her long association with him—a question she answers with all the characteristic evasiveness of a Jamesian lover—and turns again to a summary conveying Marcher's fear that he might lose her. The agony of his fear comes from his dependence on her as well as from his knowledge that "she 'knew' something and that what she knew was bad—too bad to tell him" (XVII, 92). But he is shown as having rationalized this fear into the flattering appearance of an unselfish concern for the loss *she* would suffer by her death. The irony of this subtle self-deception has been mentioned above. And of course there is the further irony that will flash out only at the end: he will realize that she died in full knowledge of his fate, a knowledge she scrupulously spared him out of tenderness. The idea that his "great accident" might after all be "nothing more than his being condemned to see this charming woman, this admirable friend, pass away from him" crosses his mind, only to be dismissed as "an abject anti-climax" (XVII, 95–96). Another thought that has begun to torment him is the dread that "it was overwhelmingly too late" for anything to happen to him (XVII, 96): "It wouldn't have been failure to be bankrupt, dishonoured, pilloried, hanged; it was failure not to be anything" (XVII, 97).

4. Tate, "Three Commentaries," p. 7. [Allen Tate, "Three Commentaries: Poe, James, and Joyce," *Sewanee Review*, LVIII (Winter 1950), p. 7—*Editor.*]

The scene in this section has an insignificant function in comparison to the summary, through which James conveys the very atmosphere of his hero's mind.

In the next section the scene is given predominance to dramatize Marcher's supreme failure in deciphering May's answer to his riddle and in grasping the sole opportunity to escape the Beast. Apart from the scene in the opening section, this is the only other scene provided with some kind of setting, although the setting in this case is more atmospheric than physical: it conveys his impression of May as he visits her "one afternoon, while the spring of the year was young and new."[5] He sees her as "the picture of a serene and exquisite but impenetrable sphinx," as "an artificial lily, wonderfully imitated and constantly kept," as someone sitting "with folded hands and nothing more to do" (XVII, 98–99). It is against the background of his alarm and bafflement that the scene is played out, with Marcher remaining blank in the presence of what she tries to communicate to him. It is a scene whose importance and terror Marcher grasps later, while the reader grasps it at the moment. It is perfectly placed in the total design of the tale and is attended by the full involvement of the author and the reader. Its reverberations remain with us throughout the rest of the tale.

This is followed by a companion scene in the next section, which in its opening paragraphs depicts Marcher's anguished efforts to read the riddle of the sphinx; he fails to do so even though she spoke "with the perfect straightness of a sibyl" (XVII, 110). The approaching death of May Bartram lends poignancy to her assurance to Marcher that his danger has passed. The scene is followed by a picture of Marcher's desolation after May's death. But as the shock of that death fades, his unlaid obsession begins to haunt him once again: "What it presently came to in truth was that poor Marcher waded through his beaten grass, where no life stirred, where no breath sounded, where no evil eye seemed to gleam from a possible lair, very much as if vaguely looking for the Beast, and still more as if acutely missing it" (XVII, 116). As the quotation indicates, the jungle which Marcher now threshes has already receded into his past: "What was to happen *had* so absolutely and finally happened that he was as little able to know a fear for his future as to know a hope, so absent in short was any question of anything still to come. He was to live entirely with the other question, that of his unidentified past, that of his having to see his fortune impenetrably muffled and masked" (XVII, 117)

This calls for a slight modification of my initial statement that

5. For the symbolical importance in this tale of the characters' names in relation to the seasons, see John L. Sweeney, "The Demuth Pictures," *Kenyon Review*, V (Autumn 1943), 527, and Edward Stone, "James's 'Jungle': The Seasons," *University of Kansas City Review*, XXI (Winter 1955), 142–144.

Marcher is haunted by his future, for at this stage the habitation of the Beast shifts and so does the direction of Marcher's obsession. Had he followed May's advice, he would not have tried to "win back by an effort of thought the lost stuff of consciousness" (XVII, 117), and he would have perhaps enjoyed the bliss that lies in ignorance. But constituted as he is, this new turn of the obsession takes an even greater hold on his mind. So far he has waited intensely but almost passively for his fate. Now his search becomes more active as well as more desperate: "The lost stuff of consciousness became thus for him as a strayed or stolen child to an unappeasable father; he hunted it up and down very much as if he were knocking at doors and enquiring of the police" (XVII, 118). This vivid image expresses the fever with which he now hunts the Beast. The encounter, however, does not take place as a direct result of his own effort of thought. Before setting out on his travels, he makes a pilgrimage to May Bartram's grave, which is pictured as a part of "the wilderness of tombs" (XVII, 118). Later, just before his final revelation, the graveyard will bloom appropriately into an image of the "garden of death" (XVII, 121). Meanwhile, however, as he kneels on the stones beside the grave, "beguiled into long intensities," his question remains unanswered and not even the "palest light" breaks (XVII, 118).

The last section rapidly summarizes his cheerless travels abroad. On returning home he makes straight for "the barely discriminated slab in the London suburb" that "had become for him, and more intensely with time and distance, his one witness of a past glory" (XVII, 119). He is mentioned as having "wandered from the circumference to the centre of his desert," back to "the part of himself that alone he now valued" (XVII, 120). The reader is conscious of no abruptness in this reported transition from a harassed hunter of the Beast to a devoted worshiper of his dead friend, the change from a tormented questioner to a stoical accepter: "Whatever had happened—well, had happened" (XVII, 120). In this new state of mind Marcher begins to visit regularly May Bartram's grave, which "had lost for him its mere blankness of expression. It met him in mildness—not, as before, in mockery; it wore for him the air of conscious greeting that we find, after absence, in things that have closely belonged to us and which seem to confess of themselves to the connexion" (XVII, 120). The wilderness of tombs has now become the garden of death, where "he settled to live—feeding all on the sense that he once *had* lived, and dependent on it not alone for a support but an identity" (XVII, 121).

The garden, however, is a place associated with knowledge, and, after a year of comparative peace, knowledge comes to him on an autumn day, not "on the wings of experience" but through "the disrespect of chance, the insolence of accident" (XVII, 125). Had it come by his own effort of thought—a course perhaps equally open to the author—the point of John Marcher's "great negative adventure" would have been somewhat blunted, though his lot would have been somewhat redeemed. But the point is not only his inability to "do" anything, but also his tragic inability to "see" anything except as he finally does see. The spectacle of his waking to the horror of this knowledge is great; layer after layer of ignorance is removed, the whole backward reach of the emptiness of his life reflected, till he stands stripped before himself. The anti-hero, instead of remaining a mere pathetic figure, becomes a tragic hero, arousing pity and terror because of the single-mindedness with which he has looked forward to his destiny and the intensity with which he experiences his doom.

Allen Tate cautiously expresses several objections to the tale, among them: "The foreground is too elaborate, and the structure suffers from the disproportion of the Misplaced Middle"; the grief-stricken stranger is introduced too suddenly and "could better be described as *deus ex machina*"; and the symbolism tends to allegory in the Hawthornian way.[6] What Tate dismisses as foreground—the first two sections—is structurally proportionate, well integrated in the tale, and very necessary to an appreciation of Marcher's obsession and his relationship with May. The middle of the tale is in the third section, where Marcher's suspicion, that May knows something he does not, first turns into a virtual conviction; this is almost exactly the dimensional middle of the tale. The grief-stricken stranger may be termed a *deus ex machina*, but his descent at the opportune moment is not at all ruled out by the tenor of the tale. Here perhaps we have the basic reason for Tate's objections to the tale: it should not be evaluated as a realistic tale or be read as a mere allegory. It is a disservice both to Hawthorne and to James to dismiss "The Beast," and "The Altar" as failures *because* they are allegories. Instead, we should perhaps revise our opinion of allegory, as well as our definition of it, in the light of "The Great Good Place," "The Altar," "The Beast," and "The Jolly Corner."[7]

As contrasted with "The Altar of the Dead," there are more scenic effects in "The Beast in the Jungle," but even here the task of creating the haunting effect of the tale falls to what I have expressed by the somewhat unimpressive, but quite Jamesian, term "summary." As used here, the term expresses those narrative resources of the story-

6. Tate, "Three Commentaries," pp. 9–10.

7. For an excellent exploration of the question of allegory, see Edwin Honig, *Dark Conceit: The Making of Allegory* (Evanston: Northwestern University Press, 1959). See also F. E. Smith, " 'The Beast in the Jungle': The Limits of Method," *Perspective*, 1 (Autumn 1947), 33–40. Smith's reading of the tale is very perceptive in several places, but his concluding judgment suffers from the same fixation on "realism": "And the final irony is that [James] has preached his lesson too well, that his method is here too specialized, too barren of action, too empty of emotion, that his characters lose what life they have in the mazes of logical inference until they have more of the nature of propositions than of human beings" (p. 40).

teller by which he both bridges the gaps between his crucial scenes and lets us hear the musings of his hero without surrendering his privilege to stand beside him and, in Knights's phrase, to fleck unobtrusively these musings occasionally with his own.

EDWIN H. CADY

[The Beast in the Jungle]†

* * * Thirty years ago there were serious, competent readers who regarded James's tale as esoteric if not opaque, but a generation of James study has accomplished something which can in part be measured by the fact that "The Beast" is today a standard anthology piece. Wholly without the traditional impedimenta, the story of May Bartram and John Marcher is a gothic tale of personal and moral sensibilities betrayed, stifled, and petrified by romantic egotism until Marcher is left facing the horror of the utter nothingness he has made of his life and May Bartram's love. The theme is in part Hawthornian: egotism alienates, alienation leads to pride, pride to petrifaction of the heart and damnation. The heroine's name snags in one's mind— why should she share the patronym of the lime-burner[1] in Hawthorne's tale of Ethan Brand, the man who thought he had committed the Unpardonable Sin?

The moral is also Emersonian. Evil, said Emerson, has no positive existence. It is privative, like cold, which is the absence of heat; like darkness, which is the absence of light; like death, which is the absence of life. The penalty of sin is the horror of nonbeing, the void. The literary power and the realism of James's tale stem from the exquisite tact and timing with which the sensibility of a great artist proceeds through ever-intensifying suspense to simultaneous moments of emotional release and revelation for John Marcher and the reader.

Working by "scene" and "picture" with an almost too easy mastery, James reveals to us that Marcher has trapped his soul in the romantic egotism, the Dionysian self-regard, of waiting, and watching himself wait, for a fated, unique, perhaps heroic catastrophe to top off his life. "You said," May reminds him,

"You had had from your earliest time, as the deepest thing within

†From Edwin H. Cady, *The Light of Common Day: Realism in American Fiction* (Bloomington: Indiana University Press, 1971), pp. 39–43. The footnotes for this selection are by the editor.
1. Bartram, the lime-burner in Hawthorne's tale "Ethan Brand," is an average man puzzled by the stranger who claims to have discovered the Unpardonable Sin in his own breast and perplexed when the stranger's marble heart is burned to lime.

you, the sense of being kept for something rare and strange, possibly prodigious and terrible, that was sooner or later to happen to you, that you had in your bones the foreboding and conviction of, and that would perhaps overwhelm you."

Subtly, gently, quietly, James lets us know that because May loves John she takes the risk of stepping into his trap with him, hoping that if she loves John enough she will turn his eyes from regard of self to love and regard of May. " 'I'll watch with you,' said May Bartram," at the end of Section I.

Section II builds to suspense and what will be, in retrospect, terrible irony. Marcher's concern, his almost professional fear, raise the question of his courage. May begins to play a role partly sibyline, partly Cassandra-like.[2]

" 'But doesn't the man of courage know what he's afraid of—or *not* afraid of?' " inquires Marcher. And then he guesses, correctly,

" 'You know something I don't. . . . You know, and you're afraid to tell me. It's so bad that you're afraid I'll find out.' "

But May, who is playing the game of death with her heart, her life at stake, playing Marcher's game in the desperate hope of getting him to turn about and take up the game of life, can only say, " 'You'll never find out.' "

With only two characters and starkly disfurnished, James's fiction presses on, irony by dread irony. At the climax of Section III, learning that May is ill and might die, Marcher feels let down at the prospect of his game's being diminished by the loss of his spectator and is delivered up to the intolerable fear that his fate might never strike: "He had but one desire left—that he shouldn't have been 'sold.' " (The word, in quotation marks like a neologism but borrowed from the lexicon of Western humor, rings with allusiveness.) In fact, of course, Marcher has gulled himself, and Nemesis[3] holds him firmly in hand. At almost their last interview May tells him that truth but also that " 'The door's open,' " and " 'It's never too late.' " But as he leaves she has another prophetic word. He will not hear or see her truly, and she exclaims in pain. What has happened? he wonders: " 'What *was* to,' she said." In their last conversation she tells him, " 'You've *had* it.' " And at the very last, " 'I would live for you still—if I could. . . . But I can't!' "

The ultimate scene is one of James's achievements. Alone, baffled, a touristic ghost, Marcher wanders at length to May Bartram's grave and there meets in "the face of a fellow mortal" the shock of revelation. A man mourning at the next grave turns, unconsciously, on Marcher a face distorted by genuine grief, "the image of scarred

2. The Sibyls of antiquity were prophetesses who spoke in riddles. The Trojan princess Cassandra also had prophetic power, but no one understood or believed her, so that her prophecies also seemed like riddles.
3. Goddess of retribution for evil deeds or undeserved prosperity.

passion." Then it appears, shockingly in this hitherto ultracivilized fiction, that the title is as organic as any of George Herbert's.[4] All at once Marcher sees, stupefied, overwhelmed, the truth of his condition. Never having known passion, he has lived in emptiness, darkness, and cold diminishing to the void:

> The fate he had been marked for he had met with a vengeance—he had emptied the cup to the lees; he had been the man of his time, *the* man, to whom nothing on earth was to have happened. That was the rare stroke—that was his visitation.

And now he can see:

> The escape would have been to love her; then, *then* he would have lived. *She* had lived—who could say now with what passion?—since she had loved him for himself; whereas he had never thought of her (ah how it hugely glared at him!) but in the chill of his egotism and the light of her use.

Seeing, remembering and re-seeing, knowing at last,

> He saw the Jungle of his life and saw the lurking Beast; then, while he looked, perceived it, as by a stir of the air, rise, huge and hideous, for the leap that was to settle him. His eyes darkened—it was close; and, instinctively turning, in his hallucination, to avoid it, he flung himself, face down, on the tomb.

James's brilliant last word is altogether symbolic, but the symbol functions after the fashion of a realist. In contrast with the butterfly of "The Artist of the Beautiful,"[5] the symbolic reference looks not outward to a general reference like Beauty (or even, in this particular case, to a generality like Death). The horror of nothingness (his nothingness, his fate) is revealed to Marcher. And he *has* had it. There is no going back, no escape or refuge. But the force of James's last word in the story presses not at all to the point that Marcher is physically dead. Worse, it is that he has no point of reference, no goal but the tomb, and the horror is that he must live while he lasts in a hell of the knowledge of his self-achieved nothingness. James's symbol, the symbol of a realist, points inward to illuminate and reinforce the work of art. It is left to us to generalize or moralize upon the experience our author's sensibility has grasped and his art made available to our ruminations.

4. English religious poet (1593–1633).
5. Allegorical short story by Nathaniel Hawthorne.

KRISHNA BALDEV VAID

The Jolly Corner†

* * *

The tale opens dramatically, with Spencer Brydon's remark to Alice Staverton, indicating his impatience with people who are constantly after him for his impressions "of everything" (XVII, 435). The scene from which this remark is extracted is resumed several pages later: "It was a few days after this that, during an hour passed with her again, he had expressed his impatience of the too flattering curiosity—among the people he met—about his appreciation of New York" (XVII, 447). The intervening pages give a compact account of the total setting of this scene. A summary of this summary cannot be accomplished without attenuating the rich picture of Brydon's preliminary confrontation with his past. At best I can only point to the range of information that is abbreviated pictorially through a fusion of the omniscient narrator's voice and the consciousness of the hero. Thus we learn about the hero's "so strangely belated return to America" (XVII, 435), about "the newness, the queerness, above all the bigness . . . that at present assaulted his vision wherever he looked" (XVII, 436), about his "house on the jolly corner" and the general purpose of his homecoming (XVII, 437), about his amused perception of his "dormant" business capacities as he supervises the conversion of his other house into flats (XVII, 438), about the "communities of knowledge" he shares with his old friend Alice Staverton (XVII, 440), about the effect on him of Miss Staverton's ironical remarks about his "real gifts" (XVII, 440), about their talk of the "ghosts" during their visit together to the jolly-corner house (XVII, 441–447), and so on. The order of this information is not exactly chronological, and the process by which it is conveyed not entirely without scenic effects. Brydon's "morbid obsession" with his alter ego clings to him in the form of the "most disguised and most muffled vibrations" (XVII, 441). The form that this obsession is to take, and the ghost it will give rise to, is foreshadowed by his image of "some strange figure, some unexpected occupant, at a turn of one of the dim passages of an empty house," an image that he further improves upon: "that of his opening a door behind which he would have made sure of finding nothing, a door into a room shuttered and void, and yet so coming, with a great suppressed start, on some quite erect confronting presence, something

†From Krishna Baldev Vaid, *Technique in the Tales of Henry James* (Cambridge: Harvard University Press, 1964), pp. 235–39, 246–47. Vaid's parenthetical page references are to vol. XVII of the New York Edition, which is reprinted here. Vaid's footnotes have been renumbered.

planted in the middle of the place and facing him through the dusk" (XVII, 441). His actual nightmare is thus anticipated by this glimpse of his acutely developed visual imagination. The "actual" ghost and his adventure with it are here preceded by a mention of the "real" ghost and his preoccupation with it, for the ghost is but a symbolical embodiment of the phantom self he must exorcise.

The scene itself is not all dialogue, much of which is reported indirectly. It gives a hint, among other things, of Spencer Brydon's ambivalence toward what he might have been. The images in which he thinks of his alter ego are informed with the tenderness of desire— an "important letter unopened" and "the full-blown flower . . . in the small tight bud" (XVII, 448, 449); the words in which he describes it, taking his cue from his interlocutress, show the extent of his dread—"Monstrous above all . . . and I imagine, by the same stroke, quite hideous and offensive" (XVII, 450). Alice Staverton's even more ambiguous attitude to his alter ego, whom she tells him she has seen twice in a dream, is contained in the various enigmatic remarks she makes to quench his curiosity: "I feel it would have been quite splendid, quite huge, and monstrous" (XVII, 450). We gather that she loves him for whatever he is and would have loved him for whatever he might have been: "How should I not have liked you?" is her twice-repeated answer to his question of whether she would have liked him "that way" (XVII, 450). With the close of this section we have all that we need to know about the nature of Brydon's obsession and his determination to see the "wretch," an appellation that beautifully indicates the interlocked knot of his desire and his dread. No further scenes between the hero and his friend are necessary to demonstrate the intensity of his obsession, and Alice Staverton is appropriately absent from the second, and central, section of the tale.

This section can be subdivided into two parts. In the first part, we have a summarized account of Spencer Brydon's "particular form of surrender to his obsession"; in the second, covering about sixteen pages, we have a scenic depiction of the climactic episode in this surrender. The first part spans the initial stages of his nocturnal adventures in the house on the jolly corner; temporally it extends over several weeks. Brydon's life in this period is mentioned as having been split into two halves:

> He circulated, talked, renewed, loosely and pleasantly, old re-
> lations—met indeed, so far as he could, new expectations and
> seemed to make out on the whole that in spite of the career, of such
> different contacts, which he had spoken of to Miss Staverton as
> ministering so little, for those who might have watched it, to
> edification, he was positively rather liked than not. He was a dim
> secondary social success—and all with people who had truly not an
> idea of him. It was all mere surface sound, this murmur of their

welcome, this popping of their corks—just as his gestures of response were extravagant shadows, emphatic in proportion as they
meant little, of some game of *ombres chinoises*.[1] He projected
himself all day, in thought, straight over the bristling line of hard
unconscious heads and into the other, the real, the waiting life; the
life that, as soon as he had heard behind him the click of his great
house-door, began for him, on the jolly corner, as beguilingly as the
slow opening bars of some rich music follows the tap of the conductor's wand. (XVII, 454–455)

I have quoted this passage to point out how, in a typical summary,
the author imperceptibly merges his own voice with the consciousness
of his central character so that the two are nearly inextricable. The
very choice of descriptive words is determined by their dual origin—
they seem to proceed simultaneously from the author's and the
character's mind. It may be postulated that this is so where the author
does not want to maintain an ironic distance between his own point of
view and that of his hero. For instance, in similar passages in "The
Beast in the Jungle" * * * we are conscious of the intended ironic
margin maintained by the author in regard to what goes on in the
mind of John Marcher * * *. Another point illustrated by the
passage just quoted is the remarkable pictorial economy of a Jamesian
summary. Thus the spectacle of Spencer Brydon's social "circulation"
and its irrelevance to his own preoccupation is inimitably caught in
the "mere surface sound, this murmur of their welcome, this popping
of their corks." Notice also the contrast of the "surface sound" with
"the click of his great house-door" and "the slow opening bars of some
rich music [that] follows the tap of the conductor's wand." The wide
distance between his waking and his nocturnal life—his "unreal" and
his "real" life—could hardly be better expressed.

* * *

The last section, then, depicts the calm after the storm. It marks the
end of Brydon's obsession and shows the salubrious effect of that end;
Brydon is reborn, and the sweetest fruit of this rebirth is the consummation of his love for Alice Staverton. The "moral" of the tale is clear:
given the type of alternative self that Brydon, or any man like him,
might have had, his wholeness and health follow an exorcization of
that other self. In other words, it does not celebrate the repudiation of
all the unfulfilled possibilities of one's past, but only of certain kinds of
unfulfilled possibilities. The supreme power of the tale, however, lies
in its avoidance of a simple didactic approach to this idea, in its
adoption of an exceptionally complex artistic approach.
* * * I have denied myself the psychoanalytical insights offered by
Saul Rosensweig and Robert Rogers. Rogers, for instance, suggests

1. Shadow theater. [*Editor.*]

that "The Jolly Corner" is "like 'The Beast in the Jungle' . . . a tragic lament for a life unlived, for deeds undone."[2] To me "The Jolly Corner," unlike "The Beast," is a joyous embodiment of a life lived, of deeds done. Again Rogers considers it "noteworthy that throughout the story Alice Staverton likes—in fact, prefers—the *alter ego* to Brydon himself."[3] This also seems to me a distortion of what Alice Staverton actually likes and prefers in the tale. The real trouble with Rogers' reading of "The Jolly Corner" is that it is subservient to the biographical-psychoanalytical ax that he wants to grind. An examination of this grinding would involve me in too detailed a refutation of all the phallic and womb symbols that he so blandly points out in the tale. Instead, perhaps, I should invoke Harry Levin's admonition of much that passes for psychoanalytic criticism: "It reduces our vocabulary of symbols to a few which are so crudely fundamental and so monotonously recurrent that they cannot help the critic to perform his primary function, which is still—I take it—to discriminate. Nature abounds in protuberances and apertures. Convexities and concavities, like Sir Thomas Browne's quincunxes, are everywhere. The forms they compose are not always enhanced or illuminated by reading our sexual obsessions into them."[4]

2. Rogers, "The Beast in Henry James," *The American Imago*, XIII (Winter 1956), 429.
3. Ibid., p. 438.
4. *Symbolism and Fiction* (Charlottesville: University of Virginia Press, 1956), p. 12. Reprinted in Harry Levin, *Contexts of Criticism* (Cambridge: Harvard University Press, 1957). [A quincunx, or five-spot, is an arrangement of five objects in a square or rectangle, one at each corner and one in the middle (like the number five on dice). Sir Thomas Browne (1605–82) wrote a learned treatise on the quincunx, entitled *The Garden of Cyrus*, which suggests its wide occurrence in nature and art. Browne saw the quincunx in leaf patterns, crosses, architecture—everywhere—*Editor.*]

Selected Bibliography

Neither the articles reprinted nor the books from which the essays in this volume were derived are listed.

CHECKLISTS

Beebe, Maurice, and Stafford, William T. "Criticism of Henry James: A Selected Checklist," *Modern Fiction Studies* XII (Spring 1966), 117–77.

Edel, Leon, and Laurence, Dan H. *A Bibliography of Henry James*. London, 1957; 2nd ed., revised, 1961; 3d ed., revised with the assistance of James Rambeau, 1982.

Franklin, Rosemary F. *An Index to Henry James's Prefaces to the New York Edition*. Charlottesville, Va., 1966.

Foley, Richard Nicholas. *Criticism in American Periodicals of the Works of Henry James from 1866 to 1910*. Washington, D.C., 1944.

Gale, Robert L. "Henry James," in James Woodress, ed. *Eight American Authors: A Review of Research and Criticism*. Rev. Ed. New York, 1971. Pp. 321–75.

Ricks, Beatrice. *Henry James: A Bibliography of Secondary Works*. Metuchen, N.J., 1975.

Stafford, William T. *A Name, Title, and Place Index to the Critical Writings of Henry James*. Englewood, Colo., 1975.

BOOKS

Beach, Joseph Warren. *The Method of Henry James*. Rev. Ed. Philadelphia, 1954.

Bosanquet, Theodora. *Henry James at Work*. London, 1924.

Bridgman, Richard. *The Colloquial Style in America*. New York, 1966.

Brooks, Van Wyck. *The Pilgrimage of Henry James*. New York, 1925.

Buitenhuis, Peter. *The Grasping Imagination: The American Writings of Henry James*. Toronto, 1970.

Chatman, Seymour. *The Later Style of Henry James*. New York, 1972.

Dupee, F. W. *Henry James*. New York, 1951.

———, ed. *The Question of Henry James*. New York, 1945.

Edel, Leon. *Henry James*. 5 vols. Philadelphia and New York, 1953–72.

———, ed. *Henry James: A Collection of Critical Essays*. Englewood Cliffs, N.J., 1963.

———. *The Prefaces of Henry James*. Paris, 1931.

———, and Ray, Gordon N., eds. *Henry James and H.G. Wells: A Record of Their Friendship, Their Debate on the Art of Fiction, and Their Quarrel*. Urbana, 1958.

Gale, Robert L. *The Caught Image: Figurative Language in the Fiction of Henry James*. Chapel Hill, 1964.

Gard, Roger, ed. *Henry James: The Critical Heritage*. London and New York, 1968.

Graham, Kenneth. *Henry James: The Drama of Fulfillment, An Approach to the Novels*. Oxford, 1975.

Hocks, Richard A. *Henry James and Pragmatistic Thought: A Study of the Relationship Between the Philosophy of William James and the Literary Art of Henry James*. Chapel Hill, 1974.

Hoffmann, Charles G. *The Short Novels of Henry James*. New York, 1957.

Holland, Laurence Bedwell. *The Expense of Vision: Essays on the Craft of Henry James*. Princeton, 1964.

Jefferson, D. W. *Henry James and the Modern Reader*. Edinburgh, 1964.

Kelley, Cornelia Pulsifer. *The Early Development of Henry James*. Urbana, 1930.

Krook, Dorothea. *The Ordeal of Consciousness in Henry James*. New York, 1962.

Le Clair, Robert C. *Young Henry James*. New York, 1955.

Levy, Leo B. *Versions of Melodrama: A Study of the Fiction and Drama of Henry James, 1865–1897*. Berkeley, 1957.

Leyburn, Ellen D. *Strange Alloy: The Relation of Comedy to Tragedy in the Fiction of Henry James*. Chapel Hill, 1968.

Matthiessen, F. O. *The James Family*. New York, 1947.

Maves, Carl. *Sensuous Pessimism: Italy in the Work of Henry James*. Bloomington, Ind., and London, 1973.

McElderry, Bruce R. *Henry James*. New York, 1965.

Miller, James E., Jr., ed. *Theory of Fiction: Henry James*. Lincoln, Nebr., 1972.

Nowell-Smith, Simon, ed. *The Legend of the Master*. New York, 1948.

Poirier, Richard. *The Comic Sense of Henry James*. New York, 1960.

Putt, S. Gorley. *Henry James: A Reader's Guide*. Ithaca, 1966.

Roberts, Morris. *Henry James's Criticism*. Cambridge, Mass., 1929.

Sharp, Sister M. Corona. *The Confidante in Henry James*. Notre Dame, 1963.

Spender, Stephen. *The Destructive Element: A Study of Modern Writers and Beliefs*. London, 1935.

Stewart, J.I.M. *Eight Modern Writers*. New York, 1963.

Ward, J. A. *The Imagination of Disaster: Evil in the Fiction of Henry James*. Lincoln, 1961.

——. *The Search for Form: Studies in the Structure of James' Fiction*. Chapel Hill, 1967.

Wiesenfarth, Joseph. *Henry James and the Dramatic Analogy*. New York, 1963.

Winner, Viola Hopkins. *Henry James and the Visual Arts*. Charlottesville, Va., 1970.

Wright, Walter F. *The Madness of Art: A Study of Henry James*. Lincoln, Nebr., 1962.

Yeazell, Ruth Bernard. *Language and Knowledge in the Late Novels of Henry James*. Chicago and London, 1976.

ARTICLES

Babin, James L. "Henry James's 'Middle Years' in Fiction and Autobiography," *Southern Review* XIII (July 1977), 505–17.

Bender, Bert. "Henry James's Lyric Meditations Upon the Mysteries of Fate and Self-Sacrifice," *Genre* IX (Fall 1976), 247–62.

Berkelman, Robert. "Henry James and 'The Real Thing,' " *University of Kansas City Review* XXXI (December 1959), 93–95.

Blackmur, R. P. "Introduction" to *The Art of the Novel: Critical Prefaces by Henry James*. New York, 1934.

Brylowski, Anna Salne. "In Defense of the First Person Narrator in 'The Aspern Papers,' " *The Centennial Review* XIII (Spring 1969), 215–40.

Cummins, Elizabeth. " 'The Playroom of Superstition': An Analysis of Henry James's *The Pupil*," *Markham Review* II (1970), [13]–[16].

Delbaere-Garant, J. "The Redeeming Form: Henry James's 'The Jolly Corner,' " *Revue des Langues Vivantes* XXXIII (1967), 588–96.

Dunbar, Viola. "The Revision of *Daisy Miller*," *Modern Language Notes* LXV (May 1950), 311–17.

Edel, Leon. "The Architecture of Henry James's 'New York Edition,' " *New England Quarterly* XXIV (June 1951), 169–78.

——. " 'The Aspern Papers': Great Aunt Wyckoff and Juliana Bordereau," *Modern Language Notes* LXVIII (June 1952), 392–95.

Fergusson, Francis. "James's Idea of Dramatic Form," *Kenyon Review* V (Autumn 1943), 495–507.

Gargano, James W. " 'The Aspern Papers': The Untold Story," *Studies in Short Fiction* X (1973), 1–10.

Griffith, John. "James's 'The Pupil' as a Whodunit: The Question of Moral Responsibility," *Studies in Short Fiction* IX (1972), 257–68.

Guedalla, Philip. "The Crowner's Quest," *The New Statesman* XII, 306 (February 15, 1919), 421–22.

Hagopian, John V. "Seeing Through 'The Pupil' Again," *Modern Fiction Studies* V (Summer 1959), 169–71.

Halverson, John. "Late Manner, Later Phase," *Sewanee Review* LXXIX (1971), 214–31.

Herrick, Robert. "A Visit to Henry James," *Yale Review* XII (July 1923), 724–41.

Martin, Terence. "James's 'The Pupil': The Art of Seeing Through," *Modern Fiction Studies* IV (Winter 1958–59), 335–45.

Matthiessen, F. O. "James and the Plastic Arts," *Kenyon Review* V (Autumn 1943), 533–50.

McIntyre, Clara F. "The Later Manner of Henry James," *Publications of the Modern Language Association* XXVII (1912), 354–71.

Mellard, James M. "Modal Counterpoint in James's *The Aspern Papers*," *Papers on Language and Literature* IV (1968), 299–307.

Pearce, Howard. "Henry James's Pastoral Fallacy," *Publications of the Modern Language Association* XC (October 1975), 834–47.

Raleigh, John Henry. "Henry James: The Poetics of Empiricism," *Publications of the Modern Language Association* LXVI (March 1951), 107–23.

Roberts, Morris. "Henry James and the Art of Foreshortening," *Review of English Studies* XXII, No. 87 (July 1946), 207–14.

Short, R. W. "Henry James's World of Images," *Publications of the Modern Language Association* LXVIII (December 1953), 943–60.

———. "Some Critical Terms of Henry James," *Publications of the Modern Language Association* LXV (September 1950), 667–80.

Shriber, Michael. "Cognitive Apparatus in *Daisy Miller*, *The Ambassadors* and Two Works by Howells: A Comparative Study of the Epistemology of Henry James," *Language and Style* II (1969), 207–25.

Stone, Edward. "James's 'Jungle': The Seasons," *The University of Kansas City Review* XXI (Winter 1954).

———. "Victor Cherbuliez and *Daisy Miller*," in *The Battle of the Books: Some Aspects of Henry James*. Athens, Ohio, 1964, 88–93.

Sweeney, John L. "The Demuth Pictures," *Kenyon Review* V (Autumn 1943), 522–32.

Terry, Henry L. "Henry James and the 'Explosive Principle,'" *Nineteenth-Century Fiction* XV (March 1961), 283–99.

Tompkins, Jane P. "'The Beast in the Jungle': An Analysis of James's Late Style," *Modern Fiction Studies* XVI (1970), 185–91.

Toor, David. "Narrative Irony in Henry James's 'The Real Thing,'" *University Review* XXXIV (1967), 95–99.

Watanabe, Hisayoshe. "Past Perfect Retrospection in the Style of Henry James," *American Literature* XXXIV (May 1962), 165–81.

Watt, Ian. "The First Paragraph of *The Ambassadors*: An Explication," *Essays in Criticism* X (July 1960), 250–74.

Wegelin, Christof. "Henry James and the Aristocracy," *Northwest Review* I (Spring 1958), 5–14.

Wellek, René. "Henry James's Literary Theory and Criticism," *American Literature* XXX (November 1958), 293–321.

Winner, Viola Hopkins. "Pictorialism in Henry James's Theory of the Novel," *Criticism* IX (Winter 1967), 1–21.

NORTON CRITICAL EDITIONS

AUSTEN *Emma* edited by Stephen M. Parrish

AUSTEN *Pride and Prejudice* edited by Donald J. Gray

Beowulf (the Donaldson translation) edited by Joseph M. Tuso

Blake's Poetry and Designs selected and edited by Mary Lynn Johnson and John E. Grant

BOCCACCIO *The Decameron* selected, translated, and edited by Mark Musa and Peter E. Bondanella

BRONTË, CHARLOTTE *Jane Eyre* edited by Richard J. Dunn

BRONTË, EMILY *Wuthering Heights* edited by William M. Sale, Jr. *Second Edition*

Robert Browning's Poetry selected and edited by James F. Loucks

Byron's Poetry selected and edited by Frank D. McConnell

CARROLL *Alice in Wonderland* selected and edited by Donald J. Gray

CERVANTES *Don Quixote* (the Ormsby translation, substantially revised) edited by Joseph R. Jones and Kenneth Douglas

Anton Chekhov's Plays translated and edited by Eugene K. Bristow

Anton Chekhov's Short Stories selected and edited by Ralph E. Matlaw

CHOPIN *The Awakening* edited by Margaret Culley

CLEMENS *Adventures of Huckleberry Finn* edited by Sculley Bradley, Richmond Croom Beatty, E. Hudson Long, and Thomas Cooley *Second Edition*

CLEMENS *A Connecticut Yankee in King Arthur's Court* edited by Allison R. Ensor

CLEMENS *Pudd'nhead Wilson* and *Those Extraordinary Twins* edited by Sidney E. Berger

CONRAD *Heart of Darkness* edited by Robert Kimbrough *Second Edition*

CONRAD *Lord Jim* edited by Thomas Moser

CONRAD *The Nigger of the "Narcissus"* edited by Robert Kimbrough

CRANE *Maggie: A Girl of the Streets* edited by Thomas A. Gullason

CRANE *The Red Badge of Courage* edited by Sculley Bradley, Richmond Croom Beatty, E. Hudson Long, and Donald Pizer *Second Edition*

Darwin edited by Philip Appleman *Second Edition*

DEFOE *Moll Flanders* edited by Edward Kelly

DEFOE *Robinson Crusoe* edited by Michael Shinagel

DICKENS *Bleak House* edited by George Ford and Sylvère Monod

DICKENS *Hard Times* edited by George Ford and Sylvère Monod

John Donne's Poetry selected and edited by A. L. Clements

DOSTOEVSKY *Crime and Punishment* (the Coulson translation) edited by George Gibian *Second Edition*

DOSTOEVSKY *The Brothers Karamazov* (the Garnett translation revised by Ralph E. Matlaw) edited by Ralph E. Matlaw

DREISER *Sister Carrie* edited by Donald Pizer

ELIOT *Middlemarch* edited by Bert G. Hornback

FIELDING *Tom Jones* edited by Sheridan Baker

FLAUBERT *Madame Bovary* edited with a substantially new translation by Paul de Man

GOETHE *Faust* translated by Walter Arndt and edited by Cyrus Hamlin

HARDY *Jude the Obscure* edited by Norman Page

HARDY *The Mayor of Casterbridge* edited by James K. Robinson

HARDY *The Return of the Native* edited by James Gindin

HARDY *Tess of the d'Urbervilles* edited by Scott Elledge *Second Edition*

HAWTHORNE *The Blithedale Romance* edited by Seymour Gross and Rosalie Murphy

HAWTHORNE *The House of the Seven Gables* edited by Seymour Gross

HAWTHORNE *The Scarlet Letter* edited by Sculley Bradley, Richmond Croom Beatty, E. Hudson Long, and Seymour Gross *Second Edition*

George Herbert and the Seventeenth-Century Religious Poets selected and edited by Mario A. Di Cesare

HOMER *The Odyssey* translated and edited by Albert Cook
HOWELLS *The Rise of Silas Lapham* edited by Don L. Cook
IBSEN *The Wild Duck* translated and edited by Dounia B. Christiani
JAMES *The Ambassadors* edited by S. P. Rosenbaum
JAMES *The American* edited by James A. Tuttleton
JAMES *The Portrait of a Lady* edited by Robert D. Bamberg
JAMES *The Turn of the Screw* edited by Robert Kimbrough
JAMES *The Wings of the Dove* edited by J. Donald Crowley and
    Richard A. Hocks
Ben Jonson and the Cavalier Poets selected and edited by Hugh Maclean
Ben Jonson's Plays and Masques selected and edited by Robert M. Adams
MACHIAVELLI *The Prince* translated and edited by Robert M. Adams
MALTHUS *An Essay on the Principle of Population* edited by Philip Appleman
MELVILLE *The Confidence-Man* edited by Hershel Parker
MELVILLE *Moby-Dick* edited by Harrison Hayford and Hershel Parker
MEREDITH *The Egoist* edited by Robert M. Adams
MILL *On Liberty* edited by David Spitz
MILTON *Paradise Lost* edited by Scott Elledge
MORE *Utopia* translated and edited by Robert M. Adams
NEWMAN *Apologia Pro Vita Sua* edited by David J. DeLaura
NORRIS *McTeague* edited by Donald Pizer
Adrienne Rich's Poetry selected and edited by Barbara Charlesworth Gelpi and
    Albert Gelpi
The Writings of St. Paul edited by Wayne A. Meeks
SHAKESPEARE *Hamlet* edited by Cyrus Hoy
SHAKESPEARE *Henry IV, Part I* edited by James J. Sanderson *Second Edition*
Bernard Shaw's Plays selected and edited by Warren Sylvester Smith
Shelley's Poetry and Prose edited by Donald H. Reiman and Sharon B. Powers
SMOLLETT *Humphry Clinker* Edited by James L. Thorson
SOPHOCLES *Oedipus Tyrannus* translated and edited by Luci Berkowitz and
    Theodore F. Brunner
SPENSER *Edmund Spenser's Poetry* selected and edited by Hugh Maclean
    Second Edition
STENDHAL *Red and Black* translated and edited by Robert M. Adams
STERNE *Tristram Shandy* edited by Howard Anderson
SWIFT *Gulliver's Travels* edited by Robert A. Greenberg *Revised Edition*
The Writings of Jonathan Swift edited by Robert A. Greenberg and
    William B. Piper
TENNYSON *In Memoriam* edited by Robert Ross
Tennyson's Poetry selected and edited by Robert W. Hill, Jr.
THOREAU *Walden and Civil Disobedience* edited by Owen Thomas
TOLSTOY *Anna Karenina* (the Maude translation) edited by George Gibian
TOLSTOY *War and Peace* (the Maude translation) edited by George Gibian
TURGENEV *Fathers and Sons* edited with a substantially new translation by
    Ralph E. Matlaw
VOLTAIRE *Candide* translated and edited by Robert M. Adams
WATSON *The Double Helix* edited by Gunther S. Stent
WHITMAN *Leaves of Grass* edited by Sculley Bradley and Harold W. Blodgett
WOLLSTONECRAFT *A Vindication of the Rights of Woman* edited by
    Carol H. Poston
WORDSWORTH *The Prelude: 1799, 1805, 1850* edited by Jonathan Wordsworth,
    M. H. Abrams, and Stephen Gill
Middle English Lyrics selected and edited by Maxwell S. Luria and
    Richard L. Hoffman
Modern Drama edited by Anthony Caputi
Restoration and Eighteenth-Century Comedy edited by Scott McMillin